Logan Hocking County

S0-AGK-488

...gary ...de *Raiders*:

"This classic quest tale begins when Lord Stephano, former-ly of the Dragon Brigade, gathers his friends to track down a missing Royal Armorer. Traveling by dirigible (shades of steampunk, but why not?), Stephano and friends meet Fa-ther Jacob just in time to be attacked by demons riding giant bats. With the help of one of Stephano's old dragon com-rades, they win. But have they won the war, or is the Apoca-lypse at hand? Tune in to future volumes for the answer, but meanwhile enjoy a great, big, fat fantasy novel with its own rollicking good story."
                                        —*Booklist*

"Longtime writer Weis joins with video producer Krammes for this first book in a new fantasy series, Dragon Brigade. Majestic dragons are just some of the fantastic creatures found in this epic tale of adventure, secrets, schemes, and plots. The characters are detailed, from actions and motiva-tions to wardrobe, and fully developed . . . . the beautiful writing flows and the intriguing characters [are] memora-ble. Of interest to Weis's fans as well as lovers of fantasy and adventure stories."
                    —*Library Journal* (Starred Audio Review)

"'The demons were flying nearer and nearer, lifting the can-nons to their shoulders and taking aim. Apparently, they had never fought a dragon before. They were in for a shock.' Readers too will be in for surprises, in their case much more pleasant, with the first volume of Margaret Weiss and Rob-ert Krammes' new Dragon Brigade series launch. The known world in this festering new microcosm floats above a thick substance similar to Earth's oceans, making it accessi-ble only by airship. An imaginative military fantasy about empires in deadly conflict."   —*Barnes & Noble*

SHADOW RAIDERS

District Library
230 East Main Street
Logan, Ohio 43138

SHADOW RAIDERS

MARGARET WEIS & ROBERT KRAMMES

DAW BOOKS, INC.

DONALD A. WOLLHEIM, FOUNDER

375 Hudson Street, New York, NY 10014

ELIZABETH R. WOLLHEIM
SHEILA E. GILBERT
PUBLISHERS

www.dawbooks.com

Copyright © 2011 by Margaret Weis & Robert Krammes.
All rights reserved.

Cover art by Tom Kidd.

DAW Books Collectors No. 1546.

DAW Books are distributed by the Penguin Group (USA) Inc.

Book designed by The Barbarienne's Den.

Map by Sean Macdonald.

All characters and events in this book are fictitious.
All resemblance to persons living or dead is coincidental.

The scanning, uploading and distribution of this book via the Internet
or any other means without the permission of the publisher is illegal,
and punishable by law. Please purchase only authorized electronic
editions, and do not participate in or encourage the electronic piracy
of copyrighted materials. Your support of the author's rights is appreciated.

First Printing, May 2012
1   2   3   4   5   6   7   8   9   10

DAW TRADEMARK REGISTERED
U.S. PAT. AND TM. OFF. AND FOREIGN COUNTRIES
—MARCA REGISTRADA
HECHO EN U.S.A.

PRINTED IN THE U.S.A.

I dedicate this book to my parents for a lifetime of love and support. I love you, Mom, and I miss you, Dad. To my wife, Mary, who has been my inspiration for a quarter century and to my dear friend, Margaret, for giving me this incredible opportunity. I sincerely thank you all.

—Robert Krammes

This book is dedicated to my Cadre: Jeffrey, Grant, Rusty, Hugh, Dennis and Marney, Bob and Mary. Thank you for your love and friendship for so many years. (And for putting out the fire!)

—Margaret Weis

Acknowledgments

We would like to acknowledge the band *Tartanic* for their recording of the old Irish folk tune, "The Jolly Beggarman," which inspired us to adopt it as the march for the Dragon Brigade. We would especially like to thank piper Mike McNutt of *Tartanic* for his help and advice on playing the bagpipes. Please visit *Tartanic*, the official band of the Dragon Brigade, at www.tartanic.net.

The *Code Duello* to which we refer was an actual document covering the practice of dueling and points of honor. The Code was drawn up and settled "at Clonmel Summer Assizes, 1777, by gentlemen-delegates of Tipperary, Galway, Sligo, Mayo and Roscommon, and prescribed for general adoption throughout Ireland." The *Code Duello* was also followed in England and America, though with variations. *American Duels and Hostile Encounters,* Chilton Books, 1963.

The quote that opens chapter thirty-seven regarding calling cards is from the book *Our Deportment or the Manners, Conduct, and Dress of the Most Refined Society*, by John H. Young, circa 1879. Rodrigo would, of course, consider such a reference guide invaluable.

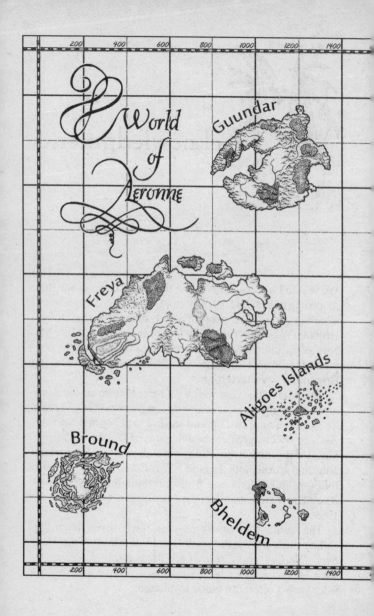

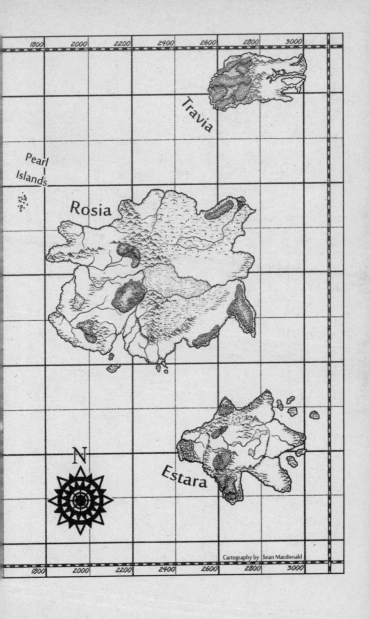

Prologue

SIR HENRY WALLACE SAT AT HIS EASE in his favorite chair—carved wood with a straight, rigid back and a worn rose-colored cushioned seat—in front of the fireplace in his bedroom. The servants had closed the heavy curtains that covered the mullioned windows and snuffed the candles and then quietly withdrawn, dismissed for the night. The fire provided the room's only light. The flames glowed warmly on the burled walnut of the headboard of the bed in which his young wife lay sleeping. She was seven months pregnant with their first child.

His gaze lingered on her fondly. She lay on her side, her hand resting on her swollen belly. Her brown hair strayed out from the lace nightcap. She was small, and was almost lost in the bed with its huge, ornately carved headboard and heavy, fringed tapestry curtains. She was faintly smiling; her dreams were pleasant. Lady Anne was no great beauty. With her brown hair and large brown eyes, small form, shy demeanor, and thin, winsome face, she was considered dull and mousy. And, indeed, "Mouse," was Henry's pet name for her.

Sir Henry had never planned to fall in love with his wife.

He had married her because she was the queen's niece. The marriage had brought him prestige and this fine manor house on an estate located in the countryside outside Haever, the capital city of Freya. The marriage was ostensibly a reward for years of service to Crown and country. In truth, the estate, the wife, and now the child made Henry the Earl of Staffordshire and solidified his ties to the Crown. Queen Mary Chessington wanted to ensure that her Master of Secrets (Sir Henry's unofficial and not particularly complimentary title) never let those secrets pass his lips.

Henry was grateful to Her Majesty, but he required none of these royal favors. Henry Wallace was a patriot to the core of his being. He was loyal to his queen. He considered her a strong and intelligent ruler (unlike her counterpart, that arbitrary egoist King Alaric of Rosia). Henry had been pleased and even moved to think that Her Majesty thought well enough of him to give him her niece's hand in marriage.

Lady Anne was seventeen. Henry was forty-two. Lady Anne was retiring and not particularly intelligent, but she was sweet-tempered. He was brusque, acerbic, and the smartest man in the kingdom. Some in court termed him cold-blooded and calculating, particularly when it came to Freyan politics. No one had been more surprised than Sir Henry Wallace to discover he loved his Lady Anne, his Mouse. Given his tall, athletic frame, thin face, hooded eyes, and long, crooked nose, he had been surprised to discover that she adored him.

Unfortunately, his love for his wife and his unborn child made him vulnerable, could make him weak.

Sir Henry sighed and frowned slightly at himself for having strayed into sentimentality and turned back to business. In one hand, he held a cut-crystal goblet in which a swallow of rare, fine brandy still remained. In the other hand, he held a plain metal tankard, such as one might find in any number of city taverns. As the Earl of Staffordshire, Sir Henry was accustomed to the finest things money and station could provide. Yet it was this ordinary tankard that kept him up past midnight, hoping for a better future for his child and, God willing, the other children to come.

The steadily burning fire wavered with a change in the movement of the air in the room. Sir Henry turned to see the arrival of his adjutant and trusted secretary, Mr. Sloan. Sloan entered the room quietly, without knocking, shielding the light of his candle with his hand so as not to disturb Lady Anne. Closing the door behind him, he walked across the thick carpet without making a sound. His given name was Franklin, but few knew that. He was known to everyone from Her Majesty on down as Mr. Sloan.

"All is in readiness, my lord."

Sir Henry did not turn around. He seemed fixated on the tankard in his hand.

"It doesn't look like much, does it, Mr. Sloan?"

"No, my lord," Sloan said softly.

Sloan was a large man, over six feet tall, with a developing paunch. He was bald, with a neatly trimmed goatee. Years of service in the Freyan army were still visible in his stance and bearing. He had been a sergeant in the Royal Marines prior to taking service with Sir Henry.

"Your instructions were fairly vague, my lord, but I believe I have fulfilled all your requirements," said Mr. Sloan, adding, hinting, "If I knew what you intended . . ."

"Assuming this tankard is all it claims to be, we are looking at the future, Mr. Sloan," said Sir Henry. He finished off the brandy, set down the crystal goblet, and rose to his feet. "We need to test these claims."

"We are going to test the future, my lord?" Mr. Sloan asked with a faint smile.

"No, Mr. Sloan, we are going to blow it up," said Sir Henry.

He lit his own candle to find the way through the dark house, left the bedroom silently and, with one final fond glance at his wife, gently and softly shut the door. The two men traversed the sitting room, walked past the many other bedrooms, drawing rooms, dressing rooms, and the nursery, all of which were located on the third floor of the manor house. A grand staircase of red-and-black marble and oak led from the third floor to the second where there was a dining room, a ballroom, a long gallery, the enormous library, and Sir Henry's study.

A smaller, more cramped back staircase took them from the second floor to the ground floor. The two men walked down a stone corridor and came to the kitchen. Mr. Sloan opened the door and stood back for Sir Henry to enter.

Henry gazed about with interest. He had never been in the kitchen, which was the province of Cook and her servants, and he was surprised by the remarkable view that could be seen from out the tall, narrow windows. Haever, Freya's capital, lay in the distance—a sea of glittering lights on a black backdrop.

When originally built, the kitchen had been separate from the main building. Kitchen fires were commonplace—given the fact that fires were burning daily in the two large fireplaces. With the two buildings kept apart, a fire in the kitchen would not spread to the main house. The kitchen walls and floor were made of stone to prevent sparks from setting them aflame.

Unfortunately, this meant that the servants had been forced to carry the food to the house through all sorts of inclement weather. So, fifty years ago, for the sake of convenience, the kitchen and manor house had been connected by a stone-walled corridor. The kitchen consisted of one large room used for general cooking and several smaller rooms designed for more specific purposes: the cold storage room, the pantry, the wine cellar, and so forth.

A fire in one of the fireplaces, usually allowed to die down during the night, had been built up by Mr. Sloan and filled the room with light. Sir Henry gazed around curiously. Tables, cabinets, and washstands occupied the central room. Large pots hung on hooks set in the timber beams that ran overhead. Other utensils stood in rows on the inner wall.

Everything was neat, clean, and well organized, reminding Sir Henry of a military camp.

"My lord, I have everything arranged over here," said Mr. Sloan.

"Allow me a moment, please, Mr. Sloan," said Sir Henry. "I have never been in this kitchen or even gave it much thought." He walked over to study with interest a copper-bottomed kettle. "Copper, you see, to better disseminate the heat."

Henry regarded the kitchen with approval. "Simple order, Mr. Sloan, designed to prepare for the coming chaos. You look amused, Mr. Sloan."

"I was merely wondering what your enemies would say if they could see you now, my lord."

Henry gave a dry chuckle. "Henry Wallace, the most dangerous man in Freya, master spy, deceiver, liar, thief, and assassin with his nose in a stewpot. Was that what you were thinking, Mr. Sloan?"

"Something like that, my lord. Although I confess to being lost at your reference to chaos."

"Breakfast," said Henry. "Picture what will happen early this morning before the sun rises, with Cook and her army rushing furiously about: baking, frying, hauling water, washing, scrubbing, kneading, mixing, pouring. From chaos comes breakfast."

"Yes, my lord," said Mr. Sloan politely.

"When what you really mean is, 'Let's get on with this, my lord.' And so we shall, Mr. Sloan."

Henry turned to look at the table where all of the items he had requested were arranged: a horn of gunpowder; three pistols and a large caliber musket, each with several rounds of lead shot; ten feet of fuse; a stoppered glass vial filled with a dark liquid, and pieces of paper impregnated with wax.

"The servants?" Sir Henry asked.

The servants' quarters were located nearby on the ground floor of the main house. He had told Sloan he did not want the servants to be alarmed or to start talking about any strange noises they might hear in the night.

"I gave Cook a message to let her know you were going to be engaged in a scientific experiment tonight, my lord. She informed the staff and then expressed her hope that the experiment did not cause the milk to sour as happened last time, in the kitchen of the city house."

"Well, then, let's get started."

"What exactly would you like me to do, my lord?" Mr. Sloan asked.

"You will observe."

Sir Henry walked over to the second of the two fireplaces, which was cold. The hearth had been swept and wood stacked preparatory for lighting in the morning.

"I have carried this tankard everywhere with me since its arrival yesterday. I slept last night with my hand upon it, to the bemusement of my lady wife."

Sir Henry stood the tankard in the middle of the fireplace. He then returned to the table, picked up one of the pistols and, sighting down the gun's barrel, fired a shot at the tankard. The force of the shot sent the tankard bouncing around the stone interior of the fireplace with a most ungodly clanging. Henry picked up the other pistol and shot the tankard again, with the same result. He fired a third time with the musket, almost sending the tankard up the chimney.

"Very well, Mr. Sloan, let us see what damage the tankard has sustained."

Sloan picked it up and stared at it.

"Good God, my lord!" said Mr. Sloan, shocked into blasphemy. He looked in amazement at Sir Henry. "There's not a scratch on it!"

He brought the tankard to Sir Henry for inspection. The metal sides were smooth and unblemished, not a dent, not a mark. Yet both men had seen the bullets strike it, seen it ricocheting about the walls of the fireplace, not once, but three times.

"Now for the ultimate test."

Sir Henry picked up the powder horn and poured gunpowder into the tankard, filling it about halfway. He carried it to the fireplace and set it, once more, in the center. He thrust six feet of fuse into the powder in the tankard and used a piece of waxed paper to pack the powder tight. He finished by placing a log on top.

"I do love science," said Sir Henry.

Mr. Sloan appeared dubious. "Before we bring the ceiling down on us, perhaps you could explain what you are trying to do, my lord."

Sir Henry did not immediately answer. He walked over to one of the windows to gaze out at the lights of Haever. Lights of the country he loved.

"We know Rosia has been raiding the treasury to build up its navy, Mr. Sloan. Our Rosian enemies will attack us some time in the not-so-distant future and when they do, we will lose."

Mr. Sloan ventured to protest. Sir Henry shook his head.

"I know our capabilities and those of our enemy. Barring a miracle, their superior ships and the vast number of troops they can hurl at us are greatly against us. Force of will and courage can stand only so long against round shot and musket fire. In the end, Freya will lose.

"Some in the government would have us sue for peace, a treaty between our two nations." Sir Henry glanced back toward the fireplace, the tankard. "You and I are realists, Mr. Sloan. We both know that as long as Rosia exists, Freya will always be in danger. No piece of paper can overcome centuries of hatred. No, Mr. Sloan, there can be no peace."

Sir Henry walked to the other fireplace where the fire was starting to die down. He took a punk from the mantel and lit it, then walked back to his makeshift bomb.

"I said, 'barring a miracle.' You are a religious man, I believe, Mr. Sloan. You may be looking at our miracle."

Sir Henry lit the fuse and then stepped quickly back.

"Might I suggest we should retreat behind that large cupboard, my lord?" Mr. Sloan said, and he had presence of mind enough to take the horn of powder with him as he accompanied his master.

Concealed behind their shield, they watched the sparks progress as the fuse burned. There was a bright light and then the explosion.

The blast echoed off the walls, shaking loose a century of dust, and sent pots and pans crashing to the floor. The two men waited a moment for the dust to dissipate, then—ears ringing—they ventured out from behind the cabinet to inspect the damage.

The log which Sir Henry had placed on the tankard was blown to splinters, some of which were now stuck in the timber beams above their heads. Utensils littered the room, along with chunks of the stone fireplace. The kitchen was in shambles.

"Cook will not be happy with me, I fear," observed Sir Henry.

The two men waded through the debris, searching for the tankard. At last, Mr. Sloan pulled it from the wreckage.

"My lord," he said, awed.

Sir Henry examined the tankard. The two men stared at each other.

The sides were slightly dented, and the bottom of the handle had come off, but the tankard itself was still intact.

"Play devil's advocate, Mr. Sloan," said Sir Henry.

"This is simple magic, my lord," said Mr. Sloan. "Some crafter has strengthened this tankard with magical constructs."

"Do you see any constructs on the vessel, Mr. Sloan? As I recall, you have some talent for magic."

"I am not a crafter, my lord," said Mr. Sloan. "I lack the power to create magical constructs. I do, however, have some small abilities as a channeler, which means I can use existing constructs to cause the desired magical effect."

Sir Henry smiled. "You are a humble man, Mr. Sloan."

"As God requires us all to be, my lord," said Mr. Sloan gravely.

"Which is your humble way of saying that if there were any magical constructs hidden on this tankard, you would see them."

"The sigils that cause the magic would be visible to me, yes, my lord." Mr. Sloan studied the tankard with narrowed eyes. He peered inside it and turned it upside down.

"No sigils, my lord." He looked at Sir Henry with astonishment. "And yet, this *must* be magic, my lord."

"Either magic or a miracle sent to us by Our Heavenly Father, Mr. Sloan. And I doubt if Our Heavenly Father is taking an unusual interest in tankards these days," said Sir Henry dryly.

He was trying to appear calm, but he heard the slight tremor of excitement in his voice and he knew Sloan could hear it, too, by his next question.

"My lord," said Mr. Sloan, after a moment's hesitation, "if this is magic and yet we see no magic what are we looking at?"

"The future of warfare, Mr. Sloan," said Sir Henry. "We have tested it and found it worthy. This simple tankard does not hold ale. It holds victory."

Mr. Sloan did not understand, but he was not there to understand. He was there to follow orders, and Sir Henry was now proceeding to issue them.

"We have much to do and very little time to do it. I am going to set in motion Operation 'Braffa,' as we discussed. A trifle earlier than I had intended to move, but I need the eyes of Rosia to be looking in a different direction, and destabilizing the government of one of her allies should do that nicely. Meanwhile I need you to ride with all speed to my good friend, Admiral Baker. He will be in bed, but you will wake him and give him a note."

Mr. Sloan was supplied, as always, with a writing kit, consisting of a pen, a small bottle of ink, sealing wax, and several blank sheets of note paper, all of which he carried in a compact wooden box tucked into the pocket of his long, black coat. He produced these and handed them to Sir Henry, who wrote swiftly, with large, bold strokes.

I require immediately a fast ship with an experienced crew and a captain who knows how to keep his mouth shut.

"Give this into the admiral's hands."

"Yes, my lord," said Mr. Sloan.

Sir Henry gazed long at the tankard, then he frowned at the letter. Taking up the pen, he crossed out the words: *a captain who knows how to keep his mouth shut* and scribbled something else. Sir Henry folded the letter. Mr. Sloan dripped the sealing wax on the fold. Sir Henry pressed a signet ring he wore in the wax. He did not sign the letter.

"The admiral will know my seal," said Sir Henry.

"Yes, my lord," said Mr. Sloan.

"When he has read the letter, you will take the usual precautions."

"Of course, my lord. The letter will be magically burned to ashes, the ashes stirred, and then mixed with wine and tossed into the slop jar."

Henry nodded and the two men parted.

As Mr. Sloan left upon his errand, he reflected that he had seen much in his thirty-five years, twenty-two of which had been spent in the service of his country. He was noted for his extraordinary calm. He was never rattled, rarely impressed. Yet now, as he hurried to the stables, he noted that his hand, which was holding the letter, was shaking with excitement.

Sir Henry had written, beneath the slashed-out words, this sentence:

I need a captain and crew who are expendable.

Chapter One

Scripture tells us the Breath of God is the echo of God's voice. The magic in the Breath is the Word of God. The Breath of God upholds the seven continents and the thousands of small islands that make up the world of Aeronne. The Breath contains a gas that gives lift to the ships that carried the Four Saints in their blessed efforts to spread the Word of God across Aeronne and establish the Church of the Breath. The Breath separates the world above from the Hell below where dwells the Fiend and Foe of God, Aertheum.

Praise God in his Greatness.

—From the writings of Father Osric Eihnhardt,
Church Historian

THE EVENTS THAT WOULD EVENTUALLY SHAKE the foundations of the Church of the Breath of God, threaten to topple two monarchies, and plunge the world of Aeronne into war began simply enough in a modest house on the Boulevard of Saints, city of Evreux, continent of Rosia, year of Our Lord, 516 DT (abbreviation for Dark Tide) at six of the clock in the evening and began with the words, "We are broke."

The words were spoken by one Monsieur Rodrigo de Villeneuve to his friend, Lord Captain Stephano de Guichen, formerly of the Dragon Brigade, and they would never be recorded in any history book.

Rodrigo placed an iron-banded heavy wooden box on

the table where the members of the Cadre of the Lost were finishing supper. He touched the box and a magical sigil flared into light, warning anyone trying to tamper with the box that he was about to meet a most unpleasant fate. Rodrigo removed the sigil by tracing another sigil over it, then thrust an iron key into the lock, turned it, and opened the lid. He removed three small cloth bags, and placed a bag in front of Dag Thorgrimson, another bag in front of Miri McPike, and a third in front of Miri's younger sister, Gythe. He then brought out a slim leather-bound ledger and thumped it down on the table.

"That doesn't bode well," said Dag, eyeing the ledger gloomily.

"Nor does the heft of this," said Miri. "So much smaller than the job we did for that bastard, Le Marc."

She measured the weight of the coins in the cloth bag with her hand, then opened it and poured the contents into her palm. The small pile was comprised mostly of large copper ten-pennies with a few small silver coins thrown in.

Rodrigo opened the ledger. "That's because we had bills to pay. I paid for the repairs on the *Cloud Hopper* and for a crafter to fix Dag's stowaway pistol and I compensated the Han brothers for their services. You know the Han brothers—payment at once for services rendered, or they break your kneecaps."

He cast a severe glance at Dag. "That gunsmith crafter friend of yours was extremely expensive."

"Better to be safe than sorry," said Dag imperturbably. "Especially with a weapon that can blow off my hand."

"I notice you and Stephano didn't take a share of the money," said Miri, frowning

"I told you," said Rodrigo, "we're broke. For the moment, Stephano and I can survive. I have my allowance. Our esteemed captain has his military pension—such as it is."

He looked at Stephano and added, with an exasperated sigh, "Would someone wake him up?"

Stephano heard Rodrigo's voice, but he wasn't attending

to the words. He had taken a sip of the Duke of Bourlet's favorite red wine and was holding the liquid in his mouth as he had been taught, detecting the various flavors: black fruit, chocolate, leather, and violets. The taste brought back memories: the smell of the herbs and spices used to marinate the roasted beef, the sound of his father's ringing laughter, the sparkle of the crystal goblets in the candlelight, the sense of warmth and camaraderie, the sense of family.

Stephano swallowed the wine, the last dregs left in the glass. He kept his eyes closed. Beneath his hand was fine linen, silver knives and forks and spoons, porcelain plates painted with dragons. Cut roses in crystal vases added their own scent to the air. He was fifteen and the fifteen-year-old Stephano looked around the table at his family and friends and knew that he was blessed . . .

"Stephano," said Miri, giving his arm a shake.

"I'm here," said Stephano.

He held a cracked crockery mug filled with beer, not wine, and not very good beer at that. Beneath his hand was the wood of the kitchen table, a tin plate, a knife that didn't match the spoon, and a fork with a bent prong. The smell of a stewed chicken, boiled greens, and warm bread filled the small kitchen. The raspberry jam and butter had ended up, once again, in front of Dag.

Miri had noted its movement and was whispering something, with a giggle, to Gythe. Her sister smiled and caught hold of Doctor Ellington just as he jumped onto the table in the fond but vain hope that no one would notice a twenty-pound, orange-striped tabby cat licking the butter. Gythe bumped heads with the cat, whose rumbling purr resonated around the small kitchen, then handed the bag of coins back to Rodrigo. She made a sign with her hand.

Miri translated, "We will contribute our share to the cause."

She tossed her bag back to Rodrigo.

"What the Hell," said Dag. "Who needs to eat?" He handed over his bag.

Thirty-four-year-old Stephano de Guichen looked around the table at this family, at those who had become his family, and knew that he was blessed.

"I heard you," said Stephano, sighing. He kicked out a chair and propped his booted feet up onto it and leaned back. "You said we were broke."

"Perhaps I overstated the case a bit to catch your attention," said Rodrigo. "Let me put it this way—we are in less crushing debt than we were before the job."

"In other words, they're not going to throw me in debtor's prison today," said Stephano.

"*Today,*" Rodrigo emphasized. "I make no guarantee for the morrow. If you would like to see the bills, we have them from the butcher, the baker, the candlestick maker—"

"Very funny," said Stephano, growling. He glanced over his shoulder at an elderly man seated in a rocking chair in a cozy corner by the kitchen fire. "We are finished, Benoit. You may clear. And I'd like another mug of beer."

"Very good, sir," said Benoit, and, reaching for his cane, he made a feeble attempt to rise from the chair.

He sank back down with a groan.

"What's wrong now?" Stephano asked testily.

"Touch of gout, sir," said Benoit. "The old complaint. But, you notice, sir, that I don't complain. If you'll give me a moment, sir . . ."

Benoit placed his gnarled hands on the arms of the rocking chair and tried again, pitifully, to heave himself to his feet. He glanced at them out of the corner of his eye. They sat at the table, waiting. Benoit gave another groan.

Miri bit her twitching lip. Exchanging laughing glances with her sister, she rose briskly to her feet, walked over to the old man, and rested her hands on his shoulders.

"Don't trouble yourself, Mr. Benoit," she said solicitously, giving him a soothing pat. "Gythe and I will do the clearing and the washing."

"Ah, thank you, my dears," said Benoit gratefully.

Stephano glared at the old man, who pretended not to

see as he settled himself comfortably back in his chair. Grabbing his mug, Stephano followed Miri into the cold storage room, where Gythe was placing the butter on a high shelf, out of the reach of Doctor Ellington.

Miri turned to face Stephano and, winking, said loudly, "I think it's a disgrace, the way you make that poor sick old man wait on you hand and foot."

"He's the family retainer! It's his job!" said Stephano, pitching his voice so that Benoit could hear. "And poor sick old man, my ass! Only this afternoon I saw Benoit running down the street in hot pursuit of one of the local lads who had snatched his wig off his head. The lad outdistanced him, but not by much."

"He'd have been sorry if I'd have caught him!" Benoit stated, shaking his cane.

Stephano and Miri looked at each other and laughed.

"And, by the way," said Stephano, grinning, "when did you ever see Benoit wait on me or anyone else?"

Stephano reached for the beer pitcher and saw that it was empty. He gave the barrel an experimental kick. The barrel rang hollow. The beer, too, was almost depleted and there wasn't money for more. His grin vanished. He heaved a sigh and handed Miri the mug for washing.

"Benoit has free room and board, and I never knew one old man could eat so much. As for drink, he always has such a pleasant beery smell about him." Stephano kicked the barrel again and muttered, "I should chuck him out into the street."

"Then why don't you?" Miri asked pertly.

She left the cold room and returned to the kitchen, where she took out the washtub and filled it with hot water from the kettle. Gythe, escorted by Doctor Ellington, returned to the table and picked up the plates and mugs and flatware.

"I'll tell you why," Miri said, answering her own question. She plunged the plates into the water and began vigorously scrubbing. "He *is* the old family retainer. The only family you have."

Stephano reached into the washtub, took hold of Miri's red, sudsy hands, and brought them to his lips. "Not the only family. I was thinking that this evening."

He smiled down into Miri's green eyes and brushed a lock of flame-red hair back from her pretty, sun-freckled face. The two had met five years ago; the night Stephano had resigned his commission as an officer in the Dragon Brigade. All he had ever aspired to do in his life was to follow in the footsteps of his father and grandfather and be a Dragon Knight. He had served proudly in the Dragon Brigade for almost ten years. But King Alaric had disbanded the Dragon Brigade, claiming his "modern" navy had no need for dragons. Stephano had resigned in furious protest, and the admiralty had been only too happy to accept his resignation.

That night, Stephano had put on his full dress uniform with the dragons embroidered on the leather flight coat and then thrown his commission into the fire. Then he sat, watching his past burn to ashes, drinking to his own misery. He was alone; his friend Rodrigo having traveled to visit his parents in the Duchy of Argonne, where they had been exiled.

Stephano had gone out for a walk, taking a bottle of wine with him for company. He had wandered the streets of Evreux, paying no heed to where he was going. He found himself near the dockyards, where a host of Trundler houseboats, notable for their brightly colored balloons and sails, and short, stubby wings, had taken up residence. In a field nearby, the Trundlers were having some sort of celebration, perhaps a wedding or a funeral. With them, it was hard to distinguish which.

The Trundlers were rovers, belonging to no country, paying allegiance to no king or queen. They were loyal only to their own people. Governments down through the years had given up attempting to impose any sort of regulation over them, perhaps out of some sort of sense of world-encompassing guilt; these nations having come together to defeat and sink Glasearrach, the island the Trundlers had once called home, with heavy, though unintentional (so the governments claimed) loss of life.

Trundlers had their own laws. They tried those who broke them in their own courts. Trundler laws differed somewhat from the laws imposed by kings and princes. Smuggling and thieving were viewed with a tolerant eye since one had to earn a living, whereas murderers could be executed on the spot.

Sometimes such small differences in the legal system did tend to cause friction between Trundlers and the local authorities, who occasionally tried to raid Trundler gatherings. Thus, the sight of Stephano, wearing his full dress uniform, with his sword at this side, had roused intense and immediate suspicion among the young men of the Trundler community.

Six young toughs, strong and muscular, armed with clubs and flaming torches, had confronted Stephano. He could have apologized and talked his way out, but he was in a mood for a fight. The next thing he knew, he had been lying on the ground, his skull cracked, pain everywhere, looking up into the flashing green eyes and freckled face of a lovely young woman.

She had examined him, then had risen to her feet and immediately began to lay into the young men, hitting and slapping them and kicking them in the shins.

"Can't you see the dragon he's wearing, you daft buggers?" she had cried.

The young toughs had crumbled beneath her fury, mumbling in their defense that: "it was dark;" "a king's man is a king's man;" "he should've said something;" and the like until the woman had grown weary and they had been able to escape her wrath.

"I'm sorry, my dear," the woman had said to him, rubbing her stinging palms. "The young fools didn't know who you were."

Stephano had smiled at her blissfully and then thrown up on her shoes.

He had regained consciousness in a houseboat belonging to the woman's uncle, where he was a guest for the next week until the young woman deemed he was healthy enough to leave. Her name was Miri, she had told him, and she was a Trundler Lore Master. Since most Trundlers could neither read nor write, Miri and those like her were responsible for keeping the Trundler history, the old tales and legends, alive.

Miri had realized that simply handing down histories from one generation to another had resulted in inaccuracies and contradictions. Most Trundlers didn't care, but Miri wanted to know the truth behind the myths, and she had decided the only way to find out was to seek the facts in books and that involved learning to read. She had taught herself, with the help of a priest, and had learned the fascinating fact that the history of the Trundlers and those of the great dragon families were entwined, though just exactly how was lost in the mists of time. Miri had longed to talk to the dragons about this and had sought an invitation into the households of the noble dragon families. They had looked down their long and elegant snouts at a Trundler and never even bothered to respond. Then Stephano, a former Dragon Knight, had come into her camp, and her cousins had beaten him senseless.

Miri had healed his wounds, and he had gained her access into the houses of some of the dragons with whom he had served. She and Stephano were close in age; both having been around thirty at the time, and it was inevitable that they became lovers.

Any number of beautiful ladies of the court would have been happy to invite the dashing young former captain of the Dragon Brigade to their salons or even their beds to listen to his troubles. For reasons of his own, Stephano did not trust beautiful ladies of the court.

He trusted Miri, who was always honest—brutally so. Their relationship had been complicated over the years. Once he had thought he was in love with her and once she had thought she was in love with him. If these periods had coincided, the relationship might have worked. As it was, there had been confusion, hurt feelings, tears, and recriminations. Then, one night, as they lay in bed talking, they came to the realization they were friends.

"So much more comfortable than being lovers, my dear," Miri told him. That night, she ended the affair.

"I want you to meet my sister," she said. "And I only invite friends to my home. Never my lovers."

Home was the sisters' houseboat, the *Cloud Hopper*.

Stephano might have smiled at this notion of Miri's that only those she considered friends were allowed to visit, but when he met Gythe, he realized that Miri had honored him with a special trust, one he would forever cherish.

Gythe was twenty-one—fourteen years younger than her sister. But she seemed more like a child of fourteen. She was beautiful, with hazel eyes and hair the color of champagne. Where Miri's eyes glinted with green flashes of laughter and merriment and her legendary temper, Gythe's eyes were wandering, searching, shadowed. She never spoke a word. She was not mute, for though she would not talk, she could sing, accompanying herself on the harp.

"Gythe's never been quite right since 'Then,'" Miri would always say of her sister. Miri never told Stephano what happened "Then . . ." When he once hinted that he would like to know, Miri said brusquely, "No good will come of talking of it." By the glint in her green eyes, he knew to let it drop.

Stephano guessed "Then" had something to do with the deaths of their parents and the fact that the two girls were on their own, but beyond that, nothing more.

He was thinking all this, remembering. Miri's laughter brought him back to the kitchen.

"If we're a family, we're the bloodiest, messed-up family there ever was, my dear," Miri told him.

"You're right there," said Stephano.

When the dishes were done and Miri had returned from

dumping the water out of the wash bin, Dag placed his large hands on the table and levered himself slowly to his feet. The table, which was made out of a butcher's block and was heavy and solid, groaned a bit beneath the big man's weight. Dag Thorgrimson was six-foot-two, a Guundaran mercenary, and he was also part of the "bloodiest, messed-up" family. He and Stephano had met on opposing sides of a battle eight years ago—a battle Stephano had always considered both sides lost.

"We should be starting for home, girls," said Dag in his deep, grave voice.

He was invariably grave, serious, and earnest; he rarely smiled. He dressed in plain black clothing. His hair was cut short in the military style, and he had the straight and upright bearing of the soldier he had been for many years. He would speak of his past only to say proudly that he had served in the army since he was eight years old, his sergeant father having made his son a drummer. Dag had fought in his first battle at the age of twelve.

Dag and Stephano would often talk of battles in which Stephano had fought. Dag would share his opinion on the strategy or the tactics involved, but he had only once spoken of his own experience, and that had been when Stephano had wanted to hire him to help with a small job.

Dag told Stephano his story, saying that it was only right "the captain" should know what had happened before Stephano put his trust in him. Dag told a horror tale of flame and blood, men dying all around him, men dying because he had ordered them to their deaths. Dag had been the sole survivor. Stephano had listened and, at the end of the recitation, which Dag had made in a low voice, never lifting his head, Stephano had taken the man's hand and shaken it and said in a husky voice that he would be honored to serve with him.

Dag had looked up, perplexed. "Perhaps you didn't understand me, Captain. I ordered those men to die!"

"I understand better than you do, seemingly," Stephano

had answered. "And don't call me 'captain.' We're neither of us in the service of any king. Neither of us will ever order any man into any king's battle again. Let Their Majesties look after themselves."

Miri took down her cloak from the hook on the wall. Gythe picked up the cat.

"If you will settle Doctor Ellington, child," said Dag, turning his back to Gythe, who, with great care, placed the cat on Dag's shoulder.

Doctor Ellington dug his claws into the quilted shoulder padding Dag had added to his coat and purred loudly. Wherever Dag went, the Doctor went with him, riding proudly on the man's shoulder, boldly challenging the world with golden eyes, his striped tail waving like a flag.

"I'll walk with you," said Stephano, taking up his hat.

Miri was fussily wrapping a cloak around Gythe's slender shoulders, Dag was putting on his hat, and Stephano was starting to open the door when Rodrigo, who had been out of the room, visiting the chamber pot, returned. He saw them preparing to leave and came to an abrupt stop.

"Where do you all think you are going?"

"Home," said Miri, adding teasingly, "to revel in our riches."

"Oh, no, you're not," said Rodrigo severely. He pulled out a chair and pointed to it. "We are all of us going to stay here until we figure out how to solve our deplorable financial insolvency."

The four looked at each other, sighed, and came trailing back. Stephano took off his hat and tossed it onto a marble bust of His Majesty, King Alaric, which graced a table. The marble bust had been a gift from a grateful nation to Lord Captain Stephano de Guichen of the Dragon Brigade for meritorious action. Rodrigo had once asked Stephano why he kept the bust. Stephano had replied that on days when he woke feeling a brotherhood with all the world, the sight of the king's face reminded him that there was still one man on this world he hated.

Dag removed his own hat and sat with it in his lap. Miri and Gythe took off their cloaks and sat down at the table. They stared at each other blankly. The only sound was Doctor Ellington's throaty purr. The cat perched on Dag's shoulder, his eyes golden slits, kneading his claws into the padding.

"Come now," said Rodrigo at last. "Someone must know somebody who is trying to smuggle jewels to his exiled family or wants to avoid paying the king's tax on a shipment of brandy. You, Miri, have you talked to your Trundler uncle and myriad Trundler cousins? Do they have any jobs for us? Dag, what about your underworld connections?"

Dag's face darkened. His brow came together. His hand, resting on his knee, clenched to a fist.

"Now, now, my friend," said Rodrigo soothingly, "it's no use pretending you did *not* once break legs for a living . . ."

Dag scowled. Stephano saw Rodrigo's life flash before his eyes and he was about to intervene when the meeting was interrupted by the sound of wyvern wings and the clatter of a carriage coming to rest on the cobblestones outside the house. The wyverns' raucous croaks were followed by the voice of the driver shouting at the beasts to settle.

Stephano and his friends all looked at one another. Judging by the sounds of the jingling harness, the scraping of claws on stone, and the wyverns hissing and snorting, the carriage had stopped right outside the front door. Someone arriving in a carriage—a large, airborne carriage—at this hour . . .

"I smell money," said Rodrigo, his nose twitching.

There was a clatter and a scraping noise. The driver was lowering a step for the convenience of the carriage's passenger. Then came the bang of the door knocker.

Stephano turned to Benoit, who was pretending to be asleep in his chair. The knock was repeated with a bit more force. Stephano cleared his throat.

Benoit blinked and opened his eyes, looked about blearily, and said, "Someone at the door, sir."

"I know," said Stephano.

He sat stubbornly in his chair.

Benoit sat in his. After a moment, the old man said wonderingly, as if the thought had just occurred to him, "Would you like *me* to answer that, sir?"

"If it's not too much trouble," said Stephano bitingly.

Groaning, Benoit rose to his feet and began to shuffle across the floor. "If I might suggest, sir, you and Master Rodrigo should remove yourselves to the sitting room. Unless you want your visitor to find you sitting in the kitchen. He might mistake you for the cook."

"By God, he's right," said Rodrigo. "Stephano—sitting room! Run for it!"

The kitchen was on the ground floor at the rear of the two-story house. A back door opened out into a small patch of ground that was meant to be used as a kitchen garden, but which had been turned into an exercise yard. Benoit's rooms were on this level, as well. On the upper floor were a sitting room, two bedrooms, and two dressing rooms for Rodrigo and Stephano, a library, and study.

"We'll stay here in the kitchen," said Miri. She and Gythe and Dag remained seated. "I don't mind being mistaken for the cook."

Stephano flushed. "You know it's not that—"

"I know," said Miri, smiling.

She meant that she and Gythe and Dag weren't "hiding" in the kitchen because Stephano was ashamed of his "lowborn" friends. The three kept out of sight because the Cadre of the Lost often found it advantageous for people to assume there could be no connection between the son of a noble family (albeit a noble family in disgrace), the son of an ambassador, and a mercenary and two Trundlers.

Dag reached into the sleeve of his coat and drew from a hidden pocket a small pistol known as a "stowaway gun." The cheaper models of these guns relied on a flint to strike a spark to fire the weapon. Dag's pistol used magical constructs—a fire sigil carved into the metal—to accomplish the same purpose. Such pistols were expensive because they required the regular services of a crafter to maintain the magic, but Stephano saw to it that his people had only the best. Dag inspected the gun, made certain it was loaded. He nodded at Stephano to indicate readiness.

The cat, Doctor Ellington, seeing the pistol, leaped off Dag's shoulder onto the table and from the table to the floor. Tail bristling with indignation, the Doctor stalked off to the cold room. He disliked loud noises.

"Move! Move!" Rodrigo yelled, grabbing his coat and hustling the reluctant Stephano from behind.

Once in the sitting room, Rodrigo put on his coat and smoothed his brocade vest. Careless of his own appearance, Stephano walked over to the window that looked down into the street. He saw the coat of arms on the door of the carriage and said, "Son of a bitch."

Crossing the room, he flung open the door, and shouted down, "I'm not at home!"

"Very good, sir," said Benoit.

Rodrigo looked out the window and quirked an eyebrow. He remained standing by the window, a smile on his lips, humming a dance tune.

Stephano walked over to the fireplace, where a small fire burned in the grate. Though the days were warm in late spring, the evenings were still chill. He listened to the sound of voices and heard the door bang shut. He smiled in relief and was on his way out the door to rejoin his friends when Benoit came in.

"May I present Monsieur Dargent," Benoit said in a loud voice. "Confidential *valet-de-chambre* to the Countess de Marjolaine."

Stephano's face flushed in anger. "Damn it, Benoit, I told you I wasn't home—"

Benoit, who had now gone conveniently deaf in addition to his other infirmities, stepped aside to allow the gentleman to enter.

"Thank you, Benoit," said Dargent, smiling at the elderly retainer. "Good to see you again."

"Thank *you*, monsieur," said Benoit, bowing. "Always a pleasure."

Stephano caught the flash of silver in the old man's hand.

"Traitor!" Stephano yelled after him as Benoit descended the stairs.

"Perhaps next time, Master, you will answer the door yourself," Benoit returned, pocketing the coin.

Stephano, pointedly leaving the sitting room door open, turned back to glare at Dargent, who smiled at him pleasantly.

"Stephano, you are looking well," said Dargent. "And you, Master Rodrigo. You seem fit. How are your father and mother?"

"In good health, monsieur, thank you," said Rodrigo.

"Your father is ambassador to Estara now, I believe," said Dargent.

Rodrigo bowed. "He was so fortunate to be called out of exile and given that assignment."

"The king's way of making amends," said Dargent.

Rodrigo bowed again in acknowledgment. "His Majesty is the soul of generosity."

Stephano snorted and went to stand by the fireplace. He rested his arm on the mantel and stared moodily into the flames.

"I'd invite you to sit down, Dargent, but you won't be staying that long. What do you want?"

"I have a letter from the countess, Captain," said Dargent. "She asked me to deliver it into your hands."

Though a creature of a court known for its elegant and extravagant dress, Dargent wore tailored clothes in somber colors, as became a man of business. His stockings were snowy white, his buckled shoes polished, and they made no sound as he walked across the carpet. He was even-tempered, quiet of manner, discreet. He handed Stephano a missive that was folded like a cocked hat and sealed with lavender wax bearing the countess' insignia—a bumblebee.

Stephano took the letter from Dargent's hand and tossed it into the fire.

Dargent reached into the pocket of his vest and drew out another letter. "Her Excellency said to give you the second after you destroyed the first."

Stephano's angry flush deepened. He was about to seize the letter and cast it to the same fate as the other one, when Rodrigo, moving with uncustomary speed, plucked the letter from Dargent's hand and withdrew to the window to read it in the failing light. He gave a long, low whistle.

"What does she want?" Stephano asked, glowering.

"You are summoned to attend Her Excellency, the Countess de Marjolaine, in her quarters at the royal palace tomorrow morning at the hour of nine of the clock," said Rodrigo.

Stephano glowered. "I'll see her in—"

"—in the palace, my friend. There's more," said Rodrigo. "It seems the countess has bought up all your debt. Either you favor her with your presence in the morning, or she will demand that the debt be paid in full."

Rodrigo handed Stephano the letter. He glanced over it, then turned to Dargent.

"And, knowing the countess, she'll send me to debtor's prison if my bill is not paid. What's this about?" Stephano asked.

"I am sorry, Captain," Dargent murmured. "I was not apprised."

"Like Hell you weren't," Stephano said, sneering. "You know all the countess' dirty little secrets."

"Perhaps it's a job," Rodrigo suggested in a low voice. "We could use the work. The countess pays well and on time."

"She might *say* it's a job for her, but we would really be working for the king," said Stephano bitterly, *not* bothering to lower his voice.

"Pays well," Rodrigo repeated. "On time."

Stephano watched the first letter dwindle to ashes, then said abruptly, "Tell the countess I will attend her at nine. I'll hear what she has to offer. I can always say no."

"And if you say no, we can always move to Estara," said Rodrigo. "Our creditors might not find us there."

Dargent bowed. "I will show myself out, Captain."

"You do that," said Stephano.

He waited until he heard the front door close, then he picked up his hat and cloak and said shortly, "I'm going for a walk."

"Want company?" Rodrigo asked.

"No," said Stephano.

"What do I tell the others?"

"What you like," said Stephano.

Rodrigo returned to the kitchen alone. Miri, Gythe, Dag, and the cat all looked at him expectantly. Benoit was again pretending to be asleep, but he had his head cocked to hear.

"Benoit told us the man was from the countess," said Miri. "Is it a job? Will Stephano take a job from her?"

"God knows," said Rodrigo, throwing up his hands. "Most of the time, Stephano de Guichen is a rational man. But he loses his head completely when it comes to his mother."

Chapter Two

If one wishes to survive in the Rosian royal court, one must first understand the external politics that drive events in the world of Aeronne. The kingdoms of Bruond and Bheldem both lack internal cohesion and ambition and are currently no threat to anyone. Guundar produces the finest soldiers in Aeronne, willing to work for anyone with the correct amount of gold, mainly because there is no gold for them at home. Travia, home of the Trade Cartel, is an economic powerhouse, yet her small size makes her dependent on others for defense. Estara, birthplace of the Church of the Breath, could be a power in her own right, but has always been overshadowed by Freya and Rosia and sulks over her lowly status. Freya, the second most powerful nation in the world, has fostered an ancient hatred for Rosia, the first most powerful; a hatred that, as one can see from the bloodstained history of these two nations, is most happily and cheerfully returned.

—*Idle Musings on Rosian Politics*
by Rodrigo de Villeneuve

THE NEXT DAY, STEPHANO ROSE AT HIS USUAL TIME. He ate breakfast, ran through his daily fencing practice, washed, and dressed. Hearing the sound of the carriage arriving at the door, he shouted to Benoit that he was leaving and descended the stairs that led to the main entryway. Stephano cast an uncaring glance at himself in the mirror, put on his hat (which he noted had been brushed, the brown plume fluffed up a bit) and was almost ready to go out the front door when Rodrigo opened it and walked inside.

"I was just on my way to join you at the palace," said Stephano. "I thought you were 'visiting a friend.'"

Rodrigo regarded Stephano's green breeches, which were tied below the knee, his dark green stockings, light green waistcoat, and dark green coat, lacking adornment, with frowning disapproval.

"I thought I might find you in this state. One reason I returned early. We are attending court, not storming the battlements at Vertin. Benoit!"

"I wash my hands of him, sir!" came the querulous response from the kitchen.

"Back to the dressing room," said Rodrigo, placing his hand on Stephano's shoulder and shoving him toward the stairs.

Seeing Stephano's rebellious look, Rodrigo added briskly, "Pays well, on time."

"You'll find his court clothes laid out on the bed, sir!" Benoit called from below.

Stephano heaved a sigh and allowed himself to be propelled up to his dressing room. "I'm only doing this for Miri and the others, Rigo. If it were up to me, I'd starve before I went groveling to my mother."

Once Stephano was properly attired, Rodrigo inspected him. "The sleeves are frayed at the cuffs. The coat is at least two years out of fashion, but the material is of the finest quality and the style is classic, so I am not *completely* ashamed to be seen at court with you. Let me tie your cravat."

With a suffering air, Stephano let his friend tie the white cravat, edged with a hint of lace, around his throat, and regarded himself in the mirror. He privately conceded that he did look good. The knee-length silver-trimmed coat was fitted at the waist, and powder blue in color with turned back cuffs that showed the lace-edged sleeves of his white shirt. His waistcoat was of blue-and-green brocade. He wore breeches of the same blue color tied with ribbons below the knee, white stockings, and black shoes. His rapier hung from an embroidered baldric draped over his shoulder.

Stephano steadfastly refused to wear the powdered wigs then fashionable in the royal court. His sandy-blond, shoulder-length hair was tied at the back of his neck with a blue ribbon. He was clean-shaven, a task he performed himself, given that Benoit's hands were too shaky these days to be trusted with a razor. Stephano's blue eyes were changeable, becoming gray with anger or determination. He was of medium height with the light-muscled, fine-boned build of a Dragon Knight and an upright military bearing. His face tended to be stern and unsmiling, except when he was around his friends, at which time he would relax and lower his guard.

Rodrigo draped his arm around his friend's shoulder and regarded the two of them in the mirror.

Unlike Stephano, Rodrigo was dressed in the latest fashion. His long, fitted coat was mauve, decorated with gold buttons and golden embroidery. His deep cuffs were a darker mulberry. His shirt was dripping with lace, and he wore a lace collar. His stockings were white. He also did not wear a wig, preferring to show off the brown curls that framed his face. Women termed his brown eyes "melting." His face was long, his chin slightly pointed. His mouth quirked with fun and good humor. He was hopeless with a rapier and terrifying to his friends with firearms. His tongue was his weapon, he liked to say.

Rigo—as he was known—was thirty-three, and he and Stephano had been firm friends from childhood, despite their contrasting natures. Stephano was energetic, resolute, disciplined (except when it came to money). Rodrigo was indolent, vacillating, with not an ounce of self-discipline (except when it came to money).

Rodrigo was also a brilliant crafter and could have risen to the top of that profession, but he had studied magic only sporadically, dabbling in what interested him and forgoing the rest. Consequently, he had been thrown out of the University, to the dismay of his parents, who, however, continued to dote on him. He was the spoiled third son, with no income other than what he earned with the Cadre of the Lost and a modest stipend from his parents. Rodrigo was most at home in drawing rooms and salons. He knew everyone in court, knew the gossip about all of them, and he acquired most of the Cadre's jobs.

Rodrigo smiled. "You would never know I was forced to pawn your dress sword to pay for the carriage."

"You did what?" Stephano demanded, rounding on his friend. "My sword with the gold basket hilt? That was a gift—"

"And we will get it back from the pawn shop," said Rodrigo soothingly. "Just mention to the countess that you could use an advance on payment, will you?"

"I haven't agreed to take this job yet," said Stephano angrily. He snatched his best tricorn hat, which was the current fashion, since it could be folded and tucked under the arm, and stomped down the stairs.

Benoit was there to see them off. The old man smiled to see Stephano and a wistful look came into the weak eyes. "I wish your father could see you, sir. You do him proud."

"He wouldn't be proud of the fact that I'm selling my soul to the king," Stephano muttered.

"He would, sir," said Benoit stoutly. "Your father, Lord Julian, God rest him, was a practical man."

"My father wasn't practical at all, you know," said Stephano somberly to Rodrigo, as they entered the carriage. "Julian de Guichen was a man who sacrificed his wealth, his lands, and eventually his life for a hopeless cause, all in the name of honor and loyalty and friendship."

"The apple did not fall far from the tree," observed Rodrigo.

"Don't try flattering me," said Stephano, glowering. "It won't work."

"Take the rest of the day off, Benoit," Rodrigo called out the carriage window before shutting it. "We will dine out."

Rodrigo told the driver their destination and shut the carriage door. The driver nodded his head at his boy, who released the mooring line that secured the carriage to the ground, then took his place at the rear. The wyvern was harnessed to the carriage by long tethers attached to breast and shoulders. Magic used in the construction of the carriage added strength to the thin wooden walls while keeping the weight as low as possible. Internal reservoirs or "lift tanks" held the refined and purified "Breath of God" that provided much of the vehicle's buoyancy, with a balloon for additional lift.

The balloon was red in color, the carriage blue. One could always tell a rented carriage by the red balloons. The driver, mounted on the seat in front of the carriage, began channeling the magical energy that existed naturally in the world into a brass control panel. A series of constructs, set into the brass itself, allowed the driver control over the levels of buoyancy in the two primary lift tanks located on either side of the carriage, and the forward and rear stabilizing tanks. From the brass panel, the driver could also control the large multichambered red balloon tethered to the top of carriage.

The carriage's passenger compartment could seat four comfortably. The leaded glass windows were covered with lace curtains to provide the occupants a degree of privacy. The blue-lacquered exterior was waxed till it shone and was set off by polished brass fixtures and lanterns.

When the carriage was clear of the ground, the driver gave three short tweets from a whistle, letting anyone nearby know that they were preparing to leave. Next, he clucked at the wyvern and poked the creature in the back with a prod.

The wyvern angrily whipped around its head and snapped at the prod. Wyverns are temperamental and stupid, but the driver was used to such behavior from his steed. He poked the wyvern again, and the beast sullenly flapped its wings and took off.

Stephano threw himself into a corner of the conveyance and sat there, brooding. As always, when he was forced to pay a visit to his mother, he was in a foul mood. His thoughts carried him back to the past. He blamed Benoit for having brought up his father, but it wasn't the old man's fault. Stephano would have thought about his father in any case. He could not help thinking about his father whenever he was forced to visit his mother.

Cecile de Marjolaine, daughter of the wealthy and powerful Count de Marjolaine, was introduced at court when she was sixteen, having the honor to become one of the ladies-in-waiting to the queen. Cecile was an extraordinarily beautiful young woman, as well as being the only heir to her father's vast fortune. Both wealthy and lovely, she was the jewel of the court. Nobles and princes cast their hearts at her feet. Even King Alaric, newly ascended to the throne on the sudden death of his father, was said to be enamored of her.

Cecile was flattered by the attention, but her own heart remained untouched until she met the handsome and dashing young Dragon Knight, Sir Julian de Guichen. The two fell deeply, hopelessly in love—hopeless because the count had determined that his only child, his beautiful daughter, would marry well. De Guichen was merely the son of a knight and not a particularly wealthy knight at that. To make matters worse, the de Guichens were loyal friends with the king's avowed enemy, the Duke de Bourlet.

The two young people knew only that they adored each other. None of the rest mattered. And then Cecile discovered she was pregnant. She was frightened, but was also ecstatic. She and Julian would run away to be married and live happily ever after. Before she could tell Julian the wonderful news, however, the Dragon Brigade was summoned to duty and he had to leave. The two had only a few fleeting moments together before he was gone.

Cecile had no mother in whom to confide; her mother having died when she was young, and she continued to dream her pretty dreams until the day she was confronted by Lady Adele, an older woman, who was also one of the queen's ladies-in-waiting. The sharp-eyed Adele had noted Cecile's swelling breasts, expanding waistline, and her unfortunate tendency to vomit on a daily basis. Lady Adele spoke to the girl in private and in a few stark words shattered the pretty dreams by making Cecile face cold, ugly reality.

Did Cecile honestly think the Count de Marjolaine would allow his only daughter, who stood to inherit one of the largest fortunes in the kingdom, to marry a penniless knight?

"Your noble father would have Julian killed first," said Lady Adele pitilessly. "And don't think he could not do it and get away with it. If you truly love Julian, you will cast him off and never speak to him again."

Cecile was forced to admit the lady was right. Her father was known by everyone to be a cold-blooded, ruthless, calculating man. She cried herself to sleep every night, Julian's letters in her hand.

Cecile was fast reaching the point where she could no longer hide her pregnancy. She had planned to travel to Lady Adele's country estate to have the child in secret, when she received an abrupt summons to return home. The count did not ask her if the rumors he had heard about her were true. One look at her swollen belly provided the answer.

He demanded to know the name of the father. Cecile steadfastly refused to tell him. He called her a whore and struck her across the face, knocking her to the floor. His large emerald ring split her lip, leaving a small, white scar visible to this day. He sent his daughter to a nunnery, where she remained in seclusion until her baby, a son, was born.

Cecile had not written to tell Julian of her pregnancy, for she knew he would come to her and that would place his life in danger. She had determined to keep the name of the baby's father a secret. But her labor was long and difficult and at one point Cecile was in such agony and was so exhausted that she feared she would die. In her despair, she confided the name of the baby's father to the Mother Superior.

Cecile gave birth to a son. The nuns allowed her to spend a day—one glorious day—with her baby. Then, on the count's orders, the child was taken away to be placed in the Church orphanage.

The Mother Superior was a woman of strong convictions. She came from a noble family herself and did not think it proper that the child of a knight should be raised in an orphanage, never knowing his father. The Mother Superior wrote to Sir Julian, telling him he had a son.

Julian was astounded and confused. He could not help but wonder why Cecile had not told him. He traveled with the family retainer, Benoit, to the nunnery and demanded to see Cecile, but was told she had returned home. She had left no message for him. All he could think was that she no longer loved him. The Mother Superior brought the baby to him. Heartbroken and bewildered, Julian took his son home.

Several months later, after she had recovered from her ordeal, Cecile returned to court. She was more beautiful than before, if that were possible, but her beauty, which had been warm and vibrant, seemed now cold and glittering. She became the open and avowed lover of King Alaric, a calculated move, meant to ward off the men her father would have forced her to marry. Whenever she received an offer, she was able to manipulate the jealous and grasping Alaric into refusing to give his consent.

Julian had secretly dreamed his own pretty dream. He nursed the fond belief that Cecile still loved him and that someday they would be together. Then he heard about the affair. Not only was she openly involved with another man, that man was the enemy of Julian's liege lord, the Duke de Bourlet. If Cecile had stabbed Julian in the heart with a dagger, she could have caused no greater pain.

Sir Julian was a chivalrous and honorable knight. He would not say a word against Cecile to anyone. Her name never crossed his lips. There were those in his household who knew the truth—or thought they did—and they were free in venting their rage against the woman who had hurt their beloved friend and master.

Only one man, Julian's friend, Sir Ander Martel, the baby's godfather, knew Cecile, knew her father, and knew or was able to guess both sides of the tragic tale. He tried at one point to tell Julian that Cecile had done this for his sake, because she feared for his life. The moment Sir Ander mentioned her name, Julian told him coldly that if he wanted to continue to be friends, he would never speak of her again. Julian de Guichen would eventually learn the truth, but, sadly, only on the night before his execution. Too late to tell his son.

Stephano, growing up, knew he was different from other children in that he did not have a mother. He was not particularly bothered by this lack. He and his father were extremely close. Sir Julian always refused to speak ill of Cecile, but Stephano's grandfather felt no such compunction. When Stephano was twelve, his embittered grandfather summoned the boy to his study and told Stephano the truth—his side of it, which had been further tainted over the years by a hatred of King Alaric and his mistress, who, on the death of her father, was now the wealthy and powerful Countess Cecile de Marjolaine.

Sir Ander, as Stephano's godfather, could have told the boy what he knew, but that was the time Julian's friend and patron, the Duke de Bourlet, had openly split from the king. The seeds of rebellion were being sown. Sir Ander did not like King Alaric, but he believed a man should be loyal to the Crown and, although he knew the duke was in the right, in that he had been goaded past endurance into fighting, Sir Ander did not join in the rebellion. He and Julian remained friends, though they were on opposing sides of the terrible conflict.

As Stephano sat in the carriage, his hat on his knee, he heard again his grandfather's bitter, hate-filled tirade against his mother, words forever seared in the boy's memory. He was jolted from his dark reverie when Rodrigo got into a heated argument with the carriage driver, claiming that the man was deliberately taking them out of their way in order to charge them more money.

"Look, Stephano!" Rodrigo cried, pointing out the carriage's glass window, "Look where this son of a goat has taken us! Out past the Rim!"

The continent of Rosia was surrounded by an ocean of air, as were all the continents—the Seven Sisters—of the world of Aeronne. The air, the Breath of God, with its magical properties, was the "sea" on which floated the continents and islands that made up the world of Aeronne.

Similar to the water in the greater inland seas and lakes, the Breath had currents and moods. The wispy, peach-colored mist of a calm day could quickly darken to the deep reddish orange of a coming water storm with winds that would whip the surface of the Breath to a froth, lifting the heavier clouds from below to wreak havoc with the controls on an airship.

The mists that were wispy and thin as silken scarves grew thicker as one sank deeper into the Breath, becoming almost liquid at the bottom, or so learned men theorized. No one knew for certain what lay at the bottom because no one had ever been able to penetrate that deep and survive.

Where the Breath met the shoreline of the continents was called the Rim. To sail beyond the Rim meant leaving land behind and venturing into the mists of the Breath.

The view out the carriage window was spectacular and, as always, caused Stephano's heart to contract with both pain and pleasure. When he had been a Dragon Knight, riding the thermals of the Breath, flying among the tendril-like mists, he would always take a moment to view the continent from this angle: the jagged edges of distant mountains, the green of hills, the smoky haze rising from the multitude of

chimneys, the airships of all sizes and types sailing in and
out of the bustling port of Evreux, the capital city of Rosia
and one of the largest and busiest ports in the world.

He and his dragon mount, Lady Cam, would always share
this moment. He would laughingly point out his family's former small estate, tucked somewhere in those green hills, and
she would, with more gravity, mention *her* family's estate in
the Montagnes Impériale, the mountain range which the
dragons called home. The two would ride the mists, knowing
themselves—in the dragon's grace and beauty and Stephano's skills as a rider—superior to those who were forced to
rely on wood and magic and silk balloons to sail the Breath.

Lady Cam was dead now. She had died in battle eight
years ago, struck down by friendly cannon fire from a ship
of their own fleet. She had died and so had the Dragon Brigade. And so had Stephano, in a way.

Stephano looked at the clouds and took note of the wind
speed and the direction the wind was blowing, and then
endeavored to make Rodrigo understand that the carriage
driver knew what he was doing. Given the conditions, he
was taking the best route to the palace.

"Otherwise, the ride would be bumpy. We would be
blown all over the sky, and you would be air sick and complain about that," said Stephano.

Rodrigo gave way with such good grace that Stephano
suspected his friend had started this row simply to shake
Stephano out of his gloomy mood. By that time, they were
once more over land and the palace was in view.

The Sunset Palace was a breathtaking sight, whether
seen by day, suspended in the air above the lake, mirrored
in the waters below, or at night, when its lighted windows,
shining in the darkness, rivaled the stars. The palace was, as
its name implied, most beautiful in the twilight, when magical constructs set in the walls reflected the colors of the sky,
causing the walls to change color from pink to orange, purple, and blue.

Simple in design, the palace was a square with a tower at

each of the four corners. The entrance consisted of another, smaller square constructed inside the first, with a smaller tower at each of those four corners. The palace's beauty lay in the graceful magnificence of the towers and the fanciful construction of the one hundred chimneys, each of which was of a different design, so that the palace, from a distance, resembled the skyline of a city.

The Sunset Palace was the largest floating structure in the known world. The construction of the palace had started during the reign of King Alaric's grandfather. He had died while the building was still on the ground. Alaric's father, the late king, had brought crafters from all over to place the magical constructs that had at last lifted the palace up to the heavens, elevating the King of Rosia to a somewhat equal footing with God.

Stephano noted that several of those fancy new warships drifted in the air near the palace, keeping constant vigil. The ships used the liquid form of the Breath, known as the Blood of God, to stay afloat. The liquid was stored in lift tanks in the hull near the base of the wings and ballast tanks on the mast, which meant the ships had no balloons, only sails. Faster and lighter, these were the ships that had replaced the Dragon Brigade. The navy stood guard because the palace had minimal defenses. Though the towers and walls were strengthened by magical constructs, they were mainly for decoration. Most of the magic went into keeping the palace up in the air. The warships and the palace guards, mounted on wyverns, patrolled the perimeter, turning away those who did not have business with the royal court.

A series of buoys, marked with different colored flags, floated in the sky, forming lanes through which carriages were funneled. The large and splendid carriages of the nobility, sometimes drawn by as many as four wyverns, entered one lane. Delivery vehicles entered another. Hired hacks traveled yet another. Stephano's carriage took its place in line with those.

When they reached the arrival point, a palace guard

looked inside the carriage and, recognizing Rodrigo, exchanged a few pleasantries and waved them on. The carriage flew to the entrance and dropped down onto the open-air paved courtyard. The wyvern rested, tucking its head beneath its wing. The driver dismounted and lowered the steps. Rodrigo and Stephano descended. Rodrigo paid the driver, who touched his hand to his hat and, prodding the wyvern into flight, sailed off.

A line of footmen stood waiting at the entrance to greet visitors and escort them into the palace, taking them where they were supposed to go, prohibiting them (politely) from going where they weren't wanted, and generally keeping people from getting lost. The palace had over four hundred rooms and a confusing number of hallways and staircases and corridors, and even Rodrigo, who visited the palace two or three days a week, found the footmen helpful.

Stephano mentioned the name of the Countess de Marjolaine and showed the footman her letter with her seal. The footman nodded and started out.

"I'll come with you," said Rodrigo.

"To make sure I go through with this?" Stephano growled.

"Yes. And I have nothing better to do until the royal levee, which is later this morning," said Rodrigo.

The halls of the palace were wide and spacious with wood-beam ceilings and parquet floors. Paintings, colorful tapestries, and deer with immense racks of antlers adorned the walls. Suits of armor from bygone days stood in niches in the walls.

"Hollow knights with no heads," remarked Stephano. "How fitting."

"*Do* keep your voice down," said Rodrigo.

Three young ladies of the court, dressed in colorful satin gowns, with the hems pinned up to reveal their decorated petticoats; long, pointed bodices and dropped shoulders entered the gallery from one of the staircases. At the sight of Rodrigo and Stephano, the young women raised their fans and drew together, laughing and whispering to each other.

Rodrigo "made a leg" as the saying went, placing one foot before the other and giving a graceful bow. The young women curtsied. Rodrigo offered to introduce them to his friend, "Lord Captain Stephano de Guichen." The young women curtsied again, clearly in admiration of the handsome captain. Stephano removed his hat and gave a stiff bow and then stood fuming with impatience while Rodrigo exchanged flirtatious banter.

"I have an appointment," said Stephano abruptly, interrupting one of the women. "If you will excuse me—"

He bowed again, turned on his heel and walked off. Behind him, he could hear Rodrigo apologizing and the low voices of the women talking behind their fluttering fans.

"That was the wife of the Count of Galiar you just insulted," said Rodrigo, catching up with his friend. "I smoothed things over. Told her you were perishing of a broken heart. I fancy from the way she looked at you that she would like to help you mend it."

"She seems much more your type," said Stephano.

"I was in love with her once," said Rodrigo in the sorrowful tones he always used when speaking of his past *amours*. "I was on the verge of proposing, but then she married the count."

Rodrigo was always falling in love and always on the verge of marrying, but the women with whom he was always falling in love always ended up marrying counts or barons or dukes or earls—anyone besides Rodrigo. He maintained that he was unlucky at love. Stephano wondered, not for the first time, if his friend was unlucky or remarkably adroit.

The Countess de Marjolaine had a suite of rooms in one wing of the palace. Although she was no longer the king's mistress, the countess remained King Alaric's most trusted adviser and confidante. She wielded great power and was respected and flattered, hated and feared.

The countess' suite was furnished with exquisite taste and every luxury, all paid for by herself. She was one of the wealthiest landowners in the kingdom and made it a point of pride to never accept money from His Majesty or anyone else. Stephano and Rodrigo were admitted to the countess' antechamber by a footman wearing a royal blue velvet coat, lace, satin, and silk stockings. Petitioners and favor-seekers sat on curved divans and chairs, decorated with the countess' bumblebee, waiting their turn to be ushered into her presence. Two noblemen, whom Stephano did not recognize, lounged in a corner, exchanging idle gossip. They stopped their talk long enough to stare in a haughty, challenging manner at Stephano, who stared back at them just as haughtily.

Stephano gave his name and presented the countess' note to the footman, who bowed and took it to a young man seated at a desk before the door to the countess' audience room. The young man—the countess' secretary—looked at the note, looked at Stephano, and said crisply, "Lord Captain de Guichen, please be seated. I will let you know when the countess is at liberty to receive you."

With a gesture, the young man indicated one of the divans. Stephano noticed that, at the sound of his name, the two lordlings in the corner inclined their heads together and started whispering. Stephano guessed that the countess' bastard son was the subject of their conversation, and his face burned. He put his hand on the hilt of his rapier and took a step toward them. Rodrigo plucked his sleeve.

"They're nobodies, my friend," he said. "Hoping for a favorable glance from your mother, which they won't get, no matter how many hours they wait here. Don't waste your time."

Stephano was annoyed. "I will *not* wait here with my mother's flunkies and ass-lickers for hours until she deigns to receive me. She stated our appointment was for nine. It is now nine. I'm going inside."

"If you try to barge through the door, the secretary will summon the footmen, who will throw you out. You see that one footman—the big brute with the shoulders whose velvet coat is starting to split at the seams? He was once a professional bear-wrestler. We can't afford to make your mother angry by starting a row in her chambers."

"Then I won't stay—"

"Yes, you will. Leave it to Rigo. I deal with the secretary. You slip inside."

Rodrigo walked up to the secretary's desk and perched his rump familiarly on one corner. The secretary had been writing down numbers in a ledger. Shocked at such rude behavior, he looked up.

"Do you want something, sir?" the secretary said in a frozen tone.

"I have a wager I'm hoping you can settle, sir," said Rodrigo in loud and affable tones.

He had by now attracted the attention of everyone in the room, footmen included. Stephano sidled closer to the door and rested his hand, covered by the lace on his sleeves, on the door handle and jiggled it. The handle gave slightly. The door was not locked.

"I have wagered that you are a fourth son," Rodrigo went on. He shook his head. "Not even a church appointment for you, eh? Not worth the family spending the money on, I suppose. The most you can hope for is to do menial work for a great lord or lady."

The young man flushed and rose irately to his feet.

"I will have you know I am the son of Viscount Telorind—"

"*Fourth* son?"

"Well, yes," the young man admitted.

"And you're new to court?"

"I have been here a month—"

"Ah!" said Rodrigo with a knowing look. "That explains a lot. You think you were sent here to learn the ways of court. In truth, you are here as a guarantee for your father's good behavior, so that His Majesty can keep his eye on him."

Rodrigo leaned forward, as if in confidence. "I'll make

another wager. All your correspondence to and from home is being intercepted and read—"

The young man gasped and began to sputter. Everyone in the antechamber was chuckling. No one was paying attention to Stephano, who pressed on the handle, opened the door, and slid inside. He shut the door on the rising voices behind him and advanced into his mother's audience room, which was like her: quiet, refined, cool, and elegant.

A woman sat behind a desk containing a number of leather-bound ledgers and other papers. She was holding a lorgnette in front of her eyes to peruse one of the papers, a slight frown creasing her forehead. Opposite her, on the other side of the desk, Dargent sat, taking notes in a small book. The countess must have heard the door, but she did not look up. Dargent glanced around and, seeing Stephano, said something to her in a low voice.

The countess continued to read a moment longer, then she lowered the paper and the lorgnette and, without a glance at Stephano, proceeded to give instructions to Dargent, who noted them down in his book. Unlike many women in her position, who gave over control of their wealth to male relatives or trusted advisers, the countess managed her estate and business concerns. The instructions she was giving Dargent had something to do with the felling and sale of timber on her land. Stephano was angry and embarrassed at being ignored and he had difficulty hearing what she said through the blood pounding in his ears.

At last, her business concluded, the countess handed Dargent the paper and nodded her head in dismissal. Dargent rose to his feet, bowed to the countess and inclined his head to Stephano, then exited the room through another doorway. The countess turned her gaze upon Stephano.

"You were not summoned," she said in mild reproof. "What have you done to my secretary? Sliced him into bits?"

The door flew open and the flustered young man burst inside. "Madame, I am sorry! I did not see the captain enter. Here, you, sir—"

The secretary reached out his hand to grab hold of the interloper and drag him out. Stephano stopped the man with a look.

The countess glanced past the secretary's shoulder and saw Rodrigo smiling from the antechamber. He placed his hand on his heart, bowed low. The countess gave a deep sigh.

"Thank you, Emil," she said to her secretary. "Remind me to teach you how *not* to be an idiot. That will be all."

Blushing, the young man cast a furious glance at Stephano, then withdrew. Rodrigo gave a wave to Stephano and mouthed the words, "Pays well!" Emil shut the door and Stephano and his mother were alone.

Stephano gave a mocking, servile bow. "I am here, Madame, your indentured servant, come to work off my debt."

"Don't be more of an ass than you can help, my son," said the countess. "I find it so tiresome."

She made a commanding gesture. "Fetch my scarf. We are going to take a turn about the garden."

"Fetch your own damn scarf. I am not your lady's maid," said Stephano angrily. "And we will talk about this here and now—"

The countess fixed her lustrous blue-gray eyes upon her son. "I said we will take a turn in the garden. Now hand me my scarf."

Stephano swallowed his wrath. He snatched up the lace scarf—made of lamb's wool, delicate as cobweb—and flung it over his mother's shoulders.

"If I refuse to undertake this job, will you really send me to debtor's prison, Mother?"

The countess raised a delicate eyebrow, gave a delicate shrug, and said coolly, "Don't ask stupid questions, my son."

Chapter Three

The king is the absolute authority in the land, but he requires the support of the great families and they require him. They feed off each other. He sees to it that they are constantly vying for his favor. Alliances and ties between the Peers of the Realm run together like the notes in a symphony. The person conducting the orchestra is not the king, but the Countess de Marjolaine.

Only the noble and ancient Dragon families of Rosia remain aloof from the politics of the royal court. Since the disbanding of the Dragon Brigade, the offended dragons have shunned court altogether. His Majesty does not appear much bothered by their absence. Perhaps because he no longer requires the dragons in his new, modern navy.

—*Musings on Rosian Politics*
by Rodrigo de Villeneuve

COUNTESS CECILE RAPHAEL DE MARJOLAINE was fifty years old and the poets of the age still wrote songs to her beauty. They spoke of luxuriant silver hair, with curls falling on alabaster shoulders. Her blue eyes were likened to sapphires, her cheeks to the damask rose. Her figure was superb. Tall and slender, she moved with a languorous grace that suited her height.

Her complexion remained smooth, perhaps because no strong emotion was ever allowed to touch her. She had never been heard to laugh. No lines of joy creased her lips or crinkled the corners of her eyes. No lines of worry or care marred her forehead. The only two flaws on her lovely face were a single deep furrow slanting between her brows that deepened when she was absorbed in thought and a small, white scar on the right corner of her lip. The only sign of her age was the skin on the back of her hands. Once white and delicate, the skin was now stretched taut and crisscrossed beneath with blue veins.

The countess did not follow fashion. She set fashion. Her gown was simply and elegantly made of sky-blue satin, the skirt falling in sumptuous folds from a pointed bodice, the sleeves tight to the elbow, then flowing and lined with lace. She wore a necklace of blue sapphires and several very fine jewels on her fingers. Among these rings, lost and unremarked amidst the rubies and diamonds and sapphires, was a plain golden band, which she never took off. When she was preoccupied, she would often absentmindedly twist this little golden ring.

The countess led Stephano from her study into a library filled with books, whose leather bindings gave off a pleasant scent. The books were not merely decorative, as were books in the homes of much of the nobility, many of whom were practically illiterate. The countess had always been fond of reading and whereas the other fashionable women of the time invited the rich and the powerful to their salons, the countess preferred to invite poets and artists, philosophers, musicians, and scientists.

She and Stephano passed through the library and entered a small and cozy sitting room. Glass-paned doors opened out onto a charming patio enclosed by a waist-high stone wall. Trees of all varieties, many of them rare species imported from other countries, had been planted in tubs made of wood and stone. The trees formed a miniature forest that effectively screened the garden from view of prying eyes peering out nearby windows.

Looking through the trees in one direction, the observer could see blue sky and the deeper blue-purple of the

mountains, green woods, and the sun shining off the crystalline surface of a distant lake. In the other direction rose the
spires of a magnificent cathedral, surrounded by a large
complex of buildings, all protected by a wall, all stuck far
below on solid ground. The bottom level of the floating palace were about even with the cathedral's bell tower.

How the grand bishop must hate that, thought Stephano,
amused.

"Shut the doors," said the countess.

Stephano complied. The countess rearranged her scarf
around her shoulders, then walked over to the wall and
gazed out into the cloudless blue sky. She began, unconsciously, to twist the small golden ring.

Stephano remained near the door, silent, waiting for her
to speak. He had never been in her garden and he was entranced by the beauty of the view. He was also, truth be told,
always a little awed and uncomfortable in the presence of
his mother, though he would have knocked out the teeth of
any man who said so.

"What do you know of the Royal Armory?" the countess
asked abruptly, turning to face her son.

Stephano was accustomed to his mother's manner of doing business; no pleasant niceties or idle talk. She went immediately to the heart of matter at hand. This was the last
subject he would have expected his mother to bring up and
he had to take a moment to think.

"The Royal Armory makes the weapons and armor for
the king and the Royal Regiment, the king's guards. When
I was Commander of the Dragon Brigade"—his voice took
on a tinge of bitterness—"the Royal Armory outfitted me
and my company with magically enhanced riding armor
and our muskets. The Royal Armory made some of the finest armor and weapons I've ever owned."

"The Armory also looks for ways to improve those
weapons and armor," said the countess.

"That's a given," said Stephano.

The countess eyed him. The small furrow dug into her brow. "Don't stand there hovering by the door as though you are ready to bolt any moment. Come closer, so that I don't have to shout."

She was hardly shouting, and Stephano realized suddenly that there was a reason she had brought him to this garden, when usually their business was conducted in her audience chamber. Here, amid the thick foliage and trailing vines with nothing except blue sky above and the ground far below, was privacy—as much privacy as one could have in a palace populated by many hundreds of people.

Stephano felt a prickling at the back of his neck. This job was starting to sound more interesting. He joined his mother at the wall, where she stood gazing down upon the cathedral and the large, squat, towered structures that clustered around it.

"The Bishop's Palace," said the countess in reflective tones, her thoughts echoing her son's. "Fixed firmly on the ground. His Grace moved his office, you know, to the other end of the building, so that he wouldn't have to look out his window to see His Majesty floating above him."

First the Armory, now the Grand Bishop Montagne—King Alaric's longtime friend, longer time enemy. Where was this conversation leading? Stephano kept quiet and waited to find out.

The countess turned to Stephano; as she did so, a shaft of sunlight, filtering through the green leaves of a flowering crab tree, illuminated the scar on her lip. He had never really noticed the scar before now. The scar appeared to be an old one and he wondered how she had come by it. Some childhood accident, perhaps? Oddly, the scar made her seem more human. Perhaps that was why she always tried to conceal it by touching her lips with carnelian, the only cosmetic she deigned to wear.

"By law, the Church of the Breath of God oversees all development of technology involving magical constructs, even at the Royal Armory," said the countess. "Any research into new uses of magic must be approved by the grand bishop. The law has stood for centuries."

"I suppose such a law makes sense," said Stephano. "Scripture says 'from the Breath of God comes His voice and the quiet whispers of his words' and that is magic."

His gaze shifted from the cathedral to the Breath as it lapped at the Rim of the bay. "The truth is, magical energy flows in the Breath. We harness the Breath with constructs and use it to lift our airships. The Breath powers our technology and augments our machines. The Breath is magic and magic is power."

Stephano turned to his mother. "And power without the divine teachings of the church for guidance is an 'open door for the darkness that lies in wait for the heathen.'"

"Your tutor taught you well," said the countess dryly.

"Actually, it was Rodrigo," said Stephano.

"In fact, your friend, Monsieur de Villeneuve, is one of the reasons I thought of asking you to undertake this job."

"If it involves the seduction of women, you'll find Rodrigo outstanding," said Stephano, grinning.

"Actually I was thinking more of his outstanding skills as a crafter. At least, I am told he has such skills," said the countess.

"And, as usual, your spies are correct, Mother. But what have crafters and Rodrigo to do with the bishop and the Breath of God and the Royal Armory—By Heaven!" Stephano answered his own question. "His Majesty has been conducting research into new weapons technology involving magic. And he has *not* shared it with the bishop."

"You always were a smart boy," the countess murmured.

"What would happen if the bishop were to discover this little indiscretion?"

"The king would be embarrassed—"

"My heart bleeds," said Stephano, his lip curling in a sneer.

The countess smiled faintly. "There would be other ramifications, as I am certain you are aware."

The sun drifted behind a tower, throwing the garden into shadow. The countess drew her scarf more closely around her shoulders. "Sit here. The air is chill in the shade."

The countess took her seat on a wicker divan, surrounded by plump cushions. There was room for Stephano, and she made a polite gesture for him to sit beside her. He chose, instead, a seat on a marble bench opposite her. His rapier rang against the stone wall as he settled himself.

Now we're coming to it, he thought.

"I had a visit yesterday morning from Douver, Master of the Royal Armory. Master Douver was quite agitated. It seems one of his journeyman, Pietro Alcazar, did not come to work the day before."

"Hardly an event likely to sink the continent," said Stephano.

"So one would think," said the countess imperturbably. "Douver assures me, however, that this journeyman is completely reliable. Alcazar has not missed a day's work since he came to the Armory six years ago. He does not chase women. He does not indulge in strong drink. He is known to be a dedicated and brilliant crafter who lives solely for his work. He is so brilliant, in fact, that he recently made an amazing discovery. He found a way to manufacture steel utilizing the Breath of God—"

Stephano laughed. "And I can turn lead into gold. Crafters have been trying to mix metal and magic for years, Mother! It can't be done."

"I am aware of this," said the countess sharply, annoyed at the interruption. "Hear me out. Douver was so excited by Alcazar's discovery he reported it to His Majesty."

"But *not* to the bishop," Stephano inserted. "As required by law."

"He went to the king first, as was proper," said the countess. "The king was thrilled, naturally, but also, like you, my clever son, he was skeptical. He demanded proof. Douver promised to bring a sample of this Breath-enhanced steel to His Majesty."

"What sort of sample?" Stephano asked.

"Something that would appear quite ordinary—a tankard, I believe. Douver was to meet with His Majesty yesterday. When Alcazar failed to come to work, Douver was concerned that his journeyman might have been taken ill or—"

"—he was, in fact, a charlatan who knew his fraud was about to be revealed," said Stephano.

"That was Douver's fear, especially as he had allowed the king to labor under the mistaken belief that he—Douver—had developed this new metal."

Stephano smiled and shook his head.

"Douver hastened to Alcazar's rooms," the countess continued. "He found the front door had been forced open. Furniture was upended. There were signs of a struggle. Alcazar was gone and so was the tankard he had been going to show to the king. Seeing this, Douver came to me at once."

"Why you?" Stephano asked, frowning.

The countess was exasperated. "You could hardly expect Douver to go to the king! What would the fool man say? That he had lied about the fact that he had created this new metal? That he had allowed the journeyman who did create it to be snatched out from under his nose? The king would think Douver had been lying all this time. He would lose his job, if not his head."

"So he hoped you could get him back into the king's good graces. Well, that should be easy for you, Mother. Just slip into His Majesty's bed . . ."

The countess sat quite still. Her eyes were gray as a winter sky, her face expressionless. When she spoke, her tone was smooth and cold.

"There is a far more important consideration here, Stephano, as you would realize if you were not constantly occupied in hating me."

Stephano realized he had gone too far. What she said was true. He was allowing his feelings to cloud his judgment. Beyond that, his remark had been unworthy of a knight and a gentleman.

"I beg your pardon, Mother," he said quietly. "I should not have said that."

The countess stood up and took a turn or two around the garden. She twisted the little golden ring on her finger. Stephano waited in silence, still feeling the sting of her rebuke. Her next question surprised him.

"Tell me, Stephano, if Alcazar had succeeded in producing steel that could be enhanced by the Breath of God, what would be the ramifications of such a discovery?"

"Astounding," Stephano answered. "Cannonballs would bounce off our warships like hailstones. Armor could withstand bullets or, conversely, bullets could punch through ordinary steel. Such a discovery would make our military invincible. But that is assuming this Alcazar actually succeeded, and I don't believe—"

"Someone does," said the countess flatly.

Stephano was brought up short. He thought this over and now understood her concern. Alcazar had disappeared, perhaps not of his own free will. Someone had snatched him. The idea of such magically enhanced steel in the wrong hands was appalling.

"I need you to discover the truth, Stephano. Go to Alcazar's lodging, search it, see what you can learn. You will be discreet, quiet, circumspect. No hint of what has happened must leak out."

"Which is why you came to me," said Stephano.

"I dare not trust any of my local agents," said the countess, nodding agreement. "Not with something this important. Here is the address."

She reached into her bosom and drew out a piece of paper and handed it to Stephano. The address was in his mother's own hand, bold and firm: *127 Street of the Half Moon.* He thrust the paper into an inner pocket in his coat.

"How flattering to know you actually trust *me*, Mother," he remarked.

"I do trust you, Stephano," said the countess gravely. "Do not let me down."

She moved to the door and stood beside it, waiting for him to open it for her. The interview was at an end.

Stephano stood up, pressing his hand against his rapier to keep it from striking the bench. "One question. You mentioned Grand Bishop Montagne. Is it possible that he could have found out about Alcazar?"

"I thought of that," said the countess. "I have made inquiries and am convinced that the bishop knows nothing. If his creature, Dubois, were in Rosia, it would be a different matter. Dubois knows, sees, hears everything. But Dubois is in Freya, attending the royal court. And now I really must go. I am late for a meeting with the Travian ambassador."

Stephano opened the door, and the countess swept past him with a rustle of satin and the faint fragrance of honeysuckle.

"I hear Travia and Estara are hurling cannonballs at one another over which of the two nations owns mineral-rich Braffa," said Stephano. "Rodrigo's father is ambassador to Estara. He writes that the situation is grim."

"They are both trying to draw us into the fight," said the countess. "I won't allow that to happen."

"Shouldn't King Alaric be handling this matter, along with his officially appointed ministers?" Stephano asked, grinning.

"His Majesty has far more important matters to concern him," said the countess.

Stephano leaned near to say, "There's not a twitch of your cobweb that you don't feel, is there, Mother?"

"You've fought the Estarans. Do you want to do so again?" the countess asked, as they passed through the sitting room and into the library.

"I would not be given the chance, as you well know," said Stephano caustically.

"May I remind you, my son, that *you* were the one who

resigned the commission which *I* had managed to obtain for you," the countess returned.

"And may I remind you, Mother, that I resigned after the king disbanded the Dragon Brigade and took away my command," said Stephano heatedly.

"His Majesty offered you a post—"

"—as a lowly lieutenant on one of his new-fangled floating frigates. I am a Dragon Knight. If you think I would stoop—"

Stephano stopped to draw in a deep breath. He was not going to quarrel with her. Not that they ever quarreled. She was Breath-enhanced steel. Words, like bullets, could never penetrate her. He came back to business.

"If I find out what you need to know about this Alcazar, you will clear all my debts?"

The countess glanced at him. "I said I would. I keep my word."

Stephano flushed. He hated to mention this next, but he had no choice. He did so with what dignity he could muster. "Rodrigo tells me that I am ... er ... rather short of funds right now. If you could advance me—"

"I have given instructions for you to receive the paperwork clearing you of your debt and I have provided money for expenses," said the countess.

They had returned to the audience chamber. She remained standing. Business concluded, she was ready to be done with him.

Stephano bowed. "I will take my leave, then, Madame. I will be in touch. Who do I see about the money?"

The countess extended her hand for him to kiss.

"My secretary, Emil," she said, adding, with a hint of a smile, "The young man you insulted."

While Stephano was back in the antechamber, forced to endure Emil's sneers while waiting for his mother's money, one of the men he and the countess had been discussing was also being forced to wait. Only this man was waiting to clear customs, not waiting for an insufferable secretary.

For once, the countess' spies were wrong. Dubois, the bishop's "creature," as the countess had termed him, was not in Freya attending the royal court. His ship had docked at the Rosian port at about the same time the wyvern-drawn carriage containing Stephano and Rodrigo had flown over the dockyards. If Stephano had looked down and Dubois had looked up, the two men would have seen each other.

Seeing Dubois would not have done Stephano any good, for he did not know the man. They had never met. Dubois knew Stephano, however. Dubois made it his business to know everyone who had anything to do with the politics of any of the royal courts.

Once he was through customs, Dubois—known by everyone simply as Dubois—did not waste time. He met with several men who were waiting on the dock for him. He heard their reports and gave them instructions. These meetings with agents concluded, he hastened to a nearby inn where he always kept a horse in readiness, mounted, and rode swiftly through the crowded streets, paying no heed to the curses of those he nearly ran down.

Upon reaching the vicinity of the Bishop's Palace, Dubois left the horse at the stables of another inn in which he had taken up lodgings, then walked the rest of the way. He did not enter by the main gate. Instead, he went to a small gate located in the wall directly behind the bishop's private residence. The gate was hidden in some shrubbery, and Dubois had the only key.

The gate led into a small walled-off terrace, still filled with last autumn's dead leaves, located at the rear of the house. A door with a lock to which Dubois also had the key opened into a long, narrow hallway.

The hall was dark, but Dubois had walked it many times and did not need a light to find his way. At the end of the hall was another door with yet another lock. He opened this door with yet another key and entered a small closet, big enough for him and a single chair.

Dubois walked over to the wall and pressed his ear to it. He could hear voices: the deep, resonant voice of the grand bishop and other voices he did not recognize. He could hear the bishop quite clearly for his chair was near the closet door, which was concealed by a thick, velvet curtain hanging behind the bishop's chair. The other voices were agitated, less distinct, but Dubois was a master at eavesdropping.

The Abbey of Saint Agnes had been attacked during the night. Many of the one hundred nuns living there had been slaughtered, the abbey burned.

Dubois was shocked at the terrible news and was surprised he had not heard of the attack from his agents, but then he reminded himself that he had only just landed. A devout man, Dubois said a prayer for the dead. He took a seat on the chair and waited with some impatience for the visitors to leave.

In his mid-forties, Dubois was hard to describe. Plain and ordinary to look at, Dubois fostered the appearance of being plain and ordinary. His dress and demeanor were that of a lowly clerk (and a poorly paid lowly clerk at that). What lifted Dubois out of the ordinary was his extraordinary mind. He had only to look at a face and he would remember that person for the rest of his life. He had merely to peruse a document once and he could later copy it word for word, comma for comma. He could repeat a conversation verbatim, though it might have lasted hours. These amazing talents had been noticed many years ago when he was a young man by his parish priest, who had brought Dubois to the attention of the grand bishop.

Ferdinand Montagne was grand bishop of a church that had been struggling with various problems for these past twenty years. Once a power in the world, as the world's only true religion, the Church of the Breath of Rosia had seen that power wane. The Church of the Breath of Freya had split off and begun calling itself the Church of the Reformation. Its

ministers preached that the Church of the Breath of Rosia
was rife with corruption, had lost its way, and should no longer be responsible for the salvation of men's souls.

As if this were not trouble enough, King Alaric, who had
once been a devoted follower of church doctrine and friend
to the bishop (who had sacrificed a great deal for His Majesty), had started to rebel, to go off on his own. Now he was
looking for a reason to end the Church's control over the
magic and take it (and the revenue it provided) for the
Crown.

Such a reason existed in the form of a terrible secret. The
bishop possessed certain knowledge about the Church,
about the Breath of God, about the magic—"the quiet
whispers of his words" that was so dreadful, so awful, that
should the king find out, he would have the excuse he
needed.

Beset by enemies without, wrestling with danger within,
the bishop had needed help. He needed to know what his
enemies in Freya were thinking, plotting. He needed to
know what the King of Rosia was plotting, if not necessarily
thinking. His Majesty left his thinking to the Countess de
Marjolaine.

The grand bishop required spies. He had a few, but they
were not nearly of the caliber of the spies in the employ of
the Countess de Marjolaine. Montagne had been impressed
with Dubois and had given him one or two small jobs, which
Dubois had handled with skill. The grand bishop had provided him with funds to set up an intelligence network. Dubois had handled the task with such success that for the last
few years, the bishop had been able to breathe freer and
sleep somewhat more soundly at night.

The visitors departed. Dubois heard the door close. He
waited another moment to make certain the bishop was
alone. The only sounds were the rustle of the bishop's cassock and the creaking of the chair as he sat down; Montagne was a large man. Over six feet tall, he was massively
built. At sixty years old, he was in excellent physical condi-

tion, looking more like a wrestler than a clergyman. He wore his gray hair short, his whitish-gray beard and mustache neatly trimmed.

Ferdinand Montagne was ambitious, political, and a true and devoted believer in God—a dangerous combination. He believed that his voice was God's voice, his will was God's will, and that everything the bishop did or ordered to be done was for God's glory.

Dubois silently opened the door of the closet, silently drew aside the folds of the heavy curtain, and silently glided out.

"Good afternoon, Your Grace," said Dubois in his deferential clerk's voice.

Grand Bishop Montagne gave a great gasp and a start that caused his pointed, gold-decorated miter to slip from his head and fall to the floor. The bishop twisted around in his chair and fixed his man with a baleful look.

"By all the Saints, Dubois, some day you are going to sneak up on me like that and cause my heart to stop beating. Damn it, you could at least cough or bump into something."

Dubois smiled slightly as he bent to pick up the miter, brush off any dust, and hand it back to the bishop. Montagne motioned Dubois to set the miter on the desk, then directed him with an irritated gesture to take a seat.

Dubois did not immediately sit down. "I might suggest it would be well, Your Grace, if you were to send the monsignor, your secretary, and his assistants on an errand."

"And what would that errand be, Dubois?"

"I need to know who has been meeting with the Countess de Marjolaine during the past few days. I need the list of visitors to date, including all her meetings scheduled for today."

The bishop's face stiffened, as always when the countess' name was mentioned. He rose to his feet, his blue, gold-trimmed cassock swishing about his ankles, and went out to speak to the secretary.

Dubois looked about the prelate's study, taking note of any changes that had been made in his absence. The room was lit by narrow windows, two stories high. Each window was set with beveled, leaded glass. The interior walls were lined with bookcases and rich paneling carved of cherry inlaid with rosewood and precious metals. Two andirons, each taking the form of an angel with sword raised and feet on the heads of writhing demons, stood before the gold-veined, white marble fireplace.

Seeing nothing of interest, Dubois flipped through the papers on the bishop's desk, his retentive memory absorbing their contents. He resumed his seat as the bishop came back into the room, closing the door behind him and turning the key in the lock.

"I assume you were eavesdropping? You heard the news about the abbey?" the bishop asked grimly.

"I could not help but overhear, Your Grace," said Dubois. "I cannot imagine who would perpetrate such an outrage."

"I have contacted the Arcanum to investigate. Father Jacob Northrup is coming to meet with me. He would have been here by now, but he and his team were in Capione, investigating reports of that Warlock and his coven."

"The Warlock? What has that evil young man done now?" Dubois asked.

"It seems he seduced the daughter of a nobleman. She ran away from home to join him and his followers. Several bodies of his young followers have been found, drained of blood, which the Warlock uses in his heinous rites. He gives the deluded children opium and lures them into orgies, then murders them."

"I ask myself, 'Why?'" said Dubois, frowning.

"What do you mean 'why?' Because he takes pleasure in killing people," said the bishop. "He's insane."

"I doubt that," said Dubois. "He does this for a reason."

"Well, whatever that reason is, pray God this time Father Jacob has managed to find him and stop him."

"If anyone can do so, it is Father Jacob Northrup," said Dubois.

The grand bishop was silent, frowning. "So what are you doing here, Dubois? Your orders were to remain in Freya until the end of the summer court."

"Might I have a glass of wine and something to eat, Your Grace?" asked Dubois. "I am famished. I have spent the last two days traveling. I came here immediately on my arrival."

The bishop indicated the sideboard on which stood a crystal decanter of wine and a collation of cold meats and bread. Dubois forked beef onto a slice of bread, devoured it in a few bites, then poured himself a glass of wine and returned to his chair.

"I fear I have more bad news, Your Grace. Sir Henry Wallace has left Freya."

Bishop Montagne's eyes opened wide. His frown deepened, his face grew dark. He said a word suited more to a dockyard worker than a bishop, then added, "Where is the bastard?"

"I have no idea, Your Grace."

The bishop gave a heavy sigh. "Tell me everything, Dubois."

"Yes, Your Grace. Ever since his marriage, Sir Henry has been seen at court on an almost daily basis. His movements have been unremarkable." Dubois shrugged. "People say he dotes upon his young wife, who is in the last few months of her pregnancy. A short time ago, however, there was a break in his routine. I was informed by my spy, a maidservant, in his household, that a wooden box had been delivered to Sir Henry by a man who had the appearance of a sailor.

"The maid got a good look at the box, on the pretext of dusting Sir Henry's study, and reported that the box was plain, with no writing on it, nothing to indicate its origins or what was inside. She assumed it was some gift for his wife and thought nothing of it. He did not give his wife a gift, however, and yet, oddly, the box vanished. The maid asked some of the other members of the staff, but no one knew what had become of it. Several days after Wallace received this box, he suddenly, without advance notice, moved his wife and household to his estate outside Haever. He stated as his reason his wife's impending lying-in."

"What happened to this mysterious box?"

"I do not know, Your Grace, but a most curious incident occurred after Wallace arrived at his estate. The staff was told that Sir Henry was going to be conducting scientific experiments in the kitchen and they were not to be alarmed if they heard any odd sounds. Such experiments are, apparently, not unusual for Sir Henry.

"That night, the maid was awakened by what she swears were gunshots, followed by a loud explosion. The next morning the kitchen smelled strongly of gunpowder and was in such a mess, with pots and pans lying on the floor, that the cook threatened to give notice. The maid found several bullets, flattened, in the fireplace. Wallace left immediately afterward, telling his wife he was bound for Haever. He never arrived there. It took me two days to learn that he was no longer in Freya."

"You think . . ."

"I think something important was in that box, Your Grace."

Montagne grunted in agreement. "Did you find out where the box came from, anything about it? You said the man who delivered it was a sailor."

Dubois paused for a sip of wine. He drank sparingly, preferring to have all his mental faculties unclouded by the fumes of the grape.

"All I could find out was that two merchant vessels had docked immediately before the box was delivered. One was from Travia and the second a free trader from the Aligoes Islands."

"Which do you suspect?" the bishop asked.

"Free traders smuggle Estaran wine into Freya, along with other contraband. Given the fact that Estara and Travia are on the brink of war on the eastern frontier over Braffa—"

"But Freya is neutral in this conflict," the bishop interjected.

"It is well known in Freya that you, Your Grace, support Estara in its claim of Braffa and that His Majesty, King Alaric, supports Travia in its claim—"

"Say, rather, that fiendish woman, the Countess de Marjolaine, supports Travia," said the bishop.

Dubois nodded. "I noted the last time I was in the Travian court that it is crawling with her operatives. But, as I was going to say, this war between Travia and Estara over Braffa has resulted in a serious rift between Church and Crown here in Rosia. It might be very tempting to Wallace to heat up the fire under this cauldron, see perhaps if he can't make it boil over."

"To what purpose?" the bishop asked.

"Ah, who knows with Sir Henry," said Dubois.

The bishop glowered. "Do I detect a note of admiration in your voice, Dubois?"

"One should never underestimate one's enemy, Your Grace. I also have the highest regard for the Countess de Marjolaine."

A rumbling sound came from the region of the bishop's stomach. He placed his hand on his belly. "Bah! This news has made me bilious. Pour me a glass of wine."

Dubois did as he was told, returning to set the goblet at the bishop's hand. As he did so, there was a knock upon the door. The bishop gestured and Dubois crossed over to the door, opened it a crack, and received a book bound in red leather. He closed the door and once more turned the key. The bishop eyed the red leather book in Dubois' hand.

"Where the devil is Wallace? I don't like it when that fiend is on the loose." Montagne gazed moodily into his wine goblet.

"That is what I am endeavoring to ascertain, Your Grace. That is why I asked to see who has been meeting with the countess."

Dubois opened the red leather book somewhere around

the middle and began to read. At the top of each page was a date. Below the date was a list of names. Dubois scanned several pages. The bishop watched hopefully, but his hopes were dashed when Dubois shook his head and closed the book.

"Nothing?"

"The usual: favor-seekers, courtiers. Only three are in any way remarkable. Yesterday, the countess met with the Master of the Royal Armory. This morning, she met with her son, Captain de Guichen—"

"What is so remarkable about that?" asked the bishop. He was in an ill humor and inclined to be petty. "She is his mother."

"The two are not on speaking terms, Your Grace, though the countess does occasionally employ her son on sensitive business. And he did fight the Estarans prior to the Dragon Brigade being decommissioned. After he left, the countess was closeted for a long time with Lord Hoalfhausen, the Travian ambassador."

"There, you see!" said the bishop in angry triumph. "That woman is meddling in this war, consorting with my enemies."

"So it would seem, Your Grace," replied Dubois. Disappointed, he tossed the book onto the desk. "Unfortunately, this tells us nothing regarding the whereabouts of Sir Henry."

He rose to his feet and prepared to take his leave.

"Keep me informed, Dubois," said the bishop. "May God speed your endeavors."

"May He, indeed, Your Grace. And may He aid the labors of Father Jacob as he confounds the Warlock and discovers who murdered our Sisters in God."

Dubois bowed, circled around behind the bishop's chair, parted the curtain, and entered the closet. A glance over his shoulder showed Montagne sitting with his shoulders hunched, his head bowed. He picked up the goblet, drank off the wine in a gulp, then rang a bell to summon the monsignor.

Dubois left the palace the way he had come, passing through the small patio, out the hidden gate, and onto the street. Returning to his lodgings for a long overdue meal, he found an agent waiting for him.

Dubois eyed him. "You're the one who has been shadowing Wallace's agent, right? You sent me word that Harrington had arrived in the city a fortnight ago and has been keeping to himself."

"Yes, sir. There has been a development. I dispatched news of this to you yesterday, but then I heard you had left Freya, so I feared you might not have received it."

"I did not. What has happened?"

"Yesterday, Harrington, dressed as a common laborer, pretending to be a drunkard, spent the day in the neighborhood of the Church of Saint Michelle. He is back there again today, sir."

"The devil he is!" said Dubois, startled.

"He was still there when I left. Sleeping on a bench with a wine jug in front of a statue of the blessed saint."

"How very strange," Dubois murmured, frowning. "Where is it?"

"Street of the Half Moon, sir. The church is at the southern end, near the bridge."

Dubois sent his agent to keep an eye on the inn where Harrington was staying. Dubois ate his meal standing and ordered a fresh horse to be saddled. While dining, he wondered what to make of this news.

The Street of the Half Moon ran through a bustling neighborhood of shops, boarding houses, and private dwellings, most of them occupied by middle-class families. What could James Harrington, one of Sir Henry's top agents, be doing lounging about Half Moon Street?

Mounting his horse, Dubois rode off to find out.

Chapter Four

Constructs are man's way of safely controlling and harnessing magical energy. Formed of sigils connected by lines of magical energy, constructs supplement the natural properties of matter. For example, a strengthening construct set in a piece of leather armor can render the leather resistant to a sword strike.

It would seem that the same process should work using strengthening constructs in metal. But placing constructs in the metal during the forging process makes the metal unworkable. It becomes brittle and breaks. Armorers have always had to wait until the metal object is finished and then set the magical construct onto the metal's surface. This process reduces the strengthening power of the magic and causes the constructs to become susceptible to damage and wear, which means crafters must constantly repair the sigils, glyphs, and lines of connection.

Armorers down through the centuries have long sought a means to combine magic and metal. Like turning lead into gold, most believe it to be impossible.

> —An excerpt from "Constructs and Their Use
> in the Production of Weapons and Armor"
> by Gaston Bondrea
> Grand Master, Rosian Armorers Guild

STEPHANO HAD MANAGED BY A GREAT DEAL of self-control to avoid running his rapier through the insufferable little twit of a secretary and been provided with funds for the work ahead. He was now free to leave the palace and he would have done so immediately, except he couldn't find Rodrigo. After an hour's searching, he and a footman discovered his friend in the music room, playing the clavichord in his usual whimsical manner for numerous laughing silk-and-satined, perfumed-and-rouged female admirers.

Rodrigo was a very talented musician and he could have won fame as a performer and composer if he'd worked at it. As with his crafting of magic, he couldn't be bothered. Running his fingers over the keys, he played snippets of popular compositions, adding some of his own, interspersing his playing with lively tidbits of scandal and gossip.

Stephano did not want to enter the room, for he knew if he did, he'd be trapped into socializing. He stood in the doorway, making emphatic gestures until Rodrigo caught sight of him and ceased playing, much to the disappointment of the ladies. Rodrigo paid charming compliments, kissed all the bejeweled hands, made promises to dine with at least half of them, and at last escaped.

Rodrigo's first question, the moment he and Stephano were alone, was, "Did you get the money?"

"I had to wait in my mother's antechamber and hold my tongue while that bastard Emil informed me and everyone else in the room that my mother was paying my debts," said Stephano, still fuming. "Then he made a grand show of counting out the silver! Even the footmen were snickering. And *I* wasn't the one who insulted him! You were the one who sneered at him for being a fourth son!"

"True, but that's not important. I am a third son and look how well I turned out. What *is* important is—did you get the money?" Rodrigo asked again.

"After I was thoroughly humiliated," said Stephano grimly. "I have the letters of mark from our debtors, which are now all paid off in my pocket and fifty silver rosuns for our expenses."

"Excellent," said Rodrigo, with a sigh of relief. He ushered his friend through the long gallery of gleaming rosewood and black-and-white marble, decorated with landscape paintings by famous artists. At the end, a staircase led them toward an exit. "Now that we are in funds, I suggest we celebrate with a bottle of claret at some small, but elegant café, and you can tell me about the job."

"I'll tell you about the job on the way home so that I can take off this bloody cravat. I feel like I'm being strangled," Stephano grumbled, tugging at the offending object.

A footman summoned one of the wyvern-drawn carriages. Once inside, Stephano explained the situation regarding the mysterious disappearance of Pietro Alcazar. Stephano kept his voice low, despite the fact that with the wind rushing in his ears, the driver was unlikely to hear anything short of a shout. The information was sensitive enough that Stephano did not want to take any chances. Rodrigo had to lean close to hear him.

At the conclusion, Stephano added, with a shrug, "The job seems simple enough. We search Alcazar's rooms, report back to my mother, and no more debts."

"The simplicity is what worries me," said Rodrigo. "The countess is paying us a large sum for doing nothing more than instituting a search for some wayward journeyman? Doesn't make sense. Your mother, unlike her son, is an astute businesswoman."

"My mother is not paying us for the search," said Stephano dryly. "She's paying us for our silence."

"Ah, of course. Well, as you say, a simple little job." Rodrigo settled back in his seat.

"A simple little job," Stephano echoed, as he thankfully pulled off the cravat.

Stephano and Rodrigo dismissed the carriage, changed into more comfortable (and less ostentatious) clothing and then walked to their destination—the lodgings of Pietro Alcazar, which turned out to be only a few miles from their dwelling. The Street of the Half Moon was located in the central part of the city of Evreux in a neighborhood that had once been fashionable, its large homes formerly occupied by wealthy merchants and minor nobility. As the city expanded and its population grew, the wealthy abandoned the city center, removing to the outskirts, away from the crime and noise and press of people. Since nature abhors a vacuum, less well-to-do people moved to Half Moon Street, taking over the large dwellings and turning them into boarding houses. Homes that had once housed a single family were now occupied by ten.

The residents of the Street of the Half Moon liked to pride themselves on their genteel roots. A worthy matron married to a greengrocer would tell friends she lived in "Lord So-and-So's" mansion in a tone that implied she was His Lordship's invited guest, staying a month or two for the hunting season.

A major thoroughfare, the Street of the Half Moon was crowded with horse-drawn carriages, cabs, wagons and riders. Wyvern-drawn carriages sailed in the air above the chimney tops and airships, with their colorful balloons, floated up among the clouds. People thronged the sidewalks, going in and out of the shops that occupied the lower floors of most of the buildings. Women sat gossiping on the steps. Children and dogs were everywhere. Cats curled up in windows, blinking sleepily in the midday sun.

The people of Half Moon Street were generally in a good mood, Stephano noted. The children were loud and boisterous and appeared well fed and as clean as could be expected of twelve-year-olds playing at stickball in the alleys.

If Stephano and Rodrigo had appeared on the Street of the Half Moon dressed in their court clothes, they would have attracted notice and received a cool reception. Stephano was once more in his comfortable coat of dragon green with its tailored military cut, and Rodrigo, dressed in an open-collared, flowing sleeved shirt and loose-fitting coat of a soft fawn color, looked like either an artist or a poet.

The two encountered some difficulty finding the address, 127 Half Moon Street, not because people were reluctant to speak to them, but because everyone they asked had a different idea of where it was located. They received a wide variety of answers and wandered up and down the street to no avail, until Rodrigo stopped to visit with an elderly woman, dressed all in black, who stated firmly that the house was located in a court across from the Church of Saint Michelle. The elderly woman knew this because she attended services at the church twice a day, morning and evening, and she passed the address on her way.

Stephano and Rodrigo walked toward the small neighborhood church. Passing a tavern, they thought they might find out information about Alcazar from the locals and entered. The patrons, gathered inside for a midday "wet," greeted the two affably enough. Stephano bought a pint for himself and Rodrigo and one for the bartender as was customary.

"I'm looking for a friend of mine," said Stephano, speaking to the bartender. "He and I were in the king's service together. A man named Pietro Alcazar. I thought perhaps he might do his drinking here."

The bartender shook his head. He had never heard of Alcazar; neither had any of the other patrons. Stephano thanked the bartender. Finishing their pints, he and Rodrigo went back out onto the street.

"Apparently he isn't a tippler," said Rodrigo.

"Douver claimed Alcazar didn't overindulge, but it never hurts to check." Stephano looked up and down the street. "This is the most likely tavern for him to frequent. There's the Church of Saint Michelle, complete with statue. If your widow is right, the address is somewhere around here."

"She said it was located in an inner court and that the building was a neighborhood disgrace," Rodrigo stated, peering about. "Ah! I believe that is it! No wonder we missed it."

The four-story brick boarding house was set so far back from the street as to almost completely escape notice. Constructed in the shape of a "U," the building featured a courtyard protected by a wrought-iron fence with a gate in front. The dwelling had probably once belonged to a wealthy man who had liked his privacy.

Whoever owned the building now had not kept it up. The courtyard was dark and filled with dead leaves and trash. The wrought-iron gate had no lock, and several children were taking turns swinging on it. The rusted hinges gave off a shrill screeching sound that seemed to go right through Stephano's teeth.

"I thought journeymen smiths in the Royal Armory were paid well," Rodrigo said, eyeing the building with disgust.

"They're paid very well," said Stephano. "Alcazar would have been paid better than most, since he was a valued employee. He wasn't married. He didn't have twelve children to feed or an aged mother to support. He could have afforded to live some place better than this."

The two waited until a wagon loaded with barrels had rumbled past, then crossed the street. Stephano took careful note of the surroundings, observing who was coming and going. Three women carrying empty baskets emerged from the building. One of the women stopped to speak to the gate-swinging children, then the three matrons, chattering loudly, continued on their way. Four boys in their teens were kicking a ball against the wall at the corner of the building.

Across the street was the church. A priest stood on the church steps, chatting with an ordinary-looking fellow, dressed like a clerk. A drunk in filthy clothes with a slouch hat pulled over his face was either asleep or had passed out on a bench beneath a statue of Saint Michelle. Several young blades rode past on horseback, talking loudly and ogling a young woman walking toward the church. A man in an apron pushing a handcart loaded with vegetables headed in the opposite direction.

While Stephano kept watch on the street, Rodrigo went to speak to the children. He pulled a copper coin out of his purse and tossed it into the air, so that it flashed in the sunlight, then deftly caught it with a snap and held it up. The children immediately clustered around him.

"I'm looking for someone, and I'll give this bright penny to the smart lad or lass who can help me find him. I've been told he lives here."

"Who you lookin' for, Mister?" asked a boy, the tallest and probably the oldest.

"His name is Pietro Alcazar," said Rodrigo.

Stephano glanced around at the people within earshot, to see if the name had any effect. The boys playing ball paid no attention. Neither did the young woman or the priest or the clerk. The drunk lying on the bench stirred, however. The man moved his arm, which had been over his head, lowering it to his chest. Stephano watched him closely, but it seemed the drunk was merely shifting to a more comfortable position. He settled the slouch hat over his face and folded his arms and did not move again.

"What do you want with Monsieur Alcazar?" the boy was asking. "Does he owe you money?"

Rodrigo and Stephano exchanged glances.

"Does he owe a lot of people money?" Rodrigo asked.

"My papa says he owes the *wrong* people money," stated the boy with a worldly-wise air.

"Monsieur Alcazar plays with rats," added a little girl, her eyes huge.

"He does what?" Rodrigo asked, startled.

"He plays baccarat," said Stephano, translating.

"Ah, yes, that would make sense," said Rodrigo, relieved. "Thank you, my friends." He handed the boy a coin and another for the little girl. "Now, which is his lodging."

"I'll show you!" said another boy, hoping for a copper of his own. "It's up the stairs."

The children began to pull Rodrigo into the dark and dismal courtyard.

"He's not there, though," added the older boy. "The door's busted. Someone took him away in the night."

"He was carried off by demons," said the little girl. "Demons took him to the Bad Place because playing with rats is wicked."

"What an astonishing imagination that child has," Rodrigo said in a low voice to Stephano. "She quite frightens me."

The children eagerly related the story, which was apparently the talk of the neighborhood. None of the children had actually seen the demons, much to their disappointment. The interesting event had happened well past their bedtimes. But the children all agreed there had been a "terrible fight." According to the oldest boy, a neighbor down the hall from Monsieur Alcazar had actually seen the demons in the act of carrying off the poor journeyman.

"I think we should have a talk with this neighbor," said Rodrigo quietly, and Stephano nodded.

The courtyard was dark, the stairs were darker. Accompanied by the children, Rodrigo began to grope his way up the stairs. Stephano lingered in the courtyard a moment, seeing if anyone was interested. At first he saw no one and was ready to join his friend. He had set his foot on the lower stair, when he saw a shadow out of the corner of his eye. He glanced over his shoulder back out into the street. The drunk with the slouch hat, who had been asleep on the bench, was now very much awake, standing in front of the iron gate and peering intently inside the courtyard.

The drunk caught sight of Stephano, tugged on his hat, slurred, "'Afternoon, Guvnor," and lounged off.

"Go on, Rigo! I'll catch up with you," Stephano called and ran back through the wrought-iron gate in pursuit of the drunk.

Stephano reached Half Moon Street in time to see the drunk in the slouch hat running down the street with a marked and fluid grace that reminded Stephano of a jongleur or an acrobat. Slouch Hat was no longer drunk either, apparently, for he motioned to a hackney cab that might have been waiting for him and hopped into it quite nimbly. The driver whipped the horses, and the cab drove off in haste.

"Now that's odd," muttered Stephano. "Damn odd."

He looked up and down the street and saw lots of people, but no one else who appeared to have a particular interest in 127 Street of the Half Moon. He went back through the gate, entered the courtyard, and was proceeding up the stairs, when he was almost swept away by a flood of children coming down. Rodrigo had been generous with his coppers and the children were running off in high glee to the local baker to buy penny buns.

Alcazar's lodging consisted of a bedroom and a sitting room. Stephano found Rodrigo examining the lock to the door that had, according to the children, been "busted." The strike plate, which was lying on the floor, was still affixed to a portion of the wall that had broken off when the door had been violently kicked in. Rodrigo crouched down to examine the plate, regarding it intently.

"Someone was keeping an eye on us," said Stephano "That drunk in the slouch hat asleep on the bench. He woke up in a hurry, seemingly. As you were going up the stairs, I caught him nosing around outside the gate."

"Did you get a good look at him?"

Stephano shook his head. "He had a hat pulled over his face. He ran off when he saw me. I went after him, thinking I'd ask him what he found so damn fascinating about this place. But before I could catch him, he hailed a cab and drove away. Looked to me like the cab was waiting for him. So what do you find so interesting about this lock? Looks ordinary to me."

"It *is* an ordinary lock," said Rodrigo. "Or it would be, if it had not been imbued with magic."

God breathed magic into everything in the world, "from mountains to molehills, men to mice" as the catechism states. Some people have the ability to see the magic, control it, guide it, construct it. These people are known as crafters, and Rodrigo was one of the best. Completely lacking in any magical talent, Stephano had always been fascinated and a little envious of Rodrigo's skill as a crafter and had never been able to understand his friend's lighthearted, flippant attitude toward his magic.

"You waste your time on frivolous pursuits," Stephano had said in exasperation after Rodrigo had been thrown out of the University for innumerable sins, among which were smuggling women into his room at night; advancing the theory that the Breath did *not* come from God's mouth, but could be produced by mixing together the right chemicals; and, the *coup-de-grâce*, using his magic to cause the bishop's miter to float off his head during a service to celebrate All Saints' Day. The miter had gone sailing about the sanctuary, much to the glee of the assembly, and Rodrigo had been expelled.

"There are men who would kill to have your power," Stephano had told his friend.

"That's just the point, Stephano," Rodrigo had replied with unusual gravity. "Men *would* kill."

He had refused to elaborate, and had gone on to make some jest of it. But Stephano had remained convinced that for once in his life, his friend had been in earnest.

Rodrigo passed his hand several times over the strike plate, taking care not to touch it.

"As you will observe," he said to Stephano, "the locking apparatus is quite simple, consisting of a metal strike plate affixed to the doorjamb with a hole for the bolt, which is attached to the door. Shut the door, slide the bolt, the door is locked. But Alcazar did not put much trust in his neighbors. See that?"

Beneath Rodrigo's hand, the strike plate began to glow faintly.

"I see light," said Stephano.

"You see light. *I* see sigils," said Rodrigo. "Burning with the magic. One sigil here and one here and one here, forming a construct, with lines of magical energy connecting them. The magic strengthens the metal. Ah, and look at this."

He murmured a word and the glow grew brighter.

"Another layer of protection underneath," said Rodrigo with satisfaction. "You could hit this lock with a hammer, my friend, and it would only dent it."

"Too bad Alcazar didn't think to strengthen the wall with magic," said Stephano, noting the splintered wood on the floor. "A lock is only as strong as the surface to which it is attached. People tend to forget that. A couple of good, hard kicks to the door, and you rip the strike plate right off the wall."

The two of them entered the sitting room. Stephano glanced at the peeling paint and the cracks in the walls and shook his head.

"Alcazar must not be a very good baccarat player. I'll take the bedroom. You search this room."

"What are we looking for?" asked Rodrigo.

"Some clue as to what Alcazar was working on in the Armory and who snatched him and why—"

"The children claim it was demons. I see no cloven hoof-prints," said Rodrigo. He sniffed the air. "Though perhaps I detect the faintest whiff of brimstone . . . Or is it boiled cabbage?"

"Be serious," Stephano said irritably.

He was suddenly sorry he'd taken on this job. He didn't like prying into the life of another man, especially when it appeared the life of this man had been a sordid and unhappy one.

"The little girl was right about him being carried off by demons," Stephano said to himself as he entered the shabby bedroom. "Demons of his own making."

The only article of furniture was a bed and a portmanteau on top of which stood a broken porcelain bowl and a water pitcher missing its handle. Alcazar had been smart not to trust his neighbors, who had apparently ransacked the place in his absence. The bed had been stripped of bed linens and blankets. The portmanteau was empty. If there had been a rug, it was gone.

Stephano stomped his foot on the floorboards, but heard no hollow sound. No loose boards suggesting a secret hiding place. He upended the portmanteau, found no false bottom. Nothing had been hidden under the bed or stuffed inside the straw mattress.

"No luck," he said, returning to the sitting room. "Strange that there's no blood."

"Why is that strange?" Rodrigo asked. His voice was muffled. He was on his hands and knees and had his head in the fireplace.

"Well, let's say that Alcazar is overly fond of playing baccarat. Unfortunately, he loses more than he wins and ends up owing money to the wrong men, as that astute little boy suggested. These bad men come to collect the debt or at least to impress upon Alcazar that he should pay up quickly."

"The sort of work our friend, Dag, used to do for a living," said Rodrigo, craning his neck to peer up the flue.

"They would have beat him up, bloodied his nose, punched him in the gut a few times, maybe cracked a couple of ribs. That's what these sort of debt collectors do."

Rodrigo sat back on his heels. "But instead of collecting a debt, they collected Alcazar. Maybe they're holding him for ransom."

"Not likely. According to my mother, who heard it from Douver, Alcazar has no relations except a brother who is a merchant sailor in Westfirth."

Stephano shook his head. "I hate to admit it, but it seems my mother is right. Alcazar was snatched because someone thinks he devised a way to use magic to strengthen metal. What was so fascinating about the fireplace?"

Rodrigo rose to his feet, brushed off his breeches, and pointed to the grate. "You'll note that piece of paper. It seems either Alcazar or someone else tried to burn it, but was in too much haste to do the job well."

Stephano bent over to take a closer look.

"The person tossed the letter onto the fire in the grate thinking it would go up in flames," Rodrigo continued. "But it was nighttime. Alcazar had gone to bed and allowed the fire to die down. The paper landed on coals that were hot enough to sear the center of the sheet, but not hot enough to destroy the paper completely. The person burning the letter either fled or was dragged off before making certain that the fire had done its work."

"I don't see how this helps," said Stephano. "All that's left of the paper are the corners and they're blank. The rest is nothing but ash."

"Never underestimate my incredible ability to snoop about where I'm not wanted," said Rodrigo cheerfully. "I need pen and ink and paper."

"If Alcazar ever had such things, they're not here now," said Stephano, glancing about.

"Oh, he had them," Rodrigo stated. "Note the ink splotches on the table. He was a learned man, our Alcazar. You can see traces in the dust on those shelves where he kept books. And he played baccarat, albeit poorly, since he appears to have lost more than he won. I played baccarat myself in University, as do many students. My guess is that he attended University himself, at least for a short time."

Rodrigo took one final look around. "Nothing more here. I think it is time we paid a visit to the neighbor. Are you armed? It might be well to take precautions."

Stephano drew a short-barreled pistol from inside his coat. The gun had been a gift from his godfather, Sir Ander Martel, and was one of Stephano's most prized possessions. The gun was unique in design and had been a present on the occasion of his twelfth birthday. The barrel was cast in the form of a dragon; wings swept back, as though the creature was diving. The clawed hands and feet wrapped around the silver inlaid stock. The dragon's tail created the spine of the handle. The gun was one of a matched pair; the other belonging to Sir Ander.

Stephano and Rodrigo walked down the dismal hall,

heading toward a door at the far end. The door was opened a crack, allowing a shaft of dusty sunlight to creep out of the room and into the hall. Whoever was inside was watching them. At their approach, the door shut, the sunlight vanished.

Rodrigo glanced at Stephano, who nodded to indicate he was ready. Rodrigo rapped smartly on the door.

Silence. Rodrigo rapped again.

"What do you want?" came a woman's voice.

"Just a friendly chat about my poor friend, Pietro Alcazar. He seems to have gone missing," said Rodrigo in plaintive tones. "I have some questions. Nothing alarming, I assure you, Madame. I will make it worth your while."

The door opened an inch. The woman peered out. Rodrigo held up a coin, this one of silver. Her eyes widened. She drew back the door, revealing a broom, which she was clutching in a threatening manner.

"You can put down the weapon, Madame," said Rodrigo.

Stephano looked past her. A little girl, a baby in her arms, crouched under a table. He didn't see anyone else.

"Is your good man at home?"

"He's my man, but there ain't nothin' good about him," said the woman, sniffing. She lowered the broom. "If you want him, you'll find him in the tavern, drinking with his layabout friends."

Stephano returned his gun to his pocket.

The woman's eyes were on the silver coin. "He don't know nothin' anyway. I was the one who saw 'em."

"Saw who?" Rodrigo asked.

"Them as took your friend away."

"If you could tell me about that night . . ."

The woman snatched the coin, stuffed it into her bosom, and told her story.

She had been awakened by a loud bang and a splintering crash, sounds of a scuffle, thumps and bumpings, and what she thought was a muffled cry for help. She had tried to wake her husband, but he had been dead drunk and had only grunted and rolled over.

Fearing for the safety of her children, the woman had grabbed up the broom in order to fight off whatever villains she might encounter. She opened the door a crack, and saw two men, clad all in black, descending the stairs at a rapid pace. She heard more thumps and bangs from the apartment, and then two more men emerged. One of the men carried a dark lantern and, by its light, she saw him holding another man by the arm, forcing him down the stairs.

She had waited a moment longer, but, seeing nothing more to alarm her, she had gone back to her bed. Early the next morning, broom in hand, she had ventured down to Alcazar's apartment "to find out what had become of the poor man." She had discovered the door open and a scene of destruction.

"Furniture tipped over, books scattered about, clothes strewn all over the floor...."

She was relating all this with relish when a thought suddenly occurred to her. She clamped her mouth shut and started to slam the door. Rodrigo blocked it with his foot.

"You've been extremely helpful, Madame," he said. "I was wondering if I could borrow a sheet of paper, a pen, and some ink."

"As if I would have the like!" returned the woman, trying unsuccessfully to dislodge Rodrigo's foot by poking him with the broom handle. "For one, I can't read nor write. For two, paper and ink is dear—"

"But Pietro Alcazar had such things," said Rodrigo, keeping his foot in the door. "You were the first in his apartment. I was thinking that perhaps you might have taken his books and his clothes and linens—"

"I never!" cried the woman angrily.

"—for safekeeping," Rodrigo finished in soothing tones. "So that no unscrupulous person would steal them, perhaps sell them at the pawn shop...."

"They would be worth a lot of money," said the woman, her eyes on Rigo's purse.

Rodrigo produced another silver coin and held it just out of her reach. "Paper, pen, and ink. You can keep the rest."

The woman wavered a moment. Rodrigo removed his foot from the door. She shut it and they heard her walk off.

"We're not *made* of silver, you know," said Stephano testily.

"Something tells me this will be worth it," said Rodrigo.

The door opened. The woman handed out several pieces of paper, a pen, and a pewter inkwell. Rodrigo gave her the silver coin. She took it and slammed the door shut.

Rodrigo and Stephano returned to Alcazar's lodgings.

"It does look as if he was snatched," said Stephano. "By professionals, at that."

"Let us see what this letter has to tell us," said Rodrigo. "If you could shut the door—or what's left of it. And we will shove the table up against it to prevent any intrusion by broom-wielding neighbors."

Rodrigo sat down cross-legged on the floor. He placed one of the blank pieces of paper the woman had supplied on the floor in front of him. Dipping the pen in the ink, he drew four sigils on the page: one at the top, one on either side, and one at the bottom. He then drew a line connecting each sigil, one to the other.

"What exactly is this going to do?" Stephano asked.

Rodrigo picked up the page and scooted closer to the fireplace. "The partially destroyed letter has two separate components: the ink and the paper on which the ink resides. If this spell works as planned, the magical construct I have crafted on *my* piece of paper should gently pull the ink from the burnt paper and transfer it to my sheet."

"Do you think it will work?" Stephano asked.

"I have no idea. Wind coming down the flue broke up the burnt paper, but we might still be able to read something. The one major problem is that the spell will destroy what's left of the original."

"So we have only one shot," Stephano said. "Just out of curiosity, where did you learn to cast a spell like this? I don't suppose reading burnt letters was part of the University curriculum."

Rodrigo smiled. "We both have the weapons we need to fight our battles, my friend. In the circles I frequent, information can be more explosive than gunpowder. Now, please be silent and let me concentrate."

Rodrigo held the page with the construct above the remains of the letter and focused his thoughts on the magic. His eyes closed to slits. His breathing slowed. He touched each of the sigils he had drawn on the paper, tracing them with his finger. After he had gone over all four of them, the constructs began to glow. The black ink shone with a golden light.

Rodrigo placed the glowing paper directly over the burnt paper in the grate. The two merged, the glowing paper seeming to absorb the burnt letter—ashes and all. The glow faded away. His paper rested on the cold stone of the hearth. The burnt letter was gone.

"Let us see what we have." Rodrigo gingerly picked up the piece of paper and turned it over. "Damn. I was afraid of this." He sighed in disappointment.

Stephano leaned over his shoulder. Very little had been salvaged. The missive had been brief. He saw a part of a word that began with "au" and another fragment that might have been "eet." Only two words in the body of the letter were clearly visible: the word "when" and a second word "Westfirth."

"The letter was signed," said Rodrigo, holding the paper close to his eyes.

"Can you read it?" Stephano asked.

Rodrigo shook his head. "All that is left are the bottom swoops of the characters. Maybe "ce" or "ca" . . . I can't be sure.

"So all we have is 'when' and 'Westfirth," said Stephano.

"A Rosian city with an unsavory reputation," said Rodrigo. He struggled unsuccessfully to rise out of his cross-legged position and finally reached out his hand. "Help me, will you? I seem to have lost all the feeling in my right foot."

Stephano hoisted up his friend, who groaned and hobbled about the room, trying to restore the flow of blood.

"Magic always takes a toll on me," Rodrigo complained.

"It wasn't the magic," said Stephano, unsympathetic. "Your foot went to sleep."

He stood gazing about the ransacked sitting room, turning things over in his mind.

"Well, that is that," said Rodrigo. "We've learned all we can learn here. Our simple little job is ended. You can report back to your mother, and then we can—"

"No," said Stephano.

"No, what? You're *not* going to report to your mother?"

"Report what?" Stephano said. "That Alcazar was a bad baccarat player? That three men broke into his rooms in the dead of night and took him away? That we found a burnt letter?"

"A letter containing the name of a city known to be a haven for criminals. *And* you saw someone keeping an eye on this place," said Rodrigo.

"I saw a man with a slouch hat," said Stephano. "There are a thousand men with slouch hats in this city, any one of whom might simply have been a drunken gawker who came to view the scene of the crime. I'm sure my mother will be agog with wonder at my investigative skills."

"So much for the simple job," Rodrigo said with a sigh. He folded the paper and thrust it into an inner pocket of his coat. "I gather we're going to be taking a trip to Westfirth."

"Miri and Gythe can talk to their Trundler friends there, find out if they know anything about Alcazar. And Dag still has some of his old underworld contacts in Westfirth. I believe it would be worth a trip."

The two left the lodging. As Stephano started to close the door, he paused, gazed thoughtfully back inside.

"You don't think that man with the hat was a gawker, do you?" Rodrigo asked.

"Drunks in slouch hats who sleep on benches don't have hackney cabs waiting to whisk them away," said Stephano.

He shut the door. Once out on the Street of the Half Moon, they turned their steps toward home.

"I'll send Benoit to court with a letter for my mother," Stephano said. "I'll tell her about what we found and where we're going."

"Admit it," said Rodrigo. "The real reason we're going to Westfirth is because you don't want to put on a cravat."

"Damn right," said Stephano, smiling.

His smile faded. He came to a sudden stop in the middle of the sidewalk and looked over his shoulder. The time was midafternoon and the street was even busier than when they had first arrived. The tavern's customers overflowed the bar and spilled out the door. Wagons and carriages rolled past. An airship floated overhead, casting a shadow that glided over the sidewalk.

"What are you doing besides impeding the flow of traffic?" Rodrigo asked, apologizing to an irate pedestrian, who had nearly run into him. "You've been as jumpy as a frog on a gridiron since we left that apartment.

"I have the feeling we're being followed."

"We are—by about several hundred Rosians. I beg your pardon, Madame. It was my fault entirely that you trod on my foot," said Rodrigo, doffing his hat. He seized hold of Stephano and tugged him along. "You'll never spot a tail in this crowd."

Stephano acknowledged this with a mutter and continued walking.

"Why should anyone be following us?" Rodrigo asked. "*I* don't owe any gambling debts."

Stephano glanced at him.

"I paid the duke last month," said Rodrigo with affronted dignity.

"And you know I don't gamble," said Stephano.

"At least not with money," said Rodrigo. "Your life is a different matter."

Stephano glanced once more over his shoulder. "I don't see anyone, but, as you say, in all this crowd spotting a tail is nigh impossible. I'm thinking we should celebrate our good fortune this evening by arranging a picnic in the park. Let's see who's keeping an eye on us."

"An excellent idea," said Rodrigo. He stopped to bow to a woman driving past in a carriage adorned with a baron's coat of arms. The woman leaned out to wave at him and blow him a kiss. "Intrigue. I love it. Who's watching who's watching who's watching whom."

"Only in this case," said Stephano, "it will be us watching them watching us."

Chapter Five

Constructs are the combination of various sigils connected by lines
of power or magical conduits to direct and control magical energy
into a pattern in order to achieve a specific and desired purpose.
— *The Art of Crafting*
Church School Primer

RETURNING HOME, RODRIGO WENT TO HIS
ROOM for an afternoon nap to recover from the fatigues of the day. Stephano sent Benoit to find Beppe, a
sharp lad of about twelve.

Stephano had first met Beppe when his mother, who
took in laundry, came to collect the clothes to be washed
while Beppe tagged along to steal whatever he could lay his
hands on. Benoit had caught the boy raiding the larder and
was teaching him a lesson with a cane applied to his backside when Stephano, hearing ungodly howling from the
kitchen, came to the boy's rescue.

Foreseeing that Beppe's current career was likely to land
him in prison, Stephano had offered to pay him to run errands. Beppe had proved invaluable. The boy could go anywhere, talk to anyone, eavesdrop, ask questions: all without
attracting notice. The boy was friends with Dag and Miri
and Gythe (Beppe was desperately in love with Miri) and
often did small jobs for them.

Stephano sent Beppe with a message to the sisters who

lived on their houseboat, the *Cloud Hopper,* and another message to Dag in his rooming house near the docks. Stephano gave his instructions to the boy verbally and made him repeat them back.

After Beppe left, Stephano wrote his mother a brief and concise account of everything they had discovered at Alcazar's apartment. He ended by saying he and the Cadre of the Lost were traveling to the city of Westfirth to follow up on the matter, then rang the bell for Benoit.

The old man came slowly up the stairs, groaning loudly with each step, and leaning heavily on his cane. He limped into the room.

"I have a letter I want you to deliver," said Stephano. Folding the letter, he dropped melted wax on the page and dipped his signet ring with its symbol of a tiny dragon into the melted wax.

Benoit gave another groan. "I'm sure I would be happy to do your bidding, sir, if I weren't in such constant misery that I can scarcely move a step—"

"You're to take the letter to the Countess de Marjolaine in the Royal Palace," said Stephano.

Benoit stopped groaning. His eyes gleamed. He stood up straight, smoothed back his long gray hair, and straightened his jacket.

"It will be hard on me, but I will undertake to make the sacrifice, sir."

"I thought you might," said Stephano wryly.

Benoit loved visiting the royal court. A trip to the palace brought back fond memories of times gone by. He would find time to dine with his friends in the servants' quarters, hear the latest below-stairs gossip. He stood his cane in the corner and reached for the letter.

Stephano eyed the old man. "What about your constant misery? I can send someone else—"

"Do not give my suffering a second thought, sir," said Benoit. "I would never dream of permitting my failing health to stand in the way of my duty to you."

Stephano hid his smile and handed the old man the letter. "Here's money for a carriage. Give the letter into the hands of the Countess de Marjolaine, not that popinjay of a secretary."

Stephano had no fear Benoit would give the letter to anyone except the countess, who always rewarded him most handsomely.

"The countess' hands, as you say, sir," Benoit said, unusually dutiful. He dashed down the stairs.

"You move damn fast for an old cripple!" Stephano called, leaning over the stair rail. "You forgot your cane!"

His answer was the door slam. Grinning, Stephano walked over to the window and drew back the curtain in time to see Benoit hurrying down the street, waving his arm to gain the attention of one of the wyvern-drawn carriages drifting by overhead. Stephano chuckled and then cast an idle glance up and down the street. His neighborhood was residential, home to men and women of the lower upper class, minor nobility like Stephano, and those of the upper middle class, such as the wine merchant who lived in the fine house across the street. Stephano saw the young and pretty nursemaid, who made eyes at Rodrigo whenever he walked past, taking the wine merchant's young son out for an airing. While the little boy played, the young woman was happily flirting with a young man paying her admiring attention.

Stephano shut the curtain. Removing his jacket, he picked up his rapier and went downstairs and out into the small yard at the back of the house where he had set up a target, which looked rather like a scarecrow. He began his daily fencing practice, performing over and over again the nine classic parries and their intricate footwork.

Lord Captain Stephano de Guichen had a reputation as an expert swordsman, a reputation he had earned. On the urging of the grand bishop, the king had made dueling illegal, mainly because too many promising young officers were being felled fighting affairs of honor. Unfortunately, the only effect this law had was to force gentlemen to settle their quarrels in the privacy of some cemetery or farmer's field, away from the notice of the watchful police, who took great delight in hauling the sons of noblemen off to jail.

Stephano disliked dueling. His father had taught him that if you *lived* the life of a man of honor, you did not need to be constantly proving you were an honorable man. But Stephano also followed his father's dictum that while a man of honor never sought a quarrel, he never backed down from one either. Stephano had fought three duels in his life, two of them over the unfortunate circumstances of his birth, where the men had presumed to refer to him as a bastard, and one duel when he accused Lord Captain William Hastind of being the cause of the death of Lady Cam, Stephano's dragon and comrade-in-arms in the Dragon Brigade.

Stephano had won all three duels. He had disarmed two of his opponents and severely wounded Hastind, who had, however, survived and returned to duty. He was now captain of the king's pride and joy, the man-of-war, *Royal Lion*. Hastind was a favorite of His Majesty. The king had been furious when he had heard about this last duel and only the entreaties of the countess had kept Stephano out of prison.

Stephano had been aware of the danger when he had challenged Hastind, but he would never, as long as he lived, forget what he owed to Lady Cam. Though dying and in terrible pain, the dragon had fought to the end to keep Stephano safe. He had expected to be arrested and was astonished when nothing had happened. He thought perhaps that Hastind, feeling guilty, had not pressed charges. Stephano never knew of his mother's involvement. If he had, he would have been furious.

Stephano practiced his fencing exercises daily, generally in the morning. He took his practice seriously; the exercise helped him keep fit and physical activity freed his mind. The blade of his rapier was a little heavier than most; the ornate basket hilt balanced that weight. While he lunged and recovered, he considered all that had happened this day. He went over every word of his mother's conversation, every detail of the visit to Alcazar's apartment. The more he thought about it, the more he became convinced that his mother was right. Someone believed Alcazar had made a world-changing discovery. Stephano wondered what this person would do to the poor wretch if they found out his "discovery" was so much hot air.

"Ah, there you are." Rodrigo opened the window to his bedroom and was leaning his head out. "Put away your toys. Nearly time for our picnic."

Stephano saluted his friend with the rapier and went inside to wash off the sweat and change his clothes. As he did so, he glanced out his bedroom window onto the street. The nursemaid and little boy were no longer visible. But the young man who had been flirting with her was still hanging around, lounging at his ease on a stone bench in a niche in a wall.

Stephano felt a tingle at the bottom of his spine. This man *might* be the nursemaid's lover, hoping for another glimpse of her, but Stephano doubted it. He dressed quickly, putting on a murrey-colored coat, white shirt, murrey breeches, and boots that came up over the knee. Going to Rodrigo's room, Stephano found his friend in hunting attire, with a long, belted red coat that extended below his knees, red breeches, black vest, and tall black boots.

Stephano stopped to stare.

"Was I mistaken, Rigo? Are we riding to the hounds? I thought we were going for a stroll in the park."

"You mock me, but this is the latest fashion," said Rodrigo, smoothing his white silk cravat. "I am told the Earl of Monte Claire dressed like this for an evening fete last week at the palace and was the object of considerable admiration. The queen was said to be in raptures. Besides, you want to 'flush' the 'bird' who is taking an unusual interest in us. Note the clever use of hunting terminology."

Rodrigo added a black hat to his ensemble and regarded himself with satisfaction in the mirror.

"I assure you, all eyes will be on me."

Stephano thought this would be quite likely, unfortunately, but, knowing his friend and knowing that further argument would probably make matters worse, he drew Rodrigo to the window and parted the curtain.

"See that man sitting on the bench in the corner? He's been hanging around ever since we returned. I'm going to leave first. You wait behind, see what he does. I'll meet you in the park. Did you find a suitable prop?"

"Not yet. I've been dressing. But I will," added Rodrigo, seeing Stephano's brows draw together. "Don't worry, my friend. I always come through for you, don't I? Go along. I'll be there shortly. You won't have any trouble finding me in the crowd."

"That's true enough," Stephano said gloomily.

Rodrigo laughed and took up his post at the window.

Stephano smiled to himself once he was out of the room. What Rodrigo said was true. He always came through. If it hadn't been for Rodrigo's courage and tenacity, sixteen-year-old Stephano de Guichen would have died on the field after the battle of Saint Bernadette in the Lost Rebellion. Rodrigo had risked imprisonment and execution by flouting the king's command that dead rebels should be left to the vultures and rats. Rodrigo, then fifteen, had searched the battlefield until he found Stephano, badly wounded. With Benoit's help, Rodrigo had carried Stephano away in the dark of night, hidden him, and had spent a month nursing Stephano in secret back to health. Rodrigo had been with Stephano, standing at his side, as Stephano witnessed his father being executed as a traitor.

No one took Rodrigo seriously. Their friends considered him a dandy, a fop, charming, witty, delightful to have around. The serious-minded Dag disapproved of Rodrigo's cavalier lifestyle. Miri and Gythe laughed at his airs and his clothes and his romances. Stephano alone knew and appreciated the depths of his friend's courage and resourcefulness. Neither of them ever talked about that terrible time—for good reason.

Rodrigo's family had not taken part in the rebellion, but they were friends with those who had, and that had been enough to damn them in the eyes of King Alaric. Rodrigo's father and mother had been exiled. His father had won his way back into His Majesty's good graces by the payment of a considerable sum of money and had been granted an ambassadorship. Even a hint that their youngest son had been involved in saving the life of a member of the de Guichen family would ruin them. Stephano had no choice but to keep his friend's valor a secret.

Sauntering out onto the street, Stephano turned his steps in the direction of the park. He walked at a leisurely pace, pausing to admire the early blooming roses and breathing deeply the late afternoon air. As he strolled along the tree-lined boulevard, he doffed his hat and bowed in polite greeting to passing ladies, who smiled and nodded in return. All the while, he felt eyes on him. The back of his neck prickled uncomfortably and he was tempted more than once to turn his head for a quick glance behind. He gritted his teeth and fought off the impulse, which might let the follower know he had been spotted. Rodrigo would see whatever there was to see.

The Park of the Four Oaks, named after the four ancient oak trees that grew in the center, was a popular place for the citizens of Rosia to visit at day's end. Here, the common folk mingled with the quality. Riders cantered along the bridle paths, exhibiting their equestrian skills. Young unmarried women walked in company with their chaperones or proud mamas, smiling at the young unmarried men. Boys sailed boats on the ponds. Girls rolled hoops and tossed coins into the fountains. Old women fed crumbs to the birds. Old men basked in the sun that warmed arthritic bones. The city police strolled about in pairs; due to the crowds, the park was also popular with pickpockets and thieves.

All this activity made the park an ideal setting for the sharing of secrets and intrigue. True privacy was difficult to come by in the city of Evreux, whether one lived in a hovel or a palace. Walls were thin. Rooms harbored closets to hide in, beds to hide under, curtains to hide behind. Neighbors eavesdropped on their neighbors. Servants were paid to betray their masters. Two people walking in the park, out in the open air, could carry on a confidential conversation and be certain that only the sparrows in the trees heard them.

Arriving at the park, Stephano went straight to the location where the Cadre generally met—a bench near the four gigantic oak trees that gave the park its name. He saw, without seeming to see, Dag wearing his mercenary uniform, in his usual place, sitting with his back up against one of the oak trees, teasing the cat, Doctor Ellington, with a piece of string. Knowing the string game amused his master, Doctor Ellington would play for a short time. When he grew bored, he would sit with his paws tucked under his chest and stare with enmity at his mortal enemy, the squirrels, daring them to come within range of his claws.

Miri and Gythe were established beneath another oak tree some distance from Dag. Gythe sat on a stool, playing a lap harp. Miri sang and collected coins in a basket from those who stopped to listen. Miri was dressed in colorful Trundler garb that she never wore except when she was performing: long, full skirt of bright red silk, with a black fringed shawl tied around her waist, a ruffled white blouse worn low to reveal her freckled shoulders. Her hair flamed in the sunlight, her golden earrings sparkled. She sang a bawdy song that had the gentlemen laughing and caused the chaperones to look scandalized as they hustled their young women out of earshot. Gythe wore a sky-blue skirt and plain blouse, her beautiful hair bound up in a scarf. As Stephano passed, he dropped a coin in the basket and Miri winked at him.

Stephano sat down on the bench and began to act the part of someone waiting impatiently for a meeting. He crossed his legs and uncrossed them. He looked at his pocket watch, rose to his feet, paced about, looked at his watch again, and sat down. He kept this up for half an hour, by which time he was no longer acting. He was truly impatient and growing annoyed and wondering what had become of Rodrigo. The sun was starting to slide into the mists of the Breath. The sky was glowing with oranges and purples. It would be dark within the hour, and the Cadre would lose their chance to get a good look at whoever was tailing them. When Rodrigo finally appeared, Stephano jumped to his feet and waved and shouted testily.

"Rigo! Over here! Where have you been?"

"There you are. I've searched all over. I found it," Rodrigo called, waving a book he held in his hand. "*The Crafter's Guide to Metallurgy*. One of my University texts. And there is something in here I think you will find very interesting."

Rodrigo pointed to a page in the book. Stephano affected to read it.

"Well?" he asked softly.

"You were right," Rodrigo said in a low voice. "After you left, the man waited a short time, then he followed you. I waited a short time, then I followed him."

Stephano glanced around. "I don't see him."

"He watched you until you sat down on the bench, then he took off at a run. I've been waiting and waiting to see if he came back, but he hasn't returned."

"He probably went to report that I was in the park."

"Report to whom? And why would anyone care where you are?"

"I don't know. None of this makes sense."

"So what do we do now?"

Stephano shrugged. "I will watch the crowds, and you will read this enlightening piece of literature."

"Must I? This book brings back unpleasant memories of the lecture hall."

"I'm surprised you have *any* memories of lectures," said Stephano, resuming his seat on the bench.

"I attended lectures," said Rodrigo, sitting down beside him. "It was the only place a fellow could get any sleep."

Rodrigo handed Stephano the book. "You read. I will study the view."

He leaned back, crossed his leg over his knee, and fixed his admiring gaze on a young woman, who was out with her chaperone. She blushed and raised her fan and turned away, and then peeped back at him from beneath the hood of her cloak.

Stephano tried to read, but he found the discussion of sigils and lines of magical energy every bit as confusing as he had when he was a boy with his tutor. Besides, it was growing too dark to read. With the sun setting, the crowds were starting to thin out, people going home to their suppers or to dress for the evening's festivities. Stephano had not noticed anyone who remotely resembled the man in the slouch hat or the young man who had followed him to the park. Dag and Miri and Gythe had not had any luck either, apparently, for none of them had given him a signal.

Their "hunting expedition" appeared to be a wasted effort.

While Stephano sat on the bench pretending to read and Rodrigo flirted with pretty women and Doctor Ellington dreamed of chasing squirrels, the bishop's agent, Dubois, was entering the Park of the Four Oaks himself. His day had been an eventful one.

Hearing news that James Harrington, one of Sir Henry's agents, was on Half Moon Street, Dubois rode swiftly to that location. He arrived in time to find Harrington asleep on a bench beneath the statue of Saint Michelle. Harrington had covered his face with a slouch hat, but Dubois had no difficulty in recognizing him.

Dubois was fortunate to encounter a talkative priest and he established himself on the steps of the church, from which location he could keep watch on Harrington while pretending to listen to the priest discuss everything from aphids in his rose garden to the lamentable lack of funds in the poor box.

Nothing interesting happened on the Street of the Half

Moon for a full hour, and Dubois was racking his brain, trying to figure out why Harrington was wasting his time here, when two men, dressed like gentlemen, stopped in front of number 127. The two men spoke to several children who were swinging on a gate, and one of the gentlemen offered the children a copper for information.

Dubois searched his mental files for the faces and pulled out two names: Lord Captain Stephano de Guichen, bastard son of the Countess Cecile de Marjolaine. The other was Monsieur Rodrigo de Villeneuve, son of Claude de Villeneuve, ambassador to Estara.

Dubois had excellent hearing, though he really didn't need to strain his ears, for the two gentlemen did not bother to lower their voices. They were asking about a resident of this run-down boarding house, a man named Pietro Alcazar. Dubois searched his file for the name, but came up with nothing. He stored it away for future reference.

Dubois gave the chatty priest a coin for his poor box and strolled over to the statue of the saint, taking up a position behind it. He noted, as he did so, that Harrington was also taking an interest in the two gentlemen, adjusting the slouch hat over his eyes so that he had a better view.

Captain de Guichen and Monsieur de Villeneuve entered the courtyard in company with the children. The moment they went inside, Harrington rose from his bench and, keeping the hat pulled low, strolled over to the iron gate and stared intently into the dark courtyard.

Harrington suddenly tugged on his cap, then wheeled and ran down the street. At the same moment, Captain de Guichen emerged from the courtyard, his gaze following Harrington, who signaled to a cab that he had apparently kept in waiting.

"Dearie me, James, you are slipping," said Dubois. "You let yourself be spotted. That was careless."

Dubois briefly considered mounting his horse and trying to follow Harrington's cab, but rejected that idea. His agents were in position outside Harrington's lodgings, and they would pick up the trail. Dubois was intrigued by the fact that Captain de Guichen was taking an interest in this Alcazar fellow.

Several boys were playing ball outside. Dubois strolled over to question them and heard the story of the mysterious disappearance of Pietro Alcazar, journeyman at the Royal Armory. Dubois waited until Captain de Guichen and his friend left the house, then entered the boarding house himself. Dubois mounted the stairs, and took a look around Alcazar's apartment. He found the open inkwell and a pen lying on the table. The ink on the pen's nib was still moist.

"Well, well, well," Dubois murmured.

He had a habit of talking to himself. As he was accustomed to saying, he liked talking to the most intelligent person in the room.

Finding nothing more to pique his interest, Dubois left the building, returned to his horse, and rode back to his own lodgings.

As he was riding, Dubois sorted through all the various bits of information he had acquired. Two nights ago, Pietro Alcazar, journeyman at the Royal Armory disappears from his dwelling on Half Moon Street. The next day, the Master of the Royal Armory is listed as a visitor to the Countess de Marjolaine. This morning, the countess' son is listed as a visitor to the countess. Also this morning, James Harrington, premier Freyan agent, is found lurking outside the residence of Pietro Alcazar. This midday, Captain de Guichen is seen entering the apartment of Pietro Alcazar. James Harrington leaves his post, rides off in a hurry.

Dubois did not waste his time trying to figure out what was going on. He had long ago learned that it was a mistake to theorize without information. He ordered in a late dinner and was finally able eat a decent meal.

A short time after, one of his agents came to report that Harrington had returned to his lodgings, where he had remained until a man arrived in a great rush. They held a brief conversation, then the man left and Harrington, dressed quite elegantly now, hailed a cab, and ordered it to drive rapidly to the Park of the Four Oaks.

Dubois went to the park, sauntered about for a short while, until he found Harrington, standing beneath an oak tree in company with another man.

Gone was the drunken Harrington in the slouch hat. In his place was a noble lord dressed in the latest style of the Freyan court. His hair was combed and powdered. He wore a sword on a finely embroidered baldric. His coat was dark wine with velvet collar and cuffs. He was talking animatedly to a young man of about twenty, who was red in the face and appeared beside himself with fury.

Dubois put a name to the young man. Escudero Juan Diego Ruiz Valazquez, son of Baron Valazquez, Estaran ambassador to Rosia.

"That is the man," Harrington was saying. "I recognized him the moment I saw him, and I dispatched my servant posthaste to fetch you."

"I will kill him!" said the young man in a strong accent, seizing the hilt of his sword. "I will slice off his—"

"You will do no such thing, my friend," said Harrington, placing a restraining hand on the young man's arm. "You will note the presence of two policeman over by the fountain. Besides, you do not want to make a scene before all these people. Consider your sister's reputation. The fewer who know about this sad affair, the better."

Valazquez contained himself with an effort. "Then what can I do? I will not allow the bastard to go unpunished!"

"You will handle this in the way most gentlemen handle such affairs," said Harrington coolly.

Valazquez glanced at him, uncertain. "But dueling is illegal."

"Only if the police find out about it. Ah, look. The policemen are walking off. Now is your chance. Remember, hold yourself in restraint."

"I will try," said Valazquez, breathing hard. "But it will be difficult. I long to rip out his lungs!"

The two men advanced. Dubois came out from around the back of the oak to observe the object of their conversation and Valázquez's wrath.

"Well, well, well," said Dubois and he raised his eyebrows—a rare display of emotion.

Harrington and Valazquez were walking over to speak to Captain de Guichen and his friend, Rodrigo de Villeneuve.

A beautiful afterglow spread over the sky. In the distance, drifting among the clouds, the Royal Palace was putting on a magnificent show. The base of the walls was a mixture of orange and pink drifting up through lavender. The tops of the palace's towers had faded to black, and the first twinkles of starlight were just starting to glimmer along the roofline.

"It's obvious we've failed. Can we leave now?" Rodrigo asked. "I'm hungry."

Stephano cast an interrogative glance over his shoulder at the other members of the Cadre. Miri, seeing him, gave a very slight shrug. Dag shook his head.

"You're right. This was a waste of time," said Stephano.

The bench was hard, and he'd been sitting there for almost an hour. Stephano stood and stretched and rubbed his lower back. Rodrigo rose with him and brushed off his red hunting coat. They were about to walk away when they saw Dag jump to his feet, spilling Doctor Ellington, who had been asleep in his lap. The cat gave an indignant yowl. Dag jerked his thumb.

Stephano turned just in time to see two gentlemen approaching. The eyes of both men were fixed on Stephano and his companion, and there was no doubt that they were coming to speak to them. Judging by their grim expressions, the subject of the talk was going to be unpleasant. Stephano elbowed Rodrigo.

"Company," he said.

Rodrigo glanced around. "Do we know these gentlemen?"

"*I* don't," said Stephano. "Do you?"

"Yes," said Rodrigo. "The young one is what you might call my opposite. I am the son of the Rosian ambassador to Estara, and he is the son of the Estaran ambassador to Rosia."

The younger man, dressed in the flamboyant style of satin coat and breeches that marked him as an Estaran, was apparently in the grip of some powerful emotion, for he tried to speak, choked on his words, and failed utterly. The second man, who was some ten years his senior, made a cold and formal bow.

Stephano looked closely at the older man, thinking something about him was familiar. The man had short-cut fair hair, flat blue eyes, high cheekbones, a square jaw, and the pale complexion of those who live in rainy climes. He was of medium height and moved with a languid kind of grace. The two made an odd-looking pair. His young companion had long black hair that fell in waves over his shoulders, a sleek black mustache, flashing black eyes, and the brown skin of those who live much of their lives in the sun.

"Captain de Guichen," the older man said. "Monsieur de Villeneuve."

"You have the advantage of us, sir," replied Stephano, with a bow equally cold and formal.

"I am Sir Richard Piefer of Dought Crossing, Freya. May I present His Excellency, Escudero Juan Diego Ruiz Valazquez, son of Baron Valazquez, ambassador from Estara."

Rodrigo was about to bow when Valazquez stepped forward, drew off his leather glove, and slapped Rodrigo across the face.

Rodrigo put his hand to his stinging cheek and stared at the man in astonishment. "What the devil did you do that for?"

"Because you, sir," said Valazquez in passionate tones, "are a most consummate villain and a scoundrel! I accuse you of having besmirched the honor of my sister and insulting my family. What have you to say for yourself, sir?"

"'Besmirched,'" said Rodrigo, opening his eyes wide. "Who talks like that these days?" He gave a light laugh.

"Admit it, young sir. This is a practical joke. Lady Rosalinda put you up to this, didn't she?" He turned to Stephano. "She has never forgiven me for the time I hid the frog in her glove box—"

Stephano had been watching the faces of the two men, and he said in an undertone, "They're not joking."

"Oh, come now," said Rodrigo, turning back to Valazquez. "You can't be serious."

"Sir Richard was a witness!" cried Valazquez in anger, indicating his friend, who bowed again in acknowledgment. "He saw you leaving my sister's bedroom in the middle of the night a fortnight ago."

"And I would ask one question of Sir Richard," said Rodrigo. "What the devil were you doing watching this man's sister's bedroom in the middle of the night?"

"Do you doubt the word of a gentleman?" Valazquez demanded vehemently.

"I beg your pardon," said Rodrigo, bowing. "I thought Sir Richard said he was a Freyan."

It took Piefer a moment to realize he had been insulted. When he did, his face darkened. Valazquez was incoherent with rage, reduced to sputtering.

"Perhaps I can settle this," Rodrigo continued smoothly. "My lord Valazquez, I recall spending a most enchanting evening a fortnight ago with a young woman who read poems to me as I rested my head on her white thighs—"

"Rodrigo!" Stephano exclaimed, scandalized.

"You lie! My sister, sir, cannot speak your language," said Valazquez.

Rodrigo frowned thoughtfully. "Her sumptuous curves, her large, round breasts—"

"My sister is slender and petite!"

"Ah, you see?" said Rodrigo, smiling. "This proves it. We are talking about two completely different young women. I bid you a good evening."

He started to turn away, as though the matter was concluded.

"All this proves is that you are a rogue and a coward!" said Valazquez, trembling with rage. "What of this?" He took from his doublet a packet of letters, tied with a red ribbon, and thrust them at Rodrigo. "Do you deny you sent these to my sister? Her *duenna* found them tucked under her pillow."

"Of course, I deny it," said Rodrigo. "That's not my handwriting. But even if I had written them, a letter beneath her pillow doesn't prove that *I* was beneath the sheets."

Valazquez flushed in fury and reached for the hilt of his sword. But before he had his sword out of the scabbard, Stephano was holding his rapier's tip at the young man's chest. Piefer hurriedly intervened.

"Gentlemen, this is neither the time nor the place," he said urgently. "The police might return at any moment!"

Stephano held his rapier on Valazquez until the young man slammed his sword back down into the scabbard, then Stephano returned his blade to its scabbard, though he kept his hand on the hilt. Out of the corner of his eye, he saw Dag standing alert, his hand beneath his jacket where he kept his stowaway pistol.

"You should not interfere, Captain," Piefer was saying. "The quarrel of Lord Juan Diego is not with you, but with your friend. There is only one way to settle this matter and that is on the field of honor."

"You make the arrangements, Sir Richard," said Valazquez. "If I stay here any longer, I will gut this wretch like a pig."

Casting a glance of utter contempt at Rodrigo, Valazquez stalked off, walking over to stand beneath one of the oak trees.

Rodrigo looked utterly bewildered. "Arrangements. But this is a jest . . .

"I'm afraid not, my friend," said Stephano gravely. "Your sins have caught up with you."

"I didn't write to the girl!" Rodrigo protested.

"Stand over there and be quiet," Stephano ordered in exasperation.

Rodrigo did as he was told, though he continued to listen anxiously.

"I will act as second for Lord Juan Diego," said Piefer.

"And I will act as second for Monsieur de Villeneuve," said Stephano. "As the challenged party, we have the choice of weapons."

"That is true," said Piefer. "What do you propose?"

"Pistols," said Stephano.

Rodrigo bounded forward and plucked at Stephano's sleeve. "Pistols! What are you doing? You remember what happened the last time I fired a gun—"

"You stand a better chance with pistols than you do with a sword," said Stephano. He turned back to Piefer. "Where shall we meet, my lord?"

"Are you familiar with the cemetery of the Church of Saint Charles, Captain?" Piefer asked politely.

"I am, my lord," said Stephano.

"The cemetery is quiet, out of the way, suitable to such affairs as this—"

"And you can just bury me while we're there!" Rodrigo groaned. "Save time, trouble—"

"I propose we meet at the cemetery at the hour of six of the clock in the morning if that is agreeable to you, Captain," Piefer concluded.

"It is most agreeable," said Stephano. He bowed. "Your servant, my lord."

"Your servant, Captain." Piefer bowed to Stephano.

Piefer did not bow to Rodrigo, but cast him a cold glance and then turned on his heel and walked away to join Valazquez.

Watching Piefer, Stephano experienced again the feeling that something about this man was familiar. Stephano had not met Piefer at court. Stephano had not been to court in months. He watched the Freyan with the disquieting feeling that the answer was important and that it was teetering on the tip of his brain.

Stephano gave up. Whatever it was, he couldn't take time to concentrate. He had to think of Rodrigo who was facing certain death.

The afterglow lit the sky, but the shadows were dark beneath the oak trees and the park was almost deserted when Stephano gave the private signal to Dag, Miri, and Gythe that he would be in touch with them later. There was nothing they could do.

The three had all witnessed the incident, and they had heard enough of Valazquez's ravings to figure out what had transpired. Stephano could tell at a glance what they were thinking.

Dag had never approved of Rodrigo, and he obviously believed in his guilt. Miri rolled her eyes and shook her head. She could never understand men and their need to settle such matters with bloodshed. Gythe was troubled and unhappy. He saw her try to come comfort Rodrigo, but her sister stopped her. The Cadre had to keep up the pretense that none of them knew each other.

Dag gathered up Doctor Ellington, put the cat on his shoulder, and waited for Gythe to pack up the harp. Always protective of the two women, he would see to it they reached the *Cloud Hopper* safely. Dag cast Rodrigo a final stern and dour glance before he left.

"Stephano," said Rodrigo when they were alone. "You have to get me out of this duel. I don't know one end of a pistol from another."

"I'm not certain I can, Rigo," said Stephano with a sigh. "I always told you something dire was bound to happen. The way you carry on—"

"But I swear to you I never touched that wretched girl! Well, perhaps I did touch her, but nothing more than a kiss on the hand."

"They have the letters you were imprudent enough to write to the girl."

"I didn't write those letters."

"No one will believe you—"

"Meaning *you* don't believe me," said Rodrigo with a faint smile. He added wistfully, "We could sail off on the *Cloud Hopper* tonight. We were going to Westfirth in the morning anyhow. Just make an early start?"

"Rigo," said Stephano, laying his hand on his friend's shoulder, "this is an affair of honor. Think what would happen if you ran. You would be branded a coward. You would no longer be admitted to court or to any of the elegant parlors or salons you love to frequent. Besides, this affair doesn't affect you alone. Your father may be an ambassador, but his favor with the king is tenuous at best. Think of the disgrace that would fall on him and your mother and your older brothers if the story circulates that you basely fled—"

"Enough, enough," said Rodrigo. He had been standing with his head lowered. He gave a thin smile. "Can you make me an expert marksman in one night?"

Stephano thought back to the one time he'd tried to teach his friend to handle a gun and he shuddered.

"It's late to be practicing with a pistol," he said evasively. "The neighbors would call the police."

"I suppose you're right. I doubt practicing would do me any good anyway. Perhaps this foul Valazquez is as poor as shot as I am," Rodrigo said hopefully.

"Perhaps he is," said Stephano, striving to be cheerful, though he gave an inward sigh. He had heard of Valazquez. The young man had fought any number of duels. He was a good swordsman and had a reputation as a crack shot.

"I tell you, Stephano, I am innocent," said Rodrigo, as they turned their steps toward home.

"I know, my friend, I know," said Stephano, glad for the darkness that hid the sorrow on his face.

There had been one other witness to the encounter in the park besides Miri and Gythe and Dag. Dubois watched

Valazquez and Harrington, in the guise of "Sir Richard Piefer" depart. Dubois had observed the signals between Captain de Guichen and the Guundaran mercenary (as Dubois judged from Dag's clothes and military manner). Dubois had watched the mercenary gather up his cat and leave in company with the two young Trundler women. Dubois saw Captain de Guichen and his unfortunate friend leave the park.

After all of them had gone, Dubois walked over to the bench where Captain de Guichen and Rodrigo de Ville-neuve had been sitting. He found the book they had left behind, forgotten in the turmoil. The title was embossed on the cover and he could just barely read the imprint of the letters in the sun's dying glow: *The Crafter's Guide to Metallurgy*.

Night's shadows closed around Dubois, both figuratively and literally. He had the feeling something of immense importance was about to happen and he was groping about in the darkness, unable to see the danger that was perhaps right in front of him.

What game was Harrington playing? Why was he now disguised as a titled Freyan noble in company with the impressionable and not very bright youth, Valazquez, the son of the Estaran ambassador to Rosia? Why had Harrington, the instigator of the challenge, seen to it that the charge was made against Rodrigo de Villeneuve? Captain de Guichen was the threat.

Dubois could not figure any of this out, but he knew one fact for certain. Sir Henry Wallace was the thread that ran through all these seemingly disparate incidents and tied them together. Harrington was Sir Henry's agent. Find Sir Henry. Find answers.

Arriving at his lodgings, Dubois collected the reports from his agents that were waiting for him. He glanced through them and tossed them irately in the fire. None were any help. He ate a quick supper, then went to his bed. He had to be up early.

Dubois had a duel to fight.

Chapter Six

Since the invention of the pistol, crafter armorers have been exploring magical means to make weapons more durable and accurate. Constructs are placed on the barrel to strengthen the steel in order to produce lighter weapons. Targeting constructs carefully set inside the barrel aid a pistol's accuracy. These constructs are melded with others to provide basic protection from the elements, keep the barrel from rusting, etc. Because of the heat and energy generated during use, weapons that are enhanced by magic require yearly examination and repair of the constructs.

—An excerpt from "Constructs and Their Use
in the production of Weapons and Armor"
by Master Gaston Bondrea
Grand Master, Rosian Armorers Guild

RODRIGO SAID NOTHING DURING THEIR WALK back to the house that evening. When they arrived, Stephano suggested they have a glass of wine.

"Since we're once more in funds," he added, trying to seem cheerful.

Rodrigo shook his head. "I'm going to my room."

"Do you want company?" Stephano asked.

Rodrigo hesitated, his hand on the balustrade, then said quietly, "I have to write a letter to my father and mother."

He walked slowly up the stairs. Stephano felt a choking sensation in his throat and turned away quickly. This letter

would be a difficult one to write. Rodrigo was the youngest
child, the spoiled child, the mischievous imp whose antics
had delighted his fond parents who could never see a fault in
their brilliant, talented son. And now he was telling them
good-bye—forever. Stephano could not imagine how the terrible news of Rodrigo's death would affect his loving parents.

He cursed stupid sons of barons and their equally stupid
and gullible sisters and hung up his baldric, flung off his
coat, and threw his hat at the bust of King Alaric. The hat
fell on the floor and Stephano left it there. He entered the
kitchen to find Benoit and young Beppe seated at the table,
finishing up the remnants of a cassoulet of white beans and
chicken.

Beppe leaped to his feet at the sight of Stephano and
gave a salute. His dearest wish, since he had met Stephano,
was to be a Dragon Knight. Benoit cast a glance at the hat
on the floor and groaned and began to rub his leg.

"Don't disturb yourself," said Stephano caustically. "I'll
pick it up later. Beppe, I'm glad you're here. I need you to
run an errand."

"Of course, Captain," said Beppe, pleased.

Stephano dashed off a note to Miri and Gythe and one
to Dag, telling them that he both hoped and expected that
he and Rodrigo would meet them the next day at the *Cloud
Hopper* and that the ship should be ready for travel. He
warned them not to come to the house, as it was likely under surveillance, though he had no idea who was watching
or why.

"Deliver these letters," said Stephano, "and then go
home. Here's some money."

"That's a lot, Captain," said Beppe, his eyes wide.

"I'm sure we owe you back pay," said Stephano dispirit-
edly.

"Yes, Captain, thank you, sir." Beppe started to leave,
then turned back. "Is anything wrong, Captain?"

"No more than usual," said Stephano, with an attempt at
a smile. "Now run along."

Beppe gave another salute and dashed off.

Stephano, knowing it would be useless to ask Benoit, went to the storeroom fetch his own beer. The barrel was once more full.

"How was court, Benoit?" he asked. "Any message from my mother?"

"Your honored mother the countess has heard nothing more about the matter at hand, sir," said Benoit. "She bids you a safe journey."

Stephano sighed and sat down. If Rodrigo survived, the Cadre would go to Westfirth to continue the search for Alcazar. The chance of Rodrigo surviving being highly unlikely, Stephano guessed he would spend tomorrow planning his friend's funeral. He drank the beer, stared into the empty mug, then suddenly swearing viciously, he flung it at the fireplace. The crockery mug shattered.

Benoit eyed the remains. "I'm not cleaning that up."

"Like I give a damn!" Stephano said savagely.

"What is wrong, sir?" Benoit asked. He rose to his feet without a trace of infirmity to face Stephano. "I have a right to know."

Benoit had ridden with his master, Sir Julian, to the convent to bring home his newborn child. Sir Julian had placed the baby in Benoit's arms and said, "Benoit, meet my son. Care for him as you do me."

Stephano rested his elbows on the table and dropped his head in his hands and dragged his fingers through his long hair. His face was pale, haggard.

"Sir," said Benoit, sounding fearful, "tell me—"

"Rodrigo's very likely going to die tomorrow," said Stephano.

"Oh, my God, sir!" Benoit grabbed hold of the edge of the table for support. "The king didn't find out about— Master Rodrigo's not going to be executed—"

"No, no, nothing like that," said Stephano wearily. "A duel. A bloody, stupid duel."

He described what had happened in the park.

"Master Rodrigo claims he's innocent, sir," said Benoit.

Stephano gave a wan smile. "Master Rodrigo always claims he's innocent."

"That's true, sir," the old man admitted. He set to work with unusual energy, filling the teakettle with water and placing it on the hob, stirring up the coals, adding wood to the fire.

"What are you doing?" Stephano asked.

"Fixing a honey posset for Master Rodrigo, sir. It will help him sleep. He will need all his faculties for the morning."

"I doubt if his 'faculties' are going to be that much help," Stephano muttered.

Benoit disappeared into the storeroom. He was gone several moments, then returned carrying a crock of honey and a small, dust-covered jug.

"I don't suppose I could have a tumbler full of whatever is in that jug?" Stephano asked.

"For illness only, sir," said Benoit. He cast Stephano a sharp glance. "*You* need to be sober. It's up to you to find a way to save him."

"There's nothing I can do this time, Benoit," said Stephano.

"You'll find a way, sir," said Benoit stoutly.

Stephano only shook his head. He watched while Benoit concocted the posset, mixing the contents of the mysterious jug with honey and boiling water.

"I'll take that to him," Stephano offered. "Save you a trip up the stairs."

"I will take it, sir," said Benoit with dignity. "It's the least I can do."

Stephano followed the old man as he hobbled up the stairs. He heard Benoit's gentle knock, saw him open the door softly and carry the steaming mug inside. Stephano sighed deeply and went to his own room.

Benoit's posset contained rum laced with opium, with the result that Rodrigo slept quite soundly, while Stephano passed a wretched night, trying in vain to think of some way to save his friend's life. He was so desperate he even considered traveling to the palace to appeal to his mother. On sober reflection Stephano realized there was nothing even the powerful countess could do. Rodrigo had made his bed, so to speak.

In the small hours of the morning, Stephano went to his bookshelf and found a small, thin volume given to all officers in the navy. It was called the *Codes Duello* and laid down the rules of dueling. Stephano was familiar with the guide, but he read it over again, hoping to find some way for Rodrigo to honorably withdraw. Unfortunately, the book only confirmed what Stephano had known from the beginning—there was nothing to be done.

According to the *Codes Duello*, Rodrigo might have been able to offer an apology to Valazquez and his sister without loss of honor except that a blow had been struck— an insult no gentleman could tolerate. The *Codes* offered only one hope and it was faint: as a second, Stephano had the right and the duty to attempt to reconcile the parties before blood was shed. Considering the hot-headed Valazquez, Stephano didn't think reconciliation likely.

The night passed slowly for Stephano and yet far too quickly. When the clock struck four, he dressed by candlelight, putting on his military-style dragon green coat and breeches with high boots and a plain waistcoat. Beneath the waistcoat he wore a lightweight, chain mail vest made of tiny riveted links of steel, each set with its own magical construct. The vest had been a gift from his Dragon Wing when he had been named commander of the Dragon Brigade. The vest weighed only ten pounds and provided better protection than a steel breastplate. A craftsman in the Royal Armory had worked three months to make it.

How ironic would it be, Stephano thought, if that craftsman had been Pietro Alcazar.

Wearing armor to a duel wasn't exactly proper etiquette, but protecting himself *was* good, common sense. Stephano didn't know either of these gentlemen and while he assumed they *were* gentlemen and wouldn't resort to any dirty tricks, he considered it wise to take precautions.

When he was dressed, he went to summon Rodrigo. Having expected his friend to be lying awake, a prey to anxiety, Stephano was surprised to find Rodrigo sleeping as soundly as a babe in arms. Stephano had to shake him to rouse him. Rodrigo woke groggy and disoriented, at which point Stephano sniffed at the mug containing the honey posset, smelled the opium, and yelled angrily for Benoit.

Between the two of them, they managed to get Rodrigo out of bed, sobered up, and dressed. The laws of dueling forbade the wearing of any clothing set with magical constructs. The duel's adjudicator—a person brought in from outside to see to it that the proceedings were handled fairly—was required to check to make certain neither opponent took such an unfair advantage. The *Codes* did not say anything about the style of clothing the combatants wore. Stephano insisted that Rodrigo put on a loose-fitting white shirt with overlarge, flowing sleeves. In any sort of breeze, the sleeves would flap in the wind, making aiming at a vital organ difficult.

Rodrigo protested against the shirt, which was old and completely out of fashion.

"He'll probably just shoot me in the head," said Rodrigo. "At least let me die in style."

"A head shot is unlikely," said Stephano briskly, determined to be matter-of-fact. "You both will stand back-to-back with your guns in the air. At the signal, you will each walk ten paces, turn, and fire. Because Valazquez has to turn, he will be forced to fire quickly, hoping to hit you before you can get off a shot at him. He won't have time to aim at your head. He'll likely try to hit you in the chest, which provides a larger target and is easier to hit."

"So I should do the same?" asked Rodrigo. "Aim for his chest?"

Stephano thought back to the first, last, and only time he

and Dag had tried to teach Rodrigo to shoot. They had all three been extremely fortunate to escape with their lives. Rodrigo had a most lamentable habit of closing his eyes whenever the gun went off.

"Just keep your eyes open," said Stephano.

"I can't help it," Rodrigo protested. "It's like sneezing. Absolutely impossible to keep your eyes open when you sneeze."

"You will have only one shot, Rigo," said Stephano quietly. "You *have* to make it count."

Rodrigo looked down at his trembling hands and smiled wanly. "I'm not sure it will matter whether my eyes are open or closed, my friend."

Stephano tried to say something reassuring, but the words wouldn't come past the burning sensation in his throat. Down below, a clock struck five. Stephano put his hand on his friend's shoulder.

"Is it time?" Rodrigo asked with terrible calm.

"It is time," said Stephano.

Rodrigo picked up a sealed letter and handed it to Stephano.

"For my father," Rodrigo said. "You will take it to him if . . . if . . ." He couldn't go on.

Stephano took the letter and tucked it inside his waistcoat. "A sacred trust."

Rodrigo nodded gratefully and the two went downstairs together. Benoit stood waiting for them at the bottom of the staircase. His eyes were red-rimmed.

"I summoned the cab, sir," he said in a shaking voice. "It's waiting."

Benoit handed them their cloaks and hats. Stephano draped his baldric with his rapier over his shoulder. Sometimes the seconds ended up in a duel themselves. Stephano hoped that happened. He found the prospect of fighting the cold and supercilious Freyan, Sir Richard Piefer, extremely appealing.

Benoit held a tray containing two crystal goblets filled

with a golden-brown liquid. Stephano sniffed at it and wondered how Benoit had managed to come by brandywine, which was very expensive. He did not ask.

"To calm the nerves," said Benoit.

"Thank you, Benoit," said Rodrigo, and he downed the brandy gratefully.

He impulsively embraced the old man. Stephano felt tears sting his eyes, and he hurriedly blinked them away. Benoit wiped his nose with a large handkerchief and then bravely stood at the door to see them off.

Stephano remembered Benoit standing in the door like that, looking brave like that, on the day his father had gone to his execution. Stephano's stomach clenched. Bile filled his mouth. He reminded himself sternly that his friend needed him to be strong, and he drank the brandy. The liquid bit into his throat and warmed his blood. He handed the glass back to Benoit, who said softly and pleadingly, as he took it, "Keep him safe, sir."

Stephano gave a sorrowful shake of his head and turned away.

The two men entered the hansom cab. Neither had shaved; neither felt his hand to be steady enough, and asking Benoit to shave them was out of the question. Stephano gave the driver directions to the Church of Saint Charles, mumbling something about attending early mass.

The hansom driver, who was about thirty, and had the jaunty air of a race-course tout, gave them a knowing smile and a wink. He took his seat up top and whistled to the horse.

Stephano, glancing back, saw Benoit standing on the door stoop, a candlestick in his hand, tears running down his dried-up, leathery cheeks. The cab was pulling away when movement on the sidewalk caught his attention.

The sun had not yet risen. The street was dark, except for Benoit's candle, and that gave only a feeble light. Yet Stephano was convinced he saw a shadow detaching itself from darker shadows. Stephano leaned out of the open-air compartment to try to get a better view. The shadow melded with the darkness. Stephano sat back, frowning.

"What are you doing?" asked Rodrigo listlessly.

"I saw a man in the alley," said Stephano. "Someone is still watching us."

"Probably to make certain I don't run off," said Rodrigo.

"Possibly," said Stephano, but he was not convinced.

Rodrigo wrapped his cloak closely about him and sat back against the cushions, staring at the world he might shortly be about to leave. Stephano tried to think of something to say that would bring his friend some comfort, but everything he thought of sounded stupid and maudlin. Rodrigo's hand, fist clenched, rested on the seat. Stephano placed his hand over his friend's. Rodrigo responded with a pallid smile. They rode in silence to the church. Once there, Stephano asked the driver of the hansom cab to wait for them until mass was over.

The driver gave a chuckle and another knowing wink. Sitting back in the seat, he tipped his hat over his face and settled himself comfortably. The horse began to graze on the dew-wet grass.

"At least, you'll save money, my friend," Rodrigo said, as they were walking toward the site of the duel. "Going back, you'll only have to pay for one fare."

Chapter Seven

Magic, according to the church, is the echo of God's voice. Magic is of God and therefore under the dominion of the church in order to make certain that crafters use their talents for God's glory. What this means is that the church oversees the use and development of all magical constructs. The church is the final authority on the creation of new constructs.

"Magic is from God and so should glorify God and serve God and his people in their work to do God's will."

I say—bullshit.

Magic is of men.

—Introduction to treatise written by Rodrigo de Villeneuve prior to his expulsion from the University

THE CHURCH OF SAINT CHARLES WAS ANCIENT, one of the first churches built in Evreux when the city was established as Rosia's capital five hundred years ago. The church stood on a low bluff at a bend of the River Counce. According to ancient records, the original structure had been simple in design. The records listed the amount of stone and wood required, the number of crafters and laborers and masons who had worked on the church, careful notations of the money the people were paid, and a faded plan of the structure drawn up by the unknown architect. The records and the plan were all that was left of the first church. It had been burned to the ground by Freyan invaders during the Blackfire War.

The Church of Saint Charles, patron saint of Evreux, had been rebuilt on a grander scale—a defiant gesture on the part of the Rosians after driving out the Freyans. With its delicate spires and stained glass windows, the church was now a beautiful edifice overlooking the meandering river.

A cemetery had been established on the grounds adjacent to the church. A quiet and private place, the cemetery with its ancient mausoleums and marble monuments, sheltering trees, trimmed hedgerows, and long stretches of green grass was a favored place for clandestine meetings, whether for love or for those of a more violent nature.

At this early hour, the pale sun was barely visible through the thick mists rising from the river. The orb looked shrunken and gave no warmth, shining with a gray-tinged light. Rodrigo and Stephano were the first to arrive, which allowed Stephano the chance to view the ground. He had not fought any of his own duels here, but he had acted as second to a fellow officer in the Dragon Brigade who had. That duel had ended as well as these things can. The two men had fought with swords. One had been grazed in the arm, the other in the chest. Since blood had been drawn, both gentlemen had pronounced themselves satisfied and had departed with honor.

Stephano had a grim feeling today's duel was not going to end as well. He walked the long, broad sward that formed a border between the old, graying tombstones and the low stone wall that stood between the cemetery and the river. A grove of oak, walnut, and maple trees stood outside the cemetery wall at the south end. Willow trees lined the bank of the sleepy river. The church itself was at the north end, some distance from this part of the cemetery. The duelers would face north and south, so that neither one would be blinded by the rising sun which, given the mists, was not likely to be a problem.

The cemetery was very old. Few people were buried here anymore; only those with family vaults, and most of the ancient families had died out. The tombstones were worn and faded; the dead slept quietly. Any restless ghosts had long since let go their tenuous grasp on the world and drifted off to a final rest. An air of peaceful melancholy pervaded the cemetery. A statue of Guardian Saint Simone, Acceptor of the Dead, stood in the center with her arms spread in welcome, her face loving and forgiving.

The mists crept among the tombstones and rolled off the river between the trunks of the trees. Rodrigo stood quietly staring at one of the tombstones as though he could imagine himself lying beneath it. Stephano pulled out his pocket watch. They lacked fifteen minutes until the designated time. Just as he was thinking that Valazquez was going to be late or might not come at all, a black coach arrived. The elegant coach with its team of four horses and two footmen riding behind rolled to a stop next to the hired hansom cab with its driver snoring in his seat.

Sir Richard Piefer descended, followed by two men, and then Valazquez. All of them wore black cloaks and looked rather like ghosts themselves as they walked through the mists. Stephano focused on the two gentlemen who accompanied Piefer and Valazquez. One of them was portly, slightly stoop-shouldered, and walked with the aid of a silver-headed cane. He wore a shoulder-length, curled periwig beneath a black, tricornered hat. His black waistcoat barely met across his broad middle. His face was fleshy, his eyes dark and flat.

Formal introductions followed. For the first time, Stephano met the notorious Oudell Chaunquler, unofficial official adjudicator of duels in the capital city of Evreux. Chaunquler was perhaps fifty years of age. His passion was dueling, and he was often invited to officiate. He always brusquely refused payment, though he would accept a gratuity pressed into his palm after the affair was over.

Chaunquler was reputed to know the *Codes Duello* by heart, upside down and backward, and was here to settle any dispute or question that might arise. Since dueling was illegal and such matters could not be taken to court, Chaunquler's judgment was considered final. Stephano had been feeling the weight of his responsibilities as second lying heavy on his shoulders, as his fear lay heavy on his heart. He was relieved that he could turn over the procedures of the duel to a man who understood what he was doing and would see that all was handled fairly.

The other man was introduced as Doctor Alabarca. A surgeon was always present at a duel, for obvious reasons. Doctor Alabarca was so bundled up in his cloak that Stephano could not get a look at him. The surgeon had brought a camp stool with him. He set it down, sat on it, rested his bag of instruments on the grass, and did not move. He said nothing to anyone, responded to no greetings, and gave the impression he was annoyed at having to be up this early.

Chaunquler walked over to a tall, broad marble tombstone that made a perfect table. He drew a black cloth from his waistcoat pocket, shook it with a loud snap that caused Rodrigo to flinch, and spread the cloth on the tombstone. Valazquez and Piefer removed their cloaks and handed them to a servant, who took them back to the carriage. The two men advanced onto the lawn.

Valazquez wore a shirt with long sleeves and a fancifully embroidered waistcoat decorated with peacocks and flowers trimmed in golden thread, gray breeches, and black boots. He stood aloof from the proceedings, as was proper. Rodrigo mechanically took off his coat and draped it over the head of a marble angel. He stood shivering in the chill mist, his face exceedingly pale. He watched the proceedings with a detached air, as though this was happening to someone else and he was merely a confused observer.

Stephano noted with interest that Piefer was openly wearing a lightweight leather breastplate inlaid with sigils—magical constructs made of thin brass. Stephano had been feeling guilty for having put on his own magically enhanced chain mail beneath his waistcoat; the implication was that he did not trust his honored second. Stephano guessed that Piefer's long coat also had various magical constructs sewn into it. Since both he and Sir Richard were acting as seconds, nothing in the rules prohibited them from wearing such protection. Apparently, Piefer did not trust his opponents any more than they trusted him.

"Bring the pistols forward for examination," said Chaunquler in cold, dispassionate tones.

Piefer motioned to one of his servants, who brought forth a beautiful case made of ebony. He placed it on the tombstone that was serving as a table and then withdrew.

"Are these your pistols, my lord?" Chaunquler asked Piefer

"They are, sir," said Piefer.

"Have you any objection to the use of pistols provided by your opponent, Captain?" Chaunquler asked Stephano.

"None in the least, sir," said Stephano. "I assume I will be permitted to examine them."

"Certainly! I *do* know the rules, Captain," said Chaunquler sharply, annoyed.

"I meant no offense, sir," said Stephano.

Mollified, Chaunquler grunted and reached out his large, puffy hands to open the ebony box, revealing a pair of matched dueling pistols, a brass powder horn, lead balls, and small patches of oiled cloth nestling beside the guns.

Stephano picked up one of the pistols and took several moments to thoroughly examine it, looking for any signs of magical constructs that might either interfere with the pistol's firing mechanism or enhance it. Rodrigo would have been better suited to the task, but permitting one of the duelists to examine the weapons was very much against the rules.

Satisfied, Stephano loaded the gun, pointed it at the ground, and pulled the trigger. Rodrigo shuddered visibly at the sound. Piefer gave a faint, disdainful smile that made Stephano long to knock it off the Freyan's face. He kept himself in firm control. He had to, for Rodrigo's sake. But Stephano resolved privately that no matter what happened today, he and the Freyan would meet again. Piefer picked up the second weapon, examined it, and fired.

Chaunquler then examined the two pistols. Satisfied that both guns were smooth bore, as the rules required; that both were in good working order; and that neither had been magically enhanced, he returned them to the seconds. Each man reloaded his pistol and placed it back in the case. Both men turned to Chaunquler, who had been watching with a critical eye.

"You are both satisfied?" he asked.

Piefer and Stephano nodded and Chaunquler continued.

"The seconds will now determine the distance," said Chaunquler.

"Ten paces," said Piefer.

"Twenty," said Stephano, thinking that the farther Rodrigo was from Valazquez the better the odds he might come out of this alive.

Piefer was not pleased. He argued that ten paces was the rule, but Chaunquler stated that such was not the case. He decreed that twenty paces was acceptable. Piefer glanced at Valazquez, who shrugged. Piefer agreed with an ill grace.

Once this matter was settled, Chaunquler motioned. "The two participants will please come forward. I will check to make sure neither is using magic to gain any advantage. Are we agreed that I may proceed?"

"Of course, sir," Piefer answered.

"We are, sir," said Stephano.

Valazquez walked to the table and began to unbutton his waistcoat. Rodrigo made no motion to walk over, and Stephano had to call his name in a low undertone. Rodrigo looked at him pleadingly, begging him to tell him this was some sort of strange mischance and they could all go home to a good breakfast. Stephano's heart ached, but he could do nothing. The duel had to proceed. He motioned to the table and Rodrigo, gently sighing, began to try to unbutton his waistcoat. His trembling fingers fumbled.

Valazquez laid his waistcoat on the table and, as he did so, he cast Rodrigo an odd glance, as though he seemed to want to say something, but couldn't make up his mind.

Stephano noticed the glance and so did Piefer. The Freyan frowned and walked up to Valazquez and said something to him in such a low voice that Stephano could not hear. Stephano watched Valazquez closely and saw the young man shake his head. He continued to appear to be undecided and Stephano had a sudden wild hope that Valazquez wanted to call off the duel. Perhaps he was afraid or perhaps he had discovered he'd accused the wrong man. Piefer appeared to be attempting to bolster the young man's resolve.

Stephano tried frantically to think of some way of speaking to Valazquez, but the rules of dueling strictly prohibited either second from talking to the opposing combatant. As for Rodrigo, he was completely oblivious to anything. He took off his waistcoat and went to lay it on the tombstone and missed. The waistcoat fell to the ground. He stared at it as though trying to figure out what it was doing there. Stephano picked it up for him and rested it on the black cloth.

Chaunquler went about his job briskly and efficiently. He turned both waistcoats inside-out, searching for magical constructs that might deflect a bullet. Finding nothing, he then asked each man to hold out his arms. Chaunquler examined the shirts each man was wearing. This done, he asked if there was a possibility that either man could be dissuaded from this course of action.

A slight breeze had risen, enough to cause the mists to swirl about the boles of the trees. The breeze ruffled a few loose strands of Rodrigo's hair, that he wore tied back. He was deathly pale, no color in his face. His brown eyes appeared unusually large. He made some movement with his lips that might have been a "no." Chaunquler turned to Valazquez, who cleared his throat.

"Before we commence, I have a sentiment I wish to express to Monsieur de Villeneuve," he said.

Stephano's heart beat fast. Rodrigo's cheek stained with a faint flush of hope. Piefer looked angry and disapproving.

Valazquez made a slight bow. "It would be unseemly of

me if I did not express my sympathy to Monsieur de Villeneuve on the death of his father."

Rodrigo stared at the man. He looked dazedly at Stephano.

"What did he say?"

"That your father is dead," said Stephano, shocked. He
wondered if this was some ploy by Valazquez to attempt to
rattle Rodrigo.

"That can't be!" said Rodrigo, shaken.

"We are both amazed by this terrible news, Monsieur,"
said Stephano sternly. "My friend has heard nothing of this.
Please explain yourself."

Valazquez looked startled. "Truly? He has heard nothing? Then I fear I am the bearer of ill tidings. My father, as
the Estaran ambassador, received the news last night. Monsieur de Villeneuve was the victim of an assassin's bullet.
The murderer escaped, unfortunately, but the authorities
are doing all they can to find him. They have evidence that
he was a Travian. Probably having to do with this lamentable dispute over Braffa."

Stephano had no reason to doubt Valazquez, but he
knew that this information, having traveled a great distance
and passed through many hands, was open to question. The
news of the death of the ambassador would have to be ver-
ified. The countess would know the facts. Meanwhile, he
saw a way to save Rodrigo, who was staring in wordless
confusion at Valazquez. Stephano turned to Chaunquler.

"Monsieur, as you can see, my poor friend is overcome
by grief and amazement. He is in no condition to fight this
day. I ask for a postponement."

Once the duel was postponed, he could take Rodrigo off
to Westfirth and then try to negotiate a settlement with the
Valazquez family.

Stephano was not pleased to see Chaunquler cast a swift
glance at Sir Richard Piefer, as though asking what he should
do. Chaunquler was here supposedly as an independent judge

and observer. What business did he have looking at Piefer for the answer?

"Well, sir?" Stephano demanded tersely.

Piefer stepped forward. "I see no reason to postpone this meeting. Lord Valazquez has acted as a gentleman in giving his condolences. He still requires satisfaction for the insult to his sister."

Stephano saw Valazquez frown at the Freyan lord's intervention.

"I would like to hear Monsieur Valazquez speak for himself in this matter," Stephano insisted.

"Of course," said Piefer. He turned to the young lord. "I would remind his lordship that the name of Valazquez is untarnished. Should his lordship agree to postpone this meeting, there are those who will put his delay down to cowardice."

Valazquez flushed in anger at the imputation.

"There will be no delay," he said shortly.

"I received a letter from my father only three days ago, Stephano," Rodrigo said, bewildered. "How can he be dead?"

"It's just a rumor. We'll find out the truth from my mother. But right now," Stephano added gently, "I fear you have to go through with this."

"I know." Rodrigo gave a faint smile. "I may not be overly burdened with courage, but I am not a coward."

His unshaven cheeks pale, his mouth tight, he walked over to the box holding the dueling pistols and picked up one of the guns. Valazquez took the other pistol.

"Very well, gentlemen," Chaunquler said. "Since you will not be dissuaded, I ask you to take your positions. You will stand back-to-back, the guns pointed in the air. Your seconds have determined that you will walk twenty paces and then turn and fire. I will commence the count."

Rodrigo and Valazquez stood with their backs touching. Valazquez pulled back the hammer. Rodrigo, hearing a sound, cast Stephano a panicked glance, asking him wordlessly what he was supposed to be doing.

"Cock the hammer!" Stephano mouthed, going through the motion.

Rodrigo lowered the gun. He was forced to use both thumbs to draw back the hammer and nearly dropped the gun in the process. Stephano was cold and sick with dread. Piefer was impassive, unconcerned. Doctor Alabarca, the surgeon, opened his bag of instruments. Rodrigo resumed his position, standing back-to-back with Valazquez.

Chaunquler began to count out the paces. "One."

Each man took a step forward, moving away from his opponent. Chaunquler continued the count. The two men walked off the paces. Stephano noted that Rodrigo was taking unusually large steps. He also saw, to his dismay, that his friend had his eyes squinched tightly shut.

"Ten," said Chaunquler.

He was about to say "eleven" when he was interrupted by a bang. Rodrigo stood enveloped in a cloud of acrid smoke staring in blank astonishment at the pistol he had been carrying, which was now lying on the ground.

"It went off!" Rodrigo gasped. "I didn't pull the trigger. I swear! It just went off!"

" 'A misfire is equivalent to a shot,' " stated Chaunquler, quoting from the *Codes Duello*. "The duel will proceed."

Rodrigo looked wildly at Stephano. "The gun went off. I didn't fire the blasted thing! What am I supposed to do now?"

"You have to keep going," said Stephano grimly.

Valazquez heard the shot and stopped walking. He remained in position, his gun raised, though he did cast a glance over his shoulder to see what had happened. The pistol's misfire meant that Valazquez could now take his aim at his leisure without the fear that Rodrigo might shoot him first. Valazquez was known to be an excellent marksman. He would not miss. Rodrigo was a dead man and he knew it.

Stephano pressed his hand against his breast pocket, against the letter he had promised to deliver to Rodrigo's family. Rodrigo saw the gesture and understood. He smiled sadly, swallowed and, lifting his chin, continued to walk steadily to his death. Stephano knew the courage this simple act cost his friend and even in his despair and grief, he was proud of him.

"Twenty!" said Chaunquler.

Rodrigo turned and stood unflinching. Valazquez pivoted, aimed, pointed, and fired. Rodrigo shuddered involuntarily at the crack of the shot and closed his eyes.

The bullet whistled by his head, so close the bullet grazed his cheek. Valazquez lowered his gun. He cast a cool glance at Piefer.

"I would not want it said that I killed an unarmed man," Valazquez stated with dignity.

Stephano gave the young man a look of gratitude, then hurried over to Rodrigo, who was still standing stiffly, his eyes closed tight, waiting.

"It's over, my friend," said Stephano.

Rodrigo didn't comprehend. Opening one eye, he whispered, "What's taking the bullet so long?"

Stephano began to laugh, and then he suddenly noticed that both Chaunquler and Doctor Alabarca were running rapidly down the road, running as though in fear of their lives.

A pistol fired. The shot half-deafened Stephano. and he turned to glare angrily at Valazquez.

"Why the devil did you shoot—"

The words stuck in Stephano's throat.

Valazquez no longer had a face. His head was a mushy pulp of blood and brains and shattered bone. His body jerked spasmodically, then plopped wetly onto the ground.

Stephano stared at the murdered man, then looked in blank astonishment at Piefer, who was thrusting one smoking pistol into his belt and coolly drawing a second. The Freyan turned from Valazquez to face Rodrigo and raised the gun, taking aim. Stephano had no idea what was going on, and he didn't have time to sort it out. He hurled himself at Rodrigo, knocked him to the ground, and flung himself on top of him.

Another bang. A sharp blow hit Stephano between his shoulder blades. The bullet knocked the breath from his body, but his chain mail and its magical constructs deflected the bullet that otherwise would have torn through his back.

"What's going on?" Rodrigo demanded in muffled tones, his face in the dirt. "Why is he shooting at us?"

"I wish I knew!" said Stephano fervently.

Piefer thrust the useless pistol into his belt and reached into his breast pocket where he had another gun, probably what had come to be known as a "corset gun," a type of short-barreled pistol small enough for a lady to tuck into her bosom.

Stephano leaped to his feet and drew his sword in the same motion. He calculated he could reach the Freyan before he had time to fire. Stephano took a step, heard another shot. A bullet struck the dirt at his feet, kicking up dust. The flash of muzzle fire came from beyond the stone wall. Another bullet whistled over his head. At least two more men were firing at them from the shadows of the trees.

Piefer had drawn his corset gun and was taking direct aim. He cocked the hammer and was about to pull the trigger when another gunshot sounded. The small pistol went spinning out of the Freyan's hand. Piefer cursed and whipped around to glare in anger and astonishment into the woods.

Stephano did not take time to wonder if someone in the forest was on his side or one of Piefer's friends was a bad shot. He grabbed hold of Rodrigo, who was staring in shock at the bloody remains of Valazquez. Stephano dragged his friend to his feet.

"We've got to make a run for the cab!"

"Wait!" Rodrigo cried and he darted forward to pick up the dueling pistol he had used. A bullet struck the ground. He snatched his hand back, then made a grab for the pistol, and ran, hunched-over, to Stephano, who glared at him.

"That thing's useless!"

"I know!" Rodrigo gasped. He thrust the pistol into his belt.

Stephano gripped his friend's arm. "Keep your head down! Use the tombstones for cover!"

Crouching low, they tried to blend in with the mists that were, unfortunately, starting to burn off, and dashed from one tombstone to the next. The bullets hit close, striking the tombstones, chipping off pieces of marble and sending the shards flying through the air. They took refuge behind a monument of a marble angel and stopped to catch their breath. A bullet struck one of the angel's wings, knocking it off. Both ducked.

Rodrigo asked in altered tones, "Do you think what Valazquez said about my father being dead is true?"

"We'll soon find out," said Stephano. "The countess will know."

Another bullet took off the angel's nose.

Rodrigo was suddenly angry. "Why is he trying to kill us?"

"Damned if I know," said Stephano, wiping the sweat from his face. He'd lost his hat to a bullet. "His friends are extremely good shots, though. They must be using those new weapons with the rifled bores. I've heard about them, but never seen one. They're supposed to be more accurate than barrels that use targeting constructs. I'd really like to get a look at one—"

"I've seen quite enough, thank you!" Rodrigo flattened himself on the ground as a bullet slammed into the angel's foot.

Stephano risked raising his head, hoping to see what had become of Piefer. The Freyan lord was nowhere in sight. Stephano didn't know if his disappearance was good or bad. He shifted about to see if the hansom cab was still there or if the driver had fled. Surprisingly the hansom cab was still there. The horse didn't like the gunfire, however. The animal was rolling its eyes and shifting nervously in the traces. Stephano was amazed the driver had not run off at the first sign of trouble. Or maybe he had fled and left the carriage behind.

"One last dash!" Stephano said.

Rodrigo nodded. The two jumped out from behind the angel and ran headlong for the cab. They were tense, expecting more bullets, but all was suddenly quiet.

"They've gone!" Rodrigo cried, elated.

Stephano shook his head. Men armed with such expensive weapons were most likely professionals. They weren't about to give up this easily. Reaching the hansom cab, he found out why the driver had not taken off. He was crouched on the floor of the cab, his eyes closed and his fingers stuffed in his ears. Stephano grabbed hold of him.

"Don't shoot me!" the driver wailed, flinging his hands in the air.

Stephano eyed the man, who was shaking all over. "He's worthless. Get inside with him. I'll drive."

"Do you know how?" asked Rodrigo dubiously.

"I've flown dragons," said Stephano. "How hard can driving a cab be?"

The hansom cab was a small two-wheeler, with room for only two passengers, both of whom sat directly behind the horse. The driver's seat was on top of the cab, in the rear. The reins ran through two supports located at the front of the roof. Stephano climbed up onto the seat and took hold of the reins. Not certain what to do, he slapped the reins and shouted, "Giddy up!"

The horse was only too glad to leave and plunged forward with a jolt that almost sent Stephano flying off the seat and flattened Rodrigo and the howling driver against the cushions. The hansom cab careened madly down the road, swaying from side to side, rattling and shaking as Stephano grappled with the reins and tried desperately to gain some sort of control over the terrified animal.

Rodrigo, who was clinging to whatever he could find to cling to, leaned his head out to yell at Stephano.

"Where are we going?"

"The *Cloud Hopper!*" Stephano shouted back.

A bullet smashed into roof of the cab. Swearing with what breath he had left, Stephano glanced over his shoulder to see the black carriage racing after them in pursuit. Piefer was seated next to the driver.

Stephano had an excellent look at one of the new rifled guns. He stared straight down the barrel.

Chapter Eight

I am saddened to find the leaders of the Church focusing more on secular politics than on the worship of God. The grand bishop must now have his own personal army, his fleet of warships, his networks of spies... Young crafters do not practice their art for the glory of God, but for the glory of the grand bishop. It was with a heavy heart that I counseled His Majesty the King to break with the Church of the Breath.

—Fifty-year-old Journal entry
by Archbishop Samuel Winton,
Church of the Restaration, Freya

DUBOIS WAS IN THE VICINITY OF THE CEMETERY well before dawn, in time to see Rodrigo de Villeneuve and Captain de Guichen arrive for the duel. Dubois was not on the grounds. He had taken up his position in a tree.

To look at Dubois, one might not think he was someone adept at tree-climbing. He had developed this skill over time, finding it useful to ascend to such perches where he could hide among the leaves, see without being seen. Dubois was also adept at climbing up trellises to sneak onto balconies or peep into windows, and he had become an expert at walking over rooftops.

Ensconced in his tree, shielded from view, Dubois settled himself comfortably. He straddled a broad limb with his legs and rested his back against the trunk.

His perch provided him an excellent view of the field of combat and the woods surrounding the cemetery. He was vastly interested to note the stealthy arrival of two other men in the woods. Both were strangers to Dubois. He watched the two slip through the mists and take up positions directly behind the cemetery wall. Both were dressed in long coats and tall boots and carried long-barreled muskets. Anyone seeing them would mistake them for two gentlemen hunting grouse.

Dubois reached into a pocket, drew out a collapsible spyglass and, extending it, put it to his eye to observe the two men more closely.

"Well, well, well," said Dubois.

One man carried a large bore musket, while the other was armed with the new weapon known as a "rifle" for its rifled bore, which gave the shooter far better accuracy than smooth bore guns, even those with magical targeting constructs. An expensive weapon for shooting grouse. In addition, each man carried several pistols.

Obviously paid assassins, but who was paying them and who were they there to assassinate? Dubois could make an excellent guess. He reached beneath his coat to draw his own pistol, which he carried in a pistol sheath he had designed himself. Much like a sheath for a sword, the pistol sheath was made of leather attached to a strap that looped around his right shoulder. The pistol sheath allowed him to wear the weapon on his body, concealed beneath his coat, providing swift and easy access.

His pistol was double-barreled, operated by magic rather than flint. The two barrels were stacked one above the other with a single firing mechanism. The hammer and the strike plate each had deeply set sigils that sparked when they came into contact, separated by a small brass shield when the weapon was not in use. A lever near the strike plate allowed him to choose which barrel to fire. On top was a longer, lower caliber barrel, set with interlocking layers of magical targeting constructs, designed for better range and accuracy. Beneath it was a large bore barrel designed for stopping power.

The gun had been given to Dubois by the grand bishop. The weapon had been made especially in the bishop's own armory, according to Dubois' instructions. He checked the pistol, particularly the magical constructs, and found all was well. Not that there was ever any doubt. He invariably checked the gun before strapping on the belt.

Dubois rested the pistol on the tree limb, placed his hand on the grip, and settled himself to watch the proceedings. The sun's rays were burning off the mists and he had a good view. His tree was only about one hundred feet away from the dueling ground. In the still morning air, he could hear most of what was being said.

Dubois smiled to see Chaunquler arrive. The old reprobate was undoubtedly in the pay of Harrington. Chaunquler was here to ensure the duel went Harrington's way, whatever way that was.

Dubois watched and listened attentively, hoping for clues that would lead him to Sir Henry Wallace. He observed the firing of the dueling pistols and Chaunquler's investigation of the clothing for magical constructs. Nothing noteworthy there. The duel was just about to commence when Valazquez said something that Dubois found to be of considerable interest.

The young man's voice, heavily accented, carried well on the still air. "I would like to express my sympathy to Monsieur de Villeneuve on the death of his father."

Rodrigo de Villeneuve had not been apprised of this news, apparently. He looked as though he'd been run over by an ox-cart.

"I regret to be the bearer of ill tidings. My father, as the Estaran ambassador, received the news yesterday. Ambassador de Villeneuve was the victim of an assassin's bullet. The murderer escaped, unfortunately, but the authorities are doing all they can to find him. They believe that he was a Travian."

Dubois was equally surprised to hear that the Rosian ambassador had been murdered. Dubois did not like surprises. His agent in Estara should have informed him immediately. Dubois made a mental note to replace his agent, even as he reflected on Valazquez's explanation of the events.

The Rosian ambassador shot by a Travian. How very convenient for Sir Henry Wallace, who was suspected of fomenting the feud between Estara and Travia over Braffa. That island nation refined a substance known as the Blood of God—a concentrated, liquid form of the Breath used to power the airships of both the Estaran and Rosian fleets.

The island and its resources had long been the subject of a dispute between Estara and Travia. The two nations had nearly gone to war over Braffa, but the Church had stepped in to conduct negotiations and brought about an uneasy truce—a truce that seemed likely now to be broken, for King Alaric could not allow the assassination of his ambassador to go unpunished.

As this young man, Valazquez, was upholding the honor of his sister, King Alaric must uphold the honor of his nation. But Alaric was now in an awkward situation. The whole world knew that the king sided with Travia, and it appeared that a Travian had assassinated the Rosian ambassador. What would Alaric do? Or rather, what would the Countess de Marjolaine tell the king to do? Dubois filed the information in one of his mind's cubbyholes and concentrated on the duel.

Captain de Guichen was attempting to use the death of his friend's father to bring about a postponement of the duel. It seemed he might succeed. Young Valazquez was a dolt, but he was an honorable dolt. But Harrington, in his guise as Piefer, goaded Valazquez into fighting. Why was Harrington *aka* Piefer so keen on having Valazquez kill the wretched Rodrigo de Villeneuve? There was no doubt Monsieur de Villeneuve would die. Valazquez was known to be a superior marksman and from what Dubois had observed, Villeneuve barely knew one end of a gun from another.

Dubois watched the two combatants stand back-to-back, raise their guns, and begin to walk off the twenty paces. Chaunquler was counting. He and the others were focused on the two combatants. Dubois was watching Harrington. Just as Chaunquler was counting "ten," Harrington lifted his hand to his face, an innocent-seeming gesture.

Dubois clapped the spyglass to his eye.

Harrington kept his hand near his face, as though scratching his jaw. Dubois could see Harrington swiftly drawing a magical sigil in the air. His lips moved, speaking the incantation. At that instant, Villenueve's gun fired.

"It went off!" he cried in dismay. "I didn't pull the trigger. I swear! It just went off!"

Villeneuve was right. He had *not* pulled the trigger. The gun had been set off by Harrington's magical spell. But no one, not even his friend, the captain, would believe him. Chaunquler judged the shot a misfire. Valazquez would now face an unarmed opponent and, by the laws of dueling, he had the right to kill him. Harrington was smiling with satisfaction. Apparently everything was proceeding according to plan.

The two men walked out the twenty paces. Rodrigo de Villeneuve turned to face certain death. Harrington stood with his arms folded, coolly awaiting the bloody outcome.

Valazquez fired. The bullet grazed his opponent's cheek. Valazquez lowered his pistol. The young man had abided by the rules laid down by the *Codes Duello*. He had satisfied his honor by drawing blood. He cast a defiant glance at Harrington.

"I would not want it said that I killed an unarmed man."

Rodrigo de Villeneuve remained in a petrified state of terror, his eyes closed, still waiting to die. Captain Stephano de Guichen ran to his friend. Neither of them saw Harrington's face flush in frustration and anger. Neither saw him reach into his coat and pull a pistol from his belt.

Chaunquler saw everything, however, and alerted the surgeon. Both took to their heels.

Young Valazquez died instantly from a bullet between the eyes. Dubois kept his gaze on Harrington, who drew a second pistol and aimed at Villeneuve. Captain de Guichen threw himself on his friend, knocking him down and shielding him with his own body. The shot hit Captain de Guichen in the back. The bullet did no damage; undoubtedly the captain was wearing magically protected armor.

Harrington threw down this pistol and drew his corset gun from the inside pocket of his coat. Captain de Guichen was on his feet, reaching for his sword, when the two assassins opened fire. Bullets kicked up the dirt around the captain. Harrington's men were hampered in their shooting because they did not want to accidentally hit Harrington, who was leveling the small, but deadly little gun at the captain.

Dubois swore softly. He had not wanted to reveal himself, but he could not permit Harrington to kill Captain de Guichen. Son of the Countess de Marjolaine, the captain was a factor in this complex situation of the missing journeyman.

Dubois could not kill Harrington, who was going to lead him to Wallace. He sighted down the top barrel of his pistol, fired, and shot the corset gun out of Harrington's hand. Harrington spun around to glare at his men, thinking that one of them had shot him. The two assassins knew better. They had heard Dubois' shot coming from somewhere off to their right and they were momentarily distracted, looking about fearfully for the unknown assailant who might shoot them next.

Captain de Guichen and de Villeneuve were wisely taking advantage of the momentary lull to run for their lives. As for Harrington, he was running, too; racing for his carriage. Dubois could not lose track of him. The two assassins were firing, reloading, and firing again. With the reverberations of the gun blasts ringing in their ears, they would not hear a thunderclap, much less the sound of Dubois hastily slithering out of his tree.

Dubois had tied his horse nearby. He had mounted and was ready to ride by the time Harrington reached the carriage and was giving instructions to the driver to follow Captain de Guichen and Villeneuve, who were haring off in a stolen hansom cab. Harrington grabbed a musket and climbed up onto the driver's seat of the carriage as it was rolling off. Looking back, he shouted urgently for his two men to join him. Dubois waited patiently in the woods until these two had mounted their own horses and ridden past him, then he urged his horse to a trot.

Captain de Guichen was in the lead in his hansom cab. Harrington, in his carriage, raced after the captain. The two assassins galloped on their horses to catch up with Harrington. Dubois brought up the end of the line.

"Like a string of baby ducks," remarked Dubois, chuckling.

Chapter Nine

The most important part of any operation is a well thought out plan.
I have sent you additional funds and several of the newly developed
weapons known as "rifles" to assist you. You will notice that the rifles
have slow curving grooves cut into the interior of their barrels. This
"rifling" provides greater accuracy than targeting constructs, but does
require some practice in order to use effectively.

—Excerpt from a letter
from Sir Henry Wallace
to his agent, James Harrington

GRABBING THE BUGGY WHIP, STEPHANO
SNAPPED IT over the horse's head, urging the beast
on. The cab went careening down the road with Stephano
rocking from side to side and bouncing up and down on the
sprung seat. Glancing back, he saw Piefer still in pursuit,
again taking aim with his rifle.

Stephano had nowhere to go. He lowered his head and
hunched his shoulders, trying to make himself as small a
target as possible. Then suddenly he had more to worry
about than being hit by a bullet.

The road made a sharp curve to the right up ahead. The
cab was heading into the turn at a frightening speed. The
driver yelled that they were going to crash and hurled himself out of the side of the cab. The last Stephano saw of him,
the driver was tumbling head over heels into a weed patch.

Stephano tried to slow the horse, but the creature was out of control. He had his ears laid back, his eyes swiveled wildly, and spittle flew from his mouth. He plunged on as Stephano braced himself. The cab took the corner on one wheel, teetered perilously for a moment, then righted itself, landing on both wheels with a bone-jarring jounce.

Stephano slapped the reins and snapped the whip, and they went rolling on. He looked back to see that Piefer's driver, fighting to maintain control of a far larger carriage, sensibly slowed to make the turn. Piefer had fallen behind, but the two assassins mounted on horseback were catching up. These were the two who had been firing at him from the woods. Each brandished a pistol.

Stephano hoped they *would* shoot. He was a moving target, the odds were likely that they would miss, and once they had fired their weapons, they would have to reload. They would have a hard time pouring in powder and thrusting home a bullet while riding a horse at a full gallop.

Unfortunately, these men were too professional to make such a mistake. Holding their pistols in readiness, they spurred on their horses. They planned to catch up with the cab and simply shoot their victims once they were close.

Stephano faced to the front, keeping his eyes on the road. The horse was starting to tire, showing signs of being winded. The two men on relatively fresh horses would easily manage to catch the cab.

Stephano considered his options. They were grimly few. When his assailants arrived, he could jump from his seat onto one of them and knock the man off his horse. But that still left the other man *and* Piefer free to kill them.

The cab was heading into another curve, but this time Stephano didn't have to worry about overturning. The weary horse had slowed his pace and they took the corner decorously. Rounding the curve, Stephano was startled to see that they had reached the outskirts of the city.

The road that led to the Church of Saint Charles was

not much traveled. But the cab and those pursuing it were now going to be running into a stream of carts, wagons, horses, and pedestrians. The two assassins on horseback could weave their way through traffic faster than he could maneuver a cab.

Stephano looked over his shoulder again. Thinking the two assassins would increase their pace, he was surprised to see them dropping behind, apparently in response to some order from Piefer. They were conferring with him as he leaned down from the driver's seat.

By Heaven, Stephano thought with elation, *we might get out of this alive after all!*

He arrived at an intersection. Several roads branched out from a single lane, all heading into the city. He needed to reach Canal Street, where the *Cloud Hopper* was docked. Stephano guided the horse onto the Street of Kings, a narrow thoroughfare that led into the heart of the city, as Rodrigo thrust open the trapdoor through which passengers communicated with the driver and shouted up at him.

"What are you doing? This street will be crowded at this time of day. You should take Cattle Market Road."

"We like crowded streets," Stephano shouted back. "The more people the better. Look behind us."

"And get my head blown off?" Rodrigo asked, horrified.

"Just look," Stephano yelled.

Rodrigo poked his head cautiously out of the carriage.

"They're still there," he reported. "They're still chasing us."

"Yes, but they're not still *shooting* at us," Stephano said. "They won't risk firing into a crowd."

At least, he hoped they wouldn't risk it.

Rodrigo held up the pistol he'd recovered from the site of the duel and waved it in the air. "I found a hidden magical sigil on the firing mechanism! That's what caused the gun to misfire! I *told* you I didn't shoot it!"

Stephano thought the matter over as he continued to try to negotiate the cab through the traffic. Rodrigo had been meant to die in that duel. Valazquez had been supposed to kill him.

"Why in the name of all the saints and all the angels and God Himself would anyone go to this much trouble and expense to kill Rodrigo!" Stephano asked himself.

The Street of Kings was of one of the most heavily traveled roads in Evreux. Stephano was doing a fair job of driving the cab, and hoped he might actually be able to reach Canal Street when the horse decided enough was enough. Exhausted, in a bad mood, wanting only its stable and oats, the animal came to a dead stop in the middle of a busy intersection.

Stephano yelled and cajoled and plied the whip—to no avail. The horse stood with his head down, stubbornly refusing to budge. Traffic in all directions rolled to a standstill. Drovers with loads to deliver swore at Stephano and shook their fists. They were joined in their ire by the drivers of cabs and coaches and by their irate passengers. One drover even jumped off his wagon and came running toward Stephano with the idea of throttling him. Several pedestrians clustered about, attempting to deal with the horse, which added to the gridlock.

Stephano had no idea what to do. The carriage belonging to Piefer was caught in the snarl. But the two assassins on horseback were steadily pushing their way toward him.

Stephano flung the whip aside, dropped the reins, jumped out of the seat, and ran to the front of the cab.

"Get out!" he yelled at Rodrigo. "We're walking!"

His friend stared at him in astonishment, wondering if he'd lost his mind, then he climbed out of the cab. Ignoring the swearing and irate shouts, Stephano and Rodrigo bolted for the sidewalk, which was now filled with interested spectators. The two elbowed and shoved and began to dodge and weave and push their way through the crowd.

Stephano looked back to see chaos had broken out in the intersection. The drover who had been going to fight Stephano was now taking on a fellow drover. Passengers were leaning out of the carriages. People were tugging on the horse. Traffic was backing up as far as he could see. Unless Piefer abandoned his carriage, he wasn't going anywhere any time soon. The two assassins on horseback were trying their best to edge their way through the confusion, but without much better success.

Stephano paused a moment to go over a mental map of the city of Evreux in his head, trying to figure out the quickest route to the *Cloud Hopper,* which was docked along one of the canals that ran through the city.

He noticed people stopping to stare at him, but he assumed this was because he was filthy from running through graveyards and driving a cab with a crazed horse, so he did not give it much thought. He was about to say, "We can continue down this street to reach Canal," when Rodrigo suddenly seized hold of him and dragged him into a dark alley.

"Why did you do that? We can't stop, they'll catch us!" Stephano said, annoyed.

"You're bleeding," said Rodrigo, pointing to Stephano's left shoulder. "You've been shot."

Stephano looked down to see a large amount of blood had soaked through both his shirt and his coat. That was why people had been staring at him.

"I'll be damned," he said.

"You didn't know you'd been shot?" Rodrigo asked, amazed.

"I was trying to control that demonic horse," said Stephano. "And thank you so much for telling me. I didn't feel anything until you said something. Now it hurts like Hell!"

"Let me look."

Rodrigo gingerly pulled aside the bloodstained coat. Stephano winced and gasped at the pain.

"I can't see anything except blood," Rodrigo told him. "Your shirt is plastered against the wound."

"That's probably stopped the bleeding," said Stephano, gritting his teeth. "Don't pull it off, or it will start again."

"How bad is it?"

"The bullet didn't hit a major artery, or I'd be dead by now," said Stephano. "I don't think it broke any bones. But, damn, it hurts! Do you see an exit wound?"

Rodrigo looked behind him and shook his head.

"Then the bullet must still be lodged in my shoulder."

"Can you keep going?" Rodrigo asked worriedly.

"I don't have much choice," said Stephano, grimacing. "Take a look into the street. See what our friends are doing."

Rodrigo peered around the corner of the building. "The two killers are now on foot, looking for us. I see Piefer's carriage, but I can't see him."

"He's probably on foot, as well. We have to reach Canal Street. I don't suppose this alley cuts through to the next street over?"

Rodrigo ran down the alley and returned to report. "It's a dead end. But I did find this." He exhibited a woman's linen underskirt and a man's wool coat. "Found these on a clothesline. Don't worry. I left a silver piece in the woman's stocking as payment."

Rodrigo tore up the underskirt to use as a sling, which he wrapped around Stephano's arm. He eased off Stephano's bloodstained coat and draped the wool coat over his shoulder.

"Now you won't draw so much attention."

"We can't stay here," said Stephano, once his arm was bandaged. "Piefer's men will assume we're hiding, and alleys will be the first place they'll look. Our best chance is out there, mixing with the people."

Rodrigo took one more look into the street. He reported that Piefer's men had split up, one taking the north side of the road and the other the south. He and Stephano plunged into the crowd. Traffic was moving on the street again, under the direction of a policeman.

Rodrigo stopped. "The police! We should report Piefer to the police!"

"And you'd be the one they'd arrest," said Stephano grimly. "Dueling is against the law, which makes the death of Valazquez murder. The honorable Sir Richard Piefer would tell them you shot Valazquez, and we can't prove that you didn't."

"My God!" Rodrigo cried, horrified. "I'm a wanted man!"

"I'll talk to my mother," said Stephano. "The countess will see to it that the right people are bribed and paid off and the murder is hushed up. She's good at that sort of thing. We'll add the cost in as a business expense related to Alcazar."

"So you think this has something to do with Alcazar? But why do they want to kill me?" Rodrigo demanded.

Stephano's mind had been grappling with this question; suddenly he had an answer.

"Because you are a crafter; a highly skilled crafter," Stephano said. "And because someone knows you are investigating the disappearance of Alcazar, also a crafter. Someone knows this because they had a man watching Alcazar's apartment . . ."

And then Stephano knew where he had seen Sir Richard Piefer.

"Piefer is Slouch Hat!" he said to Rodrigo. "*That* is why he had looked familiar to me! I remember thinking Slouch Hat looked like a jongleur, like a man who has been on the stage, an actor."

"But then who is he and why was he trying to kill us?" Rodrigo asked, bewildered.

Stephano's mind, once it got going, was now racing along. "Because Slouch Hat/Piefer was afraid you had discovered something related to Alcazar."

"But I didn't, except the possibility that Alcazar has ties to Westfirth . . ."

"Piefer couldn't know that. He tried to kill you just on the possibility that you had learned something!"

"And poor Valazquez?" Rodrigo asked.

"He was just a cat's-paw; a hotheaded young man who could be easily lured into fighting a duel. You *were* telling the truth, weren't you?" Stephano said remorsefully. "You said you didn't write those letters. I should have believed you."

"I can understand why you wouldn't," said Rodrigo with a faint smile. "You are right. My life as a reprobate was bound to catch up with me."

"As for the wretched Valazquez, he was supposed to kill you and, when he didn't, Piefer killed him so that there would be no witnesses."

"If Alcazar found a way to fully meld magic and metal, such a discovery would definitely be worth killing a few people," said Rodrigo. He regarded his friend in concern. "You don't look good. How are you doing?"

Stephano shivered. He was starting to grow feverish. "I'm all right," he lied.

Rodrigo glanced behind. "We've been spotted. Piefer's assassins are catching up. I believe that lane cuts through."

The entrance of a small, narrow street was on the opposite side. They darted recklessly in front of a cab, forcing the driver to rein in his horse to avoid hitting them. He lashed at them angrily with his whip as they dashed past. They ran down the lane, not stopping to look, hoping that their sudden movement had caught the two assassins off guard.

At the end of the lane, Stephano had to stop. He could feel himself weakening. He leaned against a wall, shaking with chills.

"Not much farther," said Rodrigo. "We're on Canal Street. I can see the *Cloud Hopper* from here."

"Just . . . give me a moment to rest," Stephano said.

Rodrigo looked back down the lane.

"We don't have a moment, my friend."

Stephano sucked in his breath. "All right. Let's go."

He tried to take a step, staggered, and nearly fell. Rodrigo put his arm around his friend and half-dragged, half-carried Stephano toward the *Cloud Hopper*.

As the name implied, Canal Street bordered the largest, longest, and oldest of the canals. Originally natural formations—deep ravines that cut inland—the canals had been magically extended by crafters, who had used their magic to blast through the rock. Although the canals resembled water-bearing canals, these canals were filled with the Breath, not water, and were used by smaller craft to enter the city. Larger craft, such as the naval ships, were not permitted into the city at all, and had to dock at the wharf, which was some distance away.

Floating wherries and barges sailed up and down the canals, delivering passengers and goods to various parts of the city. Trundler houseboats, such as the *Cloud Hopper*, docked in the stalls, paying a fee for the privilege. The Royal Barge was there, ready for use. The grand bishop and many other nobles had their own private *yachts*, as these luxurious vessels were known. The *yachts* and the Royal Barge cruised the canals on fine nights.

Canal Street was lined with warehouses, taverns, and market stalls that sold goods fresh off the barges. Stevedores loaded and unloaded cargo. Vendors in the stalls shouted out their wares. Buyers went from stall to stall, examining the vegetables, the slabs of beef, and the fish fresh-caught in the lakes in the mountains.

Stephano and Rodrigo mingled with the buyers, going from stall to stall, making their way down the street to where the *Cloud Hopper* was docked.

"My poor friend can't hold his ale," Rodrigo remarked to those who stared as they stumbled past.

Canal Street was not as crowded as the other city streets, and Piefer's assassins were closing in. Stephano kept going by sheer will alone; moving in a kind of pain-tinged daze.

He was concentrating on putting one foot in front of the other, when Rodrigo steered him to a halt. They had left the market area of Canal Street behind without Stephano even knowing it and were in a quieter area, surrounded by large warehouses.

"We're here," Rodrigo said, holding onto Stephano. "We made it. Well, almost."

Stephano could see the *Cloud Hopper* tethered to the dock. The houseboat measured close to sixty feet in length, with a raised sterncastle and forecastle and a full lower deck. She had an upper and lower mast, along with an upper boom. Short wings extended out from the hull from just behind the curve of the bow and ending in front of the sterncastle. Airscrews, used for maneuvering, were mounted into the rear edge of each wing.

A refined and concentrated form of the Breath was stored in the balloons that were tethered to the mainmast and boom. The Breath in the balloons could be magically charged to create a much greater amount of lift than was present in the Breath naturally. The Breath was also trapped inside the lift tanks built into the hull at the base of the *Cloud Hopper*'s stubby wings. The lift tanks were wooden barrels with a thin iron lining set with protective magical constructs that allowed the tank to be pressurized, thus providing even greater lift capability. Cables connected both the balloons and the tanks to the helm—a brass panel inscribed with magical constructs. The helmsman could control the amount of lift in the balloons and the tanks, as well as the magical energy that powered the airscrews from this panel. Spare tanks built into the hull contained additional quantities of the gas, should the balloons tear or the tanks rupture.

To reach the boat, Stephano and Rodrigo would have to cross the boardwalk—a promenade made of wooden planks that ran the length of Canal Street. The boardwalk was a popular place for people to take a stroll on a fine Breadun afternoon. A fence running along the boardwalk protected pedestrians from tumbling (or jumping) into the canal. Piers led from the boardwalk to the stalls where the barges and houseboats were moored.

Today being a weekday, the promenade was empty. The *Cloud Hopper* was the only houseboat currently docked in this part of the canal. The entire broad expanse of board-walk lay between Stephano and Rodrigo and the house-boat. They would be easy targets for Piefer's assassins, who had drawn their pistols and were coming toward them.

Dag paced anxiously back and forth on the prow of the *Cloud Hopper*. Miri stood beside him, both of them worried. They had not yet caught sight of Rodrigo and Steph-ano, who were keeping to the shadows. And waiting on the promenade for news was Benoit.

"Dag!" Rodrigo risked a shout and waved. "We need help!" He pointed at the two assassins.

Dag heard, looked, and understood. He had obviously been expecting trouble, because he had his blunderbuss ready, propped against the ship's rail. He picked it up and swiftly loaded it with shot and powder.

"There's going to be gunfire," he told Miri, his words booming through the quiet. "Tell Gythe to stay below with Doctor Ellington. You do whatever it is you do to get this boat airborne."

"Do you need help?" Miri yelled back. She was a fair shot with a pistol, and Dag said she was the fastest person at reloading he'd ever known.

"No," said Dag coolly. "There's only two of them. I can handle it. You get ready to take us out into the Breath."

"Mr. Benoit," he shouted to the old man on the pier, who had been gesticulating wildly with his cane at the sight of Rodrigo. "I suggest you seek cover!"

Benoit hobbled over to crouch behind a large barrel of creosote that had been left on the pier. He drew an ancient pistol.

"Who am I shooting at?" he asked, squinting his eyes to see.

"No one!" Dag shouted, more frightened of the old man's shaking hand than he was of the assassins.

Dag raised the blunderbuss to his shoulder and yelled at Rodrigo and Stephano. "Run for it! I'll cover you!"

"One last effort," said Rodrigo. "Can you make it?"

Stephano nodded. Dag took aim.

"Now!" Rodrigo said. He ran, and Stephano stumbled across the boardwalk.

A gate in the fence permitted access to the pier. The two assassins fired their pistols and Dag fired off the blunderbuss simultaneously. Rodrigo reached out his hand to open the gate. A bullet grazed it. Splinters flew. Rodrigo swore and snatched back his bleeding hand. He kicked open the gate and ran through it and onto the pier. Stephano stumbled and fell to the ground.

A peppering shot from the blunderbuss forced the two assassins to seek cover. Rodrigo ran back to grab hold of Stephano, who had managed to regain his feet. Miri lowered the gangplank. Rodrigo helped Stephano to cross to the *Cloud Hopper*.

"You're bleeding!" said Miri to Stephano, and she put her arm around him.

"I'm bleeding, too," Rodrigo said, holding out his hand.

Miri snorted. "Make yourself useful. Go cast off the line!"

Dag dropped the blunderbuss and drew a long-barreled pistol. The two assassins raised their heads. Dag fired, and they ducked back down.

"Cast off!" he yelled to Rodrigo.

Miri lowered Stephano to the deck, then ran over to the helm, which was located on the upper part of the forecastle. She stopped when she saw Gythe was already there, handling the controls.

"I told you to stay below deck!" Miri told her sister.

Gythe pointed at Stephano and then turned away. Miri regarded her in frustration, then decided that arguing would waste too much time. She went back to tend to Stephano.

Rodrigo ran along the pier to where a thick rope held the boat tethered to the dock. As he leaned down to take hold of the line, a bullet tore through the air where his head had been. Rodrigo dropped to the pier with a panicked howl.

"That was a damn fine shot," said Dag, impressed. He looked around, puzzled. "Where did it come from?"

"Piefer!" Stephano gasped. "Everyone take cover!"

He grabbed hold of Miri and dragged her down beside him on the deck. Gythe crouched behind the protective shielding surrounding the boat's controls. Rodrigo remained on the pier, hugging the wooden planks. Dag picked up another pistol.

"Dag, get down!" Stephano yelled. "Piefer's using one of those new-fangled rifles!"

"Is he?" said Dag, adding wistfully, "I'd dearly love to get my hands on one of those!"

A bullet went zinging past his head. Dag had been keeping watch for the muzzle flash and, seeing it, he aimed his pistol and fired. Realizing he'd been spotted, Piefer ran out of the shadows.

"He's on the move," Dag called. "Cast off!"

"Are you sure he's gone?" Rodrigo asked fearfully.

"Cast off!" Dag roared.

Rodrigo crawled on his hands and knees to reach the line, wrestled with it a moment, then managed to get it free. The *Cloud Hopper* started to drift away. Gythe steered the houseboat, keeping it close to the pier, and Miri yelled for Rodrigo to jump for it.

Rodrigo had just begun to run toward the gangplank, when one of Piefer's men leaped up suddenly from behind the fence line and brought his pistol to bear, aiming for Rodrigo. Dag saw the danger, but he was reloading and there was nothing he could do except shout a warning.

A shot fired, coming from the vicinity of the creosote barrel. The assassin spun around from the force of the bullet and fell onto the boardwalk.

Benoit stood up, waving the smoking pistol and shouting defiantly, "Did you see that, sir?"

"You old fool, get out of here!" Stephano yelled. "Help me to my feet, Miri! He's going to get himself killed!"

"He's taking your advice, Captain," Dag reported, keeping an eye on Benoit, who had left his creosote barrel and was making a dash for one of the warehouses. Dag added in admiring tones, "He can move damn fast for a cripple."

Rodrigo raced across the gangplank. Dag heaved it in while Gythe sent power into the helm. According to the Church, channelers could touch God's Hand as He sent magic flowing through the world and open themselves up to act as a conduit. Gythe could hear God's voice like a song and draw His strength into herself and then direct the magical energy into the control panel's constructs. The magical energy arced through the gas and caused the boat to begin to rise.

The *Cloud Hopper*'s two airscrews began to whirl; the sails billowed. Gythe turned the starboard airscrew to full ahead and the larboard screws to full reverse, swinging the bow of the boat toward the harbor. A strong breeze filled the *Cloud Hopper*'s sails and the boat drifted down the canal toward the harbor. Beyond was the vast expanse and pink-tinged mists of the Breath.

Piefer fired again as the *Cloud Hopper* began to put distance between them. Stephano was leaning against the rail, ignoring Miri's scolding and her urgent attempts to make him go below. He saw the flash and heard the report and looked around anxiously. Piefer had missed apparently; everyone was safe.

The sail billowed and the houseboat gained speed. The gap between the ship and pier widened. As Stephano watched the Freyan lower his gun, he was back in the cemetery watching Piefer lower his pistol as Valazquez's corpse, with its shattered bloody pulp of a head, sagged to the ground.

Sir Richard Piefer. Slouch Hat. Which was he? Who was he? A noble lord who could act the part of a drunken idler or an idler who could take the part of a noble lord? Whoever he was, he had the means and connections to hire spies and assassins and arm them and himself with rare and expensive rifles. Stephano stared at the Freyan, fixing his face in his mind.

"I don't know who the Hell you are," Stephano shouted. "But you and I will meet again. That's a promise."

The Freyan smiled at Stephano and shrugged with his languid grace. He thrust his pistol in his belt, tucked his rifle in the crook of his arm, and strolled off into the shadows.

Stephano's strength gave out. He felt himself falling and had the horrible idea he was falling into the emptiness of the Breath, but Dag caught hold of him and lowered him down. He saw Miri's frightened face, and he smiled to reassure her, and then he sank into a dark dream in which he was driving a hansom cab through the halls of the palace, trying to find his father . . .

Dubois had followed Harrington and the assassins as they were following Stephano and Rodrigo. Dubois had not taken part in the fight, for the crew of the *Cloud Hopper* seemed to have that matter in hand. He stood on the pier and watched the Trundler boat sail safely away. He recognized the big man, Dag, from the episode in the park, as well as the two pretty female Trundlers who manned and probably owned the boat. Dubois watched Harrington and his remaining assassin toss the body of their compatriot into the canal and then separate.

Dubois tailed Harrington back to his inn. Finding his own agent still on duty in a tavern across the street, Dubois gave him the sign that he was to continue to keep an eye on Harrington, and returned to his lodgings.

An eventful morning, Dubois thought, as he dined on roasted fowl and suet pudding.

While he ate, he read over a report, just delivered from the bishop, further detailing the incident at the Abbey of Saint Agnes where a hundred women of God had been murdered in a most horrible and gruesome manner. A lone survivor told a very strange story. Dubois didn't know what to make of it. The thought occurred to him that the massacre at the abbey might have something to do with Sir

Henry Wallace. Dubois couldn't see for the life of him how a missing journeyman could be connected to this terrible tragedy, but he resolved to keep an open mind. Dubois considered paying the abbey a visit.

His meal finished, Dubois picked up the volume, *A Crafter's Guide to Metallurgy*, poured himself a glass of port, and began to leaf idly through the pages. He had just finished drinking his wine when his agent arrived with news that Harrington had booked passage on a coach bound for Westfirth, leaving that afternoon.

"He is going to report to Sir Henry," Dubois guessed, rubbing his hands.

He hastily packed a bag and made ready to travel. Before he left, he dashed off a letter and gave it to his agent with orders to deliver it immediately to the bishop.

The letter consisted of one sentence:

Find out what happened at the Royal Armory!

Chapter Ten

The unknown frightens us. So we employ spies to learn what our neighbors are doing, as they send their spies to watch us. We want to feel safe, but by our own actions we help continue the paranoia. We sign treaties of friendship and deliver copies to our allies in the hands of our spies.

—Journal entry,
Lady Cecile, Countess De Marjolaine

THE COUNTESS DE MARJOLAINE WAS NOT HOLDING audience this day. She instructed her secretary to tell all who came to her salon that the countess was indisposed. She did admit one visitor, though not by way of the salon. Benoit obtained entry to the countess' salon via the palace kitchen, where he was well known and well liked by the staff. Word of Benoit's arrival and his urgent need to speak to the countess passed from the cook to the scullery maid to one of the footmen to a seamstress to Maria, the countess' trusted lady's maid, who brought the message to the countess.

Maria Tutolla was sixty years old. She had been in the service of the countess for forty of those sixty years, having accompanied the countess on her return to court following Stephano's birth. The countess treated Maria and all her servants well. She insisted that everyone in her personal staff learn to read and write and she employed a tutor to teach them. Her servants were well-paid; their living quarters were comfortable. Contented servants do not betray their masters. This said, the countess never permitted the slightest hint of familiarity from any of her servants. Though Maria had attended the countess for forty years, she still went in awe of her mistress.

Maria went to the kitchen, retrieved Benoit, and led him through the palace's "servant" passages — dark, narrow, hidden hallways that led to the various dining rooms and salons of the palace's inhabitants and guests. The myriad passages were intended for the use of the palace's household staff, who were expected to appear the instant the mistress' bell rang as though they had materialized out of thin air and to disappear in the same manner. Servants were not the only people who made use of these passages, however. Noble lovers found them convenient when slipping out of one bedroom and into another. The passages were often quite crowded during the night.

A plain wooden door led from the dark hallway used by the servants into the countess' wardrobe. Maria opened the door with a key and a touch on a magical sigil entwined around the lock. She led Benoit into a large closet smelling of perfume, rosewood, and cedar. Maria lit a filigree lamp that stood on one of the innumerable chests containing overskirts and underskirts, cloaks and dressing gowns, negligees, petticoats, stockings, and shawls. Dainty and elegant shoes stood in a neat and orderly row along one wall. Maria pointed to a chair and indicated in a whisper that Benoit was to have a seat. The old retainer was well-accustomed to these proceedings and he settled himself comfortably. Maria passed through another door that led into the countess' bedchamber and went to find her mistress.

The countess was in her library sorting through a stack of letters, dispatches, and reports from her agents, separating them into three piles: those of no importance which she would give to the viscount to answer, those which required further reading, and those which demanded her immediate attention.

Occasionally, the countess left off her sorting to look with fondness at a young girl of fifteen seated cross-legged on the floor, much to the detriment of her voluminous blue silk skirt and white lace petticoat that spilled around her in layers of folds and frills. The girl rested her elbows on the floor with the easy elasticity of youth. Her chin in her hands, she was studying a large and colorful map of the world of Aeronne. The girl's rich chestnut hair had begun the day beautifully curled and coifed by her maids, but a romp in the hall with her spaniel had brought the curls tumbling around her face. The spaniel, a small version of the breed, with long ears and big brown melting eyes, was named Bandit, because he was fond of stealing petit fours. The dog now lay curled up asleep on the hem of the girl's blue dress.

Her Royal Highness Princess Amelia Louisa Sophia, known as Sophia, was the third child and only daughter of King Alaric and Queen Annmarie. The king's two sons, both in their twenties, were now serving in the military. The king was pleased to have produced two male heirs to the throne and thus began and ended the extent of his interest in them. He had shipped them off to seminary school when they were little. After that, they had attended University and then gone into the military. The elder, Prince Alaric II, was now Admiral of the Royal Navy's fleet in the north. The younger, Alessandro, was captain of his own airship. Neither was exceptional, though the elder had a bad reputation among the sailors for being something of a martinet.

Sophia, the unexpected child, the late child, was the child the king adored. Alaric doted on her, gave her everything she wanted and much that she didn't. The queen, her mother, a vain and vapid woman, cared nothing for the girl herself, but only for the wealthy and prestigious match she would make for her daughter. With this end in mind, the queen was always trying to improve her daughter's looks. Her Majesty primped, curled, and fussed over Sophia's hair, rouged her cheeks and painted her lips, and laced her into corsets in an effort to plump up her small breasts.

Sophia was required to take dancing lessons and etiquette lessons. She learned to paint and to do fancy embroidery. She was not taught to read or to write for these were skills considered by her illiterate mother to be of no importance to a woman. The queen scolded Sophia when she caught her wasting time with a book, telling her daughter that men did not want clever wives.

Between the king and queen, they might have utterly ruined their daughter. Sophia's naturally sweet nature, a passion for music, an extraordinary talent as a magical crafter, and the countess' tutelage saved the princess from turning out to be a spoiled and empty-headed porcelain doll.

Early in life, Sophia had developed an attachment to the Countess de Marjolaine. No one in court could understand the attraction. The cold, cunning, devious countess and the sensitive, shy Sophia seemed an unlikely match. Their relationship had begun the day when the countess entered her music room to find the little girl of five teaching herself to play the pianoforte. The countess had recognized the child's talent and had given her lessons. Discovering that Sophia could neither read nor write, the countess had expanded those lessons to include these skills.

The countess did not relax her cold, dispassionate demeanor around the girl, never exhibited any affection toward her. On the contrary, the countess was often a stern and difficult taskmaster. Sophia knew the value of what she was learning and enjoyed her studies. She came to love the countess, though she was wise enough to keep her affection a secret. Sophia had learned at an early age that her mother, the queen, hated the Countess de Marjolaine, though it would be many more years before Sophia would come to understand the jealousy that prompted this hatred. All Sophia knew was that when she was with the countess, she was free to be Sophia, not Papa's "pet" or Mama's "darling."

As for the countess, she found that teaching the girl brought her a deep satisfaction she had never before experienced. She felt something akin to happiness when Sophia was with her, a feeling she had once thought she would never know again. The countess would not admit her affection for the girl. She told herself it was her duty to see to it that a princess of Rosia should be an educated and well-informed woman. The child would certainly not learn anything from her mother, who had all the intellect of an eggplant, or her father, a man of low cunning, but no particular intelligence.

The countess was attempting to concentrate on sorting her correspondence, but her gaze often left the letters and reports to fix upon Sophia, admiring her delicate beauty and wondering irritably, not for the first time, how the queen could ever refer to her daughter as "homely and plain."

Sophia felt the countess' eyes upon her and lifted her head to smile at her. Sophia's face—minus the rouge, which she invariably rubbed off when she was out of her mother's sight—was sweet and winsome and pale, too pale; the pallor of illness, not of fashion.

Sophia had long suffered from severe headaches. The headaches had been mild when she was young, but they were growing more frequent and more severe. The king had brought in physicians and healers from around the world to treat her. She had been examined by the best, but no one could find a cause for her ailment. Sophia did not have poor eyesight. Her vision was perfect. She had never suffered a head injury. She did not exhibit symptoms of a brain disease; no seizures, no bleeding from the nose or ears.

The physicians and healers had tried numerous remedies, everything from bleeding to leeches to potions that made her throw up. None helped. When the attacks came, her screams could be heard in distant halls and corridors. The pain was so bad the servants often had to lash her arms and feet to her bedposts to keep her from thrashing about and hurting herself.

Both parents suffered almost as much as Sophia; the king because he truly cared about his daughter and the queen because she did not know how she was ever going to find a husband for her afflicted child.

"I am glad you are feeling better today, Your Highness," the countess said with her customary cool politeness, as she continued to glance through her correspondence. "I heard you were ill last night. Was the pain very bad this time?"

Sophia flushed, pleased that the countess was taking an interest in her. She spoke somberly, yet rapidly, as though glad to talk about it. "The pain was horrible. It felt like someone had stabbed a hot, burning knife into my skull. When it comes, I can't think about anything except the pain and trying to make it stop. Mama wanted me to take that bitter medicine the latest physician gave me, but I hate the way it makes me feel, as though I'm wrapped in a thick woolly blanket, and, anyway, medicine doesn't help. I know the pain is still there, beneath the blanket, and that makes it worse. I drank the medicine to please Mama, but I spit it out after she left the room."

Sophia started to say something, then bit her lip and fell silent.

"Yes, Your Highness, what is it?" prompted the countess.

"The medicine makes me sleep, but it doesn't stop the bad dreams. I think sometimes the dreams are worse than the pain."

The countess stopped sorting to look with concern at her young friend.

"Was it the same dream, Your Highness?"

"Yes, my lady. I am in a cave lit by torches. The cave is cold. I can see my breath and I'm not wearing anything except my shift. Something is chasing me and I'm running away and the cold air makes my chest hurt. I stop because I can't breathe and hide behind a boulder, but I keep hearing the booming footsteps coming after me. I can sense its hunger. It wants me. I start running again, and the footsteps keep coming: boom, boom, boom."

Sophia's voice dropped. "What is most horrible is that it

knows my name. It calls out to me, and when it does, I wake up."

Her brow furrowed. "Even when I'm awake, I can hear the footsteps sometimes: boom, boom, boom. I can even feel them coming up through the floor."

The countess was troubled. Sophia had told her about the dream before. The dream was always the same, with little variation, as if the girl were describing something real, something that had actually happened to her. Cecile was wondering whether or not to mention this to the king, thinking it might be a new symptom, when her thoughts were interrupted by her servant, Maria, coming to whisper that Benoit was waiting in the wardrobe and that he appeared agitated.

The countess rose languidly with a rustle of silk, her skirts falling in graceful folds around her.

"I must leave you for a moment, Your Highness. While I am gone, I want you to locate Travia and Estara and the island of Braffa on your map."

"I already know where they are, my lady," said Sophia, shyly proud. She pointed out the two small continents on the map.

"Then be ready to discuss the deteriorating political situation between these two nations and how it relates to Braffa *and* to Rosia when I return," said the countess.

"Yes, my lady," said Sophia.

She picked up the spaniel and held him poised over the map.

"Now, Bandit, you must find Braffa . . ."

The countess, not expecting formal visitations, was dressed for comfort in a voluminous and exquisite white cambric chemise. Maria fetched a green moiré dressing gown, which the countess put on over the chemise, then entered her wardrobe.

Benoit rose respectfully and made an attempt to bow, staggered, and nearly fell. The countess ordered Maria to fetch brandywine. Benoit drank it, and some color returned to his wrinkled cheeks.

"Please, sit down," said the countess.

She herself remained standing, an indication that Benoit should not expect to linger.

"You've come about Stephano."

"Yes, my lady," said Benoit, seating himself.

"The last I heard my son and his 'Cadre' were planning to travel to Westfirth."

"They are on their way there now, my lady," said Benoit. "They were somewhat delayed."

He went on to tell her about the challenge in the park, how Stephano and Rodrigo had gone to the duel, how both had been certain Rodrigo would be killed, but that Stephano had hoped to be able to find a way out of it and had ordered the *Cloud Hopper* to be ready to sail, how Benoit, fearing the worst, had gone to the houseboat to await the dire news.

"I do not know what happened at the duel, my lady," said Benoit. "Master Stephano was not at leisure to tell me, what with the men shooting at us. Did I mention to your ladyship that I shot one of the assassins?"

"Twice," said the countess coolly.

She listened with her usual calm languor, evincing no emotion. "My son was wounded, you said."

"Yes, my lady. Shot in the shoulder," said Benoit, adding with a certain pride, "He was shot up worse than that during the war. He'll survive this one. The Trundler woman, Miri, is an herbalist like most of her kind. She will see to it that he pulls through."

The countess did not evince much interest and shifted to another topic. "Tell me more about this man with the gun with the rifled bore."

"Monsieur Rodrigo called him 'Sir Richard Piefer.' According to the master, he laid claim to be a Freyan nobleman. He spoke with a Freyan accent."

"Can you describe this Piefer?"

"The master would be able to do so. I regret to say that I only saw him from a distance, my lady, and he was trying to kill me at the time."

The countess' lips twitched slightly. "Is that all you have to report, Benoit?"

"Yes, my lady."

"Do you know if Monsieur Rodrigo has been apprised of the death of his father?"

"Is his lordship dead, my lady?" Benoit asked, astonished.

"I fear so, Benoit. The ambassador was gunned down as he was leaving the office of the Estaran Minister of the Exchequer. The Estarans have arrested a Travian revolutionary, who happened—most conveniently—to be in the vicinity. His Majesty King Alaric has sent a strongly worded letter expressing his outrage at the death of his ambassador and demanding a full investigation."

"I see," said Benoit. The old man's eyes moistened. "Monsieur Rodrigo will be most affected by this tragic news. I will write to him immediately."

"You may also write to Monsieur Rodrigo that he should avoid returning home. He is wanted for the murder of young Valazquez. I was wondering what this ridiculous charge was all about. Now I know. The matter will be resolved, but the negotiations may take some time. I will send you word when it is safe for Monsieur Rodrigo to return."

"Yes, my lady. Thank you, my lady."

"Is there anything else?"

"No, my lady."

Benoit finished off the brandywine, set the snifter on the table, and rose to his feet. The countess summoned Maria, who came to escort Benoit back through the servants' passage. As the two were about to leave, the countess stopped them.

"Benoit, you said you have some means of communicating with my son? You know where he is lodging while in Westfirth?"

Benoit looked wary. "I might, my lady."

"Relax, Benoit. I will not demand that you tell me. But I would appreciate knowing when you hear from him."

"I will, my lady," said Benoit, bowing once again, then exiting the closet in company with Maria.

Left alone, the countess blew out the lamp and stood in the darkness for long moments, twisting the ring on her finger, before leaving the wardrobe and going to her sitting room. Summoning her valet-de-chambre, Dargent, the countess told him to dispatch one of her agents to find out information regarding the mysterious Sir Richard Piefer.

Dargent left swiftly upon his errand, and the countess returned to the library. Sophia tried to rise as the countess entered, but the princess was hampered in this effort by the spaniel, which had once more planted himself on the hem of her skirt and refused to budge.

"Bandit, you are a bad dog," said Sophia, scolding him by kissing him on the top of his head.

The countess languidly resumed her seat. "I am sorry I was absent so long, Your Highness. Now, tell me about the situation in Braffa."

Sophia shooed away the spaniel, rose to her feet, and came over to stand before the countess to recite her lesson.

"Estara and Travia both claim the island nation of Braffa because of its valuable resource known as the Blood of God, which is a form of the Breath that has been transformed into a liquid and can be used to power airships. The grand bishop favors the claim of Estara over Braffa because the Church has more influence in that country. The king, my father, says that we have stronger ties to Travia and he favors their claim."

"What about the city-state of Braffa?"

"The Braffan council wants to refuse both claims and remain independent."

Sophia went on to describe how a city-state differed from a monarchy. As she was talking, the countess happened to glance down at the letter she had been about to read when she had been obliged to leave to speak to Benoit. The letter was from her principal agent in Freya. A name in the letter caught her attention. A chill came over the countess. She longed to read the letter, but she did not want to hurt Sophia's feelings by dismissing her. Too often the girl had been told to "run along and play."

"And what about our longtime enemy, Freya?" the countess asked. "Which side do they support and what role does the Blood of God and the Freyan Navy play in this dispute?"

Sophia's eyes widened in dismay at the question. She bit her lip. Her cheeks flushed.

"The Freyan Navy? I'm not certain, my lady . . ."

"We talked about the Freyan Navy during our last lesson," said the countess, and she added with a slight smile, "Perhaps some cakes and hot chocolate would help your thought process."

"Oh, yes, I'm sure they would!" Sophia cried, laughing and clapping her hands.

The countess rang a small silver bell and Maria appeared. The countess gave her order. Maria returned bearing a tray on which gold-rimmed plates of the finest porcelain bore small cakes decorated with sugared violets, bonbons, and spiced nuts. The tantalizing smell of coffee mingled with the aroma of hot chocolate.

"May I be hostess, my lady?" Sophia asked eagerly. "Mama never lets me pour. She fears I will spill on my gown."

The countess said she would be honored if the princess would serve her. Sophia was delighted. She took her duties as hostess quite seriously, her first task being to remove Bandit from the chair on which he had jumped with the intent of helping himself to cake. Sophia laughingly asked him which he wanted and made him choose by holding his small nose over each cake. Once Bandit had made his decision, which he did by licking a cake before Sophia could stop him, the princess hovered over the cake tray, selecting the very best delicacies for the countess and arranging them attractively on the plate. After that, Sophia had to make a decision on which cakes she wanted. All this took a considerable amount of time.

While Sophia was thus happily engaged, the countess was at liberty to read her letter, which was written in code, made to appear as nothing more than two ladies exchanging the latest gossip in case the missive should be intercepted.

Our dear friend, Honoria, has not been in attendance at the royal Freyan court recently.

"Honoria" was her code name for Sir Henry Wallace.

Honoria's unexpected absence is of great concern to her friends and has become the cause of much speculation. I have asked around, but no one knows where she is or what has become of her. I confess that I am quite worried and I know that you will be concerned, as well.

I will tell you what I know. Rumor has it that a short while ago Honoria received a mysterious package delivered to her by a merchant sailor. No one knows what was in the package, but after she received it, she departed at once for her estate. I have heard nothing of her since.

Now you know, my dear, that my curiosity is enough to kill any number of cats, and I decided to find out more about this mysterious package. I have a friend who is in the custom office and he was obliging enough to provide me with a manifest for the two merchant vessels that were in port at the time. A package recorded on the manifest was addressed to Honoria. The contents were described as: one pewter tankard! An odd gift for our elegant friend!

But here is a most strange coincidence that will amuse you. As I was reading the manifest, I came across the name of one of your friends. You happened to mention the name to me in your last correspondence: Manuel Alcazar, that merchant sailor from the city of Westfirth. Or was your friend Pietro Alcazar? I

*can't recall. Perhaps they are relatives. Isn't it funny
that I should happen to run across his name on this
manifest? A small world, as they say!*

The following was added in a postscript, obviously written in haste.

*I have just received news that is most shocking. It
seems a small boat bound for Rosia has disappeared
into the Breath in a dead calm. All hands are feared
lost. This happened about the same time our dear Honoria vanished. You don't suppose she was aboard? Ah,
it is too dreadful to contemplate! Still, she has as many
lives as the aforesaid cat. I will let you know the instant
I hear more about our missing friend.*

The countess allowed the letter to slip from her hands.
She sat staring at a porcelain figurine of a shepherdess on
the desk. She did not see the shepherdess, she did not see
the room around her, she did not hear Sophia's gentle voice.

"My lady, are you ill?"

The countess blinked and hurriedly left the dark streets
and cul-de-sacs in which her mind was wandering. She had
the impression this was the third time Sophia had spoken.
The countess put her hand to her temple and gave a wan
smile.

"I am sorry, Your Highness, but I fear that I am not feeling quite well."

"Is there anything I can do for you, my lady?" asked
Sophia in alarm, setting down the cup of chocolate she had
been holding. "Can I fetch your smelling salts? Some
wine?"

"If you could ring for Maria, Your Highness," said the
countess faintly. "I fear we will have to postpone our lesson
for the day. Besides, Her Majesty the Queen will be wondering where you are. I would not have her angry at me."

Sophia rang the silver bell. "I hope you feel better, my

lady," she said anxiously. "Please let me know if there is anything I can do for you."

"I will be fine, Your Highness," said the countess. "It is but a sudden indisposition."

Sophia nodded, her eyes soft with concern. She gathered up Bandit and, with a fond look, left the countess' chambers. When the countess could no longer hear the sound of the girl's rustling petticoats, she turned to Maria.

"Find Dargent," the countess said. "The matter is urgent."

Maria obeyed with alacrity. When she was gone, the countess picked up the letter and, lighting a candle on her desk, held the paper to the flame. Once the letter had caught fire, the countess dropped the burning paper onto a plate and waited until it was consumed, then ground up the ashes with a coffee spoon and dumped them into the silver coffeepot.

Dargent entered her room. "You sent for me, Your Grace."

"I must speak with Stephano's retainer, Benoit. He was here a short while ago. He may still be in the servants' hall. If not, go to my son's home and bring Benoit back here immediately. It is of the greatest importance that I communicate with him."

Dargent bowed and departed.

The countess rose to her feet and began to pace back and forth, clasping and unclasping her hands and twisting the little ring.

Dargent traveled swiftly to Stephano's house in the wyvern-drawn carriage kept by the countess for his exclusive use. Dargent was out the carriage door almost before the wyvern's claws had scraped the pavement. He knew the countess. He had heard the quaver of fear in her voice.

He ran to the door and raised his hand to knock, then he froze on the door stoop. He had no need to knock. The door was open, ajar. Dargent had been to Stephano's house many times, and he knew Benoit would not be so careless as to leave the entrance unlocked. Dargent drew his pistol. Cocking the hammer, he gave the door a shove.

He entered slowly and cautiously. He looked behind the door, saw no one there.

"Benoit?" he called.

No answer.

Dargent went to the kitchen, where he knew Benoit liked to reside, and found a scene of destruction. Cabinet doors gaped wide, their contents strewn all over the floor. A marble bust of King Alaric lay smashed on the floor. Sacks of flour had been slit open and dumped out. Barrels were split apart and chairs upended.

Dargent hastened through the kitchen to look out the rear door, but found no one there. He returned through the kitchen and went across the hall to Benoit's room. The bed had been overturned, clothes pulled out of the wardrobe. Still holding the pistol, Dargent made his way stealthily up the stairs. He was fairly certain the searchers had completed their work and were gone, but he was not taking any chances.

The searchers had been thorough; he had to give them credit for that. They had taken the paintings from the wall to look behind them. They had broken into locked chests, removed papers and letters from the bureau. They had even gone through all the books, taking them down from the shelves, flipping through the leaves, and throwing them down on the floor when they were finished.

Now certain that he was alone, Dargent lowered his pistol and released the hammer. He wondered what the searchers had been looking for, wondered if they had found it.

Shaking his head, he called out again, "Benoit! Are you here? It's Dargent! The countess sent me!"

There was always a chance the old man might be hiding in a closet, but, again, no answer. Dargent had not truly expected one. He went back into the kitchen and knelt down to examine the splatters he'd seen on the floor. He dipped his fingers in them.

Blood. Fresh blood.

Dargent sighed deeply. He guessed that the old man had returned from the palace to catch the searchers in the act. They had beaten him, then had either kidnapped him to see what he knew or they'd taken away the corpse. Leaving the house, Dargent told his carriage driver not to spare his whip.

The countess received the disturbing news regarding the ransacking of Stephano's house and the disappearance of Benoit with a raised eyebrow and a deepening of the frown line on her forehead.

"Thank you for trying," she said to Dargent. "You may go now."

When he was gone and she was alone, the countess sank down in her chair. She tried to think what to do, how to warn Stephano that he was about to unwittingly cross swords with Sir Henry Wallace, spymaster, assassin, a man she considered the most dangerous man in all the world.

The countess had agents in Westfirth. She could alert them, tell them to find Stephano. She ruled that out. Sir Henry had his own agents in Westfirth and his agents knew her agents, just as her agents knew his. In using any agent to warn Stephano to keep away from Sir Henry, she might inadvertently lead Sir Henry right to him.

Yet, if she did not warn Stephano . . .

Night was falling. The servants came to light the candles. The countess sent them away. She preferred to sit alone in the darkness, her head resting on her hand. She would have to apprise His Majesty of the situation regarding Sir Henry Wallace or at least some part of the situation, the part she chose to tell. Alaric would be upset, but she knew how to handle him. He was not the problem that concerned her, deeply concerned her.

Closing her eyes, the countess brought Stephano's face to mind; the face so like his father's that her heart constricted with pain every time her son smiled.

"Julian, my love, my own dear love," Cecile de Marjolaine whispered softly, "Be with our boy!"

Chapter Eleven

Man is imperfect and thus our understanding of God is imperfect.
This lack is most evident in the understanding of God's gift, Magic.
We have learned to use magic for His glory, but I fear there are those
who seek to use magic for His downfall. Beware the quiet night, when
the dark voice whispers in your ear, for the magic in his voice is corruption.

—Writings of Saint Dennis

SIR ANDER MARTEL WAS KNIGHT PROTECTOR to
Father Jacob Northrop, a priest representing that most
mysterious and greatly feared order of the Church known
as the Arcanum. As Knight Protector, Sir Ander had
pledged before God to hold the life of this priest as a sacred
trust, to lay down his own life in defense of the priest, to
protect and shield him from all harm.

Far easier pledged than done, Sir Ander gloomily reflected as he removed the cuirass, marked with the emblem
of the Knight Protectors, and enhanced with magical constructs, his helm and other accouterments before placing
them in the yacht's built-in storage locker. He kept his armor and his weapons close to hand. One never knew, when
traveling with Father Jacob, when they would be needed.

Sir Ander flung himself down in a chair and tried to
sleep, without success. Whenever he started to drift off into
slumber, lulled by the gentle swaying of the airborne yacht,

he saw again the horrific scenes of last night's bloody debacle in the town of Capione and was jolted back into unpleasant wakefulness.

Sir Ander looked with envy and some bitterness at his companion, Father Jacob, who was sleeping quite soundly. The priest slept in the same position always, lying on his back, his hands resting on his chest, fingers clasped, his body completely relaxed.

Never mind that eleven soldiers had lost their lives last night, half a city block had been destroyed, and months of careful planning had literally gone up in flames. Never mind that the yacht, specially designed for a priest of the Arcanum, was now speeding through the night in reply to an urgent summons from the grand bishop. Father Jacob could still sleep soundly and even, to add insult to injury, snore.

"The mind is the ruler, the body is the subject," Father Jacob often said. "When the mind tells the body it is time for sleep, the body should obey. The inability to fall asleep when and where you desire means your body is tyrannizing your mind; something I never permit."

Sir Ander shifted about on the chair, trying to find a more comfortable position. He could have made up the yacht's other bed, which was now a bench, but Sir Ander disliked lying down when the yacht was airborne. The swaying motion always made him feel slightly queasy.

He thrust out his long legs and settled himself in the chair, chin on his chest, and gave up the fight for sleep. He was once more in the flames and smoke of the battle last night, a battle they thought they had won, only to discover that even with all their careful plans, their quarry, a man known to his deluded followers as the Warlock, had managed to escape. . . .

The soldiers who had survived the assault and finally fought their way into the coven's hideout searched among the dead on orders of Father Jacob. They found a body in the wreckage that matched the description of the Warlock: a young man of about seventeen or eighteen years of age with blond hair, blond beard and mustache, and intense blue eyes. Those blue eyes were now wide open and staring in death. They could not tell how he had died. There was no blood on the corpse, no sign of a wound.

The soldiers set a guard over the room and sent word to Sir Ander and Father Jacob that they had found the Warlock and that he was dead. No one went near the corpse. Father Jacob had warned the soldiers that if they found their way into the Warlock's inner sanctum, they were to be careful not to touch anything—an order the soldiers were happy to obey.

The room was below ground level; the walls and floor lined with stone. Two rows of thick wooden pillars supported a vaulted stone ceiling. On the pillars were sigils of warding and protection. Brass lamps shed a dim light throughout the room. Small cells had been built in the middle of each wall. Iron bars enclosed each cell, leaving just room enough for a person to stand. Each contained the body of one of the coven's many victims. All of them had died horribly, in some depraved manner.

Sir Ander was not a crafter. He did not have a magical bone in his body, as the saying went. Yet he was able to feel the dark magic in that room hiss and sputter like the fuse of a bomb. Bodies of the Warlock's allies lay on the floor, some torn apart by bullets, others burned to death, victims of their own black magic gone awry. All the victims were young, none of them above twenty years of age. Sir Ander had seen death in many gruesome forms on the field of battle, but the horror of this sight, as he entered the room, made his stomach roil.

"God save us!" whispered a voice at his elbow.

The knight turned to find Brother Barnaby standing at his side. Sir Ander was startled. He had not realized Brother Barnaby had tagged along after them. The young monk was always so quiet and self-effacing, one tended to forget he was around.

Barely in his twenties himself, Brother Barnaby was slight of build, with intelligent brown eyes and a fine-boned face. His skin was the onyx color of those who dwell in the Galiar region, east of Argonne. His hair was blue-black, shaved in the tonsure. Despite his appearance, he was strong and capable, far stronger than he looked.

Sir Ander regarded the young monk with concern.

"Brother Barnaby, you should not be a witness to this sad scene. Go wait for us back at our lodgings."

"I have a letter for Father Jacob, sir," said Brother Barnaby, clutching a folded and sealed document. "It just arrived, forwarded to the Father from the Arcanum. And I have a message from one of the Bishop's Own, who flew to Capione on griffin-back and needs to speak to Father Jacob most urgently."

"The letter and the Bishop's Own can both wait until we have finished here," said Sir Ander, trying to find a way to keep Brother Barnaby from entering the horror-filled room. "Go tell the guardsman that Father Jacob will attend him shortly."

"I already told him, sir," said Brother Barnaby, sticking doggedly to Sir Ander. The monk smiled faintly. "You should know by now, sir, that you can't get rid of me that easily. Father Jacob might need me."

Sir Ander opened his mouth and shut it again. He knew he would be wasting his breath. Brother Barnaby was dedicated, body and soul, to Father Jacob. Sir Ander would not be able to remove the young monk, short of picking him up and carrying him out the door.

"Very well," said Sir Ander testily. "But keep close to me and don't touch anything!"

Brother Barnaby nodded and silently accompanied Sir Ander as the knight entered the bloodstained room. The cavernous chamber had no windows and was as shadowed as the hearts of those who had once inhabited it, or so Sir Ander thought. The soldiers ordered to guard the room were carrying torches, but even their flaring light could not lift the darkness that seemed to settle on the soul.

The soldiers pointed the way to the corpse. Sir Ander had brought a lantern fueled by a glowing magical sigil and by its light they located Father Jacob, on his knees on the floor of a small antechamber off the main room. Brother Barnaby stood gazing on the awful scene, his brown eyes moist with sorrow and wide with shock. Sir Ander looked very grim.

Father Jacob held his own lantern, magically enhanced to give off an extremely bright glow. He had placed the lantern on the floor near the corpse and was kneeling in the blood, studying the corpse with such intensity that he did not hear the footsteps of his comrades.

He sniffed at the cold lips and studied with minute care the victim's robes. He peered at the soles of the boots and the hands clenched to fists in the agony of the death throes. He was careful not to touch the body, Sir Ander noted.

The knight looked down sternly at the corpse of the young man.

It is a sin to be pleased at the death of any man, Sir Ander thought, particularly one so young. He could not help but feel intensely relieved that this evil young man was dead, his reign of terror ended.

Sir Ander squatted down beside the body. "No trace of blood. How did he die? Poison?"

Father Jacob did not answer. He was frowning, lost in his reflections. Sir Ander, accustomed to the priest's ways, patiently repeated the question.

Father Jacob roused himself and said abruptly, "Something damn odd about this." His voice was deep and resonating and although Father Jacob had lived in Rosia twenty-five years, his Freyan accent was still pronounced.

Sir Ander repeated his question a third time, and, since he finally had the priest's attention, he added in rebuking tones, "Brother Barnaby is here. He came to see you."

"I have a letter for you from Master Albert Savoraun, Father," said Brother Barnaby. "And the grand bishop sent a messenger saying he has urgent need of you."

Father Jacob snorted and with that snort dismissed the letter *and* the grand bishop. The priest continued to study the corpse.

Father Jacob Northrup was in his early forties. His brownish hair, shaved in the traditional tonsure, was starting to go gray. He was clean-shaven, of medium height, though he seemed taller to most people, perhaps because he was muscular and well built. He had been a prize-winning pugilist in his youth and was still fond of the sport. He wore the black cassock that marked a member of the Arcanum and a black, stiff hat made of felt. He would have been termed handsome, for he had a strong jawline and fine nose, but for his eyes, which were gray-green in color and glittered with an intensity most people found disturbing.

"When Father Jacob looks at you, he sees you—sees all of you, whether you want him to or not," Sir Ander often said.

Father Jacob's face was marked with the trials of his life; deep lines marred his brow, wrinkles webbed his eyes. He was thin-lipped, and when he smiled, the smile could be either charming or a prelude to doom.

"Father, you should send Brother Barnaby away," said Sir Andrew.

"And why should I do that?" Father Jacob asked irritably.

"Because there is no need for this young monk to have to witness such carnage. Bad enough we should have to see it ourselves. I'll have nightmares for a week and I've seen men blown apart by cannonballs and never flinched. But this . . . They were so young . . ."

Father Jacob glanced about the room, then returned his frowning gaze to the corpse. Sir Ander sighed and gave up. He knew from long experience that when Father Jacob looked at this room, he did not see the tragic ruin of young lives or think of the terror and pain these young ones must have endured. To Father Jacob's analytical mind, the dead youths were nothing more than factors in an equation he had been given the task of solving. And right now, judging by his furrowed brow and tight lips, he was not having much success.

"I'm missing something," Father Jacob said, frowning in perplexity and frustration. "Missing something. . . ."

He pushed himself to his feet and stood with his head lowered, deep in thought. When a soldier came up and seemed about to interrupt the priest in this work, both Sir Ander and Brother Barnaby hurriedly intervened.

"'How did he die?'" Father Jacob muttered. "You have a knack, Sir Ander, for hitting the very center of the target. 'How did he die?' A most intriguing question."

He bent back to examine the corpse and Sir Ander, who was growing stiff from squatting, stood up. His knees made popping sounds and he grimaced. He was fifty years old and though he was in excellent condition physically, he was at the age where his bones were starting to creak.

"So very young. So very sad," said Brother Barnaby. Murmuring the prayer for the dead, he reached down his hand to shut the staring eyes.

"Don't touch!" Father Jacob cried, striking the monk's hand with such force that Brother Barnaby stumbled and nearly fell. The young monk shrank back in dismay.

"Really, Father, there was no need to hit him!" Sir Ander began angrily.

Father Jacob looked up at the soldier who had arrived with a question.

"Get your men out of here," Father Jacob ordered. "And take Brother Barnaby with you!"

"Sir, our captain's dead," the soldier began. "I'm not sure—"

"I don't give a tinker's damn who's dead!" Father Jacob shouted. "Get your men out of here! Set a guard on the door. Don't let anyone in."

The alarmed soldier hastened off to convey the priest's command. The troops obeyed with alacrity, all of them thankful to leave that chamber of horrors. Since the door had been blown apart and battered down, the soldiers took up their positions in the hallway outside. In his haste, the soldier had forgotten about Brother Barnaby, who had retreated to the shadows, hoping Father Jacob would not notice he was still around.

The monk's efforts failed.

Father Jacob glowered. "Brother Barnaby, I said you were to leave."

"I will leave when you leave, Father," Brother Barnaby said quietly.

Father Jacob muttered something, then motioned with his hand. "If you insist on staying, Brother, walk over to that wall and stand there and do not move! Sir Ander, remain near. I may need your services."

Father Jacob knelt on the floor beside the corpse, being careful not to touch it. He passed his hand over the young man's chest and spoke words that were harsh and ugly, the language of dark magic, sounding like a screeching bat, a cawing crow. His face, mild and benign, twisted and contorted. Brother Barnaby shuddered and looked away. Sir Ander felt the hair prickle the back of his neck. His gut tightened. He placed his hand on his sword's hilt, ready for whatever might come.

Father Jacob continued to pass his hand back and forth over the dead man's chest and then he stopped. He made a gesture of summoning and spoke a word of command.

A viper reared up from where it had been lying coiled beneath the robes on the corpse's chest. The snake's hooded head faced Father Jacob. The viper's tongue flicked out of its mouth. The snake hissed at Father Jacob and seemed to want to strike, but the priest held it in thrall with his magic. The viper's head swayed back and forth, its slit eyes fixed on Father Jacob.

"You must cut off the head, Sir Ander," said Father Jacob coolly. "Quickly, man! I cannot hold sway over it much longer."

Sir Ander swallowed his inborn revulsion of all things that slithered on the ground and drew his broadsword from the scabbard slowly, trying not to make a sound that might cause the viper to attack. He held his sword in his hand, estimating the stroke.

"You're too close to the snake. I don't want to cut off two heads instead of one," said Sir Ander softly.

"I don't dare move," said Father Jacob. "If I do, I will break the spell that is holding the viper in thrall."

Sir Ander drew in a deep breath. "Then when I swing, you must pull your head back. Are you ready?"

"Ready," said Father Jacob.

Brother Barnaby was softly praying.

"Put a prayer in God's ear for me, Brother," said Sir Ander and, using a backhanded stroke, he swept the blade through the air.

Father Jacob lunged sideways. The blade whistled past him and sliced through the viper, severing the snake's head from the body. The head flew off onto the floor. The snake's body fell, twitching, on top of the corpse.

"A Tissius viper," said Father Jacob, eyeing the snake with interest. "Comes from the Kharun Dir Desert. Highly poisonous. Brother Barnaby, could you find me a sack? I should like to take the corpse back to the yacht to study—"

Sir Ander coughed and jerked his head.

Father Jacob looked up at Brother Barnaby. The young man leaned against the wall, shivering. Father Jacob's expression softened.

"I am sorry you had to witness this, Brother Barnaby," said Father Jacob with a sigh. "And I am sorry I struck you. But if you had touched the corpse, the viper would have bitten you. Death would have been inevitable and most painful."

"I understand, Father." Brother Barnaby gulped. He looked ill, but he stood steadfast. "Please do not apologize. I will find a sack—"

"Thank you, Brother, but never mind," said Father Jacob in regretful tones. "I wouldn't have time to dissect it anyway."

Sir Ander drew his handkerchief and carefully wiped his blade. He thrust his broadsword back into the scabbard and tossed the handkerchief in disgust onto the floor.

"Why did the Warlock plant the snake on himself?" asked Sir Ander. "Just to have the sadistic pleasure of knowing that he could still kill after death?"

Father Jacob was staring with perplexity at the corpse. "I'm not certain that was the reason. From what I know of him, the Warlock, though young, is highly intelligent. His actions are always purposeful. Reason and logic guide him."

He looked more closely at the corpse, then he said urgently, "Tell the soldiers to start searching the area."

"What are they searching for?" Sir Ander asked, puzzled.

"For the Warlock, of course," Father Jacob snapped impatiently.

Sir Ander had no idea what the priest was talking about—the Warlock was dead on the floor. But Sir Ander had been with Father Jacob for ten years and he knew that questioning him now would only further aggravate him. He trusted the priest implicitly and although the Warlock was most certainly dead, he went to tell the soldiers to conduct a thorough search of the building and the surrounding area for the Warlock.

The soldiers looked at Sir Ander as though he was crazy, but he was a Knight Protector and they were bound to obey. They walked off slowly, muttering among themselves. They wanted to leave this place, go back to pick up their dead. Sir Ander didn't blame them. A mug of cold ale in some noisy tavern where people were carefree and laughing seemed like Heaven to him about now.

"They're searching for him," Sir Ander said on his return. "Though they have no idea why."

"They won't find him," Father Jacob remarked, talking to

himself more than his companions. "He had his escape route all planned. A brilliant young man. He could have done great things in this world. For such a mind to be corrupted . . ."

Brother Barnaby was bewildered. "I don't understand, Father," he said hesitantly. "Isn't this dead man the Warlock?"

In answer, Father Jacob placed his hand on the young man's cheek and, with a sudden jerk, ripped off the blond mustache. Brother Barnaby flinched and gasped in shock.

"It's not real, Brother. Spirit gum," Father Jacob said succinctly, holding up the mustache. "The sort used by actors."

He tore off the blond beard, then twitched aside the collar of the red robes to reveal the breasts, bound in strips of flannel, of a young woman.

Brother Barnaby hurriedly averted his eyes. The young monk took his vow of celibacy seriously. Sir Ander drew closer to get a better look, then he remembered the snake and kept his distance.

"Oh, it's quite safe now," Father Jacob said. "The poor child will not hurt anyone anymore."

"She can't be more than fifteen!" Sir Ander knelt down to gaze with pity at the youthful face. He sighed and said quietly, "Elaina Devroux."

"Yes," said Father Jacob. "Sad news for the viscount and his lady wife."

"He murdered her and then disguised the body so that we would think it was him," Sir Ander said grimly.

"He did not murder the girl, though one might say Elaina Devroux perished the day she fell victim to him and his cult," said Father Jacob. "Note the expression on her face. The young woman died in a drug-induced state. The juice of the poppy, if I'm not mistaken. She dressed with care, even to binding her breasts to make herself appear flat-chested. She put on men's boots, which are too big for her."

He looked at the rigid, pale face with its strange and

terrible smile. "The beard and mustache are made of real human hair and were applied by someone who knew his business. Such a disguise required careful planning and forethought. She must have agreed at the outset to sacrifice herself for the Warlock should that become necessary. The Warlock was her lover. She ran away from home, to go to him and to the opium he fed her."

"How do you know she was taking opium?" Sir Ander asked.

"When her parents first found her, wandering aimlessly about the city, they thought her ravings were the result of 'demonic possession.' In truth, the seizures were brought about by the removal of the drug to which she had become addicted. I have seen the same behavior among patients in the infirmary who were given opium in honey for the pain of broken limbs. In some instances, when the opium is taken away, these patients appear to have been seized by demons."

The priest drew back Elaina's robes and pointed to two small marks on the young girl's neck.

"That is how she died. When the Warlock placed the viper on her chest and covered it with her robes, she knew that it must eventually bite her."

"But why would she do such thing?" Brother Barnaby asked, his voice soft with dismay.

"To give the man she adored the opportunity to escape, of course," said Father Jacob. "He needed time to evade our pursuit and this poor child provided it."

"He escapes, leaving her and everyone else in his cult to die. I hope he rots in Hell!" Sir Ander said savagely. "He was warned in advance of our coming."

"Yes," Father Jacob said and he added bitterly, in sudden anger, "As if we needed more proof than the fact that I walked into his trap and now eleven men are dead!"

"But who could have warned him? No one knew except you and me and the viscount . . ."

Sir Ander saw the grim look on the priest's face. "The viscount? You can't be serious! Why warn the very person he wanted us to catch? His soldiers were the ones who died in the assault."

"I doubt that he meant to," said Father Jacob. "We will probably find he has a servant in the pay of the Warlock."

The priest rose to his feet and dusted off his hands. "We are not dealing with a lunatic, Sir Ander. We are dealing with a young man who is operating with a purpose, a young man with someone even more intelligent behind him."

"You are talking about the Sorceress. But what purpose can there possibly be in torturing and murdering people? Other than"—Sir Ander glanced askance at Brother Barnaby and lowered his voice—"for sadistic sexual pleasure . . ."

"That is part of it, certainly," said Father Jacob. He glanced about at the room, at the corpses in the alcoves. "But I believe it has more to do with the terror these gruesome crimes generate among the populace. Unlike most criminals, who seek to hide their crimes, this young man performs his openly. He wants people to know what he is doing. This entire part of the country has been in a state of panic for weeks, what with the discovery of mutilated bodies in farmers' fields and a missing viscount's daughter. All designed to awaken public interest and outrage and draw attention to the Warlock. Even my arrival feeds into this frenzy."

"But why?" Sir Ander asked, bewildered. "To what end?"

"I very much fear, my friend, that the Warlock wants me to look at him because he does not want me looking at something else."

Father Jacob stood for long moments lost in thought, then he roused himself.

"Well, we have done all we can here." Father Jacob glanced at Brother Barnaby and his voice softened. "I believe you should say the prayer for the dead, Brother."

Sir Ander and Father Jacob bowed their heads and folded their hands as Brother Barnaby, his face soft with sorrow and compassion, knelt down to close the staring eyes and say a prayer for all the souls lost and wandering in darkness. . . .

Sir Ander gave up trying to sleep. He felt the need to talk, yet he knew better than to wake Father Jacob. Sir Ander opened the hatch, located in the front of the *Retribution,* and peered out.

"Would you mind if I join you, Brother?" he asked the monk.

"I would like the company, sir," said Brother Barnaby, pleased.

The driver's station on the *Retribution* was located in the front of the yacht and, of necessity, was partially open to the elements. The black-lacquered hull enclosed the cabin and storage rooms and supported a small mast and a ballast balloon. Wings swept back from the curve of the prow, running the length of the twenty-foot hull. Small airscrews were mounted at the rear of each wing, close to the hull. Polished brass rails ran along the roof of the cabin. Brass lanterns, mounted every four feet, and brass hardware for the doors and windows completed the yacht's regal look. The symbol of the Arcanum: a crossed sword and a staff over which burns a flame set on a quartered black-and-gold shield, was painted on both sides of the hull.

Brother Barnaby took pride in the yacht. He saw to it that the brass was always polished to a high sheen, though Father Jacob maintained caustically that polishing the brass every day was a waste of time.

Sir Ander joined the monk at the driver's seat and settled himself on the bench behind the windscreen.

Brother Barnaby glanced at him. "Do you mind if we talk of what happened this night, sir?"

The night air was refreshing, and Sir Ander breathed deeply. The two wyverns, barely seen in the darkness, moved their wings in tandem. Brother Barnaby held the reins loosely. The gentle monk had a way with animals. He had picked and trained the wyverns himself. Wyverns were notoriously ill-tempered and recalcitrant, but these wyverns, guided by Brother Barnaby, were submissive and eager to please.

Sir Ander watched as the monk reached out to touch a small brass helm located to his right. The helm was set with magical constructs that glowed with a golden radiance. As his fingers touched a sigil within one particular construct, correcting a list to starboard, the color shifted red.

"What would you like to talk about, Brother?" Sir Ander asked, though he already knew.

"I do not *like* to talk so much as I feel the need," said Brother Barnaby. He looked at the ballast balloon above them and frowned slightly. His fingers slid across the control panel and touched several sigils that adjusted the yacht's trim to compensate for the slight cross breeze.

Sir Ander regarded the young monk with concern. "I feared what you witnessed tonight would upset you, Brother. Father Jacob was remiss in allowing you to come with us."

"I needed to see, sir," said Brother Barnaby. "As Father Jacob says, 'if we are to fight evil, we must look it in the face, no matter how dreadful the aspect.'"

Sir Ander shook his head. He knew he would see the mutilated corpses in his nightmares for the rest of his life. He would have spared any man that sight, but particularly Brother Barnaby.

The young monk was a foundling. The monks of the Order of Saint Anton had discovered the babe wrapped in a blanket, left on the doorstep on a warm summer's night. They had taken in the child and raised him.

Brother Barnaby had grown up believing himself to be a child of God. He had been nurtured and loved by the monks, who had soon discovered the child had a talent for magical healing and a way with animals. They had taught him to read and write and cipher and how to use the magic that was God's gift. When Barnaby was older, he had studied the lore of herbs and medicines and had become adept at tending to the ills and hurts of beasts and men.

Then one day when he was sixteen years old, as he had been placing his offering of candles on the altar, Brother Barnaby's patron saint—Saint Castigan, guardian of children and animals—had appeared to him in a vision.

"Serve this man," said the saint. He had held his hand over the head of a man dressed in a black cassock denoting him to be a member of the Order of the Arcanum.

Brother Barnaby had never doubted that vision. He had told the abbot he was leaving to find the man revealed to him by Saint Castigan. The monks of the abbey had been upset and disturbed. The abbot had tried to dissuade the young man. He could hardly argue against Saint Castigan, however, and he had at last given Brother Barnaby permission to leave. The abbot had perhaps been well aware that if he had not given his permission, the determined young monk would have left anyway.

Brother Barnaby had walked the three hundred miles to the Citadel of the Voice, where the select few priests admitted into the Arcanum lived and worked. He had arrived at the gates barefoot and in rags, half-starved, thin and weary, but joyful. He had said simply he was here on orders from Saint Castigan to serve a man whose name he did not know. The young monk then provided them with the description of the man in his vision.

The Provost of the Arcanum had immediately recognized Father Jacob Northrup and summoned him at once. When Father Jacob had entered the office, Brother Barnaby smiled in recognition, though they had never before met.

"Saint Castigan sent me to serve you, Father. He said you needed me."

"Why would the saint say that?" Father Jacob had asked, regarding the young man with interest.

"I have no idea, Father," Brother Barnaby had replied humbly. "All I know is that I am here and I will serve you and the saint most faithfully."

The Provost had been dubious about accepting this obviously cloistered and naïve young man into the Arcanum and would have sent the young monk back to his abbey, but Father Jacob had found Brother Barnaby "fascinating" and insisted on keeping him, much to the dismay of Sir Ander.

"I need a scribe, after all," Father Jacob had argued. "This Barnaby is a true innocent."

"He is, indeed," Sir Ander had said sternly. "You cannot take on this young man because you want to study his brain, Jacob. Such an innocent young person should not be exposed to the evil you and I see on a daily basis."

"Brother Barnaby is stronger than you think, my friend," Father Jacob had said. "And he has a mission to fulfill in this life. I do not know what that mission is, nor does he. But Saint Castigan knows and the saint and I both believe Barnaby will find his purpose traveling with us, not sheltered behind the walls of some reclusive monastery."

And so, here was Brother Barnaby, driving the wyverns and trying to make sense of the senseless.

"This young man led his followers to their deaths. He drove them to commit terrible acts and then urged them to sacrifice themselves, while he himself escaped. What horrible force drives him, Sir Ander? Why did he do it?"

"That is not an easy question to answer," said Sir Ander. "I'm not sure I *want* to try to understand. Father Jacob believes the Warlock obeys a master, or rather a mistress, an older woman who schooled him."

"The one known as the Sorceress."

"Yes. We know very little about her or this so-called Warlock except that he preys on young people. He lures sons and daughters of peasants and of nobles to his cult. Any youth who is lonely, unhappy, and desperate falls easy victim to the Warlock's charms and blandishments. Once he has them in his clutches, he uses opiates and the lusts of the body (I beg your pardon for speaking of such things, Brother) to keep them."

"I find myself at odds ..." Brother Barnaby gazed into the darkness, fumbling for the right words. "If you and

Father Jacob had found this young man, Sir Ander, you would have killed him, wouldn't you?"

"As God is my witness, yes," said Sir Ander in grim tones. "I would have put a bullet in his skull without hesitation."

"But he is only seventeen. Just a boy!"

"He stopped being a boy when he stabbed his first victim," said Sir Ander. "This 'boy' deliberately placed that viper on the breast of a young girl, knowing she would die."

"He has turned to evil," said Brother Barnaby sadly. "But perhaps that was not his fault. Perhaps he is also a victim of this sorceress. He might be counseled, reclaimed . . ."

"You feel pangs of conscience when I swat a fly, Brother," said Sir Ander, placing his hand on the monk's arm. "Take comfort in the fact that we are not likely to confront him again, either him or his dark mistress. We now have more important matters to consider it seems."

"The summons from the grand bishop about the poor nuns of Saint Agnes," said Brother Barnaby somberly. "I have prayed for them this night."

The guardsman on griffin-back had delivered a letter from the grand bishop that told of the massacre at the Abbey of Saint Agnes, ordering Father Jacob to drop whatever he was doing and report to the Bishop's Palace at once.

Father Jacob had planned to spend the next day searching for clues, hoping to pick up the trail of the young Warlock. A man of single-minded purpose, Father Jacob was not happy to receive the bishop's summons.

"Some other member of my Order must go," Father Jacob had said brusquely.

"The bishop asked for you specifically, Father," the rider had said. "He said you were the best."

Sir Ander had waited confidently for Father Jacob to say no, he wasn't leaving his investigation until it was finished. Father Jacob never had difficulty saying "no" to anyone, be it king or commoner or grand bishop.

Father Jacob had startled his friend. "Tell the bishop we will make all haste."

Father Jacob was, in Sir Ander's opinion, the wisest, most intelligent man the knight had ever known. Among all the priests of the Order of the Arcanum, Father Jacob *was* the best. The trouble was—he knew it, which often made him very difficult to live with.

Sir Ander and Brother Barnaby were startled by a sudden shout coming from inside the yacht.

"What a fool I have been! What a bloody, stupid fool! Where is that letter?" Father Jacob yelled.

"What is the matter, Father?" Brother Barnaby called out anxiously, trying to divide his attention between the control panel and the wyverns and the priest. "Do you need me?"

"He's fine," Sir Ander said irritably. "After all, *he* had a good night's sleep."

"Where is that letter?" Father Jacob demanded again.

"On the table," Sir Ander returned, opening the hatch and pointing. "You're looking straight at it!"

"You moved it," Father Jacob said, grumbling. He dragged out a chair, sat down, and picked up the letter.

"Must be an odd sort of letter," said Sir Ander to Brother Barnaby. "He's casting a magical spell on it."

As Rodrigo had cast a spell on the ashes of the letter in Alcazar's fireplace, Father Jacob was casting a similar spell on this letter. But whereas Rodrigo had drawn sigils and lines connecting them and then physically connected the sigils and lines, using the magical energy within his own body to produce the magic, Father Jacob merely passed his hand over the letter. A shimmering light began to shine from the page.

Father Jacob Northrop was a *savant*: one of those rare persons who, as the saying went, "was born of magic." As there are some people who can arrive at the answer of a complicated mathematical equation without going through the steps of adding, subtracting, multiplying, or dividing,

Father Jacob could work magic without the need for all the intervening steps leading to the end result.

Father Jacob looked up from the letter.

"What was the name of that abbey where all those nuns were killed?"

"Saint Agnes, Father."

"That's what I thought. Come in here for a moment. I need to speak to you."

Sir Ander left Brother Barnaby and climbed back through the hatch, inside the yacht. Father Jacob was sitting at the table, the letter in his hand. The magic he had cast on it still glowed faintly.

"This letter is from our friend, Master Albert Savoraun. You remember him? He worked with us on the affair of the naval cutter, *Defiant*. Master Albert has recently been made head of the Maritime Guild chapter in Westfirth."

"Good for him," said Ander heartily.

"That is not what is important," Father Jacob said impatiently. "What is important is that he needed to review the records of the guild and discovered that they were not in the guildhall. Following a great fire that had destroyed parts of the city, the records were moved for safekeeping to a nearby abbey. The Abbey of Saint Agnes . . ."

"I'll be damned!" said Sir Ander, startled into alertness. "That's a strange coincidence."

"You know I do *not* believe in coincidence," said Father Jacob. He referred again to the letter. "Master Albert writes: 'I found the information in the abbey to be of the utmost importance. I cannot stress its value. So important I dare not write it.'"

"Not even in a letter that requires a knowledge of magic to read?" Sir Ander asked with a smile.

The letter was seven pages long and, on the surface, contained mostly news of the antics of Master Albert's ten children. The true contents of the letter had been written with a magical cipher that required a magical counter cipher to read.

"Apparently not," said Father Jacob. He indicated the date on the top of the letter. "Master Albert wrote this letter a fortnight ago. The letter was addressed to the Arcanum, the Citadel of the Voice where we normally reside. The Provost received it there and forwarded it to me in Capione, which is why it took so long to reach me. And now we hear from the grand bishop that this very abbey has been attacked and the nuns who lived there murdered."

Father Jacob sat pondering. "How far are we from the Bishop's Palace in Evreux?"

Sir Ander consulted his pocket watch. "We have been flying for about ten hours now. I would say we were within an hour of arrival."

"You and Brother Barnaby have been awake all night. You should both try to get some sleep," said Father Jacob. He stood up, walked to the hatch, and flung it open. "I will drive, Brother Barnaby."

Brother Barnaby looked at the priest in alarm.

"Uh, no, Father, that's not necessary. I'm not at all tired."

The monk cast a pleading gaze at Sir Ander, begging him not to let Father Jacob drive. The wyverns did not like Father Jacob. There was no telling what the beasts might do if the priest took the reins.

"I'm not sleepy," said Sir Ander, stifling another yawn. "Come, Father Jacob. I will let you beat me in a game of dominoes."

Father Jacob's eyes brightened. His one weakness was an avid passion for dominoes. He drew a magical sigil on the letter from Master Albert, spoke a word and the letter was instantly consumed in a flash of blue fire. Not a trace of the letter remained, not even the ashes.

Sir Ander sneezed and irritably waved away the smoke. Father Jacob brought out his cherished set of ivory dominoes in their hand-carved rosewood case. The two sat down to their game. On the driver's seat, Brother Barnaby closed the hatch and sighed in relief.

Sir Ander dumped out the dominoes. Father Jacob

turned them upside down to hide the pips. Sir Ander began to stir them around.

"Too bad you didn't receive this letter earlier," said Sir Ander.

"I was meant *not* to receive it," said Father Jacob.

Sir Ander stopped stirring to stare. "What?"

"As I suspected, the Warlock was a diversion, my friend," said Father Jacob. He picked up a domino, but he did not play it. He tapped it on the table. "Poor Lady Elaina. The viscount was frantic to recover his child. Of course, he would insist on having me investigate. I went. Master Albert's letter missed me. And now the nuns of Saint Agnes are dead."

"But why?" Sir Ander asked. "What has one to do with the other?"

He turned over the domino.

"You've drawn a blank. How very fitting," said Father Jacob. "Until I know more, that is your answer."

Chapter Twelve

The laws of kings exist to judge and punish those who sin against man. The priests of the Arcanum, God's warriors on Aeronne, are responsible for protecting the faith from those who would corrupt or destroy it. We carry the light into the dark places, ever vigilant, searching out Aertheum and his foul servants.

—Mandate of the Arcanum
Saint Marie Elizabeth
First Provost of the Arcanum

BROTHER BARNABY CAREFULLY GUIDED THE WYVERNS into the mists that drifted serenely above the extensive grounds of the Conclave of the Divine—the official residence of the grand bishop and the administrative center of the Church of the Breath in Rosia. Although his majesty's palace was far more beautiful, floating high above the Conclave, the grand bishop could take comfort in the fact that the Church owned more buildings and took up considerably more land. The Conclave of the Divine was larger than many small cities.

The grounds housed three cathedrals, each dedicated to a different saint; motherhouses for four orders of monks, two orders of nuns, and three military orders; an elementary school for children skilled in magic, and a University with dormitories to house the students.

The Grand Bishop's Palace was the largest structure and

the oldest in the Conclave. All the other buildings had been erected down through the centuries, radiating out from the Grand Bishop's Palace, which stood in the center as the sun of the small world—as was right and proper in the eyes of God and the grand bishop.

The cathedrals and other structures had been built at different periods of time with each architect attempting to outdo his predecessors and thus there was no consistency of style. One cathedral had graceful spires. Another featured a vast dome. The third was adorned with minarets, while the University had tried to outdo them all by erecting spires and minarets above a vast dome.

The Conclave's sacred grounds were always busy. By day, the gates were thrown open so that people could attend services in one of the grand cathedrals. University students played croquet on the green lawns or studied in the gardens. Monks and nuns and priests, abbots and abbesses, answered the bells that called them to their prayers. At night, the common people were shooed out, the gates closed. Those who required admittance had to enter through a single gate where they came under the scrutiny of a porter and the Grand Bishop's Own, as his soldiers were called.

The skies above the Conclave of the Divine were also patrolled by the Grand Bishop's Own. Flying on the backs of griffins, the soldiers guarded the walls and the Breath, permitting only those who could prove they had business in the Conclave to enter.

The glistening black yacht, *Retribution*, with its striking, ornamental brass work was met by three of the Bishop's Own, who flew to meet it. Upon speaking to Brother Barnaby and noting the symbols of the Arcanum painted in gold on the side, the soldiers immediately escorted the yacht to the main courtyard.

Brother Barnaby decreased the magical energy flowing into the *Retribution*'s lift tanks, a process called "cooling," and landed the vessel. Once on the ground, the wyverns hissed and snapped at the griffins, which were well trained and held themselves aloof from such inferior animals, though the griffins did take care to keep clear of the wyvern's sharp fangs and claws. Brother Barnaby soothed his wyverns and praised them and made certain they were given space in the stables and fed and watered. Once settled, the wyverns tucked their heads under their wings to rest.

"If it is agreeable to you, Father," said Sir Ander, while they were waiting for Brother Barnaby to return from the stables, "I will forgo meeting with His Excellency."

"A wise move," said Father Jacob.

Grand Bishop Montagne disliked Sir Ander Martel and the feeling was mutual, an animosity that dated back to the Lost Rebellion, the name given to the fight waged against the king by the Duke de Bourlet. Sir Ander had remained true to the Crown, but he had made no secret of the fact that he thought King Alaric and Bishop Montagne had both conspired to drive the Duke de Bourlet to rebel. The grand bishop had attempted to block Sir Ander's acceptance into the Knight Protectors, but Sir Ander had an influential friend at court—the Countess de Marjolaine. She had seen to it that Sir Ander was made a Knight Protector. The grand bishop had taken his revenge by assigning Sir Ander to protect a member of the Arcanum, one of the most dangerous assignments for members of the Order.

"I will pay my respects to my commander and see if those pistols I ordered from the Royal Armory have been delivered," said Sir Ander. "Shall we meet at noon for dinner in the dining hall of the Knight Protectors? Will you be finished with your meeting with the grand bishop by then?"

"Dear God, I hope so!" said Father Jacob. "Ah, and here is Brother Barnaby, armed for battle with his lap desk, pen and ink, and other mighty weapons."

Brother Barnaby looked slightly startled at this and glanced down at the lap desk, a hinged wooden box containing the tools he needed for recording notes of the meeting. He had no idea what Father Jacob meant, but Brother Barnaby had grown accustomed to the priest's odd way of speaking, so he only smiled in response and fell into step beside him. The priest and the monk followed the path leading to the Bishop's Palace, bidding good-bye to Sir Ander, who trod another path that would take him to the motherhouse of the Knight Protectors.

Although the day was early and the gates had not yet been opened to the public, people were coming and going through the courtyard surrounding the Bishop's Palace. Morning prayers, a light meal to break the night's fast, and then off to do the Lord's work.

Father Jacob walked among the crowd with a well-measured pace, his hands behind his back, his keen eyes taking in each and every person he encountered, much to that person's consternation. The black cassock of the Arcanum struck guilty fear into even the most innocent hearts, causing each individual to secretly run over his or her catalog of sins.

Nuns in their white habits and wimples saw the black cassock and made graceful reverence to Father Jacob, then glanced at each other with round eyes as they hurried past him. Monks in their plain brown robes, priests in their more colorful garb, eyed Father Jacob askance and kept their heads averted and stayed out of his way, fearing lest his eye fall on them.

Brother Barnaby was always offended by this rude treatment of the priest. Father Jacob did not mind. Instead, he even toyed with people by suddenly stopping and fixing his gray-green eyes on them. His victims would grow pale and shrink, some would even break into a sweat. Father Jacob would then give them a cheery greeting and go on his way, chuckling to himself. Brother Barnaby thought he would never completely understand Father Jacob.

They passed through several gates, were questioned (briefly) by the gate guards, and finally gained entry to the palace. A young priest who acted as escort led them through the echoing halls of the palace, down corridors adorned with tapestries and paintings and life-sized marble statues depicting the saints and various episodes in their lives. Brother Barnaby had been to the Conclave of the Divine before, but never to the palace. He was awed by the magnificence and enthralled by the works of art. His steps lagged. He gazed about in wonder and sometimes, forgetting himself, he would come to a halt to gaze in rapture at a mural on the wall.

Father Jacob did not chide the monk or try to hasten him. The priest would stop, rocking on his heels, patiently waiting. Their escort, however, was extremely annoyed. He would hasten back to speak sternly to Father Jacob, reminding him that the grand bishop's time was valuable.

"God works in wondrous ways, Father," said Brother Barnaby in a low voice to Father Jacob as they walked the corridors of white marble, surrounded by saints and angels. "Yesterday, seeing the terrible work evil men do, I was cast down in despair. Today I see the work created by men blessed of God and I am filled with hope."

Father Jacob smiled. Sir Ander had feared that Brother Barnaby would be wounded, his serenity disturbed, his gentle and kindly disposition destroyed by his exposure to the dark caverns, cruel wastelands and stinking swamps of the human mind. But as Sir Ander wore a cuirass enhanced with magical constructs when going into a potentially dangerous situation, Brother Barnaby went into battle accoutered in armor far stronger than the strongest, magically enhanced steel. He was armed with his faith.

Father Jacob had accepted Brother Barnaby as scribe and assistant for one reason—he was intrigued by the young man's claim to have been led to him by the command of Saint Castigan. Father Jacob was intensely interested in the study of mankind and while he did not quite add Brother Barnaby to his collection of specimens, as he might have added a rare sort of beetle, he did look forward to studying a young man driven by such intense faith.

To Father Jacob's credit, he would have immediately

returned Brother Barnaby to his monastery if he had
thought any harm could come to the young man. But as
Father Jacob had told Sir Ander, "Brother Barnaby's faith
in God is not like water in a glass that will spill if the glass
is broken. His faith will not evaporate or leak out through
a crack. Brother Barnaby's faith is the air he draws into his
lungs and the blood that pulses in his veins and the quiet
beating of his heart. His soul does not exist separate and
apart from his body. His soul is his body and his body is his
soul. You need have no fear for Brother Barnaby."

The young monk did not blame God for the evil in the
world. Nor did he rail against God or demand accountabil-
ity. He often asked questions of Father Jacob, not because
he doubted God, but for help in understanding.

"We imperfect creatures are constantly striving for perfection," Brother Barnaby said, as they traversed the hall.
"I've been thinking, Father. Perhaps men and women suc-
cumb to evil because they seek to achieve perfection too
easily, without having to work to attain it. They give up the
struggle and thus fall into the pit."

"And how do we help such people?" Father Jacob asked.

Brother Barnaby considered this question. "Some priests
would say we should stand on the rim of the pit and preach
to those who have fallen. But I believe the only way to help
them is to climb down into the pit and put our arms around
them and lift them out."

"You are a wise man, Brother," said Father Jacob gravely.

Brother Barnaby was quite startled by this compliment
and retreated into shy, if pleased, silence.

When Father Jacob and Brother Barnaby reached the
offices of the grand bishop, they were ushered into the antechamber—a large room, beautifully decorated with more
famous works of art. The ceiling was high and had been
painted to depict the Breath with its twilight-orange-and-
pink mists and white clouds, the sun, moon, and stars. The
parquet wooden floor was covered with a sumptuous carpet
into which the foot sank most pleasantly. Although the

large room was occupied by many priests, seated at desks or busy at various tasks, the antechamber was so intensely quiet that Brother Barnaby tried to hush the sound of his breathing.

"Is that the grand bishop?" he whispered to Father Jacob.

Brother Barnaby was referring to a man dressed in a scarlet cassock bound with a broad golden sash and a white stole about his shoulders.

"That is the monsignor," said Father Jacob, speaking loudly. The sudden intrusive sound caused all the priests to snap their heads up and glare at him in rebuke. "The monsignor serves His Eminence in much the same capacity as you serve me, Brother Barnaby."

Having seen all he cared to see, Father Jacob strode rapidly forward, his black cassock swishing about his ankles. The priests followed his progression through the room with their eyes. The monsignor, seeing and hearing him, rose hurriedly from his desk.

"Father Jacob Northrop," Father Jacob boomed and he added, unnecessarily, since the black cassock proclaimed him, "of the Arcanum."

"His Eminence left instructions for you to be immediately admitted upon your arrival," said the monsignor. "If you would accompany me . . ."

The monsignor placed his hands on the handles of a pair of double doors, beautifully and intricately carved of wood, and was about to open them when he saw Brother Barnaby.

The monsignor gave a delicate cough. "Your servant may wait for you here, Father Jacob," he said. "He will be well cared for, of that you may be certain."

"Brother Barnaby is *not* my servant," said Father Jacob, his brows coming together in a frown. He latched onto Brother Barnaby's arm. "He is my amanuensis and, as such, he goes everywhere with me."

Brother Barnaby clasped the lap desk in both hands and lowered his eyes in embarrassment. "I don't mind, Father."

"I do," said Father Jacob sternly, keeping fast hold of the monk.

The monsignor took a moment to consider, then said, "Very well." He opened the doors and announced, "Father Jacob Northrop and ... er ... Brother Barnaby."

Grand Bishop Ferdinand Montagne motioned for them both to enter. He was seated at his desk, frowning over a small piece of paper which had been delivered last evening, but which the bishop had only received this morning.

"Please be seated, Father Jacob and Brother ..."

The grand bishop had not caught Barnaby's name. He dispensed with formalities by waving his hand at two chairs placed directly opposite his desk.

"If you will both excuse me one moment."

The grand bishop motioned the monsignor to approach the desk and handed him a note. They both spoke in low tones, their voices soft. Father Jacob watched and listened with interest.

"Dubois sent this last night," said the grand bishop softly. "He wrote it in haste. Can you make out what it says?"

The monsignor read the note. " 'Find out what happened at the Royal Armory.' "

"That's what I thought it said. Do you know what he means?"

"No, Your Eminence, I am afraid I have no idea."

"Then do what it says. Find out."

The monsignor nodded, bowed and, taking the note, left the room.

The bishop gave a sigh and ran his hand over his head. "Affairs of state," he said by way of apology. "We always seem to find ourselves entangled in such matters, though most unwillingly."

He sat down in his chair and looked directly at Father Jacob.

"How are you, Father Jacob? It has been some time since we last met."

"I am well, Your Eminence. And you?"

"Not good, Father. Not good." The grand bishop placed his hand on his stomach. "Dyspepsia. It seems that nothing I eat agrees with me. The pain and discomfort I experience is most debilitating."

"If I might presume to suggest something, Your Eminence...." Brother Barnaby spoke up meekly.

The bishop looked at him, startled.

"Brother Barnaby is known for his healing skills," said Father Jacob. "You would do well to listen to him, Your Eminence."

"If your Eminence would mix ground gentian root with hot tea, drink this three times daily, eat only the blandest foods, and abstain from wine for at least a week, I believe you will show improvement."

The grand bishop raised an eyebrow. "And you say this gentian root works, Brother?"

"I have had much success with it in the past, Your Eminence."

The grand bishop rang a bell and a priest appeared in the doorway. "Bring me hot tea mixed with ground gentian root," the bishop ordered.

The priest appeared slightly startled at the request, but he hastened to fill it.

"Now," said the grand bishop with a heavy sigh, "we must discuss this terrible business."

"At the Abbey of Saint Agnes," said Father Jacob.

"The abbey and elsewhere," said the grand bishop.

Father Jacob raised an eyebrow, then he glanced at Brother Barnaby and nodded. The young monk placed the lap desk he had been carrying on his knees, opened it, and drew out pen and paper and a small bottle of ink. He set the ink in a hole in the desk that kept the bottle stable, dipped his pen in the inkwell, and made ready to write.

The grand bishop frowned. "Is this man intending to take notes on what we say?"

"With the permission of Your Eminence, of course," said Father Jacob. "I find —"

"You do *not* have my permission! What I am about to tell you is of a highly volatile nature! If anyone were to find out—"

"Your Eminence can rest easy," said Father Jacob in soothing tones. "Brother Barnaby writes the notes in a special code I devised. He and I are the only ones who can read it. I will show Your Eminence what he has written before we leave and if you can decipher a word of it, I will destroy the notes immediately.

He added gravely, "These notes are critical to my work, Your Eminence. I would be laboring at an extreme disadvantage without them."

"Why even bother to seek my permission," the bishop grumbled. "Oh, very well. But I will look at these notes before you leave."

Montagne wasn't happy, but he was desperate. He rose to his feet and began to pace restlessly back and forth behind the desk as he talked.

"You know my secret, Father Jacob. The secret that keeps me awake at night and eats holes in my stomach."

"The secret that magic in the world, the Breath of God, is being destroyed," said Father Jacob.

Brother Barnaby looked up, astonished. Father Jacob glanced at him and nodded slightly. Brother Barnaby's pen scratched across the paper.

"Recently, the situation has grown more dire," said the bishop. "Magical constructs have begun breaking down at an alarming rate. I am hearing reports from crafters that they require more and more time to maintain the existing constructs."

The bishop stopped in his pacing, stood frowning down at the carpet, then suddenly lifted his head and turned to face Father Jacob directly.

"To put it bluntly, Jacob, magic is failing! It is failing in all parts of Rosia, and now I have received a report of the same occurring in Freya. Magical sigils are weakening at an alarming rate. The Church has managed to stave off panic by telling people that the magic is cyclical, that every few hundred years the magic wanes as the moon wanes and waxes. We maintain that we are in a part of the cycle where the magic is weak and that it will eventually come back."

"You do realize that what you are saying is bullshit, Your Eminence," said Father Jacob crudely.

Brother Barnaby raised his head and blinked his eyes.

"Pardon my language, Eminence," Father Jacob continued, "but magic is not 'cyclical.'"

"I know that," the grand bishop said irritably. He extended his hands in pleading. "But what else can we say? That the magic is dying? That the Breath is being sucked out of our world? That God is gasping for air? Do we tell the populace that some day soon their houses will collapse? Their airships will drop out of the skies? Do we tell them that some of the continents are starting to sink and that doomsday may not be long in coming? Do we tell them this?"

Father Jacob was silent, grave. The only sound in the room was Barnaby's pen crawling across the paper and, occasionally, the tinkling sound of the nib touching the rim of the inkwell as he refreshed his ink.

"Well?" said the bishop shortly. "What do *you* have to say, Father?"

"That what I predicted eight years ago is now come to pass," said Father Jacob.

"Damn it, Jacob!" the grand bishop swore angrily and struck the desk with his clenched fist. "How can you be so goddamn cool about this? I know that I blaspheme, but if the blessed Saint Dennis himself were standing here, I have no doubt he would say the same!"

"I assume this has something to do with the massacre at the Abbey of Saint Agnes," said Father Jacob. "Since that is why you sent for me."

The bishop sighed deeply, ran his hand through his hair, belched, grimaced, and lowered himself back down in his chair.

"It does, but there is more you must know before I tell you. A few weeks ago, a watchtower collapsed. The tower was old, but the crafter mason who maintained the magical constructs that strengthened the stonework has sworn on the sacred writings of the Four Saints that the constructs were in perfect condition. Twenty soldiers were inside the structure when it fell. All of them were killed."

Brother Barnaby said a prayer for the dead beneath his breath as he made the notation.

"Was this reported to the Arcanum?" asked Father Jacob.

"Of course," said the bishop. "I asked for you, but I was told you were working to put an end to this evil young man who calls himself the Warlock. A most inconvenient time for you to be away!"

Father Jacob's lips tightened. "Yes, wasn't it," he said grimly. "I trust you sent Church crafters to investigate."

"My personal secretary, the monsignor, led the group," said the bishop. "He is a very talented crafter. The tower had been reduced to a heap of rubble. Much of the stonework on the ground was still intact. The monsignor was going to study the magical sigils on the stones, but he found that there were no magical sigils. The magic had been utterly destroyed."

Brother Barnaby gasped. "No sigils! But that is not possible!"

Catching Father Jacob's stern glance, the young monk ducked his head and went back to his recording.

"Not a single magical sigil left in the whole damn tower," said the grand bishop. "The monsignor and our crafters went over every single, solitary stone they could find. One would expect to see weakened sigils, broken sigils. The monsignor said, and I quote his words, 'It was as if someone had taken a rag and wiped away the magic.'"

"As happened with the cutter *Defiant*," said Father Jacob.

"I reread your report—" the bishop began.

"Did you, Your Eminence?" Father Jacob said with a

glint in his eye. "I was told my report had been burned as heresy, expunged from the records."

"We always keep copies, Father Jacob," said the bishop and he added sourly, "As you know perfectly well. So don't be so damn sanctimonious."

Montagne jumped to his feet with such suddenness that he knocked over the chair. His choleric face was red with anger. "I was wrong, Jacob, and you were right! Does that make you happy? Do you take pleasure in that?"

"No, Your Eminence," said Father Jacob quietly. "Given the terrible consequences of my predictions that magic throughout the world would fail, I have been praying that I was the one who would be in the wrong."

He reached out his hand to stop Brother Barnaby's pen. "You needn't record any of that."

Brother Barnaby nodded and scratched out what he had been writing. The bishop started to sit down, only to realize he didn't have a chair. Brother Barnaby laid down his desk, jumped to his feet, walked over to the chair, and picked it up. The grand bishop muttered his thanks and resumed his seat. Brother Barnaby went back to his note-taking.

The bishop resumed. "I reread your report, Father Jacob, as I said, but I would like to hear from you directly about the incidents related to the *Defiant*."

Father Jacob was silent a moment, collecting his thoughts, then began to relate the story. "Eight years ago, several merchant ships sailing the Breath near the Bay of Faighn outside Westfirth reported that they had come under attack by pirates. The pirates would pose as a merchant vessel lost in the Breath seeking directions. The pirates would sail their ship over to the other merchant ship to exchange information. Once close by, the pirates would use canister rounds to sweep the deck and then board the helpless victim, rob the merchant of anything of value, then leave the survivors adrift in the Breath. The navy was alerted to this threat and sent the cutter RNS *Defiant* to the area.

"The *Defiant* arrived to find a merchant ship under attack.

The *Defiant* sailed in to stop the attack and capture the pirates. The *Defiant* was a two-masted floating warship with sixteen twelve-pound cannons and a crew of one hundred men. The pirate vessel was a modified merchant vessel with eight six pounders. The pirates were outgunned and outmanned. I later spoke to the captain of the *Defiant*, who told me he assumed the pirates would attempt to flee.

"To the captain's immense surprise, the pirate vessel turned to attack the cutter. The captain said he and his officers actually laughed, for the pirate vessel was taking aim at them with what appeared to be a small cannon mounted on the ship's forecastle. The captain told me it 'looked like a child's popgun.'

"The pirates fired. A beam of eerie-looking green light shot from the small cannon aimed directly at the brass panel on which the *Defiant*'s starboard control constructs were inscribed. The green light disrupted the magic, causing the helmsman to lose control of the ship. The *Defiant* still managed to go about, when a second blast of green light hit the ship, this one aimed at her larboard cannons. Several of the cannons exploded, killing their gun crews and blasting holes in the hull.

"Fortunately, the *Defiant* was close to shore when the attack occurred, or she would have undoubtedly sunk into the Breath with all hands lost. As it was, the cutter managed to limp to shore, where a land-based army patrol came aboard to help protect the wounded vessel.

"Then something unusual happened. Or perhaps I should say, something *more* unusual. The pirate ship sailed close to the *Defiant*, but did not attack. The pirates had their spyglasses trained on the disabled ship. The captain told me: 'It was damn strange. Looked to me as if they wanted to see close-up the destruction they had caused.' The army patrol started firing at them and the pirate ship sailed off, vanishing into the mists.

"Word of the attack reached a nearby garrison. They sent an urgent message to the Westfirth Crafters' Guild saying they needed a Master Crafter to restore the magical constructs and make the *Defiant* airworthy as quickly as possible. The crafter, Master Albert Savoraun, boarded the cutter to inspect the damage. He was astounded by what he found and, as required by law, Master Albert immediately reported his findings to the Arcanum. Your Eminence sent me to investigate."

They were interrupted by a priest, who returned with the stomachic recommended by Brother Barnaby. He made up the concoction. The grand bishop drank the tea, grimacing at the bitter taste. Suddenly the bishop's stomach rumbled mightily and he gave a great belch. An expression of relief crossed his face. He cast Brother Barnaby a look of gratitude and told Father Jacob to continue.

"The captain of the *Defiant* and her crew had already been transported back to their base. Shocked by his discovery, Master Savoraun asked the garrison to place a guard on the cutter. He was waiting for me when I arrived, in company with Sir Ander Martel."

Father Jacob paused, then said, "Before I go into detail about what I found, I need to know how much Your Eminence knows about ships of the air."

"I know that through the blessing of God, my yacht sails the Breath," said the bishop. "I leave the workings of the vessel to the captain."

"Then, Your Eminence, I will digress a moment to explain that when an airship is built, crafters spend months putting the magical constructs into place. Magic embedded in an airship ranges from complex constructs that strengthen the wooden hull to the smaller, more delicate interlaced magical constructs on the brass helm that allow the helmsman to steer the ship through the Breath.

"Magic is in every part of the ship: the wooden planks of the hull, the metal of the cannons, the lines and pulleys of the rigging. Once set, the magical constructs will slowly degrade over time, which is why, when an airship is in dry dock, naval crafters come on board to maintain them.

"Now, Your Eminence, here is what is important to understand. Even if the constructs, which are made up of sigils, degrade to the point where they break down completely, the magic leaves behind what are known as 'burn marks.' Since the sigils have been burned into the wood or onto the metal, a crafter reading these burn marks can detect the imprint of the sigils and restore them.

"On the *Defiant*, wherever the green light struck the ship, the magic had been obliterated. Nothing was left of it. No burn marks. No sigils. No constructs. Nothing."

Father Jacob lowered his voice and said softly, "It was as if the magic had never been."

"As the good monk here says, that is impossible," said the bishop. "God's work cannot be destroyed."

"In this case God's work was wiped out. And apparently also in the case of the watchtower and the Abbey of Saint Agnes or you would not have sent for me."

The grand bishop muttered something that was unintelligible and motioned irritably for Father Jacob to continue. He did so, with a sigh.

"When I returned to the Arcanum, I spoke to the priest who is the foremost authority on constructs in the world. As you may recall, Your Eminence, Father Antonius was the person responsible for sinking an Estaran floating fortress during the war. He did so by manipulating the hundreds of constructs set into its stonework. I asked Father Antonius to try to replicate what we found on the *Defiant*. He said what you said, Your Eminence, no crafter—not even the blessed Saints themselves—could destroy God's work. 'It is impossible,' he said, 'to obliterate a magical construct.' Yet, Your Eminence, the impossible was done. I saw it for myself."

Father Jacob ceased talking so that Brother Barnaby could catch up. He wrote, then laid down his pen to indicate he was finished. The room was so silent that the ticking of the clock was quite loud, reminding them all that time was slipping past.

At length the bishop stirred. "Which was, unfortunately, precisely what the monsignor found in the tower. The impossible had come to pass. The magic had been obliterated. Witnesses to the collapse described a bright green glow that illuminated the building and then the tower fell down."

"Whoever is behind this has made their weapons more powerful," said Father Jacob. His voice hardened. "Not surprising. They've had eight years to work undeterred."

The bishop heard the note of rebuke and glowered. "Meaning we should have massed a force and sent our armies to attack Freya. You know why I didn't recommend that, and His Majesty, for once, agreed with me. An unprovoked attack on Freya would have meant war and we are not prepared for war. We ..." The grand bishop shook his head and then clamped his lips together.

"The real reason was that you didn't believe me when I told you that this green beam was capable of destroying magic," said Father Jacob.

The bishop didn't respond.

Father Jacob regarded the man for a moment, then said quietly, "I take that back. You believed me, but you didn't *trust* me. Because I am Freyan."

The bishop rose to his feet again. He strode over to the sideboard and was about to pour himself some wine. Brother Barnaby gave a gentle cough and shook his head. The bishop, sighing, resorted to water.

"His Majesty and I thought Freya was behind these attacks," the bishop said gravely. "We are being forced to reconsider that position. You see, Jacob, the tower that collapsed was in Freya."

"Good God!" Father Jacob exclaimed, caught by surprise.

"The Archbishop of Kerringdon of the Freyan Church has not communicated with us in years, but he was concerned enough by what his crafters discovered that he asked for our help—not directly, of course, but through discreet channels."

"The inimitable Dubois?" Father Jacob asked.

The grand bishop glared. "Do you know all my secrets?"

He walked back to the desk, but he did not sit down. He stood frowning at it. "I know now I owe you an apology, Father Jacob. But since you are a man of logic, I am sure you can agree that I did have some reason to doubt your loyalty. That said, I prove my faith in you by entrusting you with this secret which, if it leaked out, could bring down the Church."

"I concede that you owe me an apology," said Father Jacob coolly. "However, let us move on. If the Freyans are not the ones who have developed this weapon, then who? No other nation has the capability or the resources to develop such destructive power. You are certain it is not Freya?"

"I wasn't. Until now."

"The attack on the abbey," Father Jacob said.

The bishop laid his hand on a slender document that was rolled, bound, and sealed. "I have here the report of the attack written by the monk who was assigned as the nuns' confessor. Brother Paul was absent the night of the attack. He did not live at the abbey, but in a small hermitage some miles away. He wrote an account of what he found on his return."

Father Jacob interrupted. "I trust I will be able to speak to this Brother Paul?"

"Of course. He has been told to prepare for your arrival. The abbey—or what is left of it—is under guard. Nothing has been disturbed."

The bishop handed over the document. He glanced at the clock. "I have another appointment, Father. If you have any questions . . ." He paused, then said with some bitterness, "I don't have the answers. God be with you."

Father Jacob understood that this discussion was at an end. He said a word to Brother Barnaby, who scribbled a final note and then began to pack up his writing desk.

"Your Eminence asked to see my notes." Brother Barnaby handed over what he had written.

The bishop glanced at the page. "It looks like a chicken with inky feet has walked across the paper."

"Precisely," said Father Jacob.

The bishop shrugged and handed back the notes. Brother Barnaby carefully placed the sheets in the writing desk, along with the pen and the ink. Closing the desk, he indicated he was ready. Father Jacob rose to his feet.

"I would very much like to speak to the monsignor about the Freyan tower collapse."

"That will not be necessary," said the bishop curtly. "I told you everything. Please send a detailed report on the abbey as soon as you have concluded your investigation."

Father Jacob was not pleased. He could do nothing, however, except bow and leave the room. Once in the antechamber, he cast a swift glance about, hoping to be able to talk to the monsignor.

"I could look for him, Father," said Brother Barnaby.

"Useless. The bishop will see to it that the man is stashed away someplace where I cannot lay my hands on him," said Father Jacob irately. He rounded on their escort. "Leave us! I know the way perfectly well."

Father Jacob strode off. Brother Barnaby cast the escort a glance of apology for the father's rude behavior, then hurried after him. Father Jacob stalked rapidly through the Bishop's Palace, anger trailing in his wake like the flaming tail of a comet.

Brother Barnaby clutched his lap desk to his chest and, being shorter than Father Jacob, was forced to run to keep up.

Chapter Thirteen

It is difficult when walking in darkness, carrying a lantern, to see beyond the circle of your own light. So it is that when a member of the
Arcanum carries God's light into the darkness, we walk with them,
the Knight Protectors. We are sworn to defend our charges with our
weapons, our courage, our faith and, ultimately, our lives.

—The Journal of
Sir Edward Beauchamp
Order of the Knight Protectors

SIR ANDER WALKED SWIFTLY ACROSS THE EXTEN-
SIVE grounds of the Conclave of the Divine, taking the
shortcut that led around the University, thereby saving at
least half a mile. He eyed the students as he entered the
quadrangle and thought, as usual, that they looked younger
every year. Their faces made him recall those in Capione
who had died so young and so needlessly. He shook his
head, to shake them out of his thoughts, and continued on
his way.

The sight of the stolid, plain, unadorned motherhouse of
the Knight Protectors was comforting, reassuring. Some
things in this world never changed. He remembered coming
here after being forced to witness the execution of his
friend, Sir Julian de Guichen. He remembered going to the
private chapel and sinking to his knees and giving way to
raw rage and anger and grief, emotions he'd been forced to

hold inside or risk losing his own life. He remembered the feeling of peace and calm that had come over him.

"Your friend is in my care now," God seemed to say. "His pain and suffering are ended. He has come home."

And so had Sir Ander.

The seventh son of a Travian merchant, Ander Martel had no property to call his own. His oldest brother had inherited the family fortune and the modest house in Travia, a house Sir Ander remembered only vaguely. He had not been back to see his family since he had left them to join the Travian Military Academy at the age of twelve.

At the age of twenty, he had been granted a knighthood by the Travian king for valor in action by leading the force that had rescued a Travian frigate captured by the Freyans during one of the many minor skirmishes between the two countries. Sir Ander had been invited by Sir Edward Beauchamp, a friend of his father's, to the Rosian court. There, Ander had met the man who would come to be his best friend, Julian de Guichen. Both young men had fallen deeply in love with the young and beautiful Cecile de Marjolaine, but she had eyes and heart only for Julian.

Sir Ander had accepted his defeat with good grace. Finding it too painful to be around Cecile, he had sought a way to leave the court. Sir Edward Beauchamp was a member of the Order of Knight Protectors. He had taken a keen interest in the young knight. He helped Sir Ander find direction in his life and solace for his lost love through faith. Sir Ander had applied to join the Knight Protectors and had been accepted.

As he walked through the doors that stood open and seemingly unguarded, he remembered the youngster who had first walked through that gate over thirty years ago. Sir Ander looked back at that unhappy young man with sympathy and compassion and he said again a quiet thank you to Sir Edward Beauchamp, who had long ago gone to a well-deserved rest.

The gates led into a narrow corridor paved with stone

surrounded by stone walls. Shafts of sunlight shining through slit windows lit his way. At night, glowing sigils set in the walls lit the corridor. No guards were posted at the gate, no guards patrolled the corridor.

Sir Ander smiled to himself. Anyone who was not supposed to be here would not have taken six steps through those gates before he was challenged at gunpoint. Ander nodded to the guards concealed in "watch holes" as they termed the closetlike rooms from which the knights observed all who entered their compound.

The narrow corridor led to a large inner courtyard, open to the air, used for practicing all forms of martial arts from swordsmanship to archery (a skill in which Sir Ander had never excelled) to hand-to-hand combat. He crossed the courtyard and entered the double doors that led into a building housing the central offices of the motherhouse.

Inside the small, shadowy foyer, a knight sat at a desk, sorting through paperwork. The knight looked up on hearing the doors open. Sir Ander smiled to see him.

"Sir Conal!"

"By Heaven! Ander Martel," exclaimed Sir Conal, rising from his chair. "You're still alive? I thought those black magicks you fight would have claimed you at last."

"Ah, that's nothing to jest about, my friend," said Sir Ander, clasping his friend's hand and shaking it heartily. "And what about you? I consider black magic to be good wholesome fun compared to the politics of the grand bishop's court."

"You speak a true word there," said Sir Conal with a grimace. "Give me a moment and I will order a room made ready—"

"I can't stay, I'm afraid," said Sir Ander. "Father Jacob is being dispatched to Saint Agnes."

"I heard about that," said Sir Conal, his face darkening. "A sad business." He raised an eyebrow. "So the Arcanum is involved. That's interesting."

"*Too* damn interesting, if you ask me," Sir Ander

grunted. "Anyway, while my charge is conversing with the grand bishop, I'm here on the chance those new pistols I ordered from the Royal Armory were delivered. And to pick up my mail."

"Ah, yes, those pistols," said Sir Conal.

The two men were the same age and had fought and studied together. Sir Conal was a short, pugnacious man with grizzled hair and the neck of a bull. He had always been a rough-and-tumble kind of fellow, never happier than when he was knocking sense into the heads of young squires. Sir Conal had been in charge of teaching hand-to-hand combat. Sir Ander had been about to ask why his friend had been relegated to desk duty and then he saw Sir Conal pick up a cane and was thankful he had kept quiet.

Sir Conal limped painfully from out behind the desk. Seeing Sir Ander's look, Sir Conal gave his right leg an irritated slap.

"Damn knee keeps going out on me. Hurts like a son-of-a-bitch sometimes. Fool healers can't do anything to fix it. Just old age, they say."

"I'm sorry to hear that," Sir Ander said. "The knighthood must miss your expertise on the drill field. Or maybe they don't." He rubbed his jaw and smiled ruefully. "I can still feel a punch or two you landed on me."

"As I recall, you had an unfortunate tendency to keep dropping your right fist. Left you wide open," said Sir Conal. Seeing a squire coming down the hall, he raised his voice in a shout, "Master Arthen, watch the desk."

The squire made his obeisance to the two older knights and hastened to obey. Sir Conal and Sir Ander walked the familiar passages leading to a spiral staircase that wound down below ground level.

Once on the lower floor, they passed the iron-banded and magically protected steel doors of the treasury and those of the wine cellar, whose doors were almost as well guarded. Sir Ander looked forward to drinking one of the knighthood's fine wines with his supper. Conal halted when they came to a large chamber known simply as the "Storage House."

The large chamber was divided into numerous stalls, each with its own gate. Every active member of the Order based out of the motherhouse had his own stall. Above each was a small plate with the knight's personal arms painted on it. When a knight died, his personal effects were returned to his family, his stall was given to another knight. His arms remained on the gate.

Sir Ander picked up the key ring which hung from the wall and, sorting through the numerous keys, found the one that opened his gate. Inside was a small table and an oak chest with his name carved on the top, a gift from his mother. The chest contained all his personal items. He glanced at it, but did not open it. Too many memories: some good, more not so good. All precious, too precious to be disturbed. A few pieces of armor that he'd worn when he was young lay rusting in a corner, along with his ceremonial armor. The last time he'd worn that armor had been at the funeral of his friend and mentor, Sir Edward.

A leather pouch rested on the table along with a large wooden box stamped with the seal of the Armory. Sir Ander opened the pouch and took out his letters. Four were from his second brother's third wife and would provide him with news of his family back in Travia. Seven were written on expensive paper, sealed with lavender wax. The insignia on the seals was a bumblebee. He smiled and slid the letters into the breast pocket of his coat. He would read them in the privacy of the *Retribution*.

He looked at the box from the Royal Armory. "So the pistols are here," he said. "I didn't really expect them so soon. I only ordered them a short time ago."

He was wondering uneasily if he had the funds to pay for them. The Knighthood provided him a stipend to be used for his expenses when he was attending Father Jacob. The money was intended for food and lodging and clothes and Sir Ander had to account for every penny. The funds were not intended to be spent on such luxuries as specially designed pistols. He lifted the lid.

Six pistols lay nestled in a velvet-lined tray.

"Beautiful weapons," said Sir Conal.

"They truly are," Sir Ander agreed.

He lifted one of the pistols from the velvet-lined case. The stock was carved of burled red wood. The mechanism was polished steel. Silver-and-brass inlays swirled about the trigger lock.

"How well do they work?" Sir Ander asked his friend with a smile.

"How should I know?" Sir Conal wore an expression of innocence, belied by a gleam of amusement in his eye.

"Because this pistol has been fired," said Sir Ander, grinning. "And because you were the only person who knew I had ordered them and since you are now on desk duty, you would have been the one to receive them when they were delivered."

"You've been with that puzzle-solving priest of yours too long," said Sir Conal, snorting. "You're even starting to sound like him. I knew you'd want someone to test them, to make sure they worked and send them back to be fixed if they didn't."

"So I ask again, did the pistol work well?"

"Considering that there is not a single magical construct anywhere on it, yes, it worked very well. I have to say I was amazed. I was able to hit the target nine times out of ten and the last was my fault. Damn knee went all wobbly on me, threw off my aim."

"Excellent. But I see you didn't test all of them," said Sir Ander.

He looked over the weapons, then lifted another out of the box. On the side of one of the pistols, opposite the hammer, was a silver plate engraved with a winged wolf holding a sword—Sir Conal's device.

"For you my friend," said Sir Ander, handing over the pistol and a matching powder flask.

Sir Conal stared. "You're not serious!"

"Unfortunately, I am," said Sir Ander. "Deadly serious."

"Pistols that don't rely on magic," said Sir Conal, studying his gun with obvious pleasure, but also with a look of puzzlement. "Can I ask why?"

"You can ask, but I'm not going to answer," said Sir Ander. "And you can't tell a soul that you own one."

"You know me, my friend. I keep my mouth shut. What did you say to Master Gaston at the Armory when you put in the order for pistols that are purely mechanical? He must have been curious."

"I told him that Father Jacob tends to be irresponsible in tossing about magical spells and that I feared that if his magic went awry around the weaponry, he'd blow himself up and the rest of us along with him. Which is not exactly a lie," Sir Ander added dryly.

"I see. I've heard rumors ..." Sir Conal paused, then said, "I sometimes wonder what would happen to weapons imbued with magic if for some reason the magic ceased to work. Pistols wouldn't fire—"

"Or they would blow off your hand," said Sir Ander. He fixed Sir Conal with an intense gaze. "That's what they are, you know. Just rumors." He paused, frowning down at the guns, and then said impulsively, "I wish—" He stopped and sighed.

"Wish what?" asked Sir Conal.

Sir Ander forced a smile. "I wish I was drinking some of that remarkable old port I know you have stashed away in the wine cellar."

He took two pistols and powder horns from the box and then closed the lid, leaving three pistols inside. "I'll leave these here. In case."

He didn't say in case of what, but Sir Conal nodded gravely. Sir Ander shut the gate to his storage cell and locked it and returned the keys to the ring on the wall.

"We'll pick up a bottle of port on our way past the wine cellar," said Sir Conal.

"I'll meet you in the dining hall," said Sir Ander. "First I want to stop by the chapel and pay my respects to God. Then I need to go to the Bursar's to make arrangements to pay for these pistols." He gave a shrug. "Good-bye military pension."

"I am certain God will be glad to hear from you," said Sir Conal, "but you need not bother the Bursar. The pistols are a gift, it seems. Someone else has paid for them."

"A gift?" Sir Ander repeated, astonished.

"The bill came in from the Armory marked 'Paid.'"

"But who?" Sir Ander asked, puzzled. "Not Father Jacob. He doesn't know anything about them."

"You must have a secret admirer," said Sir Conal.

Sir Ander remembered the letters with the lavender seal, and he flushed. He knew who had paid for the pistols and was pleased, at first, to think that Cecile de Marjolaine was thinking of him. On reflection, he was not so pleased. He was glad he did not have to impoverish himself in order to pay for the pistols, but he didn't like the thought that the countess was spying on him.

Sir Ander had not seen Cecile de Marjolaine in years, although they did frequently correspond. Sir Ander had been to court. He knew the ways of the court and he knew Cecile de Marjolaine. Thinking of her, he remembered the desperate battle she waged all alone and regretted his twinge of resentment. He thought he knew why she was watching him, why she had given him the pistols.

Sir Conal had been observing his friend's face and said with a grin and a wink, "Ah, these pistols came from some lady."

"A very great lady," said Sir Ander gravely, and he and Sir Conal left to pursue their reunion over a bottle of port, which was every bit as good as Sir Ander had remembered.

Father Jacob arrived at the motherhouse of the Knight Protectors in a foul mood. He barked at the startled young squire on desk duty, demanding where to find Sir Ander. The squire said politely that he didn't know, but he would go look. Father Jacob told the squire he was a blithering idiot and began shouting Sir Ander's name in a thunderous voice that echoed off the rafters.

Confronted by the fearsome black cassock of the Arcanum and a priest who appeared to be more than a little insane, the squire bolted from the desk and ran in search of Sir Ander. He had already heard the commotion and, sighing, drank the last of his port. He hurried down the stairs to find Father Jacob pacing back and forth impatiently.

"*There* you are!" Father Jacob snapped in a tone that implied that he'd been waiting for Sir Ander for weeks.

"Here I am," said Sir Ander imperturbably. "I was thinking we might take supper—"

"The devil with supper! We are leaving now. I have sent Brother Barnaby to ready *Retribution*. I will meet you at the landing site. And don't dawdle!"

The priest glared at him, turned on his heel, and stalked out.

Sir Ander heaved a deep sigh, then shrugged and gave a rueful smile.

"Something's up, seemingly," he said to Sir Conal, who had limped after him. "So much for supper and another glass of that wonderful port. Farewell, Conal. Use the gift in good health."

"Farewell, my friend," said Sir Conal. He cast an apprehensive glance after Father Jacob. "And good luck!"

The two friends shook hands and then embraced. With the taste of the port, like drinking honeyed chocolate, warming his mouth, Sir Ander departed the motherhouse, new pistols tucked into his belt, the letters in his inner coat pocket.

Arriving at the landing site, he found Brother Barnaby fussing over the wyverns. Father Jacob was nowhere to be found.

"He's inside the yacht," said Brother Barnaby in a low

voice, "writing a dispatch to be sent to Master Savoraun by swift courier. He's in a terrible state!" he added in a whisper.

"What happened with the bishop? Why the rush?" Sir Ander asked, glancing askance at the yacht and keeping his voice down.

"I will let Father Jacob tell you himself," said Brother Barnaby circumspectly. "You know that I sometimes misspeak."

"I know that you strictly observe your vow of secrecy," said Sir Ander with a smile. "Even when it comes to me. And I honor you for it."

Brother Barnaby's dark skin darkened further with pleasure and embarrassment. The young monk scratched one of the wyverns on its head between its eyes. The wyvern gave a rumbling sigh of pleasure, while its partner attempted to shove its head under Brother's Barnaby's soothing hand. Sir Ander reflected that if he tried petting a wyvern, he would end up missing an arm.

"The wyverns haven't had nearly enough rest," said Brother Barnaby with a fond and worried look for his beasts. "They can travel only a couple of hours before we will be forced to stop. I tried telling Father Jacob ..."

"Useless," said Sir Ander. "When he's in this sort of mood, a sixty-four-gun ship of the line couldn't stop him. Don't worry. Once he's stomped around the yacht for an hour and aired his frustrations, he'll calm down. Of course, we'll have to listen to him—"

The hatch banged open and Father Jacob came bounding out. He looked around, then glowered.

"Where's that godforsaken courier!" he demanded, waving his letter. "Why isn't he here by now?"

"You only just sent for him—" Brother Barnaby began.

"The man is on the way," said Sir Ander, seeing the wyverns bristle at the priest's strident tones. "I'll take charge of your letter, see that the courier gets it."

"Complete incompetence!" said Father Jacob, scowling. "I'll be inside the yacht. Let me know when he comes."

He disappeared. The hatch banged shut.

"Perhaps I should go look for the courier," Brother Barnaby said worriedly

"No, you won't, because then he'd be in an uproar as to where you'd gone," said Sir Ander. "Just keep pampering your wyverns. I'll take this opportunity to read my mail. Let me know when the courier arrives."

Brother Barnaby nodded and continued fussing over his charges. Sir Ander walked over to a bench beneath a shady maple tree and sat down. He quickly scanned the letters from a family he scarcely knew (he could never keep track of the various nieces and nephews) and then, with a feeling of pain mixed with pleasure, he drew out the letters with the lavender seals.

He was aware of a faint scent of jasmine as he broke the first seal. The scent evoked memories. He could envision Cecile quite clearly; even hear her voice speak from the firm, feminine handwriting on the pages.

She wrote to him often, at least once a month and sometimes more. He wrote to her sporadically. Sir Ander disliked writing letters. He wasn't any good at it. He never knew what to say. Most of his work for the Arcanum he was forbidden to talk about, and the rest of his life was mundane. He was aware that his lapse in responding to her letters did not bother Cecile. She wrote to him for one reason and that was to keep him informed about his godson, Stephano.

Always mindful that letters could be intercepted, Cecile buried any information of true importance in a mire of the trivial. Indeed, examining the seven letters, Sir Ander noted signs that the latest one, dated only two days ago, had been opened. Someone had passed a hot knife under the wax seal, leaving the seal intact but permitting the snoop to read the letter's contents. The snoop had been careless, however, having allowed the seal to partially melt.

The snoop had wasted his time. Cecile's letter to Sir Ander was that of one old friend to another, filled with news of the court, talk of the latest fashion, a witty description of a party given aboard the royal barge, expressing admiration for a young musical prodigy who was taking the court by storm, and discussion of her problems managing her estate. He enjoyed her writing; he would take time to savor the letter later, in the lonely hours of the evening. For now, he was curious as to why someone had gone to so much trouble to intercept this particular letter. He read it before reading the others.

Sir Ander found nothing in it that would mean anything to anyone else and he decided the letter had probably been opened at random: just someone checking on the countess. The last sentence meant a great deal, but only to him.

When all else fails, know that you can still rely on my friendship and this small token of my esteem.

"When all else fails," Sir Ander softly repeated the words.

All else—including magic. She was letting him know she was aware of Father Jacob's investigations. But then, of course she would know. Probably the king himself had told her.

And Cecile had told Sir Ander. She trusted him; perhaps he was the only person in the world beside Stephano she could trust. Her friend and her son.

The thought warmed him.

Sir Ander was tall and well-built with an upright, military bearing. Years ago, when he had courted the young and beautiful Cecile de Marjolaine, he had been considered handsome. Over the years, his strong-jawed face, that had once exuded rakish confidence, had softened, becoming graver, more serious. His smile was generous and lit his eyes. Father Jacob was volatile, a bomb liable to go off at any moment, leaving debris and destruction in his wake. By contrast, Sir Ander was reliable, steady. Women were drawn to him. He was fifty years old and he knew many women who would have happily and proudly called him "husband." He had never married. He would never marry. He would always remain faithful to his own true love.

Sir Ander carefully folded Cecile's letter (more valuable to him than the pistols) and placed it along with the other unread letters in the inner pocket of his coat. He then rose to his feet to greet the courier.

The Abbey of Saint Agnes, located about four hundred miles north and west of Evreux, near the Bay of Faighn, and one hundred miles east of the city of Westfirth, would require a good twelve days to reach traveling by land. Sailing the skies, the *Retribution* could make the journey in two days. Even this was too slow for the impatient Father Jacob and much too slow for Sir Ander and Brother Barnaby, who had to put up with him.

Sir Ander spent his time performing routine maintenance on the yacht's arsenal of weapons, a task made difficult by Father Jacob's restless stompings about the yacht and his attempts to point out to Sir Ander that he was doing everything wrong. Sir Ander had learned early in their relationship that it was far easier to agree with Father Jacob than be drawn into an argument. Sir Ander, who was an expert on firearms, as well as being an excellent shot, nodded when Father Jacob attempted to tell him how to load the canisters that were fed into the swivel gun, and chuckled to himself when Father Jacob stalked off to instruct poor Brother Barnaby how to manage wyverns in flight.

As Barnaby had predicted, Father Jacob was incensed when the monk insisted that his wyverns had to be rested and fed after only four hours of flight. The monk suggested they spend the night in the coastal town of Predeau.

"We will waste eight hours!" Father Jacob stated angrily. "I insist we keep going. We can hire wyverns from one of the inns—"

"Fly with hired wyverns!" Brother Barnaby repeated, appalled.

His wyverns were his love, his pride and joy. They were like children to him, and the thought of abandoning his wyverns, leaving them behind in a strange place to be cared for by strangers, was too much to bear. He cast a desperate glance at Sir Ander.

"I thought you might use this time to question the sailors in some of the local taverns, Father," said Sir Ander. "Find out if they saw anything odd or unusual in the Breath the night of the attack on the abbey."

Father Jacob glowered and appeared about to make some caustic comment, then he relaxed and gave a wry smile.

"I do believe you are trying to get rid of me, Sir Ander."

"All I'm trying to do is get a good night's sleep," replied Sir Ander. "And I can't do that with you stomping about."

"Talking to the sailors is a good idea," said Father Jacob. "Brother Barnaby, land some distance from town. I don't want anyone to see us. I will change clothes," he added, opening one of the chests built into the bulwarks. "Can't go roaming about the docks looking like the Angel of Death. Scare people half out of their wits."

Brother Barnaby cast Sir Ander a grateful glance.

They camped by the Rim, close to where the Rhouse River emptied into the Bay of Faighn, a magnificent sight — water roaring over the edge of the continent, cascading into the Breath in a cloud of mist and rainbows. The river was swollen, for now was the rainy season, the time of year when rains fell incessantly in the continent's interior for days on end, replenishing the water in the rivers and lakes and in land seas. The water fell off the continents into the Breath, creating the mists and the clouds that would then rise up and cause the rains. God's everlasting miracle.

Just as the magic is his everlasting miracle, thought Sir Ander. Except now not so everlasting.

Brother Barnaby released the wyverns to hunt. Father Jacob, dressed in a disreputable shirt and trousers topped by a shabby jacket, headed off for the docks. On these occasions he refused to take Sir Ander, saying he would be a hindrance. The knight had no gift for acting and always

looked and sounded exactly like what he was, no matter
how much he tried to disguise himself.

Sir Ander did not overly worry about Father Jacob going
off on his own without a Knight Protector. Dressed in
shabby clothes, the priest would not be a target for thieves.
The worst that might happen was that he would end up in a
barroom brawl, which, knowing Father Jacob, he would actually enjoy.

Sir Ander and Brother Barnaby both slept soundly; neither of them awoke when Father Jacob returned in the wee
hours with bruised knuckles and a wide grin. He had, indeed, enjoyed himself, which made up for the fact that the
sailors he questioned had not seen or heard anything untoward in the Breath. He did hear rumors about Trundler
houseboats coming under mysterious attack, but such tales
had been circulating for years, and were generally held to
be nautical ghost stories.

The next day, with the wyverns well-fed and well-rested,
Sir Ander and Brother Barnaby well-rested, and Father Ja-
cob once more in a good mood, *Retribution* set sail for the
Abbey of Saint Agnes.

Chapter Fourteen

People term us thieves and vagabonds. Their Church would see us banned from Heaven. Their communion with God is not our way. We are the Trundlers, children of a world gone by.

Ours is a culture of two halves, the half we show the world and the half we hold in our hearts and in our words. Our people remember the old ways, the old songs and lore and the true pathway to God, long since corrupted by their church.

I am a Trundler and I am a Guardian of the Past, a Keeper of the Word.

—*The Story of the Trundlers*
by Miri McPike, Mistress of Lore,
Never Published

THE *RETRIBUTION*, DRAWN BY WYVERNS, sailed the skies above Rosia, heading for the ill-fated Abbey of Saint Agnes. Lost in the Breath, the *Cloud Hopper* wasn't going anywhere. Or rather, it was going somewhere, just not where anyone on board wanted to go.

It was Stephano who made the discovery that the last shot fired by Sir Richard Piefer had not missed. Piefer had not been aiming his new gun with the rifled bore at the people on board the *Cloud Hopper*. He had aimed at the boat, and Piefer was a good shot. Stephano, recovering from the bullet wound in his shoulder, could attest to that fact.

Piefer's shot had struck the starboard airscrew's propeller.

Undoubtedly, he had been hoping the bullet would cause the propeller to shatter, immediately disabling the *Cloud Hopper* and forcing the boat to return to the docks, where he and his men could finish them off. Piefer's plan had been foiled by the myriad powerful magic constructs set into the metal propeller. According to Rodrigo, the magic held the propeller together, kept it from breaking when the bullet struck it.

"Fortunately, the magic allowed us to escape into the Breath," Rodrigo stated. "Unfortunately, the magic allowed us to escape into the Breath."

"What does that even mean?" Stephano demanded.

"What it means is that we are in a good deal of trouble," said Rodrigo. "We have drifted off course. We've lost sight of land. And we have no way to steer the ship."

"But you said the bullet only dinged the propeller blade," Dag pointed out.

Rodrigo pointed to the propeller. "Please observe. There is the 'ding' left by the bullet. The dent appears harmless, right?"

"Right," said Dag warily. He knew from past experience with Rodrigo he was being led into a trap.

"Wrong!" Rodrigo said triumphantly. "The dent is not only in the metal. The dent is also in the magical constructs that strengthen the metal and keep the propeller turning. And that's why we're adrift."

"A dent in the magic caused us to break down?" Stephano asked, baffled. He started to rub his aching shoulder, caught Miri's eye, and pretended instead to scratch. "Damn bandages itch."

He'd been lucky. The bullet had lodged in the muscle, and had not broken any bones. Miri had taken advantage of the fact that he'd been unconscious to dig out the bullet. Then she'd applied her famous poultice, a noxious yellow in color, bound the shoulder with bandages, trussed up his arm in a sling, dosed him with some sort of foul-tasting liquid, and told him to stay below and keep to his hammock.

Miri had learned her healing skills from her mother, who had learned them from her mother and so on back through generations of Trundler women. Miri was knowledgeable in herb lore and grew many of her own herbs in small containers that had their own special place either on the deck or below deck and must not be moved, no matter how many times people tripped over them.

She used some of the herbs fresh, particularly for cooking, and cut and dried others. Lavender and rosemary hung in fragrant bunches upside down below deck. She stored the rest in crockery containers in the large pantry Dag had built for her near the galley.

One jar was filled with catnip for Doctor Ellington. The cat was of two minds regarding catnip. He was extremely fond of it, but he was well aware that the herb robbed him of his dignity. Within seconds of sniffing a pinch, he would be rolling about the floor with his four large paws in the air, cavorting like a kitten. After the effect wore off, Doctor Ellington would glare at everyone in the vicinity, daring them to suggest he had made himself look foolish, and stalk off with his tail bristling.

Some people claimed the Trundlers used magic in the brews and concoctions and regarded them with suspicion. Rodrigo, in particular, was convinced Miri laced her concoctions with a pinch of magical sigil and he badgered her constantly to teach him the rituals.

Miri always refused, not so much because she was determined to keep her secrets, it was because to her what she did wasn't magic. It was a part of being a Trundler. The little rhymes Miri whispered as she mixed the potions were rhymes she had heard her mother recite, as were the little songs she sang. Each concoction had its own rhyme, its own song. Perhaps they were magical, as Rodrigo claimed. Perhaps the rhyme caused the poultice to stop the wound from putrefying. Perhaps her song caused the beef tea to strengthen the blood. If that was magic, she didn't know how it worked and she didn't care.

Stephano had rested in his hammock only a few hours before he was once more up on deck.

"How can I get any sleep when the lot of you are clomping back and forth above my head," he said fretfully. "I'll just doze here in the sun."

Dag and Rodrigo and Miri looked at each and rolled their eyes and grinned. The reason Stephano was up on deck had nothing to do with clomping. He was their captain. He was in charge. He was responsible. He could no more lie in his hammock and let the world go by than Doctor Ellington could ignore the lure of catnip.

"You owe me five copper rosuns," Dag told Rodrigo. "I said he'd keep to his bed for four hours. You said six."

"You should have given him a larger dose of that funny smelling stuff," Rodrigo grumbled at Miri.

They had docked for the night at a site regularly used by Trundlers, who were called "Trundlers" because their little boats were said to "trundle" through the air. Several other Trundler houseboats, of similar make and design, were docked, tucking in for the night. Trundlers did not sail after dark, believing this was the time demons and other evil beings roamed the Breath.

Trundlers were rovers with their own close-knit society, made up of clans. Each clan was loosely governed by the eldest member of the clan, be that person male or female. Trundlers had their own laws, which sometimes did not accord with the laws laid down by governments. Trundler laws tended to be more easygoing, taking into account human nature and human foibles.

The Trundler's tragic history had taught them to be wary of outsiders, known as "chumps." Rodrigo, Dag, and Stephano had been admitted into Trundler society only because Miri, a Lore Master and much respected, had vouched for them. They had spent a pleasant time last night exchanging tales and stories, food and drink with the Trundlers, and had set sail when the morning sun turned the mists of the Breath pinkish orange.

All had gone well until catastrophe struck. Miri had been steering the boat when suddenly sparks of blue fire had danced over the brass helm, followed by a horrible grinding sound and a wild flapping of sails. Miri had thought at first they'd been struck by lightning, though no storm was in the Breath. She had used some colorful Trundler swear words and frantically tried to reestablish control, but the boat was unresponsive. Nothing like this had ever happened before on any boat she had ever sailed. She had no idea what had gone wrong.

"Think of this dent in the magic as a large boulder dropped into a small stream of water," Rodrigo said, explaining. "The water tries to find a way around the boulder and a small amount of the water will manage to slip past. Thus we had a small amount of magic to keep us going all day yesterday.

"The dent acts like a dam. Some magic flows past, but more magic begins to back up behind it. The constructs in the propeller were not able to handle the buildup of the magical energy and began to fail. That set off a chain reaction throughout the boat. Like tipping over a line of dominoes, more and more constructs failed and then everything failed and now here we are, adrift in the Breath without any way to steer the ship."

"So fix it," said Dag. "You're a crafter. You must be good for something besides causing men with guns to shoot at us."

"I would love to fix it, I assure you," said Rodrigo earnestly. "I don't want to be marooned in the Breath any more than the rest of you. The problem is—the magical constructs are in such a tangle I can't figure out where one begins and another leaves off. It's the odd way the constructs are interwoven that allowed the chain reaction failure in the first place."

He turned to Miri. "Who laid these constructs on the boat for you? I've never seen anything quite like it."

"I don't understand what you mean," Miri said uneasily. "The boat belonged to my parents ..."

"Whoever laid the constructs is highly skilled in magic. *Highly* skilled," Rodrigo emphasized. "I'm impressed. But the crafter was an amateur, untrained. No idea what he or she was doing. If you like, I can draw you a diagram."

"Oh, God!" Stephano groaned. "If he's reduced to drawing diagrams, we're really in trouble."

Miri glanced around for Gythe and couldn't find her. She thought for a moment her sister had gone below, then she saw Gythe huddled underneath a table. She sat hunched there, her knees drawn up to her chin, her arms around her legs.

Stephano followed Miri's gaze. "Oh, no," he said softly. "Not again."

Gythe was pale, her face strained. She stared fearfully into the swirling mists.

"She's always like this out of sight of land," said Miri, regarding her sister with concern. "Leave her there. She feels safe."

"Why does she do this?" Stephano asked, as he'd asked before when this happened.

Miri looked into the mists closing thickly around the houseboat and shook her head and frowned. "Now's not the time to talk about it."

Doctor Ellington jumped from Dag's shoulder onto the table and then from the table to the deck. The cat rubbed his head underneath Gythe's arm. She picked him up and buried her face in his striped fur.

Rodrigo had gone below for pen and ink. Returning, he spread the paper on the brass helm and began to draw. Miri left her sister in the care of the Doctor and joined the others to look curiously over Rodrigo's shoulder.

"Let us say I am a crafter wanting to imbue this paper with magic. I lay down sigil A." Rodrigo drew an A on the paper and drew a circle around it. "I next lay down sigil B." He drew another sigil across from A and labeled it B. "In order to cause the magic to work, I draw a line from A to B. I now have a construct. Magic flows from A to B.

"But let us say that I drop water in the middle of the line. Like this. The ink smears, leaving a large blot on the paper. The construct is broken. No more magic. Ordinarily, a crafter would repair the break by redrawing the line, or a channeler would bridge the line. With the magic on board the *Cloud Hopper*, the crafter did not repair the break. The crafter bypassed the break altogether by adding more lines and sigils. So that now we have not only A and B, but also C, D, E, and F."

Rodrigo drew sigils all over the page and lines that ran every which-way. "All very original. I've never seen these types of sigils before. Some of them actually elevate the magic to the level of genius," said Rodrigo in admiring tones. "But the crafter who laid down the magic was not trained in the art, and now our boat is burdened with such a mishmash of magical sigils and constructs that I have no idea how to untangle them. If the crafter who did this was on board, I might possibly—"

"The crafter is on board," said Miri flatly.

They all stared at her.

"Not me," she said, raising her hands. "Heaven forefend! I'm a fair channeler. I can channel the magic through my hands from one construct to another. But I cannot create a sigil."

She glanced at Gythe, crouched beneath table. "My sister is a crafter and she has a rare gift for the magic, or so I've been told."

"But she's never been trained," said Rodrigo.

"She *was* trained," said Miri. "By our parents. By my uncle."

"Drop it," said Stephano beneath his breath.

Rodrigo ignored him. "Trundler magic . . ."

Miri rounded on him angrily, her fist clenched. "And what do you mean by that remark, sir?"

"Told you to drop it," said Stephano.

Rodrigo tried to reason with her. "All I meant was that Gythe never went to school—"

"And who needs bloody schooling!" Miri cried, seething.

"Judging by the confused mess I've found on board this boat . . ."

Miri seized a belaying pin.

Stephano grabbed hold of Rodrigo. "Apologize!"

"What? Why?"

"Before she cracks open your skull! Apologize!"

"Ah, yes, well, I apologize, Miri," said Rodrigo. He gave her his best charming smile. "I meant no offense. Truly. Tell me about Gythe and the Trundler magic. I need to understand so that I can fix this."

Miri grew calmer. She lowered the belaying pin, much to Rodrigo's relief, and glanced anxiously at her sister, who was still hiding beneath the table.

"Gythe loves to work the magic. Nothing makes her happier, except maybe playing the harp. She sings to herself while she works. She has such few pleasures. I encourage her. The magic soothes her, like the music."

"Do you know what she is doing with the magic?" Rodrigo asked.

Miri shrugged. "I assumed she repairs broken constructs. I couldn't see that she was doing any harm. Like I said, I'm no crafter."

The mists of the Breath were gray, shifting and whirling around them. The damp clung to their clothes, made them feel cold and clammy.

Rodrigo wiped his face.

"She was not doing any harm," said Rodrigo. "Far from it. These magical constructs are meant for protection. Over and over, she laid down constructs designed to protect this boat and those in it. From stem to stern and back and again, the *Cloud Hopper* is festooned with webs of magical protection constructs."

Miri's eyes shimmered with tears. Her lips trembled. "My poor sister."

"But protection magic is good, isn't it?" Stephano argued.

"Yes and no," said Rodrigo. "Yes, because the protection

magic is what kept the propeller from being shot to bits. No, because there are so many layers of spells I can't figure out how to unravel them in order to repair the damage. Our situation is this: we have no way to operate the sails or the rudder or energize the gas that keeps the balloons inflated and the lift tanks working. Soon the gas will start to cool and lose its magical energy. The balloon will deflate and the lift tanks will fail and we will sink into the Breath. The mists of the Breath grow thicker as one descends, the temperature drops. It is theorized that eventually the Breath at the lowest altitudes turns to a liquid form, which means we will all drown. Though by that time it won't matter, since we will have already frozen to death."

Stephano regarded his friend grimly. "There must be some way you can get this boat up and running!"

"I might be able to repair the constructs enough to get us as far as Westfirth, but only if Gythe helps me," said Rodrigo. "A lot of these sigils are new to me and, trust me, I know my sigils. This is Trundler magic"—he glanced apprehensively at Miri—"no offense, Miri."

She shook her head, too alarmed at the terrible prospect they were facing to angry.

"We have always kept our magic a secret," she said.

Stephano glanced over at Gythe. "This goes back to what happened to her, doesn't it? The reason she won't speak. Miri, you need to tell us what happened. Maybe we could help her. I know you don't like to talk about it—"

"I vowed I would never talk of it," said Miri fiercely. She stood with her arms folded across her chest, staring stubbornly down at the deck. "My uncle made me take an oath. He said if we talked about it, it would only make things worse for us. People call us thieves and swindlers. If they knew that something out there in the Breath was killing our kind, they'd say the horror came because of us and they'd set fire to our boats and drive us out. . . ."

Miri began to cry. She tried to stop, but she couldn't help it. Stephano put his arm around her and drew her close.

"We won't tell anyone, Miri," he said. "We'll keep your secret. We'll take any oath you ask of us." -

She smiled bleakly and hurriedly dashed away the tears. Dag fished out his handkerchief and handed it to her. His big, ugly face was soft with concern. She blew her nose and cast Dag a grateful glance and, slightly flushing, squirmed out of Stephano's grasp.

"Swear by our friendship," she said. "That will be good enough for me."

Each of them made the promise. Miri gazed around at them and swallowed. "There's not much to tell. My sister and I were away visiting my uncle and his family. He has children our age and all of us cousins grew up together. We lived as much on his boat as we did on ours. When it was time to join up with our parents' houseboat, we knew immediately something was wrong.

"Our boat wasn't at the meeting place. We waited, but our parents never came. My uncle, thinking there might be a problem with the boat, sailed out to search for it. We came across our boat not far off, adrift in the Breath, like we are now.

"Our father and mother should have both been on deck, working to fix whatever was wrong. But they weren't. There was no one. The deck was empty . . ."

She was shivering. It was cold out here on deck, with the mists of the Breath closing in. Dag draped a coat about her shoulders, and she drew it around her. The coat was huge on her and the shoulder yellow with cat fur. She nestled into it and found the courage to finish her tale.

"My uncle guessed that something terrible had happened, and he tried to stop us from going aboard. But we were kids and didn't know anything. The world was all sunshine to us then. Before he could catch her, Gythe had jumped from his boat onto ours. She was light as a bird and seemed to almost float through the air. She landed on the deck and shouting, 'Mam' and 'Pap,' she ran down into the hold."

Miri paused, then said in a low voice, "I will hear her scream until the day I die. She only screamed once and then she never spoke a word after. My uncle tried to make me stay on board his ship, but I would have fought a bigger man than him to reach Gythe, and at last he let me go with him.

"Our snug cabin, where we all had lived so happily, was awash in blood. The blood was so deep it sloshed back and forth with the movement of the boat. Gythe was standing in it, staring. Just staring. We never found the bodies. Not whole bodies. Only . . . pieces . . ."

"I guess we know the reason for the protection spells," said Rodrigo somberly.

Dag awkwardly patted Miri's shoulder. She gave him a wan smile of thanks. "Pirates," he said.

Stephano shook his head. "Why would pirates attack a Trundler houseboat? It's not like they're stuffed with gold . . ."

"It wasn't pirates," said Miri. "I told you before. It was something terrible that came out of the Breath. There were marks on the walls—like giant claws. The bodies had been ripped apart. And the magic was gone."

"What do you mean, the magic was gone?" Rodrigo asked.

"The magic on the boat. It was just gone," said Miri.

Rodrigo shook his head. "But that's not—"

Stephano elbowed him in the ribs. "Let it go."

Her story had unnerved them. They looked into the thick mists and then back at Gythe, shivering under the table. They thought about the protection constructs she had laid down, layer upon layer upon layer.

"You swore you wouldn't tell," Miri reminded them.

"I won't," Stephano said. "But someone should. The navy could help . . ."

Miri snorted her disbelief. "Help Trundlers?"

"There have been rumors," said Dag. "I've heard them. The sailors talk about ghosts in the Breath."

"We now know why Gythe worked her magic," said Rodrigo. "She can't help me while she is still under the table."

"I think Dag should talk to her," said Miri.

"Me?" Dag looked astonished.

"Gythe loves you. She trusts you," said Miri simply.

Dag's face went red. He shook his head, embarrassed, and mumbled, "Don't leave it up to me."

"We're starting to sink," Rodrigo warned, looking up at the balloon. "We don't have much time."

"Dag," said Stephano. "Miri's right."

"But what do I say?" Dag asked helplessly.

"Whatever is in that big heart of yours," said Miri softly.

Dag's face went redder than ever. He stood for a moment, looking uncomfortably at Gythe. Her head was buried in Doctor Ellington's fur. She was shivering with fear. Dag's expression softened. He managed, with considerable effort, to sit down awkwardly on the deck and, by means of scooting and scrunching, squeezed his way beneath the table.

The Breath dampened sound. All was eerily silent.

"Girl dear, I want you to look at me."

Gythe very slightly raised her head to peep at him over the Doctor. Her fair hair straggled wetly around her face.

"I was born ugly," Dag said cheerfully. "Came by it naturally. Neither my pa nor ma were anything to look at. But God made up for my ugly face by making me big and strong. I've been shot at by every conceivable type of gun. I've had cannonballs thrown at me. I've been stabbed with swords and cut with knives and struck with fists. I've even been attacked by our captain and his dragon." Dag glanced at Stephano, who smiled at the memory of their first encounter.

"And I'm still here, Girl dear," Dag said simply. "Nothing's been found that can kill me yet."

He rested his hand on her hand and said quietly, "Anything out there that wants to do you harm will have to go through me first. You know that, don't you?"

Gythe nodded and lifted her head to smile at him. She leaned over and kissed him on the cheek. Miri, turning away, wiped her eyes. Stephano looked at her. He looked at Dag, and something seemed to strike him.

"Miri loves him! I'll be damned," he said to himself, and he didn't know if he liked that or not.

"It seems that Master Rigo is having trouble sorting out what you've done with the magic. He needs your help to fix it, or the boat won't sail. Let me take the Doctor." Dag reached for the cat, who was loath to leave and, with much yowling, had to be pried loose. "While you go help Master Rigo. He's not very bright, you know."

Gythe smiled tremulously at that. She hesitated only a moment, then slid out from beneath the table and stood up, smoothing her skirt. She indicated with a little nod that she was ready to assist. Miri went to her sister and hugged her.

"I am in awe of your work, Gythe." said Rodrigo. "Truly in awe. What you've done is quite marvelous. But your magic is causing a bit of a problem. If you could just show me what you did, we might be able to fix it."

He steered Gythe to the helm. The two bent over it, Rodrigo explaining and Gythe listening with grave attention. Miri hurried over to assist Dag, who was floundering about on the deck, unable to stand up.

"Damn leg went to sleep on me," he grumbled.

"Let me help," said Miri.

She managed to hoist Dag, grimacing, onto his feet. She stood a moment with her arm around his broad back. She smiled at him. "Thank you, Dag."

He blushed and lowered his eyes and mumbled something, then he hobbled off, trying to get the feeling back into his leg. Doctor Ellington flounced across the deck, tail flicking angrily. He turned up his nose at a piece of smoked fish Stephano held out as a peace-offering, and ran down the stairs into the hold, determined to punish them by depriving them of his company.

Stephano ate the smoked fish himself. Miri was gazing after Dag with a fond, exasperated look.

"So it's that way with you, is it?" said Stephano.

"What way?" she asked, startled.

"You're in love with Dag."

"I suppose I should blush, but I'm too old. Yes, I love the big lummox." She paused, then faltered, "Do you mind?"

"A little," Stephano admitted.

"You know we always said we would just be friends."

"I know what we *said*," Stephano replied. "But saying and feeling are two different things. Face it," he added in teasing tones, "you'd be mad if I *wasn't* jealous."

Miri laughed. "I guess I would." She sighed and cast a rueful glance at Dag, who was pacing the deck as though he was walking guard duty on the top of a redoubt. "Though there's no need for you to be jealous. He won't give me the time of day."

"He's been wounded, Miri," said Stephano quietly. "And unlike a bullet wound or a sword slash, this wound is deep in his soul. It won't be easy to heal."

"Something happened to him. Tell me what," said Miri.

Stephano gazed out into the swirling mists. "Dag will tell you himself when he's ready." He turned to smile at her. "And when he does, you'll know he loves you."

"And if he doesn't . . ."

Stephano shook his head. "Dag hates himself for something that happened long ago, Miri. Right now, that hatred is so big it's squeezing out every other feeling. You have to be patient. Loving and patient."

"If that's what I have to do, then I guess I'll do it," said Miri.

She looked over at the helm. Gythe was making rapid gestures with one hand and jabbing her finger at the helm with the other. Rodrigo was staring at her in helpless bewilderment.

"I guess I had better go translate," Miri said. She started to leave, then looked back at Stephano. "Thank you."

"For what?" he asked.

"For being jealous."

She gave him a pert smile, then went to the helm, where

she was immediately confronted by Gythe and Rodrigo, both talking at once; Gythe with hands flying and Rodrigo saying plaintively, "I think I upset her ..."

Miri explained to Rodrigo what Gythe meant with her gestures and tried at the same time, to explain to Gythe that Rodrigo didn't mean what he'd said with his mouth. The three of them began to laboriously try to untangle the overlapping strands of magic.

They had a difficult time of it. Gythe was at first adamantly opposed to removing any of the magical constructs she'd laid down to protect the *Cloud Hopper*. Rodrigo tried to tell her that one of her magical constructs was so powerful she did not need twenty more on top of it.

"In fact, the others have weakened the entire construct. Think of your first construct as a mighty river, with the water all flowing in a one direction. When you added additional constructs, you essentially siphoned off the water, sending it flowing into ditches and creeks and streams, with the result that your river is down to a trickle. If you remove all these other constructs, the magic will flow strong again."

Stephano listened and watched and tried to imagine what it must be like to see the glow of sigils and the lines of energy connecting them and to know you had the power to manipulate such a miraculous force. Perhaps the feeling was akin to flying through the air on the back of a dragon, with the wind in your face, knowing the freedom that comes when you leave the world and all its problems far behind.

There were those like Hastind who claimed they felt the same striding the deck of one of the large ships of the air, but Stephano knew better. On board ship, he was one of many junior officers, all vying for the attention of the godlike captain, who rarely, if ever, deigned to listen to a lowly lieutenant. Being a ship's captain meant you had to deal with the politics of the Royal Navy, suck up to some dunderhead of an admiral who didn't know his starboard from his port. When you were a Dragon Knight, you only had to talk to your dragon, and Stephano had often found dragons far more sensible and intelligent than people.

The *Cloud Hopper* was now starting to sink deeper into the Breath. The lift tanks were cold; the magical sparks that energized them were flickering, ready to die. The mists were so thick that now Stephano could barely make out the balloon, which was starting to deflate, as were their spirits. Stephano's wound had begun to throb painfully, but he kept quiet, not wanting to take Miri away from her work.

Night wrapped around the boat. Dag gave up keeping watch. He apologized to Doctor Ellington, which apology, accompanied by smoked fish, was graciously accepted. Stephano tried to light a lantern, but the wick was too damp to catch. He and Dag and the Doctor sat in the deck chairs and watched Gythe and Rodrigo and Miri work. Stephano felt helpless. All he could do was listen to the dismal flapping of the sails and feel the cold water drip off the ratlines onto his head. Every so often, flashes of magic arcing from one sigil to another flared in the night and gave them hope. But then the light would fail, Rigo would sigh and shake his head. Gythe looked like she was going to cry. Miri drooped from exhaustion.

They had to keep working. The *Cloud Hopper* was sinking fast.

Chapter Fifteen

Most of us have no true understanding of just how little of Rosia we inhabit. We fly from city to city, over vast stretches of unexplored wilderness and rarely look down to marvel at the deep green forests, jagged shorelines, and tall snow-covered mountains. A few have sought to live in these places, untouched by man, so as to be closer to God.

—Unknown priest in a letter to his family describing his pilgrimage into the wilderness

AS THE DISABLED *CLOUD HOPPER* SANK SLOWLY into the Breath and her crew struggled desperately to rekindle her magic, the *Retribution* continued flying through the night, planning to reach the Abbey of Saint Agnes by dawn.

After finally obtaining a good night's sleep, Sir Ander wakened in a somber state of mind, thinking sorrowfully of the murder of a hundred innocent souls and wondering about the evil that had committed such a heinous crime. He should have been relieved to find Father Jacob in a cheerful mood, for life with the priest when he was in a good humor was far more comfortable than when Father Jacob was on a rampage. But the priest's good mood clashed with Sir Ander's, who found himself resenting the Father's smile and hearty "good morning."

Ander dipped the shaving razor in the water basin and then held it poised, waiting for the rocking motion of the yacht to steady enough that he didn't have to worry about cutting his own throat.

"Whose nose did you bloody last night?"

Father Jacob looked up, startled. Then, glancing at his split knuckles, he began to laugh—loud, booming laughter that apparently startled the wyverns, for the yacht took a sudden lurch. Sir Ander braced his leg against his foot locker.

"You will be pleased to know that I did not take out my frustrations on some poor innocent fisherman," said Father Jacob, slicing cold roast beef and eating it off the edge of the knife. "Quite the contrary, I was almost swept up in a press gang."

The yacht was relatively steady, and Sir Ander scraped at his jaw quickly.

Father Jacob looked quite pleased with himself. "Some naval vessel must have come up short-handed. A lieutenant was rounding up the local fishermen to 'offer' them a life in the navy, which meant that he was sending them back to his ship in legs irons and handcuffs."

"Didn't you tell him who you were?"

"And miss out on a grand brawl?" Father Jacob grinned and ate beef with enthusiasm. "Instead of bloodying a fisherman's nose, I bloodied the lieutenant's and then took to my heels."

Sir Ander grunted and, when the swaying eased again, he swiftly completed his shaving. He mopped his face with a towel.

"Well, I'm glad the fight has improved your mood."

Father Jacob was indignant. "What do you mean, improved my mood? I am always in the best of humors, despite the fact that my patience is constantly tried to the limit by dunderheads like the grand bishop, who insists on trying to keep political plates spinning in the air while his world is literally crashing down around his ears."

"His Eminence doesn't have much choice," said Sir Ander. He put on his dress uniform, consisting of a long coat in the dark red of the Knight Protectors, white trousers, white stockings, and polished black knee-high boots.

Father Jacob only grunted. His gaze grew abstracted. He chewed thoughtfully on a hunk of beef and said suddenly, "Do you know what strikes me as odd about this atrocity we've been sent to investigate?"

"I have no idea," said Sir Ander, finally sitting down to breakfast. "Has Brother Barnaby eaten anything?"

"I offered to drive while he ate, but he said he wasn't hungry."

"God forgive the good monk the sin of lying," Sir Ander said to himself, inwardly smiling. Aloud he remarked, "What do you find odd?"

"Dubois," said Father Jacob.

"Dubois? Who is Dubois?" Sir Ander asked, startled.

"A remarkable man. One might say, a *very* remarkable man. He has a mind like a rat terrier. Once he sinks his teeth into the meat of a problem, he never lets go. Dubois is the bishop's most valued agent. Dubois is to the bishop what the Countess de Marjolaine is to His Majesty."

Sir Ander felt his face grow warm at the mention of the countess, warmth radiating perhaps from the letters in his breast pocket. He hoped Father Jacob wouldn't notice. Fortunately, Father Jacob was engaged in holding a loaf of bread on the table in an attempt to slice it without slicing his fingers.

"The bishop mentioned Dubois' name as Brother Barnaby and I were in his office."

"He mentioned it to you?"

"Well, no," said Father Jacob. "He was talking to the monsignor—"

"—and you were eavesdropping."

Father Jacob smiled slightly and shrugged. "Dubois and I worked together many years ago, before your time. He was low in the ranks then, but he has since advanced to become the bishop's right hand, his ears and, in some cases, his brain. Dubois sent a note to the bishop wanting to know about something happening in the Royal Armory. And it has something to do with Henry Wallace."

"Wallace?" Sir Ander was alarmed. "He's not still after you, is he?"

"I'm sure Sir Henry would be extremely pleased to hear of my demise," said Father Jacob cheerfully. "But, no, I don't think the man is pursuing me. Not after all these years. He has moved on to more important matters."

"Something happening at the Royal Armory?" Sir Ander looked exasperated. "We're investigating the tragic murder of one hundred nuns. What could the Royal Armory possibly have to do with that?"

"Nothing that I can fathom," said Father Jacob. "And that's what I find odd."

"You've lost me," said Sir Ander.

"The grand bishop calls upon Dubois to deal with matters which are of the utmost importance," said Father Jacob. "One would think a hundred murdered nuns would fall into that category. And, yet, Dubois is poking about the Royal Armory. Although if Wallace is involved . . ."

Father Jacob fell into a musing silence.

Sir Ander eyed the priest, saw he was drifting off course. Sir Ander forked cold beef on a slice of bread and said sternly, "What could be more important than this terrible attack on the abbey?"

"Something happening at the Royal Armory apparently," said Father Jacob in thoughtful tones. "I can't help but wonder what. Ah, well." He shrugged. "No sense wasting time worrying about it."

He says that, Sir Ander thought, but I know better. This Dubois fellow isn't the only terrier who doesn't know when to let go. Though Father Jacob might be considered more like a bulldog in that respect.

"I read through this report the bishop gave me on the abbey. The report from the unknown Brother Paul." Father Jacob shoved over a sheet of paper covered with close, jagged handwriting. "Read that. I want your opinion."

Sir Ander smoothed out the paper. Whoever Brother Paul was, he had obviously written the report in a state of great agitation—portions were scratched out, notes had been scrawled in the margins. Sir Ander had considerable difficulty deciphering the brother's hysterical penmanship. Fortunately, the report wasn't long.

"I pray to God we find the bastards responsible for these atrocities!" Sir Ander said grimly when he had finished reading. "One survivor, and that poor young woman driven out of her wits by the horror."

"Out of her wits." Father Jacob raised an eyebrow. "You believe she is crazy?"

"Don't you?" Sir Ander gestured to the report with a bit of bread. "She talks about demons riding on the backs of gigantic bats with glowing eyes of fire . . ."

"Brother Paul doesn't think she is crazy. I quote: 'Demonic legions of Aertheum the Fallen attacked the nuns in response to their godly work.' Demons 'hurling balls of glowing green flame' . . ."

Father Jacob tapped his knife on the table. "Does that put you in mind of something? A certain cutter, maybe?"

Sir Ander stopped with the bread halfway to his mouth. "The *Defiant*? The cutter was attacked by a ship armed with a weapon that fired a green flame, but those were pirates, not fiends riding giant bats."

"His Eminence noted the connection. That's why he sent for me to investigate."

"But, still, giant bats?" Sir Ander appealed to reason.

"The nun said one thing that I found particularly instructive. See if you come to the same conclusion."

Sir Ander read back through the report and shook his head. "I don't know what—"

"'The demon yelped . . .'" Father Jacob repeated the words with relish, seeming to savor them.

Sir Ander looked blank. "I don't understand. What is so important about that?"

"You don't find it interesting? Ah, well, perhaps I'm

jumping at shadows," said Father Jacob. "No use speculating. I look forward to talking with our sole witness. According to Brother Paul, the nun's injuries were not severe."

"Injuries to her body, maybe," said Sir Ander gravely.

"We are coming up on the abbey, Father," Brother Barnaby relayed from the driver's seat. "You can see the two spires of the cathedral. And"—Brother Barnaby caught his breath—"there's a dragon, Father! Flying over the abbey!"

Sir Ander bolted a last bite of bread and beef and hastened to join Father Jacob, who had gone out the hatch to sit with Brother Barnaby.

Below the yacht the land was wild and untamed—jagged hills covered with brush and scrub trees from which rose strange and grotesque rock formations. The sun sparkled on streams and glinted off a river winding back and forth upon itself through hollows and ravines.

The abbey had been constructed centuries ago on a large promontory that jutted out into the Breath. The twin spires of the cathedral stood in lonely, haughty isolation, dominating and defying the wilderness.

The Abbey of Saint Agnes was ancient; its history murky. The decision to build their abbey in this remote part of Rosia had been made by an order of monks who had vowed to shun the world, spend their days and nights in worship. The early buildings had consisted of a single large, crude wooden structure where the monks slept and a small and humble church. The monks built a high stone wall around their compound and lived their lives behind it.

The monks did not venture into the world, but they could not escape it. The world came to them. King Alfonso the Third, who ruled over eight hundred years ago, was involved in secret and delicate negotiations with the foreign minister of Travia. Surrounded by spies in the royal court, the king contacted the Prince-Abbot of the Abbey of Saint Castigan, as it was known then, to ask if he could meet the minister at the abbey. The prince-abbot reluctantly agreed. The meeting was successful, and both His Majesty and the minister gave substantial donations to the order by way of thanks.

Word went round among the princes of all nations that if they wanted a secure place for any type of secret liaison or assignation, they could find safe haven in the Abbey of Saint Castigan. Kings and nobles who visited the abbey made donations to the abbey's coffers. The order spent their wealth on building a beautiful cathedral, a dortoir, a comfortable guesthouse with stables for wyverns, griffins, and horses and carriages, and docks for airships.

When the Dark Time fell, bringing catastrophic upheaval to the seven continents, princes, kings, and nobles were caught up in the daily struggle to keep their people alive from one day to the next. The Breath churned and boiled and was far too dangerous to travel. All trade between nations and continents ceased. The Abbey of Saint Castigan was forgotten.

When the world finally emerged from darkness, Rosia basked in the sunshine of wealth and power. The grand bishop came across old records from the Abbey of Saint Castigan and wondered why nothing had been heard from the monks for many long years. He sent representatives to the abbey and found it empty, abandoned. They could find no trace of the monks, no records left behind to indicate what had happened. There did not appear to have been any sort of catastrophe. All had been left in order: beds made, dishes washed, treasure coffers—still full—safely locked.

No one ever learned the fate of the monks, though there were many theories. The most logical of these was that the monks, near starvation, had been forced to take to their airships and sail into the stormy Breath, where they had perished. The Abbey of Saint Castigan was given to an order of nuns, who rededicated it to Saint Agnes. The nuns lived quietly in far more reduced circumstances than the monks. No more wealthy nobles came to the abbey. The nuns' visitors tended to be of a humbler nature.

Every night, the nuns would climb the spiraling stairs to

hang lights in the twin spires to guide ships sailing the
Breath. Oftentimes occupants of these ships and boats—
sailors and Trundlers—sought shelter at the abbey's docks,
which were located in an inlet several miles distant from the
abbey's walls. The nuns would give the sailors food and water and tend to any illnesses or injuries they suffered. In
addition, scholars would sometimes come to the abbey to
do research in the famed library. Among these was Master
Albert Savoraun, who lived in the nearby city of Westfirth.

Master Albert Savoraun had traveled to the abbey to
track down old records of the Maritime Guild. Some guildmaster had decided the records would be safer behind the
abbey walls than in the guildhall in Westfirth. Given that
the guildhall had twice in its history been destroyed by fire,
this decision had undoubtedly been a wise one.

The guild owned a ship and several yachts, all of which
were used to conduct guild business. Albert had sailed himself in one of the small yachts to the abbey. While going
through the library, he had found something there that had
astonished him greatly. Thinking Father Jacob Northrop
would find this discovery interesting, Albert had sent a letter to the Arcanum.

Albert had been in the vicinity of the abbey the night the
attack took place. Sleeping aboard his yacht, he had been
awakened by what he had thought was lightning. He believed a storm was coming, and he had gone out to make
certain his yacht was securely tied down. Once he was outside, he realized that the eerie green light did not emanate
from a storm, but was flaring around the abbey. He could
smell smoke in the air and he saw, to his consternation, that
the lights in the cathedral's spires had gone dark.

Alarmed, Albert dressed swiftly and, taking up his lantern, hastened to the abbey to see if he could help. During
his walk, which took him about half an hour, he watched
the green flashes of fire diminish and then cease altogether.
The smoke grew thicker; he could see plumes roiling above
the abbey walls, blotting out the stars. He could not hear

any sounds, no screams or voices calling or shouting as one would expect to hear if the nuns were battling the fires.

The odd silence struck fear into Albert's heart, and he began to wish he'd brought his musket. His fears were realized. He found the abbey's gates shattered. He entered cautiously, only to come upon a scene of such nightmarish destruction that the veteran sailor who had witnessed ship battles—blood running from the scuppers—was overwhelmed with horror and blacked out.

He was roused by the priest who had been the nuns' confessor. Brother Paul was a hermit who resided in a rude shack in the wilderness about five miles from the abbey. He had seen the green fire and come to see what was going on. Together, the two men entered the compound and began to search for survivors.

They had found one—a young nun who had escaped detection by hiding beneath a pew.

Brother Paul had insisted, quite rightly, that word of the attack should be immediately sent to the grand bishop. He had urged Master Albert to carry the message to the abbot in Westfirth to be dispatched to Evreux by swift courier. Albert agreed the message needed to be sent, but he was loath to go himself. He had seen much to trouble him about this attack. Trusting that Father Jacob was already on his way, Albert did not want to leave the abbey unguarded.

He had been trying to figure some way out of this dilemma when he was startled to hear a loud voice, coming down from the sky. Albert looked up to see two dragons circling overhead. His nerves were raw, his mind unsettled and the thought came to him that the dragons had committed this atrocity. Then one of the dragons, landing ponderously among the scrub trees, had introduced himself as Sergeant Hroalfrig, formerly of the Dragon Brigade.

"Now retired," Hroalfrig said.

He and the other dragon, his brother Droalfrig, also a former soldier, raised sheep and goats on a wretched piece of land provided to them by the Crown in return for their military service. They had seen the smoke and had come to find out what had happened. The nuns, it appeared, had been good to the dragons and the brothers were both appalled and angered by what had occurred.

Albert had enlisted the aid of the dragons to keep watch over the abbey. The dragons had sailed to Westfirth, carrying Brother Paul's account, and had then returned to the abbey to await the arrival of Father Jacob.

One of the dragon brothers was now flying in large, slow, dignified circles above the abbey, keeping watch.

The sight of the dragon, who weighed six thousand pounds and measured seventy feet from nose to tail, with a wingspan of over one hundred and forty feet, alarmed the *Retribution*'s wyverns. They began to shriek and flail about in their traces, giving Brother Barnaby all he could do to try to soothe them and maintain control.

The sight of the black yacht likewise alarmed the other dragon, who came flying over ponderously to take a look. The Church emblem on the yacht reassured the dragon, who dipped his wings in salute. Seeing that he was upsetting the wyverns, the dragon flew off to resume his patrol.

"There are the docks. Should we land there, Father?" Brother Barnaby asked.

"Too far away from the abbey. I need to be close by."

"We need to put down quickly somewhere," said Brother Barnaby, who was continuing to have a difficult time with the wyverns.

Sir Ander pointed to a small patch of grassland outside the abbey walls. He handled the helm, adjusting the yacht's buoyancy and trim, as Brother Barnaby continued to assure the wyverns that the dragon was not going to harm them. He brought the yacht down safely. Master Savoraun, who had been watching for their arrival, hurried to meet them.

"Albert Savoraun! It's good to see you, my friend," said Father Jacob, reaching out his hand to his longtime friend.

Sir Ander gripped Master Albert's hand. "I suppose I

should call you Guildmaster Albert now. Congratulations. You have done well for yourself."

"Thank you, Father. It's good to see you, though I wish it were under better circumstances," said Albert. He was haggard and pale, his eyes bloodshot. He turned to Sir Ander. "You are looking well, sir."

"A little grayer than the last time we met, but otherwise in good health, thanks be to God," said Sir Ander.

"We're all grayer, sir," said Albert and he ran his hand over his thinning hair. "I've added a good many gray hairs over this, I can assure you."

Albert Savoraun was in his mid-thirties, with the weather-beaten face of a lifelong sailor. He was short, with a stocky build and a take-charge attitude. Born into a family of seafaring crafters in Rosia, he had been brought up in his trade and served on board his first ship as apprentice to his father at the age of thirteen.

"I've never seen anything like this, Father," said Albert. "And I hope I never do again."

Father Jacob introduced Brother Barnaby, who was still concerned for his wyverns.

"Is there a place where I can stable them?" he asked anxiously. "The dragon makes them nervous. So long as they can't see him, they'll feel safe."

"The stables are still standing," said Albert. "I have no idea why the fiends didn't burn them, too. Maybe they were spared because they were far from the main compound. You can't see them from here. They're on the west side of the abbey, outside the walls—three large stone buildings. You can house your wyverns there, Brother."

Brother Barnaby refused all offers of assistance, saying apologetically that the wyverns were in such a state he did not trust them around anyone. Sir Ander maneuvered the yacht into position, placing the back of the yacht against the abbey's walls, with the front facing west, looking out across a flat expanse of windswept granite into the swirling mists of the

Breath beyond. A low wall had been built at the cliff's edge, serving to keep people from falling over the precipice.

"I've never seen any place so lonely and forgotten," Sir Ander remarked, shaking his head.

Brother Barnaby unharnessed the wyverns and led them to the stables, leaving Father Jacob and Sir Ander to talk to Master Albert. Their desolate surroundings and the sad nature of their business oppressed their spirits and made idle conversation difficult. Father Jacob did not want to discuss the tragedy until he had seen the site for himself. He asked Albert about his numerous children back in Westfirth. Albert cheered at the thought and began to talk about his brood. His oldest son, age fourteen, was already serving with the navy as an Apprentice Craftsman.

When the wyverns had been housed and calmed, fed and watered, Brother Barnaby came to join them, carrying his portable writing desk which he had brought from the yacht.

"Would you like to rest after your journey, Father?" Albert asked.

Father Jacob shook his head. "We should view the site while there is still plenty of daylight."

"In that case, you will need these." Albert produced several handkerchiefs.

"Ah, yes," said Father Jacob.

He took one of the handkerchiefs for himself and offered the others to Sir Ander and Brother Barnaby. The young monk looked confused.

"The stench," said Father Jacob gently.

Brother Barnaby accepted the handkerchief and tucked it into the belt of his plain brown monk's robes. Sir Ander, looking grim, signaled that he didn't need one.

They walked around the outside of the abbey, the wind whipping them and blowing sand in their eyes. They could not see anything beyond the abbey's high stone wall except the twin spires of the cathedral soaring to Heaven.

As they walked, the dragon's shadow flowed over them. The dragon dipped his wings, gave a wheezing cough. The dragon's advanced age was apparent in the color of his scales. Once shining blue-green in his youth, the scales were now a dull greenish gray. His beard was hoary, but his eyes were still fierce and proud.

"That's Sergeant Hroalfrig," said Albert, seeing Father Jacob's interested gaze closely observing the dragon. "Formerly of the Dragon Brigade. He and his twin brother, who was also a member of the Brigade, live on a small farm some twenty miles inland. When they heard of the tragedy, they flew here to offer their help."

Master Albert gave a wry smile. "Neither of the old boys can stay up in the air too long, so they take turns flying patrol."

He was silent a moment, brooding, then said abruptly,

"I'm glad you were able to come with such speed, Father. Brother Paul has been insisting on burying the dead. After what I saw, I knew I had to keep everything just as it was until you could see for yourself."

"You mean, the dead have not been given proper burial, sir?" Brother Barnaby was shocked.

"I'm sorry to say, Brother, that there is not that much left to bury," said Albert.

Brother Barnaby's dark complexion paled and he murmured a prayer beneath his breath.

"Please relate your story, Albert," said Father Jacob briskly. "I'd like to hear it before we enter the walls."

"The night of the attack," Albert began. "I was asleep—"

Father Jacob interrupted. "Everything in the proper order, please. A fortnight before the attack, you sent me a letter coded in magic saying you had found something of interest in the abbey. What was it?"

Albert was impatient. "That's of little consequence in view of this tragedy, Father."

"I will be the judge of that," said Father Jacob mildly.

Albert paused to mop his forehead with his coat sleeve. The sun shone brightly. No clouds drifted in the sky, save the misty haze of the Breath on the horizon. The day was going to be a hot one.

"Guild members have long complained that they couldn't get access to guild records, which had been stored in the abbey for safekeeping. That included the guild charter and bylaws, membership rolls and legal documents and such like. I proposed that we have the records brought back to the guildhall and have copies made.

"When I arrived at the abbey, I asked the nuns where the guild records were kept. They weren't much help. Poor women. They lived in poverty. It was all they could do to keep body and soul together. When they weren't praying, they were tending to their crops and their livestock. They told me the records were likely in the library, which was in the cathedral. Brother Paul had the key. He used the library as his office when he was visiting the abbey."

"He was the nuns' confessor and priest, but he would not reside at the abbey, of course," said Father Jacob. "That would not be seemly."

"He's a strange one, is Brother Paul. He wouldn't reside at the abbey, seemly or not. He's a hermit, lives in the wilderness somewhere."

"Where was he when the abbey was attacked?"

"He was in his dwelling, asleep. The attack happened long after he'd left for the night."

Father Jacob nodded. "Well, for the moment, we can dispense with Brother Paul. What did you discover in the abbey library that you thought I would find interesting?"

Master Albert paused to look around, which Sir Ander thought an odd precaution, considering the fact that they, Brother Barnaby, and Brother Paul were likely the only in a hundred-mile radius.

"Brother Paul's office consisted of little more than a stool and a desk where he did his writing. He paid scant attention to the books in the library. He has weak eyes and finds it difficult to read for long periods of time. He had no idea where the guild records were located. He told me I could 'rummage around.'

"As it turns out there was no need to 'rummage.' The

library is well-ordered, with church records in one place, theological texts in another, books on crafting in yet another and so on. I found the guild records easily enough, and I put them aside. Since no one minded my being there, I poked around some more and ended up in the section where there were books on crafting."

Albert gave a rueful smile. "As you know, Father, I've always regretted that I was never able to study the art properly. My father didn't hold with reading about magic in school. He taught me crafting as he had learned it from his father who had learned it from his father and so on. I've always been interested in finding out more on the subject and here I was, surrounded by books on crafting. I was like a kid in a bakery.

"I roved among the stacks and came across an entire section given to seafaring magic. The books were on the very top shelf. I had to fetch a ladder to reach them. I was taking out one of the books when I noticed a wooden chest on top of the bookcase. The chest was tucked well back from the edge, so it hadn't been visible from below.

"The chest was heavy, covered with dirt and cobwebs. I managed to haul it down, though I nearly fell off the ladder in the process. I set it on the floor and dusted it off as best I could. The chest was magic-locked and cost me considerable effort to open it.

"Inside were five slim volumes, all bound in leather with no title on the covers. I opened the first one to a frontispiece, very elaborate art, which appeared to be have been drawn by the author, consisting of his name and title all done in fancy lettering. The name was: Cividae. The year was 721 GF (Grand Founding)."

"Interesting," said Father Jacob.

"Why? Who was this Cividae?" asked Sir Ander.

"Prince-Abbot of this abbey during the war with the Pirate King and the subsequent descent into the Dark Time," said Father Jacob. "The Abbey of Saint Agnes was then known as the Abbey of Saint Castigan—Brother Barnaby's patron saint."

Brother Barnaby smiled and shifted the writing desk he was carrying to a more comfortable position. They had rounded the north corner of the wall. The front gate faced south, so they had a considerable way to walk before they reached it.

"The reason you sent for me was something you found in the prince-abbot's journals, or so I'm guessing," said Father Jacob.

"Yes, Father. The journals were written in the old Church language, Rosaelig. I couldn't read a lot of it. But one word kept appearing over and over—a name, as if this prince-abbot were writing about this person."

"And this name was—"

"Dennis, Father."

"Dennis!" Sir Ander exclaimed, taken aback. "You don't mean . . . *Saint* Dennis?"

"Of course, he does," said Father Jacob. His tone was cool, but his eyes gleamed with suppressed excitement. "We have long known that after Saint Dennis left his home in Travis, he traveled to Rosia. We always wondered where he went. It makes sense that he would have come here to this reclusive place to pursue his studies of magic in solitude."

"I found another word I could read, Father. A word that wasn't written in Rosaelig and was easy to spot, because the writer consistently underlined it. I was rocked back on my heels so to speak when I saw this word, Father. I went all over gooseflesh. Here." Albert reached into his coat and brought out a small piece of paper. "I was so struck by it that I used my magic to lift the word off the paper and set it down on another sheet. I dared not write it in the letter."

He opened the paper and held it out. Sir Ander and Father Jacob and Brother Barnaby gathered around, gazing down at the word that was written in a neat and precise hand and, as Albert had said, had been underlined.

Contramagic.

Sir Ander looked at the word, then looked at Father Jacob. The knight's expression was dark. Brother Barnaby looked at the word and involuntarily moved back a step and raised his hand to ward off evil.

"'Contramagic.'" Father Jacob read the word in a murmur, scarcely heard. "Yes, it was wise you did not write this down, Master Albert. You could be tried for heresy."

He drew in a deep breath, then let it slowly sigh out. "I must see this journal, Albert."

"I wish you could, Father," said Albert in an unhappy tone. "At the moment that's not possible. The journal disappeared."

"What do you mean 'disappeared?'" Father Jacob asked sharply. "Was it lost in the attack? Destroyed?"

"No, Father. The journal wasn't in the abbey when it was attacked. The theft occurred long before the attack, the day after I sent the letter to you. I was alarmed by what I had found. If anyone knew I was reading about such forbidden knowledge I would be arrested. I removed the journal from the library to my yacht. I asked permission of the abbess first, of course. I told her and I told Brother Paul that I was interested in the abbey's history, about Saint Dennis and the fact that he'd spent time here ..."

Father Jacob frowned and shook his head. "That was a mistake, Albert."

"I did *not* tell anyone about this ... word, Father!" Albert looked haggard. "I've been terrified to even think it, much less speak it!"

"You mentioned nothing about contramagic," Father Jacob said, thoughtful. "Only Saint Dennis. What did the abbess say?"

"She had worries enough of her own and wasn't the least bit interested in Saint Dennis. She readily gave me permission to study the journal, provided that I returned the volume when I was finished."

"Brother Paul?"

"He said only that my time in this world would be better spent in doing good works than in reading about them. I translated part of the journal that day, then my eyes gave out and I needed a break. I had found a trout stream not far from here and I decided to go catch my dinner. I left the door to my room key-locked and magic-locked *and* magic-sealed and a protective spell on the journals. When I came back, the lock on the door had not been tampered with. The magic-lock had not been broken. The magic seal remained intact. The journal was gone."

Father Jacob frowned. "If it were any other crafter, I would say you had been careless in your spell-casting. But I know your work, Albert, and I know you. You are one of the best. Obviously it was stolen."

Albert gave a sigh of relief. "I am glad you trust me, Father. I was afraid you would think I had been negligent."

"But who would steal it?" Sir Ander demanded. "The nuns? This Brother Paul? They were the only people around. Why would they steal a book that had been in their own library for centuries?"

"Because they didn't know it was there," said Father Jacob. "Because someone knew or suspected that the blessed Saint Dennis was here seeking forbidden knowledge."

Brother Barnaby was distressed. "You cannot believe Saint Dennis was a heretic, Father."

"Of course, not. He was seeking the truth. And knowledge should not be forbidden, Brother," said Father Jacob, his brows coming together, his fist clenching. "No grand bishop, no king, no authority in the world has the right to dictate what we think, to prevent us from studying, from learning, from discovering!"

Brother Barnaby shrank back, dismayed by the priest's passion. Sir Ander drew him to one side.

"You touched a sore spot, Brother. I'm sorry. I should have warned you."

"He's very angry with me, I fear," said Brother Barnaby unhappily.

"Not with you, Brother," Sir Ander sighed and repeated quietly, "Not with you."

Father Jacob had lapsed into deep thought, his brow furrowed, his head bowed, his hands clasped behind his back. When Albert started to speak to him, Sir Ander shook his head, warning him to keep silent. Father Jacob walked on, preoccupied, absorbed, until at last they arrived at the broken remains of the gates of the Abbey of Saint Agnes.

Father Jacob raised his eyes at last. He looked at the twin spires, pointing to Heaven.

"God, grant us courage. What happened here at the Abbey of Saint Agnes could forever change our world."

Chapter Sixteen

In the places where God's voice cannot be heard, his fallen children, cast from Heaven, have found refuge. They seek forever to destroy that which God has created. Beware the quiet. Beware more the terrible voices.

—Anonymous

THE GATES THAT PIERCED THE TALL GRAY GRANITE WALL encircling the abbey compound were made of oak studded with bronze rosettes and banded with iron. The gates were extremely heavy, their hinges rusted. The nuns would not have been able to open them and, fondly believing themselves safe from any enemy, they had never closed them.

"Not that the gates would have stopped the assault," Albert added bitterly. "Their attackers came out of the Breath, flew over the walls."

"Demons on giant bats," Sir Ander said, shaking his head. "We read the account of that poor girl."

"Yes," said Albert in subdued tones, "Brother Paul told me what she said."

"You did not see her?"

"I helped carry her to the infirmary, but she was unconscious. I have not spoken to her since she woke up. Brother Paul says she needs rest and quiet."

"I would like to interview her," said Father Jacob. "I want to hear her account in her own words."

"She is in the infirmary, Father," said Albert. "One of the few buildings that was not extensively damaged. Brother Paul has been nursing her. She's only sixteen. As for demons attacking the abbey . . . After you've seen the horror for yourself . . ." Albert sighed and shrugged. "I believe it. No human could be so depraved."

"You'd be surprised," said Father Jacob, exchanging glances with Sir Ander.

"The writings of the Saints speak of angels and their evil counterparts," said Brother Barnaby and he added quietly, almost to himself, "I saw paintings depicting demons on the walls of the Grand Bishop's Palace."

"I will hear her and judge for myself," said Father Jacob brusquely.

The shadow of the dragon, still circling overhead, had been expanding as the dragon flew lower and lower. The dragon was so low now that he had to be careful not to brush one of the cathedral's spires with his wing tips.

"I believe Master of the Flight, Sergeant Hroalfrig, would like a chance to meet you, Father," said Albert, as the dragon's scaled belly passed overhead.

"Of course," said Father Jacob. He rubbed his hands. "I would like nothing better."

Sir Ander shot Brother Barnaby a warning glance. The monk gave a slight nod in response. When Father Jacob had been a University student in Freya, his area of study was dragon magic, with particular emphasis on a dragon's innate ability to deconstruct human-crafted magical constructs. This ability was the reason dragons had once been highly valued by the militaries of all the major powers. A dragon attacking a ship could use his breath to cause the magic of the constructs in the hull to break apart. A dragon could not erase the magic, but he could do serious damage.

Father Jacob had become so interested in his studies, he had expanded them to include dragon lore, dragon culture, and dragon history. If his life had not taken the near-disastrous turn that had caused him to flee Freya, he might have become one of the world's foremost experts on the subject.

Thus, whenever Father Jacob encountered a dragon, he had a most unfortunate tendency to completely forget the task at hand. He would engage the dragon in endless conversation, delving into the dragon's family history, find out where and how the dragon lived, and so forth. One of Brother Barnaby's tasks was to remind Father Jacob of his duty without hurting the feelings of the dragon.

This was the first dragon Father Jacob had met in some time. The great dragon families of Rosia had served proudly in the Dragon Brigade for over two centuries and they had been deeply angered and offended when King Alaric had disbanded the Dragon Brigade. Relations between the noble dragon families and the Crown had grown strained. Dragons no longer attended the royal court, but kept to their estates in the mountains.

Hroalfrig made a lopsided and decidedly ungraceful touchdown. The elderly dragon shook himself, lifted his head, folded his wings against his flanks, and advanced, with a slight limp in his right leg, to greet the newcomers.

"Master of the Flight, Sergeant Hroalfrig," said Albert, introducing them. "Father Jacob Northrop, Sir Ander Martel, and Brother Barnaby."

The dragon's head reared high over the abbey walls. The towers were about one hundred fifty feet in height. The dragon could have looked into the windows about a third of the way up with ease. He had landed on his heavier and more muscular rear legs, but he walked on all four. Father Jacob noted the beast's stubby mane, his short snout, and thick neck and knew him to be a dragon of the lower class. Dragons of the noble families had long manes, slender and graceful necks, and elongated, elegant snouts.

Hroalfrig took care to keep a polite distance from the humans, not wanting to risk accidentally stepping on them. He gravely inclined his head in greeting to each in turn.

"Honored, Father, honored, Sir Knight," said Hroalfrig in a deep voice. "Honored, Brother."

Dragons had long ago learned human speech, though it came more easily to some than to others. Humans had never been able to speak the language of dragons. The human throat and tongue were not capable of forming the words. Some, such as Father Jacob, had learned to understand it.

"Master of the Flight Hroalfrig served with the Dragon Brigade, Quartermaster Corp," said Albert.

"Retired," said Hroalfrig, adding in gruff tones with a growl, "Forcibly."

Hroalfrig was apparently a dragon of few words.

"I heard about the disbanding of the Brigade," said Father Jacob. "A serious mistake. I wrote most strongly to His Majesty to protest."

"Thankee, Father," said Hroalfrig, obviously pleased. "Call me Hroal and my brother Droal."

Brother Barnaby attempted at this moment to draw Father Jacob away from the conversation, but the monk's attempt was foiled by his own ally. Sir Ander was now regarding the dragon with interest.

"You served in the Dragon Brigade. Perhaps you knew my godson, Lord Captain Stephano de Guichen."

"My commander, m'lord. Good man," said Hroal. The dragon flicked a wing in salute.

"How were you wounded?" Sir Ander asked.

"Siege of Royal Sail," Hroal replied. "Barrel gunpowder. Explosion. Too close."

"Did you fly in that battle?"

"Never flew, m'lord. Would have liked to. Not my job. Hunting. Meat. Lots of it. Keep 'em fed."

"An army of dragons flies on its belly," said Sir Ander. "So you were at the Siege of the Royal Sail. Captain de Guichen lost his dragon in that battle. I have often wondered—"

Brother Barnaby was now forced to enter the fray. He

fixed Sir Ander with a reproachful gaze, indicative of his
disappointment. "I am sorry to interrupt, Sir Ander, but I
fear you and Father Jacob are keeping Master of the Flight
Hroalfrig from his duties."

"That is true. Forgive me, Sergeant," said Sir Ander. "I
forgot myself in the pleasure of our talk. I will let you return
to the skies. I hope we have a chance to speak again."

"And I would very much like to speak to you, Sergeant
Hroal," Father Jacob said. "To you *and* your brother. Later
this afternoon, if that is convenient. I would like to hear
your account of this tragic event."

The dragon's eyes flickered. He gazed at the priest a moment, then gave a brief nod of his head.

"Honored, gentlemen, all," said the dragon, and he again
flicked his wing in salute.

Mindful of his bulky body and long tail, Hroal politely
waited until the humans had moved a safe distance away,
then he turned ponderously and hobbled back across the
field. He lifted his wings and leaped off his back legs to "gain
air" as the dragons put it. Everyone on the ground could hear
the dragon's grunt of pain and see him wince before Hroal
was once more airborne.

"He's tough, that one," said Albert. "He's been on duty
all night, but he'd fall out of the sky before he'd admit he
was tired. His brother, Droal, will be along soon to relieve
him. You won't be able to tell them apart."

Albert cast a worried glance at Father Jacob. "As I said,
Father, the two dragons are doing an excellent job. They
came when they saw the smoke—"

"Don't be concerned, Albert," said Father Jacob. "I won't
offend them. I just want to ask them a few questions."

The morning sun was bright, too bright, making the
shadows seem sharp-edged, deep and dark. The chill winds
blowing out of the Breath glanced off the surrounding cliffs
and struck at them from unexpected directions. Sir Ander,
in his dress uniform, wished he'd thought to add his fur-
lined cape. Brother Barnaby stood with his back and shoul-

ders hunched against the wind. Master Albert had to hold onto his hat. These three stood in front of the gates, watching Father Jacob, whose black cassock billowed and flapped, as he made an inspection of the gate and the ground surrounding the entrance.

"Too rocky to tell much, but, as Albert says, the attackers did not come this way. We will proceed inside."

He clasped his hands behind his back and strode through the gates, his sharp-eyed gaze going from the posts to the hinges to the walls, to the grounds. The others followed more slowly, reluctant to enter.

"It's like walking through the gates of Hell," Albert said, his voice muffled by the handkerchief he was holding over his nose and mouth.

Father Jacob turned back to regard them with impatience. "You're dawdling. Albert, please go tell Brother Paul we are here and ask him when would be a good time to interview his patient. Sir Ander, Brother Barnaby, I need you both with me."

The great cathedral with its twin spires, each topped by an ornate cupola, towered above them. The spires were known for their red-orange stained glass windows. When lit from behind, the windows glowed with flame that could be seen even through the thick mists of the Breath. The stained glass windows were gone, the leaded glass panes smashed. Father Jacob stared at the destruction for a long time, then turned away, his expression thoughtful, somber.

The towers framed a central bell tower, smaller than the other two, topped by a dome. The church bell might have summoned help if there had been any ships passing in the night, but, according to Albert, the bell had been silent. Death had come upon the nuns too swiftly for them to call for help.

The bell tower also featured an enormous clock, said to be the largest in the world. The clock chimed the hour and the half hour; its distinctive music, known as the Chimes of Saint Castigan, was mimicked by other clocks throughout

the world. According to Albert, the clock had been silent
since that night.

Albert hurried off to find Brother Paul, heading for the
infirmary, which was about a half mile from the cathedral,
close to the dortoir where the nuns had lived.

Father Jacob and his companions crossed a paved courtyard that surrounded the cathedral. Beyond the courtyard
lay ornamental gardens that once must have been beautiful;
with marble fountains, statues of saints, clipped hedges,
shade trees, and broad swards of green grass. These gardens
had been a marvel, astonishing all who saw them, completely out of place with the abbey's wild surroundings.

The monks of Saint Castigan had discovered early in
their occupation of this rugged land that little would grow
in the rocky soil. What did grow was stunted by the wind.
The monks shipped in immense quantities of rich, black
dirt, hauling it to the abbey by the barge load. They worked
for years developing and designing their gardens. The high
walls had protected the roses and flowering trees and grass
from the wind, and the plants had flourished. Father Jacob
did not go immediately to the cathedral. He turned his steps
toward the gardens.

Brother Barnaby cast Sir Ander an interrogative glance.
Sir Ander shook his head in reply. Who knew why Father
Jacob did anything? Sir Ander began to think he should
have accepted that handkerchief. He had smelled the stench
of death on the fields of battle, but this was far worse.
Brother Barnaby held his handkerchief over his face. Father Jacob had forgotten his entirely. Brother Barnaby later
found it lying on the ground.

The practical nuns had taken over the gardens, digging
up the rosebushes and planting vegetables and herbs. Much
of the vast gardens had been left unattended and were now
overgrown by grass and weeds.

The gardens had been destroyed, the dirt churned up,
new plants and seedlings trampled. Large divots of sod had

been gouged out of the ground. All of the statues had been pulled down, smashed, and lay in ruins.

"Senseless, wanton destruction," said Sir Ander.

"On the contrary, the destruction was far from wanton," said Father Jacob. He was down on his hands and knees on the ground, studying what looked and smelled like a pile of manure. He rose to his feet, dusting his hands, and glanced around. "This was deliberate savagery."

"Please take a sample, Brother Barnaby." Father Jacob added, indicating the manure. "I want to study it further. Be careful not to touch it."

Brother Barnaby had been gazing around in grief-stricken awe. He looked startled at the request, but he hastened to obey. Placing the writing desk on the ground, he opened it, removed one of several small glass vials and, using a wooden spatula, gingerly scooped a small portion of the manure into the vial and stopped it up with cork, then put it back into the writing desk.

Father Jacob's next request was for a measuring tape such as tailors used. Brother Barnaby supplied the tape, retrieving it from the desk. The priest measured the pile of manure, taking care to keep from soiling his hands. Sir Ander watched with rising impatience until he could contain himself no longer.

"A hundred women are dead! Why are you wasting time on a pile of sheep droppings!" he said angrily.

"No sheep dropped *that*," said Father Jacob. "Unless I am much mistaken, it is bat guano."

Sir Ander stared. His jaw sagged. "Bat guano! You're not serious!"

"I am, I assure you, my friend," said Father Jacob. "Deadly serious. Look around. You will see more of these piles. And where are the sheep? Here, I'll show you."

Father Jacob walked off a short distance and picked up a hunk of wool stained with blood. The skin and flesh were still attached. "The sheep were torn apart, probably devoured."

"But how is that possible?" Sir Ander demanded. "To carry off a full-grown sheep, a bat would have to be the size of a horse . . ." His voice trailed away.

" 'Demons with glowing eyes of fire riding gigantic bats,'" said Father Jacob, repeating what he had read in Brother Paul's report. "This proves the young nun is *not* crazy. She reported exactly what she saw."

" 'And the Gates of Hell will open and Aertheum the Fallen will send forth his evil legions,'" Brother Barnaby quoted.

"Evil legions . . ." Father Jacob shook his head. "I need to interview that young woman. What can be keeping Albert? Well, we have learned all we can here. Let us move on to the cathedral and the grounds."

They left the gardens and walked across the courtyard. Sir Ander had a great many questions, but he dared not ask them. He had been with Father Jacob so long he knew the signs. When the priest walked slowly, his head bowed and his hands clasped behind him, he was a fox hound running round and round, trying to find the scent. When, as now, he walked briskly, his head up, his cassock flapping about his ankles, his eyes glinting, he had picked up the scent and was on the trail.

As they approached the cathedral, Sir Ander looked curiously at the paved area immediately in front of the entrance. He wondered why the paving stones here were black, when the rest of the courtyard was white. And then he realized, the hair prickling on the back of his neck, that the stones were not black in color. They were stained black. Black with blood. And as he drew nearer, he saw lumps lying scattered about.

Not much left to bury, Albert had said.

Lumps of flesh, parts of bodies.

Sir Ander was shocked to feel himself grow queasy. He sought the shelter of the shaded portico and leaned against a column until he felt better. He had seen the grass of battlefields red with blood, seen men disemboweled, heads severed. This was worse. Men went to war for a reason. Maybe not a good reason, but still a reason. This was butchery—horrible, senseless.

If he had been so affected, he wondered suddenly what Brother Barnaby must be feeling. Sir Ander went in search of the young monk and found him seated on one of the stairs leading into the cathedral, the writing desk on his lap, his pen in his hand, hard at work. He'd managed to sit on a portion of the stairs that was not stained with blood. Father Jacob was off on his own, walking slowly around the north side of the cathedral, his gaze fixed intently on the ground.

Sir Ander sat down beside him. "Are you all right?"

Brother Barnaby sighed softly and kept writing.

"Well, I'm not," said Sir Ander. "I want to run out that gate and keep running."

Brother Barnaby looked up. "Father Jacob requires me to make notes. I don't mind, sir. Really. I'd rather be busy."

He went back to his work.

Sir Ander stood up and walked off. He met the priest coming around the corner of the cathedral.

"A ghastly scene," Father Jacob said.

Sir Ander nodded. He did not feel himself capable of speaking.

"The attack occurred at the conclusion of Midnight Prayers. You noticed, of course, the time on the clock when it stopped working."

Sir Ander had *not* noticed, but he nodded again anyway.

"The nuns were just coming out of the sanctuary after prayer service when they were attacked. The assailants knew what they were doing," Father Jacob added, his tone grim. "They waited to strike until most of the nuns were in the open. The yard is trampled, churned, soaked in blood. Death came at them from the sky. They looked up to see gigantic bats swooping down on them. I doubt if they knew what was happening. The bats were merciless. They tore their victims apart with sharp, rending claws, ripping their flesh from their bones while the poor women were still alive, and then devouring them."

"For God's sake, why?" Sir Ander asked angrily. "Why kill with such cruelty? I thought at first the foes might be Freyan soldiers, but why would Freyans attack an isolated abbey and slaughter every living being inside it? And riding giant bats? Doesn't make sense. None of this makes sense!"

"This atrocity was *not* committed by Freyans or the soldiers of any other nation," said Father Jacob with finality. "The assault on the women was an act of hatred, a hatred so deep we cannot even comprehend it."

"The fiends came simply to murder these nuns?"

"Interestingly enough, they did not come to kill. They came for something else. The murders were an afterthought, a crime of opportunity. I want you to look at something."

Father Jacob squatted down. Sir Ander ran a trembling hand over his face, wiping the chill sweat from his brow. Drawing in a deep breath, he knelt down beside the priest.

"See this. And this."

Sir Ander bent closer. "Footprints!"

"Not footprints," said Father Jacob.

"No, you're right. Paw prints!" Sir Ander stared, amazed. "Like the paws of a bear!"

"Similar," said Father Jacob. "But a bear walks on all fours. Whoever made these walked upright on two legs like a man. And a bear has five toes ending in claws. Note this has four toes ending in claws in front and one larger claw in back. See how deeply that back claw gouged into the ground. Remind you of something?"

"A spur on a riding boot . . ." said Sir Ander doubtfully.

"Exactly what I was thinking," said Father Jacob. "These prints were left by the attackers. They are all over the ground. All heading in that direction." Father Jacob gestured to the cathedral. "The bats had riders."

"Men with clawed feet. You mean . . . demons . . ." Sir Ander was aghast.

"Just like the paintings by the old masters that so impressed Brother Barnaby. Judging from the evidence, it would seem the riders turned their bats loose to feed, while they entered the cathedral."

"The inhuman savage beasts killed the nuns and then went to the cathedral to destroy it like they destroyed everything else." Sir Ander paused, then said in a low voice. "These *were* demons, Father. Bent on the destruction of all things holy!"

"Except they didn't destroy the cathedral," Father Jacob pointed out.

Sir Ander considered this. "That's true. They set fire to the dortoir and some of the outbuildings. Why leave the cathedral standing?"

Father Jacob rose to his feet, absent-mindedly wiping his dirty and bloody hands on his cassock.

"Isn't the reason obvious?"

"Not to me," said Sir Ander irritably.

Father Jacob smiled and walked off, shouting for Brother Barnaby to draw a diagram of the paw print.

Sir Ander removed his helm, let the wind cool the sweat running down his face. None of this made sense to him. He was glad it made some kind of sense to Father Jacob. The knight took a moment before entering the cathedral to silently pray, asking God for strength and for wisdom, then he joined Father Jacob in the sanctuary.

The scene was gruesome. The floors and walls were covered in blood. The same paw prints that they had seen outside were all over the floor, only these were outlined in the blood. Statues of saints had been destroyed, the altar hacked to pieces, tapestries shredded, stained glass windows broken. Yet, as Father Jacob had said, the demons had left the cathedral standing.

Brother Barnaby entered some time later. He looked about the sanctuary in mute grief and dismay, then sat down in a pew to take notes as Father Jacob dictated.

"The fact that the bodies were consumed accounts for the absence of corpses," Father Jacob was saying. "From the smears of blood on the floor, it appears that the nuns who had remained inside the sanctuary were attacked by the riders, probably tortured for information. The riders then dragged the women outside and fed them to the bats."

Brother Barnaby blinked his eyes rapidly to try to stop the flow of tears, but to no avail. A drop fell onto the page, smearing the ink. He hastily wiped his eyes with his sleeve. Father Jacob was not paying attention. He was staring intently at a marble column, running his hand up and down the marble, still dictating.

"—burned the dortoir, but did not set fire to the cathedral—"

Sir Ander rested his hand on Brother Barnaby's shoulder, offering quiet comfort. Brother Barnaby sat still for a moment, then he put away his pen, laid down the writing desk, rose to his feet and left the sanctuary.

Father Jacob stood with his head tilted back, staring up at the marble column, following its graceful lines to the high, vaulted ceiling.

"Brother Barnaby," said Father Jacob, "come over here. I want you to make a diagram—"

"Brother Barnaby left," said Sir Ander.

"Oh?" Father Jacob glanced vaguely around. "Where did he go?"

"I don't know." Sir Ander snapped the words. "He's upset, Father. This has been terrible for him."

Father Jacob was too absorbed in his work to take notice. "You come look at this."

Sir Ander heaved a sigh and stalked over.

Father Jacob pointed to the column. "What do you make of that?"

The column with its fluted shaft was typical of churches of that period. What wasn't typical was that in places, the ridges and grooves of the fluting had been destroyed. He could see blast marks on the column, like a castle wall struck by cannon fire.

Father Jacob passed his hand over the column. "Let us

take a look at the magical constructs embedded in the stone. See what they tell us. A castle wall hit by cannon fire would still retain traces of the magic that had strengthened the walls."

Sir Ander hoped he would see the faint blue glow of magic. He hoped Father Jacob was wrong. Unfortunately, the priest was right.

"No blue light. No magic. *This* is why the grand bishop sent for you," said Sir Ander. "The magical constructs have been erased."

"Remember the nun who survived said that 'the demons threw balls of green fire and cast beams of green light.'"

Sir Ander looked down the long double rows of columns, probably twenty-five or more on each side.

"Without the magic, the columns will be too weak to support the roof. The cathedral is liable to fall down around our ears. So why are we standing here discussing it?" Sir Ander demanded. "Why aren't we standing *outside* discussing it? Where it's safe?"

"We're in no danger," said Father Jacob complacently. "At least not for the moment. Only a few of the columns I've studied were hit with the green fire. The assailants did not want to destroy the cathedral until they had found what they came for. Instead, they weakened the columns. The magic will continue to fail and, in a month or two, the cathedral will come crashing down."

"When it would be filled with masons and crafters and priests and others working to repair it," said Sir Ander grimly. "They would all be killed."

"I fear so," said Father Jacob and he added in an undertone, "Demonically clever."

Sir Ander grunted. "So turning the cathedral into a death trap was the reason they didn't destroy it during the attack."

"No, I believe that was an afterthought," said Father Jacob. "Another crime of opportunity. They left the cathedral standing because of the library."

Sir Ander blinked. "The library?"

"Well, of course," said Father Jacob. "That was the real reason they came. The library is inside the cathedral. The attackers could not destroy the cathedral because they needed to search the library."

"Demons came for the library? But why?"

"Ah, that is the question. I need to ask Albert—" Father Jacob looked around impatiently. "Where *is* Albert? He has been gone far too long. You better go search for him. I will investigate the library—"

They were both stopped by the sight of Brother Barnaby entering the sanctuary. The monk carried a large wooden bucket filled with water and a bundle of rags.

"Are you finished with your work here, Father?" Brother Barnaby asked.

"Yes, Brother," said Father Jacob. "I am finished. What are you doing?"

"The sanctuary has been defiled, Father. With your permission, I will clean it."

He set the bucket on the floor, kilted up his robes, and knelt down on his hands and knees and began to mop up the blood. Father Jacob watched a moment, then he walked over to where the young monk was scrubbing the blood off the floor and wringing the soiled cloth in the bucket. The water was already stained red.

"You are my conscience, Brother Barnaby," Father Jacob said, rolling up the sleeves of his cassock. "I think that is why the blessed Saint Castigan sent you to me."

Brother Barnaby looked astonished at the thought that he could be anyone's conscience, much less Father Jacob's. He gave a self-deprecating smile and shook his head as he continued his sorrowful task.

"Sir Ander, return to the *Retribution* and fetch my sacred vestments," Father Jacob continued. "When we have finished the cleansing, I will say a mass for the dead."

He hiked up his cassock, got down on his hands and knees, and began scrubbing.

Sir Ander stood watching the priest and the monk working together to cleanse God's House, and he reflected on the fact that there were times—many times—when Father Jacob could be arrogant and insufferable, insensitive and demanding, stubborn and infuriating and so on and so forth. More than once, far from protecting Father Jacob, Sir Ander could have cheerfully throttled him.

And then there were times like this when Sir Ander saw the Father Jacob he had come to revere and admire, the brilliant, gifted Freyan crafter who had been offered fame and fortune if he would only renounce his faith; the priest who had risked his life and fled the land of his birth to remain true to his beliefs.

As Sir Ander left to fetch the vestments and see if he could find Albert, he again affirmed the vow he had taken when he had become the priest's Knight Protector.

"'If Death reaches out for Father Jacob,'" said Sir Ander, "'I will step in between.'"

He added quietly, "And the same holds true for Brother Barnaby!"

Chapter Seventeen

There are many paths to Heaven. The Martyr walks a dark path holding her faith like a candle that lights her way but also attracts those that hunt in the darkness. Some on that path would hide their candles until the evil has walked by, but the Martyr holds her faith dear, her candle bright, no matter the outcome.

—The writings of Saint Marie,
who was martyred three years later

"WHAT DO WE DO WITH THE WATER we used for cleaning, Father?" asked Brother Barnaby somberly, wringing a bloody cloth into a bucket. "We cannot simply dump it in the yard, as if it were waste."

"You are right, Brother. This water contains the blood of martyrs," said Father Jacob and he sat back on his heels to give the matter serious thought.

They had worked for over two hours, and the sanctuary was finally almost clean. Brother Barnaby had found additional buckets in the stable. He had placed the buckets filled with water red-tinged with the blood of the murdered nuns before the altar. Another bucket, this one covered with a white cloth, contained the gruesome remains recovered from the ground outside the cathedral. Father Jacob had attended to this heartbreaking task. As for the blood on the ground, the tears of the angels and the saints falling from Heaven would eventually wash it away.

"The first abbess is buried in the cathedral, Brother Barnaby," said Father Jacob. "Her tomb is in the catacombs beneath the cathedral. We will pour the water around the tomb. We will bury the remains in the abbey cemetery."

Brother Barnaby was content and went back to washing away the last vestige of blood. Father Jacob spent a few moments quietly observing the young monk. His expression was solemn, sorrowful, troubled.

"You must have questions for God, Brother," said Father Jacob abruptly. "Perhaps you find yourself doubting in His love and mercy?"

Brother Barnaby looked up from his task. "I *do* have questions, Father. With God's help, you and Sir Ander will find the answers."

"And with your help, Brother Barnaby," said Father Jacob. "Our triangle is equilateral."

Brother Barnaby smiled. "All I do is drive the wyverns, Father."

"There, you see? That's more than I can do," said Father Jacob. He rose to his feet, grimacing at the pain in his knees and back. He reflected that he had not scrubbed floors since he was a novice, some twenty years ago.

He remembered that time. He remembered that person—the man he had been. A young man with a dazzling gift for magic, Jacob had been proud and arrogant—a real bastard, he could now admit. He had always felt God's calling, but he had tried to ignore it. He had harangued and questioned, fought and bullied, tested God's patience every step of the way. He had turned his back on God, run to the edge of the precipice, stared into the blackness and had been ready to leap when he had felt God's hand gently drawing him back. He had been guided by the touch of God's hand ever since.

Father Jacob glanced about the sanctuary. "I will hold the service when Sir Ander returns. See if you can find some candles, Brother, though I have no idea where we will place them."

The beautiful golden-and-silver candlesticks that had graced the altar had been hit by the same ruinous green fire that had melted the stone. Father Jacob recalled what he had said to Sir Ander about the hatred that had driven these attackers to destroy what they could have stolen for gain. The candlesticks alone were easily worth fifty gold rosuns. Whoever attacked the abbey did not raid it out of greed. They came for something far more important than gold.

"I am going to the library," said Father Jacob. "Let me know if anyone finds Master Albert— Ah, speak of the man and here he is! Albert, where have you been? You have been gone for hours. I was growing worried. Now that you are here, when will I be able to speak to this nun who survived? I have a great many questions. It is more important now than ever that I talk to her . . ."

Albert stood in the door that led into the sanctuary. His face was flushed and he was breathing hard, so hard he had to wait a moment to catch his breath before he could respond.

"As to that, Father, I fear you will never be able to talk to her this side of Heaven. The woman is dead."

The echoes of his voice reverberated off the walls, sounding hollow in the empty chamber.

"Dead?" said Father Jacob, regarding Albert intently. "You said her injuries were not severe."

"The injuries to her body were not serious," said Master Albert with a sigh. "But those of the mind could not be cured, seemingly. She took her own life, Father. She threw herself off the cliff."

Brother Barnaby gave an exclamation of pity and grief.

Father Jacob was very thoughtful. With an abrupt gesture he motioned Albert to accompany him into a hallway.

"Tell me what happened," he said when he and Albert were alone.

"I went to find Brother Paul. When I reached the infirmary, the monk was in a terrible state. He said that his patient had fallen into an exhausted sleep. Weary himself from watching over her, he dozed off. When he woke, she was gone. He asked me to help him find her.

"Her trail was easy enough to follow. She had taken no care to hide it. We came across her tracks on the path leading up the cliff. They led to the edge of the cliff. No footprints led back. Brother Paul and I searched for her body on the rocks below—" He shook his head.

"Damn and blast it to Hell and back!" Father Jacob swore, causing Albert to stare at him in astonishment. "Poor child. May God grant her ease."

He sighed deeply, his brow furrowed. Whatever he was thinking, he did not share. "Show me the way to the library."

Albert escorted the priest through a door that opened into a narrow corridor leading to the other areas of the cathedral. They passed schoolrooms, the office of the abbess, a communal room where the nuns ate their meals, the kitchen, and eventually arrived at the library.

They had no need to open the door. It lay splintered on the floor. Father Jacob stepped over the shambles and paused to survey the damage. Shelves had been knocked down, their contents strewn about. The floor was covered, ankle-deep in some places, with papers and parchments and books.

"A real mess," Albert said unhappily. He started to right a bookshelf.

"Please, Albert, have I taught you nothing?" Father Jacob said sharply. "Don't touch anything. Go stand by the door and don't move. You told me that the library was well-organized. Church records in one place—"

"Over there, Father," said Albert, pointing.

Father Jacob waded through the piles of books and papers, careful to disturb as little as possible.

"To your right were the books on theology," Albert continued. "That bookcase, the one on the floor, held hymnals and sheet music."

"I see, yes."

Father Jacob took note of some of the titles of the books, then roamed on. One of the shelves was still standing, though all its contents had been pulled down and scattered about. He happened to come upon one of the few spots on the floor not carpeted with books or paper and saw what he had expected to see: bloody paw prints, the same that had left marks on the ground outside and tracked blood through the sanctuary.

Father Jacob carefully shifted a pile of books and found more paw prints. He straightened and looked around, but he was not looking at his surroundings. He was seeing, in his mind, the attack.

"The demons—we will call them that, for the time being—flew over the walls as the nuns were leaving the sanctuary. Probably they had been lying in ambush. They left the bats they were riding to kill the women outside and entered the sanctuary, where they tortured and murdered the women they found inside. Some of the demons remained behind to defile the cathedral and drag away the bodies, which they fed to their bats. The rest came here, to the library. The true reason for the attack. They spent their time searching . . ."

"Searching for what, Father?" Albert asked.

"The writings of the blessed Saint Dennis," Father Jacob said, sitting down on a toppled bookcase and gazing about. "The books mentioned in the prince-abbot's journal."

Albert gave a horrified gasp. "Are you saying, Father, that this . . . this terrible tragedy happened because of *me*? Because *I* found that journal? But I don't understand! If all the demons wanted was to search the library, why murder the nuns?"

"Hatred and rage, for one reason. But there is another. Picture this: two men stage a fight on a busy city street. A crowd gathers. While people are watching the fake fight, a third man picks their pockets."

Albert was bewildered. "I'm sorry, Father, I have no idea what you're talking about."

"The term is 'misdirection.' We are meant to focus our

attention on the murder of the nuns and not on the fact that the demons were truly here to search for the books written by the saint. Fortunately, the demons made two mistakes that led me to look in the right direction."

"Mistakes . . ." said Albert weakly.

"The first was the theft of the journal," Father Jacob went on. "The demons had to steal it, you see, because they needed clues as to where the prince-abbot might have hidden the work of the saint."

"But who stole it, Father? There were only the nuns and Brother Paul and myself —"

Father Jacob gave a wry smile. "Think about it. That makes one hundred and two people, not counting you, Alfred, and maybe more. The abbess might have mentioned the information in a report to the grand bishop, for example. Or she could have told any number of sisters over dinner, perhaps. They could have told any Trundlers who had stopped to seek refuge with the nuns. Brother Paul might have mentioned it to any sailors whose ships docked here. And so on."

"I don't think the nuns would have talked about it —"

"Ah, but you don't know for certain! As for the theft, you were gone from your yacht at least an hour, probably longer. Trout fishing is a leisurely sport. There are unscrupulous crafters who make their living by thieving. A talented thief could have entered the yacht, removed the magical spells, stolen the journal, replaced the spells . . ."

"It's all my fault, then." Albert stood with his arms crossed, leaning back dejectedly against the wall. Father Jacob stood up and made his way back through the mess, stepping carefully over the piles of books, trying not to dislodge anything.

"Do not take the blame upon yourself, my friend," said Father Jacob gently. "All you did was find a journal."

"I know what you say makes sense, Father," said Albert. "Still, I can't help but wish my eyes had been gouged out before I ever saw that thing. What do demons want with writings of the saints?"

" 'Know thy enemy,' says the wise man," said Father Jacob. "You mentioned Saint Dennis and that was enough to pique someone's interest. The thieves broke in, read the journal, and found that one single word: *contramagic.* That was why they stole it."

"I know it is forbidden by the Church to even speak that word, Father, but can you tell me why demons would be interested in it?"

"Because they are using contra magic, Albert. The green light that destroys magic." Father Jacob cast Albert a rueful glance. "You are aware, my friend, that no hint of this must get out. I may have to place you under Seal."

"Meaning you take me to the Arcanum and hold me there so I won't tell anyone else what I've seen." Albert gave the ghost of a smile. "I might enjoy the rest. I need to know the truth, Father. I know you say I shouldn't, but I do feel responsible—"

"If it will ease your mind, I will tell you what I know. Especially," Father Jacob added with a sigh, "since there may soon come a time when the Church can no longer hide it. After much study, I reached the conclusion that *contramagic* had been used to disable the cutter. The sailors spoke of seeing green light, you remember."

"My God!" Albert exclaimed, staggered.

"The bishop refused to believe me or even admit such magic existed. He very nearly had me arrested for even thinking such an idea. Montagne believes me now. He has no choice. And now here we have the abbey's lone survivor talking of the demons hurling balls of green fire—"

"But she was mad," Albert protested feebly.

"She was *not* mad," said Father Jacob sternly. "She was their second mistake. They let her live. They wanted a survivor to talk about demons and giant bats, to make us so terrified of Hell's legions that their raid on the library would go unnoticed. But she said something that gave them away. When I arrived and asked to talk to her, they feared what she might tell me. She had to die."

"But she killed herself!"

"We are meant to think she killed herself."

"But what about Brother Paul? He was with her?"

"He had fallen asleep. They waited for their chance."

Albert grew pale. "That means they are out there, watching us . . ."

"I think it likely. Especially since they did not find what they came for."

"How do you know, Father?"

"They would have burned the cathedral, destroyed all the evidence. As it is, they need to come back to continue the search. The prince-abbot risked his life to save these books. He would have hidden them with care. The books of Saint Dennis will not be easy to find."

"You don't believe the attackers were demons from Hell, do you, Father," said Albert.

"I think it highly unlikely Aertheum the Fallen would be interested in the writings of a saint," said Father Jacob.

"I saw the paw prints," said Albert. "The claw marks left by the fiends that ripped those poor women apart. I think you are wrong, Father."

Father Jacob gazed somberly out a broken window. He didn't see bloodstained grass or fire-torched trees or the shadow of the dragon, passing over the bleak land. He saw the future, and he sighed deeply.

"I almost hope I am wrong, my friend. I think I would rather face the immortal hordes of Aertheum the Fallen than the terrible foes who flew over these walls that tragic night . . ."

———◆———

Sir Ander did not hurry his errand to the *Retribution*. He walked slowly, taking his time, trying to come to grips with the tragic sights he had witnessed. In the skies above, the faithful Hroal was still on patrol. Or perhaps that dragon was Droal, his brother. Sir Ander waved, and the dragon dipped a wing in return.

When Sir Ander finally reached the yacht, he looked out into the Breath and saw the balloon and sails of a naval cutter. Had the navy been sent to assist in the investigation? If so, Father Jacob would be furious.

The cutter drifted slowly among the light mists, sailing close enough to be able to keep watch on the shoreline, but apparently not intending to dock.

The cutter must be on routine patrol duty, searching for pirates who liked to hide in secluded coves and inlets. The grand bishop might have hinted that the navy pay more attention to this section of coastline, but he would not have told them to start looking for demons riding giant bats! No one is more superstitious than a sailor and no one more talkative when they go ashore. The grand bishop would keep the details of this attack secret as long as possible.

Father Jacob had both key-locked and magic-locked the yacht door. The key Sir Ander used to unlock the door was inscribed with a magical sigil that broke the spell. He entered the yacht and first checked to make certain all his weapons were cleaned and loaded. He then unlocked and opened a cabinet hidden beneath one of the beds, took out a swivel gun, and, climbing up to the yacht's roof, mounted it on top.

He then went to the chest where Father Jacob kept his vestments. Drawing out the alb, the stole, and the chasuble, Sir Ander held the sacred garments, smoothing the fine fabric with his hand and thinking of the battle that he, like Father Jacob, saw coming.

On his way back to the cathedral, Sir Ander paused to scan the gray cliffs and jagged rock formations. A grim landscape, bleak and desolate. The demons could hide an entire army among those crags, he thought, and he was thankful the dragons were keeping watch from the skies. Hroal and Droal might be well past their prime, but dragon eyesight was still much keener than that of humans—even the eyesight of elderly dragons. The brothers would have been quick to notice any sign of enemy movement.

Sir Ander shifted his head to look once more into the vastness of the Breath with its swirling mists. Nothing much to be done to stop an enemy that came from the mists. He was glad to have the cutter with its cannons out there. He hoped it stayed around.

He returned to the cathedral and found the sanctuary cleansed of blood. Candles glowed on the altar. Brother Barnaby was carrying the last few buckets containing the blood of the martyrs. Another monk was assisting him in this sorrowful task.

Brother Barnaby smiled to see Sir Ander, took the priestly vestments, and went to find Father Jacob. Barnaby made introductions before he left.

"Sir Ander, this is Brother Paul of the Holy Order of Saint Ignatius."

"I am pleased to meet a Knight Protector," said Brother Paul, straightening from stooping over the buckets and turning to face Sir Ander. "God honors your selfless service."

"Thank you, Father—" Sir Ander began.

"I prefer to be known simply as 'Brother Paul,'" said the monk, with a grave smile. "I joined the Order of Saint Ignatius several years ago and have since dedicated my life to his service."

Brother Paul was not ill-favored, but he was certainly unusual in appearance. So much so that Sir Ander found himself staring. Brother Paul was slim, of about average height with a wiry build. What struck Sir Ander was the monk's excessively pale skin, almost alabaster. His hair, cut in the tonsure, was dark black and curly. His face was smooth. He had no facial hair. He was not too young to grow a beard. He looked to be at least thirty-five. Sir Ander could not tell the color of the monk's eyes; they were hidden behind spectacles made of dark glass.

"You find these curious," Brother Paul said, touching his spectacles.

"I didn't mean to be rude," said Sir Ander, flustered.

"I've seen spectacles before, but never ones made of dark glass."

"No need to apologize. They are specially made for me. My eyesight is weak. I am subject to headaches, and I find these help."

Sir Ander muttered something about that being good, then asked, "Can I do anything to assist you?"

"Our sad task is finished," said Brother Paul. His voice was deep, with a musical tone that had a pleasant, soothing quality. He staggered at that moment, and almost fell.

"Sit down, Brother," said Sir Ander. "You seem weary to the point of dropping."

"I have slept little in all the nights since the attack," said Brother Paul in an apologetic tone.

"No one could blame you," said Sir Ander, assisting the monk to a pew.

He sat beside the monk, noting as he did so that the hem of his robes was covered in mud and stained with blood.

"You were nursing that young woman who survived," said Sir Ander. "I heard she died."

"Thanks be to God, she is at peace," said Brother Paul somberly. "The demons did not rend her flesh, but they sank their claws into her soul and dragged her down into Hell's pit. I pray for God's love and mercy for her tormented soul."

"Then you believe Hell's legions were responsible for this attack?" Sir Ander asked.

"I do not have the slightest doubt, sir!" Brother Paul seemed astonished at the idea that anyone could think otherwise. He regarded Sir Ander sternly. "You *do* believe in Hell, Sir Knight."

Sir Ander didn't know quite how to answer. He and Father Jacob had often held discussions regarding the nature of Hell and Heaven. Sir Ander didn't like the thought of a wrathful God who doomed souls to eternal torment.

"We are commanded *to* believe in Hell, sir," Brother Paul added in rebuking tones.

Sir Ander saw the road ahead littered with theological

caltrops and wisely reined in the conversation and switched subjects, asking questions about the grand organ whose pipes gleamed in the afternoon sunshine. Did it still work, did anyone play?

Brother Paul answered readily, and the uncomfortable moment passed. Astonished by the monk's fervor, Sir Ander made a mental note to tell Father Jacob.

There was no more talk of Hell, for Father Jacob, robed in his vestments, entered the sanctuary, accompanied by Brother Barnaby. Both made a reverence to the altar, then Father Jacob took his place before it. Master Albert joined Brother Paul in a pew in the front. Sir Ander retreated, finding a pew by himself in the back. He felt in need of solitude.

Father Jacob's voice resonated through the sanctuary.

"Eternal rest grant to them ..."

The sun shone through the broken glass. Sir Ander felt its warmth ease the chill that seemed to have struck to his heart. Outside, he could hear birdsong, making up for the lack of music, for the sister who had played the organ was dead. The song of the birds, accompanying the words of the mass, comforted Sir Ander. Simple souls, the birds gave no thought to Heaven or Hell. They sang for joy because the sun shone.

He brought his mind back to the service and was kneeling to pray when, to his immense astonishment, he caught sight of a man also seated at the very back, in a pew a few rows over. The man was short and nondescript. Dressed in a plainly made traveling cloak well-splashed with mud, he looked like a clerk on holiday. He was on his knees, his hands clasped, as Father Jacob prayed for the souls of the dead.

Sir Ander dared not interrupt the sacred sermon by calling attention to this stranger who had appeared seemingly out of nowhere. He cast a glance at Father Jacob, to see if he was aware of the stranger. If so, the priest gave no sign. Sir Ander wondered how the man had slipped past the dragon, who was apparently keeping such careful watch. The Knight Protector clapped his hand on his dragon pistol and kept his gaze fixed on the interloper. If the man noticed, he gave no indication. He sat listening to the service reverently.

The moment the service ended, Sir Ander bounded to his feet, crossed over to the pew, and seized hold of the man by the arm. He searched him for weapons and pulled an odd-looking gun from a leather holster. The man offered no resistance, but smiled placidly at the knight.

"Who are you, sir?" Sir Ander demanded. "What are you doing here?"

"Sir Ander Martel," said the man. "I am glad to see the Knight Protectors take their vows seriously. My commendations."

"I take my duty seriously, sir, as you will find out to your sorrow if you do not answer my questions," Sir Ander said grimly.

"His name is Dubois," said Father Jacob, walking down the aisle. "He is the bishop's agent, Sir Ander. One might say we are on the same side." He regarded Dubois with a slight smile and added, "Or one might not."

Sir Ander released Dubois reluctantly and handed back his weapon. Dubois tucked the gun into its holster.

"All of us are on the side of the angels," Dubois said gravely. He cast Father Jacob a keen glance. "I would very much appreciate a moment of your time, Father."

"I rather suspected you might," said Father Jacob wryly.

The two walked off toward a shadowy alcove. Seeing Sir Ander moving to accompany them, Dubois stopped and said politely, "You are not needed for the moment, Sir Ander. Your charge is safe with me."

"I am here to ensure the safety of you both," said Sir Ander gravely. "We have reason to believe that whoever committed these atrocities may still be in the area."

Dubois appeared rather disconcerted by this statement. He looked around uneasily, as though suspecting murderers hiding beneath the pews.

"My time is short," said Father Jacob irascibly. "As I am

certain your time is as well, Dubois." He glanced at the mud-stained cloak. "My guess is that you are hot on the trail of someone. Sir Henry Wallace, perhaps?"

Dubois gave a great start of astonishment. Then he smiled and twirled his hat in his hands. "You do like to have your little jests, don't you, Father? But since you bring up the topic yourself, you won't mind my asking if you have seen any signs that might lead you to think Henry Wallace had anything to do with this terrible tragedy?"

Father Jacob regarded Dubois with narrowed eyes. He did not immediately answer, but asked his own question.

"Do you have reason to think he does?"

Dubois gave a little cough. The two stood staring intently at one another.

Like a pair of duelists, Sir Ander thought.

"No," Father Jacob said at last. "I have not."

"Do you have any idea where Sir Henry Wallace might be?" Dubois asked.

"The last time I saw Henry Wallace was some twenty years ago. He was firing a gun at me at the time in an attempt to kill me. Needless to say, we do not keep in touch," Father Jacob answered gravely.

Dubois inclined his head, then put on his hat. "That is all I needed to know. I should warn you, Father, and you, Sir Ander, that I have reason to believe Sir Henry Wallace is in Rosia. You should be on your guard."

"Thank you for your concern, Dubois, but since I have nothing to do with the Royal Armory, I doubt if Wallace would be much interested in me."

Dubois again looked startled, then he wagged his finger. "Ah, Father Jacob, you are a caution. You will have your little jest. And now, I must be going. God be with you, gentlemen, and speed your holy work to find those who committed this unholy crime."

Dubois gave a bobbing bow and took his leave, looking more like a clerk than ever, Sir Ander thought, as he escorted him out of the cathedral. Sir Ander kept an eye on

Dubois until he exited the gate, where a wyvern-drawn carriage was waiting for him. The shadow of wings passed overhead. Hroal was also keeping an eye on Dubois.

He waited until the carriage had taken to the skies, then walked back inside the cathedral. He found Father Jacob standing with his head bent, deep in thought.

"You think Wallace is behind this, Father?" Sir Ander asked.

Father Jacob shook his head. "Henry Wallace may be many things and most of them bad, but he is first, last, and always a Freyan patriot. He has worked all his life to one end and that is for Freya to rule the seven continents. He has no motive. The slaughter of these poor women has nothing to do with politics."

Sir Ander shook his head. "Still, I don't like the fact that Wallace is in Rosia."

"The man is up to some mischief, you may be certain," said Father Jacob. "But let us leave Wallace to Dubois. We must lay to rest the blood of the martyrs."

* * *

Master Albert, Brother Barnaby, Father Jacob, and Sir Ander each picked up the buckets of bloodstained water and carried them to the back of the cathedral. Brother Paul led them to the entrance to the catacombs—a long row of stone stairs that had been cut into the ground, leading down to a wrought-iron gate.

Beyond the gate, the dead slept in silent darkness.

The gate was not locked and, though the hinges were rusted, it opened easily enough. Brother Paul brought two lanterns. Guided by their light, they entered the catacombs.

Dating back hundreds of years, the catacombs had likely been constructed at the same time as the abbey, built far below ground level. The men entered a long corridor with an arched ceiling made entirely of bricks. Magical constructs would have been placed on the bricks to keep the catacombs dry and preserve the structural integrity. When the magic constructs started to fade, crafter priests would have renewed them.

Many bodies, shrouded in white linen, had been placed in niches in the walls. Due to space considerations, only high-ranking members of the Church had been buried in tombs. During the Dark Time, the abbey had been abandoned and there had been no more burials. When the world emerged from the Dark Time, burial customs and practices had changed. The idea of placing bodies out in the open covered only by a shroud was considered distasteful. The Abbey of Saint Agnes, like many other churches, established a cemetery where the sisters were laid to rest. The abbesses were entombed in the cemetery's mausoleum.

The catacombs were not forgotten. Once a year, the abbess and the sisters entered to pay their respects to the dead in a reverent ceremony, saying prayers and placing flowers on the tomb of the first abbess.

The men walked single file in respectful silence through the narrow corridors. They found the abbess' tomb—a large and elaborately carved marble sarcophagus—in a large niche covered with dust and remnants of dead flowers. The effigy of a woman graced the top of the sarcophagus; her stone face seemed grave, sorrowful.

"She grieves," said Brother Barnaby softly.

Beyond, the corridor grew narrower. Dimly seen in the lantern light were the tombs that dated back to the time of the prince-abbot. The men placed the buckets on the floor, gathered around the tomb, and bowed their heads.

Father Jacob led them in prayer, then Brother Barnaby slowly and reverently lifted a bucket and poured the water stained with the blood of the martyrs onto the stone floor around the tomb. The red-stained water slid over the bricks that had been worn smooth by time and seeped down through the cracks. One by one, each man said a soft prayer, then poured the water around the tomb. Brother Barnaby placed the bucket carrying the remains on the altar.

Their sad task accomplished, the men stood a moment in

silence, broken by Brother Paul saying softly, "The martyrs shine with glory, safe in the arms of God."

Brother Paul turned to leave. Albert, carrying one of the lanterns, accompanied him. Sir Ander was about to go with the other two, when Father Jacob softly called his name. Turning, Sir Ander saw the priest standing beside the tomb, his head bowed, his hands clasped behind his back.

"I feel the need to remain here a moment," said Father Jacob. He shot Sir Ander a glittering glance from out of the corner of his eye.

Sir Ander tensed and slipped his hand inside his coat, to the pocket where he kept his stowaway pistol.

"Leave the lantern with Sir Ander and go with the others, Brother Barnaby," said Father Jacob. "I know your wyverns will be hungry."

Brother Barnaby's face brightened at the mention of his beloved wyverns, then constricted with concern. "You are right, Father. Poor things. They must be starving. I have neglected them. I will go to them at once."

Brother Barnaby handed over the lantern, then hurried off.

Sir Ander played the light on the stone walls, sending it jabbing into dark niches. "He is safely gone. What is wrong?"

"I hear something," Father Jacob said, cocking his head.

Sir Ander cocked the pistol's hammer and listened.

"I don't hear anything," he said after a moment.

"You must!" said Father Jacob testily. "Unless you've gone deaf."

"Nothing but dripping water . . ."

"That's it!" Father Jacob exclaimed. "The sound of dripping water!"

Sir Ander sighed wearily, let down the hammer and slid the pistol back into his pocket. "Is that all?"

"Why do we hear the sound of dripping?" Father Jacob stood staring at the bricks. "Don't you find that curious?"

"It's late, Father. We still have work to do. You need to interview Brother Paul and the dragon brothers."

Father Jacob shook his head turned away. They walked back down the narrow corridor and emerged into the bright sunlight, blinking their eyes. Sir Ander checked his pocket watch and was surprised to see that it was almost four of the clock in the afternoon. The day had been long in some respects and passed by far too swiftly in others.

"I have decided on second thought that *you* should go talk to the two dragons," said Father Jacob. "They are more likely to be open with you—a fellow soldier—than with me."

"What do you want me to ask them?"

"I want to know the truth about what they saw the night of the attack."

"But they weren't even here at the time," Sir Ander said, puzzled. "They live twenty miles away. They couldn't have seen anything."

"I think they *were* here. I think they *did* see something," said Father Jacob. "Something that scared them enough to volunteer for patrol duty."

"If you say so," said Sir Ander. "I'll go speak to them now."

"And I will talk to Brother Paul."

Father Jacob started to walk away, then paused and turned to stare, frowning, into the darkness of the catacombs.

"Why is the water dripping?" he muttered.

Father Jacob spent the next two hours in a most unsatisfactory interview with Brother Paul. He came out of the meeting thinking he might as well have spent ten minutes. Brother Paul was of little help. He knew that Albert had found a journal and had taken it back to his yacht. That was apparently all he knew or even cared about. Brother Paul had not read the journal.

"Reading is very difficult for me, due to my poor eyesight, Father," he said.

Brother Paul wasn't the least bit interested in the writing of a prince-abbot or the fact that Saint Dennis had spent time here.

"The words of God are the only words that have meaning," said Brother Paul.

As for the person who could have stolen the journal, "I have prayed for the thief's soul," said Brother Paul.

Father Jacob asked the monk about the night of the attack. Brother Paul had been sequestered in his dwelling in the wilderness. Weary from his day's work helping the nuns by working in the fields, he had fallen into a sound sleep. The first he knew of the attack was when he had been awakened by flashes of green fire in the sky.

Regarding the young woman, the sole survivor, he said he had found her in a pitiful state. She had been in the sanctuary when the demons entered. One of them struck her. She fell to the floor, stunned, and waited to die. The demons surged past her and she realized they assumed she was already dead. He had recorded in his report to the grand bishop everything she had said to him. He had nothing to add.

"According to what you wrote," said Father Jacob, referring to the report, "the nun said that when the demons were smashing the windows, one of the demons was hit by shards of glass and 'the demon yelped.' Do you remember that?"

"I am afraid I don't, Father," said Brother Paul. "I was shaken by the terrible events of that night as you might expect."

"Yet you were able to write this report . . ."

"It was my duty, Father," said Brother Paul simply. "God guided my hand."

He blamed himself for the young woman's death. "I had not slept in many nights and I dozed off. When I woke up, she was gone."

Father Jacob continued probing and prodding, but Brother Paul never wavered in his account. He did not grow confused, frustrated, or angry. He answered every question readily, patiently. At the end of the interview, he thanked Father Jacob.

"I want to do everything I can to help," said Brother Paul.

He declined an offer to partake of their evening meal and spend the night with them.

"You realize, Brother, that you could be in danger," Father Jacob warned. "It would be safer for you to remain here with us."

"God is my sword and my shield, Father," said Brother Paul as he departed. "He protects me."

Twilight tinged the mists of the Breath pinkish red, reminding Father Jacob of the bloodstained water in the buckets. He clasped his hands behind his back and walked slowly through the fading light, leaving the abbey compound, heading for the yacht and an early bedtime. He planned to spend tomorrow sorting through the mess in the library.

One of the dragons was back on patrol in the skies. In the distance, Father Jacob could see the sails and ballast balloons painted with the Rosian flag of the naval cutter as she took up a station out in the Breath.

"Father!" Sir Ander called. "Wait for me!"

Father Jacob turned to see his friend coming around the corner of the wall. He waited for him to join him and noted that he was alone.

"What did you do with Master Albert and Brother Barnaby?"

"Albert went back to his yacht. He was falling asleep on his feet. Brother Barnaby is with his wyverns. He says something is still bothering them. He thinks it's the presence of the dragons. He asked if he could spend the night in the stables. I gave him permission. I hope that's all right. It means I'll have to do the cooking."

"Fortunately, I have little appetite," said Father Jacob. "How did your talk with the dragons go?"

"You were right, Father. The brothers *had* been flying

close to the abbey that night. They usually eat the goats they raise themselves, but every so often they develop a taste for venison. In essence, they were poaching. The deer they were hunting happened to be on the abbey's land. That's why they didn't want to say anything."

"I am certain the grand bishop can spare a few," said Father Jacob dryly. "I hope they know we will not turn them in."

"I assured them we would keep quiet. And you were also right. They did see the attackers," said Sir Ander.

"Excellent news!" Father Jacob exclaimed, excited. "Dragons are creatures of good common sense and practical turn of mind. They do not believe in our God or in our Heaven or our Hell. No demons or giant bats for them. What did they see?"

"Demons," said Sir Ander. "Riding giant bats."

Father Jacob heaved a sigh.

Chapter Eighteen

God's voice pours forth the Song of Magic. Man has learned to create constructs some liken to a symphony. But what if that symphony were written in a minor key? What dread voice would sing the counter notes?

—*On the Nature of Magic*
by Saint Dennis

THE BENCHLIKE BED IN THE YACHT SEEMED UNUSUALLY comfortable to Sir Ander, or perhaps he was just uncommonly weary. Brother Barnaby's chicken stew, cooked in a kettle over an open fire, lay pleasantly on the stomach. Sir Ander and Father Jacob had not been forced to rely on the knight's cooking after all, though his cooking wasn't bad, as far as he was concerned. He liked boiled beans and salt pork. Brother Barnaby had fixed supper, then returned to the stables to be with his wyverns, which remained uneasy. The dragons did not fly at night, but took turns resting in a nearby field in case they should be needed.

Sir Ander stretched out on the wooden plank bed with its goose down mattress, closed his eyes, and sighed deeply. It was good just to lie still and let the sad events of the day sift through his mind, like sand between the fingers. He listened with drowsy amusement to Father Jacob fidgeting and rolling about restlessly.

"Your body tyrannizing your mind?" Sir Ander asked.

"There is nothing wrong with my mental discipline. Something is bothering me, that's all," said Father Jacob irritably.

Sir Ander smiled in the darkness and, rolling onto his side, he dragged the blanket over his head and fell asleep.

He was awakened by an explosive shout from Father Jacob. Whenever Sir Ander accompanied the father on a dangerous investigation (and most of the investigations performed by members of the Arcanum fell into that category), he slept in his trousers and shirt, his boots by the side of the bed, one of his pistols within easy reach beneath his pillow.

Sir Ander was instantly awake, his hand sliding beneath the pillow to take hold of the gun. "What? What is it?"

Light flared, magical light that half-blinded him. He had a glimpse of Father Jacob's face, eager and excited, bent over a "glow worm"—a type of lantern whose light came from magical sigils embedded inside the glass panels. When he could see, Sir Ander found Father Jacob buttoning his long black greatcoat over the black cassock.

"You'll need your coat, as well," said Father Jacob. "The night air has a definite nip to it."

Sir Ander yawned. "What time is it?"

"Near midnight. I'm sorry to wake you, but this is important."

Sir Ander sighed and swung his feet out of bed. "Where are we going?"

"Back to the abbey. Bring the pickax."

Sir Ander stared. "What for?"

"I'm not sure yet," said Father Jacob. "We'll need a shovel, as well."

"The ax and shovel are in the storage compartment in the rear." Sir Ander thrust his feet into the boots, struggled into his coat, tucked his pistol into the inner pocket, buckled on his sword belt, ran his hand through his hair, thought about wearing a hat and decided against it, and yawned again.

Father Jacob snapped his fingers and another glow worm

lantern burst into light. Leaving one lantern for Sir Ander, Father Jacob opened the door and went out. Sir Ander could hear him rummaging about in the storage compartment. Picturing the havoc the impatient priest was causing in his search, Sir Ander grabbed the lantern and hastened outside.

He found the pickax and shovel and picked up the other tools the priest had hurled onto the grass. Father Jacob did not wait but headed for the abbey. Sir Ander could see the bright white light of the glow worm swinging back and forth from the priest's hand.

He hefted the pickax and shovel and followed. The night was clear, the mists of the Breath shredded to wisps and tatters by a chill wind coming down from the distant mountains. Stars crusted the sky. A sliver of moon glimmered palely on the horizon.

The two dragon brothers, slumbering in the field, were bulky black hulks against the starlight. One slept on his side, like a horse, his legs stretched out, his head on the grass. The other slept on his belly, legs tucked beneath him, his neck curled about his feet, his head almost touching his tail which was wrapped around his hind legs.

"So why haul me out of my warm bed?" Sir Ander asked.

Father Jacob made an impatient gesture for him to be quiet and kept walking. Sir Ander was accustomed to the priest's sudden after-dark escapades and he said nothing more, knowing he would be wasting his breath. He spent the time trying to goad his sleep-fogged mind into wakefulness.

Father Jacob did not enter the cathedral, as Sir Ander had expected, but went swiftly around to the back. Sir Ander thought now he knew where they were going and why. When they came to the gate that led into the catacombs, he called a halt.

"It's the dripping water, isn't it?"

"The sound of the water kept nagging at me. That's the reason I couldn't sleep," said Father Jacob. "Then I figured out why."

He thrust open the gate and walked inside. Sir Ander

remained standing at the entrance. He threw the pickax and shovel on the ground.

"I'm not going to desecrate a tomb, Father," Sir Ander said.

Father Jacob scowled, displeased.

Sir Ander faced the irate priest calmly and shook his head. "Not for you or the Arcanum."

Father Jacob stood silently regarding his friend for a moment, then he bent down to retrieve the ax and the shovel.

"I know you will think I am being irrational, Ander," Father Jacob said earnestly, "but I believe the murdered nuns are trying to tell me something. Keep watch. See that I'm not disturbed."

He entered the catacombs alone. Sir Ander watched the light of the glow worm until it disappeared into the darkness. He stood outside in the whipping wind, pulling his coat collar up around his ears and wishing he'd worn his hat. After several moments, he heard the faint sounds of a pickax ringing against stone. Sir Ander could stand it no longer. He entered the catacombs.

Sir Ander did not believe in ghosts, but he conceded that there were far more pleasant places to take a midnight stroll than a dark burial chamber. The white-shrouded figures shone with an eerie pallor in the lantern light. The dark eye holes in the skulls seemed to be watching him. The sounds of the pickax grew louder. He came upon Father Jacob raising the ax over his head, prepared to bring it down. He was not attacking the tomb—to Sir Ander's vast relief. The priest was chopping up the floor beneath the tomb.

The floor was lined with bricks, as were the walls and the arched ceiling, making it difficult to determine where the brick floor left off and the wall began. The bricks beneath the tomb were still wet and glistening from the bloody water they had poured around it.

Father Jacob brought the ax down so near his boot that Sir Ander winced.

"Here, Father, I'll do that," he said, hurrying forward. "You're liable to cut off your foot."

Sir Ander took hold of the pickax. "I don't suppose you'd like to tell me why we are down here in the middle of the night breaking up bricks."

"There's your answer," said Father Jacob in satisfaction. "Look."

He held the lantern over the portion of the broken brick floor. Sir Ander peered down and for a moment saw nothing except cracked and broken pieces of brick. Father Jacob pushed aside some of the rubble, then thrust his hand into the opening. His hand disappeared up to the middle of his forearm.

Sir Ander stared down into the hole.

"All right, Father, I'm baffled. How did you know there was a false floor?"

"I heard the water dripping," said Father Jacob triumphantly. "Water poured onto bricks set into the ground might drain through the rock and could make a dripping sound. I didn't pay much attention at first. But then the water kept dripping. You can hear it still dripping even now."

Sir Ander listened and, sure enough, he could hear, very faintly, a drip and then another, like raindrops falling from the eaves after a summer shower plopping monotonously into the grass.

"And look at this!" Father Jacob spoke a word and passed his hand over the bricks. They began to shine, though very, very faintly. "These are laced with magical sigils. Masonry sigils, designed to give added strength. The sigils are very old. There is almost nothing left of them now."

Father Jacob rose and walked over to a different portion of the floor and did the same thing, passing his hand over the floor. No light shone.

"These bricks have no sigils. They did not need extra strengthening. If you were to look beneath them, you would find dirt."

Father Jacob pointed to the base of the tomb. "When you

slide your fingers in here, you can feel the bricks crumbling. That's where the water seeped through and made the dripping sound. The blood of the martyrs. The nuns trying to tell me something."

Sir Ander shivered in the darkness. "But why reinforce bricks used in a floor?"

"Because if you are down below, these bricks are no longer the floor. They are the ceiling."

"Of course." Sir Ander grunted. "I'm still half asleep. So you've found a chamber hidden beneath the tomb. What do you think it is? The abbey treasure vault? The monks were said to have amassed great wealth."

"Enlarge the opening," said Father Jacob. "Enough for us to shine our lights down there."

Sir Ander went to work and had soon chopped open a large hole. He and Father Jacob lay on their bellies, flat on the ground, and lowered their glow worm lanterns into the hole as far as their arms would reach.

In a child's tale, Sir Ander reflected, we would be rewarded with the sight of our lights gleaming off stacks of gold and piles of rubies and diamonds and emeralds.

But this wasn't a child's tale. This was Father Jacob. What they found appeared to be a classroom. The light from their lanterns illuminated a rectangular-shaped chamber, containing four writing desks and a large wooden table that was empty save for six leather-bound books stacked neatly one atop the other. Book shelves lined two of the four walls. They were empty, as well. The other two walls were made of slate planed flat and smooth. Floor, books, table, desks, and walls were all covered with thick dust. Sir Ander could see rivulets of water running through the dust on the floor from where it had dripped from the ceiling.

"Damned odd place to build a classroom," said Sir Ander.

"Not if you are working on a project that will forever change the Church and its teachings," said Father Jacob. "You would want to work somewhere in private. And if you are a prince-abbot and you desperately need to hide something, what better place."

Sir Ander let out his breath in a soundless whistle. He stood up, took hold of the pickax, and began to enlarge the hole. The floor of the class room was about ten feet beneath them, a short drop. Father Jacob was about to jump for it, when Sir Ander took hold of him.

"Perhaps someday humans will devise the ability to fly like birds, Father, but we have not managed to do so at present. Once we are down there, we will need a way to get out."

"Ever practical," said Father Jacob. "You will find rope in the stables."

"I don't like the thought of leaving you here alone."

"I'm not alone," said Father Jacob. "The nuns brought me here. They will keep me company."

Sir Ander gave up the argument. He left the catacombs and made his way to the wyvern stables. Brother Barnaby was fast asleep in one of the stalls, lying on a blanket spread over straw. The two wyverns were as near him as they could crowd. One had his head draped over the monk's legs. The wyverns woke when Sir Ander entered, raised their heads, and glared at him balefully. So long as he didn't come near, they were quiet. He found a coil of rope and left. Brother Barnaby never stirred. Looking back, Sir Ander saw the wyverns still watching him.

He carried the rope into the catacombs and fastened it around the tomb. He felt a twinge of guilt, and hoped the abbess wouldn't take offense. Father Jacob cast a magical spell on the rope to make certain it held secure. He lowered himself first. Sir Ander sent down the lanterns, then descend.

Father Jacob went straight to the books. He held out his hands, murmured some words, and gave a satisfied nod. "As I thought. Cividae cast spells of protection on them. Very powerful spells. He was a good crafter, our prince-abbot. It will take time to dismantle them."

Father Jacob set to work, moving and shifting and plucking at sigils and constructs, which was tantamount to dismantling a cobweb strand by silken strand. Sir Ander walked around the room, flashing his light on the writing desks. Brushing away the dust, he looked at the ink splotches and found initials carved in each desk: D, C, M, M.

"So they were *all* here," Father Jacob murmured, awe-struck. "The Four Blessed Saints: Saint Dennis, Saint Charles, Saint Michael, and Saint Marie."

"And an 'X,'" said Sir Ander, pointing to a fifth desk that had been shoved into a corner.

"X," said Father Jacob, frowning in puzzlement. "Why would there be a desk marked with X?"

"X marks the spot," said Sir Ander. "Perhaps this desk has something hidden in it?"

"Perhaps," said Father Jacob, though he didn't sound convinced.

Sir Ander studied the desk with the X, but couldn't find any hidden drawers or secret nooks. He shrugged and turned away. Another thought had occurred to him.

"This was a monastery not a nunnery back then," said Sir Ander. "How did Saint Marie manage to live in an abbey inhabited solely by men?"

"Marie was reputed to have been such a brilliant crafter that she was granted permission to attend the University at a time when only male students were accepted," said Father Jacob. "Popular myth has it that she dressed in men's robes and shaved her head in a tonsure in order to fit in. Perhaps the myth was true."

Sir Ander could well imagine her three friends and colleagues sneaking her into the abbey, especially if the prince-abbot was aware of the deception. *But if the X was for Marie then who did the other M represent?*

Looking at the desks, Sir Ander had the strange impression that time had gone backward. If the four saints had walked through that door, he would not have been much surprised. He could see the four so clearly, each sitting at these very desks, working in comradely silence or gathered around the long table discussing their research.

When he found himself almost seeming to hear their voices, he shook the fancies out of his head and muttered, "I've got to get some sleep!"

He inspected the slate walls and was surprised to find chalk markings—diagrams of what he assumed were magical constructs. He was about to mention these to Father Jacob. The priest was deeply engrossed in his work and Sir Ander decided not to interrupt him. Thinking he'd leave the father to his work and see what lay beyond this curious room, Sir Ander went over to the door, opened it, and gasped.

"Good grief!" he said, startled, nearly walking into a plaster wall.

Father Jacob glanced around. He halted in his work, his brows raised.

"Interesting," he said.

Sir Ander rapped on the wall. "Not very sturdy."

"It wasn't meant to be. It was intended to conceal the existence of this room."

Father Jacob walked over to the diagram. Sir Ander joined him. "I saw you looking at these. Do you know what they are?"

"Some sort of magical constructs—"

"Constructs such as I have never seen. Magic used in a way I have never seen. I will have to study them further, but I believe we are looking at the constructs of contramagic," said Father Jacob. He breathed a soft sigh. "You were right when you said this was a treasure trove, my friend. It holds a wealth of knowledge."

"Dangerous knowledge," said Sir Ander grimly. "Some people would say it should have never been brought into the world."

"That is where some people would be wrong," said Father Jacob, flaring in anger. He slammed his hand on the table, sending a cloud of dust into the air. "Damn it, when will mankind learn to stop fearing knowledge? Fools believe that by burning books they can burn away the truths the books hold! God knows what He is about. Every action has its equal and opposite reaction. The same applies to the science of magic. I say to you now, Ander, we would be far better off if we had been studying contramagic all these years instead of denying its existence. We would not now be facing utter ruin!"

Father Jacob was literally shaking with the force of his passion. Sir Ander felt himself properly reprimanded.

"I am sorry, Father. You are right. I wasn't thinking."

"That is the problem, my friend," said Father Jacob with a weary smile. "The Church never permitted you to think. And I am sorry. I didn't mean to yell at you."

"Do you want me to knock down this wall?" Sir Ander asked.

Father Jacob shook his head. "Not tonight. We must transport these books to the yacht where I can study them. We will return first thing tomorrow morning and then you may knock down the wall."

"So are these the writings of Saint Dennis the prince-abbot mentioned in the journal, Father? The writings the demons were searching for?"

"We are about to find out."

Like a bard striking the strings of a harp, Father Jacob strummed the air with his fingers. He blew on the dust-covered book and then gently brushed off more dust with his hand. The cover was plain, devoid of decoration or title. He carefully opened the book's cover and looked at the writing on the first page.

"Bring the lantern closer."

Sir Ander held the lantern over the book. Light spilled on the pages. The title and subtitle were written in Rosaelig, which he did not know. But he could read the four names penned beneath: Dennis, Charles, Marie, Michael, and one word: *Contramagic*.

The two men were silent, both of them thinking of the impact this revelation would have upon a church which taught that contramagic did not exist, could not exist.

"You were right, Father. What does the rest of the writing say?"

"Notes and Collective Thought on the Science of Contramagic." Father Jacob paused, then continued reading, "Silencing of the Voice of God."

Sir Ander felt a shiver go through him. Father Jacob stared off into the darkness.

"*This* is why the demons want the books!"

"What do you mean?" Sir Ander asked tensely.

"They want to silence the Voice of God," said Father Jacob. "They want to find a way to utterly destroy the magic. And since almost everything in this world is built using the magic, this means they are trying to find a way to utterly destroy us . . ."

Father Jacob continued to study the book, staring intently at the title, minutely examining each letter, frowning over it and muttering to himself.

"I need more light," he complained. "It looks as if some of the writing on this page has been magically expunged."

"Then let us go back to the yacht," said Sir Ander, with a jaw-cracking yawn. "You can read and I can sleep."

Sir Ander climbed the rope first, waiting up top for Father Jacob to attach the books to the rope. Sir Ander hauled them up. Last came Father Jacob, climbing the rope nimbly.

"Wait a moment before we go," said Father Jacob, frowning at the hole in the bricks. "I don't like to leave that unguarded."

"No one's likely to come down here," said Sir Ander, who wanted only to crawl into his bed.

"Still, you never know," said Father Jacob. "Someone *was* here poking about. I saw the traces when we first arrived."

"Probably the nuns. Caring for the dead."

"Perhaps, but the prints were recent. Someone tracked in mud and bits of grass. The mud was still damp."

"All right, but if we're going to make it look as if nothing had been disturbed, we shouldn't leave this mess lying about," said Sir Ander. He picked up a chunk of brick and threw it down into the hole.

"An excellent thought, my friend," said Father Jacob.

"I have one or two on occasion," said Sir Ander.

Father Jacob helped toss the evidence that they had been digging down into the hole. When they had cleaned up, he knelt down on the edge of the hole, spoke several words, and traced a pattern in the air with his hand. The hole vanished. Sir Ander found himself looking at dirt. His magical construct laid, Father Jacob picked up a rock and threw it at the center of the hole. Blue light flashed. The rock bounded off.

Sir Ander and Father Jacob left the catacombs. Father Jacob placed another magical spell on the rusted gates, a spell that would give anyone who tried to enter a most unpleasant shock. They carried the books back to the yacht and placed them on the table. Sir Ander undressed down to his shirt and trousers, slid his pistol beneath the pillow, hung his sword belt on a hook, pulled off his boots, and lay down with a contented sigh.

"I suppose you're going to stay up all night reading," said Sir Ander.

"Will the light bother you?" Father Jacob asked.

Sir Ander grabbed his tricorn, placed it so that the brim shielded his eyes. He took one last look at Father Jacob, sitting in the lantern's glow, the book open on the table before him. He seemed to devour, rather than read.

Sir Ander smiled and closed his eyes. He slept so deeply that when he heard the boom of cannon fire, he did not wake at first.

He thought it was still part of his dream.

Chapter Nineteen

That portion of the Breath that provides lift for our world can be isolated, purified, and concentrated. We can then charge that gas using constructs to evenly distribute magical energy throughout. This process creates considerably more lift than found in nature and allows us to build large flying ships capable of carrying men and goods. Our constructs safely manage the level and consistent flow of magical energy into the various devices used for holding the lift gas, giving the helmsman full control over his vessel's buoyancy.

—Basic Marine Crafters textbook

WHILE FATHER JACOB AND SIR ANDER WERE ENTERING the catacombs, following the call of the blood of the martyrs, Stephano and his comrades were looking forward to spending a second uncomfortable night aboard the *Cloud Hopper*, lost in the Breath.

At least the houseboat was no longer sinking. Miri was a "channeler" of magic, and twice that day she had made the perilous climb up the swaying mast to reach the main balloon and used her channeling abilities to keep the magic flowing into the constructs, to keep the balloon from deflating.

A channeler was a person who could "channel" magical energy, send the magic flowing through existing constructs. A channeler was not gifted enough in magic to be able to draw sigils and create new constructs. Some channelers could act as a conduit for the magic, transfer it from one sigil to another by touch. If Rodrigo had drawn one of his famous diagrams, it would have three sigils, A, B, and C in a line. If B was broken, a channeler could form a bridge between A to C, keep the magic flowing.

The climb up the wet mast in the dark, by feel alone, was dangerous even for Miri, who had spent her childhood racing up and down the mast just for a lark. Once up there, she had to cling to the slippery wood with one arm, while she reached up to the balloon to channel magic directly into it. Since the constructs that evenly distributed the magical energy were set inside the balloon, charging the lift gas in this manner would have only limited, short-term success.

Dag, his face creased with worry, stood beneath the mast, peering upward in a vain attempt to see Miri through the thick mists. Perhaps he had some thought of catching her if she fell, though they all knew that if she did fall, she would likely pitch straight into the Breath.

"Miri's skills are really what's been keeping the *Cloud Hopper* afloat all these years," Rodrigo told Stephano. "She was able to use her channeling abilities to reroute the magic around, above, over, and under all of Gythe's protection spells."

The two were down below in the hold, where Stephano was rooting around in the trunk Benoit had packed in preparation for his master's journey. A lantern, hanging from a hook in the ceiling, swayed back and forth as the boat rocked in the currents of the Breath.

This night was going to be colder than the night before and he was digging out his old flight coat. Benoit had, of course, dumped the coat at the very bottom, hiding it beneath frilly shirts and dress coats and trousers, stockings and underwear. Benoit had packed as if Stephano was making a grand tour of the continents, not a trip to the unsavory city of Westfirth.

Stephano didn't answer. He was in a bad mood. He knew he was in a bad mood and he knew why—his friends were in danger, he couldn't get them out of danger, and it was his fault they were in danger in the first place. And he was jealous.

He needed to be doing something. He had never been the kind of officer to lead from the rear. He had been at the head of the charge, fighting the foe head-on. Dag was working to repair the damage done to the propeller. Gythe and Rigo were working to fix the magic. Miri kept the ship afloat. Stephano was reduced to pacing the deck in company with the cat. And even Doctor Ellington played his part, boosting morale by rubbing around their ankles.

As for Miri, Stephano had no reason to be jealous. He loved her as a friend; his closest friend next to Rodrigo, but still a friend, not a lover. Dag was like a brother to him, a good man worthy of any woman's love. Stephano wanted both his friends to be happy, so why wasn't he happy for them? Perhaps, Stephano admitted sourly to himself, he had fondly imagined Miri loved him. It had come as a shock to find out that she was in love with someone else. His heart was bruised, his pride wounded.

Because he was in a bad mood, he needed someone to blame, and Rodrigo was close at hand.

"There's something I don't understand," Stephano said, pulling out linen drawers and lace-edged shirts and tossing them onto the floor. "We've been sailing on the *Cloud Hopper* for four years, and I can't help but wonder you never noticed until now that the magic on this boat was in such a bloody mess!"

"But, my dear fellow, why should I have paid any attention to the magic?" Rodrigo asked, picking up the clothes Stephano was hurling about. He looked truly astonished at the thought, and that irritated Stephano even more.

"Because you're a bloody crafter!"

"A mere dabbler in the art," said Rodrigo. "A theorist, a philosopher. When I set sail, I watch with pleasure the panorama of the passing shoreline. I admire the picturesque little villages, the grandeur of the mountains. I do not spend my time dissecting magical constructs on the hull."

"Well, maybe you should!" Stephano said angrily. "Make yourself useful!"

"Like I'm doing now?" said Rodrigo with quiet dignity.

Stephano remembered belatedly that his friend had been awake all last night, working with Gythe to try to find a way to solve their predicament. They had worked all that day, taking a break only for meals.

"I'm sorry," Stephano muttered. "It's just . . . I feel so damn useless!"

"You are our captain," said Rodrigo. "You give us guidance, inspiration. You boost our spirits—"

"Oh, go jump in the Breath," Stephano told his friend, though he couldn't help but smile.

Rodrigo found Stephano's flight coat at the bottom and handed it to him. He then folded Stephano's clothes and carefully repacked them.

"I may have thought of a way out of this," he said as he worked. "I'm going to go to my hammock and sleep on it. I sent Miri and Gythe to bed, as well. You should get some rest yourself."

"I napped some this afternoon," said Stephano, adding bitterly, "I didn't have anything else to do. I'll stand watch."

Rodrigo nodded and left, rubbing his eyes and heading for his hammock.

Stephano picked up the flight coat. The smell of leather seemed to warm the dank air of the hold, brought back memories of the best and happiest time of his life. Putting on the green coat, meant to blend in with the greenish-blue scales of a dragon, was like reuniting with a dear friend. The calf-length garment, made of the finest quality leather, was slightly fitted at the waist, though loose enough to hide several inner pockets and a sheath for a small pistol.

Brass buttons, engraved with a winged sun with a vertical sword thrust through the center of it—the emblem of the Dragon Brigade—adorned the front. The padded coat had a high collar and a mantle that covered his shoulders. The mantle was deliberately designed to flap in the wind when he rode, throwing off the aim of anyone shooting at him.

The coat was split in back, allowing the wearer to sit in a saddle and keep his legs covered.

Two dragons made of contrasting colors of leather had been appliquéd on the coat, one on each breast. Trimmed in gold thread, the dragons faced each other. The workmanship was exquisite, detailed down to the scales and claws and done in deep red, gold, and purple. Only the Lord Captain of the Dragon Brigade could wear a flight coat with dragons of those colors.

The coat had cost him dearly. Upon his promotion, his mother had offered to commission a coat for him as a gift. Stephano had proudly refused. He had spent every last silver rosun he possessed to have this coat made to his specifications, including magical constructs to keep the wearer warm and protect against enemy gunfire, flying shrapnel, and the like.

The coat was worn, well-worn. He'd noticed a month ago that the stitching was wearing thin and one of the buttons was loose. He had told Benoit to see to the mending and, looking at the coat, he was astonished to find out that his old retainer had actually done what he'd been asked to do.

Or rather, Stephano realized, looking at the small, neat stitches and the expert manner in which the button had been reattached, Miri had mended his coat. It was like her to do the work and say nothing to him about it.

Before he put it on, he gently touched a patch of gold scales on the dragon over his left breast. The scales were stained, but that was one place on his coat he never cleaned. The stain was blood—the blood of his dragon and partner, Lady Cam.

He slid his arms into the sleeves, remembering the first time he'd worn the coat, on parade at his promotion ceremony. His men had cheered; the dragons of the Brigade had lifted their voices in a raucous shout. He could have never imagined at that moment wearing his flight coat to keep warm on a Trundler houseboat stranded in the Breath.

Taking the lantern, he went up on deck, where Dag was

pacing back and forth, his hands stuffed into his pockets, trying to keep warm. He was wearing a padded leather coat of Guundaran make and design, from his days in the military. Miri had knit him a pair of gloves, but he was not wearing them. Difficult to pull a trigger with gloves on.

The night was so cold, Stephano could see his own breath mix with God's.

"You should get some sleep," he told Dag.

"The back of my neck itches, sir," said Dag. "I've had the feeling before. When I'm walking sentry duty and I know the enemy's somewhere around, but I don't know where."

"Yeah, I've been feeling the same," said Stephano, staring into the thick and heavy darkness, into the ghostly mists that flitted past the lantern light. "I keep thinking about that story Miri told, about what happened to her parents."

"It sounds crazy, sir. If it hadn't been Miri telling the tale, I wouldn't have believed her."

Stephano knew what he meant. Sailors and Trundlers down through the centuries had told tales of monsters lurking in the Breath, reaching up gigantic tentacles to snatch the unsuspecting sailor off a deck or dragging down entire ships. Stories of ghost ships sailed by dead crewmen and ships simply vanishing.

He had never put much stock in such tales. But then, he'd never before been stranded in the dark in the Breath. He'd never felt it closing in around him, moving and shifting like a restless spirit, dampening sound, muffling voices, causing the boat to rock and lurch unexpectedly.

Dag reached up his hand to pet Doctor Ellington, who was also standing guard duty, his claws dug into the padding on Dag's shoulder. The cat's eyes gleamed gold in the light.

"The Doctor hears things, too," said Dag.

The cat kneaded his claws into the padding and looked very fierce.

"What time is it?" Stephano asked. He could have looked at his own watch, but he wanted to change the subject.

Dag pulled out his pocket watch, opened it, and held it

to the lantern. "Nineteen hundred hours, sir. Five more to midnight."

Stephano hunched his head into the high collar. "Seems a lot later. Like it should be two in the morning."

The two walked the deck together in companionable silence, instinctively marching in step. They were comfortable with each other. Stephano glanced sidelong at Dag: big, stalwart, an excellent shot, confident in his ability to fire a weapon, if in nothing else.

Once an officer, a leader of men, Dag had made a decision, given an order in battle that had cost the lives of men who had trusted him. Dag blamed himself. The next battle, he found he couldn't give an order at all. He'd frozen, unable to move or speak. He had been brought up on charges of dereliction of duty and drummed out of the mercenary company in disgrace.

Depressed and caring nothing about where he went or what he did, Dag had ended up in Westfirth, a city where it was easy to hide one's past. He had fallen in with one of the local criminal gangs, whose business enterprises included operating opium dens, houses of pleasure, gambling and prostitution, and selling local shopkeepers protection. He'd been a bodyguard and helped to collect gambling debts and protection money. His criminal career had ended the night he had been forced to kill his partner.

Dag and a new partner had been sent to "persuade" a shop owner to pay his debt. Dag had gone on such missions before. A punch in the kidney, a black eye, a bruised jaw, and the shopkeeper usually found the silver. Unfortunately, this time, Dag's new partner had turned out to be a bloodthirsty maniac. In order to keep his partner from beating the victim to death, Dag had broken his partner's neck.

Dag had carried the shop owner to his rooms, which were above the shop. Dag sent for a physician, who examined the man, said there had been extensive internal damage, and there wasn't much he could do. Dag nursed the shop owner, day and night, to no avail. The man eventually died, but not before he had forgiven Dag and asked him a final favor—take care of his beloved pet cat. Dag had made the promise. He and Doctor Ellington had since been inseparable.

Dag had resigned from the gang, only to find that the boss wouldn't accept his resignation. The gang came looking for him. He moved to Evreux and went to work on the docks, loading and unloading cargo. He had met Stephano five years ago, after extricating Benoit from a fight with the dockworkers over perceived negligence in regard to a shipment of wine. Dag had escorted the old man home and been introduced to Stephano, who had invited Dag in for a glass of the aforementioned wine. The two former soldiers had fallen to talking of past battles, only to discover that they'd both been at the Siege of the Royal Sail, though on opposite sides. Stephano had offered Dag a job with the Cadre of the Lost.

No one knew the full history of Dag's past except Stephano. The others knew only that Dag was a former soldier and small-time crook, now reformed.

He asked Dag about how the repairs to the airscrew and propeller were coming. Dag had good news. The repairs were finished.

"That shot Piefer made was one hell of a shot, sir. You said he was using one of those muskets with the new rifled barrel. I'd love to see one. What did it look like?"

Stephano replied that he hadn't really gotten a close look at it, but from what he had seen, it looked similar to a musket except the barrel was thicker, which would make sense; the grooves were cut directly into the metal. They spent the next hour walking back and forth to keep warm, discussing modern weaponry. Neither lowered his guard, however, and when they heard footsteps on deck, both whipped around, reaching for their guns.

"Don't shoot!" said Rodrigo, lifting his hands in the air. "I surrender!"

"You sound awfully damn cheerful," Dag grumbled, lowering his blunderbuss.

"That is because I have a solution to our predicament," said Rodrigo. He was wearing a coat made of sheepskin with the woolly fleece on the inside for warmth, and matching sheepskin gloves. "I dreamed of chocolate layer cake."

"What does cake have to do with anything, except remind me that I've had nothing to eat but smoked fish for the last two days and not much of that," Stephano said irritably.

Dag grunted. "I'll toss him overboard, if you want, sir."

"It wouldn't do any good. He'd only come back to haunt us," said Stephano.

"I've been going about repairing the magic in the wrong way," Rodrigo explained. "Gythe placed layer after layer of protection spells over the ship, one on top of the other, like the layers of a chocolate cake. Now, any professor at the University will tell you that magic simply does not work this way. Her spells should have gotten all mixed up with the construction spells laid down by her uncle when he was building the boat. In other words, we should have chocolate pudding, not cake."

Dag's stomach rumbled loudly.

Stephano could almost taste the chocolate, and his mouth watered. "I don't suppose you could use a different analogy."

Rodrigo grinned. "This is the only way I can explain it to you lay people so that it will make sense. Gythe's protection spells are stacked on top of the original magic. In order to reach that magic, I've been trying to punch a hole through the layers. That doesn't work. What I need to do is to have Gythe remove the layers, take them off one by one until I can reach the constructs underneath and repair them."

"Can that be done?" Stephano asked.

"Not according to the textbooks," said Rodrigo blithely. "According to the so-called wise, what Gythe did can't be done. And yet, she did it. I have reached the conclusion, my friends, that our Gythe is a savant."

Dag glowered. "Is that an insult?"

"Far from it, I assure you," Rodrigo said hastily. "The term 'savant' refers to a crafter who is a genius in magic, someone who 'has magic in the blood, not just in the fingertips' as one of my professors termed it. Savants are very rare in this world. And that is why she was able to create a veritable layer cake of magic."

"Did I hear someone mention cake?" Miri asked eagerly, opening the hatch and coming out on deck. She was wearing a wool hat and a thick wool coat over pantaloons made of soft, supple lambskin tied at the ankles so as not to get tangled in the rigging.

"Only in regard to magic," said Stephano.

Rodrigo explained his plan. Miri listened, her head cocked to one side.

"It might work," she said. "The problem is Trundler magic is secret. We don't let Outsiders see or hear how any Trundler casts spells."

"We're not Outsiders, Miri," said Stephano. "We're friends."

"I trust you. *I* would tell you if I knew. But the magic is Gythe's . . ." Miri hesitated.

"And by the looks of these protection spells, she doesn't trust anyone. She's terrified of removing them," said Rodrigo. "But that's the beauty of my plan. She won't have to remove them. All she has to do is pick them up long enough for me to repair the damage on the original constructs. Then she can let them fall back in place. Picture a chocolate cake with sugar icing and almond paste in between in each layer—"

"For God's sake, sir, make him stop!" Dag pleaded.

Miri looked at Rodrigo in helpless confusion. "Is that even possible?"

"Oh, yes." Rodrigo gave a firm nod of his head.

"I'll go talk to her."

She entered the hatchway leading to the cabin where the two sisters berthed. Doctor Ellington was either bored with sentry duty or hoping to persuade Miri that he was a cat deserving of smoked fish. He bounded off Dag's shoulder and ran after her, his tail frisking.

"You're a damn liar, aren't you, Rigo?" said Stephano. "Moving layers of magic around is not remotely possible."

"Anything's possible," said Rodrigo, shrugging. "Just not very probable."

Stephano sighed. Dag muttered beneath his breath. Rodrigo hummed a few bars of a sonata. At last they heard footsteps. They turned to see Miri coming on deck, followed by Gythe with Doctor Ellington.

"She'll do it," said Miri. "But she doesn't think it will work."

Gythe affirmed this with a shake of her head. She was wearing a long fur cape with a woolen dress and flannel petticoats for warmth. She had wrapped Doctor Ellington in the fur cape, holding him close, her chin nestled into the top of his head. Engulfed in the cape, warm and happy, the cat gazed at them, eyes blinking drowsily.

"Imagine that you are playing your harp," said Rodrigo. "The magical protection constructs are the strings. You pluck one, then another, then another . . ."

Gythe stared at him, her blue eyes widening. Her hair, damp from the mist, straggled down out of the snug hat she wore. She rubbed her face in the cat's fur. Doctor Ellington began to purr loudly, a low rumble in his chest. Keeping fast hold of the cat, Gythe walked over to Stephano. She touched his lips with her fingers, then touched his heart.

"She's telling you to keep her secret," said Miri.

"As God is my witness, I swear," said Stephano.

Gythe did the same with Rodrigo, who readily took the oath. She went to Dag and touched his lips.

"You know I'll keep your secret, Girl dear," said Dag.

Gythe gave the Doctor a kiss and then placed him on Dag's shoulder. Dag and Doctor Ellington returned to sentry duty. Rodrigo and Miri and Gythe debated for a moment where to begin, finally deciding to start with the brass helm.

Stephano trailed after them. "Is there anything I can do?"

"You can hold the lantern," said Rodrigo magnanimously.

Seeing the dour look Stephano gave him, Rodrigo added, "Honestly, I need someone to hold the lantern!"

Stephano took the lantern. Rodrigo posted him beside the helm and showed him where to shine the light.

"Explain to me what's going on," said Stephano. "In words of a single syllable."

Rodrigo gestured to the helm. "The constructs set in the brass allow the helmsman to control the amount of magical energy sent to the lift tanks and the balloon. Internal constructs arc that energy through the lift gas 'charging' it, creating buoyancy. Braided leather cables, set with additional constructs, act as conduits leading from the helm to the lift tanks and the balloon. Each of these symbols inscribed on the panel allows the helmsman to control a different part of the boat. You could increase the amount of lift in the tanks by sliding your finger up the arrow symbol on the panel, decrease it by sliding your finger down. The surge of magical energy caused by the bullet disrupting the magic blew up some of the sigils that form the constructs. I can repair them, but I have to physically touch and reconstruct them. And these are buried at the bottom of the chocolate cake."

"They're Trundler magic," said Stephano. "You said you'd never seen some of them before."

"True, but I spent most of yesterday studying them. With Miri's help, I think we can get the boat up and running again."

"When?" asked Stephano.

"Dag has fixed the propeller," said Rodrigo. "Once we can reach the constructs, repairing them shouldn't take too long. It all depends on Gythe," he added somberly.

Gythe looked uncertainly at Miri, who gave her an encouraging smile. "Like playing your harp," she said.

Gythe drew in a deep breath. She placed her hands, fingers spread, on the brass panel and began to sing.

Stephano had heard Gythe sing before, mostly when she was singing softly to Doctor Ellington, sometimes when she was puttering about the houseboat or at his house, helping Benoit peel potatoes or washing dishes or in the park for money. She had a sweet voice, perfect pitch. He had come to recognize some of the tunes over the years, for they were simple and easy to remember, and she sang the same ones over and over. He'd often catch himself humming one or two of them.

The song she sang now was far different from her "Doctor Ellington" song or her "housework" song. This song was ancient, primitive and wild, harsh and discordant, plaintive and sorrowful. A song of yearning and seeking and finding. A song of power that Stephano could feel in his own body, a tingling, shivering sensation that went through him in waves, raising the hair on his arms.

Dag stopped dead, turned to stare. Rodrigo gazed at Gythe in slack-jawed astonishment. Miri watched her sister with fond pride. And then Stephano saw the magic. He saw what he'd always longed to see. He saw sigils, simple and complex. He saw the lines connecting them, myriad lines, myriad sigils, blue-and-purple shining lights, dazzling and beautiful. And confused. Like a spider spinning web over web over web …

Down below the blue-and-purple spiderwebs, he could see sigils set into the brass helm and the sigils with the lines connecting them dancing along the braided leather cord. These sigils were brown in color, nothing pretty about them. They were working sigils. He saw large gaps between some of the sigils. No lines ran between them. These sigils were damaged.

As he watched, awestruck, Gythe reached out with her hands and, still singing, she took delicate hold of one strand of blue-and-purple shining magic between her fingers, like plucking a harp string, and lifted it up into the air. Letting it hang, shimmering with light, she picked up another and another. Stephano counted seven in all. They arched over the brass panel, quivering and fragile as a rainbow.

Miri nudged Rodrigo with her elbow. "You can get to work now."

Rodrigo blinked his eyes and drew in a deep gulp of air. "Right. Sorry. Forgot to breathe there for a moment. Now, let's see what we have here."

He bent over the helm, with Miri working to channel the magic when he instructed her. Gythe continued to sing, her voice sweet and sad, young and lovely, old and wise. Stephano noticed Dag wiping his nose and brushing his sleeve across his eyes. Stephano felt his own eyes burn and a lump in his throat.

Rodrigo touched the brass panel, drawing sigils with his fingers at Miri's direction. He waited a moment for the sigils to sparkle to life and when they didn't, he swore softly in frustration, deconstructed them and began again. This time, the magic worked. The sigils began to gleam beneath his hand. He gave a whoop of joy and flung his arms around Miri, who laughed delightedly.

Rodrigo quickly returned to his work and, now that he knew what he was doing, he drew a great many sigils in rapid succession. He spoke several words and drew lines connecting them. As these began to glow, Rodrigo performed a few dance steps in celebration and went to work extending the sigils along the braided leather.

Gythe stopped singing, perhaps for lack of breath, but the magic continued to shine. She held the blue-and-purple arrays of lines and sigils and they floated out from her hands and drifted over the boat like radiant banners, encircling the balloons, sparkling on the sails, glimmering on the propeller blades.

Stephano watched, fascinated. The bright light of the flaming sigils illuminated the night. He might have worried that they were now a well-lit target, but Gythe's song seemed to ease the disquieting feeling that there was something sinister out there in the mists.

Rodrigo flung off his coat and began to climb the mast to reach the sigils on the balloon.

"Where did you learn to climb like that?" Stephano asked him.

"Crawling up trellises to reach ladies' bedrooms," Rodrigo returned.

"I've never seen the like," said Dag in solemn tones. "If a man didn't believe in God, he would surely believe in Him now."

"If a man didn't believe in Rodrigo, he would believe in him now," said Stephano.

"I suppose the rascal does have his uses," Dag conceded with a grudging smile. He reached up to stroke the cat on his shoulder. "He does more tomcatting than the good Doctor here. Perhaps his brush with death has taught him a lesson."

Stephano hoped that was true, though he had the feeling that the first sight of smiling lips, blonde curls, and a buxom bosom would erase the terrors of the dueling field from Rigo's mind.

The sigils on the balloon began to glow. Lines flashed between them.

"Gythe, you can let go of the protection spells. Dag!" Rodrigo yelled from where he was clinging precariously to the mast. "You say the propeller is in working order?"

"It is!" Dag shouted. "Not much to fix, really," he added in an aside to Stephano. "The bullet knocked the blade askew. I had to take off the blade, reposition it. We were damn lucky."

"Not luck. Well protected," said Stephano, glancing at Gythe with a smile.

She let go of the spells, and they settled like layers of wool blankets (Stephano refused to let himself think about cake) onto the boat. Rodrigo slithered down the mast and landed on the deck below.

"I've done as much as I can do, Miri. Let's see if we can bring the *Cloud Hopper* back to life."

Miri gave a nod and walked over to the brass helm. Gythe came to stand close beside her. Too nervous to speak, she reached out to squeeze her sister's chill hand.

Stephano waited tensely, arms crossed over his chest. Beside him, Dag muttered something in his own language, Guundaran. Either he was swearing or praying, Stephano could not tell which. Stephano said a prayer of his own, making it short and to the point. "Lord God, let this work!"

Rodrigo leaned over the helm. He had forgotten to put his coat back on and he was shivering and too tense to notice. Miri placed her hands on the brass panel. Her fingers spread wide. Gythe slid her arm around her sister's waist and began to sing. Everyone on board stopped breathing except for Doctor Ellington, who sneezed.

Miri placed her fingers on the symbols inscribed on the brass, her hands darting over them with loving, practiced skill. And then, as if God Himself were breathing life into the little boat, the sigils caught fire. The houseboat blazed with magical light. The balloons swelled. The sails billowed.

Gythe stood gazing upward, the light shining on her face. She seemed radiant as an angel at that moment. An instant later, the magical light died. Stephano could no longer see the sigils, but they continued to work. He could feel the warmth in the air as the *Cloud Hopper* started to rise.

Dag gave a mighty shout that startled Doctor Ellington, who leaped off his shoulder and ran to his favorite hiding place beneath one of the cannons. Rodrigo and Miri were dancing together, capering up and down the deck. Gythe grabbed Doctor Ellington, hauled him out, and began to dance with the cat in her arms.

Stephano felt giddy with elation. He turned to Dag. "Shall we join them?"

Dag grinned. He took hold of Stephano's hands and the

two of them began to lumber clumsily about the deck, arguing about who was leading, until Stephano tripped over Dag's feet and fell on his backside, rendering everyone helpless with laughter.

The mists parted. They could see the stars shining in the heavens and their laughter died away. They stood together and gazed upward in silence.

Miri returned to the helm. Using the stars as guide, she was able to calculate the ship's position. "We're near the Abbey of Saint Agnes," she reported to Stephano. "The nuns are friendly to Trundlers. They'll give us safe harbor and a hot meal. We can rest up and then sail on for Westfirth. I don't usually like to sail at night, but Rodrigo says the fixes are only temporary. He needs to do more work. We should reach the abbey by dawn."

Dag and the Doctor went down below to get a few hours of sleep. Rodrigo, exhausted, had fallen asleep in a deck chair. Stephano draped his coat over his friend.

"Thank you," he said.

"Don't mention it," Rodrigo murmured and rolled over.

The *Cloud Hopper* sailed near to the shoreline. They could see the running lights of other vessels: houseboats like theirs, a convoy of merchant ships traveling together for fear of pirates.

Stephano caught himself about to yawn and managed to close his mouth on it. He was too late, however. Miri had seen him.

"Go to bed," she told him. "You're still not fully recovered from your wound. There's nothing more you can do," she added, seeing him about to argue. "Gythe and I will take turns steering the boat."

Stephano felt weariness seep through him, starting at his feet and spreading upward. He gave Miri a brotherly kiss on the cheek and another for Gythe, who only grinned at him and shook her head, then he headed for his hammock.

He paused in the hatchway to look back. Miri and Gythe stood together at the helm, the wind blowing their hair wildly. They were sharing some private joke, apparently, for both were laughing softly.

Stephano thought how much he loved them, loved all of them. His family. Safe. He lay down in his hammock. The rocking motion of the boat lulled him to sleep.

When Stephano heard the cannon fire, he thought, like Sir Ander, that the booming noise of battle was part of his dream.

Chapter Twenty

We surround ourselves with wood and stone walls imbued with magic to keep us safe. Behind these walls, we cower. But walls do not make us safe, nor does sword or musket. It is the men and women who wield these weapons, standing shoulder-to-shoulder, that fight back the darkness.

—General Roberto Estaban,
Grand Army of Rosia, Ret.

SIR ANDER SAT UP IN BED, BLINKING IN THE LAMPLIGHT. Cannon fire. The booming sounds were real. Not a dream. He reached beneath his pillow, pulled out his pocket watch. The time was five of the clock, five hours past midnight.

"Father Jacob!"

The priest was sprawled across the table, sound asleep, his head resting on his arms. The lantern burned brightly, lighting the interior of the yacht. Making them excellent targets. Father Jacob sat bolt upright.

"They're here . . ." he said softly.

"Douse that light!" Sir Ander hissed.

Father Jacob spoke a word, and the lamp went out. In the darkness, Sir Ander reached up his hand to one of three ornate brass hooks fixed to the wall above his bed. His cloak hung on one of these hooks, his sword belt on the second. One hook was bare. He took hold of this hook and gave it a yank. The wall slid open, revealing a hidden cabinet. Inside were four pistols, including Sir Ander's favorite, his dragon pistol; bags of shot and gunpowder, and two long knives. He grabbed the dragon pistol.

"Use your new pistols!" Father Jacob said urgently. "The ones that don't require magic."

Sir Ander glared at him. "Am I never to have any secrets?"

Sir Ander couldn't see Father Jacob's smile in the darkness, but he could picture it. He pulled on his boots, grabbed one of the new pistols, and hurried over to the window. He parted the curtain and looked out to see winged shapes silhouetted black against the stars flying toward the yacht. Riding on their backs were creatures from a bad dream, men of darkness with orange glowing eyes.

"You're right, Father," said Sir Ander grimly. "They're here."

Green balls of flame, aimed at the yacht, showered down from the sky. The balls of green fire hit the "boarding net," his term for the defensive magic Father Jacob had embedded within the yacht's hull. The fire struck the magical net. Blue-and-red fire arced. Father Jacob cried out in pain.

Sir Ander reached the priest's side in a bound. Outside the yacht, green fire burst and blue fire sparked. Father Jacob had doubled over, groaning.

"Father, are you hurt? Were you shot?" Sir Ander had not heard a pistol go off, but that seemed the only explanation.

Father Jacob raised his head. His face, eerily reflected in the flaring green light, was wet with sweat and contorted with pain. He spoke in shuddering gasps.

"Contramagic . . . Destroying my spells . . ."

A large burst of green fire caused the yacht to shudder. Father Jacob cried out again. His body went into spasms, his hands jerking and twitching.

"Destroying your spells! It's destroying you!" Sir Ander cried. "What is happening?"

Father Jacob sat up, breathing heavily. The spasm had passed.

"They're trying to break into my mind!" he said, awed. He pressed his hand over his chest. "Erratic heartbeat, racing pulse, pain, and difficulty breathing ... Being a savant means my magic is physical ... a part of me ... They're trying to destroy my magic to see inside ... find out what I know ... I must ... make notes ..."

A flash of blue light was followed by a loud crackling sound and a horrible screeching. One of the bats had apparently flown into the magical netting. The net was still holding.

"Not for long," Father Jacob murmured, grimacing. "The contramagic is burning up sigil after sigil. My constructs are starting to break down, fall apart...."

Sir Ander had a sudden, terrifying thought. "Brother Barnaby! He's in the stables with the wyverns!"

"We must pray for him," said Father Jacob. "There is nothing we can do to help ..."

Sir Ander said an agonized prayer for the monk and returned to the cabinet. Every day, he unloaded and reloaded the pistols, making certain they were always ready to fire. He laid the four new pistols on the table, along with his dragon pistol. Catching hold of his sword belt, he looped it over his shoulder. He turned to find Father Jacob hurriedly gathering up the books they had taken from the abbey.

"Are the demons after those?" Sir Ander asked, astonished. "How could they? No one knows we found them!"

"They're here for us," said Father Jacob. "Because they know we're looking for the books, they want to find out what we've discovered."

A tapestry depicting the Four Saints hung on a wall at the back of the yacht. Father Jacob passed his hand over it, and the tapestry dissolved, revealing a second hidden compartment. Father Jacob thrust the books into the opening, closed it, then replaced the tapestry which itself was magical. He spoke a few words of magic, and sigils with connecting lines flared at his command, forming an additional complex spell of protection over the tapestry.

Another burst of green fire lit the interior of the yacht. The blast penetrated the net, striking one of the windows. The glass cracked. Father Jacob staggered beneath the blow and nearly fell. Sir Ander caught hold of him and lowered him into a chair.

Sir Ander was reminded of the time he'd been in a fortress under siege. The Guundarans had fired round after round. The din had been so constant he hadn't heard it after awhile. He and his men could do nothing but pray and endure the pounding and make ready for the attack that would come when the walls crumbled.

"I assume they're planning to kill us," said Sir Ander.

"They'll try to take us alive. Torture us first," said Father Jacob.

"You're such a comfort," Sir Ander growled.

More blasts rocked the yacht. Another window cracked. The hatch shivered, but the wood was magically reinforced, and it did not break. Sir Ander held two of the plain, unmagical pistols, one in each hand. A massive green burst of light struck the yacht, blowing out a window, sending shards of glass flying. Father Jacob clenched his fist and closed his eyes. Sweat rolled down his forehead. Blood dribbled from his mouth.

Sir Ander stood at the broken window, hoping to get off a good shot. The green fire blinded him, seemed to burst in the back of his eyeballs, leaving a blazing image imprinted on his eyes. The bats flitted past almost faster than he could see. He had no idea how he would hit one. He could not get a clear view of anything except the glowing orange eyes of the riders. He fired his pistol at one of the dark shapes, more out of frustration than with any hope of hitting it. He was rewarded with a shriek of pain that came either from the bat or its rider.

The shriek was heartening to Sir Ander.

"Damn fiends *are* mortal!"

He hadn't liked to admit it, but he'd had his doubts.

"Of course," Father Jacob said. "The demon yelped . . ."

"Ah, so that's what you meant," said Sir Ander. He threw the empty pistol on the table and picked up the third, then looked back with concern at Father Jacob. "You should go to the coffin."

"A bit premature, don't you think?" Father Jacob asked with a faint smile.

"You know what I mean," Sir Ander said tersely, peering out the window, watching for a shot.

The coffin was a compartment built into the floor of the yacht large enough to hold a man. It had been designed for occasions such as this. Father Jacob had given it the name after he'd been forced to use it once several years ago when the yacht had been attacked by a Freyan privateer lurking around outside the port of Marklin in Bruond, hoping to snap up the *Retribution*, the yacht belonging to the traitor, Father Jacob Northrop, to collect the bounty on the priest's head. He had boarded the yacht and searched it, but found nothing. The approach of a frigate bearing the Rosian flag had driven the Freyan off.

Father Jacob shook his head. "I can help you."

"How?" Sir Ander demanded. "You're so weak, you can barely stand up!"

Father Jacob raised an eyebrow. "I am perfectly capable of working my magic sitting down—"

"Damn it, Jacob, this isn't funny!" Sir Ander said angrily. He glanced around. "You could reload."

"I can do that," said Father Jacob and he picked up one of the spent pistols and began to pour in the powder.

One of the bats—this one riderless—dove straight at the window, screeching horribly, wings flapping. Sir Ander fired at its mouth. The bat slammed into the side of the yacht. Blood and bits of fur and flesh spewed through the broken window.

"The net's been destroyed," Sir Ander reported.

The demons were hurling green fireballs at the hatch, trying to batter it down. Reinforced with iron and magical spells, the hatch continued to hold, but it wouldn't stop them for long. Father Jacob handed Sir Ander two pistols, both reloaded. Through the broken window, the knight could see the stars starting to fade with the coming of dawn. Green fire blazed. He heard the sound of claws raking the wood. He tried not to think about how the nuns had died.

Cocking the hammers of each pistol, he aimed them at the hatch. He spoke over his shoulder. "Jacob, please go to the hiding place. If not for your sake, then for my own. I took an oath before God to protect you with my life. If I am to die, do not let me die with the knowledge that I failed."

Father Jacob gasped, shuddered, and gripped hold of the table. He gave a fleeting smile. "I have always wanted to study the effects of contramagic . . . This is my chance . . ."

Sir Ander turned, met the priest's eyes. He saw in them faith in God, trust in God's plan, and deep affection for himself.

"You are my friend," said Father Jacob simply.

"And you're a pain in the ass," Sir Ander said gruffly. "You know that."

Father Jacob chuckled. Several blasts struck the hatch. The priest cried out and slumped over the table, clutching it in agony.

Sir Ander could hear the bats screeching and raking the hatch with their teeth and claws. Father Jacob managed to straighten. He gritted his teeth and inscribed a sigil on the back of his hand and faced the hatch and waited.

"This is it," said Sir Ander.

The hatch shattered in a blinding ball of green flame. The riders surged inside. Sir Ander fired both pistols at the mass of seething bodies. Father Jacob raised his hand, fingers outspread, and spoke an arcane word. Five streams of pure white fire flared from his fingers. The holy fire of God's wrath burst on His foes. The demons screamed and fell back. More took their places. A blazing comet of green fire burst near Sir Ander, throwing him back against the wall and filling the yacht with choking smoke.

Father Jacob slumped over the table. Sir Ander staggered to his feet. The demons were waiting for the smoke to clear before they entered to finish them off. He threw down the useless pistols and reached for his last gun, his dragon pistol. He held the gun in his left hand and gripped his sword in the right.

Four demons stood in the hatchway, their orange eyes glowing, their faces hideously contorted in skull-like grins. They were about to surge inside when a fearsome roar, coming out of the sky, stopped them.

"Take cover!" Hroal shouted.

Flames blazed down from the sky, engulfing the demons. They died screaming, burned alive, their bodies shriveling in red-orange fire that poured from the dragon's mouth. Sir Ander had no time to heed the dragon's warning, and he was driven back by the intense heat. One of the demons, his body ablaze, staggered inside the yacht. Sir Ander fired his pistol at the fiend, and it fell back through the hatch.

Suddenly the night was quiet. Horribly quiet. Greasy smoke floated in through the hatch, bringing with it the sickening stench of burnt flesh and singed bat hair. He stepped cautiously over wreckage—nothing was left of the hatch. Peering through the greasy smoke, he looked out on a hellish scene. The blackened bones of bats and demons mingled together in smoldering heaps.

"Still alive, sir?" A voice shouted the question from above.

Sir Ander looked up to see the first rays of sunlight sparkle on gray-green scales. The dragon circled overhead, peering down in concern.

"Thanks to you, Flight Master Hroal!" Sir Ander returned, coughing. "Are there more out there?"

"Rest flew off. Didn't see me coming." The dragon appeared inordinately proud of himself. "Probably went for reinforcements."

"Keep watch!" Sir Ander shouted.

The dragon dipped a wing in salute and began flying over the yacht in circles.

Fighting down a wave of nausea, Sir Ander hurried back inside. Father Jacob was breathing, but he was unconscious.

Sir Ander was baffled. Trained in tending battlefield wounds, he knew how to dig a bullet out of a man's chest, set a broken leg, apply a tourniquet to stop bleeding. The priest's injuries were beyond him. He had no idea how to help Father Jacob, because he had no idea what was wrong. He recalled something the priest had said about the magic attacking him physically . . .

"I need Brother Barnaby," Sir Ander said to himself. 'He's a healer. He'll know what to do."

He ran back outside and yelled up at the dragon, circling overhead. "Hroal, I need you to carry a message to the monk, Brother Barnaby. He's in the stables! Tell him to come—"

"Stables?" The dragon shook his head. "Fire."

Sir Ander stared at him, a cold qualm twisting his gut.

"Bats," said Hroal, further elaborating. "Stables on fire."

Sir Ander remembered Father Jacob's words.

They're here for us . . . We know too much . . .

"They're going to torture Brother Barnaby, too. Oh, God, no! Hroal!" Sir Ander shouted. "Can you help the monk?"

Hroal was dubious. "More demons on the way, sir. I shouldn't leave."

Logic dictated that Sir Ander should ask the dragon to remain here to help him protect Father Jacob, but logic had not met Brother Barnaby. Nor did Sir Ander want to hear what Father Jacob would have to say if he survived at the cost of the life of the gentle monk.

"You go to the monk, Hroal!" Sir Ander shouted. "I'll stay here."

Hroal dipped his wings in acknowledgment and flew off. Sir Ander remembered the cutter, remembered the boom of cannon fire and he looked hopefully in the direction of the naval ship. The cutter, too, was on fire. The bats were a black swarm around it, far too many to count. And now, in the predawn light, he could see a large number of the bats flying inland, heading for the yacht.

Sir Ander hastened back inside. Father Jacob was still unconscious. His skin was cold and clammy to the touch, but his breathing was regular. Sir Ander lifted the priest and carried him to his bed, wrapped him warmly in blankets, and rested his hand on the priest's shoulder and said a prayer, commending himself and his friends to God. Then he picked up the sturdy table where they worked and ate and carried it to the rear corner of the yacht. He climbed up on the table, opened the trapdoor that led to the yacht's stern where he had mounted the swivel gun on the stand and loaded the first canister.

Now all he could do was wait and watch and pray.

The abbey stables were constructed of stone and timber; good solid construction dating back to the time of the abbey's glory days when the prince-abbot entertained members of the nobility residing in the abbey's comfortable guesthouse. At that time, the stables' occupants might have numbered thirty or more, including horses, wyverns, and griffins.

The stables were large, narrow buildings, three in number, and were designed to comfortably house each of the species. Not only did wyverns and griffins require different types of lodging, this practice was also useful for keeping the wyverns and griffins from dining on horsemeat. All the stables consisted of two rows of stalls with large doors at either end. The floor was of brick with drainage channels running down the center. The stalls in the wyvern and griffin stables were much larger than those for the horses in order to accommodate room for the wings.

The practical nuns, who kept no horses or wyverns, had no need for the stables. They housed their sheep and goats and cows in one building during the winter and used the other two for storage.

The stables were located some distance from the main

part of the abbey complex (to keep guests from being offended by the smell). The demons might not have seen them during the first attack or, if they had, did not think it worth their time to set fire to them. Brother Barnaby's wyverns were happy with their accomodations, which were much airier and more open than those of the inns where they were often forced to reside. Wyvern stables at inns tended to be small and cramped.

Brother Barnaby fed his wyverns hunks of meat soaked in brine which he kept stored in barrels beneath the yacht. The wyverns preferred fresh meat, but they would not hunt with the dragons flying overhead. They gulped down the large chunks hungrily.

Worn out from the emotional and physical rigors of the day, Brother Barnaby hung the leather harnesses and halters used to tether the wyverns to the yacht on iron nails driven into the walls. He said his prayers, adding a special prayer for the souls of the martyrs, and then made himself a bed in an empty stall and wrapped himself in his blanket. He sank into a deep sleep.

He was wakened by the wyverns restlessly prowling about their stall, making loud screeching sounds, clawing at the floor, and hitting their tails against the sides of the stall. Such behavior was unusual, especially after a long and tiring journey. He ascribed their nervousness to the proximity of the dragons and he went into their stall to try to reassure them that they were safe. The wyverns could not see the dragons, nor hear them, yet they seemed unable to settle.

The wyverns calmed down for the moment, curled up on the straw-strewn floor, their tails wrapped around their bodies, their heads buried in their tails, and closed their eyes. Brother Barnaby returned wearily to his bed, only to be roused again by their screeching. He was certain the noise must be disturbing Father Jacob and Sir Ander, even though the *Retribution* was on the other side of the wall, some forty yards distance from the stables. Wyverns have carrying calls.

Fearing they would rouse Father Jacob, Brother Barnaby picked up his blanket and went to stay with his wyverns in their stall. His presence soothed the beasts—at least they quit screeching and lay down. But the wyverns remained exceedingly nervous. They could not sleep. He could see their reptilian eyes glittering in the darkness.

Their nervousness began to affect Brother Barnaby. Wyverns were believed to be distantly related to dragons (who indignantly refuted this claim) and, though wyverns were not nearly as smart as their more advanced cousins, wyverns had good instincts. Brother Barnaby recalled the time his wyverns had stubbornly refused to fly, going so far as to rip the leather halter out of his hands when he'd tried to put it on. Father Jacob had been incensed and suggested darkly that they have wyvern stew for dinner. Within a matter of hours, a fierce storm came out of nowhere, with hail, hurricane-force winds, and torrential rain. If the *Retribution* had been caught in the storm, the yacht would have crashed. Brother Barnaby gently pointed this out to Father Jacob, who grumbled, but eventually apologized to the wyverns, though he was still heard to refer to them as "witless lizards."

Near dawn, Brother Barnaby and the wyverns both heard the cannon fire. The wyverns' heads reared up, yellow eyes gleaming in alarm. Brother Barnaby knew the naval cutter was flying routine patrols. Sir Ander had pointed it out to him. The monk did not have much experience with navy ships or naval customs. He had no idea why the ship would be firing its guns. He wondered if it was some sort of salute.

The stable had windows on both sides of the building, allowing for the flow of fresh air through the stalls. Brother Barnaby walked over to the window and looked out. He could not see the naval cutter. The abbey wall blocked his view.

The cannon fire continued unabated and now even someone as naïve about naval warfare as Brother Barnaby realized this was no salute. The ship was engaged in battle.

The wyverns were on their feet, tails twitching. Their nostrils flared. They turned their heads this way and that, sniffing the air and not liking what they smelled, apparently, for their lips rolled back in snarls, exposing sharp fangs.

Green fire suddenly lit the night. The fire came from the other side of the abbey wall in the direction of the *Retribution*. Brother Barnaby could hear shrill, ear-piercing shrieks mingled with the sound of crackling explosions. He heard a bang, the report of a pistol.

Green fire—the demons.

Father Jacob and Sir Ander were under attack by the same demons who had slaughtered the nuns. Brother Barnaby's first reaction was to go to the aid of his friends, do what he could to help. He was turning from the window when he heard whirring sounds. He bat wings blotting out the stars and the glowing orange eyes of their demon riders.

The orange eyes saw him.

Shocked and appalled, Brother Barnaby sprang back from the window. He now knew what had been upsetting his wyverns, who were crazed with fear, flapping their wings and stomping their feet and lashing out with their tails. Trapped inside, they might break bones or tear the membrane of their wings. Brother Barnaby flung open the gate to the stall and tried to drive the wyverns out.

The panicked beasts were flustered and afraid. He shouted and waved his arms and finally they obeyed him and ran from the stall. Still shouting, he drove the wyverns down the long aisle toward the large stable doors that were standing wide open.

A ball of green fire flew through a window into one of the stalls. The timber posts and straw burst into flames. The fire and smoke spurred on the wyverns. They shrieked in terror and made a dash for it. Running out of the stable door, the wyverns spread their wings and were about to take to the air when they were attacked by the bats and their demons riders.

Brutish, sullen, and not very smart, wyverns are notorious bullies and cowards. They will kill deer, sheep, horses, cows, or humans—any prey not likely to put up a fight. Confronted by a dragon, a griffin, or even a good-size eagle, wyverns will turn tail and run for their lives.

The wyverns had never encountered such creatures as these gigantic bats, which dove and darted at their heads in an attempt to claw out their eyes. The wyverns had no intention of fighting this strange and terrifying foe. Shrieking in terror and pain, the wyverns kept trying frantically to escape by taking to the air. The bats clustered thick around them, striking at their wings, preventing them from getting off the ground.

Green fireballs burst in the stables. The building was now fully engulfed in flame. Half-blinded by smoke, Brother Barnaby heard his wyverns' frightened screams and saw them surrounded by the darting bats. He grabbed a length of flaming timber and ran out of the stables.

The bats had no riders. Brother Barnaby did not stop to think about what that might mean. His one thought was to save his wyverns. He waved the flaming brand at one of the bats. The bat snarled and shrieked at him, but the creature did not like the fire and veered off.

Heartened, Brother Barnaby drove away two more bats and one of the wyverns managed spread his wings and fly off the ground. A bat clung to the neck of the second wyvern, biting at the wyvern's head and trying to dig its claws into the scales. The wyvern was frantic with pain and terror, shrieking and flinging its head about, trying to dislodge the bat. Brother Barnaby struck the bat with the flaming timber. Burning cinders set the bat's hair ablaze. The bat snarled and let go its hold on the wyvern and flew off, trailing smoke.

Barnaby slapped the wyvern on its flank and yelled at it, urging it to fly. The wyvern at last managed to leap into the air. Now that the wyverns were airborne, they could attack with their claws. The bats hung back, wary.

"Fly!" Barnaby yelled at the wyverns. "Fly away!"

Something caused him to turn around. He did not know what. Perhaps he heard something. Perhaps it was nothing more than primal instinct, the prickling of the hair on the back of his neck. Brother Barnaby felt the foe behind him and whipped around. He saw glaring orange eyes and the reflection of their hideous light on the blade of an ax poised to strike him.

Brother Barnaby had never received martial training. The monk was a healer and had vowed to never take a human life. He acted out of instinct, thrusting the flaming wood straight at the glowing eyes, striking the demon in the face. The glowing orange light went out. The demon dropped the ax and clasped its hands over its face. Three more pairs of orange eyes emerged from the stables. The demons were closing in on him.

He saw suddenly these same fiends attacking the helpless nuns, their axes cutting off their limbs, chopping up the bodies, feeding them to their bats. Anger blazed inside Brother Barnaby, anger such as he had never known before. He had read about the wrath of God. He knew then how God felt.

Yelling wildly, he flung himself at the demons, battering them with his timber, hitting them on the head, shoulder, back, whatever was near. He startled them with the ferocity and suddenness of his attack and for a moment he actually drove the demons back. Then the demons saw that he was armed with nothing but a wooden stick, and they fell on him. He was bleeding and crying out in rage, knowing he was bound to fall before his foes, for he was outnumbered with no weapons now except his fists. All he wanted before death came was to make these fiends suffer.

Shrill shrieks came from above him and the demon standing in front of Barnaby disappeared, hit by a lashing wyvern tail that lifted the fiend off his feet and flung him into the stable wall. The same wyvern lit on top of another demon, flattening it beneath its claws. The second wyvern caught up a demon in its mouth and shook it like a sheep, breaking its neck.

Brother Barnaby fell to the ground. The fire of his fury had died down as suddenly as it had blazed up. A wound in his arm was bleeding profusely. His head ached from a blow. He could taste blood in his mouth. He felt unbearable cold steal through him and knew he was going into shock.

Dawn was gray in the heavens. Looking up, he saw silhouetted against the sky, more bats and more demons with their orange glowing eyes. They were hurling green fire down on the wyverns, his beloved wyverns, who, instead of flying off to save themselves, had come back to fight for him.

The fire hit the wyverns on the neck and back and wings. Wherever the fire touched, flames bubbled and boiled like acid, eating away their scales and burning through to their flesh. The wyverns screamed and flailed about in agony. They tried to fly away, but the green fire was burning holes in their wings. Barnaby tried to go to their aid, but he was too weak. He heard himself shouting curses at the demons. He heard himself shouting curses at God.

The wyverns' screams changed to gurgling gasps and they sank feebly to the ground and lay there, thrashing about in their death throes. Barnaby managed to drag himself over to the head of one of his wyverns. The wyvern saw him and gave a pitiful moan. Barnaby gathered the wyvern's head in his arms and held the dying beast close to his breast, rocking and murmuring until he felt the head droop in death.

The demons were coming for him now. Barnaby closed his eyes and gave himself into God's hands.

Chapter Twenty-One

Trundler tradition says approach your destination from the west whenever possible. This way you greet the sun in the morning. And always keep your eye on the Breath. Her moods are reflected in the color of the mist.

— The Story of the Trundlers
by Miri McPike

"STEPHANO!" THE BOOMING VOICE SHATTERED dreams of battle.

Hearing the urgency in the voice, Stephano rolled out of his bunk ... only to find that he hadn't been in a bunk. He had been in a hammock suspended from a beam overhead and he was now lying on the deck, swearing at the pain in his injured shoulder.

Cognizance returned a second later. Stephano staggered to his feet. He'd been sleeping in his clothes for warmth. Clad in shirt sleeves and trousers, he thrust his feet into his boots and started to reach for his coat, only to realize that the air was warm again. They had risen up out of the depths of the Breath. He grabbed the small pistol he'd tucked into the inner pocket of his coat and raced up to the top deck.

Dag was at the rail, staring intently at the twin spires of a large cathedral silhouetted against the light gray-blue of approaching dawn. The boat itself was still in darkness. The stars above shone brightly. The balloon was fully inflated. The sails billowed with God's Breath.

Miri, at the controls, was also gazing out into the east. Rodrigo was sitting up in the deck chair in which he'd spent the night, groaning and rubbing his neck and back and demanding querulously to know why no one had awakened him.

All seemed right with the world.

"I must have been dreaming," Stephano said. "I thought I heard cannon fire."

"You weren't," said Dag, adding grimly, "You did."

A flash of orange in the distance was followed by a loud boom. Stephano rubbed his eyes that were bleary with sleep.

"Sounds like a four-pounder," he said, referring to the cannon.

"So I'm guessing," said Dag, with a nod.

Miri reached down below the brass control panel to a small storage area to retrieve the ship's spyglass. Stephano held the glass to his eye and, after a moment's search, made out the two masts and ballast balloons of a navy cutter. As he watched, the ship's starboard cannons fired raggedly. The gun crews were being told to fire as they found their targets, not to wait for all to be fired in a broadside. The navy ship was under attack, but by who or what was the question. Bursts of strange green fire illuminated the cutter. Stephano was frankly puzzled by this sight.

"What the hell is making those green flashes?" Stephano asked Dag.

"Damned if I know, sir," Dag replied. "Some sort of signal flare?"

"No," said Stephano, staring through the glass until his eyes began to water. "The green fire is not coming *from* the cutter. It appears to be aimed at it."

Miri took the glass from Stephano and put it to her eye. "Is that navy ship firing on the Abbey of Saint Agnes?"

"Perhaps His Majesty has finally declared war on the grand bishop," said Rodrigo, coming to stand alongside Stephano.

Miri's eyes flashed, her brows constricted.

"He's teasing, Miri," said Stephano and hastily changed the subject. "I could use a cup of hot tea. Anyone else?"

"Gythe and the Doctor went to put on the kettle," said Miri, still glowering.

"Rigo, go help," said Stephano.

Rodrigo grinned and departed.

Stephano assured Miri that the king would never declare war on the nuns and also pointed out that the cutter was aiming at something in the Breath, not on shore. He and Dag continued to watch the orange flashes and green flaring lights blaze in the distance. Miri, not entirely convinced, went back to her steering.

"Pirates?" asked Dag.

Stephano shook his head. "No pirate in his right mind would be fool enough to attack a navy cutter that carries fourteen four-pounders. Might be a Freyan privateer . . ."

They watched for another few moments, then Stephano said, "Miri, is it my imagination or are we sailing closer to the battle?"

"We are sailing closer to the Abbey of Saint Agnes. We were going to stop there to get a hot meal, remember?" said Miri with a look of innocence.

"Uh-huh." Stephano grunted. "Our meal's liable to be a bit hotter than we can swallow if we end up in the middle of a naval battle with the Freyans."

"The nuns were always good to Gythe and me," said Miri. "If anything *is* wrong, we might be able to help."

She glanced at him and Dag from out the corner of her eye. Her red hair was damp from the mist and clung to her face. Her eyes narrowed. "Do either of you have a problem with that?"

Dag cleared his throat, rubbed his grizzled chin, glanced at Stephano, and said in a low voice, "Sorry, sir, but you're on your own." Dag moved off to take cover behind the mast.

"Miri, be sensible. We don't want to get caught in the middle of a naval bombardment—"

"So now you're calling me daft," Miri said.

"I never said any such thing!" Stephano returned.

"You said I wasn't being sensible. That's the same as daft."

"It is not—" Stephano began, then he stopped, drew a deep breath, and started over. "If one stray cannonball hit the balloon or the lift tanks or took down a mast, the *Cloud Hopper* would be finished. We're only a few hours from Westfirth. We'll sail there, report what we saw—"

A billowing mass of red flame suddenly lit up the sky. Stephano forgot Miri, forgot everything.

"I'll be damned! That's dragon fire!" Stephano said excitedly. He seized hold of the spyglass and brought it to his eye. "There's a dragon in this battle! Maybe a dragon from the Brigade!"

Miri glanced at him from beneath her long lashes and said demurely, "Too bad we're sailing for Westfirth." She held her hand poised over the helm.

"We might move in a little closer," said Stephano. "Just to get a better view."

"Now who's daft," said Miri, jabbing him in the ribs with her elbow.

An offshore breeze carried the *Cloud Hopper* landward. The sky and mists were now a pale pink. The orange flashes were no longer as bright as they had been in the darkness. The cannon fire was more sporadic. The strange green lights continued to flare. Rodrigo and Gythe brought up crockery mugs filled with steaming tea and handed them around. Doctor Ellington jumped up to his usual place on Dag's shoulder.

"What is going on?" Rodrigo demanded suddenly. "Do you know we are sailing closer to the battle? Why are we sailing closer?"

He jabbed his finger at the cutter, that could be seen quite clearly now. "People are shooting at each other out there!"

Stephano was searching the skies. "There he is!" he

called, and he pointed at the cathedral spires. The dragon could be seen flying over the cathedral. Wings spread, he was soaring upward, gaining altitude.

"He's spiraling around for a dive!" Stephano said. His brow creased in a frown. "He's not climbing very fast, though."

"He's an elder dragon," said Miri, looking through the glass. "I can see the silvering of the scales on his head and mane. I don't think he was in the Brigade, Stephano. This dragon is not a trained fighter. He has no idea what he's doing."

"Things are not going well for the cutter," said Dag, shaking his head. "I've been watching the flashes, and I count only nine cannons firing. That means five of their guns have been knocked out. Has to be Freyans, sir."

Stephano took the spyglass and aimed it at the cutter. He drew the glass away, rubbed his eyes.

"I must be seeing things."

He handed the glass to Dag. "You take a look."

"I have narrowly escaped certain death three times in as many days," Rodrigo was saying. "That's way over my limit. Can we please turn around and get the Hell out of here?"

"Just a bit closer," said Stephano. "We can always slip away without being noticed. Dag . . ."

"You weren't seeing things, sir. Those black creatures flying around the cutter. The green fire seems to be coming from them."

"That's what I thought," said Stephano. He hesitated a moment, then asked, "What do those creatures look like to you?"

Dag scratched his jaw. "You're going to think *I'm* daft, sir . . ."

"If you are, then so am I. Bats?"

"Bats the size of a bloody horse, sir," said Dag.

Rodrigo snorted. "Oh, come now, you two—"

"You look," said Dag, and he handed over the spyglass. Rodrigo set down his tea mug on the table, took the glass, stared through it for a long moments, then handed it back to Dag. "I need something stronger than tea. Where's the Calvados?"

"That's for medicinal purposes only!" Miri called after him, as he dove into the hold.

"This *is* medicinal!" Rodrigo's voice floated up from below. "I'm seeing giant bats!"

"Oh, for mercy's sake!" Miri said in disgust. "I think you've *all* gone daft."

Stephano raised the spyglass. "The beasts fly like bats, that's for certain. The way bats dart and flit about."

He stared, eyes squinting, trying to see. "It looks as though the bats have riders . . ." He lowered the glass. "Riders with glowing eyes. Like demons . . ."

They were all startled by a crash. Stephano turned to see Gythe, white to the lips, staring at him in horror. She had dropped the mug she was holding. It lay broken on the deck.

"This isn't funny! You're scaring her! Stop it, Stephano!" Miri cried. "Gythe, dear, they're not serious. I'll prove it. Stephano, give me the glass!"

Wordlessly, Stephano handed her the spyglass. Miri brought the glass to her eye. Her face paled. She watched a moment, then took the glass away and returned it to Stephano.

"Dag, take the helm," said Miri. She walked over to her sister. "Gythe, come below . . ."

Gythe shook her head. Crooking her fingers into claws, she made a motion of tearing at flesh. Then she pointed at her eyes and pointed in the direction of the battle.

"My God!" Miri said in a low voice. "Is *that* what you saw? Gythe, tell me . . ."

Gythe shook her head wildly and began to sing. Her song was frantic and wild and desperate. She flung out her hands and strands of brilliant blue magic streamers arced and flared around the ship.

Rodrigo emerged from the hatch, Calvados bottle in hand, and stared about, appalled.

"Gythe, what are you doing? Gythe! No! Stop!"

Gythe kept flinging magic into the air. The bright blue coils twined about the masts, sparked on the balloon and danced over the deck.

"What was that about slipping away without being noticed, sir?" Dag asked worriedly. "We're lit up like the palace on His Majesty's birthday."

The others stared in shock and amazement at the dazzling display, the magical blue light reflected in their faces. Gythe's song ended in a strangled cry. She collapsed, sobbing, onto the deck.

Rodrigo handed the bottle to Stephano, then knelt down beside her, took hold of her in his arms, patting her and soothing her. She clung to him, sobbing. He looked at the others, who were standing, transfixed.

"What happened?" Rodrigo demanded. "What did you say to her?"

"It's what she said to us," Miri replied, her voice quivering. "Giant bats! That's what she saw on board our ship. Blood and claw marks and . . ." She choked and covered her mouth with her hand.

"Giant bats with demon riders," said Stephano.

"I suggest we leave *now!*" said Rodrigo in stern tones. "This isn't our fight, Stephano."

"The dragon is attacking the bats, breathing fire at them." Dag reported, keeping an eye on the battle as he steered the ship. He suddenly began swearing. "Bloody Hell! The dragon flew too close to the cutter. He set one of the masts on fire. The balloon will go next. The cutter's liable to sink, sir."

Stephano ran to the rail to try to see better. "Damn it! Miri was right. That dragon has never been trained for battle."

He watched a moment longer, then said, "Dag, turn over the helm to Miri. We need to get out of here."

"We can't just leave, sir! There are over sixty sailors on that cutter," Dag protested. "We can't let them die!"

"We are five people on a houseboat," said Stephano. "We can't do anything to help them. Besides, there's Gythe to consider."

Dag glanced at Gythe, who was sobbing and shivering in Rodrigo's arms, and he reluctantly relinquished the helm to Miri. She touched the sigils on the brass panel and sent the magic flowing out to the sails and the airscrews. The *Cloud Hopper* was starting to veer away when Miri, looking to the north, gave a cry and a gasp.

The mists of the Breath, generally wispy, peach in color and calm, drifting on gentle breezes, had changed. Thick clouds, black and turbid and shot with spiky, white-purple lightning, were rumbling across the sky.

"What the Hell is that?" Stephano gasped. He'd flown the Breath since he was a child through rain and snow and every type of weather and he'd never seen anything like this.

"They call it a wizard storm!" Rodrigo cried. "The magic in the Breath has gone berserk. Take cover! There's nothing we can do except ride it out."

He dragged Gythe through the hatch. The wind slammed it shut behind him.

"Grab hold of something and hang on!" Miri cried.

Stephano flung his arms around the mast. Dag thrust Doctor Ellington under one arm and wound his other arm around one of the ropes securing the cannons. Miri glanced around, nodded, and remained standing at the helm.

"Miri! Get down!" Stephano shouted.

Miri shook her head. Her red hair streamed out from her head, her skirts whipped around her. She was bent nearly double, her hands gripping the helm. Stephano could do nothing to help her. He tried letting go of the mast and was slammed back against the bulkhead. Dag battled the wind and managed to drag open the hatch. He tossed the terrified, spitting, and yowling cat down the stairs, then struggled over to Miri.

He braced her with his body, reaching his arms around

her—one strong arm on either side—and took hold of the top of the helm. Gripping the brass helm with all his strength, he shielded Miri's body with his own just as the wizard storm hit.

Black clouds, dark as night, engulfed the boat. Buffeting wind came at them from every direction. The boat heeled violently and Stephano thought for an agonizing moment that they were going to flip over. He couldn't see anything until the lightning sizzled, and then everything was lit for an instant and then went dark. Thunder rolled over the boat. He clung to the bottom of the mast to keep himself from sliding across the canting deck. He heard a crash from below and he thought he heard a scream, but he couldn't tell if the howl was a voice or the wind. His biggest fear was that one of the two cannons would break loose and go careening about the deck, crushing everything in its path. Another blast of wind hit the ship, this time from a different direction. One of the deck chairs flew across the deck, slammed into Stephano's shin, and then went skittering off.

As quickly as the storm struck, it was gone. The clouds rumbled past. The wind was no longer wild and erratic, but no one was relieved at the change. A strong, steady breeze was blowing the *Cloud Hopper* directly into the line of fire.

Stephano jumped to his feet and looked around. Miri was safe, held fast in Dag's arms. He released her and she remained at the helm, both of them flushed and breathless and unable to look at each other.

Stephano opened the hatch. "Rigo! Gythe! Are you all right?"

Rodrigo came up onto the deck, followed by Gythe, holding fast to Doctor Ellington. Rodrigo was bleeding from a cut on his forehead. Gythe was unharmed and so was the cat, though he was howling and spitting angrily, all "furred out," his tail bristling like a bottle brush.

Gythe deposited the cat onto the deck. The Doctor ran immediately to his hiding place beneath one of the cannons and glared at them, certain they were responsible. The houseboat was being carried straight toward the battle. The wizard storm evaporated. The sun shone on the twin spires of the cathedral, the burning cutter, and the attacking bats.

Stephano whipped out the spyglass and brought it to his eye.

"Miri," he said, keeping his voice deliberately calm, "you need to take us away from here."

Miri's hands flew over the sigils. She turned her head, glared at him.

"I'm trying, damn it! We're being sucked into a vortex—"

"It's the magic," Rodrigo said, dabbing at the cut on his head with his handkerchief. "This storm wasn't caused by atmospheric changes in air pressure. This storm was caused by a disruption in the magic of the Breath."

Dag was frowning. "Remember the writings of Saint Marie. 'And on that day the Gates of Hell will open and the fell legions of Aertheum will fly forth on hideous beasts and the Breath will erupt in fire and the stars fall. . . .'"

"Ah," said Rodrigo, looking at the blood on the handkerchief. "Hit by a falling star. That explains it."

Dag glowered. He was a devout man and took his faith very seriously.

"Not the time for jesting, Rigo," said Stephano quietly.

Rodrigo nodded his head toward Gythe. "Look at her if you don't believe me. She feels the magic. And so can I. I've gone all gooseflesh and it's not because I'm shivering with terror—even though I am. Our little boat is caught in the wild, foaming waters of a magical rapids."

Rodrigo pointed to the giant bats and their demonic riders. "Wherever they have come from, that green fire is not 'fire.' It's magic of some sort. Very powerful magic. So powerful that it is fomenting this wizard storm. Which must mean . . ."

He paused, his brows drawing together in thought.

"But it can't be . . . It's not possible!"

"Rigo—"

"Not now. I have to think."

Rodrigo went back down belowdecks. They heard a thud and a crash and a "Bloody Hell! Where are my books?" Followed by, "Oh, never mind, I found them," and then silence.

Stephano was only half-listening. They were being sucked rapidly closer to the coastline. The abbey and its walls were now visible through the mists. Bats swarmed over the walls. The abbey itself was under assault. On board the cutter, the sailors had managed to douse the flames, but the mast was gone. The captain had ordered chains dropped over the sides, to keep the bats from attacking the ship from below. A few cannons continued to fire. The cutter, though crippled, was gamely fighting on. But as Stephano watched, the cutter fired a distress signal.

The dragon flew in circles above the ship, no longer fighting the bats. Naval officers had small use for dragons, anyway, and Stephano could imagine the captain's rage at the dragon who had accidentally set the mast on fire. The captain must have furiously ordered the dragon to keep his distance.

And yet, Stephano thought, the dragon has a much better chance of killing these monsters with his fire than the naval gunners have of hitting one of the swift flying creatures. The *Cloud Hopper* was being drawn ever closer.

"They've seen us," said Stephano.

Several bats had veered off from the attack on the cutter. The demon riders, with their strange fiery orange eyes, seemed to be staring straight at him. He hurriedly lowered the spyglass and turned to Gythe.

"Those spells of yours. Will they protect the boat?"

Gythe cast a frightened glance at the bats and shrank away. Shaking her head, she put her hands over her ears.

"She is afraid of the ... er ... demons," said Miri with a glance at Dag. "Gythe says their words hurt her. They're trying to get inside her head."

"Words? I don't hear any words. And how can they get inside her?"

Miri gave a helpless shrug. "I don't know what she means."

Stephano took hold of Gythe's hands and drew them away from her ears, forcing her to listen to him.

"Gythe, dear, we don't have a choice. Those demons or whatever they are have seen us. They may attack us at any moment. Those spells of protection you cast ... *This* is the reason you cast them! Does your magic work?"

Gythe looked uncertain, then she gave him a tremulous smile and tilted her head and made a gesture with her hand as of something coming out of her throat.

"She needs to sing the magic," said Miri, translating. "If she sings, the protection spells will work."

"Good," Stephano said. He paused, struck by a sudden, unwelcome thought. "These spells won't stop us from firing our guns at the bats, will they? I mean, the cannonballs won't bounce off the magic and hit us ..."

Gythe flashed an indignant look at him and made a rude gesture. Miri started to translate. Stephano grinned.

"No need. I understand. I'm sorry, Gythe. It *was* a stupid question. Dag—"

"Yes, sir."

Stephano cleared his throat, uncomfortable. "If those creatures *are* demons ..."

"'The righteous will be called upon to drive them back through the gates,' sir," said Dag.

"Yes, good," said Stephano, relieved.

"We'll use the swivel guns," said Dag. "No time to load the cannons."

The swivel guns were small, breech-loading cannons mounted on the rail of the boat. The guns had removable chambers that could be preloaded with powder and grape-shot and then inserted into the breech. Once the gun had been fired, all the gunner had to do was to remove the spent chamber and ram home another. The four swivel guns also had the advantage of mobility. The gunner could pick one up and carry it to another part of the ship, whereas the cannons were mounted on trucks that were roped in place.

Dag headed down below to fetch the chambers. The *Cloud Hopper* had two four-pounder cannons, mounted on the main deck, one on the starboard side and one on the port, and one "frog," so-called because the cannon's squat body and wide mouth resembled the reptile. The frog was positioned on the sterncastle, placed there to protect the helm. The frog fired an enormous cannonball, twenty-four pounds, or a variety of other types of shot, but had limited range.

Few Trundler vessels were so well armed. Most could not have afforded such expensive weapons, and there was generally no need for Trundlers to have to defend themselves. The biggest danger in the Breath was from pirates, and they almost never attacked Trundler houseboats, for the Trundlers carried little of value. A Trundler boat might be armed with a single swivel gun or an old-fashioned ballista. Most relied on muskets and pistols for defense.

"Dag!" Stephano shouted down the hatch. "While you're there, bring your pipes!"

Dag stopped on the stairs and stared up at him in astonishment. "My what?"

"Bring your bagpipes! And tell Rigo to quit reading and start helping!"

Dag shook his head in bewilderment and continued on down.

"Why do you want him to play the pipes?" Miri asked tersely. "A funeral dirge as we're dragged into Hell?"

Stephano didn't answer. He was gazing at the cutter, measuring the distance between them with his eye.

"Miri, there must be *some* way for you to steer this boat." He looked up at the balloon. "We have lift. We're not sinking . . ."

Miri sighed, then, and shook her head. "Only in the direction the magic is taking us. We can't maneuver or change course."

"All you need to do is aim for the cutter. That's more or less sailing in a straight line." Stephano pointed in the direction they needed to go. "If we can reach the cutter, we can team up to protect each other."

Sixty sailors defending the cutter, five on the *Cloud Hopper*. Six counting the Doctor, who had been forcibly removed from beneath the cannon by Gythe. Judging by the cat's dismal howls, the good Doctor was now locked up in the storage closet.

Dag emerged onto the deck, carrying a large wooden case in one hand and a gunnysack filled with preloaded canisters in another. Rodrigo followed, staggering beneath the weight of a similar sack, which he flung with a sigh onto the deck, narrowly missing his own foot, and turned to Stephano.

"I found what I was looking for. An early Church edict banning—"

"Rigo, where's the water?" Dag demanded. "I told you to fetch water!"

"In a moment. This is important—"

"So is our need for water," said Stephano. "In case we need to put out the fires. Dag's right, Rigo. You can explain all this magic stuff to me later."

"If there *is* a later," said Rodrigo in ominous tones, and he ran back down below to the hold where they stored the water barrels.

Stephano looked back through the spyglass at the demons. He could see them more clearly, and he had to admit that they looked exactly like the fiends in the paintings on the walls of his father's chapel, paintings depicting the torments of the damned. Fiends with snarling faces and those strange fiery eyes, as though Hell's flames burned inside them. Like most children, he had been fascinated by the demons, more interested in the fearsome looking creatures than in the angelic beings singing among the clouds. His father had been a religious man, but not demonstrative about his faith. He kept no chaplain. What was between him and God, he liked to say, was between him and God.

Was there a Hell? Did some fallen soul rule over it? Stephano had always believed men made their own Hell.

The demons were staring in his direction, perhaps trying to analyze the threat. The *Cloud Hopper* was partially obscured by the mists, which was perhaps the only reason the demons hadn't flown to attack them already.

"What are you?" Stephano asked them silently. "Who are you? Where did you come from? Freya? Or some place hotter . . ."

Gythe had talked of hearing voices. If so, they weren't answering him. Stephano shook off his metaphysical musings. The righteous and not-so-righteous aboard the *Cloud Hopper* were preparing for battle.

While Dag was loading the swivel guns, Stephano explained his plan. "Miri, position our boat directly above the cutter. That will keep the bats from attacking us from below and the cutter from above. We'll be able to fire on the bats without risking hitting the cutter."

"I'll do my best," said Miri

"Once you're in position, you can go help Dag. Rodrigo can reload—"

"He is not touching my guns," said Dag firmly. "He'd end up blowing us all to Freya."

"Rigo should stay with Gythe," said Miri. "He understands what she does with the magic. She might need him."

"We all have *our* jobs. What will *you* be doing, sir?" Dag asked, eyeing Stephano curiously.

"Bring out the pipes, my friend," said Stephano, watching the dragon circling the cutter. "Play 'Jolly Beggarman.' The Dragon Brigade is going to fly again."

Chapter Twenty-Two

Constructs degrade dependent upon the medium in which they are set and the processes they facilitate. Targeting constructs set in a cannon require monthly servicing, whereas strengthening constructs set in the stone wall of the Opera House in Galiathe, for example, require little maintenance. Only dragon breath is known to accelerate magic degradation, breaking down a construct in a process know as deconstruction.

—*The Art of Crafting,*
Church School Primer

WHILE DAG WAS REMOVING HIS BAGPIPES from their carrying case, Stephano ran down to his berth. He put on his flight coat and grabbed his sword belt, his saber, and the dragon pistol that had been a gift from his godfather. He flung the sword belt with the saber over his shoulder, tucked the loaded pistol into the pocket in his flight coat, then ran back up on deck.

Rodrigo ended a one-sided conversation with Gythe and glanced at Miri, who was still at the helm, looking with distress at her sister.

"How is she?" Miri asked worriedly.

Rodrigo shook his head.

Stephano watched the two of them and groaned inwardly. "What's wrong now?"

"Gythe," said Rodrigo.

Stephano glanced back at her. She was smiling, relaxed, and happy. Seeing Stephano looking at her, she grinned at him and laughed like a child and waved.

"Oh, no!" said Stephano softly. "Not now."

"I'm afraid so," said Rodrigo. "She's having one of her spells. As bad as I've ever seen her."

"Miri was hoping she was better." Stephano ran his hand through his hair in frustration. "What is she doing?"

"She thinks she's a child again, steering her parents' boat. She's laughing and giggling, singing old nursery rhymes. . . ."

"Can you help her?" Stephano asked.

Rodrigo shrugged. "In a way, she's helping herself. She's so terrified she's gone into hiding, so to speak. She's gone back to being a little girl."

Rodrigo looked out at the strange battle going on between the cutter and the bats—a battle the *Cloud Hopper* would soon unwillingly join—and he shook his head. "I can't say that I blame her. I wish *I* had somewhere to hide."

"But the protective magic," said Stephano urgently. "It only works if she's singing . . ."

"Not necessarily. It works better if she's singing, but it will work. I don't know what to tell you," Rodrigo added, with a helpless shrug. "She may come out of this state. She may not. Perhaps if Miri talked to her . . ."

Miri had been listening to their conversation. She shook her head. "I've tried before. When she's like this, she doesn't even know who I am."

Stephano swore softly. The rocky shoreline loomed ever closer. The cathedral had sustained serious damage; the walls were burned and charred and in some places completely breached. The beautiful stained glass windows had been broken out. He could smell the acrid stench of the smoke from the still smoldering rubble and another smell more horrible, like burning flesh.

"Bagpipes are ready when you are, sir!" Dag announced, arranging the chanter and the drone over his shoulder and placing the blowpipe in his mouth.

"You're really doing this," said Miri gloomily. "Flying off and leaving us."

"I'm not leaving you. Not exactly," said Stephano, putting on his leather. "I think it's our best chance. Stay with Gythe. Try to help her."

Rodrigo gave a nod and shook his head at the same time and went back to talk with Miri, who was standing at the helm, watching over Gythe, who thought she was a child steering her parents' boat.

"Go ahead, Dag," said Stephano.

Dag drew in a deep breath and blew into the pipe, filling the bag with air. He began to "skirl," referring to the high, shrill, wailing tone made by the pipe known as the chanter. Soon the lively music of "Jolly Beggarman" sounded from the deck of the *Cloud Hopper*.

Dag knew the tune well, for Stephano often asked him to play it in the evening hours when the members of the Cadre would sit on the deck of the houseboat on a fine summer's evening or were snug around the fire in Stephano's house on a winter's night. The moment the music of the bagpipes started, an irate yowl sounded from down below emanating from the storage closet. Doctor Ellington took strong exception to bagpipe music.

The march made Stephano's blood tingle, bringing with it a flood of memories. He watched the dragon, who was still flying above the cutter, waiting for him to react.

Dragons are passionately fond of music. A dragon's greatest sorrow is the inability to make music, the one skill in which dragons concede humans are superior. The wealthy dragon families often hired human musicians, bringing them to live in their immense castles, where they were treated like royalty.

Stephano hoped the dragon would be able to hear the sound of the pipes over the noise of battle. Dragons have excellent hearing, far better than humans, and they especially love the sound of the bagpipes. Unfortunately, the demon bat riders also had very good hearing, apparently, and perhaps they did *not* like the sound of the pipes. At the first notes, the demons who had been conferring about whether or not to attack the *Cloud Hopper* made up their minds. Three bat riders began flying toward them. The dragon, so far, was oblivious.

Dag cast a sharp glance at Stephano, requesting permission to stop playing and man the guns.

"Just a few more bars," Stephano urged.

Dag continued to play, and at last the dragon heard the music. Hovering in midair, he turned his head, searching for the source of the sound. Stephano had no way of knowing whether this dragon had ever been part of the Brigade, but all dragons knew the march, which was ages old, going back to the days when noble dragon families had signed the first nonaggression treaty with the human king of Rosia.

The dragon turned his head in the direction of the houseboat. Stephano waved his arms. The dragon dipped his wings in a signal of acknowledgment used by the Brigade and altered course. The dragon flew toward them.

"All right, Dag! You can stop now," Stephano shouted over the music. "He's seen us!"

Dag took time to hastily repack his precious pipes and stow them in the compartment beneath the helm, then went to man one of the swivel guns. Stephano was already readying the other. He made certain the powder charge was set, his slow-burning match smoldering in its bucket, one chamber loaded, more ready to load. Rodrigo and Miri were talking earnestly, both of them looking with worried concern at Gythe, who had been singing a song to the music of the pipes.

"We're too close to shore, Rigo," Miri was saying, "I have to stay at the helm. We'll end up on the rocks if I don't. Dag has to man the guns. You'll have to help Gythe. I'm worried sick. She's hasn't been as bad as this in long time!"

Rodrigo patted Miri's shoulder, said something meaningless and soothing, and went to be with Gythe, who greeted him with an eerie laugh. Rodrigo started talking to her in cheerful tones and even joined in her singing.

Stephano felt helpless—again. The three enormous bats with their demonic riders were closing rapidly on the *Cloud Hopper*. Stephano had never known any creature to fly so fast. The bats were little more than a black blur. A sleek young dragon might have given them a race, but this elder dragon with his graying mane, heavy girth, and lumbering flight could not hope to reach the *Cloud Hopper* before the boat came under attack. Stephano could see that the fire in the old soldier's eyes still burned bright, however. Stephano hoped the same would prove true of the fire in the dragon's belly.

As the bats and their demon riders drew near, Dag muttered a prayer. Miri shivered, but she remained at her post, her hands moving with Gythe's over the sigils on the helm. Rodrigo stared at the bats intently, then swiftly shifted his position so that he blocked Gythe's view.

As Dag had said, each bat was the size of a "bloody horse," with a wingspan of about forty feet, large pointed ears, and small, glistening eyes set on either side of its snout. The bat's gaping mouth had four long, curving fangs in front used for ripping apart its prey. The body was covered with rusty black fur. Clawed feet thrust out from the gray-black membrane that spread wide between gigantic "arms," allowing the bat to fly. Large hooks were visible on the upper part of the wings.

The gigantic bats were hideous to look at, but at least they appeared to be mortal, made of flesh and blood. He wondered uneasily if the same could be said of the demon riders.

Stephano believed in God, a belief he had been taught as a child, a belief he had abandoned in anger when he was a youth. How could he have faith in a God who had allowed his father to die such a terrible death? Stephano remembered that dark time in his life. He had finally struggled through it to find his faith again, with the help of Lady Cam, his dragon.

Being very private, dragons rarely discuss their beliefs

with humans. Lady Cam and Stephano had been unusually close; she had often talked to him of her God, a God who watched lovingly over dragonkind, who hoped they would live courageous, noble lives; a God who grieved when they fell short, as all mortals do, a God who understood.

Stephano could believe in such a God; though the relationship between him and God was still a bit rocky. He did *not* believe in the God of the Church of the Breath. That God, according to the grand bishop, had consigned Julian de Guichen to eternal torment in Hell.

A Hell populated by creatures such as these. . . .

Stephano banished that thought from his head. Lord Captain Stephan de Guichen had fought many enemies in his lifetime. He'd known fear as he rode into battle and had found the strength and courage to overcome it. But he had never before been confronted with an enemy that had sprung from an artist's rendition of the torments of the Damned, and he felt his gut twist and a shiver crawl up his spine.

The three demon riders were built like humans, though they were extremely thin. They rode the bats with ease, sitting forward of the wings, their legs straddling the furry bodies. The demons' skin was blood-red in color, with black spikes rising along their arms and shoulders. They wore what appeared to be some sort of leather armor. Their faces were red and wizened. Their mouths were thin, dark slits. Gaping holes formed the nostrils. What was most horrible was that the faces were expressionless, impassive, uncaring. Only their eyes were alive and that life was hideous. The eyes glowed orange, as though lit from within by Hell's fire.

Stephano grabbed the portfire and held it ready. He was filled with loathing and horror, and he fought an impulse to fire before the bats were in range and waste a shot. Glancing around, he saw his feelings reflected on the faces of his friends. Miri was deliberately not looking at the creatures. She was concentrating on flying, sometimes casting a glance of loving concern at her sister. He saw her hands shaking.

Rodrigo's face was pale. He sat quite still and rigid, staring at the bats in disbelief. He was still mindful of Gythe, however, keeping one arm around her. Gythe sang softly to herself with childlike abandon. Dag, manning the other swivel gun, stared straight at the bats, his face stern and grim, his jaw clenched, his brows drawn together in a frown of concentration. Dag was a deeply religious man. Did he believe he was about to fire on fiends sent from Hell? If so, did he think this fight was hopeless?

Dag looked over. "Hold steady, sir!"

Stephano nodded. The dragon was drawing near the *Cloud Hopper*, but he would not reach the boat ahead of the bats. Stephano held the smoldering match poised over the vent.

"Wait," he counseled himself softly, "Wait just one moment more ..."

The demons held in their hands what Stephano first thought were large blowguns, such has he and Rodrigo had made as children and used to fire darts in an effort to bring down rabbits (until Rodrigo accidentally fired a dart at Stephano, which brought down the wrath of Benoit). As he watched, one of the demons lifted the weapon to his shoulder. It was not a blow dart. It appeared to be some sort of handheld cannon. Balancing with ease on the bat, holding on with his thighs, the demon aimed the cannon at the *Cloud Hopper*'s helm.

"Take cover!" Stephano yelled, but he ignored his own command.

A ball of green fire erupted from the cannon. Time seemed to slow. Stephano could hear Dag yelling at Miri to duck and Rodrigo urging Gythe to sing the song she had sung the other night, the song of her magic. He could hear Gythe's wild laughter.

Green fire burst on the helm and blue light flared, half-blinding Stephano. He saw for one dazzling moment the sigils and constructs, layer upon layer, of the protective spells Gythe had cast on, around, and over the boat. She had wrapped Miri and the helm in a kind of cocoon of spun blue magic. The green fire struck the blue glowing sigils and constructs of the outer threads of magic. Wherever the green flames touched, they began to devour the magic. It was like watching Gythe's spells being eaten away by green fiery acid. The green flames died swiftly, however, leaving the protection spells damaged, but intact.

Gythe screamed. Stephano turned to see Rodrigo holding her in his arms. She was writhing in pain, moaning and crying out.

"Gythe! What's wrong?" Miri cried, unable to leave the sails. "Rigo, what happened to her?"

Rodrigo could only shake his head. "I don't know!" he said helplessly.

Stephano had no time to help either Gythe or Rodrigo, for Dag was telling him, "Make ready, sir! Here they come!"

Stephano tore his gaze from Gythe and tried to sight in his gun on the bats that were about thirty feet away and closing. He was having trouble finding a target. Reddish smoke flowed from the demonic riders, as though their flesh were on fire, wrapping them in a hellish fog and making it difficult for him to see.

Stephano aimed the swivel gun where he'd last spotted the bats and touched the portfire to the vent. The gun banged. Grapeshot flew. Dag's swivel gun went off a second or two later. Stephano could not see anything through the fog, but he heard a shrill screech, as if one of the bats had been hit. Picking up one the preloaded chambers, Stephano rammed it into the breech.

"Stephano!" Miri was pleading. "Go to Gythe!"

With Miri's attention on Gythe and not on the airscrews, the strong winds left over from the wizard storm were pushing the *Cloud Hopper* closer and closer to the heart of the battle.

"Take over firing!" Stephano yelled to Dag, who nodded as he reloaded his own gun.

Stephano looked about for the dragon, but had lost him in the reddish smoke. He could not see the demons either, but apparently the demons could see them because a wave of green fire washed over the boat. The *Cloud Hopper* rocked. Blue sparks burst; sigils and constructs seemed to wither and melt away. This time, Stephano could feel the heat of the blast.

Gythe screamed again and doubled over. Her fists clenched in pain. She shuddered and Rodrigo clasped her tightly. He seemed to be holding her together.

Stephano knelt beside her. "Is she wounded? Where? I don't see any blood . . ."

"The demon magic," said Rodrigo. His face was pale and strained and covered with a sheen of sweat. "The green fire is destroying, layer by layer, Gythe's protection spells. It's also destroying her for some reason. Oh, and by the way," he added, "your dragon friend is about to roast us!"

The dragon flew out of the reddish smoke, shredding it with his wings. Only two demons remained; Stephano must have hit one. The dragon's gaze was fixed on the demons and their bats. His mouth opened. He was sucking in a deep breath, ready to breathe a blast of fire that would incinerate everything it touched: demons, bats, and the *Cloud Hopper*.

"No!" Stephano bellowed, waving his arms in a signal that meant to break off the attack. "Stop!"

The dragon heard the shout and looked down at the boat which lay beneath him.

"Use the Hawk Attack!" Stephano yelled and held up both hands, fingers crooked, like claws.

The dragon understood. He shifted his body in midair, and—claws extended—dove like a stooping hawk. He struck one of the bats before it could escape, sinking his claws into its back. The bat made a horrible screeching sound then went limp. The dragon shook it off. The demon rider, straddling the neck, leaped from the falling bat. The rider made a desperate attempt to seize hold of the dragon's claw. The demon missed and fell into the Breath, vanishing silently, without a scream.

The dragon pulled up out of his dive and soared over the

Cloud Hopper. Dag fired his gun and then ran over to fire Stephano's at the surviving bat. The demon rider apparently decided he didn't like the odds, for he turned his bat and fled, heading back to join his fellows, still attacking the cutter.

Stephano motioned for the dragon to come up underneath the *Cloud Hopper.* As the dragon was circling around, Stephano bent down to examine Gythe. She was shivering in Rodrigo's arms, her head buried on his breast. Her body was drenched in sweat. She shuddered and moaned, gripping hold of Rodrigo tightly.

"Dag!" Miri yelled. "Take over. Keep the helm just as I have it."

Dag grabbed hold of the lines. Miri ran to her sister, knelt beside her, and spoke her name. Gythe lifted a tear-streaked face and, making a low, animal sound in her throat, she flung her arms around Miri's neck and clung to her.

"I'll take her below," Miri said.

She put her arm around her sister's waist and helped her to her feet. Gythe kept her face hidden in Miri's shoulder. Stephano held the hatch open for them as Miri helped Gythe slowly descend the stairs. He could hear Doctor Ellington, locked in the storage closet, howling dismally.

For a moment, there was a lull in the battle. The bats were clustered around the cutter. They would be back, and next time they would come in greater numbers. Dag yelled for Rodrigo to come look at the helm. Rodrigo held his hand above the shining brass panel. His lips moved in what Stephano assumed was some sort of incantation.

"How's Gythe?" Dag asked, his face creased with worry.

Stephano shook his head. "I don't know. I don't know what's wrong with her."

Rodrigo stood up. He looked very grim. "I know what's wrong with her. The green fire."

Stephano stared at him in perplexity. "But it didn't hit her. Did it?"

"The green fire wiped out two layers of Gythe's protection magic above the helm and let some of the green fire seep through. Here"—he pointed at places on the brass panel—"and here and here. Wherever the green fire struck, the sigils and constructs are gone."

"Like dragon fire," said Stephano. "Dragon fire hits the sigils and weakens them until they eventually break down."

"I did not say 'break,' did I?" Rodrigo returned testily. "I did not say 'weaken.' I said 'gone.' Wiped out. Vanished. Obliterated. *As if they had never been*," he added with biting emphasis.

"That's not possible," said Stephano. "Even I know that much. The magic in a sigil inscribed in a block of stone might fade, but the sigil will always be there."

"Except when it isn't," said Rodrigo, gesturing to the brass. "The magic is gone. And not only is the demon fire destroying her magic, the fire is hurting Gythe through her magic."

"But it's not hurting you."

"I'm not a savant. With me, the magic is in my brain. With Gythe, the magic is a part of her, like her skin and her blood . . ."

Stephano ran his hand through his hair that was wet with sweat.

"You'll have to put the sigils back," he said. "How long will that take?"

Rodrigo raised his eyebrows. "Let's see, I would be required to start as an apprentice to a shipwright crafter. That would take me about two years . . ."

"Be serious!" Stephano snapped.

"I am serious!" Rodrigo snapped back. "The sigils that are gone are wiped clean! I don't have the skill to lay down new ones. Neither can Miri. Only a crafter who is trained in this sort of magic can replace them. My dear friend, you don't seem to understand—"

"You're damn right I don't understand!" Stephano shouted angrily. "Giant bats and demonic green fire disabling the helm and hurting Gythe and there's nothing anyone can do!"

He realized he was losing control and stopped to draw in

a deep breath. He said more calmly, "Dag, can you and Miri fly this damn boat?"

"I can steer, but it's the magic from the helm that is keeping us afloat. If the fiends wipe that out . . ." Dag shook his head.

"I might be able to bridge the gaps," said Rodrigo.

Stephano assessed the situation. The *Cloud Hopper* was adrift, being drawn toward the naval cutter that was still bravely fighting the swarm of demons. Two cannons remained in operation out of fourteen. The number of bats and riders attacking had decreased considerably, but those remaining were bombarding the ship with green fire. The *Cloud Hopper*, caught up in a magical tide, was being swept along at a rapid rate and the cutter was now almost within hailing distance; Stephano could see the deck without need of his spyglass. The captain and another officer were too busy trying to save their ship to pay them much heed. The *Cloud Hopper* was, after all, only a Trundler houseboat. Still, he must have heard them firing on the bats. Stephano turned his gaze toward the abbey, which was also under attack. He could see bats darting about the walls.

Stephano needed to talk to the captain. He needed to find out what was happening at the abbey. He needed to protect his people. And he couldn't do any of that where he was. He made up his mind.

"Dag, you're in command while I'm gone."

Dag shook his head. "No, sir."

"Dag, you're in command," said Stephano harshly, his voice grating. He turned his back, pretending he didn't hear Dag's protest, and crossed the deck to the forecastle. Rodrigo went with him.

"Dag in command," said Rodrigo, shaking his head. "The man who swore he'd never give an order again."

"I know." Stephano was having second thoughts. "Maybe I shouldn't leave."

"This is why you formed the Cadre, my friend," said Rodrigo, putting his hand on his friend's shoulder. "Each of us has a job to do. We'll do ours. You do yours. Dag will come through. He always does."

"I know. Fix the helm, will you?"

Rodrigo nodded. Stephano motioned for the dragon to fly closer, come up under the ship. The dragon's head lifted up over the hull.

"Lord Captain de Guichen!" the dragon exclaimed with a gasp.

Stephano looked more closely at the dragon. "Droal, isn't it? Master of Flight Droalfrig."

"Yes, sir!" The dragon was immensely pleased, though he was now eyeing the small houseboat in some confusion. "Begging your pardon, sir, but what are you doing on board a Trundler—"

"I'll explain later!" Stephano cried. "Come closer!"

The dragon floated upward, taking care not to hit the boat's keel with his wing. Stephano reached over the rail, caught hold of the very last spike on the dragon's long neck and, hoping he still remembered the knack of boarding dragons and trying not to think of what would happen to him if he didn't, he took firm hold.

"Ready when you are!" he cried.

The dragon, Droal, eased away from the boat, taking Stephano, hanging onto the spike, with him.

"Mind your tail!" Stephano yelled.

Sometimes dragons misjudged the distance from a ship and would accidentally smack the hull as they flew off.

Droal, both proud and extremely nervous at the honor of carrying on his back the famous Lord Captain of the Dragon Brigade, was so terrified of doing anything wrong that he was practically flying with his tail between his legs.

"We're clear," Stephano called urgently, for they were rapidly losing altitude. "You can relax!"

Droal flapped his wings, rising into the air, and Stephano settled himself on the dragon's back. Ordinarily he would have been sitting in one of the specially designed saddles made for dragon riders. All dragon riders are taught to fly bareback first before they are given saddles. Feeling the movement of the dragon's muscles provides a rider with a better knowledge of the art of dragon flight. And riders never knew when they might encounter an emergency situation when, like now, they might be forced to fly without benefit of a saddle.

Stephano kept hold of the dragon's spike and flung one leg over the neck, then settled himself firmly on the broad back at the start of the curve of the spine. He gripped the dragon's scales with his knees.

"Orders, sir?" Droalfrig asked.

"Fly me close to the cutter. I need to talk to the captain."

"Captain won't like it, sir. I started a fire," said Droal unhappily. "Accident. Never flown combat."

"We won't stay long," said Stephano. "I only need a few words."

The dragon veered around and began to fly toward the cutter. Stephano looked down on the *Cloud Hopper*. Miri had come back on deck. She saw him and waved her hand, then she hurried over to relieve Dag at the helm. He went back to manning the swivel guns. Rigo looked up at Stephano and gave a jaunty salute.

"They'll be fine," said Stephano to himself. "Rigo's right. We each have a job to do and this is mine."

As the dragon veered around, the wind struck Stephano full in the face, whipping his hair, stinging his eyes. He buttoned up the flight jacket, hunched his shoulders, and tried to keep from grinning like a kid on Yule. After five years with his feet on the ground, he was flying again.

He knew now how much he missed it: the freedom, the exhilaration. Dear God, how he had missed it!

As it was, he was not particularly comfortable. His flight coat protected him from the wind, but he was not wearing a helm with the protective eye-screen, and his eyes were starting to water from the wind in his face. And many years had gone by since he'd flown bareback. He hadn't been on the dragon ten minutes and already his posterior was aching.

The bats and their riders swarmed the cutter, hitting it with green fire. Between the red smoke flowing from the demons and the smoke rising from the fires on board the cutter, it was difficult to see anything clearly. Stephano wondered if the demons had caught sight of him and the dragon.

"What can you tell me about these giant bats and their riders?" Stephano bent forward to shout in the dragon's ear.

"I'm two hundred years old, Captain," said Droal. "Never seen the like."

"Ever heard any stories about demons?"

"Just from humans, sir." Droalfrig looked faintly disdainful. "Dragons don't believe in such things."

Their conversation was interrupted by an ear-piercing whistle. Three of the demons immediately broke off their attack on the ship and turned to fly toward Droal.

They're acting on orders, Stephano realized, which means they have a commander. He searched among the demons, hoping to find out which was in charge. Commanders typically wore some sort of insignia or badge that distinguished them as officers, something that could be easily seen by their troops during battle.

Stephano searched among the group of demons that were attacking the cutter, looking for the leader and he finally spotted him—a demon flying over the cutter, directing the battle from above. The fiend looked like all the others, but as he and his bat made a sweeping turn, Stephano saw the demon's armor was emblazoned with intertwining knot work set in a triangle. The insignia glowed red, probably so that it was visible through the reddish clouds that trailed from the demons.

"Orders, sir?" Droal yelled. "Claw or fire?"

Stephano thought this through swiftly. The bats were flying too fast for the lumbering dragon to attempt to outflank them or circle around to attack from the rear. From what he had observed of their green-fire cannons, the demons had to come within musket range of the target. Whereas a dragon in good physical condition could blast the demons with his fiery breath from a much greater distance.

All three of the demons carried the handheld cannons. Stephano had seen the damage the demon fire inflicted on the *Cloud Hopper*'s magic. He no idea what the green fire might do if it struck the dragon or himself and he wasn't about to chance it. He noted the position of the cutter to make certain Droal was not likely to accidentally hit it again and calculated the direction of the wind, not wanting the dragon's flaming breath to blow back and engulf him, then gave the order.

"Fry them, Flight Master!"

The demons were flying nearer and nearer, lifting the cannons to their shoulders and taking aim. Apparently, they had never fought a dragon before. They were in for a shock.

Droal sucked in an immense breath. Stephano could feel the dragon's rib cage expand beneath his legs. Droal exhaled. Orange-red fire washed over two of the demons, who blazed up like torches. The bats screeched in agony as they spiraled down into the Breath, trailing smoke, taking their hapless riders with them.

"They died," said Stephano, watching the smoldering corpses trail downward until they vanished.

"Burnt to a crisp, sir," said Droal in satisfaction.

"They can be killed," said Stephano.

He was suddenly vastly relieved. He had been harboring the fear that these fiends were immortal. The fact that these demons could be killed was comforting, although, Stephano had to concede, the knowledge that these demons were mortal didn't really tell him anything about them. He still had no idea who they were or what they wanted or where they came from.

He heard again the demonic commander's piercing whistle and saw the third bat break off the attack and fall back. Stephano was certain now that the demon wearing the knot work insignia was the source of that piercing whistle. He kept an eye on this demon and ordered Droal to fly over to the cutter.

"Come in straight," Stephano told the dragon. "Keep the ship at eye level."

The name of the ship was painted on the stern: *HMS Suspicion*. Stephano had not heard of it. He did not know its captain, who was glaring balefully at the dragon, waving him off and shouting obscenities. Then the captain noticed Stephano mounted on the dragon's back and stared in astonishment.

Stephano raised himself up on the dragon, so that he could be seen and heard.

"I am Lord Captain Stephano de Guichen of His Majesty's Dragon Brigade. What is your status, sir? Can you still fight?"

The captain continued to stare, dumbstruck, at Stephano, all sorts of questions undoubtedly running through his mind. Stephano didn't have time to explain. He pointed at the *Cloud Hopper*, sailing toward the cutter. Rigo must have patched the helm because Miri had steered the little boat into position some twenty feet above the cutter.

The captain saw and finally understood. His first reply was cut short by a blast from his sole remaining cannon. Smoke drifted over the deck.

"What's wrong with your guns?" Stephano shouted.

The captain was grim. "When that damn green fire hits them, they blow up."

"Can you hold on, sir?" Stephano asked.

The captain glanced about his ship. He was an older man, with grizzled hair and a jaw like a bulldog. Captaining a small cutter at his age meant he had been passed over for command of the larger, more prestigious ships. Either he'd made enemies at court or he was inept. Judging by the fact that he had fought a valiant and intelligent battle against an enemy that must have seemed to fly straight from a nightmare meant that he'd made enemies.

"Two guns are gone and the others are disabled!" the captain shouted. "But we can hold on, sir."

Stephano saluted in acknowledgment and then told Droal to make a wide, swinging circle that would take him close to the demon commander. If Stephano had been riding Lady Cam, he would have been able to communicate the direction they should take through a shifting of his body in the saddle, the pressure of his legs. Droal had not been trained to carry a rider, so Stephano had to tell him where to fly. Droal was an old soldier, and he immediately understood Stephano's plan. The loss of the demon commander would hopefully throw the rest of the troops into confusion.

The demon saw the dragon coming for him. The *Cloud Hopper* was in position and its swivel guns were firing, two at a time. Now that she could leave the helm, Miri must be assisting Dag. The swivel guns were finding their marks, dealing damage to the demons. Stephano heard the screeching of wounded bats and he saw one go tumbling into the Breath.

With his force reduced to about fourteen, plus a few bats that had lost their riders, the commander had to know he could not hope to battle a dragon who could wipe out at least six bats with one breath. In the commander's place, Stephano would have pulled his troops from the cutter and flown off to join the assault on the abbey. Stephano planned his attack accordingly, telling Droal to fly into position to kill the commander and then attack the demons who might try to retreat back to the abbey.

The shrill whistle sounded. Stephano was close enough to the commander to see the details of the insignia on his armor. The bat hissed and screamed at the dragon. The demon turned his frozen, hideous, expressionless face to stare directly at Stephano. Reaching around to his back, the demon seized hold of an ax. The bat carrying the commander made a steep, sudden, darting dive, flying off so swiftly that by the time Droal breathed his fiery breath, the commander had flown safely out of range.

Droal rumbled angrily and was preparing to chase after him when Stephano called to the dragon to halt. The commander had not given his troops the order to fly back to the abbey. He had given them the order to make a last, desperate assault on the *Cloud Hopper* and the *Suspicion*.

Bats darted and swooped at the two vessels. Green flames spread over the ship and the little houseboat. The cutter fired its last working cannon. The ball whistled harmlessly past its target and fell into the Breath. The swivel guns on the *Cloud Hopper* continued their firing. Dag was managing to keep the bats and their riders at bay.

Catching sight of Stephano, Dag pointed to the preloaded chambers for the swivel guns and then held up one hand, fingers spread. Only five rounds left.

The demons flew low, firing their strange cannons. Green fire burst on the protection spells. They were still holding; the *Cloud Hopper* was not yet badly damaged. But each shot weakened them, weakened Gythe. Dag fired and missed. One round gone. Miri fired and winged a bat, causing it to veer off with a screech. Two rounds gone.

The demon commander left his troops to continue the assault. Flying his bat perilously close to the *Cloud Hopper*, the demon looked straight at Stephano. The orange eyes flamed in derision. He jumped off the bat and landed on the deck of the boat. Two more demons joined him, leaping from their bats and landing on the deck. They had abandoned the green-fire guns and carried axes.

They had no thought of retreat. They had boarded the *Cloud Hopper* with the intent to kill.

Two of the demons raised their axes and ran across the deck, one heading for Dag, the other for Miri. The commander ran for the hatch that led down into the hold. The demon would find Gythe and Rodrigo. Gythe helpless, Rigo unarmed, unable to defend her or himself. Dag was sighting in the swivel gun. Intent on his aim, he did not see the demons. Miri saw them and cried a warning.

Stephano swore savagely. He could order Droal to incinerate the demons, but the dragon could not do that without incinerating the *Cloud Hopper*.

Stephano drew his dragon pistol.

"Take me in close," he ordered Droal.

Chapter Twenty-Three

Aertheum the Fallen knows that God has given mankind free will,
the choice between good or evil. With honeyed words and false promises, he entices us to leave God's side and join with the foul legions.
Some listen; the choice is theirs. Never turn your back on the Fallen
for that is when he drives home the knife.

—"Thoughts on the Nature of Evil"
from the writings of Saint Michael

DAG HEARD MIRI'S CRY AND TURNED to see one
demon coming at him, ax raised and a demon running
at Miri. The demon was right behind her. Dag had his pistol
in his hand, but the demon was too close to Miri for him to
risk shooting it without hitting her. He roared a warning.

Miri reached beneath the helm, seized a pistol, turned,
and fired all in the same motion. The blast struck the demon
full in the chest and sent him flying backward. The fiend
smashed into the base of the mast and crumpled over in a
heap. Miri stood trembling, her face and clothes covered
with blood and gunpowder.

Dag fired at his demon, aiming for the hideous face. The
demon's head exploded and the fiend dropped to the deck.
Dag threw down the spent pistol and was drawing another
when he heard Miri scream. He looked over to see the demon with a gaping hole in its chest had regained his feet
and was coming at her again, a knife in his hand.

Horror-struck by the awful sight, Miri could not move. Dag shot the demon again, this time in the legs. The demon crashed down almost at Miri's feet. Still the demon tried to stand up. Miri grabbed a boat hook and began beating it, hitting it again and again until the fiend finally stopped moving.

Dag turned to look at the one he had shot and was thankful to see he was still dead. The third demon had almost reached the hatch. Stephano and the dragon soared past, the dragon's belly gleaming in the sunshine.

"I've got this one, Dag!" Stephano shouted, aiming his gun at the demon commander.

Droalfrig made a steep banking turn, wings narrowly avoiding taking out the boat's main yardarm. Stephano fired. His shot struck the demon commander in the back just as he reached the open hatch. The demon commander either jumped or tumbled through the hatch and disappeared. The dragon flew past, shouting as he went something about his brother being attacked at the abbey. Dag had no idea what the dragon was talking about. He lost sight of both the dragon and Stephano in the smoke.

Another demon leaped from his bat and charged straight at Dag, sending the bat to attack Miri. Dag fired the blunderbuss at the bat and the creature was a mass of blood and bone and fur. Dag swung the empty blunderbuss like a club and caught the demon in the midriff. The demon doubled over. Dag smashed the stock down on its neck.

"Reload!" he shouted at Miri.

She dropped to her knees and picked up a pistol and put in the powder and shot. She thrust that pistol into her belt and grabbed a musket.

"Dag, behind you!" she yelled, jamming the ramrod into the musket.

Dag turned to see the demon he'd shot in the face getting to its feet. Blood oozed from the demon's cracked helm. The orange eyes glowed. The demon reached out his hands and foul-smelling reddish noxious smoke began to flow from the demon's limbs. The smoke roiled around Dag. He covered his mouth and nose with his hands, but he could not filter out the fumes. He began to feel giddy, light-headed.

Dag had been raised by a deeply religious mother who believed in a God of wrath. People who did bad things in this world were forever damned. Dag had done many bad things in his life. He had since repented and worked hard to make amends, but he feared in his heart he could never right the terrible wrongs. He was doomed to spend eternity in Hell and as he watched the demon coming toward him, reaching for him with bloody hands, he heard his mother's voice crying that he was doomed, the fiends were coming to claim him and drag him into the Pit. Dag stood helpless, staring transfixed at the fiend.

Miri saw Dag was in trouble. She had no idea what was wrong with him. He was just standing there, making no attempt to stop the demon that was about to kill him. The ramrod was still in the barrel of the musket she had been reloading. She didn't have time to take it out. Hoping the weapon would not blow up in her hands, she aimed and pulled the trigger. The recoil knocked her sideways. The long wooden rod flew out of the musket and drove like a spear through the demon's back.

Blood spewing, the demon fell to the deck and this time did not get up. Miri ran to Dag, He was in a daze, his eyes wide and unseeing. The reddish smoke was starting to dissipate, shredded by the gusting winds, but she caught a whiff and tasted the bitter flavor of what might have been some sort of opiate. She cried Dag's name and flung her arms around him, pleading with him to come back to her. She felt a shudder go through his body and then he blinked and looked up at her. He seemed about to say something when a wail of terror and a frantic shout came from below.

"The demon Stephano shot went down into the hold!" Dag said. "Are any of the guns loaded?"

"Two," said Miri, pointing to the pistol in her belt and

another lying on the deck. She drew the pistol from her belt and handed it to Dag.

"I'm going below. You stay here. If one of those fiends lands on the boat, shoot it."

He disappeared down into the hold, leaving Miri alone on the deck. Several bats without riders flew around the *Cloud Hopper*. They screeched at her, but didn't attack. She picked up the pistol and looked down over the rail at the cutter. Demons had boarded it, as well. Captain and crew were fighting them off.

Three demon riders were still in the air. Miri kept a watch on them and gripped the pistol in her hands. She tried to find Stephano and the dragon. She had lost track of him during the battle, and now they were nowhere in sight.

Three more demons, armed with the green-fire cannons, flew toward the *Cloud Hopper*. Miri heard yelling and shouts coming from below and her sister's terrified screams and then green fire dazzled her eyes. She felt the heat of the flames wash over her, and she flung open the hatch and dove through it, shutting it behind her as the green fireballs burst on the *Cloud Hopper*.

The dragon was pulling out of his dive after Stephano had shot the commander when suddenly Droalfrig lifted his head and roared out his brother's name. He made a steep, arcing turn that forced Stephano to fling his arms around the dragon's neck and hold on tightly.

"Droal!" Stephano yelled. "Don't throw me off!"

"Sorry, Captain," Droal returned. "Forgot."

Stephano waited for his stomach to resume its proper place in his body, then asked, "What's wrong?"

"Brother Hroalfrig, sir! Demons! Attacking the abbey!"

Stephano could now see another dragon, flying over the spires of the cathedral, valiantly fighting off a horde of demons. Splotches of green fire burst in the air around the dragon. Smoke coiled into the air.

"I have to go to him, sir," Droal yelled. "Should I set you down?"

Stephano looked back at the *Cloud Hopper*. Dead demons lay sprawled on the deck. Dag and Miri appeared to have killed the boarders. He didn't see any other demons and he was worried about the nuns in the abbey. He turned back to the dragon.

"I'll come with you!" Stephano shouted.

If he had waited a moment, Stephano would have seen that the demons lying dead on deck weren't all that dead. Droal spread his wings and took off with such speed that Stephano had to flatten himself against the dragon's neck to avoid being swept off. He didn't have time to look back at his friends.

"Is anyone at the abbey helping the nuns?" Stephano yelled.

"Nuns dead," said Droalfrig grimly. "Demons slaughtered them. Days ago."

Stephano was shocked. The demons might have killed the abbey's nuns days ago, but the fiends had not finished their horrible work, apparently, for they had returned to complete the abbey's destruction. Was the Fallen One sending his minions to launch an all-out war on those who served God?

Stephano looked over his shoulder again to see the *Cloud Hopper* was still afloat and no longer under attack. The deck was empty, however. Dag and Miri were both absent, and that was worrisome. Dag would not leave the deck with a battle still raging. Perhaps they had gone below to be with Gythe.

"I should go back . . ."

"Brother Hroal not quite fit, Captain," said Droalfrig. "Bad leg. Explosion. Too much to ask, I know. If you could help . . ."

Stephano could see the dragon's brother being surrounded by bats, diving and swooping at him, attacking from all sides. The *Cloud Hopper* appeared secure.

"Let's go help Hroal," Stephano said.

Gythe was very ill and Rodrigo had no idea how the magic was harming her. He carried her to the small cabin below deck she shared with Miri, placed her in her bed, which was built into the bulkheads, and wrapped her warmly in blankets. He fetched water and moistened her lips and cooled her feverish skin.

That was all he could do. He sat beside her and watched her moan and shiver. Her body twitched painfully every time a blast of green fire struck the ship. He washed away the blood when it began to trickle from her mouth.

He wondered what was happening. Looking out the porthole, all he could see was smoke. All he could hear was the sound of gunfire coming from above and the enraged howls of Doctor Ellington, in the storage closet. The cat was so frantic that he began hurling himself at the door, beating on it with his large paws.

Fearing the good Doctor would hurt himself and feeling the need of company, Rodrigo freed the cat, who shot out of the closet as though his tail was on fire. The frantic cat evaded Rodrigo's grab and ran straight to Gythe. Doctor Ellington jumped into bed with her and began licking her face.

Gythe flung her arms around the cat, moaned and held him close, and began singing to him, as she often did. Her voice was raw and shrill and discordant. Doctor Ellington gave her hand a swipe with his tongue.

Rodrigo and the cat both jumped at the loud report of a pistol going off near the hatchway. The gun shot was followed by a loud thudding sound, as though someone large was tumbling down the stairs. Rodrigo froze, terrified, waiting for the sound of footsteps, but nothing happened.

He opened the door a crack and called out, "Dag? Is that you?"

No answer. Rodrigo called again, "Miri? Did you fall? Are you all right?"

Still no answer. Drawing in a deep breath, Rodrigo grabbed hold of a hairbrush to use as a weapon and ventured out to see what had happened. He was unpleasantly amazed to find a demon lying in a pool of blood at the bottom of the stairs.

Rodrigo was just thinking he was going to be sick when reddish smoke began to waft from the corpse. He caught a whiff and was immediately transported back to his wild days at University when he'd once rashly agreed to visit an opium den. Already nauseous, he covered his nose and mouth. Not knowing what else to do, he seized a blanket and flung it over the smoldering demon, as one might fling a blanket over a fire. He ran back to Gythe's cabin, shut the door, locked it, and then stuffed blankets in the crack to keep the noxious fumes from seeping inside.

He was about to cast a spell of protection on the door and then he remembered the green fire eating away Gythe's protective spells.

"Why waste my time?" Rodrigo sat down nervously on the end of the bed and addressed himself to the cat. "The demon is dead." He then added, as an afterthought, "But it's a demon. Demons can't die. Can they?"

He brooded over this a moment and tried to reassure himself. "That thing has a great bloody hole in its back. There's blood all over the deck. Of course, it's dead. You agree with me on this, don't you, Doctor?"

The cat appeared to be about to express his opinion when their conversation was interrupted by the sound of claws scrapping over the wooden deck. Rodrigo prayed he was imagining things or that it was Dag or Miri coming down to tell him the fight was over and they were all safe. He could see that his prayers weren't going to be answered. The cat was staring, wide-eyed, at the door.

"Oh, God!" Rodrigo whispered, rising to his feet.

He tried to shout for help, but his mouth was so dry that nothing came out. He coughed, moistened his lips, and was about to yell again, when a wailing scream from Gythe almost made him leap out the porthole. She had backed into the corner, clutching the blankets around her, whimpering in terror.

Rodrigo found his voice. "Help! I need some help down here!"

The sounds of clawed feet walking on the deck drew nearer. Doctor Ellington jumped from the bed onto a shelf and crouched there, hissing, his hackles raised, his tail furred out and waving slowly from side to side.

The footfalls stopped. Something struck the door. Splinters flew. The wood split apart. An ax blade appeared briefly, then was gone. The ax hit the door again. Rodrigo looked down at the hairbrush he was clutching, shook his head sadly, and tossed it aside. He cast a swift and desperate glance around the cabin. The water pitcher stood on a table. The pitcher was still almost half full. He had used only a little for Gythe and he himself never drank the stuff. He picked up the pitcher and hurriedly drew three sigils on the base, connected them with a line, and a stammered few words.

This was one of his favorite constructs. He used it to make afternoon tea for the ladies of the court, who were always charmed and delighted.

The ax struck the door again, and though more splinters flew, the door held. Rodrigo flattened himself against the bulkhead near the door and waited tensely, staring into the pitcher, urging the water to boil. He was certain the magic never took this long, and he wondered if he'd made a mistake. Then he recalled that a watched pot never boiled and he looked away—just in time to see the ax smash through the door not six inches from his head. The door fell to pieces. The bolt snapped. The demon commander, who should have been dead, walked through the wreckage and into the cabin.

Rodrigo practically crawled into the bulkhead. He did not move. He did not even breathe. The demon walked past him, never noticing him. The demon was staring at Gythe.

The fiend was a hideous sight. He had red, wizened skin;

his eyes glowed orange. Blood from his ghastly wound dribbled onto the deck. Reddish smoke flowed in wisps off his
arms like morning mists. Doctor Ellington, on the shelf,
hissed and spat. Gythe shrank into the corner and covered
her head with the blankets.

The demon's attention was completely focused on
Gythe. He appeared to be more curious than threatening,
for he held the ax loosely in his hand. A part of Rodrigo
wondered why he was so interested in Gythe, even as most
of Rodrigo was quaking with fear. He braced himself, drew
in a deep breath, and hurled the boiling water at the demon

The steaming water splashed over the demon's head,
shoulders, and arms. The demon flinched and grunted and
turned, swinging the ax, but missing Rodrigo, who had
dropped to the floor.

The demon raised the ax again and walked closer.

Rodrigo was hastily tracing a construct with shaking fingers in the palm of each hand. Trying not to look at the
demon's orange eyes or the blood or the ax, Rodrigo
gulped, swallowed, closed his eyes, and tickled the demon's
ankles.

When Rodrigo performed this act for the lady of choice,
the small electrical tingle dancing from his fingers over the
skin and running tantalizingly up his lover's legs never
failed to make her shudder with pleasure. The demon shuddered, but not with pleasure. Electricity, connecting with
the water, gave the demon a horrific jolt. The demon fell to
the floor, his body thrashing and flailing.

Rodrigo stared at the electrified demon and wondered
what to do with it. The ax lay on the floor, but he could not
bring himself to pick it up and finish the job. He had to do
something, though. He was reaching gingerly for the ax,
fighting down a wave of sickness when Dag burst through
the door, aimed his pistol at the demon's head and fired.

The demon jerked and then, finally, lay still. Dag stared
at it in awed wonder, then he bent over it.

"Look at these boots—" he began.

The body began to glow green.

"Get back!" Rodrigo shouted and he seized hold of Dag's arm and dragged him away from the corpse.

Gythe screamed horribly. The green glow died. Gythe collapsed and lay unconscious.

All that remained of the demon were scorch marks on the wooden floor. No ashes, no trace of the corpse. Nothing.

"I'll be damned!" Dag breathed, catching Doctor Ellington as the cat jumped from the shelf onto Dag's shoulder.

"I think I'm going to throw up," said Rodrigo faintly.

He staggered over to the slop bucket.

Dag held the yowling cat and, petting him soothingly, looked down with helpless anxiety at Gythe.

"What's wrong with her?" Dag asked, his voice cracking. Rodrigo came back, white-faced, wiping his mouth with a handkerchief.

"She's leaving us," he said with brutal frankness. "And I don't know how or why . . ."

Some distance away, in the abbey stables, Brother Barnaby was preparing himself to die. He was not afraid of death. He knew God was waiting to receive him. Brother Barnaby clasped his hands and asked God to forgive him his sins and then he waited for the demons to kill him as they'd killed his poor wyverns.

But the demons did not kill him. A horrible smell filled his nostrils and mouth, leaving him sick and disoriented and too weak to help himself. Rough hands seized hold of him and dragged him off.

Brother Barnaby was vaguely aware of his surroundings. He saw grass and mud and blood, the legs and feet of the demons, a stall in the stables. He was aware of vomiting, choking, fighting to breathe. Strange visions filled his head: fiends and fire, blood and torment and death.

A hand touched his shoulder. He flinched and lashed out in panic.

"Brother Barnaby!" said a ragged voice. "Don't be afraid. It's me. I'm not going to hurt you."

Brother Barnaby stopped fighting and blinked up to see a face reflected in the gray light of dawn. He knew the face. He gasped in amazement.

"I am sorry," said Brother Paul. "I didn't mean to frighten you. I wanted to see if . . . if you were alive . . ."

"I am . . ." said Brother Barnaby, bewildered.

"Thank God!" Brother Paul said.

Brother Barnaby looked at his fellow monk with shocked concern. Blood oozed from a vicious gash on the top of Brother Paul's head. His face was bruised and battered. His robes were soaked in blood. Barnaby saw, to his horror, that the back of the monk's robes were torn, his flesh was stripped with the marks of the whip. He had lost the dark lenses that shielded his eyes, and they were almost swollen shut.

"Let me tend to your wounds, Brother," Brother Barnaby said, his heart wrenching. "God has given me the gift of healing."

He looked about the stall to see if he could find water. The air held a lingering odor, but the smoke, the noxious smell was gone. Except for an annoying buzzing sound in his ears, Barnaby's head was beginning to clear. The sun had risen, morning light filtered dimly through the smoke-filled air. He and Brother Paul were in the stall of one of the abbey stables. Not the stables where he had housed his poor wyverns; that stable must be a heap of charred rubble. This stall had no windows. The stall door was shut. He could hear the screeching of bats and movement outside, so he guessed the demons were not far off.

Brother Barnaby rose to his feet and nearly fell down again. He waited until the dizziness passed, then he walked unsteadily to the stall's gate and pushed on it. The gate would not open. He stood on tiptoes and looked out. At the far end of the stables, he could see three demons, silhouetted in the sunlight, standing guard. More demons stood at the opposite end.

Barnaby considered the possibility of escape. He could probably climb over the gate, but then what? He was still weak, and his mind was foggy. He was not a trained warrior, not like Sir Ander. He thought to back to the murderous rage that had consumed him at the deaths of his wyverns and went hot with shame. Besides, even if he could flee, he could not leave Brother Paul, who was grievously wounded. Barnaby walked back to Brother Paul, who was mumbling prayers through his bloody lips.

"We are prisoners of Aertheum," Brother Paul was praying. "Father in Heaven, please help us!"

There is a time to ask for God's help and a time to ask God to help you help yourself: the Word according to Father Jacob. Brother Barnaby could almost hear the priest's voice, and he could hear Father Jacob say further, *Seek the truth. Never be afraid. You have questions. Ask them!* Brother Barnaby said a fervent prayer that Father Jacob and Sir Ander were safe, then knelt down beside Brother Paul.

"Did the demons do this harm to you, Brother?" he asked, placing his gentle hand over the monk's bloody wounds. "Tell me what happened."

Brother Paul nodded his head and then sighed to feel his pain ease. "I was on my way to the abbey for morning prayers when I heard the sound of cannon fire and saw the demons flying over the walls. I feared for you and Father Jacob, and I came running to help. Suddenly there were demons all around me. They seized hold of me and dragged me here. They . . . began hitting me . . ."

Brother Paul moaned and buried his head in his hands. Barnaby put his arm around the monk's quivering shoulders.

"Why didn't they kill you?" Brother Barnaby muttered, more to himself than to Brother Paul. "Why didn't they kill me? They murdered the nuns. Why leave both of us alive?"

"The books," Paul mumbled. "They kept asking me about the books. When I didn't tell them what they wanted, they hit me."

Brother Barnaby was startled. "Books? What books?"

"Can't you hear them?" Brother Paul asked, shivering. "The voices in your head. 'Books' over and over."

Brother Barnaby had been trying to ignore the terrible buzzing sound in his ears, but now that Brother Paul mentioned it, he did seem to hear words. *Books. The books. Books. The books.*

Brother Paul suddenly cried out and clutched his ears. "I don't know! I can't tell you! Stop tormenting me!"

Brother Barnaby whispered a prayer and sent the soothing warmth of God's grace flowing from his body to Brother Paul's. The monk relaxed again at the healing touch and gave a shuddering sigh.

"What do they mean—books?" Brother Barnaby wondered, mystified. "What books?"

Brother Paul raised a haggard face and sighed wearily. "All I can think of are the books of Saint Dennis. Those mentioned in the journal."

"But I don't know where they are," said Brother Barnaby. "Do you?"

"No," said Brother Paul, shaking his head. "But since we were with Father Jacob . . . Perhaps they think he told us . . ."

"Father Jacob has nothing to tell," said Brother Barnaby.

The buzzing in his ears seemed to be growing louder and it was no longer annoying. It was starting to be all he could think about.

Books. The books. Books. The books.

And then, beneath the buzzing, Barnaby heard someone moving outside the stable door. Brother Paul heard the noises, as well. He choked and clasped his hands and began to pray. Brother Barnaby rose to his feet and stood protectively in front of his fellow.

The gate opened. Two demons walked inside, one of

them holding a scourge in his hand. This was the first time Barnaby had seen the demons in the daylight. Sir Ander always said one must look fear in the face. Brother Barnaby fought down his revulsion and looked the demon in the face. Father Jacob had taught Barnaby to be observant and he was surprised to note that the demon was wearing a helmet made to resemble a hideous face and that the glowing orange light actually emanated from the helm. A visor made of glass gave off the strange light.

Brother Paul cried out in terror and shrank back against the stable wall. Barnaby moved swiftly to interpose his body between the demons and the monk.

"Don't hurt him anymore," said Barnaby. "He can't tell you about the books of Saint Dennis. He doesn't know."

The books. The books. The books.

The words were now like a hammer in Brother Barnaby's head, pounding on his brain. The demon swung the scourge, striking Brother Barnaby on his shoulder. The scourge seemed made of fire; the pain was excruciating. Barnaby gasped. Tears sprang to his eyes.

Books books books books!

"I don't know!" he cried or at least he thought he had cried out the words. He could no longer hear his own voice. He couldn't hear anything except the horrid buzzing.

Chapter Twenty-Four

The first time I sat on Lady Cam's strong back and felt the play of her muscles as she took to the air, I knew I would never truly be happy on the ground again. I had ridden dragons before but this was the first time as a member of the Dragon Brigade. She and I were battle companions and I was a Dragon Knight and that made everything different.

—Sir Stephano De Guichen,
in a letter to his friend, Rodrigo.

DURING THE BRIEF RESPITE BETWEEN THE FIRST WAVE of demons and the second wave he knew would be coming, Sir Ander made certain the swivel gun was in working order, the chambers ready for loading. Then he went back down into the cabin, reloaded the pistols, took two short barreled muskets from a hidden compartment near the hatch to the driver's station and readied himself for the assault. As he worked, he kept a worried eye on Father Jacob. He had carried the priest to his bed and wrapped him warmly in a blanket. He had not regained consciousness. His lips moved and he made sounds, as though he were speaking, but the words made no sense.

The sun shone through the broken windows. His pistols loaded, Sir Ander went to the front of the yacht where there had once been a door and looked out the gaping hole into the Breath to see if the naval cutter was still afloat. He was surprised to see a smaller boat had joined the cutter. He recognized the boat as one of those Trundler floating houses. Bats swarmed around both vessels. Green fireballs burst in the air. The fireballs looked smaller and paler than they had appeared in the dark of night, but he assumed they were still just as deadly.

Hroal's brother, Droalfrig, was out there, as well, flying around the houseboat. Sir Ander looked up to see if he could find what had become of Hroal, saw the dragon battling in the skies over the cathedral, fighting off the attacks of three bats and their riders.

The dragon was fighting for his own life and would not be able to help Sir Ander.

Smoke was still rising from the area of the stable. Sir Ander pictured Brother Barnaby, trapped by the flames, fighting off demons, lying there hurt . . . dying.

Sir Ander asked God to help them all, then climbed up on top of the yacht where he had mounted the swivel gun. More bats were flying his way. He was ready for them, as ready as he could be. While he was on the roof, he gave the yacht a cursory glance, surveying the damage.

Most of the demon's fire had been concentrated on the center of the yacht. The hull on the port side of the main cabin was badly burned. The fireballs had blasted through the outer and inner bulkheads in three places. The hatch was so much kindling. The roof was charred and burned to such an extent that a good rain would cause at least two places to give way. Sir Ander made a mental note not to step on those.

He caught sight of movement out of the corner of his eye and turned around, pistol drawn. He could see, through the haze of smoke, someone running toward him. He raised the pistol, then saw to his relief that the figure was human, not demonic. He recognized Albert. The guildmaster had come armed; he held a musket in one hand and a pistol in the other.

Sir Ander dropped back down inside the yacht, took a

look at Father Jacob and, seeing no change, hastened out to meet his friend.

"You come in answer to a prayer!" Sir Ander cried.

"Thank God, sir, you are alive!" Master Albert gasped. He stood staring in dismay at the destruction, the greasy piles of ashes, the wrecked yacht. "Is Father Jacob all right?"

"He is not," said Sir Ander grimly. "He's hurt and I don't know what's wrong, so there's nothing I can do."

Master Albert looked stricken. "How can I help, sir?"

Sir Ander had been thinking this through and he had made up his mind. "The one person who might be able to save Father Jacob is Brother Barnaby. He is in the stables—"

"But they're on fire, sir," Master Albert said, alarmed. "They're crawling with demons!"

Sir Ander was tucking the pistols into his belt. "I'm going to leave Father Jacob in your care. I've mounted the swivel gun on the roof. Preloaded chambers for the gun are up there, as well. The roof's been damaged, so be careful where you walk."

Master Albert nodded. "I understand, sir. I will not fail you or Father Jacob.

Sir Ander gripped his friend by the hand, then, picking up one of the muskets, he ran to the wicket that pierced the abbey's wall and entered. The smoke was thicker behind the wall, stinging his eyes and stealing the breath. He cursed it and peered through it, trying to get his bearings, trying to see the stables or what was left of them.

Only one building was on fire, but the stable yard was filled with demons. Their heinous bats darted about or perched on the roof. He saw no sign of the wyverns or Brother Barnaby. Recalling the gruesome and horrifying deaths of the nuns, Sir Ander was sick with dread. He longed to rush in and kill every demon in sight. Sir Ander was an experienced soldier and he knew better than to let hatred and vengeance guide him. He told himself not to give up hope. Brother Barnaby was quick-thinking and intelligent. Sir Ander pictured his friend hiding somewhere, waiting for help.

In that case, help needed to arrive in one piece.

Sir Ander was thinking he would circle around the cathedral, using the smoke for cover, and come up on the demons from behind. A roar caught his attention. He looked up to see a dragon soaring over the abbey walls. Droalfrig coming to his brother's aid. The dragon was about twenty feet above the walls and the direction of his flight would bring him near Sir Ander.

He had only seconds to make a decision. A gunshot would alert the demons to his presence. He decided to risk it and fired the musket into the air—taking care not to hit the dragon—and used his best battlefield bellow to call Droalfrig's name.

The dragon heard the gun blast and saw the flash of fire. He snaked his head around and Sir Ander saw a dragon rider seated on the dragon's back, near the neck. Sir Ander waved his arms, threw down the musket, and broke into a run.

The dragon rider coolly looked in the direction Sir Ander was indicating and saw the demonic force surrounding the stables. The dragon rider waved his arm in return and bent forward to speak to the dragon. Sir Ander cast a glance at Hroal, who was fighting his own battle. Hroal had slain one of his foes. He had only two to contend with now and, though he had a bloody gash on his chest, he was holding his own. Droalfrig shifted the direction of his flight toward the stables, roaring a challenge as he went.

The demons could both see and hear the dragon bearing down on them. Those on the ground summoned their mounts, while the demons in the air flew to the attack, raising their handheld cannons to their shoulders. Green fire burst around Droalfrig. Sir Ander had lost sight of the rider, but assumed he was flattened against the dragon's neck, keeping his head down.

Sir Ander wondered about this reckless rider; a man rash enough to jump on the back of a dragon. Perhaps he was a

sailor from the cutter. Whoever he was, Sir Ander was
grateful to him and to Droalfrig. Most of the demons and
their riders had taken to the air to fight the dragon, leaving
only a couple on the ground, standing near the smallest of
the three stables. The thought came to Sir Ander that these
demons had been left behind, perhaps to guard something.
Or someone.

The smoke that he had cursed was now Sir Ander's ally.
Concealed by the smoke and the deep shadow of the stable
building cast by the morning sun, he counted three demon
guards near the entrance to the stable, all of them gazing
into the sky, intent on the battle between the dragon and
their comrades.

Sir Ander was certain these demons had been left behind to stand guard duty and he looked around. What he
saw made his heart leap with hope and then constrict with
fear. Two monks—Brother Barnaby and, astonishingly,
Brother Paul—were on their knees on the ground. Their
hands were bound behind them. They had ropes looped
around their necks.

Overhead, Droalfrig was roaring and breathing out his
flaming breath. A burning bat tumbled out of the sky, almost
crashing down on Sir Ander, who ducked beneath an awning.
The dead bat landed on its rider, who was also on fire. Sir
Ander was amazed to see the rider suddenly flare with green
light and then vanish. He wrenched his gaze away from this
astonishing sight and looked back at the two monks in time
to see a fourth demon emerge from the stables.

The demon raised a scourge, its tips crackling with fire,
and brought the whip down across the back and shoulders
of Brother Barnaby. The young monk sank to the ground.
The demon stood over him and raised the whip again.

Sir Ander's experience and training went up in flames of
rage. Never mind that he was outnumbered four to one, not
counting the bats. Holding one of the nonmagical pistols in
his left hand and his dragon gun in the right, he broke cover
and ran to save Brother Barnaby.

Stephano, riding on Droalfrig's back, flew directly over the black yacht adorned with the symbol of the Arcanum. He saw the damage done to the yacht, as well as the smoldering remains of bat carcasses. A person on the roof manning a swivel gun looked amazed to see a dragon rider. Stephano waved at him and the man waved somewhat hesitantly back.

Stephano was not surprised to find the Arcanum had come to investigate the attack on the abbey, nor was he surprised the Arcanum's representatives had come under attack. The Arcanum was a force to be reckoned with. Even the Fallen One must hold them in respect. Stephano knew his mother certainly did. He was curious to know what the priest had discovered about these demons.

As Droalfrig flew over the abbey walls, Stephano saw a large group of demons and bats gathered in what appeared to be a stable yard. He wandered what they were doing. Droalfrig was not interested. He was flying straight to his brother, when he and Stephano both heard the report of a musket and saw the flash of fire. They looked down to see a man on the ground obviously trying to attract their attention.

The man wearing armor was pointing at the demons. As Stephano watched, the man broke into a run, heading for the demons. Stephano understood. He shouted at Droalfrig.

"Demons! By the stables! They've taken prisoners!"

Droalfrig turned his head. Sighting the demons, he glanced at his brother, saw that Hroal was holding his own in his battle and could manage. Droalfrig gave a rumbling growl and switched the direction of his flight.

Demons flew to meet them. Stephano raised his dragon pistol, but he did not fire. Droalfrig could do far more damage with his breath. The demons fired their hellish cannons, but they were disorganized and unprepared, and their aim was off. Green fireballs soared far above the dragon's head.

Droalfrig's breath was right on target. He spewed out a great gust of flame that engulfed the lead bats and their riders. Seeing their comrades go down in flames, the other demons hastily flew out of the dragon's range.

If the demons are smart, Stephano reflected, they'll attempt to flank us, come at us from the rear.

Droalfrig soared over the stable roof and made a banking turn. Stephano had been keeping an eye on the man on the ground, saw him take cover beneath an awning. Stephano noted the demons standing guard, and he guessed immediately that the man, who had the bearing of a soldier, was attempting to rescue the captives.

"Set me down!" Stephano yelled to Droalfrig.

The dragon would be far more effective battling demons in the air without having to worry about dumping his rider. Stephano would be of more use on the ground.

Beyond the stables was pastureland where the horses and other occupants would have been turned out to graze. Droalfrig swooped down low, slowing his flight as much as possible. Stephano slid off the dragon's back and landed with a bone-jarring thud on all fours in the grass. Droalfrig soared into the sky. Two more demons had joined in the battle against Hroal, who was clearly starting to tire.

"Go help your brother!" Stephano yelled, jumping to his feet.

Droalfrig dipped his head in acknowledgment and flew off. Stephano drew his dragon gun. He had reloaded after killing the demon on the *Cloud Hopper*. He had one shot and then it would be saber work.

The demons and their captives were at the north end of the stables. He entered the stables from the south, gun drawn, searching the stalls as he ran for more demons who might be lurking there. Through the gate at the end, Stephano saw two monks on the ground and a demon standing over them with a whip in his hands.

A pistol report and the demon with the whip went down. The man with the soldierly bearing came into view. The three demons standing guard had been watching the dragon. They now turned at the sound of the gunshot. Before they could react, the man raised a second pistol and fired at point-blank range, hitting one demon in the face. As this demon fell, the man reached into his belt to grab another pistol.

He did not have time for a shot. The demons had been caught by surprise, but they swiftly recovered. Two of them leaped on the man and pummeled him with their fists. The man fell to the ground. Stephano leveled his pistol, but did not have a clean shot. A demon seized an ax and was about to swing. Stephano aimed his dragon gun and fired. The bullet struck the demon in the back. Stephano thrust the dragon pistol in his belt and drew his saber.

The demon who had been holding the whip was only wounded, apparently, for it was trying to regain its feet. Stephano thrust his sword through the demon's throat and it went down with a gurgling scream, choking on its own blood.

He turned to see the demon with the ax aiming a blow at him. Stephano ducked. The ax blade whistled over his head and he drove his saber into the demon's gut, drove it hard, to penetrate the strange-looking leather armor that covered the demon's body. The demon jerked horribly. Stephano dragged his sword free and the demon fell to the ground.

The two remaining demons were coming for him. He shifted his saber to his left hand, picked up the demon's ax, and threw it. The ax hit a demon in the head and, although the blade did not pierce the helm, the blow knocked the demon off its feet. Stephano jumped forward and drove the saber's point into the stunned demon's throat. He twisted the blade as he pulled it free, taking no chances on the thing getting back up.

Stephano shifted his saber back to his right hand and turned toward the last demon, but he was too late. He could see the ax blade flash in the sunlight above his head. A pistol went off. The demon shrieked. The ax flew out of its hands and the demon toppled over. Stephano drove his saber into the twitching body, just to make sure it stayed down. He looked around to see that the man who had run to the rescue of the monks had managed to sit up long enough to fire. He was staring at Stephano in dazed puzzlement.

Stephano stood breathing hard, saber in hand, looking swiftly around for more foes. All was quiet. No sign of any more demons. Even the bats had flown off. He lowered his saber and went to the two monks. One of them, a younger man, had his arm around the older monk and was speaking words of comfort. Their robes were bloody and torn. Both of them had been beaten and whipped.

"Are you all right, Brothers?" Stephano asked.

"We are, sir, thanks be to God," said the younger monk. His face creased in anxiety. "I will stay with Brother Paul. Please go to my friend."

Stephano nodded and hurried over to tend to the man whose shot had saved his life. He was bleeding from a jagged, ugly wound that had split open his forehead. Stephano regarded the wound in concern.

"I fear your skull is cracked, sir. You should lie down."

The man gazed at Stephano, blinking. Then he smiled.

"Julian? . . ."

Stephano started back, amazed.

The man sat on the ground, staring at him. "Julian . . ." he said again.

"Is your name Julian, sir?" the young monk asked.

"No," said Stephano, lost in wonderment. "Julian was my father."

A pistol lay on the ground where the man had dropped it. Stephano reached out and picked it up. He drew his dragon pistol and held the two side-by-side. One was the exact match of the other.

He had never met this man before, but he was as his father had often described him—brave and selfless and loyal.

"What is this man's name?" Stephano asked.

"Sir Ander Martel. Do you know him, sir?"

"He is my godfather," said Stephano.

On board the *Cloud Hopper*, Rodrigo sat on the bed at Gythe's side, bathing her forehead and calling her name gently, hoping to rouse her. Doctor Ellington had jumped back on his shelf. Dag stood by the door, ready to repel another invasion. When he heard footsteps, he drew his pistol. Rodrigo, his eyes squinched shut, shielded Gythe.

But it was Miri who appeared. She stood in the ruined doorway, staring at the burn marks on the floor and then at Dag and Rodrigo.

Dag grunted in relief and lowered the pistol. "What's happening topside?"

"The demons are gone," Miri said wearily. "What happened here?"

Rodrigo sat up and Miri saw her sister. Dropping the pistol she had been holding, Miri ran to her. "Oh, Gythe! Oh, my God!" She knelt beside her and kissed her. "What happened? What is wrong with her?"

Rodrigo shook his head. "She's been hurt by this strange magic."

"What can I do?" Miri asked frantically. "I have to do something!"

"We could take her to the abbey," Dag suggested after a moment's thought. "Perhaps the nuns can heal her."

Miri grasped the idea thankfully. "Yes, we'll take her to the abbey!"

"Can the *Hopper* still sail?" Rodrigo asked.

"I hope so!" said Miri fervently. "I wasn't on deck during the last attack. I ran down and shut the hatch." She looked out the porthole. "At least we're not sinking . . ."

"Always a good sign," said Rodrigo gravely.

Miri rose to her feet. "I'll go—"

"You stay with Gythe," said Dag gently, resting his hand on her shoulder. "I'll take a look."

He started to remove Doctor Ellington from his shelf.

"You should leave the cat," said Rodrigo. "He seems to soothe her."

Dag nodded and placed the cat gently on the bed, then went up to investigate the damage. Doctor Ellington rubbed his head against Gythe's limp hand, trying to make her pet him. Rodrigo watched anxiously, but she did not respond. He sighed and shook his head.

Miri sat down beside her sister and took over placing wet cloths on her forehead and tucking the blankets around her. Rodrigo dragged a rug over to hide the scorch marks, then climbed the stairs to join Dag at the forecastle. He was standing at the helm, his hands running over the sigils on the brass control panel.

Rodrigo looked up at the sails. They were intact, as was the balloon. He smiled sadly. Gythe's final protection spell had held, kept the *Cloud Hopper* safe.

"The boat seems airworthy," Rodrigo said. He ran his hand over the brass panel.

"We have suffered minor damage. The magic is still keeping us afloat. Some of the rigging lines burned and one of the yardarms snapped. We can run some plain ropes and control the sails by hand and splice the yard until we can replace it. Thanks to our girl, we fared better than they did, poor bastards," said Dag, indicating the cutter.

The *Suspicion* was listing badly. Several sailors were working frantically to make repairs to the mast. Another group had laid out the bodies of the dead and carried the wounded below. The captain stood on deck, shouting orders. Hearing the *Cloud Hopper*'s propellers start to whir, the captain of the cutter looked up and saluted. Dag returned the salute and went to the helm.

"Looks like the abbey came under attack, as well," Rodrigo said. "I've cobbled some magic together. We'll see if this works. Any sign of Stephano or his dragon friend?"

Dag shook his head. Rodrigo bent to examine the deck. There were no bodies, only scorch marks like those below.

"Some sort of magic in their armor deliberately destroyed the corpses," he reported. "Not a trace left behind. You started to say something about the boots."

"They had claws sticking out of them," said Dag. "Strangest damn thing I ever saw. One in back like a spur—"

"Now what have we here?"

Rodrigo squatted down. He found in the midst of the scorch marks what looked like a small round object, about the size and shape of a dessert plate, only made of brass. The brass plate was badly charred, but here and there Rodrigo could make out what appeared to be sigils, though they were like no sigils he had ever seen. In the center of the brass plate was a chunk of faceted crystal.

He reached out his hand and gave the brass plate a gingerly poke with the tip of his finger. Nothing happened. It didn't burn him or jolt him. He poked it again and again it just lay there. He picked up the plate and turned it over and found more sigils on the underside. He examined these and could make nothing of them. He turned his attention to the crystal, studying it with the eye of one who had noted that Lady Katrina De Burg's famous diamond necklace, reputedly worth a king's ransom, was actually paste, starting a scandal that had rocked the royal court. Rodrigo raised his eyebrows.

"A diamond! Not a very good diamond," he remarked to himself. "Poor clarity and color. But a diamond nonetheless."

"What's that you've got?" Dag asked curiously.

"I believe I have found some sort of fiendish frippery," said Rodrigo. "A Hellish bijou. A demonic diamond."

He held the brass plate out to Dag, who examined it with interest.

"This appears to be some sort of grenade," said Dag.

Rodrigo backed nervously away. "How could you possibly know that?"

"I got a good, close look at those cannonlike weapons the fiends were using." Dag ran his hand over his singed head. "A little too close. Singed off half my hair. I saw one of the fiends load something that gleamed like brass and was about this shape and size into the back of the cannon. My guess is that the crystal—"

"It's a diamond," Rodrigo pointed out.

"The diamond holds some sort of magical charge that sets off the green fire like the spark that ignites the gunpowder that fires a bullet. The sigils on the brass medallion surrounding the diamond might be there to focus the fire or protect the diamond or to keep the green fire from melting the cannon or all of that together."

Rodrigo came to take another look at the strange plate.

Dag shrugged. "You would know more about that than I do. Magic is in your line not mine."

"True," said Rodrigo, "except that I've never seen sigils like these."

"Aren't sigils sigils?" Dag asked.

"My dear linguistically deprived friend, is the Guundaran language the same as Rosian? Is Freyan the same as Estaran? Sigils form the language of magic and as far as I knew, there was only one language. Even Gythe's Trundler magic uses the same sigils, just arranges them in different patterns. Apparently I and thousands of magical scholars down through the ages have been wrong. The language of these sigils is completely unknown to me."

Rodrigo drew cautiously nearer to stare intently at what he was mentally terming the "green grenade." He made no move to touch it, however.

Dag noted this reluctance and was disturbed. "Do you think it's likely to go off? If so, we should get rid of the damn thing."

"Are you mad?" Rodrigo snatched the brass plate out of the big man's reach. "This demonic grenade of ours could be highly valuable. It might tell us more about the crafter who made it, for example."

"More about the Fallen One?" Dag scowled and shook

his head. "Who wants to know more about that? I say we throw it overboard, send it back to Hell where it came from."

"Do you really think we were attacked by the spawn of Aertheum," Rodrigo asked. "Fiends from Hell? I find that hard to believe."

"That's because you *don't* believe," said Dag sternly.

Rodrigo opened his mouth and then shut it again. Before the duel with the young Estaran, Rodrigo would have made a glib and lighthearted answer. He had been doing some soul-searching since then and, while not yet ready to embrace the idea of an omnipotent, omniscient Master of the Universe, Rodrigo had acquired new respect for those who did. He thought about his father, perhaps dead by an assassin's bullet . . .

You don't know if that is true yet, Rodrigo told himself for the hundredth time. The news could be rumor, speculation. Don't go borrowing trouble.

"I must admit," Rodrigo said with a shiver, "the sight of that fiend walking around with half his body blown off is difficult to explain rationally."

Dag gave a grave nod. "I saw these demons suffer deadly wounds and get back up and keep fighting. I saw them hurt Gythe without touching her. I saw their corpses vanish in a flash of green flame. I saw their orange glowing eyes. I'm not a scholar like you and Stephano. I can't explain what I saw. But I know I saw it."

Rodrigo had been standing all this time holding the grenade in his hand. A startled expression suddenly crossed his face.

"What?" asked Dag, who had been eyeing the grenade uneasily.

"I can feel the magic, like a buzzing bee in my palm," said Rodrigo. "It must be residual magic. I need to study this." He started to go below, then stopped and turned. "Unless you need me on deck?"

"Go below and take that infernal thing with you!" said

Dag, scowling. "I'll need you when we dock, but that won't be for awhile. I'll call you."

Rodrigo opened the hatch and was going down the stairs as Miri was coming up.

"How's Gythe?" he asked.

"No change," said Miri. "Could you stay with her? I feel so helpless. I need . . . I need to be doing something."

Rodrigo entered the cabin and startled Doctor Ellington. The cat leaped up, hackles raised.

"It's only me," said Rodrigo.

The Doctor glared at Rodrigo in annoyance, and curled up again by Gythe's head. She was still unconscious, but Rodrigo saw there had been a change, albeit a subtle one. She had more color in her face. Her breathing was easier. She was clearly better now that the attacks had stopped. But she remained unconscious. He called her name softly and patted her hand. All attempts to rouse her failed.

Rodrigo drew up a chair near to the bed and sat down. He was reminded of the last time he had kept watch at his friend's bedside, eighteen years ago, when he and Benoit had rescued the badly wounded Stephano from the battlefield of the failed rebellion. Rodrigo had stayed with his friend throughout the night, listening to Stephano's feverish ravings, fearing he was going to die.

Rodrigo looked at the object in his hand—a brass dessert plate with a diamond in the center. Dag had said this was what created the green fire. Rodrigo looked at Gythe and pondered.

━━━━◖━━━━

Miri climbed up onto the deck and came over to stand beside Dag.

"I'll take over," she said.

"Are you sure?" he asked, regarding her with concern. "If you want to stay with Gythe—"

"No. I can't do anything for her," said Miri brokenly. "This way at least I feel like I'm doing something to help."

She put her hands to the helm felt the *Cloud Hopper* respond to her touch. The walls of the abbey were in view. She and Dag both stared in dismay at the wreckage done to the cathedral, the broken windows, the rising smoke.

"The demons attacked the abbey!" Miri said. "The last I saw of Stephano, he and that dragon were flying in that direction."

"The demons are gone," said Dag reassuringly. "Likely Stephano and that dragon of his drove them off. We'll find him there, safe and sound, and we'll find help for Gythe there, too. You'll see."

Miri nodded, unable to speak for the choking sensation in her throat. She could not take her hands from the helm, so she rested her head against Dag's broad shoulder. She felt his warmth, his body, solid, firm, and stalwart.

"You are a comfort to me, Dag," she said softly.

Dag wanted to put his arms around her and hold her to him tightly forever, but he kept his arms stiffly at his sides. He loved Miri with a love that was vast as the vault of Heaven above and as deep as the fathomless depths of the Breath below. He meant to keep his love to himself, never, never to tell her.

He had her friendship, her sisterly affection, and that was enough. More than he deserved. He stood rigid, trying to keep from trembling at her touch.

He didn't succeed. Miri felt his body quiver. She saw his jaw clench, his hands balled to fists.

Dag, you're in charge . . . Stephano had told him.

No, sir, Dag had answered.

Miri did not know what had happened to him. All she knew was that she loved him. She was almost certain he loved her. She could tell him she loved him and she knew quite well what would happen. She would never see him again. She had to wait for him to heal.

The two stood at helm of the *Cloud Hopper*, close together and so far apart.

Chapter Twenty-Five

Julian often said the bravest thing he ever saw a man do was to turn and walk away from his own true love, as Ander walked away from Cecile, calling it an act so selfless, God himself must have wept. And then sixteen years later, Julian asked Ander to walk away from his own true friend. I am not sure about God, but I wept for us all.

—Rudolpho Benoit,
Steward to the de Guichen family

STEPHANO RELOADED HIS DRAGON PISTOL and stood guard over the stable yard while the young monk, who said his name was Brother Barnaby, tended to the wounds of the knight and the other monk. The battle was over, at least for the moment. The bodies of the demons had been magically consumed by some sort of unholy green fire, much to the dismay of Brother Barnaby. Stephano had to drag the young monk away from one of the blazing corpses.

"What is happening? Some of them are still alive," Barnaby said. "I might have been able to save them."

"Nothing you can do for them now," said Stephano.

"I can at least pray for them," said Brother Barnaby.

The other monk, Brother Paul, sat huddled in the grass, his robes torn, his back a bloody pulp from being whipped, his face battered. Brother Barnaby had a deep cut on one arm, a split lip, a bruise on his temple, and the marks of the scourge on his back. Stephano recalled what Droalfrig had told him about the horrible deaths of the nuns. He remembered Gythe, screaming in pain.

Stephano shook his head. "These fiends murdered innocent women. They beat Brother Paul and tortured you. Why are you praying for them?"

Brother Barnaby seemed astonished at the question. "We are all God's creatures, sir."

"Not if they are lost souls, Brother," said Stephano.

"Do we abandon the little child lost in the forest, sir," asked Brother Barnaby gently. "Or do we expend all our energy trying to reclaim her."

Stephano knew better than to be trapped in some sort of religious tangle, especially one to which he had no answer. He left the monk to his prayers and his healing and made a thorough search of the stables and the stable yard, looking for demon stragglers or stray bats.

Satisfied that none of the enemy was still lurking about, Stephano went to check on the dragon brothers, Hroalfrig and Droalfrig. They had defeated their foes and were now resting in a nearby field. Hroal was bleeding from a deep gash in his chest. Dragons had remarkable powers of healing, however, and he would soon recover. The dragons were concerned about him and the others. Stephano assured the two brothers that all was well, at least for the time being. He thanked them both for their valiant service and asked if they could remain on guard. Droalfrig, looking pleased, flicked a wing in salute.

Stephano returned from his reconnaissance to find Brother Barnaby trying to examine Sir Ander's head injury. The knight waved away the monk's attention.

"A bump on the head, nothing more. My own damn fault. I should have been wearing my helm. We need to get back to Father Jacob," Sir Ander said impatiently. "He's been injured."

"I will go to him immediately," said Brother Barnaby, then he faltered, "But there is Brother Paul—"

"Do not let me deter you," said the monk. He had

managed to rise and was standing, though somewhat unsteadily. "You should go to Father Jacob. He needs you,
Brother. I am in God's care."

"Bring Brother Paul along," said Sir Ander, chafing at
the delay.

"An excellent idea," said Barnaby, relieved. "Come
along, Brother. I have medicines at the *Retribution* to treat
your wounds."

Brother Paul at first demurred, protesting he did not
want to be a burden, but he was too weak to put up much
of an argument. He went on ahead with Brother Barnaby,
leaving Sir Ander and Stephano to follow along behind, pistols reloaded and ready to fire.

The two men walked for a time in silence, both at a loss
to know what to say to each other. Stephano had never met
his godfather and Sir Ander had met Stephano only once
and that when he was barely a week old. Stephano was confused and embarrassed. His feelings toward his godfather
were complicated, not easy to sort out. He and the knight
had carried on a correspondence through the years, exchanging letters that were warm on Sir Ander's part and
stiff and formal on Stephano's.

Sir Ander had been Julian's closest friend. Both Stephano's father and his mother had always spoken well of the
knight. His mother's praise of Sir Ander was more damning
than helpful, however. Stephano had never been able to
forgive Sir Ander for his continued close friendship with
the countess and for the fact that the knight had sided with
the king during the rebellion that had cost Julian de
Guichen his life.

At the end, facing execution, Julian had counseled his
son to turn to his godfather if he ever needed anything.
Stephano had refused to listen. Angry and grieving and bitter, Stephano was convinced Sir Ander had betrayed and
abandoned his father. Stephano had torn up Sir Ander's
letter of condolence and then burned it to ashes. He would
have destroyed the dragon pistol that had been his godfa-

ther's gift, but he hadn't been able to find it. Benoit, as it turned out, had hidden it away, restoring it years later, when Stephano had been granted his commission in the Dragon Brigade.

He was old enough then to admire the craftsmanship, recognize the quality, the value of such a gift. But when he looked at it, he saw only the man who had turned his back on his father.

"Put it back," Stephano had said. "I don't want it. Sir Ander betrayed my father."

"He did no such thing," Benoit had told him. "Your father wrote to him, urged him not to take up arms against his country. I know. I carried the letter to him myself."

"But why would my father do that?" Stephano had asked, not believing. He eyed Benoit. "And how do you know what my father wrote?"

"Because I read the letter, of course," Benoit had replied. "Keep the gun, you young fool. It was your father's wish you should have it."

Stephano had kept the dragon pistol. He often thought about what Benoit had said, wondered if it was true. Sir Ander had patiently continued to write to his godson over the years, giving the young man counsel as befitted a godfather, urging him to find solace in faith and relating stories about his father in the days of their youth, stories that spoke of his father's courage and honor.

Stephano came to value the correspondence, though his own responses tended to be cool and impersonal. He even went so far as to take Sir Ander's advice and make a somewhat shaky peace with God. He never spoke of this to anyone.

As they walked together, the two soldiers unconsciously fell into cadence, strides equal and matching. When the silence grew uncomfortable, both men felt driven to speak and both spoke at once. Both looked even more uncomfortable.

"I beg your pardon, sir," said Stephano, with a stiff bow. "Please continue."

"I was only going to say that you are very like your father," said Sir Ander and he added, with a smile, "Though you have your mother's eyes."

Stephano's brow furrowed and the eyes that were like his mother's eyes hardened and went steely gray, making the resemblance even stronger.

"I understand, sir, that you are a friend of my mother's," said Stephano in frozen tones.

"I have that honor," Sir Ander replied gravely.

He was reloading the dragon pistol as he walked. Stephano looked at the knight's pistol, then looked at his own, a gift from his godfather, a gift he had come to cherish. He was ashamed of his churlish response, but excused it by reminding himself he had good reason to be angry at this man.

""I held you in my arms the day you were baptized." Sir Anders was saying. "You screamed bloody murder the entire time and lashed out with your little fists at the priest when he flicked the holy water in your face. Julian burst out laughing. He said it showed you had fighting spirit. The poor priest was so shocked, your father had to donate a pair of silver candlesticks to the saint to make reparation."

Stephano gave a grudging half smile. "Benoit often tells that story, particularly when he wants to embarrass me."

"Benoit!" Sir Ander turned to face him. "Is that old man still alive?" When Stephano nodded, the knight added in softer tones, "I am glad to know it."

Stephano cast sidelong glances at his godfather as they walked together, noting with approval his military stance, his firm and muscular body, his strong jaw and forthright appearance. Stephano was disposed to like the man, but there was that one lingering doubt. He was brooding on this and only half-listening to Sir Ander saying something about being astonished to see a soldier come to his aid, riding a dragon.

"But, of course, you served in the famed Dragon Brigade. Julian wrote to me of the first time he put you on dragon back. You were three, I believe. He held you on the saddle in front of him as the dragon soared through the air. You were not the least bit afraid, he told me. He was so proud of you."

Stephano remembered that moment, one of his earliest recollections. He remembered that he *had* been afraid until he felt his father's strong arm encircle him. He remembered his father calling to the dragon that they were ready and the beast taking to the air and the wind rushing past his face and the thrill and elation of leaving the ground and flying to the skies. His heart constricted with pain as he lowered his head and made no answer.

They reached the wicket in the wall, and their conversation came to an end. Thus far, they had not seen any demons or their bats, but no one knew what might be waiting for them on the other side of the high wall. Musket held at the ready, Sir Ander entered the gate first, while Stephano remained guarding the two monks.

"Looks like they've gone," Sir Ander reported, and he motioned the monks to enter. Stephano brought up the rear.

He was pleased and heartened to see the *Cloud Hopper* sailing bravely toward the docks which were in a small inlet located about three miles from the abbey at the bottom of a steep hill. He cast a critical eye over the houseboat and was relieved to see that it had not suffered much damage. A yardarm had been snapped and hung tangled in the rigging. He wondered worriedly how Gythe was faring.

He was eager to go to his friends, but he felt a responsibility to the two monks and Sir Ander, who had, after all, saved his life. The knight tried to brush off the effects of his head wound, but Stephano saw Sir Ander wince every so often and guessed that it pained him more than he was letting on. And there was something he desperately needed to ask him.

The two men walked on for a moment in silence, then Sir Ander said, "I know this must be awkward for you—"

"Will you answer a question for me, sir?" Stephano asked abruptly.

"Of course," said Sir Ander.

"Why did you refuse to join my father in the rebellion? You believed in his cause. He told me you did."

"Your father wrote to tell me not to," said Sir Ander.

So Benoit was telling the truth, Stephano thought. He said nothing, however, but waited for the knight to continue.

Sir Ander gave a deep sigh. "I knew King Alaric had goaded the Duke of Bourlet into rebelling. The duke did not want to go to war. He suffered insult after insult in silence. But when his outposts were attacked, his property illegally seized, his friends and supporters threatened, he could take no more. But you know all this. You were fifteen, old enough to understand."

"Old enough to fight at my father's side," said Stephano proudly. He would have added, "unlike you, sir," but he swallowed the words. He might as well have said them, for they hung in the air.

"You fought while I sat at home," Sir Ander said. "Or rather, I sat in prison."

"I was told you refused to take up arms and that you were imprisoned for your refusal. I credit you with that much, sir. But you were set free, while my father . . ."

Stephano could not go on. He stared moodily out into the Breath.

"Yes, I was set free," said Sir Ander. "I was a Knight Protector and subject to the laws of the Church, not the Crown. The Knighthood saw to it that I was freed, but I was still punished. I was suspended for a time and then assigned to Father Jacob Northrup, a duty no one else wanted. Two Knight Protectors had threatened to resign rather than undertake to risk their lives guarding a Freyan priest—a man most believed to be a traitor. As one of my Order was overheard to say about me, 'They set a traitor to guard a traitor.'"

"Admit it, sir," Stephano said, his voice burning with anger and resentment, "you were set free because of my mother!"

"No, Stephano," said Sir Ander quietly. "At the time, the Countess de Marjolaine was herself walking on a precipice. Her enemies had arrayed themselves against her, all striving to bring about her downfall. She had all she could do to save herself and her son . . ."

Seeing Stephano glower darkly, the knight did not finish his sentence. "But you don't want to hear her trials, do you?"

"No, sir, I do not," said Stephano coldly.

Sir Ander was silent a moment, then he said quietly, "The Duke de Bourlet was your family's patron. Not only that, the duke was a good friend to your father. Your father fought and died for his friend, Stephano. Julian de Guichen did *not* die for the duke's cause."

Stephano set his jaw and kept grimly silent.

Sir Ander gave a sad smile. "When I wrote to tell Julian I was considering siding with the rebels, he wrote back to urge me to remain loyal. Not loyal to a cruel and avaricious king. Loyal to Rosia, the country he loved."

How many times Stephano had heard his father say almost those exact words! Julian de Guichen had said them to his own son when he had tried to deter Stephano from joining in the fighting. The hot-headed fifteen-year-old had refused to understand his father. Or rather, Stephano had refused to *want* to understand. Julian had said the same during his trial for treason. Facing a cruel and painful death, Julian de Guichen had yet proudly and steadfastly proclaimed his love and loyalty for his country. Stephano had never forgotten. His father's loyalty to Rosia was his son's loyalty, the reason he had accepted the commission into the Dragon Brigade.

Stephano had wept then and he felt the bitter tears sting his eyes now. He blinked rapidly and walked on.

"I am glad to see the dragon pistol has proven useful to you," said Sir Ander, glad to change the subject.

"The pistol has never failed me, sir," said Stephano. He added grudgingly, "I fear I never thanked you properly for it. And for the letters and the advice you have given me over the years."

"As to the pistol, you used it to save my life back there," said Sir Ander. "I guess that is thanks enough." He paused, then said, "I am glad to finally meet you at last, Stephano. Julian would have been very proud of you."

"Thank you, sir," said Stephano. "I am glad to meet you, as well."

Politeness dictated he say that. He wondered if he meant it. He could not forgive, but perhaps he could now begin to understand.

They reached the yacht without incident to find Master Albert still manning the swivel gun.

"How is Father Jacob?" Sir Ander called.

"I just checked on him, sir," Albert called back. "He is much improved." He cupped his hand around his mouth, and added quietly, "And, just between us, sirs, in a foul mood."

Brother Barnaby stared in shocked and horrified amazement at the damage to the yacht. He helped the exhausted Brother Paul through the wreckage and hastened inside to tend to Father Jacob, who could be heard demanding loudly to know where the monk had been all this time.

"I must remain with my friends," said Sir Ander, halting in front of the *Retribution*.

"And I must go to my friends," said Stephano.

The *Cloud Hopper* was now sailing into the docks, along with the ravaged cutter, so badly damaged the ship was barely able to remain afloat.

The two men saluted each other. Stephano walked down the hill toward the docks, emotions churning.

Sir Ander watched his godson walk, taking those long, impatient strides that were exactly like his father's. Not waiting for life to come to him, but striding forth eagerly to seek it. Sir Ander touched Cecile's letters, secreted in his pocket, and renewed to her a sacred promise. Then, bracing himself for the worst, he hurried to the yacht to deal with Father Jacob.

The priest was up and moving about, much to the consternation of Brother Barnaby, who was trying to persuade Father Jacob to lie down and rest. Instead he was bent over a washbowl filled with water, cleansing the bloodstains from his face.

Brother Barnaby stood near him. "Father, you are weak—"

"This from a man who sticks leeches on people!" Father Jacob said irritably. "Stop hovering! Tend to yourself."

"I have suffered only minor injuries, Father," said Brother Barnaby. "And I have seen to them already."

"Then help Brother Paul. He needs you. I do not. God has already ministered to me."

Brother Barnaby cast Sir Ander a long-suffering glance as the knight entered. Sir Ander gave a rueful smile and shrugged. Brother Barnaby shook his head, then went to Brother Paul, who lay stretched out on the knight's bed.

Father Jacob straightened and turned around. His face was dripping wet, his eyes squinched shut against the water. He groped about for a towel. Sir Ander brought over the towel and gave it to the priest.

"You should be in bed," said Sir Ander.

"Nonsense," said Father Jacob. "I'm fine now that I'm not being bombarded with . . ."

He paused, glanced at Brother Paul, and said abruptly, "I'm fine."

Father Jacob dried his face and then threw the towel aside and said briskly, "I want you to take a look at the damage to the *Retribution*. Master Albert tells me the yacht is not air worthy. That is not acceptable."

Sir Ander patiently pointed. "Did you happen to see the gigantic hole in the front?"

Father Jacob waved the hole away as unimportant.

"Albert also tells me that the damaged naval cutter has limped into the docks. That presents a problem. I can't have sailors running around Rosia telling tales about demons riding giant bats. I will have to place them under Seal. I will need to speak to the dragon brothers, as well—"

"Father, I can deal with the dragons and the yacht *and* the navy. You should rest—"

Father Jacob looked pointedly at the jagged, bloody gash on Sir Ander's head and said testily, "Look in a mirror. You are in worse shape than I am."

Sir Ander glared at the priest.

"I know," Father Jacob said, suddenly grinning, "I'm a pain in the ass. Where is Master Albert?"

"Outside, but—"

Father Jacob cast a significant look at Brother Paul and said, "Walk with me."

Sir Ander accompanied the priest outside. Father Jacob stood for long moments gazing gloomily at the charred patch of ground in front of the yacht and the clumps of greasy ash that was all that was left of their attackers.

"Dragon fire does not leave many clues." Father Jacob said bitterly.

"Nor does holy fire," Sir Ander pointed out. "You were the one who called down God's wrath and incinerated them."

"I was attempting to exorcise them, not kill them," said Father Jacob. "As you see, that did not work."

Sir Ander's head throbbed, his stomach heaved from the horrible smell of burnt flesh and hair. He shut his eyes against the bright sunlight and thought back to the horrific attack and how they had both been within moments of death or worse—capture and torment. And now Father Jacob was saying he had been trying to exorcise evil spirits! Sir Ander could only stand and marvel.

Father Jacob was now yelling up at Albert, who was crawling over the roof of the yacht.

"How bad is the damage, Master Albert?"

Albert looked down from the roof. "The control conduits on the both sides of the yacht have been reduced to cinders. Both of the primary lift tanks are intact, but there is no way of setting buoyancy levels or maintaining the ship's trim. There is impact damage all across the hull, but the main structure should hold together as long as you don't get caught in a storm."

"And both our wyverns are dead," Sir Ander added.

"Ah, yes, poor Brother Barnaby," said Father Jacob somberly. "He told me the beasts died trying to save him. Remarkable. I've never known wyverns to show such courage and loyalty. I promised him that we will give their remains a proper burial. What was I saying? Oh, yes." He turned back to Albert. "How soon can we get to work?"

"On what, Father?"

"On repairing the *Retribution*, of course?"

Albert had to struggle to keep a straight face. "You need a shipyard to handle extensive repairs like this, Father!"

"Damn and blast it, man, I must return to the Arcanum at once!" exclaimed Father Jacob in loud and angry frustration. "The matter is vital! I won't be marooned—"

Father Jacob stopped suddenly and turned to look in the direction of the docks. Sir Ander thought he was looking at the cutter, perhaps contemplating the meeting he would have with the captain. He was therefore surprised when Father Jacob said suddenly, "The Trundlers."

"What about them?"

"Master Albert, could the *Retribution* be towed?"

"A short distance, maybe," said Albert. "Not as far as to the Arcanum."

"I assume you have shipyards in Westfirth. That city is not far."

"You could probably make it to Westfirth, yes, Father."

"We will ask the Trundlers if they can tow us," said Father Jacob.

"What about the Seal of the Arcanum?"

"I know Trundlers," said Father Jacob with confidence. "They will keep quiet about this if I ask them."

Sir Ander smiled. "As it happens, my godson is aboard that houseboat."

"Your godson?" Father Jacob was amazed. "Captain de Guichen? Son of the Countess de Marjolaine? He's here?"

"He is not only here, he saved my life," said Sir Ander with quiet pride.

"Then I am deeply indebted to him," said Father Jacob warmly. "But why is the son of a countess sailing the Breath in a Trundler houseboat?"

"You can ask him yourself," said Sir Ander, who had caught sight of someone running up the hill. "If I am not mistaken, that is Stephano coming this way."

Father Jacob touched Sir Ander's arm, drew him close. "A quick word while we are alone, my friend. The demons asked both Brother Barnaby and Brother Paul about books."

"Books?" Sir Ander was troubled. "What books?"

"Undoubtedly the books mentioned in the Prince-abbot's journal."

"And *that* is why the demons didn't kill them," said Sir Ander. "I was wondering. So the fiends can talk. What did they say?"

"Brother Barnaby reported all he heard was a buzzing in his head repeating the words, 'books, the books' over and over. Brother Paul told me the same. I believe them. I heard it myself."

Sir Ander was troubled. "But this doesn't make sense, Father. Brother Barnaby wasn't with us when we found the books of Saint Dennis. He doesn't know about them. Nor does Brother Paul."

"And we must keep it that way. No one must know about what we found, Ander. I will not place such a burden on Brother Barnaby or anyone else, including your godson."

"Whether they know or not, we're all still in danger,"

said Sir Ander. "And we will bring that danger down on everyone who comes into contact with us."

"I will find a way to tell your godson as much of the truth as I can," said Father Jacob. "Give him the choice of aiding us or not."

"You know perfectly well he will."

"Of course, I do," said Father Jacob. "He's your godson."

Stephano had run all the way up the hill and was gasping for air by the time he arrived. Sir Ander made introductions, giving Stephano time to catch his breath.

"Lord Captain Stephano de Guichen, this is Father Jacob Northrup . . ."

"I need . . . a healer," Stephano spoke between gasps, "A friend . . . a young woman . . . gravely ill . . ."

"Sir Ander, send Brother Barnaby to me," said Father Jacob at once. "He and I will tend to this young woman. You stay with the yacht and Brother Paul."

He cast Sir Ander an expressive glance, reminding him about their precious cargo, the books of Saint Dennis, hidden in the secret compartment. Sir Ander nodded in understanding. He lingered to speak a few words to Stephano, expressing his confidence in Brother Barnaby and his hope that the young woman would fully recover, then returned to the yacht, where he found Brother Paul saying his farewell.

"I pleaded with Brother Paul to remain here," said Brother Barnaby. "But he insists on returning to his own dwelling."

"I need to be alone with my God," said Brother Paul.

The monk had his cowl drawn over his head, his face hidden in the shadows. Sir Ander recalled the monk saying he suffered from headaches without his tinted glasses and those had been lost in the fight with the demons. Sir Ander also recalled that Brother Paul was a hermit, who had chosen to live in this desolate place by himself. Still, he couldn't be allowed to depart. He had seen too much.

"I think you should stay here, Brother," Sir Ander said gently. "Father Jacob will want to speak with you again."

The hooded head turned toward him. Brother Paul's pale face was a glimmer of white in the shadows.

"Then I will remain, of course," he said with ready compliance.

Sir Ander told Brother Barnaby he was needed at the Trundler houseboat. Barnaby went to fetch his medicines. Master Albert was busy working on the yacht, attempting to make it ready for towing. Sir Ander went inside the yacht to keep an eye on their "guest." He found Brother Paul on his knees, praying.

Sir Ander sat down, lowered his aching head into his hands, and wondered if a dram of brandy would help or make the pain worse. He was tired enough already. The brandy would only put him to sleep and he had to stay awake to keep an eye on Brother Paul. Feeling fatigue start to overwhelm him, Sir Ander took out pen and paper and occupied himself in writing a letter.

Countess Cecile de Marjolaine,

My Dearest Friend,
  I write to tell you that I have finally had the very great pleasure of meeting your son . . .

Chapter Twenty-Six

The Trundlers' homeland was sunk when the seven kingdoms defeated the notorious Glasearrach Pirates in the War of the Pirate King. The Trundlers lived in a city on the opposite side of the island, and according to history, sided with and supported the pirates. The island had a terrible reputation as being a haven for murderers and worse. Some say Aertheum himself walked the hills and valleys of that fell place. The Church teaches that God's hand dragged the island and all her people into the Breath. That was when the Trundlers who survived turned their back on Him.

"The History of the Trundlers"
by Professor Angus McFarland

STEPHANO INDICATED HE WOULD ESCORT Father Jacob and Brother Barnaby to the *Cloud Hopper*. Stephano was uncomfortable in the presence of this black-robed priest with the intense, glittering eyes. Stephano believed in God, but not in his representatives here below. The Church had betrayed his father, and Stephano had never set foot in a house of worship since. He distrusted priests and didn't like having to rely on them, especially a priest of the mysterious and powerful Arcanum and one with a Freyan accent no less.

But I would make a pact with the grand bishop himself if he could help Gythe, Stephano thought as they were waiting outside the yacht for Brother Barnaby to fetch his medicines.

"What is wrong with the young woman, sir?" Father Jacob asked.

"I don't know, Father," Stephano replied. "She has no visible wounds, yet when the demons were hurling that green fire at the boat, she was in terrible pain. Now she lies in a deep sleep from which we cannot wake her."

"I trust we can help her, sir," said Father Jacob. "Is this young woman by any chance a crafter?"

"My friend says Gythe is more than a mere crafter, Father. Rigo termed her a 'savant.'"

"I myself am a savant," said Father Jacob. "The green fire affected me much the same way. As you see, I am a little weak in the knees, but otherwise recovered. Ah, here is Brother Barnaby."

Stephano said he was sorry disturbing the monk, who must be in pain from his own wounds. Brother Barnaby assured him that he was feeling much better and he was pleased to think he might be able to help. The three began the long walk down the hill toward the docks.

Stephano glanced sidelong at his two companions. He had already formed a favorable opinion of the monk, Brother Barnaby, though he considered the young man sadly naïve, one of those God-smitten individuals who see a halo around the head of every living being. Still, there was no harm in this gentle monk and a great deal of good.

The young monk's brown robes were torn and stained with blood. Stephano winced at the sight of the lash marks on the slender back. Brother Barnaby walked swiftly, his weariness and pain apparently forgotten in his concern for a fellow being, for he asked Stephano questions about Gythe as they walked and nodded his head in thoughtful concern. Looking at the dark-complected face, Stephano saw openness, honesty, caring, and compassion.

At one point, when Stephano was talking about Gythe singing, Father Jacob interrupted. "You say she doesn't speak, but she does sing."

"She sang the magic that protected our boat," said

Stephano, remembering that night on the *Cloud Hopper* when the magic danced and blazed before his eyes.

"Interesting," said Father Jacob. "I was affected by the demonic green fire in a similar manner. Yet I am up and moving about, much to the dismay of Brother Barnaby."

"You should be in bed," said the monk firmly.

Father Jacob merely smiled and continued, "Yet your friend still suffers."

"She was terrified by the demons," said Stephano. He hesitated. In her worry for her sister, Miri had relieved Stephano of his oath to keep their secret. He felt uncomfortable talking about it, however. "This is not the first time she has encountered these fiends."

"It isn't?" Father Jacob asked in surprise.

"When she and her sister were young girls, their houseboat came under some sort of mysterious attack. Both their parents were brutally murdered. Gythe and Miri had been staying with their uncle. Gythe jumped on board before anyone could stop her, and she saw what was left of the bodies. We think she also saw the attackers."

"She saw demons . . ." said Father Jacob.

"She seemed to recognize them when they attacked the *Cloud Hopper*," said Stephano. "She suddenly became a little child again. Laughing and singing to herself. Nursery rhymes . . ."

"The sisters' surname name wouldn't be McPike, would it?" Father Jacob asked.

Stephano stopped dead and turned to stare at him. "Gythe and Miri McPike. How did you know that, Father? Do you know them? How?"

But the priest did not answer. He walked with his head bowed, his hands clasped behind his back, his black cassock flapping about his heels. Stephano asked again, this time with some impatience. Father Jacob still did not reply.

"Do not be offended, Captain," said Brother Barnaby. "He is not deliberately ignoring you. He simply doesn't hear you. When he is like this, he wouldn't hear a cannon if it went off beside him. As to how he knows your friends, Father Jacob has been making a study of these strange attacks on the Trundlers."

"So there have been more such vicious, brutal murders, Brother," Stephano said.

"I fear so, sir," said Brother Barnaby. He added with a frown, his usually mild voice hardening. "No one in power except Father Jacob pays attention because the victims are Trundlers."

Stephano was more impressed with both the monk and the priest. "I hope you can help Gythe, Brother. I feel responsible for what happened to her. She and the others came on this accursed journey because of me."

"You take a great deal of responsibility upon yourself, Captain."

"You think God brought me here?" Stephano asked, half serious, half in jest.

"Sometimes we do not arrive at the place where we want to go, but where God needs us to be," Brother Barnaby said with serene faith and confidence.

Stephano looked curiously at Father Jacob. He thought what an odd pair these two made: one whose heart was laid bare to all the world; the other watchful, keen, sharp, secretive, solitary, seeing all, telling nothing.

Father Jacob was pale, and his face was haggard from pain and fatigue. His strong jaw was set, his eyes bright and even now, while he was abstracted, he appeared keenly aware of everything going on around him.

A savant, Father Jacob had termed himself. One to whom magic comes easily, naturally, unlike Rodrigo, who had to work at the magic and mostly didn't bother. For Gythe, magic was like the music she loved. She had a talent for magic as she had a talent for music. No one had ever taught her to play or sing; she had not studied with some great master at the University. She could not read the notes; she did not understand musical theory. Gythe cast magic as she played the harp—by ear, doing what she liked or, as in the protection spells, she acted instinctively, out of fear.

Father Jacob was different. He knew magic, understood magic. The magic was in his heart and his soul, yet also in his brain. He was disciplined, controlled, and that made him powerful and dangerous.

"But only to those with evil intent," said Father Jacob.

Stephano gave a start, amazed and not at all pleased.

"Do not be alarmed, Captain," said Father Jacob with a chuckle. "I cannot see into your head. I simply followed your thought process on your face. We were speaking of your friend as being a savant. I said I was a savant. You then began to compare the two of us, and I could see by the narrowed eyes and the dark glances you gave me that I come up short."

By this time they had arrived at the docks—three large piers extending into the Breath. The large ships would dock at the piers, while smaller ships that flew primarily over land would tie off onto one of the tall wooden posts that had been built for that purpose on top of the cliff. Half a dozen buildings served to store cargo and provide lodging for sailors. All stood empty now.

The *Cloud Hopper* was docked at the far pier. The naval cutter had docked at the first pier, though "crashed" would be a truer description. The *Suspicion*'s crew worked frantically, trying desperately to find some way of keeping the battered ship from sinking. Father Jacob stopped, saying he needed to speak to the captain.

Stephano hurried onto the *Cloud Hopper*. Dag and Rodrigo were waiting for him.

"So a priest of the Arcanum is paying us a visit. This should be interesting," said Rodrigo with a quirk of his eyebrow that Stephano knew all too well.

"It better not be," Stephano said in warning tones. He was about to add more when Dag seized hold of his arm and dragged him off to the forecastle.

"That priest is from the Arcanum," Dag said. His eyes were wide. His hand trembled.

"He's here to help Gythe," said Stephano, wondering what all this was about.

"Maybe not," said Dag in a low voice. "Maybe he's come for me."

"Why?" Stephano asked, baffled.

"Because of . . . you know," said Dag, his eyes cast down. "I'm going to Hell. Maybe he's come to take me."

Stephano heaved a sigh and ran his hand through his hair. He was feeling exactly the way he'd felt when he'd been desperately trying to control that blasted runaway horse. Some strange malady was affecting Gythe, an Arcanum inquisitor was coming aboard, Rodrigo was up to some sort of mischief, and now Dag—known for his courage and coolness under fire—had completely lost his mind.

Stephano gripped his friend's arm tightly. "Dag, all Hell is breaking loose—literally. I need someone I can count on, someone to watch my back. I need *you*. Don't let me down."

Dag blinked at him and then gave a rueful, half-ashamed smile. "Sure, Captain. I'm sorry. I don't know what came over me."

By now the monk was coming on board. Stephano hurried over to greet him. "Dag, this is Brother Barnaby. Take him down to Gythe, will you?"

Dag escorted the monk below to where Miri was keeping watch over her sister. Stephano went back to talk to Rodrigo, who was lounging against the ship's rail, gazing at the priest.

"Whatever you are plotting, forget it," said Stephano. "I want that priest on and off this boat without incident."

"Trust me. It won't be that easy, my friend," said Rodrigo.

Father Jacob had gone first to visit the naval cutter, whose crew had been working feverishly to keep the ship from sinking. Their efforts had been in vain. The crew had given up the fight to save their ship and were now hastily unloading what stores and supplies they could salvage, hauling them down a gangplank to the dock. The dead still lay on the deck. The captain and sailors had not had time to tend to them.

Father Jacob waited until the sailors had rolled a barrel down the gangplank, then he boarded the ship and went to speak to the harried captain, who was the last man remaining.

"Father, you shouldn't be here!" the captain said, seeing him approach. "*Suspicion* is sinking beneath us! She'll go down any moment!"

"I came to say a prayer for your dead," said Father Jacob coolly.

The ship was, indeed, sinking slowly beneath them. The crew on the dock were shouting for them to come off, they couldn't keep the gangplank in place much longer. Father Jacob paid no heed. He went to stand in front of the row of bodies: the youngest, a powder boy, age nine; the eldest a grizzled veteran with a pegleg.

Father Jacob raised his voice in prayer. The crew on the docks fell silent. Hats off, they stood with their heads bowed. The captain removed his hat, held it over his breast. Amazingly, the ship remained steady. One of the sailors would swear later he saw God's hand beneath it, holding it up.

"He's got guts, that priest," said Rodrigo.

Stephano grunted.

His prayer concluded, Father Jacob raised his hand in blessing, and then he and the captain literally ran for their lives across the faltering gangplank. The captain, the last to leave his ship, was standing on the gangplank when it gave way. He was saved from falling into the Breath by Father Jacob, who caught hold of him and dragged him bodily onto the dock.

Father Jacob spoke a few words of comfort and prayer to the sailors who had been wounded and lay on the ground on litters. The ship's doctor, a healer, was busy among them. Seeing they were in good care, Father Jacob said a final word to the captain, who looked at him grimly and then shrugged and went back to work.

As Father Jacob walked toward the *Cloud Hopper*, he looked suddenly very tired.

"I wonder what that talk with the captain was about," said Stephano.

"He put them under Seal," said Rodrigo.

Stephano frowned. "What does that mean—being put under Seal?"

"That refers to the Seal of the Arcanum. Those men will be hauled off to the Citadel, kept locked up."

"But why?" Stephano demanded.

"My dear fellow, you can't have sailors roaming about the world claiming their ship was sunk by demons," said Rodrigo.

"So *that's* why he came with the monk," said Stephano grimly. "He's going to try to muzzle us. Well, he can't. We have to get to Westfirth. We've lost time enough already. Which reminds me," said Stephano, fixing Rodrigo with a stern eye, "I'm putting *you* under Seal. You are not to say a word about Alcazar or the duel or anything related to our job."

"Stephano, you wound me," said Rodrigo, offended. "You know that I am the soul of discretion."

Stephano had no time to respond. In the absence of Miri, he had to greet Father Jacob as he boarded the houseboat. The priest stood looking about with a casual air that did not fool Stephano. He saw Father Jacob's gaze go to the helm, the scorch marks on the deck, the damage done to the houseboat.

"Welcome aboard, Father," said Stephano in not very welcoming tones.

He had a mind to confront the priest immediately, demand to know if they were going to be placed under Seal. He decided to hold his peace, at least for the time being. What was important now was Gythe.

"Rodrigo de Villeneuve," said Stephano, introducing his friend, who came up behind him. "Father Jacob Northrop."

Rodrigo gave a graceful bow and said, with a mournful air, "I owe my dismissal from University to you, Father Jacob."

"Indeed?" The priest raised his eyebrows.

"Yes. It had to do with that book of yours, the *Metaphysics of Magic: How Magic relates to Being, Knowing, Substance, Cause, Identity, Time, and Space.* Our professor was expounding upon it and making a complete pig's breakfast of it. When I pointed out where he had gone wrong in his thinking—if one wants to call it thinking—he ordered me to leave and never darken the door of his classroom again."

"And were you right?" Father Jacob asked, his lip twitching.

"Oh, yes," said Rodrigo. "That is what galled him."

"De Villeneuve," Father Jacob repeated the name thoughtfully. "I seem to recollect hearing something about an incident involving you and the grand bishop's miter . . ."

"The man has no sense of humor," said Rodrigo.

Father Jacob smiled. "I must go see how Brother Barnaby fares with his patient. But I look forward to hearing your views on the *Metaphysics of Magic*."

He gave a friendly nod and was going below when Rodrigo said airily, "Or perhaps you and I could talk about a new theory I was thinking of writing about. I plan to call it, *The Metaphysics of Green Fire Destroying Magic*."

Father Jacob stopped walking and turned to look back at Rodrigo.

"You know, Monsieur, that such a thing is not possible. Magic is the Breath of God and cannot be destroyed. You are talking heresy," said Father Jacob.

The priest's manner was not threatening. His voice was calm and his eyes mild, yet Stephano felt the danger, like lightning in the air. The hair rose on his arms, a shiver went down his spine. Rodrigo heard the danger. He glanced at Stephano, looked away, kept quiet.

"I trust, however," Father Jacob continued, "you were jesting. You *are* known for your sense of humor, I believe."

"No one takes Rigo seriously, Father," Stephano assured him.

"That's true," said Rodrigo, gulping.

Father Jacob smiled. "I would have given a great deal to see the grand bishop's miter go sailing about the dining room."

He proceeded down below.

"I'll be with you in a moment, Father," Stephano called after him.

He turned to Rodrigo, who was gazing after the priest with a certain amount of awe.

"What a terrible old man! I know exactly how people feel when they encounter a basilisk. Those eyes of his froze my feet to the deck."

"Too bad he didn't freeze your tongue!" Stephano said furiously. "Soul of discretion, my ass! I don't know what you were talking about, but I'm guessing that if we weren't going to be put under Seal before, we sure as Hell are now. I have to go. Just keep that mouth of yours shut!"

Rodrigo gave a doleful nod. Stephano dashed down the stairs to find Father Jacobs staring at a smeared puddle of blood on the floor. Stephano was sweating, and he realized he was still wearing his heavy flight coat. He took it off and tossed it on a crate.

"That blood belongs to a demon," said Stephano, hoping to turn the subject away from Rodrigo. "I believe this particularly demon led the attack."

"How do you know that?" Father Jacob asked curiously.

"He wore some type of knotlike device on his armor, and he was using whistles to direct the troops. He tried to board our boat. We think he was after Gythe. I shot him, but he didn't die. Rigo killed him."

"I don't suppose there's a body I could examine," asked Father Jacob eagerly.

"Not anymore," said Stephano. "The body was incinerated by the same green fire that destroyed our magic. Dag said it appeared to be generated by the armor the demons wore."

"An interesting theory your friend, Villeneuve, has advanced," said Father Jacob, staring fixedly at the blood. "Green fire destroying the magic."

Stephano wished he'd kept his mouth shut.

"Relax, Captain," said Father Jacob. "I am not such 'a terrible man' as your friend seems to think. Where is the young woman who is ill?"

"Gythe's quarters are this way, Father," Stephano said.

As they continued down the passageway, Stephano heard Gythe's voice, singing softly. A chill went through him. She was singing a nursery rhyme. He found Dag standing in the doorway of the room where the sisters slept. His hands and face and uniform were black with gunpowder residue and red with blood, some of it his own. Doctor Ellington was curled up on Dag's shoulder. Seeing the priest, Dag whipped off his hat and ducked his head, muttering something no one could hear. He flattened himself against a bulkhead, allowing Father Jacob to squeeze past him.

"A very handsome cat," said Father Jacob, pausing to regard the Doctor, who was regarding the priest with slit-eyed dislike. The cat's hackles rose, he sank his claws into the padding on the coat. "What is the name?"

Dag hastily reached up his hand to try to soothe the ruffled cat. "Doctor Ellington, Father."

"Doctor Ellington," Father Jacob repeated in admiring tones. He wisely made no move to pet the Doctor. "Interesting name. There's a story involved, I'll wager. I look forward to hearing it."

Stephano and Dag exchanged grim glances. The priest sounded as though he intended to stick around for awhile.

Father Jacob entered the room with silent and measured tread. Stephano went in after him. The cabin was crowded. Despite having removed his coat, he was still sweating.

Gythe sat huddled in a corner, her knees drawn up to her chest, playing with some of Doctor Ellington's yarn, twining the strands around her fingers to form a Cat's Cradle and singing to herself in a high, shrill voice.

Brother Barnaby knelt down in front of her. "May I play your game with you?"

Gythe looked at him and laughed and held out her hands with the yarn twined around them to him.

Brother Barnaby took hold of yarn that was in the shape of the Cat's Cradle, tugged at the crossed strings, and pulled them out from the center. He twined the yarn around his fingers to form the Soldier's Bed. Gythe clapped her hands and then took hold of the yarn and plucked it off and held up the configuration known as the Candle.

Miri sat on the bed. Her face was drawn and strained with fear. Intent upon Gythe, she hadn't heard Father Jacob enter. The priest kept his distance, silently watching, assessing.

"At least Gythe is conscious," said Stephano.

"The moment the good Brother put his hands on her, she stopped twitching and moaning," said Dag. "She relaxed and woke up and smiled. But when Miri tried to talk to her, she climbed out of bed and ran to sit in the corner."

Miri heard them talking and looked around. Seeing the priest, she rose to her feet and stretched out her hand.

"Papa Jake!" she said, her voice breaking. "You're here. Thank God!"

Stephano stared in astonishment. He dimly remembered hearing Miri talk about a priest who defied Church law by administering sacraments to the Trundlers. The nomadic people had been declared apostates, after openly rebelling against the Church centuries ago, following the deliberate sinking of their island homeland. Some wondered why the Trundlers wanted the blessing of a God in which they didn't believe, but though they may have renounced their faith, they had retained a superstitious trust in the sacraments, especially those that marked passages in life such as baptisms, marriages, and the last rites.

A priest known affectionately as Papa Jake often visited the Trundlers to perform the rites. He was one of the few priests welcome among them, for he did not preach at them or harangue them or threaten them with hellfire and brimstone if they didn't change their wicked ways.

Father Jacob greeted Miri in her own language, speaking soothing words of comfort. When she began to cry, he embraced her, patting her on the back until her sobs lessened and she grew quiet. Miri blinked her shimmering eyes and looked up at him.

"I am so glad you are here, Papa," she said. Her clothes were stained and torn; her face smeared with tears and gunpowder. "You must say a prayer for Gythe. Give her your blessing."

"We will all pray together," said Father Jacob.

He cast a glance over his shoulder, including Dag and Stephano, and knelt on the scorched planks where the demon had died. Miri sank down beside him, her hands clasped, her disheveled hair falling about her shoulders. Dag hurriedly removed Doctor Ellington from his shoulder and dumped him on deck. The cat stalked out into the passageway. Stephano could see yellow eyes gleaming in the shadows. Dag, with some effort, managed to lower himself to his knees. He clasped his hands and bowed his head.

Stephano was the only one still on his feet, and he had the feeling Father Jacob knew it, though the priest had his back turned and his head bowed. Stephano joined the cat in the shadows of the corridor. He and God were on speaking terms, but Stephano was not yet ready to kneel to Him or anyone. He did bow his head and, in his heart, he joined in the prayer. Father Jacob spoke in the Trundler language, of which Stephano knew only a smattering. He couldn't understand the words, but he could hear in the priest's rich, mellifluous voice his compassion, his steadfast faith.

Stephano did not know what to make of the enigmatic Father Jacob.

The prayer ended. Miri rose to her feet, wiping her eyes and unwittingly smearing gunpowder residue across her face.

"Thank you, Papa," she said, resting her hand on his arm.

He put his arm around her shoulders and spoke a few soft words to her. She smiled and went to sit on the floor beside Brother Barnaby. Father Jacob assisted Dag to his feet. The big man's face was flushed; he didn't seem to know where to look.

"Thank you, Father," he mumbled.

"Let us leave them," Father Jacob said, herding Dag out into the narrow passageway where they encountered Stephano and the Doctor. The cat hissed at the priest. Dag made a grab for the cat. He missed. Doctor Ellington dashed into the cabin where Brother Barnaby was still playing Cat's Cradle with Gythe, each of them taking turns forming the yarn into various configurations.

The cat ran to Gythe and, lifting his paw, began batting at the yarn. Brother Barnaby reached out to pet the Doctor, who arched his back beneath the monk's touch and purred loudly.

"I'm sorry, Father," said Dag, flushing even more deeply. "The Doctor's making a nuisance of himself. I'll fetch him—"

"The cat is trying in his own way to help her," said Father Jacob, halting Dag. "Never discount love, no matter how small the heart that offers it."

Miri accompanied them into the passageway.

"Papa, you look ill and tired. Don't return to the abbey. You must spend the night with us."

"Thank you, my dear," said Father Jacob. "But I must report back. If not, Sir Ander will be certain to come looking for me."

"We will see you tomorrow?" Miri asked.

"Oh, yes," Father Jacob replied cheerfully. "You'll be seeing a good deal of me."

Stephano didn't like the sound of that. Miri went to her sister and Brother Barnaby. Stephano and Dag escorted the priest to the top deck. The sun was sinking into the twisting coils of the Breath. The twilight was murky, unsettled. Wind gusts rose unexpectedly, singing in the rigging with a mournful sound that echoed Gythe.

The *Suspicion* was gone. The captain and crew of the sunken vessel were straggling up the hill to the abbey, carrying their wounded with them on litters. Rodrigo leaned on the rail, gazing down into the swirling mists that had swallowed up the ship. He looked up, saw Father Jacob, and looked away.

"If you please, Monsieur de Villeneuve," said Father Jacob. "I am going to be returning to my yacht. I would appreciate it if you would walk with me."

Rodrigo cast Stephano an alarmed glance.

"He can't help you, I'm afraid," said Father Jacob.

"I'll just go . . . fetch my cloak," Rodrigo said faintly.

Stephano, looking out into the inky sky, saw one of the two dragon brothers circling above the cathedral spires. "Do you think the demons will be back tonight, Father?" Stephano asked quietly.

"At a guess, I would say no," said Father Jacob. "They found what they came for. Or rather, they *didn't* find it, but they no longer believe it is here."

"I don't understand," said Stephano.

"You're not meant to," said Father Jacob. "Just in case, you should move your boat near the abbey walls, close to *Retribution*. And your proximity to my yacht will save us time in the morning."

"Time for what?" Stephano asked suspiciously. "Time to put us under Seal? I have important work to do in Westfirth. I give you my word of honor, Father, that none of us will say anything—"

"I accept your word, Captain," said Father Jacob gravely. "You are Sir Ander's godson. No more need be said on the subject. And, that reminds me, I have been remiss in offering you my sincere thanks. You saved the day, Captain de Guichen. You and our friends, Hroalfrig and Droalfrig."

Stephano brushed aside the praise. "So we can sail to Westfirth?"

"You can sail, Captain, if you will permit us to accompany you," said Father Jacob. "The *Retribution* needs extensive repairs. Master Albert says that the yacht can be taken under tow to the shipyards at Westfirth. I was thinking the *Cloud Hopper* could handle that job. The journey requires only a few hours, as I understand it."

Stephano was not certain he wanted to spend even a few hours with Father Jacob. He needed to reach Westfirth, however, to pursue the hunt for information regarding the kidnapped journeyman, Alcazar—almost forgotten in the dramatic events of the past few days.

"Brother Barnaby can remain with Mistress Gythe," Father Jacob continued. "I think that would be wise. The two have been through similar experiences. The demons spoke to him, as well."

"You think the demons spoke to Gythe?" Stephano asked, astonished.

Father Jacob sighed and gave a grave nod. "I believe they did. They spoke to me. I didn't answer, but I think she did."

Stephano was doubtful, incredulous.

"You said the demon commander came for her, Captain," Father Jacob explained. "Even though she was down below, locked in her cabin, the demon still found her. He was guided by her voice, as it were."

"I will have to speak to Miri about towing the yacht," said Stephano, troubled. "The *Cloud Hopper* is her boat. But I am certain she will be more than happy to assist you."

"Excellent!" said Father Jacob. "I trust I will have the pleasure of seeing you and your friends later this evening after you've moved the boat. And now, Monsieur de Villeneuve, I await your convenience."

Rodrigo pressed Stephano's hand. "You will think of me from time to time, my friend, as I sit chained to the wall in some forgotten oubliette . . ."

"By far the best place for you," Stephano said firmly. "If you say a word to him about Alcazar, I'll chain you up myself."

Rodrigo reached inside his coat. "I almost forgot. I found this. Dag says it's a demonic grenade." He held out the brass plate with the diamond to Stephano, who regarded it with disgust and made no move to touch it. "He says this is what the demons used to shoot off their green fire—"

Father Jacob swooped in with a flurry of black, plucked the brass plate from Rodrigo's hand, and tucked it into the bosom of his cassock. The priest's movements were so fast that Rodrigo stood staring blankly at his empty palm.

"A remarkable find, Monsieur," said Father Jacob. He slapped Rodrigo on the shoulder. "Perhaps I won't have you burned at the stake as a heretic after all."

"He's jesting, isn't he?" Rodrigo asked nervously, looking back at Stephano over his shoulder. Stephano only waved and Rodrigo turned to the priest, "You're jesting, Father, right?"

Dag sailed the *Cloud Hopper* to the abbey, landing the houseboat on the ground close to *Retribution*. Dinner was a somber affair and didn't last long. Brother Paul insisted that he was well enough to go minister to the captain and crew of the sunken ship, who had taken refuge in the one stable that had not been burned. Father Jacob warned everyone to keep out of the cathedral, due to the extensive damage.

Droalfrig had flown off, at Father Jacob's request, carrying urgent dispatches to the Arcanum. Hroalfrig's wound was healing well. The dragon had offered to stay at the abbey, assist in its defense and make certain the sailors under Seal did not try to leave.

"The Arcanum will send a fast ship to pick up the survivors from the *Suspicion* and Brother Paul and take them to the Citadel for their own protection," Sir Ander told Stephano. "Don't worry. They will be treated well. They won't be thrown into an oubliette."

"Rigo has a vivid imagination," said Stephano.

He had asked Rodrigo what Father Jacob had spoken to him about.

"He questioned me about Gythe and her magic and the demonic magic and my thoughts on it," said Rodrigo. He paused a moment, then said, "He recommended most strongly that I keep such thoughts to myself. Then he asked if I would like to come to the Arcanum."

"By God, if he tries to take you—"

"No, no," said Rodrigo soothingly. "He wants to know if I'd like to become a priest."

Stephano burst out laughing.

"Yes," said Rodrigo. "That was *my* answer."

Dag brought over his tools and offered to assist Master Albert with the repair work on the yacht. Stephano went to check on Gythe and found her lying asleep on the floor beside Brother Barnaby, who had also fallen asleep. Her head rested on his shoulder, her hands were twined around his. Doctor Ellington slept with them, his large furry body stretched out across the monk's ankles. Miri kept watch over them all.

Stephano and Sir Ander had agreed to take turns on guard. Stephano took first watch. He had never minded guard duty. He liked being alone with his thoughts, and although he was bone-tired, he knew from experience that even if he went to bed, he would not be able to rest. He would relive the battle with the demons over and over, seeing it in his mind in bright flashes like strikes of lightning.

Hearing footsteps, he turned to find Father Jacob, his black cassock tinged with silver in the moonlight, coming toward him.

"I couldn't sleep," he said by way of explanation. "I didn't want to disturb Sir Ander and so I thought I would come disturb you, Captain de Guichen. If you don't object to some company?"

"Not at all, Father," said Stephano politely. "My own thoughts aren't very good companions."

Father Jacob joined him in his pacing. They walked for a few moments in silence, then Father Jacob said, "I know you have a great many questions, Captain. You and your comrades are risking your life to help me without knowing why. I wish I could explain, but I cannot. It seems unfair."

"I do have one question," said Stephano.

"I cannot promise to answer it," said Father Jacob.

"I know. But I'd feel better asking."

Stephano paused, staring out into the Breath, where strands of mists were casting nets around the moon.

"Did the gates of Hell open this day, Father?"

The priest regarded Stephano intently for long moments. Then he turned his gaze toward the abbey with its shattered windows and blood-soaked ground and gave a soft sigh.

"That depends on your definition of Hell, Captain," replied Father Jacob.

Chapter Twenty-Seven

They say fortune favors the bold, the foolish, and the prepared. Here, fortune favors the heavily armed.

Welcome to Westfirth.

—Graffiti, Anonymous

LIFE HAD NOT BEEN EASY FOR SIR HENRY WALLACE these past two weeks. While Stephano and Father Jacob were battling demons, Sir Henry was battling inanity. Given a choice between fighting demons and trying to figure his way out of the present accursed predicament, Sir Henry might well have chosen the demons. At least he could have ended his problem on the blade of a sword. Which is what he was seriously considering at the present moment. As he now stood glaring at Pietro Alcazar, Sir Henry was tempted, sorely tempted, to slice the journeyman's scrawny throat.

Alcazar was undoubtedly a genius. He had discovered the greatest invention of the last several centuries: how to combine metal with the magical Breath of God, rendering steel strong enough to withstand bullets, gunpowder, and cannonballs. His invention would revolutionize warfare. Unfortunately, the inventor was not only a genius, he was a whimpering, whining, stubborn, piss-yellow Rosian dog of a coward.

Sir Henry had known from the start that Pietro Alcazar

was not what one might term a shining example of honor and nobility. Alcazar had, after all, offered to sell his invention to Freya, his country's most implacable foe, dedicated to Rosia's utter annihilation. Still, Sir Henry had expected the man to have more backbone than your average *blanc-mange*.

Having received the pewter tankard from Alcazar's brother, Manuel, and having tested the tankard with the help of Mr. Sloan, Sir Henry had left his pregnant young wife to make a dangerous trip to Rosia in order to meet with Pietro Alcazar and personally transport him safely back to Freya.

The agreed-upon meeting place was the city of Westfirth, that cesspool of corruption, much loved by smugglers, pirates, and spies. Westfirth was an old city, founded by Freyans some seven hundred years ago and had remained loyal to Freya during the Black Fire War, fighting to the end before going down to defeat. The victorious Rosian army had not been kind to Westfirth's citizens. Whether they were Freyan or Rosian, all were considered traitors. Bitter memories still lingered.

Upon his arrival in Westfirth, Sir Henry sent a note to Alcazar, who lived in Evreux on Half Moon Street, arranging their meeting. Using one of his many disguises, Sir Henry had secured a suite of rooms in an inn and then waited for Alcazar.

Alcazar received the letter, but he was having second thoughts and he tossed the letter in the fireplace—which was where Rodrigo would later find it. When Alcazar failed to arrive at the meeting place, Sir Henry, seething, acted promptly. He sent his agents, under the leadership of James Harrington (alias Sir Richard Piefer), to procure Alcazar. Harrington was to handle Alcazar gently but firmly and send him on his way, under escort, to Westfirth. Harrington was then to linger on Half Moon Street to see who took an interest in Alcazar's disappearance and to deal with them as circumstances warranted.

Harrington had of late proved to be troublesome. The man had begun to think too highly of himself, leading him to indulge in rash and reckless behavior. Sir Henry had more than once thought of cutting Harrington loose, but the man had two qualities that made him valuable: his ability to masquerade as anything from a chimney sweep to an ambassador and his skill with firearms.

In this instance, Harrington delivered the goods. He and his associates swept up Alcazar in the middle of the night and carried him off. When Alcazar was escorted into Sir Henry's presence by his captors, the first thing the journeyman saw was Sir Henry cleaning his pistols. Alcazar collapsed, senseless.

Sir Henry revived the wretched journeyman and assured him that he was not only safe from the moneylenders, he was about to take a trip to Freya where he would become a very wealthy man. He would have his own armory, his own journeymen, everything he needed to continue his work.

"But I don't want to go to Freya, Monsieur Russo," said Alcazar.

(Henry had not, of course, given Alcazar his true name. He had told Alcazar that he was Monsieur Russo, a mere agent of the famous spymaster, Sir Henry Wallace.)

"Of course you want to go to Freya," Henry snapped.

"No, I don't, sir," Alcazar said, trembling. "I just want my money."

It seemed that the genius Pietro Alcazar had spent a lot of time reflecting on what he had done and had—somewhat belatedly—come to the horrifying realization that if he was caught fleeing to Freya, he would be branded a traitor. Alcazar knew what happened to traitors. He had witnessed their cruel deaths and seen their heads mounted on pikes on the palace grounds and watched the crows peck out their eyes. And not only would he be branded a traitor, his brother would be executed as his accomplice, his brother's young family turned out into the streets.

"All I want is my money," Alcazar kept whining, apparently having some idea that if he merely took money for the secret formulae, he was not betraying his country.

Sir Henry could have locked up Alcazar in a trunk and hauled him to Freya bodily, but his invention of magically infused steel was so vitally important that Sir Henry did not dare upset the genius. A browbeaten, terrified Alcazar might decide to take his revenge on his captor by sabotaging the project. Sir Henry needed Alcazar to come willingly, gladly, enthusiastically.

Sir Henry endeavored to explain to Alcazar that once he was in Freya, he would be under Freyan protection. The Rosians could not harm him and he at last persuaded Alcazar to agree to go to Freya, if his brother and his family could accompany him.

Sir Henry spent several days making careful arrangements. He and Pietro Alcazar were to travel to Freya on board the merchant vessel, *Silver Raven*, on which Pietro's brother, Manuel, served. Manuel's wife and children would be smuggled out on a different ship, so as not to arouse suspicion, and transported to the Aligoes Islands. From there, they would be taken to Freya.

Since Alcazar's brother, Manuel, was currently on board the *Silver Raven* and it was somewhere between Bheldem and Westfirth, he could not be reached. Sir Henry discreetly approached his wife. With a passel of small children to feed, she was living on the meager earnings of a sailor and was only too happy to agree to leave Westfirth, especially with wealth in the offing.

All Henry had to do now was await the return of the *Silver Raven*. The manifest the captain had filed with the port authorities stated the ship was expected back in port in approximately a week, give or take a few days due to uncertain weather.

Sadly, the genius, Pietro Alcazar, remained in a state of perturbation. He was certain the Rosian guard was on his trail and feared that any moment they would break down the door and arrest him. He trembled whenever he heard a footstep in the hall and this morning he had nearly fainted when a troop of soldiers came marching down the street on their way to the Old Fort. It was at this juncture Sir Henry seriously considered skewering the journeyman. Instead he had to appease him, keep him happy.

"You are in no danger whatsoever," Sir Henry assured the wretched Alcazar. "But it is true that we have stayed in one place too long. We are going to switch to a new location."

He and Alcazar had moved from the inn to a seedy boarding house much like the one in which Alcazar had lived in Evreux. Sir Henry had been alarmed that morning when the old biddy down the hall tried to engage him in conversation. Probably quite innocent, but he wasn't one to take chances.

Henry often used the city of Westfirth as his base of operations when he made his secret trips to Rosia. He had loyal people in his employ and vast and extensive connections with the Westfirth criminal underworld. Smugglers and assassins and thieves knew him by a different face, a different name ("the Guvnor"). He had money, disguises, documents, and weapons of all kinds stashed in various locations throughout the city. He went out the next day, made the necessary arrangements, and returned that night to collect Alcazar.

Sir Henry spent long moments observing the dark street from the window of his room, making certain no one was loitering in the shadows. The street was empty. He and Alcazar, both heavily cloaked, left the boarding house in the dead of night and walked to another house with a "For Let" sign in the window. Sir Henry had procured a key and the two entered.

Drawing the heavy curtains, Sir Henry lighted a lantern and placed it on a dust-covered table.

"I brought you a change of clothing," he said, opening a large portmanteau.

Alcazar stared, astonished, at the contents.

"You want me to dress as a woman?"

"An excellent disguise, don't you think?" Sir Henry said coolly. "I have rooms for us at the Blue Peacock. I went there in the guise of a servant and told the proprietor that my master, a noble gentleman of substantial means, is planning a secret assignation with a married woman whose husband must not know of the affair. I will be the noble gentleman. You will be my mistress."

Pietro Alcazar was a slender, lithe man with long, soft brown hair and large brown eyes. His hands were working man's hands, not the soft hands of a lady, but gloves would hide that defect. His effeminate build and features had given Sir Henry the idea for the disguise.

In an age where marriages were arranged for either monetary or political convenience, men and women of the noble classes often indulged in affairs. All parties knew what was going on; husbands knew about their wives' lovers; wives knew about their husbands' mistresses. The only rule was that the affair was to be conducted with secrecy and discretion so as not to compromise the family's honor. Such an arrangement as Sir Henry had proposed was not at all unusual. The innkeeper of the Blue Peacock was accustomed to entertaining wealthy guests who gave false names and arrived heavily cloaked, veiled, and masked.

Alcazar started to protest, but the expression on Henry's face, especially the glint in the flat, cold eyes, caused Alcazar to shut his mouth and put on his petticoats.

Sir Henry also changed clothes. He had that morning gone to the Blue Peacock dressed in the somber attire of a gentleman's gentleman. Henry the Manservant had been soft-spoken, retiring, with lowered eyes, not daring to look upon his betters. Sir Henry the Rosian Nobleman wore a silk waistcoat, embroidered vest, tight trousers banded at the knee with velvet rosettes, silk hose, buckled shoes, and an overlarge, frilly lace collar. He applied a black goatee and mustache with spirit gum, put on a periwig, slid several flashy rings onto his fingers and, smoothing his mustache with the tip of his finger, transformed himself into the flashy and arrogant count.

Henry spent the rest of the night drilling Alcazar how to walk in the voluminous silk skirt and petticoats and dainty shoes without tripping over the hem or turning an ankle. He showed him how to hold his fan in one hand and catch up his skirts in the other, then marched Alcazar ruthlessly up and down the empty room until he was satisfied that on-lookers would take Pietro for a lady, albeit a clumsy one.

The "count" and his "lady" arrived at the Blue Parrot at midmorning. They descended from a coach, decorated with a false coat of arms, and driven by one of his agents. The propri-etor was on hand to greet them. The two were immediately whisked up to their suite of rooms at the top part of the inn. Alcazar stumbled over his petticoats while ascending the stairs. Sir Henry covered this by laughing boisterously and teasing his lady about imbibing too much champagne.

Sir Henry's Rosian was flawless, his accent unimpeach-able, no matter what accent he chose to use. He could con-verse as a dockworker with a dockworker or discuss religion as a monk with the Archbishop of Westfirth and no one would guess he wasn't who he claimed to be.

Confident he had not been followed, Sir Henry did not grow complacent. He was far too skilled for that. But he did allow himself to relax a little, take some champagne with his breakfast, and reflect on the fact that the next few days should pass peacefully enough and then he and Alcazar would be on the way back to Freya.

He lay down for a nap and rose refreshed in the after-noon. He changed his clothes and demeanor to those of Henry the Manservant, left the inn, and went to take his daily stroll through a quiet churchyard. The exercise cleared his mind; he ran over his plans and found no flaws. As he walked through the old, picturesque cemetery, he went to pay his respects to a certain grave.

Sir Henry stopped, stared. The tomb was quite old and weather beaten. The carving was mostly worn off. The frag-

ment of a name, "Henri," was all that was visible. Lying on
the tomb was a bunch of purple clover tied with a bit of
black ribbon.

Sir Henry stood gazing down at the clover for long moments, then, frowning, he walked on, his peace of mind shattered.

James Harrington left Evreux heading for Westfirth on the
afternoon of the day the *Cloud Hopper* sailed out into the
Breath. Harrington had not been planning a journey to
Westfirth. Quite the contrary, his orders from Sir Henry had
been quite clear—he was to remain in Evreux. The arrival
of a letter, however, caused Harrington to change his plans.
A ship would be the fastest way to reach Westfirth, but
there was not time to book passage. He acquired a seat on
the post chaise—wyvern-drawn carriages that carried the
mail to various locations throughout Rosia.

The carriages had room for up to four riders and were
the fastest way to travel overland from one point to another. The carriages stopped at posts along the way to
change wyverns and deliver the mail. Mindful of the need
for speeding the post on its way, the changing of the
wyverns was accomplished with such rapidity that passengers were permitted to get out only to stretch their legs
before the whip cracked and they were off again. Since the
carriages were noted more for speed than for comfort,
those passengers who took the post chaise generally did so
because they needed to be somewhere in a hurry.

Harrington arrived in Westfirth two days ahead of the
Cloud Hopper. He took up residence in an inn and did as
Sir Henry had taught him. He enjoyed the pleasures of
Westfirth. Harrington frequented taverns and gambling
dens, strolled along the docks, walked about the shops. He
mingled with the crowds in the park and took a stroll to
view the wondrous new cathedral, which was being built on
the old church grounds. He bought a bunch of clover from

a pretty flower vendor. He walked through an old cemetery and read the names on the tombs. Everywhere he went, Harrington struck up conversations, bought drinks for the patrons, surrounded himself with people.

And everywhere Harrington went, either Dubois or his agents were right behind him, waiting for Harrington to meet with Sir Henry. Dubois knew Sir Henry by sight, of course, but Henry Wallace was a consummate actor who changed identity as often as another man changed his stockings. Wallace would never allow himself to be spotted on the street.

"These places are too public for the two to meet. Harrington is letting Sir Henry know he's in town," Dubois told his agents. "He's setting up the rendezvous."

Dubois had followed Harrington from Evreux in his own carriage, making certain he kept on the trail of his quarry by asking at every stop if they had seen a man matching Harrington's description and, if so, what route he had taken. Dubois had arrived in Westfirth the same time as Harrington, tracked him to his inn, and then arranged with his most trusted agents to keep an eye on him around the clock while Dubois made a fast trip up the coast to visit the site of the massacre at the Abbey of Saint Agnes to speak to Father Jacob Northrup. When Dubois returned, he took the day shift himself.

Dubois believed he now knew why Henry Wallace had risked his neck traveling to Rosia. Dubois had received a letter from the grand bishop relating the disappearance of a journeyman armorer named Pietro Alcazar, a journeyman rumored to have been working to develop steel infused with the power of the Breath. The day after the journeyman had not shown up for work, the Master Armorer had paid a hurried visit to the Countess de Marjolaine. She had subsequently summoned her son, Stephano de Guichen, who was known to be involved in many of her intrigues. Stephano had gone to Alcazar's lodgings and had been seen by James Harrington. Some hours later, Stephano and his friend, Rodrigo de Villeneuve had been lured into a duel by Harrington in the guise of Sir Richard Piefer. Dubois arrived at the same conclusion as had his counterpart in spy craft, the Countess de Marjolaine: Sir Henry Wallace had come to Rosia to abduct Alcazar.

Dubois did find it odd that Sir Henry had not yet left Westfirth with his prize. Why was Wallace still on Rosian soil? He must know that the hounds were on his trail and that every moment he remained brought him closer to the executioner. There were times when Dubois told himself that Sir Henry must have left. But, if that were true, why was James Harrington in Westfirth?

"No, no, never doubt your instincts," Dubois told himself as he sat reading his mail in a park next door to the inn where Harrington was staying. "The pieces fit. Sir Henry is here in Westfirth. He has Alcazar. And sooner or later James Harrington will lead me to him."

Unless the Countess' son finds Wallace first. Stephano de Guichen and his friends were traveling to Westfirth. The murder of the poor pawn, Valazquez, had been hushed up: a tragic accident while loading a pistol. . . The Countess de Marjolaine had attended the funeral. . . . The family was grateful for her support. . . . Most grateful . . . No mention of Monsieur de Villeneuve or Captain de Guichen.

Dubois had abducted Benoit, de Guichen's family retainer, then searched the captain's house. He had discovered from Rodrigo's accounts that the countess had paid all of her son's debts. Clearly, she had hired him to find and recover Alcazar. Benoit had claimed to know nothing about anything. He wouldn't even admit to the fact that he worked for Captain de Guichen. Dubois had set the old man loose and then had him followed. He had been interested to hear that Benoit had gone immediately to the palace and then disappeared.

Dubois sat in the park, reading a letter he'd received that morning from the grand bishop, all the while keeping a watch out for James Harrington. The letter informed Dubois that he was to listen for any strange rumors in connection with the tragic murder of the nuns of Saint Agnes.

Particularly any rumor of demonic influence, the grand bishop had written in his own hand.

"Well, well, well. Demonic influence!" Dubois shook his head. Having visited the site of the killings, he could well imagine that Hell in some form had taken part.

Father Jacob of the Arcanum is on the scene, the grand bishop wrote in conclusion. *Everyone involved will be placed under Seal.*

The bishop can rest easy then, Dubois thought to himself. No word will leak out. The Arcanum could be trusted to see to it that all were silenced. Strange, though, that the deaths of these nuns under such mysterious circumstances should happen while Sir Henry Wallace was on Rosian soil. Once again, Dubois tried every way he could to fit that particular piece into his puzzle, but Henry was the wrong shape and size. As much as Dubois wanted to think that Sir Henry was acting under "demonic influence," he, like Father Jacob, could not see how the Freyan spy master was involved.

Dubois folded the letter and thrust it in his inner pocket. He sat in the park, listening to the twitter of the birds, eavesdropping on conversations, throwing crumbs to the squirrels, and watching and waiting for Harrington to leave his inn.

Chapter Twenty-Eight

Ghosts are said to haunt the places they once loved so much they are unable to leave. If that is true, Westfirth is filled with ghosts from her past. Westfirth was the last Freyan city on Rosian soil to be conquered by her enemies at the end of the Black Fire War. The ghosts of the dead still walk the streets. The stone in the Old Fort still bears the scars. The city and people of Westfirth still remember and will always remember. The ghosts make it impossible to bring these people to God.

—Father Roger Lousea, Former Archbishop of Westfirth,
in his letter of resignation
to Grand Bishop Montagne

THE *CLOUD HOPPER* SAILED INTO WESTFIRTH with the *Retribution* in tow behind. As they entered the harbor, Stephano pointed out the famous landmark known as the Dragon Bastion, a fortress built on top of a mountain peak by the dragons of the Dragon Brigade. The Bastion had been occupied by the Brigade during the glory days when the dragons and their riders had guarded the city of Westfirth and its important harbor. Stephano stood at the rail, gazing at the walls of the abandoned Bastion, a place no one ever visited now, due to the long and arduous climb required to reach it. He pointed out its features.

"For the tenth time," Rodrigo remarked.

"What does that mean?" Stephano demanded.

"Every time we sail to Westfirth, you regale us with the history of the Bastion," said Miri.

"I, for one, find it most interesting," said Father Jacob, who was currently a passenger on the *Cloud Hopper*. "I should like to visit there someday."

With the *Retribution* in tow, the *Cloud Hopper* sailed past the Bastion and the Old Fort with its battlements and towers and shore batteries.

"We're coming up on the dockyards, Captain," Dag called from his position as lookout.

The Westfirth Dockyards, located near the heart of the bustling city, were crowded with ships. Though all insignia and emblems of the Arcanum had been painted over, the sight of a Trundler vessel towing a yacht was sure to cause comment and perhaps even arouse suspicion, especially given the damage suffered by the yacht. Sure enough, the moment the *Cloud Hopper* sailed into port, a white-painted boat with a green-and-gold pennant belonging to the harbormaster headed straight for them.

"Damnation," said Stephano, coming to stand beside Dag. "I suppose we'll have to stop?"

"Unless you want them shooting at us," said Dag.

Miri set the airscrew to reverse and brought the *Cloud Hopper* to a halt. Father Jacob was standing at the rail, observing their entry into Westfirth. Rodrigo lounged against the rail, preparing for his version of "fishing." Rodrigo had been oddly quiet, oddly subdued ever since his talk with Father Jacob. Stephano had been worried about his friend, but their arrival in Rodrigo's favorite city appeared to be having a cheering effect on him. Brother Barnaby was still below with Gythe and Doctor Ellington. Stephano had been to check on them and was heartened to hear from Brother Barnaby that Gythe had spent a restful night.

Master Albert had been following the *Retribution* in his own boat. Sighting the harbormaster, he steered alongside the *Cloud Hopper*.

"I know this fellow," Albert called. "He'll have all manner of questions and he'll expect to be paid well for *not* asking them."

"Wonderful," said Stephano grimly. "Here we are with a priest, a monk, a knight, two gentlemen, and a cat on board a Trundler houseboat—"

"Sounds like a joke I once heard," said Rodrigo.

Stephano ran his hand distractedly through his hair. "And both the houseboat and the yacht have obviously been in a fight. This is going to cost us plenty. Rigo, where's the cash box?"

"You know I never like spending money on bribes," Rodrigo protested. "Plays merry hell with my accounting. I never know how to record it in the ledger."

The harbormaster sailed alongside and requested permission to come aboard. Once on deck, he glanced about at the motley group assembled to meet him in considerable astonishment, his eyebrows almost flying off his head at the sight of a priest in the black cassock of the Arcanum.

"Who is the owner of this vessel?" the harbormaster demanded, trying to sound stern, though the sight of the dreaded black cassock was clearly making him nervous.

Miri came forward to proclaim herself the owner. Rodrigo reached for his purse. Father Jacob stopped them both by walking over to the harbormaster, putting his hand on his shoulder, and leading him off to the stern. They stood in hushed conversation. After a few moments, the harbormaster, hat in hand, walked up to Stephano.

"I am sorry to hear you were attacked, Monsieur," he said. "These pirates are really getting out of control. I should lodge a strongly worded protest with His Majesty's Royal Navy if I were you, sir."

"Thank you, sir, I shall do that," said Stephano politely.

"I hope you enjoy your stay in our fair city," the harbormaster added, looking flustered. He started to say something more, cast a glance at Father Jacob, thought better of it, and made a hasty departure.

"You do come in handy, Father Jacob," said Stephano, as they watched the harbormaster sail away.

The *Cloud Hopper* headed for the piers on the south side of the city where the Trundlers had established a floating community known as the Flats.

On the way, the *Cloud Hopper* prepared to part company with the *Retribution*, dropping off the yacht at the shipyard. Stephano stood on the deck of the *Cloud Hopper*, preparing to say good-bye to their guests. Now that the Cadre was safely in Westfirth, Stephano was eager to get on with the secret business that had brought him here—the search for the journeyman, Alcazar.

Stephano was surprised to find he was sorry to part company with his godfather. He had Miri to thank for that. She knew the story of Sir Ander, for Stephano had often expressed his anger at the knight. He had started up his rant again, prior to the knight boarding the *Cloud Hopper*.

Miri had stopped him cold.

"You were there to save Sir Ander's life when the demon was going to kill him. He was there to save yours. Did it ever occur to you, Stephano de Guichen, that your father is looking down on both of you?"

Stephano gave serious thought to her words and determined that for his father's sake, he would learn to forgive, if he could never forget. Stephano and Sir Ander had spent the time during the brief journey from the abbey to Westfirth getting to know each other. One barrier remained between the two of them, a barrier that could not be crossed—the Countess de Marjolaine.

When Sir Ander tried, once more, to speak of her, Stephano said quietly, "I do not wish to quarrel with you, sir. Let us therefore change the subject."

Sir Ander did not mention Cecile's name again, and the two parted on relatively good terms.

"I feel that I have come to know you, sir," Stephano said,

shaking hands. "I regret that I did not value your friendship as I should have all these years."

"We will not let another thirty years pass until we meet again," said Sir Ander. "That is for damn certain!"

The knight shook hands with Rodrigo, said a few words, and shook hands with Dag. Sir Ander sent Miri into fits of laughter by kissing her hand with a courtly bow, then he and Master Albert transferred to the *Retribution* to set about unhooking the towline and setting the yacht down in the shipyard.

Stephano was wondering if Brother Barnaby would stay with Gythe when he turned to see Brother Barnaby assisting Gythe to come up from below and walk out onto the deck.

Doctor Ellington led the way, bounding out onto the deck and strutted about proudly, his tail in the air, taking credit for everything from the defeat of the demons to Gythe's recovery. Gythe stood blinking in the late afternoon sun, a shy and abashed smile on her face, sorry she had caused them so much trouble. She held fast to Brother Barnaby's hand. Miri gave the helm to Dag and hurried over to ask Gythe if the air was too cold, if she wanted a shawl, something to eat or maybe a glass of wine . . .

Gythe shook her head and pointed emphatically to the brass helm, indicating Miri was to quit fussing and return to the helm, so Dag could assist with the *Retribution*. Miri kissed her sister and embraced her, then, wiping her eyes, went to relieve Dag.

Stephano embraced Gythe and then said a few words of heartfelt gratitude to Brother Barnaby, adding, "Is she going to be all right?"

Before Brother Barnaby could answer, Gythe punched Stephano in the arm and pointed indignantly at herself.

"I'm standing right here," she told him silently.

"I'm sorry," Stephano said, laughing. "Are *you* all right, Gythe? You gave us quite a scare, you know. We thought we were going to lose you."

Gythe looked to Rodrigo, who was been leaning on the rail, now devoting himself to his favorite pastime whenever the *Cloud Hopper* came into port—fishing.

Rodrigo did not fish for fish. He fished for hats and wigs. As the *Cloud Hopper* was sinking down near the ground in order to dock, he would cast a line with a hook over the ship's rail and endeavor to snag hats or periwigs with the hook, give them a yank, and snatch them from the heads of astonished pedestrians. He would always return the object with a wave, laughing heartily at the oaths and fist-shaking outrage.

But though Rodrigo was now engaged in his endeavor (much to the annoyance of Dag), Stephano noted that his friend did not appear to be enjoying himself as before. At times, a somber, reflective expression would come across Rodrigo's face. He would gaze abstractly at nothing for long moments until someone would say something to divert his attention and then he would flash the same cheerful, careless smile.

Stephano mentioned his worry to Miri.

"Rigo's like that cat," she said, indicating the good Doctor. "He always lands on his feet. Remember, Stephano, he's been through a lot. He had to stop that demon from hurting Gythe and he did a damn fine job."

"I guess you're right," said Stephano. "For the first time in his life, Rigo is a hero."

But when Stephano tried to praise him, Rodrigo passed off the incident by saying that he hadn't done all that much.

"I merely gave the fiend a jolt," Rodrigo had said.

Stephano let it go. But he still couldn't help wondering what was wrong with his friend.

Gythe put her hand over her heart and then pointed at Rodrigo, who, at that moment, was reeling in a man's curly wig.

Stephano understood her gesture. "He saved you from the demon. Don't tell him how wonderful he is. He's already insufferable enough. Which reminds me, do you have any idea why the demon would have come after you?"

Gythe turned to Brother Barnaby, asking him with a gesture to explain.

"I am not sure, but perhaps because she was singing the magic," Brother Barnaby said. "None of you realized it. You thought she was singing nonsense songs from her childhood. On some level, she thought that herself, but deep down she knew what she was doing. She used her songs to try to keep the magical protection spells from failing as the demons bombarded it with the green fire."

"How do you know this?" Stephano asked, skeptical.

"The demons spoke to me, as well," Brother Barnaby replied. "I did not answer them because I couldn't. But Father Jacob theorizes that with her singing, Gythe was able to speak to the demons."

"What did they say to you?" Stephano asked Gythe.

She looked frightened and wrapped her hands tightly around Brother Barnaby's arm and drew nearer to him. He placed his hand over hers and patted her soothingly.

"She doesn't remember what they said."

Or it was so horrible she chooses to not to remember, Stephano thought. He was sorry he'd asked.

"I had to go a long way to find her," Brother Barnaby added in a soft, low tone.

Gythe gave him a wavering smile. She still bore traces of tears on her face; her clothes were stained, her hair wildly disheveled, falling over her face. Her blue eyes were soft and glistening, their gaze never straying long from the monk. Gythe touched her hand to Stephano's mouth, indicating that the conversation was at an end. Tugging Brother Barnaby with her, she drew him over to where Rodrigo was throwing his line over the rail. He smiled at her.

"Glad to see you up and about, my dear."

In answer, she took Rodrigo's hand in hers, turned his hand palm up, and, using the tip of her finger, drew something in his palm. Then she closed his fingers over it and smiled and, bringing Brother Barnaby with her, went to the forecastle to join her sister.

Rodrigo blew her a kiss and went back to his fishing.

"She gave him a Trundler good luck charm," Father Jacob said, coming up behind Stephano. "Your friend is greatly honored. The Trundlers do not bestow such charms lightly."

"I would have said before now that Rigo was the last person to need a lucky charm," said Stephano. "He's always been Fortune's favorite. Lately, though it seems Fortune's turned against him."

"On the contrary," said Father Jacob dryly. "He's extremely fortunate I am not taking him back to the Black Citadel. Not as a prisoner," he added, seeing Stephano's alarm. "I have been trying to persuade him to become one of us. He's quite brilliant, your friend. Too brilliant for his own good."

Stephano didn't like that comment. He took it to be a veiled threat. He didn't understand what any of this was about; he was in the deeps, way over his head when it came to magic. He was thankful beyond words that the priest was leaving the boat and he prayed to God and all the saints that he and Father Jacob would never meet again.

"You'd be wasting your time, Father. Rigo refuses to wear black. He says it makes his complexion look sallow."

Father Jacob smiled, but the smile was inward, thoughtful, knowing, and it made Stephano uncomfortable. He quickly changed the subject. "I want to thank you, Father, for bringing Brother Barnaby to help Gythe—"

"God brought Brother Barnaby," said Father Jacob, his smile warming. "I merely provided the means of transportation."

He stood regarding the three of them. Miri was explaining the workings of the helm, to Brother Barnaby, who was asking questions and telling her about the helm aboard *Retribution*. Gythe had let go of his hand, but she had hold of a fold of the monk's sleeve. She did not take her eyes from his face.

"He went into her darkness to find her," said Father Jacob quietly. "He fought *her* demons and brought her safely home."

"And now it's time Brother Barnaby went safely home," said Stephano, not sure he liked what he was seeing.

He turned to Father Jacob and held out his hand.

"Father Jacob, it has been a—" Stephano started to say "pleasure" but couldn't quite get that word out. "It's been interesting meeting you."

Father Jacob shook hands. "I do not need to remind you, Captain, that you and your friends are under Seal."

Stephano started to end the handshake, but Father Jacob placed his other hand over Stephano's and held him fast.

"We will, please God, be leaving for the Arcanum soon. I value your judgment, Captain de Guichen. I value it highly. If you hear of anything you think I should know, seek me at once. Come to me day or night, either here in Westfirth or in the Black Citadel of the Arcanum. I will give orders that you are always to have access to me."

Stephano was startled by the priest's words and his earnest tone. Stephano did not know how to respond, especially since he had just been thinking he would be glad to see the back of this priest.

"Thank you, Father," said Stephano, trying unsuccessfully to withdraw his hand. Father Jacob had a very strong grip. "But I doubt if I would ever come across anything of interest to the Church."

Instead of letting him go, Father Jacob tightened his grasp. He drew near to Stephano and said in soft tones, "What you saw at the abbey, Captain, has nothing to do with the Church, nothing to do with bishops and kings, princes and politics. I believe it has everything to do with the survival of all we hold dear."

His gaze shifted to Miri and Gythe and Brother Barnaby, to Rodrigo and his fishing line, to Dag and Sir Ander and Master Albert, who were conferring on board the yacht.

Stephano was startled and uneasy. There was no doubting the priest's sincerity or the ominous import of his words.

"I'm not sure I understand, Father," said Stephano, troubled.

"I hope you never do," said Father Jacob. "God bless and keep you, Captain."

Father Jacob let go of Stephano's hand after a bone-crushing shake that left his fingers tingling. Calling out to Sir Ander to join him, he went to the forecastle to say good-bye to Miri and Gythe and retrieve Brother Barnaby.

The shipyard was located close to the docks. The yard was surrounded by warehouses, and there were a number of taverns on the Rim that catered to the dockworkers, stevedores, crafters, and sailors; many of whom had come loitering over, ale mugs in hand, to observe the yacht and freely speculate about what had happened to it. Men in the shipyard and Master Albert were shouting back and forth; the men telling him to drop lines so that they could guide the ship into the yard and bring her down without harm. He and Dag were uncoiling lengths of rope, getting ready to toss down the lines.

Stephano had nothing to do and he was thinking that a mug of cold ale sounded very good right about now when he heard a voice from the ground shout out his name. He looked over the side and saw Benoit come dashing out of one of the taverns, waving his cane in the air in one hand and what appeared to be a letter in the other.

Stephano's first thought was that this sudden appearance of the faithful family retainer who was supposed to be hundreds of mile away, comfortably settled in front of the family fireplace, couldn't be good. His second and even more alarming thought was that Sir Ander knew Benoit. The Knight Protector would recognize him, want to be reunited with an old friend, and introduce Benoit to Father Jacob.

So far, Stephano had managed to avoid any mention about the job they were doing for his mother. To give him credit, Father Jacob had not asked what two gentlemen were doing aboard a Trundler houseboat, but Stephano knew the priest was curious. Father Jacob was the sort to be curious about everything and would probe and prod until he found the answer, if for no other reason than to satisfy himself. Benoit was loyal and trustworthy, but he had always been fond of Sir Ander; God only knew what the old man might decide to tell him.

Rodrigo had also spotted Benoit. He was staring down, openmouthed, and appeared just about ready to call out a greeting. Stephano ran across the deck to collar his friend.

"Shut up," Stephano hissed in Rodrigo's ear. "Not a word! I'll go see what's up. You get rid of that goddamn priest!"

Rodrigo glanced over his shoulder to see Father Jacob chatting with Gythe and Miri.

"Will do," Rodrigo said and hurried off.

Stephano looked over the rail. Master Albert and Dag had thrown down the lines. Men below had hold of them. *Retribution* was starting to sink. Sir Ander was just now starting to release the tow rope.

Stephano vaulted over the rail of the *Cloud Hopper* and landed in the driver's compartment of the *Retribution*. He dashed past Dag, who stared at him in astonishment.

"No time to explain!" Stephano shot out of the corner of his mouth. "You never saw me."

Dag nodded coolly, not in the least surprised that some new crisis had arisen, and went back to work. Stephano hopped down onto one of the wings and leaped to the ground below. The shipyard workers gave him some startled glances, but they were too busy trying to bring the *Retribution* down to pay attention to some mad fellow jumping off a boat. Benoit had been watching his progress and was following him on the ground, waving the letter in his hand.

Stephano caught up with him.

"Oh, Master Stephano, I'm so glad to find you," cried Benoit, nearly weeping with relief. "I've been waiting and waiting—"

"Not here!" Stephano snapped and he seized hold of Benoit, almost lifting the old man off his feet, and hustled him into the nearest tavern. Benoit kept trying to talk and Stephano kept shushing him. The tavern had a few customers who glanced at Stephano and his companion without much interest and went back to their mugs and conversations. Dockyard taverns, unlike neighborhood taverns, were accustomed to strangers.

Stephano escorted Benoit toward a table in the back, away from any windows, and sat down in a shadowy corner. He caught the eye of the barkeep, held up two fingers, indicating they wanted two mugs of ale, and ordered Benoit to keep quiet until the ale was delivered and paid for.

"What are you doing here?" Stephano demanded, once they were alone. "What's happened?"

"I was kidnapped, sir, the house was ransacked, and I have an urgent letter from your mother."

"Good God!" said Stephano.

He had picked up his ale, but now he set it down untasted. He gazed gloomily at the letter, not eager to read it, certain that it meant trouble. There was no help for it. He picked it up, broke open the seal.

Benoit was indignant. "Didn't you hear me say that I was kidnapped, sir? It was quite harrowing, I assure you."

Stephano continued reading. "You appear to have survived."

"Well, yes, that's true, sir, but—"

"Who snatched you?"

"I couldn't tell, sir," said Benoit. "They dropped a gunnysack over my head."

"What did they want?"

"A man asked me about your dealings with the countess."

"What did you say?"

"That I was not in your confidence, sir."

Stephano looked up from his letter. "Did they beat you, pull out your fingernails, and tie you to the rack?"

"I'm glad you find this funny, sir," said Benoit stiffly. "As it turned out, the man made me sit in an extremely uncomfortable chair. I lost all feeling in my lower extremities."

Stephano hid his smile. "I'm glad you weren't hurt. What happened after you told them you didn't know anything?"

"They put the sack over my head again and drove me back to the house. I found that in my absence someone had broken in. The place was a mess, sir. Furniture upended, books pulled off the shelves, Master Rodrigo's undergarments strewn about —"

"I don't want to hear about Rigo's undergarments," said Stephano. "Was anything stolen?"

"Not that I could tell, sir, but I didn't have much time to look. I had only been home a short while, when I received an urgent summons from the palace. When I arrived, I was given this note and told to board a private vessel that I would find waiting for me. The vessel brought me here. I went to the Trundler village where you usually dock, but you weren't there. I asked about, but the Trundlers claimed they hadn't seen any sign of the *Cloud Hopper*. I heard from some sailors that there had been terrible storms in the Breath the last few days and, figuring you might have been delayed, I came here to wait."

"You did well, old man," said Stephano absently, his thoughts on the note.

"Thank you, sir. I assume I will be recompensed for the ale I was forced to buy during the last two days."

Stephano looked up from his reading and raised a skeptical eyebrow.

"I had to have some explanation for why I was loitering about, sir," said Benoit.

"I see. What happened to the money I'm certain my mother gave you to cover your expenses?" Stephano asked.

"Your honored mother was kind enough to provide me with money for my travels. But there is a matter of my food and lodging, sir," said Benoit with dignity. "In addition I was forced to buy several rounds of drinks before I could induce the sailors to speak with me. Then there was the pain I suffered during my kidnapping. Did I tell you how I lost all feeling in my extremities? Then the mental distress when I feared you might be lost in the Breath and finally the joyful shock of discovering you were alive—"

Stephano grinned. "Yeah, you were in raptures. All right, you old rascal. Give your bill to Rigo."

"Yes, sir. Thank you, sir. If you're not going to drink your ale, sir—"

Stephano waved his hand and Benoit, who had already downed his, drank his master's. Stephano ordered another round for both of them and, after the ale had been delivered, he read the letter again. Judging by the handwriting, the note had been written in haste and was short and to the point.

My son,

I trust you are in good health. Regarding that lost shipment of brandywine you were good enough to offer to try to locate for me, I have received information that it has arrived in Westfirth and is in the hands of a most notorious and dangerous band of smugglers. The shipment is of immense worth, though not at the cost of your life. I would urge you to abandon the search, but I know your brave and adventurous spirit and I fear you would ignore my wishes. If you insist on proceeding, please do so with extreme caution.

Stephano grimaced and shook his head. How like his mother. Warning him of the risk inherent in continuing the search for Alcazar and yet reminding him of the vital importance of locating the missing journeyman. Urging him to abandon his pursuit of information regarding the kidnappers and advising him to use caution when pursuing them. Telling him about the danger and not giving him the slightest hint what that danger might be.

Still, he reflected grudgingly, the letter also proved how well his mother knew him. He thought back, irritably, to Sir Ander saying he had his mother's eyes. Stephano crumpled the note in his hand and dunked it in his ale. He watched the ink fade off the paper, mingling with the ale, turning the golden liquid faintly purple. He looked up to find Benoit regarding him intently.

"What now?" Stephano growled, in no mood to hear more about the old man's extremities.

Benoit glanced about. The two of them were the only people in this part of the tavern. A group of young men, apparently students on holiday, had just entered and were raucously demanding service. He and Stephano could have shouted at each other and not been heard.

Benoit motioned Stephano near. "Your honored mother—"

"Quit calling her that," said Stephano.

"—entrusted me with information she did not want to write down," Benoit continued, ignoring the interruption.

Stephano tensed. "Tell me."

Benoit whispered two words in Stephano's ear.

"Henry Wallace."

Stephano felt the tingle at the base of his spine run up his back and twist his gut.

"Do you know the name, sir?" Benoit asked.

"Unfortunately, I do," said Stephano.

Sir Henry Wallace, spy master, assassin, was perhaps the only person in the world his mother truly feared. The countess had spoken of him only once, in connection with rumors of a failed assassination attempt against King Alaric who had been going to conduct a royal inspection of the mysterians damage done to the newly commissioned naval cutter, *Defiant*. Stephano had been with the Dragon Brigade then and there had been some talk of sending the Brigade in pursuit of the assassins. She had told him her belief that Sir Henry was involved and she had gone on to tell him what she knew of the Freyan spy master, whom she had met many years ago, when he had come to court in his capacity as the Freyan Ambassador.

Stephano dredged up the memory of his mother's words. He had never heard her speak of any man the way she talked of Sir Henry.

"Henry Wallace is a man of superior intellect, rapier-sharp wit, and cold-blooded calculation. He is ruthless, clever, and cunning and a Freyan patriot to the core of his being. He hates Rosia and would sacrifice anything, anyone to see us lie crushed and defeated beneath the Freyan heel. His reach is long. He has spies in every court, agents hiding in every closet, and assassins underneath every bed."

Stephano remembered he had been impressed, but he had wondered, if this man was so amazing, why he had failed in the attempt to kill the king.

He could see the countess standing in her room, twisting the ring on her finger. He could hear her bitter and enigmatic reply. "I am not certain he did fail. It is my belief that he wasn't truly out to kill the king."

As it happened, the Brigade had not been called up. The entire matter had been abruptly and mysteriously dropped. His mother had refused to discuss it and had forbidden him to ever refer to it. She had never again spoken of Sir Henry Wallace.

The fact that Wallace was mixed up in the disappearance of Alcazar drastically altered the situation. His involvement made it a safe bet that Alcazar had succeeded in his experiment. Stephano allowed himself to picture what would happen if such magically-infused metal were to fall into Freyan hands. Rosian ships firing every gun they had and doing little damage, as Freyan vessels pounded the Rosian Navy into kindling. The war would be over in a matter of days.

He looked back at how the events had unfolded after he'd begun his investigation into Alcazar's disappearance and he could now begin to explain what had previously been inexplicable. The man with the slouch hat who had been lurking outside Alcazar's apartment, the same man—the supposed Lord Richard Piefer—who had arranged the duel, murdered Valazquez, and tried to murder them must be an agent of Sir Henry Wallace. He had probably given instructions that anyone who took too great an interest in Alcazar was to be removed. That did not explain the other person who had been present at the duel, the person whose timely shot had saved Stephano's life, but Stephano assumed now that this must have been an agent sent by his mother.

He pondered what to do now. First and foremost, he had to protect Benoit. He was angry at his mother. She had no right to get the old man involved in such a dangerous and potentially deadly affair.

"Were you followed here?" Stephano asked.

Benoit sat up very straight. His rheumy eyes flashed with indignation. "I should hope you know me better than that, sir!"

Stephano rested his hand over the old man's. "I have no doubt you managed to shake off pursuit, but I need to know if you were pursued. Were you?"

"As a matter of fact I was, sir. A man followed me when I left the palace. I made sure I lost him before boarding the vessel that brought me to Westfirth. I have kept an eye out since, but I have not seen anyone take any particular notice of me."

"Good. I want you leave Westfirth tonight and go back to—"

"Beg pardon, sir, your honored . . . that is to say your lady mother instructed me to return to her with word that I had found you. She was worried when she heard you had been shot—"

Stephano's eyes narrowed, and Benoit suddenly ceased talking.

"How did my mother hear I was shot?" Stephano demanded.

Benoit buried his nose in his ale mug and pretended to be extremely interested in observing the tavern's clientele.

"There was no one on the dock that day but you and the man who tried to assassinate me," Stephano continued in grim tones. "And I somehow doubt that the assassin was the one who went and told my mother! Which means you've been spying on me for her!"

"A mother's love, sir—" began Benoit in plaintive tones.

"Bullshit!" Stephano glowered and shook his fist. "I should wring your scrawny neck—"

Benoit suddenly leaped out of his chair.

"Good God, sir! Look who just walked in! Sir Ander Martel! Your father's dear friend. I must go pay my respects—"

Sir Ander was entering the tavern, accompanied by Father Jacob, Master Albert, and Brother Barnaby. Father Jacob, he noted, was carrying an extremely large bundle. He saw that Sir Ander was being unusually watchful; he had his hand on his sword hilt and he was staying very close to Father Jacob.

The light outside was bright; it would take the three a few moments for their eyes to adjust to the dim light of the tavern. Stephano had already located another way out. Seizing hold of Benoit, Stephano hustled him, kicking and sputtering, to the back door which was behind and to the right of the bar, a good distance from the front door. He cast a few coins on the bar as he ran past. The barkeep gave them a bored glance as they made their hasty exit. He did not say anything or even seem much interested. In a tavern frequented by smugglers, customers bolting suddenly out the back were an everyday occurrence. So long as they paid their bill, they could fly up the chimney for all he cared.

The back door led to a storage room lit only by a single, filthy window. Stephano tumbled over a few barrels and bashed his knee on a packing crate before he reached the door. He thrust it open, peered out cautiously into a dingy side street. Seeing no one, he shoved Benoit, still protesting vociferously, through the door and after a glance behind, went after him.

Stephano had to take time to assure Benoit that he had met up with Sir Ander and that they were now the best of friends before the old man would calm down.

"I know you would like to visit with Sir Ander," said Stephano, as he hurried Benoit down the street. "But trust me. Now is not the time. You have passage on a ship? You know where you're going?"

"Yes, sir, your lady mother was kind enough—"

"Yes, yes. Then take your ship, go back to the palace, tell my 'lady mother' I am not dead, at least not yet. And you can add that I thank her for her concern, but I took a job and I intend to see it through. You understand."

"Yes, sir," said Benoit.

They stopped at a street corner. Stephano had to get back to the *Cloud Hopper*, which must be about ready to depart. He eyed Benoit, realized suddenly that the old man was, well, old. No one could call him frail, but he should be back home sitting peacefully in front of the family fire nursing his blasted extremities, not running down side streets and shaking off tails.

"I'm sorry as hell you were dragged into this, Benoit," said Stephano ruefully. "Take good care of yourself going back to Evreux. Don't get yourself kidnapped again or that gray head of yours blown off. You know that Master Rigo and I can't manage without you."

"I tremble at the thought of either of you attempting to do so, sir," said Benoit with feeling. "Don't worry about me. I've come through worse than this. I do, however, find myself a bit short of funds—"

Stephano had handed over all the money he had left and Benoit went safely on his way. Returning to the *Cloud Hopper*, Stephano found everyone waiting eagerly for his return. They crowded around him the moment he set foot on deck, demanding answers.

"Rodrigo told us you went after Benoit," Dag said. "What's he doing here?"

"Where is the old man?" Miri asked, peering fondly over Stephano's shoulder. "Didn't you bring him with you?"

"Your mother sent him," Rodrigo guessed. "Something's gone wrong. Or maybe I should say something *else* has gone wrong."

Stephano cast a glance over the rail. The *Retribution* was

now in the care of the shipyard. Crafters and carpenters were swarming over the yacht, discussing the repairs, making notes. He could see some of the crafters shaking their heads over the strange scorch marks. He wondered what Father Jacob had told them about the attack. Certainly not the truth.

'I'll explain everything later," said Stephano. "For now, let's just get out of here."

Rigo put away his fishing gear. Dag went to clean and reload the guns. Stephano walked over to stand by Miri, who was once more at the controls, maneuvering the houseboat through the crowded shipping lanes of the harbor. The sun was setting, the light fading. Fortunately, the Trundler village was not far away. They would be there before darkness fell.

"Where's Gythe?" Stephano asked, looking around in alarm. "She's not sick again, is she?"

"Not sick as you mean," said Miri. "Oh, Stephano, the worst thing has happened to her!"

"What now?" Stephano asked, alarmed, preparing for some new crisis.

Miri gave a deep sigh. "Gythe's fallen in love with that monk!"

Chapter Twenty-Nine

Trundlers are a friendly lot so long as the sun is up. A floating village becomes a market, the houseboats market stalls, where all are welcome to come and spend your rosuns. When the sun sets, the Trundlers close up shop and raise the barricades. Trundlers do not take kindly to strangers and anyone not a Trundler is a stranger.

—Lord Captain Stephano De Guichen

BY THE TIME THE *CLOUD HOPPER* HAD SLIPPED into its berth alongside the other houseboats in the floating Trundler village, night had fallen. The Trundler houseboats had lit their lanterns and the glowing lights, dancing up and down or shifting from side to side with the rocking motion of the boats at anchor, made it look as if the village were populated by fireflies.

Even though most on board were "outsiders," they were welcomed by the Trundlers. Miri's uncle was leader of the McPike clan and well-liked by all except the McGonagalls, a clan with whom a feud had been raging for about three hundred years or so. Miri in her role as Lore Master was honored and highly valued, and Gythe was universally loved. Their entry into the Trundler village took on the aspect of a triumphal march. Running lights shining and lanterns lit, the *Cloud Hopper* sailed among the houseboats, with Miri calling out greetings to those they passed, asking about her innumerable relatives and whether they were "in town" and acknowledging invitations for her and Gythe to come visit.

Once they docked, Miri and her sister made ready to depart to pay their respects to their uncle, hear the latest news of the family, and make inquiries about the missing journeyman. Dag was also leaving the *Cloud Hopper*, to find out if any of his former underworld connections knew anything about Alcazar. Before everyone went their separate ways, Stephano called them together. He told them about his mother's letter, shared with them what he knew about Sir Henry Wallace, emphasized the danger, and gave them a description of Wallace.

"My mother saw Wallace many years ago, so this description is probably not much good. And he's adept at disguising himself. For what it's worth, Henry Wallace is tall, slender in build, with finely chiseled features except for his nose, which was broken in his youth and did not heal properly. Pietro Alcazar is addicted to gambling and could possibly be found at the baccarat tables if he's off his tether, which is unlikely. We want to know if anyone has seen either of these men or if anyone has been asking about them."

He also told Miri and Gythe to find out if there had been any more attacks on Trundler houseboats and, if so, if those attacks had been similar in nature to the attack on their parents' boat. Finally, he reminded them that they were all under Seal and that he had given his word to Papa Jake that they would say nothing about the demons. Everyone nodded solemnly at this.

Stephano watched Dag carefully arm himself, tucking two pistols beneath his coat and sliding a pistol and a knife into his boot.

"Are you sure you want to do this?" Stephano asked, watching Dag assemble his arsenal. "Maybe I should go with you."

Dag chuckled as he slid a second knife into his belt. "Begging your pardon, Captain, but you'd be more trouble than you'd be worth. You're a gentleman born, sir, and you can't hide it. The places I'm going don't take to gentry. You'd end up in the gutter with your throat slit, your watch missing, and your pockets turned inside out."

"You and Rigo can come with us," said Miri. She cast a sidelong look at her sister, who was staring up dreamily at the stars. "You can help me take Gythe's mind off Brother Barnaby."

Stephano was about to agree, and he was startled to hear Rodrigo decline, claiming that he was going to bed; he had to be up early the next day.

"Early for what?" Stephano asked, astonished.

"My dear fellow, I have to see my tailor," said Rodrigo, sounding shocked that he would even ask. "I have nothing to wear."

"You have a chest filled with clothes," said Stephano.

Rodrigo only smiled and shook his head. Miri rolled her eyes and whispered something to Gythe, who giggled. Dag snorted in derision. Picking up the Doctor, Dag settled the cat on his shoulder and descended the gangplank. He walked out onto the long pier that led to shore.

"You could come with us," said Miri to Stephano, as the sisters were about to leave. "Uncle likes you."

"He likes me *now*, since we've finally convinced him I have no intention of trying to worm my way into the McPike clan by wedding his niece," said Stephano. "When do you plan to tell him about Dag?"

"When I've told Dag about Dag," said Miri crisply. She glanced with concern at the back of the big man, who was walking away from them. Doctor Ellington's tail stuck straight up, looking like a furry feather in Dag's hat. "I hope he'll be safe."

"Worry more about anyone who tries to cross him," said Stephano. "Thanks for the invitation. Give your uncle my regards. I'll stay with Rigo."

He had given his friend the sad news about his father; the countess had received confirmation from her sources that Ambassador de Villeneuve had been assassinated. Rodrigo had received the news with equanimity, going a bit pale, but only saying calmly that he was thankful to be no longer in doubt. Stephano remembered his own soul-searing grief over the death of his father and he had felt helplessly that he should be doing or saying something more.

"We could find a way to send you home for the funeral..." he had begun and then he had remembered. "Damn! You can't go home. We're under Seal. I promised Father Jacob we'd all remain here in Westfirth. Never mind the priest. If you want to go home, Rigo, you should go home."

Rodrigo had smiled and shaken his head. "My dear fellow, have you forgotten that we spent days lost in the Breath? The funeral will be over and done with by now. I'm fine, really. Don't worry about me."

But Stephano was worried. Rodrigo loved Trundler gatherings. It wasn't like him to miss one.

After Rodrigo had gone to bed, Stephano sat down with a bottle of wine given to them by one of their Trundler neighbors. He went over everything that had happened these past few days and made plans for what was likely to happen in the future.

Stephano did not worry about setting the watch. They were surrounded on all sides by Trundler houseboats. The Trundlers set their own watch over the entire village; they did not take kindly to strangers. For the first night in many nights, Stephano slept deeply and woke to the sun shining and the smell of sausages.

The morning of Chardus, the fourth day of the week, was a fine one, not a cloud in the sky. Even the mists had dissipated. Peering over the hull, Stephano could see quite a distance down to the dark and murky depths of the Breath below. Stephano thought of the demons that had come up out of those depths and he shifted his gaze landward, which provided a far more pleasurable view of the city of West-firth.

He looked out over a veritable sea of gaily painted balloons. Trundler houseboats bobbed in the harbor, thin trails of smoke rising from their galleys bringing with it smells of fresh-baked bread. The morning was brightened by the laughter of children as they scrambled up and down the masts or jumped perilously from boat to boat in games of tag while parents called irritably for them to stop or they would break their fool necks or tumble into the Breath.

Beyond the Trundler village was the southern end of the city of Westfirth; a veritable forest of chimney pots. The two spires of the archbishop's grand cathedral, currently under construction and covered in a maze of scaffolding, was a new and interesting feature on the skyline.

"A sign the Church is exerting authority in Westfirth at last," Stephano reflected. "Or trying to."

Like parents endeavoring to curb the excesses of a child they had ignored for many years, the Church was finding it difficult to alter the city's bad behavior. The new archbishop was an energetic and zealous man, however; firmly determined to make his unruly city into a model of deportment.

According to Dag, who had returned to the *Cloud Hopper* in the early hours, the archbishop was not having much luck. Criminal organizations still flourished, operating brothels and gambling and opium dens, waging wars over territory and conducting running battles with the members of the Constabulary. A militaristic police force organized and financed by the Church, the Constabulary had replaced the corrupt and ineffective city guard and was doing its best to bring law and order to Westfirth. Theirs was an ambitious task. Smuggled goods were still being sold openly in the city market. The murder rate was so high the constables were forced to conduct a sweep every morning to gather up the bodies. The crackdown was having some effect.

"Watch yourselves when you're in town," Dag warned.

"The Constabulary is well-armed, and they have a fondness for hauling people off to jail to make it look like they're doing something useful."

Dag had managed to run into a few people who still remembered him—some of them fondly. He had not encountered any trouble, though the same could not be said for the good Doctor, who had returned with a swollen eye, a chipped tooth, and part of an ear missing.

"But you should see the other cat," Dag said with a proud grin.

Dag had spread the word that he would pay well for information regarding Alcazar or Henry Wallace. His silver rosuns had garnered something, though not much that was useful. About a week ago, a young man of about seventeen or eighteen years of age had appeared in the high-class brothels and gambling dens, making inquiries about a Freyan gentleman by the name of Henry Wallace.

The young man was handsome, well dressed, soft-spoken. He told people he had been sent by his mistress, Lady Wallace, to find her husband, who had gone missing. He had a description of Sir Henry, which matched in many respects the description given by the countess. No one had seen such a man, however, at least so far as Dag was able to determine.

Stephano found this odd, but not particularly enlightening, beyond the fact that someone else was searching for Sir Henry. This young man might be what he claimed to be—a member of Wallace's household. Or he might be an agent sent by a foreign government, the grand bishop, or even his mother, though Stephano doubted that. The countess had told him she could not trust any of her agents and whatever other faults Cecile de Marjolaine might have, she had never lied to him. Since any number of people could be looking for Sir Henry for any number of reasons, Stephano did not give the matter further thought.

Dag's questions about Alcazar had drawn a blank. Alcazar was a fairly common name in Westfirth, and while many people knew men named Alcazar, none were journeymen and none matched the description.

"There are three Alcazars residing in Westfirth," Dag said. "One is a middle-aged baker, another a farrier, and the third is a sailor."

"What about the warrant for my arrest?" Rodrigo asked anxiously. "Am I a wanted murderer for killing Valazquez?"

Dag shook his head. "I asked. If there is a warrant, no one here has word of it."

"I told you. My mother took care of it," said Stephano.

Rodrigo gave a faint smile and a shrug. Stephano gazed thoughtfully at him, then asked Miri what she had found out. She reported even less success than Dag. She had questioned her fellow Trundlers about Sir Henry. None of them had ever heard the name. They had not seen anyone resembling his description. The same with Alcazar.

Stephano shoved away his empty plate and sat back in his chair, frustrated.

"Not much to go on. Still, one of these Alcazars might be a relative of Pietro's. Miri, you and Dag pay a visit to the baker and the farrier. I'll go to the docks and ask around about the sailor. Gythe, you stay here to mind the boat. What's wrong now?"

Gythe was shaking her head and indicating she was accompanying her sister.

Stephano frowned. "You've been really ill, Gythe. I'm not sure you should be going—"

"Gythe, dear," said Miri, fussing with her hair, "I need another pin for this cap. Would you be a love and run fetch one for me."

Gythe ran down below. When she was gone, Miri said with a grimace, "She hopes to run into Brother Barnaby. I tell you, she's besotted with that man."

Rodrigo was incredulous. "Impossible. With that dreadful haircut!"

"I don't think love has anything to do with his haircut," said Stephano dryly. "I know Trundlers don't know much about the Church. Does Gythe realize that Brother Barnaby is a monk and that monks take vows not to . . . uh . . ."

"Frolic beneath the sheets," said Rodrigo.

"I'm not sure. I've tried talking to her," said Miri, sighing. "She either doesn't understand or refuses to understand. I'm really worried about her, Stephano. Gythe seems well enough, but she's changed. She stops dead in her tracks sometimes and stares off into nothing. She'll frown sometimes and wince and put her hand to her head, as though she's in pain."

"Sounds like love to me," said Rodrigo. He tapped Stephano on the shoulder. "It's time we were going—"

"Maybe this has something to do with her magic," said Stephano, getting to his feet. "Is that possible, Rigo?"

"If so, I have no idea what it could be," Rodrigo said. "Ask Father Grim and Dreadful."

"His name is Father Jacob," said Dag in stern and rebuking tones. "You shouldn't make fun of a priest."

"Trust me, my friend, I find nothing at all funny about that man," said Rodrigo.

"I don't know what else to tell you, Miri," said Stephano. "I can plan a raid on a heavily fortified castle, fly a dragon through cannon fire, and even battle demons from Hell. A young woman in love with a monk is beyond my capability. All I can tell you is to keep clear of the area around the Old Fort. Father Jacob said they would be staying there as guests of the archbishop. He's taken over the residential part of the Fort."

Gythe returned with the hairpin, which she gave to her sister, along with a look that said plainly she knew they had been talking about her. Gythe adjusted Miri's hair, patted her own cap in place. Miri and Gythe were dressed as servants from a well-to-do household, wearing neat gray dresses and frilly white caps. In such disguises, they could claim to be anything from parlor maids to seamstresses to cooks as the situation warranted.

"Dag, you and the Doctor go with Miri and Gythe. Do you have money?" Stephano asked.

Miri exhibited a small leather purse she carried around her wrist.

"Are you armed?" Stephano asked.

Dag indicated his weapons. Miri reached into her bosom and drew out a corset gun, then hiked up her skirt to reveal a knife in her stocking.

"And the hairpins," she said, grinning. "Amazing what damage you can do with a hairpin."

"Very well, good luck," said Stephano. "Take care of yourselves. Rodrigo and I will visit the docks—"

"*After* I've been to my tailor," said Rodrigo.

Stephano sighed and went below to dress. He wore his brown, military-cut coat and a plain shirt, no frills and no cravat. He put on his tricorn, draped his sword belt over his shoulder, slid the dragon pistol into his belt and a smaller pistol into a loop in the top of his boot. He came up on deck prepared to face Rodrigo's scathing criticism of his clothing. Rodrigo scarcely gave him a glance and said nothing beyond the fact that he had a spot of mustard on his shirt collar.

The two left the Trundler village, taking the road that led into the central part of the city. The time being midmorning, the road was crowded with people of Westfirth coming to visit the Trundler village, and Trundlers taking their goods to market. Trundlers were tinkers and craftsmen, tending to excel in weaving, embroidery, and fine leather and metal work. A few traded in gems, while others sold charms and herbal potions and remedies. Trundler villages—closed up at night—were open to the public by day.

Rodrigo wanted to take a cab to their destination. The day being a fine one, Stephano felt in need of exercise after being cooped up on the boat. He had always been fond of Westfirth, wild and lawless as the city might be, and he proposed that they walk.

Rodrigo agreed, though with obvious reluctance.

"God forbid you should have to appear wearing the same lavender brocade coat trimmed in ermine you wore in

Evreux," Stephano teased, as they continued down the street. "I suppose there *would* be a warrant out for your arrest."

"My dear fellow," said Rodrigo with a faint smile, "even you must concede that my clothes are not suitable for mourning."

"Mourning . . ." Stephano came to a sudden stop, much to the annoyance of several people behind him and regarded his friend in remorse. "Oh, my God, Rigo, your father! I'm sorry, damnably sorry! What with all that's been happening, it never occurred to me—"

"Keep moving," said Rodrigo, drawing Stephano along. "You're impeding traffic."

"We can take a cab . . ."

"No, no, I don't mind walking. See the sights. I need to stop at a stationer's if there is such a thing in this city. I have to write a letter to my mother explaining why I was unable to attend the funeral. I'll have to make up some tale. I can hardly plead fighting giant bats as an excuse—"

"Rigo, stop playing the clown!" said Stephano. "You should have said something. You don't need to hide your grief. Not from me or the others. We're your friends."

Rodrigo was silent long moments, then he said in a muffled voice, "I wasn't trying to hide from you. I didn't . . . want to think about it. Then, last night, I realized I would have to appear in public today and I had nothing that was suitable. My father is dead. He was murdered, and I have nothing to wear except lavender . . ."

Rodrigo lowered his head. Blinking his eyes rapidly and walking very fast, he blundered into a costermonger, who threw down his cap and doubled his fists and challenged the "gentlemun who thinks he's better'n the likes of us" to a fight. Stephano hailed a passing cab, and bundled Rodrigo into it before the wheels had stopped rolling. He gave the address of the tailor shop, which was on Threadneedle Street. Rodrigo sank into a corner and sat with hand over his face.

Stephano knew that no words of his could help ease Rodrigo's pain, but he also knew that the words didn't matter. What mattered was the warmth of a friend's voice, the touch of a friend's hand. By the time the cab rolled to a stop, Rodrigo had recovered his composure. He hastened into the tailor shop. Stephano paid the driver and, as was his habit, cast a routine glance up and down the street.

Rodrigo was a longtime customer of this particular tailor's shop, which happened to deal in fine-quality silks at prices much lower than anything he could buy in Evreux; mainly due to the fact that the silks entering Westfirth entered the city through unconventional means. Stephano, who detested going to the tailor's and did so only when forced, had always managed to avoid accompanying his friend on these trips. He had never been to this shop or even to this part of Westfirth.

There had been a time in the city's history when streets had been named after the nature of the shop owners' occupations. Thus there was Market Street, Butcher's Row, Smith Street, and so forth. The needs of a burgeoning population, especially a growing upper middle class (or lower upper class as they liked to think of themselves), had brought about changes. Threadneedle Street was still known as a place where one could find tailors, milliners, and dressmakers. Now one could find lodging on Threadneedle Street, as well. An inn, newly built, had opened across the street from the tailor's shop. A café known as the Four Clovers was next door.

Stephano, loath to go into the tailor's, where he was certain to be accosted by the tailor trying to sell him new trousers or the latest fashion in waistcoats, remained outside, observing the people. His mother, the Countess de Marjolaine, would have never been seen on Threadneedle Street. Her dressmaker came to her in the palace. The wife of the wealthy ironmonger who had recently been knighted for his ironmongering services to the country came to Threadneedle Street. "Lady Ironmonger" was shown pen-and-ink drawings of the dresses worn by the Countess de Marjolaine and she would then instruct her dressmaker to make a dress exactly like that worn by the countess only "it was so plain" and to add a few more feathers and a lot more ribbons and perhaps plunge the bosom and raise the hem.

Stephano also saw what were termed "men of affairs" hastening along the street, engrossed in their own business which was all about money and the making of it. Meeting other men of affairs, these gentlemen would stop to talk in urgent voices for the making of money always demands urgency.

A group of priests passed him, hands in the sleeves of their robes. Stephano gave them a sharp glance, prepared to bolt, but none wore the black cassock. He did bolt when he saw several naval officers from one of the navy ships patrolling the harbor near the Old Fort. One of those ships was the *Royal Lion*, commanded by Stephano's old enemy, Captain Hastind. None of these men were Hastind, but Stephano might know them from his days in the Dragon Brigade, which had been part of the navy, or they might know him from his notorious duel with Hastind. Either way, a meeting would be awkward. He ducked into the tailor's shop.

The "Sew On and Sew Forth" as the shop was named, was a large establishment employing many workers, some engaged in cutting the cloth, others in creating the patterns used for the apparel, and others doing actual sewing. Many of the workers sat at tables placed in front of the windows to take advantage of the daylight.

Rodrigo had been an excellent customer over the years, and the owner of the Sew On and Sew Forth came out personally to greet him. The tailor was deeply saddened to hear of Rodrigo's loss and immediately drew him over to view the somber-colored cloth worn by gentlemen in mourning.

After selecting the fabric, Rodrigo next had to decide upon the pattern for the coat, and he and the tailor were soon absorbed in leafing through the pattern book, talking of the styles being worn in court, determining the proper trimmings, and then taking measurements.

Stephano sat on a tall stool, watching his friend, glad to see Rodrigo finding comfort in the familiar routine and remembering with a pang when Benoit had brought Stephano his own suit of mourning clothes. He had flown into a rage, slicing up the black coat with his sword until he fell onto his knees sobbing—painful gasps of grief and rage. He remembered Benoit putting his arms around his shaking shoulders and saying, "I can't take his place, lad, but I will always be here."

Stephano stood up and walked over to one of the windows where he stared out, unseeing, into the street. He was forced to turn back to assist Rodrigo in deciding whether to add velvet trim to the collar or stay with satin. When all was finally concluded and the suit had been ordered and paid for, with strict instructions to have it completed as swiftly as possible, Rodrigo pronounced himself ready to leave.

"Feel better?" Stephano asked, as they emerged into the bright sunlight and began to walk down the street.

"I do," said Rodrigo. "I have only to write to my mother with an explanation. God knows what I'm going to say to her."

"There's a café across the way," said Stephano. "Let's discuss it over a bottle of wine."

"And they make an excellent roast capon served with new spring potatoes and the first crop of asparagus," said Rodrigo.

The two walked across the street.

The café, known as the Four Clovers, was near the inn that was called, unimaginatively, Threadneedle Inn. The café catered to the patrons of the inn, as well as to the tailors, the wives of ironmongers, and men of affairs. On fine days, the owner placed tables and chairs on a patio in a garden that separated the inn from the café. Trees provided shade. Flowers scented the air. The small wooden tables were crowded close together to provide room for as many customers as possible, which meant that diners were seated so close they sometimes knocked elbows with their neighbors.

The café was crowded, for it was dinnertime. Many of the shops and businesses in Westfirth closed at noon, allowing owners and employees to dine at their leisure and then refresh themselves with a nap. The shops would reopen in the late afternoon and remained open until the lamps were lighted.

Dubois sat in the park beneath a linden tree. His bench faced the street and the entrance to the inn where Harrington was staying. He was astonished beyond measure to see Stephano de Guichen and Rodrigo de Villeneuve enter the tailor shop, the Sew On and Sew Forth, which was directly across the street from the inn.

Far from being glad to see them, Dubois swore beneath his breath and consigned Stephano de Guichen and his friend to the bottomless pits of Hell. James Harrington, alias Sir Richard Piefer, lodged in the inn.

At that moment, James Harrington, wearing the fashionable clothing of a man-about-town, left the inn. Dubois prayed to God and every saint in the calendar that the captain and his friend would not look out the window. Dubois' prayers were answered, apparently, for Harrington entered the Four Clovers café without attracting any notice.

Four Clovers café. Dubois shifted his thoughts from Captain de Guichen as the report of one of his agents came to mind—Harrington had purchased a bouquet of clover from a street vendor and left them on a gravesite.

The clovers were a message for Sir Henry! This café was the meeting place!

Feeling a thrill of anticipation, Dubois watched until Harrington had found a seat, then he had hurried to the café and entered and asked for a table. He located James Harrington, sitting by himself. Dubois cast a glance around the people in the café and recognized the elderly priest with a hunched back seated at the table next to Harrington as Sir Henry Wallace.

Sir Henry had deliberately selected a table in the back near the garden wall with few other tables around it, which meant that Dubois could not acquire a table near enough to the two to eavesdrop on their conversation.

He found a table as close as possible and gazed with envy at the sparrow pecking at crumbs beneath Wallace's chair, wishing he could change places with the bird. That being impossible, Dubois ordered a plate of cold meat and a flagon of wine and settled himself to wait for Sir Henry to leave, at which point Dubois would track his quarry to his lair.

Dubois had not forgotten about Captain de Guichen and his friend. He saw them leave the tailor shop with relief that was short-lived, soon replaced by horror.

Captain de Guichen and Rodrigo de Villeneuve were coming to the café.

Dubois had once witnessed a runaway wagon crash into a carriage containing a wedding party. He had seen the wagon rattling down the street; he had watched the carriage driving straight into its path. He had known a disastrous wreck was imminent, and he had been helpless to prevent it.

He felt the same way now as he had felt then.

Captain Stephano de Guichen was going to walk into this café and the first thing he would see was the man who had tried to kill him and his friend.

And all Dubois could do was sit there and watch.

Chapter Thirty

Rule 23. If the cause of the meeting be of such a nature that no apology or explanation can or will be received, the challenged takes his ground, and calls on the challenger to proceed as he chooses; in such cases, firing at pleasure is the usual practice, but may be varied by agreement.

—*Codes Duello*

SIR HENRY SAT AT THE TABLE IN THE CAFÉ in his guise as a benign old priest and dunked bread into his beef-and-barley soup with a palsied hand. He liked the disguise mainly because the fake infirmity of a bent spine allowed him to take inches off his height, while his mild and gentle demeanor earned "Father Alfonso" much goodwill from customers and wait staff. Sir Henry had already established the character of the elderly priest in the Four Clovers. He had dined there several times before in this guise, telling the owner in his best Rosian accent that he had traveled to Westfirth from Caltreau to observe the building of the new cathedral.

"I won't live to see it finished," he said cheerfully. "But I wanted to see it started."

The elderly priest had immediately become a favorite. He was given his usual table and a glass of dandelion wine, compliments of the house. At his feet was the worn leather satchel he always carried everywhere with him. He said the satchel contained notes on a biography of Saint Stanislaus, notes he would drag out and read during his meal, offering gladly to expound upon the life of the saint if anyone made the mistake of asking. Concealed in the satchel, beneath the pages and pages of documents, was the pewter tankard. Sir Henry carried the tankard with him wherever he went by day and slept with it beneath his mattress at night.

The Four Clovers was known among Sir Henry's agents as a place where they could meet with him if an emergency arose. The sign was a bunch of clover left at any one of several locations throughout the city. Every agent had his own color of ribbon. A black ribbon around the clover indicated the request for a meeting came from James Harrington, who was supposed to be in Evreux, but who was at this moment now in Westfirth.

Harrington was in his guise as Sir Richard Piefer, wealthy and rakish Freyan nobleman. He doffed his hat and made a graceful bow to a party of three ladies and two gentlemen seated at a table beneath a rose tree. He stared balefully at several Rosian naval officers and gave them a cold bow, which the officers returned just as coldly. Rosia and Freya were nominally at peace, but the wounds from the last war were still raw and bleeding.

Harrington sauntered over to the table near Sir Henry, sat down with a languid air, and adjusted the long and frilly lace at his cuffs so that it would not come into contact with his food. He flirted with the serving girl, who gave the handsome nobleman a sweet smile, and brought him a flagon of red wine.

Harrington then exchanged a friendly greeting with his closest neighbor, the elderly priest, who smiled upon him beatifically. Harrington inquired politely what the priest was studying so intently. Sir Henry asked if the "young gentleman" would be interested in hearing about the life and travails of Saint Stanislaus. Harrington, with a wink for the serving girl, indicated that he would like nothing better.

"But I believe, Father," said Harrington, "that you have mislaid one of your documents."

Sir Henry glanced down to see a sheet of paper lying at his feet. The paper was covered with handwriting—not his, Harrington's. A written report. Henry reached a shaking hand to pick it up. Harrington politely intercepted the elderly man, picked up the report, and gave it to Sir Henry, who felt, hidden beneath the single sheet of paper, a folded, sealed note.

"From Sloan," Harrington said in a low voice.

Sir Henry knew immediately something was wrong. Sloan, his confidential secretary, would not have risked writing unless the matter was of the utmost importance. Sir Henry's first concern was for his pregnant young wife. Had something happened to her? He longed to read the note, but he dared not in such a public place. And he needed to know why Harrington was here in Westfirth. Sloan could have sent the letter by courier.

Sir Henry, shuffling and rattling papers, began to ramble on in a cracked voice. He was, in fact, reading the report that Harrington had just handed him. Harrington flung himself back in his chair and drank his wine, affecting to listen. As Sir Henry read, he began to frown. He stammered to a halt, pretending to have lost himself in his notes. Harrington heard the ominous silence and shifted uneasily in his chair and ordered more wine.

"Won't you join me, my son?" Sir Henry asked with a smile. "I have something here I think will be of interest."

Harrington did not evince any great pleasure at accepting this invitation, but he did not have much choice. He shifted his chair to the old priest's table. Sir Henry shuffled papers and leaning close said in a tone of barely controlled fury, "What the Hell were you thinking?"

"I initiated part two of the Braffa scenario as you ordered, sir," said Harrington. "The assassination of Ambassador de Villeneuve went as planned."

"Of course it did," Sir Henry stated coldly. "Because *I*

planned it. I did *not* plan for you to murder young Valazquez and try to murder the son of the Countess de Marjolaine!"

He flicked his hand at the report. Harrington squirmed, his attitude became defensive. They both stopped talking as the serving girl brought a plate of cheese, grapes, apples, and walnuts and set it down in front of Harrington. He began ripping grapes off their stems and tossing them moodily into the bushes.

"You told me, sir, I was to act on my own if I saw anyone snooping around about Alcazar. When I saw that she-bitch of a countess set her whelp on the trail, I figured you'd want him off it. At the same time, I could remove Villeneuve, who might prove to be a nuisance if he started asking questions about his father's death. My idea was that a duel involving Villeneuve would have solved everything—take him from the picture and upset the countess' son. He'd forget he'd ever heard the name Alcazar. That damned imbecile Valazquez ruined everything."

"*Valazquez* ruined it," said Sir Henry.

"Yes," said Harrington sullenly, hearing the sarcasm. "If he hadn't gone softhearted—"

"—then you wouldn't have gone softheaded," Sir Henry finished.

The elderly priest leaned close to the young nobleman, as if about to enlighten him on a discovery of immense importance about Saint Stanislaus. The old man wore a smile on his lips, but the look in his dark eyes caused Harrington to shove aside his plate and fiddle nervously with his fork.

"Who was the third man?"

"What third man?" Harrington asked uneasily, his eyes on the fork.

Sir Henry referred to the report. "The man who shot at you from the woods, knocking the gun from your hand as you were about to kill the captain."

Harrington again shrugged. "I assumed he was one of my hired guns who was a bad shot or maybe of the countess' agents looking after her bastard son. How should I know?"

"It is your business to know," said Sir Henry. "Especially as you have undoubtedly led this man right to me. He could be sitting in this café this moment."

Harrington looked shocked. "No, sir! I swear to you, sir—"

"Shut up and listen to me." Sir Henry rattled his papers and held them up to his face and peered over them, concealing his lips.

"Your plan might have succeeded, but you lost your nerve. You have imperiled an operation on which I've worked for years, laying the groundwork so that Rosia would be sucked into war over Braffa, expending money and resources while Freya remains neutral. We watch Rosia bleed and when she is weak and gasping, we strike."

Sir Henry touched the satchel containing the tankard reassuringly with his foot. The time for Freya to strike might be closer than even he had anticipated.

"So much depends on this and now . . . Now, because of your bungling, the son of my most implacable enemy, who was only moderately interested in Alcazar before you shot at him is now intensely interested in finding him and probably more in finding you! And what do you do? You come straight to me!"

Sir Henry was about to continue when he caught sight of the very man they had been discussing. Stephano de Guichen, accompanied by Rodrigo de Villeneuve, entered the Four Clovers.

Not unnaturally, Sir Henry leaped to the conclusion that Stephano was on the trail of Harrington and that Harrington had led the captain to him. Henry was somewhat comforted by the fact that the captain and his friend appeared astonished to see Harrington. Rodrigo de Villeneuve gaped at Harrington in astonishment and went quite pale. Stephano de Guichen flushed an angry red.

Harrington was sitting with his back to the door and had

not seen the two come in. Sir Henry rose to his feet and began hastily gathering up the papers on the table.

"God has an amazing sense of irony, my son," said the elderly priest.

He thrust the papers into the satchel and pushed back his chair. Bending over Harrington, Henry whispered, "If you survive, you know how to reach me."

Stephano and Rodrigo had entered the café when Stephano saw the three naval officers he'd previously avoided enjoying their after-dinner port. He made a face and started to leave.

"We'll eat somewhere else," he said and then he saw Rodrigo's eyes widen, his face go white. "Rigo! What's wrong?"

"It's . . . him," said Rodrigo in a strangled voice. "Piefer."

The patio was filled with people, but Stephano saw only one—the man he knew as Sir Richard Piefer. He was seated at a table with an elderly priest, who was shoving papers into a satchel. The priest had apparently observed the fact that Rodrigo was staring fixedly at his dinner companion, for he said something to him which caused Harrington to shift in his chair.

Harrington saw Stephano and rose to his feet.

The patio was crowded with tables and chairs, some empty, others occupied. A table occupied by several ladies and gentlemen was between Stephano and Sir Richard. The three naval officers were to his right. A group of students was seated at a table near the back and to his left. A fellow who looked like a clerk was seated in the shadows of a hibiscus.

Stephano laid his hand on the hilt of his rapier.

"You, sir! I promised we would meet again!" cried Stephano.

"Are you mad?" Rodrigo gasped. He seized hold of his friend's arm, trying to prevent him from drawing his weapon. "Leave him alone! They'll send for the constables—"

"Let them!" Stephano said grimly.

James Harrington cast Stephano a glance of contempt. He began to adjust the lace at his cuffs. "If you have a quarrel with me, sir, let us settle the matter in some less public place."

Stephano did not see Harrington. He saw young Valazquez, missing his face, lying in a pool of blood. He relived that nightmarish chase through the streets, a bullet in his shoulder. He remembered how near he and his friends had come to sinking into the Breath.

"Stay out of this, Rigo," said Stephano harshly and he took off his coat, tossed it to the ground, and drew his rapier.

By now, of course, everyone in the café was watching. The ladies were whispering in thrilled horror behind their fans. Their gentlemen stood up, looking uncertain. The naval officers had all lowered their glasses of port. One of them tried to intervene.

"Gentlemen, please—"

"This son of a bitch is no gentleman, sir," Stephano said. "He is an assassin who murdered a man in Evreux and tried to murder me. If one of you will oblige me by calling the constables, I will see to it that he does not escape justice."

Harrington had been keeping his own hand near his sleeve, smoothing the long lace that fell over his wrist. His hand darted swiftly into the cuff of his coat and came out holding a small pistol.

Stephano saw the flash of sunlight off metal. He stiff-armed Rodrigo, giving him a shove that sent him reeling backward into one of the serving girls. They both went down together with a crash of crockery.

Harrington fired. Stephano ducked. The bullet whistled harmlessly over Stephano's head and smashed into a post.

The café was in an uproar. One of the women fainted. Her companion cried out that she had been shot and then she fainted. The third woman screamed and went into hysterics. The two gentlemen had taken cover under the table, where they were endeavoring to assist the ladies. A serving girl ran to the aid of the elderly priest, who seemed on the verge of collapse, while the other patrons made a mad scramble, overturning chairs and upending tables. The clerk tried to leave, but found his way blocked by an upended table to his right and the naval officers on his left.

The owner of the café dodged around Rodrigo, who was floundering amidst broken crockery, and ran into the street, shouting for the constables. People in the street, attracted by the commotion, hurried over to see what was happening, adding to the confusion. The students, having taken cover, were exchanging bets.

Harrington threw down the useless pistol and reached for his sword. Stephano jumped onto a chair, from the chair to a table, and back to the ground, landing in front of Sir Richard. The naval officers had all drawn their weapons and advanced with the intention of trying to stop the fight.

"Stay out of this, gentlemen!" Stephano cried. "This bastard murdered a young nobleman in cold blood and he tried to kill me and my friend in the same cowardly manner. He is mine!"

The naval officers glanced at each other. If Harrington had been a Rosian, they might have stayed to try to prevent bloodshed, but he was a Freyan, and therefore not worth their trouble. The officers thrust their swords back into their sheaths. One of them saluted Stephano, and then they hurriedly left the café, well aware that the Constabulary was probably already on the way. Now that the officers were gone, the clerk made his way out from behind the overturned table.

"Sir!" the clerk called to Stephano. "For the love of God, don't kill him! Wait for the constables!"

Stephano paid no heed, but drove the point of his rapier at Harrington's throat. Harrington parried, and Stephano managed to nick the man's chin. Stephano followed with a series of attacks—slash and thrust, moving rapidly, his blade darting and jabbing, trying to force Harrington onto the defensive.

Harrington was a skilled swordsman, however, and all Stephano managed to do was slice open his shoulder. He pressed Harrington, who had the garden wall behind him. Harrington leaped lightly up onto the wall and ran along it, keeping the tables between him and Stephano.

Stephano took hold of a table, pitched it over, and lunged at Harrington, who jumped down off the wall and seized hold of one of the serving girls and flung her into Stephano's arms. Stephano tried to sidestep in order to miss hitting her, but he was not quick enough. He collided with the girl. Harrington used the advantage to drive his blade through the girl's upper arm and into Stephano's left shoulder—the same shoulder that was still stiff and sore from Harrington's bullet. Pain shot through Stephano's arm and his hand tingled.

Harrington yanked out his sword and made ready for another strike. The girl collapsed at Stephano's feet, screaming in pain and terror and further impeding his ability to reach Harrington, who scored a bloody gash down Stephano's side.

Stephano grabbed a wine glass from a table and flung the contents into Harrington's eyes, half-blinding him. While Harrington tried to wipe away the stinging wine, Stephano hurled the glass at him. Harrington lifted his arm to block the blow and managed at the same time to parry Stephano's vicious stab. Stephano sliced through the cloth and into Harrington's left forearm. The lace at the man's wrist was immediately drenched in blood. Harrington feinted to the right, fell back, and seized a knife that had been left in a saddle of beef. He threw the knife at Stephano, hitting him in the thigh.

Stephano yanked out the knife and backed up. Blood oozed from the wound, and he flung the bloody knife back at Harrington, more out of rage than with the hope of hitting him. Harrington had to dodge the knife, however, and that gave Stephano a moment's respite. For a moment, both men stood staring, each calculating the next move.

Blood trickled down Stephano's leg. His shirt was wet with blood and sticking to his ribs. Harrington was bleeding, too, but only from a few gashes here and there. He smiled. He must think Stephano was nearly finished. He came at him.

Stephano cast what he hoped looked like a panicked glance behind him, as though judging the distance between himself and the exit. He began to retreat, gasping for air, moving slowly, limping heavily. He kept his rapier raised, defending against Harrington's quick jabs. Stephano, appearing to weaken, let the tip of his blade waver and drop.

Harrington had been waiting for this. His blade slid over Stephano's, aiming for his heart. Stephano hooked his foot under a fallen stool and kicked it, sending it rolling into his foe. The stool struck Harrington in the shins. He stumbled and fought to keep his balance, but his feet were entangled with the legs of the stool and he fell to his knees.

Stephano attacked while the Freyan was on the ground, hoping to end the fight. Harrington fended off the attack with his sword as he twisted back to his feet with the same feline grace and athleticism that had caused Stephano to place him as the man in the slouch hat. Again, Harrington drove the tip of his blade at Stephano's heart, turning his wrist so the flat of the blade would slide between his ribs.

Stephano sidestepped and Harrington's momentum carried him past Stephano, who jabbed his rapier into Harrington's back. Harrington gasped in shock. He looked down to see the bloody tip of a sword sticking out of his breast.

"Valazquez, I hope you are watching," said Stephano.

He yanked out the blade and James Harrington fell onto an overturned table, bounced off it and rolled to the ground. He lay on his back, eyes wide and staring, blood dribbling from his mouth.

Stephano fell back, gasping for breath. What with the heat and excitement and loss of blood, he felt suddenly giddy. As he leaned back against a table and tried to keep from passing out, he was vaguely aware of the clerk who had begged him not to kill Harrington kneeling by the corpse. Stephano and he didn't pay much attention, though he wanted to tell the fellow not to waste his time. Harrington was most certainly dead. He did think it odd that the pudgy man was frantically searching Harrington's pockets.

The clerk yelled something at Stephano and then jumped to his feet and was gone. Stephano stared after him, wondering if he'd heard right. Before he could react, whistles sounded in the street and Rodrigo was beside him.

"Constables," he said. "We have to get out of here."

"Which way?" Stephano asked.

"Over the garden wall," said Rodrigo. He looked at Stephano's bleeding leg. "Can you manage?"

"Do I have a choice?" Stephano returned, hobbling along beside his friend.

"This or prison," said Rodrigo.

The stone wall proved to be more decorative than functional. They clambered over it, Stephano wincing and grunting and Rodrigo doing what he could to help. They floundered through some ornamental hedges, trampled flower beds, and dodged rose trees in tubs.

"First you get shot, now stabbed," Rodrigo grumbled. "If you're going to keep this up, I will have to start bringing along a wheelbarrow to haul your sorry ass back home."

"Don't make me laugh. My ribs hurt!" Stephano pleaded.

They floundered their way through the park. People stopped to stare at Stephano, who was covered in blood. Such sights were not unusual in Westfirth, however, and most shrugged and went on about their business.

Stephano and Rodrigo emerged from the park onto Haymarket Street, which ran parallel to Threadneedle, and was one of the busiest streets in Westfirth. Rodrigo hailed a cab. A hansom cab rolled to a stop. The driver looked down at Stephano, noted the blood on his clothes, and shook his head.

"He'll ruin the h'upolstery," he said indignantly.

Rodrigo looked into the cab, saw that the "h'upolstery" was faded, cracked, ripped, and disgorging stuffing.

"A little blood might be good for it," he told the driver. "I'll pay double."

The driver gave a nod. Rodrigo opened the door and pushed Stephano inside. The driver whipped up the horses before Rodrigo had the door shut, and the cab rattled off through the streets.

"Sorry about your lavender coat," said Stephano, eyeing the blood smears on the fine fabric.

Rodrigo smiled. "Good thing I just ordered a new one." He began to inspect his friend's wounds, opening Stephano's shirt and peering at them.

"They don't look very severe to me."

"What do you know?" Stephano groaned. "My ribs hurt like hell."

"Don't be such a baby. The bleeding in your shoulder has stopped. There's a big gash down your side, but the blade didn't penetrate to the bone." Rodrigo took out a handkerchief, wadded it up. "Here, press that against your leg. I'm getting to rather like bandaging wounds. Perhaps I'll study to be a surgeon."

Stephano did as ordered and held the handkerchief against the gash in his leg. "Speaking of surgeons, did you see that man kneeling over the body?"

"I didn't see the body," Rodrigo answered. "I was trying to reach you, which wasn't easy, given the fact that I had to wade through a sea of overturned furniture and hysterical women. Why? What did he do?"

"I thought he was trying to save that bastard," said Stephano. "But then he began to rifle the man's pockets and he started swearing. I heard him say, 'You bloody fool, you just killed any chance of finding Henry Wallace!' And then he was gone."

"He mentioned the name Henry Wallace?" Rodrigo asked, astonished. "Did you see what the man looked like?"

"He had on a big hat and a gray cloak," said Stephano.

"That describes about half the population of Westfirth," said Rodrigo. He was silent a moment. They were both silent, thinking, and not much liking their thoughts.

Rodrigo spoke first. "I guess we know now that Henry Wallace is here in Westfirth, probably with Alcazar."

"And I'm guessing Wallace now knows we're here," said Stephano. "And that we're looking for Alcazar."

"And that someone else is looking for him, too."

Stephano grinned. "Just as long as they're not riding giant bats."

"Amen to that, my friend," said Rodrigo.

Dubois had never in his life been so frustrated. He had tried to keep sight of the elderly priest, but Wallace had been too quick for him. When Dubois saw one of the serving girls assisting the priest to leave the scene of the fight, he had attempted to go after them, but by then bullets were flying, tables and chairs and stools were in his way, naval officers interfered, swords flashed. When Dubois next looked, the priest had vanished.

Dubois' only hope had then been to keep track of James Harrington; Captain de Guichen when killed Harrington, all Dubois' plans and efforts were gone with the jab of a rapier.

Dubois took a chance searching through Harrington's pockets, with Guichen standing over the body, but Dubois was desperate to find a note or a key or anything that might lead to Sir Henry.

Harrington had nothing on him. Frustrated, Dubois lost his head and gave voice to his anger.

"You are an idiot," he said furiously to Guichen. "You just killed any chance of finding Henry Wallace!"

Dubois scuttled out of the café, exiting through the rear door just as the constables were entering the front. In the street, Dubois looked about for the elderly priest, but, of course, Sir Henry was long gone.

Dubois sighed and reflected that Captain de Guichen, who was also on the trail of Alcazar, was once again his only hope. Dubois regretted his uncharacteristic outburst in the café. He did not often lose his self-possession, but he'd been going for days on little sleep and less food. Dubois rubbed his aching head and plotted his next move.

There was no need to follow Captain Guichen. The man had sailed from Evreux on a Trundler houseboat with his Trundler friends. They would be docked in the Trundler village.

Dubois hailed a cab.

Chapter Thirty-One

Bitter End: the last part of a rope or chain. The term has passed into common usage so that: "One hangs on until the bitter end."

—Anonymous

SIR HENRY WALLACE, IN HIS GUISE AS THE EL-DERLY PRIEST, hobbled slowly across Threadneedle Street. He paused a moment in a doorway, leaning on his cane, pretending to rest as he watched the commotion outside the Four Clovers. The constables arrived with much blowing of whistles and a great show of energy. They promptly arrested several people who had nothing to do with the affair, including the two gentlemen who had been attempting to revive the fainting ladies, and the serving girl who had crashed into Rodrigo on the grounds that she had helped the miscreants escape. The crowd lingered in hopes of seeing the body and eventually the constables emerged from the café bearing the corpse on a shutter. Although his face had been decently covered with a handkerchief, Sir Henry recognized James Harrington. He watched impassively as they carted his dead agent away, most likely to a pauper's grave, since he had little money and no one would claim the body. Certainly not Sir Henry, who pronounced James Harrington's epithet.

"Bloody fool!"

Sir Henry had entered the Four Clovers that day in a

good mood. Alcazar's brother's ship, the *Silver Raven*, was
due to sail into port tomorrow. He and the journeyman
could at last leave Westfirth. Sir Henry had heard from one
of his underworld contacts that inquiries were suddenly being made around Westfirth regarding a man named Sir
Henry Wallace. A well-dressed, well-spoken, handsome
young man and a former mob enforcer were both looking
for Wallace.

Henry had no idea who these people were—agents of
the countess, agents of the grand bishop? It didn't much
matter. He cursed Harrington, whose stupidity had set the
hounds on his trail. He did not think they would be able to
find him, for he had taken excellent precautions, but his
good mood had evaporated.

Henry waited a moment hoping to see if the constables
were going to arrest Captain de Guichen. He did not see
them hauling the captain away, and he thus gathered gloomily that the captain had escaped.

Sir Henry resumed his walk. He hobbled down the street
until he found a small, neighborhood church and went inside. The church was empty except for two old women in
black shawls who were lighting candles for the dead. Both
made a reverence to the elderly priest as they passed him
on their way down the aisle and out the door. He waited
until they were gone, then sat down in a pew near an open
window and fished out the folded letter sent to him by
Sloan.

Sloan's handwriting, usually so neat and precise, was in
some places almost illegible.

> *My lord, I run the very great risk of writing to you,
> which I would never do were the matter not of the
> greatest importance. A dire and most terrible event has
> occurred. Before I relate the circumstances, I want to
> assure you that your lady wife and unborn child are
> both safe. By the grace of God, the family was not in
> residence. Your lady wife, feeling lonely in your absence,*

decided on a whim to accept the long-standing invita-
tion of Her Majesty the Queen to return to court for
her lying-in. If she had not made this sudden decision,
I would not be writing this to you. I would be dead.

As it was, I traveled with your lady wife to court.
Seeing her safely settled in the palace with every com-
fort, I returned to the manor alone. I arrived before
dawn to find a horrific sight. The roof of the manor
house was ablaze. The exterior walls were charred and
blackened as though they had been struck by cannon
fire, which was what I first thought had occurred. And
then I beheld the real cause—demonic looking crea-
tures with eyes of orange flame riding on gigantic bats,
hurling green fire at the walls. (The words "green fire"
had been heavily underscored.)

My horse was crazed with terror and nearly threw
me from the saddle. I managed to regain control and
rode into the woods before the creatures saw me. I re-
mained in hiding, watching, until the bats and their rid-
ers left with the rising of the sun.

Once I was certain the attackers were gone, I rode
to the manor house to see if there was anyone who
could tell me what had transpired. I am not a squea-
mish man, having seen much in the service of my
country. Yet the horrible sight that met my eyes nearly
caused me to lose my senses. The people who had not
died in the fire had been slaughtered in a most grue-
some manner. I found limbs and even heads scattered
about the blood-soaked grass. The bats had torn apart
the bodies and undoubtedly devoured them.

We were fortunate, my lord, that there has not been
much rain and that the grass was dry. I helped the
flames spread and saw to it that the fire consumed the
bodies and wiped out all traces of the true nature of
the attack.

News spread quickly, however. Everyone in the vil-
lage had seen the flames and smoke and rushed to view

*the destruction. I rode swiftly to Haever to apprise
your lady wife and Her Majesty of what had occurred
before they heard any wild rumors. Though I pleaded
ignorance as to the attackers, I hinted at the Rosians.
Her Majesty is already blaming them, and there is talk
of war.*

*Finally, I paid a call upon your former associate.
You will know of whom I speak and also why I mention her in connection with this tragedy. Her house is
still as it was eight years ago — closed, empty, vacant. I
made discreet inquiries and learned that a young associate of hers, a depraved young man of about seventeen, who calls himself the Warlock and is wanted in
connection with a string of gruesome murders, is
known to be in Westfirth and is making inquiries regarding you.* <u>I urge you to take precautions</u>*, my lord.
(*That was also underlined.*)*

I await your orders.
Franklin Sloan.

The letter slipped from Sir Henry's nerveless fingers.
Sweat broke out on his neck and chest. He stared, unseeing,
into the chancel. His first thoughts were of his wife and
child and he found himself trembling at the thought of how
narrowly they had escaped a horrible death. Sir Henry muttered a heartfelt prayer of thanks and then, chastising himself for his weakness, pulled himself together and began to
think about the incident coldly and rationally. What did this
portend? Who had attacked him? He discounted Sloan's
incredible tale of demons. The man had ridden all night.
He'd been short on sleep. Sloan's final paragraph at the end
of the letter hinted at an answer — a very disturbing answer.

Ten years ago, Sir Henry had met an extremely attractive
and mysterious woman named Eiddwen, a Trundler name,
though she was not a Trundler. With her blue-black hair,
gold-flecked black eyes, and olive complexion tinged with
dusky rose, she appeared to be of Bruond extraction. An

orphan raised by nuns in a Freyan orphanage, she did not know her parents. Judging by her way of shrugging off the matter, she did not care to know them. She had been given her name by the nuns, who told her that Eiddwen meant "blessed" or "holy." She had no surname.

"I am a child of every man," she said. She always smiled when she said it, but by the arch in her black brows and the shimmer of the golden flecks in her eyes, she was more than half serious.

Sir Henry was introduced to Eiddwen at the hunting lodge of the Baron of Gahllendale, Lord Brobeaton, during the shooting season. Like many single young women of no family and no means, Eiddwen was serving as a hired companion to the baron's mother, an elderly woman confined to her wheeled chair. The old woman had been passionately fond of hunting in her youth and though she could no longer ride to the hounds, she enjoyed listening to the horn calls and the baying of the dogs and reliving her most memorable moments. Eiddwen's duties were light; she read to the old lady, pushed her about the garden in her wheeled chair, and listened patiently to her tales.

The baron had invited a great many guests to his lodge and the men were united in their opinion that Eiddwen was one of the most beautiful women they had ever seen. The women were united in their jealousy of her, but that soon faded. The twenty-six-year-old young woman was not flirtatious. She evinced no interest in "catching" a rich husband, nor was she prone to stealing the husbands of others. Men and women alike thought her too severe, too serious-minded. Some proclaimed her "dull."

Eiddwen's clothes suited her station in life. Her dress was simply cut of black, serviceable cloth, with tight sleeves to the wrist, a form-fitting bodice that buttoned from the waist to the neck unrelieved by even a hint of lace, and a long skirt that fell from the V-shaped bodice. Her plain attire served to emphasize her striking appearance.

Eiddwen did not "do" her hair, for she had no ladies'

maid. She twisted it in a chignon. During the day, long tendrils of black curls would often escape from their captivity
and twine down her long, slender neck. Her only adornment was a slender golden chain she wore around her neck
from which hung some sort of pendant that appeared to be
a sea-going knot done in gold. She termed it a good luck
charm.

Eiddwen was not a flirt, but she did have the ability to
fascinate, and Sir Henry found himself fascinated. He was,
at the time, unmarried. He was considered an eligible catch,
and he was prepared to be caught by Eiddwen, for he was
rich and powerful enough to overlook the fact that she had
no family and no money. He was pleased to find out that she
was interested in him, then astonished to discover that her
interest had nothing to do with matrimony.

The old lady spent the afternoon napping, which left Eiddwen free to pursue her own interests. She arranged a tryst
with Sir Henry, inviting him to take her rowing upon the
lake. When they were alone in the rowboat, she laid out her
plan. Sir Henry listened in amazement.

Eiddwen explained coolly that she had managed through
various means to become acquainted with the baron and to
be hired as the old lady's companion for one purpose—to
arrange this meeting with Sir Henry, a meeting that would
appear to be accidental.

"I am not what I seem," said Eiddwen. She sat in the
stern of the rowboat, facing him, her black hair blowing
about her. While she talked, she would sometimes reach up
to play with a curling tendril.

"I am a member of a group of people who have a single
goal and that is the utter destruction of Rosia. To this end,
my associates and I have developed a weapon that has the
power to destroy magic. Ah, you laugh, Sir Henry, but I assure you I am quite serious. I would prove it to you, but we
lack the funds to build it. We were wondering if you might
be interested in assisting us."

Sir Henry was interested, though cautious. The two ar-

ranged a meeting in Haever in a house located at the end of
the street in a quiet, upper middle class neighborhood. Court
gossip had it that Eiddwen had been established in this house
by Sir Henry as his mistress. That was true, in part. Sir Henry
paid for the house, but Eiddwen was not his mistress. She had
repulsed his advances with a firmness that left no doubt she
wanted a business relationship, nothing more.

As time passed, he found himself wondering how he had
ever thought her desirable. Eiddwen was ruthless, single-
minded, determined. One might say she was a female version of himself, but with a dark, underlying passion for
something unknown that chilled even Henry's blood. He
recalled vividly the night she showed up with the plans for
the weapon and explained the theory behind it.

"The weapon is powered by contramagic," she said.

Henry frowned in displeasure. "That is nothing to jest
about, Eiddwen. Even to speak the word is to risk imprisonment and death."

In answer, Eiddwen lifted a strange-looking weapon and
fired. Green flame struck the cellar wall. The fire left burn
marks on the brick.

"Examine it," said Eiddwen. "You will find that the sigils
placed on the bricks by the crafter masons have been obliterated. The contramagic does not merely break sigils. The
beam erases them, as though they had never been."

Sir Henry had examined the wall and discovered that
she had indeed destroyed the magic. She was not only talking heresy. She was *practicing* heresy. If he were caught listening to her, nothing could save him—neither wealth,
rank, nor power. The queen herself would be forced to dis-
avow him. He would be proclaimed a warlock and burned
at the stake.

Yet, if this contramagic could be transformed into a
weapon as she claimed . . . He could see in his mind's eye
the destruction of the ships of the Rosian Naval Fleet: masts
falling, hulls breaking apart, balloons exploding in green

fire, men plunging to their deaths in the Breath. Rosia humbled, ground into the dirt.

After much serious thought, Sir Henry decided that the development of this weapon was worth the risk. He funded the project; within two years, they were ready to test it. Their choice of target was the naval cutter, *Defiant*. Disguised as pirates, Eiddwen and her "people" attacked the cutter with devastating results. The green beam weapon almost completely disabled the ship. They did not sink the cutter. They deliberately left it afloat in order to later sneak aboard it to study the damage.

Henry was there with two of his most loyal associates: Admiral Randolph Baker and the famous Freyan privateer, Captain Andrew Northrop, (brother to Father Jacob Northrop of the Arcanum, a relationship neither cared to acknowledge). Mr. Sloan was there because Mr. Sloan was always there.

Sir Henry and Admiral Baker and Captain Northrop were all enthusiastic about the contramagic weapon, seeing it as the salvation of their country. The next day, Sir Henry paid Eiddwen an immense sum of money, practically a king's ransom. Several days after that, Eiddwen vanished.

Sir Henry went to visit her and found the house vacant. He let himself inside, hoping to find some clue as to her whereabouts, but the rooms were bare. She had left behind nothing but dust. He had been duped by this woman, who had taken his money and then fled. Baffled and furious, Sir Henry spared no expense trying to find Eiddwen. All he could discover was that she had an alias as vague and mysterious as herself. She was called the Sorceress by some of her associates. He could find no trace of her, however.

The years passed. Sir Henry had not forgotten Eiddwen nor had he forgiven her. He had come to believe the experiment on the *Defiant* had been some sort of hoax, an event staged to induce him to hand over the money. And then he began to receive reports of watchtowers crumbling for no apparent reason. He visited one of the sites and saw for himself the scorch marks, so similar to those on the *Defiant*. He knew the cause, but he dared not tell anyone, for he would have been forced to admit his involvement in contramagic.

And now this murderous attack. Demonic creatures riding giant bats. If any man other than the practical Sloan had written this, Sir Henry would have dismissed him as a lunatic.

I am a member of a group of people, Eiddwen had told him. Were those people fiends? Was she in league with the forces of Hell? Sir Henry could have believed this if he had believed in Hell. As it was, the prospect was dire enough without involving the Evil One. Yet, if not the Devil, who?

Eiddwen had lashed out at him, and he had no way to strike back. For the first time in his life, Henry was helpless. He did not like the feeling. It made him angry. Eiddwen had attacked his family. He wondered why. Why come for him after all these years? If she had wanted to kill him because he knew about her and her connection with the contramagic, she could have done so before this. Her timing could not possibly be worse.

"Not now!" Henry muttered, his hand closing, crushing the letter. "I can't deal with this woman now!"

He rose to his feet, picked up the satchel containing the tankard, and limped slowly out of the church. He walked through the graveyard, pausing here and there as though fondly remembering old friends. He stopped at the tomb bearing the Rosian version of his name, "Henri," and glanced down.

A bunch of violets lay in the grass.

Other agents besides Harrington knew to leave messages for him here, yet none of his agents used violets. He picked them up. They were bound with a green ribbon and there was a note tucked beneath the stems.

By now you have heard about the destruction of your manor house. Are you impressed? Come to Bitter End

*Lane this evening when the clock chimes six. We need
to talk.*

No name, but a knot had been drawn on the bottom of
the note. He had seen that knot before—on the pendant
that hung from the golden chain around Eiddwen's neck.

He sniffed at the violets and carried them back with him
into the church. Henry took his seat in the pew and remained there to hear the afternoon service. After the service, he entered the confessional. Once inside, Henry took
off his clerical robes. The well-dressed Rosian nobleman
who emerged from the church that afternoon bore no resemblance to the elderly cleric who had entered it with one
exception—he was still carrying the satchel.

Returning to the inn, Sir Henry pondered the instructions in the note. The dockyards at that time of evening
would be deserted, though there would still be some light
for the sun did not set until after seven. Eiddwen would
know, of course, that he would have refused to meet her in
the dead of night.

On his arrival at the Blue Parrot, he told the jubilant
Alcazar that his brother's ship was due in tomorrow and
that he should start packing.

Late that afternoon, a tall man dressed as a lawyer, with
a white periwig sitting slightly askew atop his head, left the
Blue Parrot. The lawyer, like most lawyers, was carrying a
leather satchel.

As a guest of the Archbishop of Westfirth, Father Jacob
Northrup had taken up residence in the archbishop's temporary residence, a stolid and imposing structure known
among the city's residents as the Old Fort.

Father Jacob disliked staying anywhere as a guest of anyone, but with the *Retribution* being refitted at the ship yard,
he didn't have much choice. He could have taken lodgings
at an inn, but he required a secure room in order to protect

the books of Saint Dennis. Much to the amusement of Sir Ander, Father Jacob was forced to swallow his pride and accept the invitation of the archbishop, who was honored and delighted to have such a renowned priest as Father Jacob of the Arcanum stay with him.

The archbishop was less delighted when Father Jacob arrived. Father Jacob was not a good guest at the best of times. Impatient to return to the Arcanum, where he could study the books on contramagic at his leisure and not worry about their safety, the priest was irritable and demanding. He insisted on changing the location of his rooms three times before he found one that suited him.

Fortunately, the archbishop was an energetic, enthusiastic, zealous man who was so busy cleaning up the disreputable city of Westfirth and building his new cathedral that he had little time to fret over the peccadilloes of his eccentric guest. The archbishop was away most of the day, supervising the construction or marching into opium dens proclaiming the Word of God, leaving Father Jacob, Sir Ander, and Brother Barnaby to themselves.

The Old Fort was located at the bottom of a mountain that towered one hundred feet above the north entrance to the bay. At the top of the mountain was the Bastion, where dragons of the defunct Dragon Brigade had once resided. Once home to a local marquis and later to the Admiral of the Western Fleet, the Old Fort consisted of a castlelike structure with a great many drafty rooms that looked imposing, but which were actually cheerless, cold, and uncomfortable. The battlements extended out from the castle, running along the edge of a cliff, broken by watchtowers. Gun emplacements made of concrete had been built into the cliff face beneath the battlements. Ten forty-two-pound, long-barreled cannons guarded the entrance to Westfirth Bay, and a full score of sixty-four-pound, short-barreled cannons, known as frogs guarded the long guns.

At the very hour Stephano and Rodrigo were entering the café where they would encounter James Harrington,

Father Jacob and his friend, Sir Ander, were strolling the parapets overlooking the Breath. The view was magnificent, as Sir Ander noted.

Father Jacob paid no attention to Sir Ander or to the view. He walked the length of the parapet — from one guard tower to the other — then turned and walked back. His head was bowed, his hands clasped behind his back, his expression grim, his thoughts grimmer. Sir Ander had tried to keep up with him, but after the third time back and forth, the knight gave up. He leaned against the wall and gazed out at the naval gunboats patrolling the harbor.

The archbishop had stated gloomily that he'd heard from the grand bishop that war with Freya was imminent. The death of Ambassador de Villeneuve made war a certainty. The arrival of a large squadron of naval vessels two days ago meant that the king was about to declare war and was planning to shut down the port. Four thirty-two gun frigates were anchored near the mouth of the bay, along with one of King Alaric's new battleships, the *Royal Lion*, boasting two full gun decks. The lower deck mounted twenty cannons that each fired a twenty-eight-pound iron ball. Twenty cannons on the upper deck fired eighteen-pound balls. Twenty-four twelve-pound cannons were located on the main deck, the quarterdeck and the forecastle.

It was true King Alaric had sent the *Royal Lion* to West-firth, but not because he was about to declare war on Freya. The Countess de Marjolaine had urged the king to send the ships to Westfirth because she believed Sir Henry and the kidnapped journeyman were in that city. She had wanted King Alaric to shut down the port immediately, but the king was reluctant to take such a drastic step. Although the mere mention of the name of Sir Henry Wallace was enough to put him in a dark mood for days, Alaric could not justify shutting down the most lucrative port in the country. Nor was he ready to go to war with Freya.

The countess discovered a most unexpected ally in her arguments for shutting down the port: the grand bishop.

Montagne was fearful that ships sailing the Breath would
be attacked by the same demons that had attacked the abbey. The grand bishop had not told the king about the assault on the abbey. The grand bishop was not ready to do so
and he could always use as his excuse the fact that the Arcanum had placed the attack under Seal. Hearing that the
countess recommended closing the port of Westfirth, the
bishop astonished the king by agreeing with her. Beset from
both sides, Alaric still could not make up his mind.

Sir Ander watched the ships sailing through the light
morning mists and thought about his godson, Stephano. The
knight was curious to know why Stephano and his interesting and diverse collection of friends had come to Westfirth.
Sir Ander wondered if Stephano was here on some mission
for his mother. That led him to the thoughts of Cecile.

The musings of both men were interrupted by Brother
Barnaby, who came hastening along the parapet, his robes
blowing in the light breeze, his tonsured head glistening in
the sunshine. Brother Barnaby waited in patient silence until Father Jacob, pacing the parapets, became aware of the
monk's presence, which he did only when he almost stepped
on him.

"What?" Father Jacob demanded, scowling.

"This came for you, Father," said Brother Barnaby, holding out a note.

Father Jacob took the note, unfolded it, scanned it. His
brows rose. He read the note again, then handed it to Sir
Ander.

> *You seek the Warlock. I can tell you where to find*
> *him. Meet me at Bitter End Lane this evening when the*
> *clock chimes six. Bring the knight if you are distrustful,*
> *but no one else.*

The note was not signed.

Sir Ander grunted and handed it back. "You know what
I would say to this."

"Yes," said Father Jacob. "And you know what I would say in return, so let's move on from there."

He examined the note carefully. "This was written by a woman. Note the feminine nature of the curling tails of the 'g's' and the grace of the 'm's' and 'n's.'"

"Another of the Warlock's conquests," Sir Ander suggested. "Perhaps a young woman who managed to escape him."

"Perhaps," said Father Jacob, still studying the missive. "But I don't think it likely. There is evidence of a forceful personality in the firm pressure on the paper. Bold courage flows from the capital letters and self-confidence abounds in her sentence structure."

"We both know of one woman who fits that description," said Sir Ander.

Brother Barnaby looked from one man to the other and his expression grew grave.

"You mean the Sorceress, Mistress Eiddwen," said Father Jacob.

"But if that is true, Father, you must not go," Brother Barnaby said anxiously. "It might be a trap."

"Bah! Not in broad daylight in a public place," said Father Jacob. "And she says I may bring Sir Ander with me."

"But if it is her, why this meeting? Why betray her young disciple?" Sir Ander asked, frowning.

"I can think of many reasons," said Father Jacob. "For one, he may be on the verge of betraying her."

"Or perhaps she feels the heat of the Arcanum's fire and wants to try to make a deal," said Sir Ander.

"Or perhaps she wants to kill you, Father," said Brother Barnaby unhappily.

"We can stand here and speculate all day," said Father Jacob. "Or we can go this evening and find out."

He rubbed his hands and smiled broadly. "What time is it? Near dinnertime, I hope. I'm starving."

He thrust the note into the sleeve of his black cassock and walked rapidly and energetically along the parapet, his black robes whipping in the wind.

"Don't worry, Brother," said Sir Ander, resting a reassuring hand on Brother Barnaby's arm. "I'll be with him. Let us count our blessings. This mysterious assignation has cheered him up. He'll be much easier to live with now that he has something else to think about besides demons and giant bats."

"He'll be easier to live with only if he lives," said Brother Barnaby. "Can't you stop him, sir?"

Sir Ander extended his arm. "See those naval warships out there in the Breath, Brother. You could line them all up, open their gunports, and aim their cannons at him, and you still won't stop Father Jacob once he's set his mind on something."

Brother Barnaby conceded, with a sigh, that this was true. "At least you'll be with him, sir. I will pray for you both."

"Ah, you know, Brother, I sometimes wonder if God himself doesn't shake His head in despair over Father Jacob," said Sir Ander.

Brother Barnaby was shocked by this statement, but he reflected that Sir Ander was a military man. Allowances must be made.

Chapter Thirty-Two

Love that steals your breath away, leaves you trembling at the lover's touch, soul-gripping passion: I celebrate love. Love is sometimes life-changing, occasionally mind-altering, and very often painful, but let us admit it, the tumble is always so delicious it is worth a broken heart.

—"Song to Love"
by Rodrigo de Villeneuve

RODRIGO HELPED THE BLOOD-COVERED STEPHANO along the pier that led to the *Cloud Hopper*, which was docked at the end of a long row of Trundler houseboats. The other Trundlers eyed them curiously as they passed, but no one said a word; Trundlers believing strongly that every person has a right to secrets. If questioned by the constables, the Trundlers would have sworn they had never seen a wounded man walking past their boats, even as they were mopping up the bloody trail he left in his wake. Fortunately, Rodrigo and Stephano had managed to evade the constables and no one thought to come questioning the Trundlers about two men who had, according to witnesses, been of gentle birth.

Miri, Gythe, and Dag had returned from their own errands and were already on board the houseboat, making repairs. When the ever-watchful mercenary saw his friends come limping toward the boat, Dag threw down his tools and drew his pistol and went to cover them.

"Anyone chasing you?"

"Undoubtedly," Rodrigo said cheerfully. "We seem to run into assassins at every turn. But no one is currently shooting at us, if that's what you mean."

Dag thrust his weapon back into his belt and helped assist Stephano on board.

"Good God, not again!" Miri exclaimed, glaring at him in exasperation. "What are you this time? Shot or stabbed or both?"

"Stabbed," said Rodrigo. "It is my considered medical opinion that his wounds are not serious. He was attacked with a steak knife."

"It was a sharp steak knife," Stephano said, grimacing as Dag and Rodrigo eased him into the chair.

"So you got into a fight with a butcher, did you?" Miri said. "Set him down and let me take a look."

Doctor Ellington strolled over to sniff at the blood. Dag, looking grim, gathered up the cat and tossed him down into the hold.

"It was that bastard who shot me and killed Valazquez and damn near sank the *Cloud Hopper*," said Stephano.

He caught his breath as Miri began to peel back his blood-stiffened shirt.

"I hope that son-of-a-bitch looks worse than you do," Dag said.

"Trust me, he does," Rodrigo assured him.

Gythe hovered near Stephano. She touched Miri's arm to draw her attention and began flashing hand signals.

"No, Gythe, dear," Miri answered her sister's silent communication. "I don't think we need send for Brother Barnaby—"

"We most certainly do not," said Stephano. "Oh, for the love of— Dag, stop her!"

He was too late. Gythe had caught up her skirts, run across the deck, and jumped off the boat onto the pier.

"She's gone to fetch the monk," Miri said. "She's clean out of her mind over that man! Dag, go with her, will you?

There'll be no reasoning with her, but you can at least see to it that she comes to no harm."

Dag thrust his pistol into his belt and ran to catch up with Gythe—not an easy task, for she was swift and light as a sparrow.

"Rigo, help Stephano down the stairs," said Miri. "Put him in my bed."

"He has all the luck," said Rodrigo with a sigh and a languishing gaze. "Would that it were *I* who had been stabbed with a steak knife."

"Keep up such nonsense and I'll accommodate you," Miri returned.

Stephano protested that he was feeling fine. Miri was adamant and ordered him into her cabin.

"You have to save me, Rigo. She's going to put that stinking goop on me," Stephano said in a low voice. "I avoided it the last time I was wounded because she didn't have the ingredients. But she's been shopping since then."

"Yes, well, maybe next time you and your little friends will think twice about playing with sharp objects," said Rodrigo.

Stephano sat down on the bed, still protesting. Miri ignored him and sent Rodrigo to fetch water. She took a mortar and pestle down from the shelf and began crushing leaves and seeds, whispering words in her own language as she worked to concoct her famous healing poultice.

"Did you find out anything about Alcazar?" Stephano asked, watching the proceedings with a gloomy air.

"Alcazar the baker has no brothers and his children are all daughters. Not a journeyman among them. The farrier is an orphan with no living relations. You were going to the docks to talk to the sailors. I don't suppose you made it that far."

"Rigo wanted to visit his tailor first," said Stephano.

"As if that man didn't have enough lavender waistcoats!" Miri said, sniffing in disdain, pounding the concoction vigorously.

"He ordered a suit of mourning clothes," said Stephano quietly.

Miri stopped her work and turned to face him. Her voice was soft with pity and remorse. "There now! I had forgotten. His poor murdered father."

"Don't say anything to him, Miri. He doesn't need us moping about."

"I won't. Still it must be hard—him not able to go to his own father's funeral."

Stephano shook his head. "All my fault."

"It's not, love," said Miri, leaving her work to go comfort him. She rested her hand on his shoulder. "You know that."

"I'd like to blame my mother, but it was *my* decision to come to Westfirth. And what good has it done us? We find out that Alcazar was most likely nabbed by Sir Henry Wallace and then I go and kill his agent, the one man who might have led us to Wallace. And now I'm not sure I want to find him or if I want him to find us. Even my mother fears him, and she fears nothing this side of Hell. Maybe we should give up, sail home."

"As if you'd ever go back to your mother and tell her you failed."

Miri gave Stephano a pat, then returned to her mixing, only to find Doctor Ellington with his head in the bowl and yellow poultice on his nose and whiskers.

"You wicked cat, get out of there!" Miri cried angrily, grabbing up a wooden spoon.

The Doctor saw Miri coming and lunged for safety. Miri made a swipe at him with the spoon, but missed. The cat landed on the deck, sneezed violently, and began rubbing frantically at his face with his paw. He sneezed again and dashed wildly from the room.

"You daft beast!" Miri called after him.

"Talking to me?" Rodrigo asked, wrestling with the water bucket and almost falling over the cat.

In answer, Miri put her arms around him, gave him a tender hug, and kissed him on the cheek.

"What is that for?" Rodrigo asked, astonished.

"For being a daft beast," Miri said.

She picked up the bowl and carried it over to Stephano, who was eyeing it grimly. "Bring the water over here, Rigo. And fetch the bandages."

Rodrigo set down the bucket and, gagging, used his sleeve to cover his nose. Miri pulled off Stephano's shirt and scooped up a glob of yellowish-gray goo.

"This is going to sting," she warned.

"Don't worry, Stephano" said Rodrigo in muffled tones. "You won't feel a thing. The smell will knock you unconscious first."

In the corridor outside the door, they could all hear the unmistakable sounds of a cat throwing up.

Gythe and Dag returned with Brother Barnaby late in the afternoon. Clocks all over the city were striking the hour of five when Miri and Rodrigo, who were entertaining Stephano, heard footfalls on the deck above. Stephano was sitting up in bed, playing a game of draughts with Rodrigo. At the sound of the monk's voice, he grimaced.

"I'm already covered in yellow stinking goop. I don't need God," said Stephano irritably. "Send the monk away."

"And hurt Gythe's feelings? I will not and neither will you," said Miri. "You'll behave."

"The good brother could say a prayer for Doctor Ellington," suggested Rodrigo.

The cat sat huddled in an orange ball on the floor, his fur all askew. Hearing his name, he gave a pathetic meow.

"Greedy animal," said Miri severely. "Serves him right for eating my poultice!"

The Doctor gave another pitiful yowl and began to heave, just as Brother Barnaby entered. He looked from the vomiting cat to Stephano, swathed in bandages and stinking to high heaven, to Rodrigo who had tied a handkerchief over his face to block out the smell.

"Which is the patient?" Brother Barnaby asked.

Rodrigo and Stephano pointed to the cat.

Gythe entered the room and, picking up the poor Doctor, she pointed emphatically at Stephano.

"I'm fine, Gythe, really—"

Gythe looked to Brother Barnaby and then gestured again at Stephano, who opened his mouth, caught Miri's eye, and meekly submitted to the monk's examination.

"He has no fever. Your poultice is doing its work well, Mistress Miri," said Brother Barnaby. "I could say a prayer . . ."

Stephano snorted. "If you're going to say a prayer, Brother, say it for the black soul of the bastard I killed today."

Brother Barnaby looked startled. A shadow crossed his face.

"He's trying to shock you, Brother," said Rodrigo. "The fight was a fair fight. The man he killed drew a pistol and tried to kill us."

"I will pray for all of you," Brother Barnaby said. Seeing Stephano grimace, the monk added with a gentle smile, "It won't hurt, I promise."

Stephano submitted to being prayed over with no very good grace. Miri stood close to him, ready to pinch him if he started to say anything untoward. She listened to the monk's prayer, to him pouring his soul out to God, his voice fervent and passionate, and she stole a glance at her sister. Gythe was watching Brother Barnaby, pouring her soul out to him from her lustrous eyes.

Miri sighed deeply. She was a skilled healer. She could heal almost every kind of ache known to man except the terrible pain of a broken heart. Some men who had taken vows of celibacy might be tempted to break them for love of a woman. Brother Barnaby was not one of them. Her sister was going to be hurt. There was no way to avoid it.

"There, that wasn't too bad, was it, Captain?" Brother Barnaby said soothingly when the prayer ended.

Stephano grunted and scratched.

"Damn stuff's starting to itch," he said.

"Your turn to draw a card," said Rodrigo. "Would you like to join us, Brother?"

Gythe touched Brother Barnaby's hand, making a sign to thank him. He gave her a smile and assured her the captain was going to be fine. She seemed about to say something else and Miri was wondering how to get the monk alone to talk to him when Dag provided the excuse.

"Hey, who poisoned my cat?" he yelled from the deck above.

"Go see to the Doctor, Gythe," said Miri. "Tell Dag the wicked beast ate some of my potion and he will be fine once he gets it out of his system."

Gythe cast a last, shy look at Brother Barnaby and then ran up the stairs to placate Dag and do what she could for the suffering cat. Stephano and Rodrigo went back to their game of draughts. Miri led the monk into the passageway. She noticed that he seemed downcast, preoccupied. His brow was furrowed, his eyes shadowed. He was about to climb the stairs leading to the deck above when Miri stopped him. She thought she knew what was wrong.

"Brother, I want to apologize for my sister," said Miri, embarrassed. "I know she is making a nuisance of herself. She means no harm, truly. I will see to it that she does not continue to annoy you—"

She stopped talking because Brother Barnaby was regarding her in astonishment, clearly perplexed by her words.

"Your sister is not a nuisance, Mistress Miri. I was glad to come with her—"

"My sister is in love with you, Brother," said Miri bluntly.

He stared at her in round-eyed disbelief. His dark-complected face flushed darker in wonder and confusion.

"In love . . . with me." He gave a shy smile and shook his head. "You must be mistaken, Mistress. How could Mistress Gythe be in love with me? She is as beautiful as an angel in a painting and I am . . . I am not well-favored."

"You found Gythe in the darkness when she was lost and afraid, Brother. You must have looked very beautiful to her then."

Brother Barnaby considered her words for his expression grew somber. Miri heard the pain in his voice.

"I am honored by your sister's love," he said at last. "Honored and undeserving of the honor."

He raised his eyes to meet hers. Miri saw his faith, heard his commitment, deep and steadfast.

"I am given to God, Mistress Miri."

Miri, who had been holding out a little sliver of hope, sighed deeply.

"I did not mean to wound you, Brother. I thought you should know. Gythe has never fallen in love with any man before. She is bound to be hurt."

"I'm sorry," he said in soft agony.

"No need to apologize, Brother. The good God knows it is not your fault," said Miri.

They both walked up to the deck. Gythe was holding the miserable Doctor in her arms, petting him and rubbing her cheek against his. Her fair hair ruffled in the breeze and shone in the sun, gleaming like a halo around her head. Like an angel in a painting.

"It would be best if you did not see her again, Brother," said Miri.

"I understand," said Brother Barnaby unhappily. "I want to assure you that I truly never meant to be the cause of any harm to her."

A bad business, Miri thought to herself. The monk has not escaped unscathed. He is hurt, knowing that he has inadvertently hurt her. Gythe saw her sister's troubled gaze resting on her and looked from Miri to Brother Barnaby. She knew that they had been talking about her. Perhaps she even guessed what they had been saying. She kissed Doctor Ellington on the top of his head, handed him back to Dag, and then, with a defiant expression on her face, walked over to confront them. Brother Barnaby's confusion increased as she approached.

"Captain de Guichen is doing well, Mistress Miri," he said, his eyes on the deck. He began to sidle toward the gangplank. "I should take my leave."

"Of course, Brother," said Miri, hurrying him along. "Thank you for coming."

Gythe planted herself in front of them. She gave Miri a reproachful look and, pointing to Brother Barnaby, she began to gesture, making signs with her hand. She placed her fingertips on his mouth and then touched her ears and then touched her forehead. She made the sign for "papa." She clasped her arms around her, shivered as though in fear. She pointed again at Brother Barnaby.

"What is she saying?" he asked.

"Gythe tells me that you are afraid, Brother. Not for yourself. For Papa Jake. You're afraid he is in danger."

Brother Barnaby stared dumbfounded at Gythe. "That is true. I *am* afraid for Father Jacob. I believe him to be in great danger, but how could she know?"

"Who's in danger?" Dag asked, coming to join them.

"Papa Jake," said Miri. "At least, that's what Gythe says."

"It is true," said Brother Barnaby. "Father Jacob received a note summoning him to a mysterious meeting at a dock-yard near a street with a strange name—Bitter Taste or something like that—"

"Bitter End Lane," said Dag, his expression darkening.

"Yes, that's it. Why?" Brother Barnaby faltered. "What's wrong?"

"Bitter End Lane is aptly named," said Dag grimly. "People who go there have a bad habit of meeting a bitter end."

"Then it *is* a trap!" Brother Barnaby said in dismay.

"It might be. Is Sir Ander with the priest?"

"Yes, of course. He would never leave him, and the note said Father Jacob could bring a friend."

"Then there's probably nothing amiss," Dag said, though he was still clearly worried. "I'm thinking I should go check on them. . . ."

He looked questioningly at Miri.

"A good idea," said Miri. "What time was the meeting, Brother?"

"When the clock chimes six."

Dag squinted at the sun. "We have time, then. Bitter End Lane is not far. I'll fetch my musket. Gythe, dear, see to the Doctor for me."

Gythe removed Doctor Ellington from Dag's shoulder. The cat's poor stomach was rumbling louder than he could purr, but the Doctor undoubtedly knew he was destined to go back in the storage closet and he dug his claws into the big man's shoulder. Gythe was finally forced to seize hold of the cat by the scruff of the neck and pry him loose. He squirmed free of her grasp, jumped to the deck, and made a dash for his hiding place beneath the cannon.

"How could your sister know what I was thinking?" Brother Barnaby asked.

In answer, Gythe walked up to him and touched her fingers to his forehead. Taking up his hand, she placed his fingers on her forehead and smiled tremulously. Tears shimmered in her eyes. She made a motion as of leaving, and another as of staying.

"It's called 'sympathetic magic,'" said Rodrigo, coming up the stairs in time to overhear the end of the conversation. "A bit out of the ordinary, but not uncommon, particularly when you take into account the fact that Gythe is a savant and you, Brother, are an extremely talented healer. She formed a connection to you. It's all about electricity, really."

Gythe blinked her eyes, bemused by this explanation, while Brother Barnaby seemed to find the part about electricity more alarming than helpful. They were interrupted by Dag coming up on deck with his musket, powder horn, bullets, and Stephano.

"I couldn't stop him," said Dag, catching Miri's accusing look.

Stephano walked across the deck. He was favoring his bandaged thigh, but the wound had not been deep and he could walk easily enough. He was wearing only his trousers and more bandages wrapped around his ribs and his shoulder. He reeked of poultice. Rodrigo coughed and moved downwind.

"Dag says the priest could be in some sort of trouble," said Stephano.

"It's probably my imagination," said Brother Barnaby, abashed.

"The brother and I will just go take a look," said Dag.

"Fine," said Stephano. "I'm going with you. Give me half a second to fetch my shirt and sword—"

He ran down below. Miri, her expression grim, walked over to the door, shut it, locked it, then planted herself in front of it and leaned against it. They could hear Stephano's muffled swearing as he began beating on the door with his fists.

"Best hurry," said Miri coolly, not moving.

Dag grinned and picked up his musket. He was already carrying two loaded pistols in his belt. He and Brother Barnaby left in haste. Miri watched the two depart, whispering a heartfelt prayer for their safety and for Papa Jake.

"And, Daiddo," she added, referring to God by the Trundler's affectionate term for "grandfather," which is how she tended to think of Him, "if you could see to it that Brother Barnaby goes back to his monastery and stays there forever more, I would be eternally grateful."

She opened the hatch. Stephano glared furiously at her. She herded him down the stairs.

"There, now," she said, pointing to a splotch of blood spreading on the bandage around his shoulder. "You've broken open the wound. Gythe, I need your help."

"The monk prayed over me," Stephano said, as she began to strip off the bandages. "I'm fine."

"Gythe," Miri called, "I need you."

No response. No sound of skirts rustling and feet running down. Miri's heart lurched. She left Stephano and ran back up the stairs, shoving aside Rodrigo, who had been coming down to join them.

"Gythe!"

Her sister was not on deck.

Miri dashed back down the stairs. Stephano was arguing with Rodrigo, who was trying to persuade him to go back to bed.

"Stephano, you have to stop her!" Miri cried. "Gythe's gone after Brother Barnaby!"

Chapter Thirty-Three

We are all born with a spark of God's grace within our souls. Those who follow the path of the Fallen have found ways to steal that spark and corrupt it to their dark purposes. Those who practice blood magic use the spark of life to power their evil spells.

—Saint Marie Elizabeth,
First Provost of the Arcanum

THE ARCHBISHOP LOANED SIR ANDER AND Father Jacob his carriage and driver to take them to the mysterious rendezvous. Father Jacob would have told the driver outright to take them to Bitter End Lane. The more prudent Sir Ander insisted that they find some place near the lane so that they could approach with caution, not leap straight into an ambush. The knight made inquiries among the soldiers manning the walls of the Old Fort and came up with a suitable location.

"Take us to the *Dirk and Dragon* on Silk Street," Sir Ander said, assisting Father Jacob into the carriage.

The driver looked startled. "But that's a tavern, sir."

"A tavern filled with sinners needing to be saved, my son," said Father Jacob solemnly.

The driver was dubious. The archbishop certainly never went near such places. He had no thought of questioning a priest of the Arcanum, however. He whipped up the horses, and the carriage rattled off.

Inside the carriage, Sir Ander sat bolt upright, perched on the edge of his seat, his back straight. He kept fast hold of the hand strap and stared grimly out the window. He was armed with his dragon pistol and one of his nonmagical pistols and his broadsword.

"You know I don't like this," he stated.

Father Jacob was relaxed, leaning back against the comfortable cushions, his legs crossed beneath the long, black cassock, his arms crossed over his chest. He was gazing out the window.

"You think I do?" he asked.

"Yes," said Sir Ander bluntly. "Anonymous notes. Mysterious assignations. Streets with ominous-sounding names. You damn well know you're enjoying this!"

Father Jacob gave a smile. "Perhaps I do—a little. And for your information, the term 'Bitter End' is not ominous. It is a nautical term referring to the end of a rope."

Sir Ander snorted, clearly not placated. "And we may have reached the end of *our* rope. I've asked around. Bitter End Lane has an evil reputation. It is only a block long. It runs between an abandoned warehouse on the south side and a balloon maker on the north. This time of night, the neighborhood will be empty. Ideal location for an ambush."

"Or a meeting with someone who doesn't want to be seen," said Father Jacob. He saw Sir Ander's frown and he added in mollifying tones, "I agree with you about the danger, my friend. But if there is a chance this woman might lead us to the Warlock, we must take the risk."

Sir Ander sighed, shook his head, and reassuringly slid his hand inside his magically reinforced coat to touch the dragon pistol resting in its holster. Father Jacob was armed, as well. His weapons were his magic.

The carriage rolled up in front of the *Dirk and Dragon*. Work had ended for the day. The crafters and sail makers, rope makers and balloon makers, stevedores and wood wrights, naval engineers and architects filled the dockyard taverns. The clientele in the *Dirk and Dragon* actually spilled out into the street, with working men and women lounging in the shadows cast by the westering sun, pledging each other's health in foaming mugs of ale and discussing the day's events.

The crowd recognized the seal of the archbishop on the side panel of the carriage and met the carriage with wide grins and crude comments. The archbishop's plan to "clean up" the city was not being well received among the tavern owners and their customers. For the moment the archbishop was more concerned with shutting down the opium dens and houses of prostitution, but the members of the Tavern League were certain they were next.

Sir Ander and Father Jacob told the carriage driver not to wait, for which he was thankful, given that the carriage was now surrounded by what he considered a drunken mob. He was off before the priest and Sir Ander had fairly set their feet to the ground. The remarks from the onlookers ceased at the sight of the priest and the knight. Sir Ander swept aside his coat to reveal the butt-end of the dragon pistol. The broadsword clanked against his thigh. But it was Father Jacob in the black cassock of the Arcanum that caused the crowd to bury their noses in their ale mugs and sidle off.

Silk Street ran north and south, parallel to Canal Street, which was a block over. Father Jacob and Sir Ander proceeded down the street, which was named for the warehouses where the silk fabric needed in the construction of balloons was stored. The warehouses were almost identical, about four or five stories tall, built of brick and mortar and magic. The front of the warehouses opened onto the street. The back faced the canal, where the bales of silk—double wrapped in jute—were loaded onto barges.

The warehouses blocked out the sunlight and though night had not yet fallen, Silk Street was dark with shadows. The doors to the warehouses were padlocked. Sir Ander tried peering into several windows, but they were coated with dirt and grime and apparently never opened. Sir Ander could see very little. Whenever there was a gap between warehouses, they could catch a glimpse of the busy canal, crowded with barges, and the mists of the Breath beyond.

Sounds of talk and laughter from the tavern faded away. The street was silent save for their footfalls that echoed in the chasm formed by the buildings. Sir Ander followed their progress by the street names which were located on the corners of the buildings. Bitter End Lane was only a block long and ran east-west to Silk Street that ran north-south. Silk Street continued on, eventually ending at the canal.

Keeping to the shadows, Father Jacob and Sir Ander stared intently down the length of Bitter End Lane. They had deliberately arrived early, before the proposed meeting time. They watched and listened, but saw nothing, heard nothing out of the ordinary.

Clocks throughout the city began to chime six times. Sir Ander drew his dragon pistol and indicated with a nod that Father Jacob was to precede him. Father Jacob walked into Bitter End Lane, moving confidently and slowly, allowing himself to be seen. Sir Ander came behind, his gaze sweeping the street ahead and behind.

A figure, murky in the twilight, entered from the opposite end of the lane. Father Jacob could not make out much in the indistinct light, but he judged by the person's height and the way he walked this was a man, not a woman. The stranger wore a greatcoat, a tricornered hat, and carried a leather satchel. The man saw Father Jacob at the same time the priest saw him and halted.

Father Jacob cautioned Sir Ander, who had also seen the man, to keep his distance. Sir Ander slowed his pace, but he kept within firing range and made certain the stranger got a good look at his pistol. Father Jacob advanced cautiously to meet the man, who advanced cautiously to meet him. The two came face-to-face in the gathering gloom and stopped.

Each spoke a single word. "You!"

Father Jacob and Sir Henry Wallace stood staring at each other in profound astonishment for a split second, both of them wondering what was going on. The answer was, sadly, simple to figure out.

"This is a trap," said Father Jacob.

"I believe you are right," said Sir Henry.

A woman's voice, frightened, terror-stricken, called out, "Mister, please help me!"

Sir Ander heard the voice and turned to see a young woman running toward him from the direction of Silk Street. Her bodice was ripped, her skirts torn. Her hair was unbound and flew around her pale face. Her eyes were wide and filled with fear. Her hands were outstretched, beseeching his aid. She had blood on her face and her bosom, her hands and her arms.

"Help me!" she cried. "Please help me!"

"Ander, no!" Father Jacob cried, but he was too late.

The wraith, shining with an eerie red incandescence, flung her arms around Sir Ander, sending jolts, like a thousand fire-tipped needles, surging through the knight's body. He could not scream, for the pain was in his lungs and his throat. He could not move. The wraith held him fast, paralyzing him. The cocked pistol fell from his twitching fingers to the street and fired the bullet, causing it to glance off the paving stones. Sir Ander crashed to the ground, as two orange-eyed demons appeared on the warehouse rooftop where they had been hiding.

Sir Henry Wallace had changed out of the black robes of a lawyer on the way to the meeting. Not trusting Eiddwen, he had put on a magically protected vest beneath a magically protected knee-length coat and covered that with a magically protected greatcoat. Thus attired, he had gone to the meeting site, where he was astounded and most seriously displeased to encounter his old enemy, Father Jacob Northrop. Sir Henry's first thought was to wonder how the priest knew Eiddwen. His second thought was the realization this did not matter since they were both about to die.

Their assailant had taken care to attack the well-armed knight early in the assault. The use of a wraith was suggestive; their foe was a wielder of dark magic. Eiddwen's underlings sometimes referred to her as the "Sorceress," but she had told him she did not like to use magic, terming it "messy" and "wayward."

"I like to be in control of a situation," Eiddwen had said. "Once you let loose a magic spell, you have no idea what is going to happen. I much prefer shooting people."

Sir Henry looked up and down the lane to see if he could find the wielder of the dark magic. Was it Eiddwen herself or one of her minions? Undoubtedly a minion. She wouldn't want to dirty her hands. The dark magic user needed to keep the victim in sight in order to control the wraith. Sir Henry caught a glimpse of movement coming from his left, near where he had entered Bitter End Lane.

A young man, handsome, wearing a long night-blue leather coat, stood with his back against the building. This must be the Warlock of whom Sloan had spoken, terming him "depraved." Judging by his smile, the Warlock was pleased with himself. He raised his hand, controlling the magic, guiding the wraith. His fingers had been dipped in blood. The conjuration of a wraith required a blood sacrifice. The knight lay where he had fallen, his body twitching.

"Take cover!" Father Jacob shouted.

Henry looked up to see a ball of green fire heading straight for him. He ducked behind his leather satchel, holding it over his head to shield his face from the blast.

The green fireball struck the satchel in a cascade of sparks that rained down around him. The satchel burst into flames, the leather dissolving as though it had been hit by acid. The leather had been covered inside and out with sigils and constructs. The magic would withstand gunfire, white magic, and even blood magic. Every sort of magic except contramagic.

"Shit! Bloody hell!" Sir Henry swore angrily when the flames reached his fingers, burning him. He flung the blazing satchel to the street. It landed with a metallic clatter. The pewter tankard that had been inside the satchel clattered onto the cobblestones. Henry risked burnt fingers to snatch it out of the flames. He was about to hide the tankard beneath his greatcoat, then realized it was on fire.

Tearing off the great coat, Henry looked up at the top of the warehouse and saw what appeared to be two fiends from Hell staring down at him. "Demons with glowing orange eyes shooting balls of green fire." Sir Henry muttered an apology to Mr. Sloan for not believing him as he searched for cover. Of course, there was none. Not a barrel, not a recessed doorway, nothing. Eiddwen had chosen the site for the ambush well. Henry drew his pistol. Beside him, Father Jacob was waving his hands, surrounding himself with blue light.

"Here! With me!" Father Jacob shouted, motioning to Sir Henry.

If there was one man Sir Henry was glad to have at his back during a fight with the forces of Hell, it would be Jacob Northrup. Henry had gone up against the priest enough times to know his worth. Keeping hold of the pewter tankard, Henry dove behind the protective shield of the blue light as another blast of green fire flew from the rooftop.

The fireball hit the blue glowing shield with a concussive force that left Henry half-blind, dazed, with ears ringing, but otherwise not injured. The same could not be said of Father Jacob. He was doubled over, gasping in pain. Henry noted that the blue light no longer glowed quite as brightly.

"Who are these fiends?" Henry demanded.

"I was going to ask you the same question," Father Jacob gasped.

Henry grunted. "So that is why you saved my life?"

"All life is precious in the eyes of God," said Father Jacob and he added, with the hint of a smile, "Even that of the snake."

Sir Henry drew his pistol and searched for a target on the rooftop, but the demons were well out of range. He could see them at work up there, perhaps reloading their infernal weapon.

"I'm going to try to reach Sir Ander," said Father Jacob, straightening. "I must counteract the wraith's spell, or she will kill him."

"I'll cover you," Henry offered.

Father Jacob gave a grim chuckle. "How many times have you tried to kill me? I lost count at six."

"The enemy of my enemy . . . all that rot," said Sir Henry.

Father Jacob shook his head, still skeptical, but he didn't have much choice if he wanted to save the knight. As the priest prepared to make a run for the spellbound knight, Henry was at his back.

"Wait!" Henry yelled.

Another fireball sizzled down from the roof and slanted off the blue glowing shield. The blast shook the ground, cracking the paving stones. Father Jacob cried out, staggered and almost fell. Henry steadied the priest with his hand. The blue glow was definitely fading.

"How long can you keep this up?" Henry asked.

"Not long, I'm afraid," said Father Jacob, wiping his mouth on the sleeve of his cassock.

"That last blast took out the wraith, at least," Sir Henry observed.

"So it did," said Father Jacob with interest. "Though I don't think it was meant to."

The wraith had vanished. Henry glanced at the Warlock. The young man had emerged from the corner of the building and was shouting angrily at those on the roof.

The two demons behind their cannon paid no heed. They were taking aim, and Henry braced himself for the next attack. Green fire burst on the blue shield. The blue light vanished. Father Jacob cried out, fell to the street, and lay there, moaning.

The blast knocked Henry off his feet and left him with an unpleasant buzzing sound in his ears. His knees were bruised and bleeding. He had dropped the tankard, but he was still clutching the pistol. His hand was covered in blood where a sharp edge on the trigger had cut deeply into the fleshy part of his palm. He looked over at the priest. Father Jacob lay unmoving, either unconscious or dead.

"Thank you for saving my life, Jacob," Henry said, rising to his feet. "Sorry I can't return the favor."

He grabbed the pewter tankard, cast a glance at the roof-top, and began running.

The Warlock was still standing at the end of the street, peering out from behind the corner of a building with some intention of attempting to recast his spell. Tendrils of energy curled from his hands, sparking and shining. But the tendrils were going nowhere and he was growing frustrated. Engrossed in his magic, he did not see Sir Henry. The Warlock's two demon bodyguards saw him, however. They stepped out from behind the building.

Henry swore and skidded to a halt and raised his hands—one holding the tankard, the other the pistol. This was his first close look at the demons. Sir Henry stared entranced at their hideous faces, the orange-glowing eyes, the leather armor that covered them from head to toe. He had to use all his considerable self-control to drag his attention back to the Warlock.

"I need to talk to Eiddwen!" Henry called. "I have vital information! Tell these fiends to let me pass."

"Eiddwen would like to talk to you," the Warlock said. He was obviously frustrated, unable to understand why his magic wasn't working. He glanced at the demons. "Seize him. Take him alive."

The two demons had other ideas, apparently. They lifted some sort of cannon-type weapons and aimed them at Henry. Henry hurled the tankard at one demon and shot the other. One demon went down. The other demon fired. The green blast hit the tankard and seemed to evaporate. The demon began to reload.

"Duck, sir!" a deep voice shouted from behind.

Henry dropped to the ground and hugged the cobblestones. He heard a boom and the hiss of a bullet whizzing past. The demon toppled over backward, half its head blown off. Henry glanced around to see a big man dressed like a mercenary lowering a smoking musket.

Henry did not stop to thank his benefactor. He was on his feet before the echoes of the blast had faded away, grabbing the tankard that had save his life, and leaving the useless pistol in the street. Drawing the stowaway gun he had stashed in his belt, he aimed it at the young man.

The Warlock smiled, almost laughing. He wiggled his blood-covered fingers. His lips moved. Tendrils of magic snaked out toward Henry. He was going to become the victim of another wraith unless he acted quickly.

The Warlock wore a long blue leather coat that covered him from head to toe and fairly crackled with magical energy. His head was protected by a wide-brimmed leather hat, adorned with intertwining sigils. Bullets fired at him from the small gun did little damage. The Warlock was amused, confident, looking forward to watching his wraith envelop Henry in her lethal grip.

"Balls!" said Henry, and he shot the young man in the foot.

The magical tendrils disappeared. The wraith wavered and dissolved. The young man stared in disbelief at the blood seeping out from his boot onto the pavement.

"Next time, fool, remember to protect your boots," Henry said.

He drew his last pistol, another stowaway gun, snatched off the Warlock's protective hat, and placed the barrel on the young man's temple.

The Warlock's face flushed an ugly red spotted with white. He was quivering, not with fear, but with constrained fury. On the ground behind the Warlock was a body of a young woman. Her throat had been slit from ear to ear. Her mouth gaped, her eyes stared at nothing. Henry recognized her—the wraith. She had been the blood sacrifice. He was thankful he was carrying the gun.

Henry heard more explosions and saw flashes of green fire. Smoke filled the street and he could not see what had become of his old foe, Jacob Northrop. Henry assumed the priest was dead, but he didn't count on it. Father Northrop had a most annoying habit of coming back from the grave.

"Start moving!" Henry ordered the Warlock. He tapped him with the gun. "That way, down the alley."

"You shot me. I can't walk," the Warlock whined.

"It's only a toe. You've got nine more. Move," said Henry, and he cocked the pistol.

The Warlock heard the click near his ear and he began to limp off slowly, dragging his injured foot. Henry followed the Warlock down the alley, the muzzle of the gun pressing against the back of the young man's skull. Henry watched for glowing orange eyes, but apparently the demons were all engaged in the fight on Bitter End Lane. The alley was empty. When he reached Canal Street, Henry called a halt.

"On your knees," he ordered.

The young man did not obey. Instead, he turned boldly to face him. The sun had set. A pink afterglow lit the sky. Night had already come to the alley. The Warlock's white skin glimmered palely in the twilight. His mouth curled in an eerie grin. The lips were black, stained with blood, as were his teeth.

Henry was not a squeamish man, but his stomach clenched in revulsion. The young man had drunk his victim's blood. Henry placed the pistol on his forehead between his eyes.

"On your knees!"

"Go bugger yourself."

Henry kicked him, hard, in the kneecap. The Warlock groaned, staggered, and sank to the pavement. Henry pressed the muzzle of the gun against the young man's forehead.

"If you're going to kill me, then kill me," he said, his voice calm, strangely uncaring.

"Believe me, you little prick, I would like nothing better

than to kill you. But I need someone to take a message to Eiddwen and you're all I've got," said Henry. "First, what does she want with me?"

The Warlock's answer was a sneer.

Henry regarded him grimly. "Very well. Then tell her this. I'm no threat to her. I have no interest in her twisted affairs. And you can also tell her that if she ever tries to harm my family again, I will track her to the farthest ends of the seven continents. I will track her to the very depths of Hell if I must. And when I find her—and I *will* find her—she will be very, very sorry. You tell her that—when you wake up."

Henry slammed the pistol into the Warlock's face. He heard the crunch of bone. The young man fell unconscious. The next problem was what to do with him. It would never do for the constables to discover him.

The sight of a heavily laden barge creeping along in the canal gave Sir Henry an idea. He dragged the unconscious young man over to the side of the canal, waited for the barge to draw near. When the barge was directly underneath him, Henry tipped the Warlock over the side and watched him fall. The young man landed on a tarp-covered pile of whatever goods the barge was hauling. He lay there, unmoving, as the barge drifted slowly on its way. Sir Henry continued down Canal Street.

All this time, through smoke, green fire, and blood, Henry Wallace had kept hold of the pewter tankard, his key to the destruction of Rosia, providing proof that Alcazar had succeeded in producing magic-reinforced steel. Henry had a sudden, terrible thought. The tankard had taken a direct hit from the green fire. The magical sigils that reinforced the steel would have been destroyed, like the sigils in the leather satchel or those in his greatcoat—or those on board the ill-fated cutter, *Defiant*, when the ship had been attacked by the green-fire weapon. The tankard was now worthless. A prey to gloom, he stopped beneath a gas lamp and drew out a monocle set with magical sigils. He flicked the sigils with a fingernail, and they burst into glowing light. He held the monocle to the tankard.

"I'll be damned!" Sir Henry breathed, awed.

He did not believe his eyes. He ran his hands over the tankard's surface, the pewter's cold, smooth, unblemished surface.

The contramagic that had sunk a naval cutter and toppled a stone watchtower had no effect on this pewter tankard.

The astounding possibilities burst like a skyrocket in Sir Henry's brain. He did not have time to consider them. His cover was destroyed. Eiddwen knew he was in Westfirth. Father Jacob knew he was in Westfirth. The countess' bastard son, Stephano de Guichen, undoubtedly by now knew Sir Henry was in Westfirth.

Time to leave Westfirth, whether Pietro Alcazar liked it or not.

Dubois could have also been added to Sir Henry's list, because he knew Sir Henry was in Westfirth and he was elated. His persistence in following Stephano de Guichen had paid off, though not quite in the way Dubois had expected.

Fearing that time was running out and the chance to nab Sir Henry Wallace on Rosian soil would slip through his fingers, Dubois had made the desperate decision to take Stephano de Guichen into custody. Dubois would use the "murder" of James Harrington as an excuse to arrest Lord Captain de Guichen and interrogate him. Dubois was well aware that arresting the captain would be difficult, if not downright dangerous. He knew the captain's "Cadre" of comrades and their readiness to defend him. He also knew that the countess would shake Heaven and earth with her rage when she found out that her son had been arrested. Dubois spent the afternoon assembling a group of agents, all the while keeping watch on those who came and went from the *Cloud Hopper*.

When Gythe and Dag left the boat to go fetch Brother Barnaby, Dubois saw them depart, but paid no heed. He was still waiting for his agents to arrive to launch his assault. He had his men assembled and was just about ready to make the arrest, when Dag and Gythe returned with the monk in tow. Dubois recognized the monk. That morning, Dubois had gone to pay a visit to the archbishop, to deliver the grand bishop's orders, and he had observed the monk in company with Father Jacob Northrop of the Arcanum.

Dubois was startled and not pleased. Here was a question he could not answer. How did Father Jacob know Captain de Guichen? Were they friends? Was the captain working for the Arcanum now? If so, what would the Arcanum do if Dubois arrested Captain de Guichen? Dubois was prepared to deal with the fury of the Countess de Marjolaine, but he did not want to offend the Arcanum.

Brother Barnaby was a healer. The captain had probably sent for him to treat his wounds. That much, at least, made sense. Dubois was trying to make up his mind whether or not to proceed when the captain's mercenary friend and the monk left the boat, going somewhere in haste. The monk looked worried. The mercenary looked very grim and was armed to the teeth.

Dubois' nerves tingled. Something dire was happening and it might be connected with Sir Henry Wallace and the missing journeyman. Dubois was not quite sure how the monk fit into all this, but he would worry about that later. Leaving a number of his men to keep an eye on the *Cloud Hopper*, Dubois took with him one of his most trusted agents, a man known as Red Dog. The two followed Dag to Bitter End Street, arriving in the midst of the ambush.

Hearing explosions and the sound of gunfire and smelling smoke, Dubois and Red Dog took cover. Dubois peered out from behind a building and did not believe his eyes. He actually rubbed them to make certain he was not seeing things.

"God save us!" Red Dog gasped, joining him.

Father Jacob Northrop, priest of the Arcanum, his Knight Protector, and Sir Henry Wallace, the man for whom Dubois had been long searching were under attack—by fiends from Hell.

Dubois' neatly organized mind reeled, incapable of belief. He even wondered for an agonized moment if someone had slipped opium into his mutton stew. The sight of the calm and cool soldier, Dag, lifting his musket to his shoulder and firing at one of the demons, the sound of the shot and the acrid smell of gunpowder was all very real and prosaic and comforted Dubois. One look at his agent, whose eyes were bulging and mouth gaping, and Dubois realized that if this was a drug-induced dream, then they were both dreaming it. Knowing this to be impossible, Dubois felt better. His mind reverted back to its normal logical operation. He ignored everything else and concentrated on Sir Henry Wallace.

"He's on the move!" Dubois said, indicating Sir Henry. He shook his dazed agent, who was still staring at the demons. "Be quick!"

Sir Henry was at that moment marching the Warlock down the alley. Dubois and Red Dog followed from a safe distance. They watched Henry pistol-whip the young man and dump him onto the passing barge. They kept to the shadows as Sir Henry paused beneath the gas lamp to look at an object he'd been carrying; an object Dubois thought at first was another pistol. The light gleaming on pewter proved Dubois mistaken. Of all the amazing events of the evening, this was the most puzzling. Sir Henry had waded through hellfire and blood, and instead of fleeing for his life, he had stopped to study a pewter tankard. Dubois could make nothing of this, and it bothered him.

Sir Henry appeared extremely pleased with his tankard. He smiled all the way down Canal Street and chuckled to himself as he turned onto the Street of Saints. Every so often, he would glance behind to see if he was being followed. Dubois made certain Henry didn't see a thing.

Sir Henry came to a halt at the head of the Street of Saints. He removed the coat he'd been wearing, folded it carefully, and placed the coat over his arm, deftly using it to conceal the pewter tankard. Beneath the coat, he was wearing evening clothes, such as a gentleman might wear to pay a visit to one of the gambling houses: black velvet coat discreetly trimmed in dark red, black stockings with dark red aiguillettes at the knees, a white silk cravat. He had lost his hat in the battle. He drew a black silk mask from a pocket and tied it around his face, then walked briskly for about six blocks until he arrived at one of the city's more exclusive bordellos.

The clock in a nearby church chimed seven times. The hour was early; the house's clientele would not arrive until much, much later. Henry did not enter the house. He spoke to the doorman, who greeted him familiarly, despite the fact that Henry was wearing a mask. Those visiting such establishments often concealed their true identities.

Dubois moved closer, gliding behind a hedge in order to eavesdrop on the conversation. Sir Henry told a tale of having been waylaid by thieves. The doorman listened in shock and deprecated the lack of police vigilance in the city. Sir Henry wondered if he could be given a ride to his lodgings. The doorman replied that the bordello's carriage was always at the disposal of their favorite clients. The doorman summoned a page, who was sent round to the stables. Within moments, an enclosed carriage drove up to the front.

"Blue Parrot," the doorman told the driver, who was assisting Sir Henry to enter.

"He's getting away! Let's grab him now," said Red Dog, spoiling for some action.

"We can't. He has not broken any law," said Dubois.

"He's a goddam spy!" said Red Dog.

Dubois explained. "Henry Wallace is also a diplomat. We are not at war with Freya. Sir Henry would say he was here on business for his government and would claim diplomatic immunity. We need to catch him with the journeyman trying to flee the country. I'll follow Sir Henry. You go back, assemble the men, and meet me ..."

Dubois paused, thinking.

"At the Blue Parrot?" Red Dog asked.

"No, not there. Wallace might see us and give us the slip. We will meet at the Masons' Guildhall. It's a block north of the Parrot."

"What about Captain de Guichen? Should I leave people to watch his boat?"

"Forget him. He has served his purpose."

"What about them demons?" Red Dog asked.

Dubois had actually forgotten the demons in his excitement. He brought to mind the report the grand bishop had sent him. The nun had described the abbey's attackers as "demons hurling balls of green fire."

"We will deal with them later," said Dubois. To his mind, Sir Henry was the primary devil.

"I guess the boss'll take care of 'em," said Red Dog, referring to one of the heads of the criminal gangs that ran Westfirth.

Red Dog left to assemble his comrades. Dubois, who was *not* an exclusive customer of the bordello, had to summon his own cab. As he rolled off toward the Blue Parrot, Dubois reveled in his victory. At long last, he would have enough evidence to send Rosia's most dangerous foe, Sir Henry Wallace, to the gallows.

What were fiends from Hell compared to that!

Chapter Thirty-Four

In my years serving the Arcanum, I have seen enough evil in this world to know that we do not need the Devil to create Hell. Hell is the destruction of hope and the loss of faith brought on by man's inhumanity to man.

—Father Jacob Northrop

DAG AND BROTHER BARNABY WERE ON THEIR WAY to Bitter End Lane and were still several blocks away when they heard the first explosion and saw green fire light the sky.

"Demons!" Brother Barnaby gasped.

Dag shook his head and muttered, "Damn!" He had been planning to approach cautiously, holding back, not wanting to make his presence known until he first ascertained that Father Jacob was truly in danger.

No need for caution now. Dag broke into a run.

"Stay put, Brother!" he shouted behind him.

Brother Barnaby had no intention of staying anywhere. He paused only long enough to hike up the skirts of his long robes. Frantic with fear for Father Jacob and Sir Ander, he fumbled at the cloth. Suddenly other hands were helping him, deft fingers tucking folds of the hem securely into his belt.

Brother Barnaby looked into Gythe's blue eyes. Startled, he seized hold of her.

"Child, you shouldn't be here!" Brother Barnaby said in dismay.

Gythe's fingers were cold. She was shivering with fear. She shook her head, however, and gave him a tremulous smile. Wrenching free of his grasp, she ran after Dag.

"Gythe, come back!" Barnaby shouted.

Dag heard the monk's shout and glanced over his shoulder. Seeing Gythe running toward him, he scowled and motioned peremptorily that she was to keep out of the fight. Gythe stopped and stood in the middle of the street, staring in horror at the demons. Brother Barnaby caught up with her. Not knowing what else to do, he shoved her into a recessed doorway.

"You will be safe here," Barnaby said, praying he was right. "Stay until we come for you."

Gythe gave a shuddering nod and Barnaby left her to follow Dag into the smoke and fire.

Gythe remained crouched in the doorway where Brother Barnaby had told her to stay. She saw bright flashes of green light, but this time the magic didn't hurt her, not like when the magic was hitting the protective spells she'd woven around her boat. She had trusted that she and Miri and the others were safe on the boat with the spells wrapped around them, like silkworms in a silken cocoon. But then the cocoon had caught fire.

She ran away from the fire, hoping to find the time she had been happy and unknowing. But the world was dark. She couldn't find the path. And she could still feel the pain, no matter how far she ran. When the pain finally stopped, Gythe realized she didn't know how to get back. She huddled in the darkness, alone and terrified, and then she heard a man's voice, gentle and soothing, calling her name.

She was afraid to answer, but she hoped the man would find her, for he sounded warm and caring. She began to hum a little song to keep up her spirits, and the man heard the song and found her in her hiding place. A monk held out his hands to her, and she took his hands and he led her safely home.

But the monk had not been the only one to hear her song. Far, far, far away was a drumbeat, soft as a heartbeat, but not as steady. The beat was slow and erratic and frightening. And there were the voices far away as the drumbeat. The voices were not gentle. They were terrible voices: hurtful and cruel and filled with hatred.

The voices ebbed and flowed like the currents of the Breath. Here in the street the voices were suddenly strong, voices of fury and rage. Voices of killing. Blood and death and hatred.

Gythe began to hum a song, a little song. Whenever she sang in the park and played her harp, people stopped talking. They fell silent to listen. She hummed desperately, hoping the voices would fall silent and they would stop hurting her friends.

The voices didn't grow silent, but they changed. They sounded bewildered. They called to her. Like the demon who had come on board the ship. The demon had been trying to find her.

Gythe hummed her little song to try to drown out the sound of gunshots. She put her fingers into her ears and closed her eyes, and the voices were again talking about pain and death and hatred.

Accusing voices. "You left us to die here below!"

"It wasn't our fault!" Gythe wept, her silent voice answering all the others, those who were also silent. "We couldn't hear you. We didn't know . . ."

When Dag saw Father Jacob and Sir Ander lying in the street, he was certain they were dead. He could not see them clearly, with the smoke swirling about, but neither man was moving. Dag had made a swift assessment of the situation as he came up on it. Two demons were on the rooftop of a warehouse with what appeared to be a mounted swivel gun. They had not yet seen him. At the end of the lane, a man stood with his hands in the air. Two demons were in front of him, their weapons aimed at him. He was obviously pleading for his life. In a bold move, the man fired at one of the demons and threw whatever he'd been holding in his other hand at the second demon.

Dag did not know this man, but any enemy of the demons was a friend of Dag's. He shouted for the man to duck. The stranger reacted with a speed which indicated he'd done this sort of thing before. He hit the pavement. Dag fired his musket and had the satisfaction of seeing half a demon's head dissolve into a bloody mess. The man was on his feet before the smoke cleared. The man fired another pistol at someone who had apparently been hiding in the alley and then kept on going, leaving Dag and his friends to fend for themselves.

Dag shrugged. He supposed he couldn't blame the gentleman. He looked up to see the demons training their swivel gun on him and made a backward scramble to take cover against the same warehouse the demons were using to mount their assault. Expecting grapeshot, Dag was startled to see the swivel gun shoot a ball of green fire. The flames struck the pavement right where he had been standing. The blast flattened Dag back against the wall. Smoke stung his eyes; chunks of cobblestones slammed into him. Fortunately, his steel breastplate protected him from the worst.

Dag swiftly and expertly reloaded the musket and looked up to see what the demons were doing. They had mounted the swivel gun on the roof directly above him. The demons could look down and see him, but they could not bring their weapon to bear on him. Dag had counted on this when he chose his cover. Seeing their heads poking over the edge, Dag fired the musket. The heads vanished.

Dag reloaded. So long as he stood in this place, directly beneath the swivel gun, the demons could not hit him. The moment he moved, the green fireballs would blow him apart. He was considering his options when suddenly he didn't have any.

Brother Barnaby came running into Bitter End Lane, heading straight for Father Jacob. Dag looked up to see the gun's muzzle swinging about, taking aim at the monk. Dag swore roundly and fired the musket at the demons. Not waiting to see if he'd done any damage, he slung the gun by its strap over his shoulder, lowered his head, and charged across the street. He slammed into Brother Barnaby and they both went down. Dag shielded the monk with his body as a green fireball exploded in the air above them. Dag could feel the heat radiate through his armor.

He scrambled quickly to his feet. Brother Barnaby was dazed, probably wondering what had hit him. Dag seized hold of the monk by the collar of his habit and dragged him into the shadows of a building, hoping without much hope that they were out of range of the swivel gun. Once there, Dag let loose of the monk and took the opportunity to re-load the musket.

"You all right, Brother?"

Brother Barnaby was bleeding from a gash where his head had hit the stones. He winced when he tried to stand. His body would be one massive bruise tomorrow. If they lived that long.

Barnaby nodded and said shakily, "I have to go to Father Jacob."

Glancing up at the roof, Dag saw the two demons huddled over the swivel gun. They should again have fired by now. Perhaps there was something wrong with it. Nice to know Hell was fallible.

"Go, Brother, if you must! Be quick. I'll keep you covered."

Barnaby ran to Father Jacob while Dag kept an eye on the demons. He was cheered to see the priest lift his head at the sound of the monk's voice. Brother Barnaby put his arm around Father Jacob and helped him to stand. Both came running back to the building where Dag was standing with his musket, watching the demons.

"How is Sir Ander?" Father Jacob asked.

"I don't know," said Dag. "I thought I saw him move—"

"I'll go to him," said Brother Barnaby.

"Wait!" Dag grabbed hold of Brother Barnaby's arm.

The swivel gun was still on the roof, but the two demons were not.

"Maybe they've run off," said Brother Barnaby hopefully, eager to go to Sir Ander.

Dag grunted and kept fast hold of the monk.

It was well he did. Four demons emerged from the side street next to the warehouse. All four were armed, each of them carrying the hellish green-fire cannons they'd used to attack the *Cloud Hopper*. They walked purposefully toward the little group huddled by the building.

Dag had one shot with his musket, one shot each with the two pistols in his belt. He would not have time to reload and that left him one demon short. Dag eyed Sir Ander. The knight lay in the street; his dragon pistol—the match of Stephano's pistol—near his hand.

"Father Jacob, is Sir Ander's gun loaded?" Dag asked. "Did he fire it before he was attacked?"

Father Jacob thought a moment, then shook his head. "I wish I could tell you for certain. I don't *think* he did, but I can't remember."

If the pistol was loaded, that gave Dag his fourth shot. If it wasn't . . .

"Guess I'll find out," Dag muttered philosophically.

He rose to a kneeling position, fired the musket, dropped it, ducked his head, ran in a crouch to the fallen knight and snatched up the dragon pistol. Dag rose and pulled the trigger. Flame flashed, the pistol fired. Dag thanked God and threw it down. He drew the first of his two pistols with his left hand, flipped the gun from his left hand to his right, raised it, and fired.

He had one more shot, one more pistol left. All this time,

he'd been thinking only of firing. He had no idea if he'd hit anything or not. He hadn't dared take the time to look. What he did know was that, inexplicably, none of the demons were shooting at him.

Dag dropped to his belly, grunting as the metal breastplate dug into his ribs. Two of the demons were down; he didn't know for how long. The other two stood with their weapons in their hands, but they weren't looking at him. Their hideous faces were turned away; they were staring at something off to their left. One pointed. The other started to walk in that direction.

"Gythe!" Brother Barnaby cried.

Dag could see Gythe crouched on the door stoop, her arms covering her head. The demon was heading straight for her.

"I'll go to her," said Father Jacob. "Cover me!"

"Father, no—" Dag began, but before he could finish, the priest was running across the street.

"Son of a bitch!" Dag swore and raised the pistol, not wanting to fire unless he was certain he had a shot. After this, his only weapon was his knife.

The lane was thick with smoke. Dag could barely see the priest, and he was hoping the demon would have the same trouble. But apparently the fiends could see, for a demon was tracking Father Jacob with his gun. Dag shouted and yelled and stood up. Seeing the threat, the demon shifted his aim.

Dag dropped to the ground again and buried his head in his arms. Green fire swept over him, searing his legs and buttocks and burning through the leather coat he wore beneath the breastplate. The green fire enveloped his pistol, heating the metal, burning his hand, forcing him to drop the weapon. He picked it up, and was dimly aware of Brother Barnaby kneeling beside him, beating on him frantically, trying to put out the flames. Dag lifted his head.

"Stop hitting me, Brother!" Dag roared.

"But you're on fire!" Barnaby gasped.

"Never mind! You're throwing off my aim!"

Brother Barnaby drew back. Dag pulled the trigger. To his horror, green fire raced down the length of the muzzle toward his hand, like fire racing along the length of a fuse attached to a barrel of gunpowder. He flung the pistol away just as the gun exploded. A split second more and the blast would have taken off his hand.

The demon who had fired at Dag was reloading. The other demon was still going after Gythe. Dag reached his hand into his boot for his last weapon—his knife. He could feel the pain of his burns now, and he grimaced and stifled a groan as he pushed himself up off the charred cobblestones. He had no idea if his knife would penetrate the fiendish armor. He took aim with the knife when a large chunk of stone coming from behind him struck the demon, knocking the cannon from his hands. Another rock hit the demon in the head, sending him reeling backward.

Dag looked back to see Brother Barnaby picking up broken chunks of cobblestone and hurling the chunks in rapid fire succession, one after the other, at the demons. Dag watched in admiration. Brother Barnaby was a good shot. The monk kept up the barrage, and the demon could do nothing except try to keep his feet.

Father Jacob had by this time reached the demon closing in on Gythe. Coming up from behind, Father Jacob grabbed hold of the fiend by the shoulder, wrenched the demon around and slammed his fist into the demon's jaw. The demon went down in a heap. Father Jacob ran to Gythe, who was huddled in the doorway, her arms over her head. He took hold of her, soothing her.

"Dag!" Stephano's battlefield bellow reverberated through the smoke and darkness.

Dag grinned widely, relief flooding through him.

"Here I am, Captain! I'm still standing!" Dag shouted.

Stephano emerged from the smoke. He aimed his pistol at the demon who was the target of Brother Barnaby's assault.

"Brother Barnaby!" Dag yelled. "Fall back!"

Barnaby scrambled to get out of the way. Stephano fired,

and the demon flopped about and fell to the street, a hole in its chest. Miri was with Gythe and Father Jacob. Rodrigo stood protectively over them, holding a lantern in one hand. His other hand was glowing; presumably he was going to cast some sort of magical spell. Dag hoped Rigo handled his magic better than he handled a gun, and then he had other things to worry about. He caught sight of orange eyes on the roof of the warehouse. The demon was back, training the swivel gun at them.

"Take cover!" Dag yelled, and once more he hugged the pavement.

Stephano dropped to the ground. Brother Barnaby flung himself on top of Sir Ander. Father Jacob shielded Gythe. Miri grabbed hold of Rodrigo, who was standing in the open, staring at the gun with his mouth open. She dragged him down. The gun went off with a shattering boom that shook the buildings. Dag smelled the stench of burning flesh and he looked about in terror, fearing his friends had been caught in the blast.

He stared in shock. The demon hadn't been aiming at them. The green fireball had struck the bodies of the four demons. The heat of the blazing corpses was so fierce Dag had to avert his face. He was astonished to catch a glimpse of the priest running past him, heading toward the flames.

Father Jacob spoke what sounded like gibberish and made a circle with his hand, opening a hole in the flames, like one opened a door into a room. He reached his hand into the fire to seize hold of something. The object was hot, for Father Jacob said a most unholy word and dropped the charred and blackened object on the ground and wrung his burned fingers.

The swivel gun turned and fired again, blasting apart the bodies of the demons Dag and the stranger had killed. Within moments the flames had gone out, leaving a large gaping gash in the street and piles of black and greasy ash. The demon on the roof mounted a giant bat and flew off in the direction of the Breath. The fiend had left the swivel gun behind and Dag was just thinking he could at last get a look at the weapon when it blew apart.

The night was still. All of them listened intently, but the only sounds were Miri's soothing voice and Gythe's sobs.

"We should get out of here before the constables come," said Stephano.

"Take your time," said Dag, picking up the pistols, planning to reload. He limped over to inspect what was left of the bodies.

"But someone must have heard the gunshots—" Stephano began.

"Nothing new, around here," said Dag. "Trust me, the police won't be in a hurry to investigate."

Sir Ander had regained consciousness and was sitting up, ignoring Brother Barnaby's pleas and remonstrations. The knight looked shaken and pale. Stephano walked over to join Dag, shouting for Rodrigo to bring the lantern.

"Turn around," Stephano ordered Dag.

When the lantern arrived, Stephano inspected Dag's back. He looked at the leather coat with the large holes burned through it and shook his head. Dag gingerly removed the breastplate, stifling a groan.

"You look as though you've been slow roasted," said Stephano. "You should go back to the boat."

"And let Miri slather me with yellow goo?" Dag said, grimacing. "No, thank you, Captain. You're not in much better shape yourself."

He pointed to the patch of blood staining Stephano's pants leg.

"I'd say you need more yellow stuff," Dag observed.

"I'll keep quiet if you will," said Stephano.

"A deal. How is Gythe?" Dag asked.

Stephano shook his head gloomily and ran his fingers through his hair. "She's more scared than hurt. She keeps telling Miri that the demons were talking to her in the

Trondler language. Doesn't make sense to me, though it seems to make sense to *him*."

He jerked his thumb at Father Jacob, who was squatting on the pavement, examining the grisly object he had rescued from the flames.

"What is that he's got there?" Stephano asked.

"Looks like the head of that demon I shot," said Dag. "He saved it from the fire. Damn near burned his hand off trying to get it."

"So now he's a ghoul," said Stephano, scowling.

Rodrigo raised the lantern. "What *do* you have against that man?"

"I don't trust him. He has secrets—"

"So do we," Rodrigo pointed out.

"You don't like him because he's a priest," said Dag in accusing tones.

"Oh, just shut up, both of you," Stephano said irritably. "I've been stabbed and shot at by demons today. I don't need to be lectured."

Father Jacob put the object he'd recovered in Brother Barnaby's script, first dumping out the contents. This done, the priest gave the script back to Brother Barnaby with orders to handle it gently, keep it safe.

"How is Sir Ander?" Father Jacob asked the monk.

"He says he is all right," said Brother Barnaby worriedly. "The wraith did not have time to drain his life. He says the green fire from the demons destroyed the wraith."

"Of course, it would!" said Father Jacob. "The wraith is a creature of blood magic. The contramagic would put an end to it."

"Your hand, Father," said Brother Barnaby, as the priest started to walk off. The priest's knuckles were burst and bleeding and his fingers were burned.

"I'm fine," said Father Jacob.

"What was that thing you grabbed out of the fire, Father?" Stephano asked, coming over to join them.

"I'm not sure," said Father Jacob.

"Looked like the demon's head," Stephano said.

The priest shook his own head impatiently and turned to Dag.

"That man who was here," said Father Jacob. "The tall man. You saved him from the demons. I saw him join the Warlock who sent the wraith to kill Sir Ander. They both disappeared. Did you see which way they went?"

"Down that alley, Father," said Dag, nodding with his head, while reloading his weapons by the lantern's light. "Who were they, Father? Did they bring the demons here to kill you?"

"The tall man was not here to kill me, not this time. He was caught in the same ambush. As for the other—"

"The Warlock," said Sir Ander grimly, walking over to them. He glanced at the smoking remains of the demons. "So the Warlock and the Sorceress are now in league with the Devil. I'm not surprised."

"I am," said Father Jacob. "What surprises me is that they know Henry Wallace—"

"Wallace!" Stephano had been listening and he gave a start. "What was that you said? What about Henry Wallace?"

Father Jacob regarded Stephano with interest. "Do you know him?"

"Do you mean *Sir* Henry Wallace? *The* Sir Henry Wallace? Are you saying he was here?" Stephano demanded.

"He was the tall man whose life your friend saved."

Stephano cast Dag a glance.

"How was I to know?" Dag demanded.

"You're certain it was him, Father?" asked Stephano.

"He is one person I am not likely to forget," said Father Jacob dryly.

"I came to Westfirth in search of Wallace," said Stephano. "It is vital that I find him! Can you tell me where he might have gone?"

Father Jacob rested his hand on Stephano's forearm. "Listen to me, Captain. You are a brave man. You are a fine shot and an expert swordsman. And I say to you that if you see Sir

Henry Wallace walking toward you, turn and run as fast as you can. Wallace is a dangerous, a deadly, an implacable foe. Don't cross him. Don't meddle in his affairs. If you came here to find him, leave immediately and pray you are not too late. Pray you are gone before he finds you."

Stephano was startled by the priest's intensity.

"I thank you, Father," said Stephano, uncomfortable. "I will take your warning to heart. But it is important that I find this man."

Father Jacob glanced at Sir Ander. Stephano knew what they were thinking, that he was here on business of the countess. He could almost hear his mother's name resonating between the two of them, and he smoldered with anger.

"If you know of any way to locate him, Father," Stephano said coldly. "I would take it as a great favor. And if Wallace *does* kill me, I absolve you of any responsibility."

Dag looked shocked. Even Rodrigo was mildly taken aback. Sir Ander only smiled, however, and said something quietly to Father Jacob.

"I see," said Father Jacob. "I suppose you are right." He turned to Stephano. "I do not know where Sir Henry is and even if I did, I doubt he will be there long. He knows I recognized him. I pose a serious threat to him and whatever nefarious scheme he is plotting."

Seeing Stephano look downcast, Father Jacob smiled; albeit gravely. "If you insist, I can devise a means for you to track him. Wallace was carrying a leather satchel that was destroyed during the fight. He seemed very attached to it. Hand me that light."

He took the lantern from Rodrigo and flashed it around on the cobblestones. "Pick up those bits of burnt leather, will you, Monsieur de Villeneuve? Sir Ander, if you would fetch me the remains of that pistol I see lying over there. The gun that blew up after the green fire hit it. I will make use of it."

"For what?" Stephano asked.

"I am going to make a compass," said Father Jacob.

"I know what direction north is, Father," said Stephano. "We're wasting time—"

"No, we're not," said Rodrigo excitedly. "I know what he's doing. Why do you need the pistol, Father?"

"The presence of other constructs might interfere with my magic. The demon's green fire erased the constructs that had been laid upon the gun."

"I didn't think erasing constructs was possible, Father," said Rodrigo coolly. He squatted down to get a better view. "Aren't you talking heresy?"

The priest glanced at him. "I see that we will have to build a special dungeon at the Arcanum to hold that mouth of yours, Monsieur."

Rodrigo grinned and watched as Father Jacob took up a bit of scorched leather and placed it on the flattened piece of metal. He touched the leather with his finger three times, at three different points. The priest set no construct or sigil, yet all three points began to glow with a soft golden light. Father Jacob drew a line connecting the three points to form a triangle of light.

While Father Jacob was constructing the compass, Brother Barnaby came over to ask if he was needed. If not, he wanted to go back to the houseboat with Gythe and Miri.

"Mademoiselle Gythe heard voices again, Father," said Brother Barnaby, deeply troubled. "And . . . I have been hearing them, too."

Father Jacob paused a moment in his work to look at the monk. He did not ask any questions, but gave him permission to accompany the sisters. "Give Sir Ander the script containing the demon remains."

Brother Barnaby handed over the script with the mysterious object inside.

"Dag," said Stephano, seeing his friend gritting his teeth against the pain of his burns, "Go with Miri and Gythe and the brother. Keep your musket handy."

"And have Miri see to your back," Rodrigo said loudly. "I hear that yellow goo is excellent for burns."

Dag cast Rodrigo a baleful glance, then went off with Brother Barnaby. Miri had her arm around Gythe. She walked slowly by her sister's side, clinging to Miri and holding fast to Brother Barnaby's hand. Dag walked behind, his musket in his hand. The clocks in the church steeples began to strike seven times.

"Sir Ander, could you find me a sliver of metal from the pistol?" Father Jacob asked. "Just a small piece will do."

The knight quickly complied and handed his friend the metal splinter. Father Jacob wrapped the splinter in the bit of leather from the satchel and held it directly above the glowing triangle. A thin stream of light rose from each point and touched the splinter, which began to glow brightly and shifted its direction.

"The priest could also use part of the fabric from Sir Henry's coat for this spell," Rodrigo was explaining to Stephano. "Anything that the person handled or wore on his body. The 'needle' makes the connection using latent magical energies—"

"Of course it does," said Stephano impatiently. "The question is, will it lead us to this man?"

"It will," said Father Jacob. "But the connection fades quickly, so make haste."

Father Jacob handed the device to the fascinated Rodrigo. Following the compass' point, the four men walked swiftly to the end of the lane and found a trail of blood. Stephano had his pistol in hand, keeping watch for trouble. When they reached the alleyway, they came to a sudden halt.

The light of the lantern shone on the body of a young woman, no more than fifteen or sixteen, lying dead on the street. Her throat was cut. Her blood ran in gruesome rivulets among the cobblestones. Rodrigo gasped and covered his mouth and turned away. Stephano gazed down in shock and horror.

"The wraith!" Sir Ander exclaimed.

"Poor child. The Warlock used her blood for his conjuration." Father Jacob sighed deeply. "May God in His mercy take her to her rest."

He knelt beside the body and reached out his hand to close the staring eyes.

"Did Henry Wallace do this?" Stephano asked, shaken.

"No, Captain," said Father Jacob, rising to his feet. His face was drawn. He seemed to have aged in the space of moments. "This is dark magic, blood magic—the work of the young man, the Warlock. He killed this girl, then drank her blood, and used her life force to create the wraith that attacked Sir Ander."

Stephano seemed stunned. "I can't believe that any-one . . . Is that even possible?"

"Sadly, yes," said Rodrigo in muffled tones. He kept his eyes averted from the corpse.

"We've seen this young man commit such murders be-fore," said Sir Ander, his voice burning with anger. "He se-duces these young women and then makes them believe that by dying for him, they're proving their love. You'll note there is no sign of a struggle."

"Good God!" Stephano said softly. He swallowed hard.

"There's more blood down here, Father," Sir Ander re-ported, flashing the lantern light about on the pavement. "Not the young woman's. It might belong to the Warlock."

"How do you know it's not her blood?" Stephano asked.

Sir Ander squatted down. "See how the blood is smeared? Looks as if the person was shot in the foot. He was dragging his boot in his own blood. And here he trod in it. You can see bloody footprints. And so did Wallace. You can see faint traces of his footprints walking along behind. Probably holding a gun on the young man. I'll follow them, see where they lead."

He continued down the alley, shining the light on the cobblestones.

"I take it from what Sir Ander says that the two of you have been working to stop this Warlock," said Stephano.

"For many long months," said Father Jacob.

Kneeling beside the body, he began to pray. Rodrigo

bowed his head. Stephano didn't want to pray. He wanted
to lash out, hit someone—God, maybe.

Sir Ander was not gone long. He waited for Father Jacob
to finish his prayer to make his report.

"The bloody smear of the Warlock's trail ends at the canal.
Wallace's prints continue down the street. Maybe he threw
the young man into the Breath," Sir Ander said hopefully.

"I doubt it. Wallace took him hostage. If he'd wanted to
kill him, he could have just shot him. With all the barge traffic, Wallace probably dumped him in a passing boat. There
is something between Wallace and the Warlock, that much
is clear."

"The Sorceress," said Sir Ander. "We know she spent
time in Freya."

"I fear you may be right, my friend," said Father Jacob.
He paused, then said, "And I believe I know how she and
Wallace might be connected. We long suspected he had
something to do with the attack on the *Defiant*."

Father Jacob started to stand, caught his foot in the hem
of his cassock and staggered. Stephano reached out his
hand to steady the priest. He was eager to start on Wallace's
trail, but there was something he needed to say first.

"What will happen to this young woman?" Stephano
asked, gesturing to the body.

"Sir Ander and I will take care of the poor child," said
Father Jacob. "There is a convent nearby. The nuns will tend
to her until we can learn her name and give the sad news to
her family."

Stephano coughed, cleared his throat. "After seeing
this . . . Well, um, I may have misjudged you, Father. I'm
sorry if I've been . . ." He paused, uncertain.

"An ass?" Rodrigo suggested.

Stephano flushed. "Not exactly the word I was going to
use in front of a priest."

Father Jacob smiled. "I understand, Captain—perhaps
better than you think. May God go with you." He held out
his hand.

"And with you, Father," said Stephano. He accepted the priest's handshake.

Sir Ander lifted the young woman in his arms, cradling the lifeless body as gently and tenderly as a father. Rodrigo drew a lace-edged handkerchief from his pocket and laid it over the cold, pale, blood-smeared face. Father Jacob gave both Stephano and Rodrigo his blessing and told them to take the lantern.

"We walk with God's light," said Father Jacob, as he fell into solemn step alongside Sir Ander.

Stephano waited to see them safely on their way with their sorrowful burden, then turned back to the business of tracking Sir Henry.

"I'm amazed," said Rodrigo. "A priest blessed you, and you didn't sneer."

"Because I have a feeling we're going to need it," said Stephano. "Let's see if that compass-thingamajig works."

The compass worked, apparently, for it led them down the alley in the same direction as the faint trail of bloody footprints. When they came to the end of the alley, the compass indicated that Sir Henry Wallace had continued along Canal Street. Rodrigo walked on, delighted with his new toy, then stopped when he realized Stephano wasn't with him.

"Hey," he said, glancing around. "What are you doing? Father Jacob warned us that the magical connection wouldn't last long."

Stephano stood in the darkness that seemed thick and heavy with evil, hard to breathe.

"You heard what Father Jacob said about this man, Wallace," said Stephano. "The priest was serious. My mother calls Henry Wallace the most dangerous man in the world. She told me I should quit looking for him. Even she's afraid of him."

The two were quiet, somber.

"My mother *does* pay well," said Stephano.

"And on time," Rodrigo said with a deep sigh. Looking down at the compass, he pointed. "Wallace went that way."

Chapter Thirty-Five

In a city where "watch your back" means you get stabbed in the chest and you can't even trust your own shadow not to kill you if the money's right, the Blue Parrot is known for offering privacy, respectability, damn fine brandy, and a rear exit.

—Dag Thorgrimson

THE COMPASS LED RODRIGO AND STEPHANO down Canal Street. They turned left onto the Street of Saints, where the compass led them straight to an exclusive bordello known as the Dovecote. The trail ended on the walkway outside the bordello's ornately carved and gold-leaf-trimmed door as they discovered when they walked past the house and continued down the street about a block. The compass did not react.

"He must have taken a cab," Rodrigo said, not knowing whether to be relieved or disappointed.

"I don't think so," said Stephano. Turning around, he studied their location. "Cabs don't frequent this street, at least not this early. He came here for a reason."

"To the Dovecote? You can't be serious," Rodrigo said, carefully tucking the compass in an inner coat pocket. "He's been ambushed by demons, involved in dark magic and the murder of a young girl. A priest from the Arcanum knows he's in Westfirth, and Wallace decides to go play slap and tickle?"

"If he's a member, he would ask the doorman if he—"

"—could make use of their carriage," Rodrigo finished, catching up with his friend's thinking. "That makes sense. I wonder if Dag's friend is still the owner?"

"We have the priest's blessing," said Stephano. "Let's see if it's worth anything. Do I look presentable?"

"No," said Rodrigo, twitching Stephano's long coat in place to hide the fact that his trousers were grimy and blood-stained and shaking his head over the sorry state of his friend's shirt. "But, then, you never did, so no one should be surprised."

The two retraced their steps back to the bordello and walked down the paved path that ran from the street to the entrance. The grounds were pleasant. They walked beneath the overarching limbs of graceful poplar trees and through a rose garden. The house was quiet at this time of evening with only a few lights in the windows. The women would be dressing, putting on their jewels and powder and perfume, preparing for the night's work. In the back rooms, the owner would be preparing the tables for baccarat, dice, and other games of chance. The doorman stood in a well-lighted portico adorned with tubs of geraniums and lilies. He had been keeping an eye on the two gentlemen and, as they ascended the stairs, he advanced to meet them. He was a shortish man, almost as wide as he was tall with broad shoulders, arms thick with muscle, and no neck. He touched his hand to the brim of his hat.

"Good evening, gentlemen," he said polite, but firm. "I fear you have made a mistake. This is a private club, for members only—"

"Thomaso," said Rodrigo warmly. "Don't tell me you have forgotten old friends?"

"Monsieur de Villeneuve!" the man exclaimed, looking at them more closely. "And Captain de Guichen! God bless my soul, but it is good to see you both. And to think I tried to send you away!"

He shook his head ruefully, then gestured toward the

door. "Come in, sirs, come in. Maudie will be so pleased. We were talking of you only the other day. We can never forget, Captain," he added, his voice growing husky, "what you and your Cadre of the Lost did for us. We would have been the ones who were lost!"

"I take it no one else has tried to run you out of business," Stephano said, wincing slightly as Thomaso engulfed his hand in a grip that was a bit too heartfelt.

"No, sir, no. Thanks to you and your friends. How is Dag? He didn't come with you?"

"He's a trifle indisposed," Rodrigo said. "Nothing serious."

"Ah, I see." Thomaso grinned and looked wise. "Send him round when he recovers. Now, do come in, sirs."

"Sorry, Thomaso," said Stephano. "Maybe another time. We're looking for a friend of ours. We're afraid he may be in trouble. He would have stopped by here in the last hour, perhaps asked for a ride—"

"You must mean Sir Robert Beauchamp," said Thomaso. "Your fears are right, Captain. Sir Robert said he'd been attacked by thieves."

Stephano and Rodrigo looked at each other.

"The assassins found him," said Rodrigo in grim tones. "Maybe we're too late!"

"I fear we are," said Stephano. "Was Sir Robert badly hurt?"

"Just a gash on his hand," said Thomaso. "He didn't stay long. He asked if we could give him a ride to his lodgings. Sir Robert's a member of long-standing. Of course, I was happy to accommodate him."

"Just to be sure this is *our* Sir Robert, could you describe him?" Stephano asked.

"A tall gentleman, well-spoken," said Thomaso. "Freyan exile. Came here after the war. That's about all I can tell you, Captain. I've never seen the man's face. Like many of our members, he always wears a mask."

"Well, it seems he's safe for the moment," said Rodrigo.

"Yes, but for how much longer," Stephano argued. "The hounds are on his trail—"

"If only we knew where he's gone," Rodrigo said helplessly. "We could warn him."

Thomaso looked from one to the other. "Generally such information is kept in strict confidence, but seeing that it is you, Captain, Sir Robert asked the driver to take him to the Blue Parrot."

"The Blue Parrot!" Rodrigo repeated in alarm. "They'll be waiting for him!"

"Thomaso," said Stephano urgently, "we haven't a moment to lose. Would it be possible for your driver to take us—"

"Of course, sirs, of course," said Thomaso. He summoned the page and ordered him to the stables.

"The Blue Parrot is not far, Captain," Thomaso said, when the carriage arrived. He assisted them to enter. "By the Masons' Guildhall."

"Thank you, Thomaso," Rodrigo called, as the carriage rattled away over the cobblestones. "You may have saved a life this night!"

Stephano sat back in the seat, flexing his hand. "I'd forgotten that man's handshake. I've lost all feeling in my fingers."

"You note I avoid personal contact," said Rodrigo. "I'm glad he and Maudie are doing well. We'll have to remember to tell Dag. So, now, what is our plan? Do we storm the Blue Parrot? If so, I must remind you that I'm not much good at storming."

"Don't you find it odd that Sir Henry is still in Westfirth?" Stephano asked. "If I'd kidnapped a journeyman who'd made an astounding discovery that would revolutionize warfare, I'd be on the first ship out."

"Maybe Wallace knew that people would be searching for him and he's lying low to wait for the furor to die down."

"Maybe," said Stephano, unconvinced. "But now he knows that Father Jacob recognized him, and while he probably hopes the demons killed the priest, Wallace can't count on it. He'll have to leave tonight."

"Perhaps he's already gone," said Rodrigo.

"Don't sound so hopeful," said Stephano. "Wallace went back to the Blue Parrot. Let's say he has Alcazar stashed there. He has to pack up his things, collect Alcazar. That could take some time."

"If I am not mistaken, here we are," said Rodrigo as the carriage rolled to a stop. "Too bad we don't know what Wallace looks like. Thomaso's description could fit almost any one."

"From what my mother told me, a description wouldn't help," said Stephano. "He'll be disguised and he'd have Alcazar disguised, as well."

"Fine establishment, this Blue Parrot," said Rodrigo, as they emerged from the cab. "A hotel suitable for intrigue, secret assignations, lovers escaping the eyes of jealous spouses. *Not* the sort of place one hides kidnapped journeymen."

The Blue Parrot was obviously a well-to-do establishment, catering only to the finest clientele. The windows of the upper levels were discreetly sealed and shuttered, while the windows on the ground floor were ablaze with light. The neatly painted sign featuring the bird for which the inn was named hung above the well-lit entryway. Through the windows, they could see serving maids bustling about in little frilly caps and white aprons waiting on elegantly dressed ladies and gentlemen.

"You're right," said Stephano, frowning. "Still it won't hurt to ask—"

He started toward the door. The scandalized Rodrigo dragged him back.

"My dear fellow, you can't possibly think you're going to go bounding inside and demand to see the guest register?"

"I was going to ask the landlord if he'd seen a man resembling Wallace's description—"

"And you would be escorted to the street and tossed out on your ear," said Rodrigo.

"So what would you do?" Stephano asked, exasperated.

"Take a room," said Rodrigo. "Wash off the gunpowder residue and have supper. I'm thinking a nice bit of fish, followed by broiled squab, new spring peas and a dry white wine, moderately chilled."

"*You* have to explain this bill to my mother," Stephano grumbled.

Sir Henry Wallace arrived at the Blue Parrot without incident. Ordinarily he would not have risked giving a carriage driver his true destination, but he was in haste and he had no reason to think anyone had followed him. He did take the precaution of ordering the carriage to drive around to the back alley and came in through the rear entrance. He opened the door to his room with his key and walked in, expecting to find Alcazar there, whining as usual.

Alcazar was nowhere in sight.

"Pietro?" Sir Henry called softly, looking about.

No answer. The suite was empty. Swearing beneath his breath, Sir Henry searched all the rooms twice, even looking under the bed. He was trying to think what might have happened, when there came a timid knock on the door.

Sir Henry flung open the door and found Alcazar in the hall. Henry grabbed hold of the journeyman and dragged him, stumbling, inside.

"Where the devil have you been?"

"I . . . I went to visit Louisa, my b-brother's wife," Alcazar stammered, shriveling beneath Sir Henry's withering eye.

"You went to *visit*?" Sir Henry said, his voice shaking with fury. "You left this hotel and went to visit your brother's wife, who is undoubtedly under surveillance—"

Alcazar went exceedingly pale. "I . . . I w-wore a hat."

"You wore a hat. God give me strength not to murder you," said Sir Henry, his fists clenching.

"I have good news, sir!" cried Alcazar faintly, backing

into a corner. "The *Silver Raven* is in port. We can leave tomorrow . . ."

"We're leaving now, tonight," said Sir Henry. "Go get dressed."

"But I'm already dressed—"

"As a woman, you blithering idiot. You came here in petticoats. You're damned well going to leave in petticoats."

The chastened Alcazar hurried meekly into his bedroom, stripped off his clothes, and began to wrestle with his corset. Henry blew out the lights, walked over to the window, parted the velvet curtain a crack and looked out onto the street. He was certain *he* had not been followed from the bordello, but that fool Alcazar, traipsing about the city in his blasted hat could have picked up any number of tails.

Sir Henry saw a group of men congregating down the block in front of the Masons' Guildhall. The men were drinking ale and relaxing after a hard day's labor. Such gatherings were commonplace and he gave them only a cursory glance and then dismissed them. No one else was about.

He left the window and went to pack his things in a portmanteau. He would give orders for the portmanteau to be delivered to one of any number of locations in the city, to be retrieved at a later date. Henry deeply regretted the loss of his leather satchel, but Alcazar had his satchel, in which he carried valuable notes relating to his experiment. Sir Henry buried the pewter tankard in the satchel under the papers and then went to wash off the blood and dirt and change into elegant clothes that suited the count.

He was putting on his white, gold-embroidered weskit when he heard the clatter of horse's hooves and the sound of wheels rolling to a stop in front of the hotel. Henry parted the curtain for a look. Two men descended from the carriage and stood in the light of a streetlamp, conversing.

Sir Henry recognized them both. He let the curtain fall.

"Son of a bitch!" Henry muttered.

Coincidence might have brought Captain Stephano de

Guichen to this hotel, but Sir Henry had learned long ago to never trust in coincidence. He had to assume, therefore, that Captain de Guichen was on his trail. Henry ran through his plans.

He had purchased tickets for himself and his "lady" for the evening's performance at the Opera Bouffe. His coach, driven by his agent, was going to take them to the crowded theater. Inside the coach were two more of his agents, dressed as the "count" and his "lady." Wallace and Alcazar would enter the coach, but his agents would enter the theater. They would mingle with the crowd, go into their box while the lights were up, wait until the lights went down, and then disappear. All the while Sir Henry and Alcazar would be boarding the ship and sailing back to Freya.

Wallace looked back out the window to see Captain de Guichen, and his friend Monsieur de Villeneuve entering the hotel. Wallace knew what they would do, which was what he would do. They would request one of the elegantly appointed tables in the dining room, eat supper, drink wine, and observe all who came and went. He did not fear that either of them would penetrate his disguise as the count, nor were they likely to recognize Alcazar in his face powder, rouge, and curling love locks.

"But should I take that chance?" Henry reflected, pacing the room, talking to himself. "We could leave the hotel by the rear entrance. I'll have to order the coach to be brought around to the back and that will seem odd, but I can tell the landlord that my lady's jealous husband is looking for her."

About to summon the page to carry a message to his coachman, Henry once again looked out the window. The lamplighter had been making his rounds and the streetlamps shed bright pools of light up and down the block. Sir Henry's eyesight was keen. He knew what to look for, and although the pudgy man in the long cloak and hat was careful never to step directly into one of those pools of light, Sir Henry saw him lurking near a doorway.

Henry drew in a hissing breath. "Dubois!"

The arrival of Dubois, the bishop's agent, at the Blue Parrot was definitely *not* coincidence. Wallace now understood everything that had puzzled him. Dubois was the third man at the duel, the mystery man who had shot at Harrington. Dubois must have kept on Harrington's trail, followed him to Westfirth, and stayed on him until Harrington had led him to Henry, undoubtedly at the café. The countess' bloodhound and the bishop's bulldog—both hot on Sir Henry's heels and closing in for the kill. Henry hoped Harrington was suffering every torment Hell had to offer.

Two men joined Dubois. They spoke together for a moment, then the two men left, heading for the hotel's rear entrance. So much for sneaking out the back.

Henry turned from the window. He had been in tough situations before, but nothing as dire as this. If he was caught on Rosian soil with the missing journeyman, he would be tortured for information (which he would steadfastly refuse to divulge) and then what was left of him dragged to a public execution. His queen would be seriously embarrassed and compromised. His agents left out in the cold. The work of many years would be for nothing. The cunning fox had been run to ground. Henry Wallace was trapped and cornered, surrounded by dogs panting to rip him apart. Worse even than losing his life, he would lose Alcazar and with him the opportunity to give Freya the power to crush her enemies.

Henry eyed the satchel containing the tankard thoughtfully, then he grabbed the tankard, thrust it into the portmanteau, closed the lid, and locked it.

"Alcazar! We've been discovered!" he said.

The journeyman came running out, half-naked, tripping over his chemise. He looked ready to faint.

"Don't worry," Henry continued coolly. "I'm going to get us out of this. I need you to place a magical construct on the lock." He pointed to the portmanteau.

"What sort of construct?" Alcazar asked, trembling with fright.

"Something that will make the lock impossible to open for anyone other than the two of us. Put a spell on the trunk, as well, just in case someone should try to hack it apart with an ax. And be quick about it!"

Alcazar cast his constructs swiftly and assured Sir Henry that the trunk was now safe from any thief. He gave Sir Henry the key to breaking the magical seal, which was a short combination of finger taps and swipes, and hurried back to finish dressing. Henry stood frowning at the portmanteau.

"Was this *my* fault?" he asked himself. "I knew Harrington was likely to do something stupid. And I knew I should have taken Alcazar out of the country immediately. I understood I might well be walking into an ambush this evening and yet ... What else could I have done? Harrington, with his charm and acting ability and skill with guns and sword, was the best man for the task. I could have forcibly removed Alcazar, but then the unhappy journeyman might have refused to work for the Freyan government and there is no way I could force him. Whereas now, I have him, his brother, and his brother's family under my control.

"And I could never have anticipated going to a meeting with the Sorceress only to find my nemesis, Jacob Northrop, there. Nor could I have foreseen that I would be attacked by fiends from Hell. If I had it to do over again, I would undoubtedly do exactly the same. I have to leave the Blue Parrot now. I have to leave Westfirth this night. A ship is waiting for us. The only question is: how to slip past the dogs?

"My Lady Luck," said Henry, "this is for you, you fickle female. Do I go out the front or the back?"

He took out a coin and flipped it. The coin landed on the floor. Henry picked it up, eyed it, and tossed it on the table as recompense for the maid. He rang the bell to summon the footmen to take away the portmanteau. He ordered it delivered to the merchant ship, the *Silver Raven,* and sent word to the agent who served as his coachman.

The Blue Parrot Hotel had been named for the large blue parrot that squawked loudly from its gold-gilt cage in the front entryway. The hotel was known for the parrot and for the beautiful marble staircase that flowed in polished and lemon-oiled majesty from the first floor to the lobby. Several pages stood at their post near the staircase, ready to rush to perform the guests' bidding. The office of the innkeeper was off the lobby to the right. The small and elegant dining room was to the left. One of the amenities for the occupants of the dining room was to be able to watch the arrivals and departures of beautifully coifed and bejeweled ladies and silk-caped aristocratic gentlemen.

Rodrigo and Stephano had both obtained rooms. Within fifteen minutes, Rodrigo had endeared himself to half the maidservants and made bosom friends of the Boots. Rodrigo had explained their somewhat rakish appearance, lack of luggage, and the unfortunate state of Stephano's trousers with a thrilling tale of having been set upon by highwaymen. He and Stephano had received sympathy and towels, copious amounts of hot water, and gossip about all the guests.

After they had both hastily cleaned up and were downstairs dining on turbot and broiled squab, Rodrigo reported that several of the gentlemen currently residing at the Blue Parrot matched the description of Sir Henry Wallace, but none of the guests came close to resembling Pietro Alcazar.

"Maybe my mother is wrong," said Stephano as the dishes were cleared away. "Maybe Wallace has nothing to do with Alcazar."

"A possibility, I suppose," said Rodrigo, ordering a snifter of brandy. "Though I might venture to remind you that your mother is never wrong."

Stephano only grunted, then asked, "So what do we do now?"

"Sit here and drink brandy," said Rodrigo.

Stephano shifted restlessly in his chair. "I don't want to sit here. We should be doing something!"

"We *are* doing something," said Rodrigo. "We are watching for Sir Henry."

"Who might be disguised as anyone from the blue parrot in the lobby to that venerable old woman haranguing the wait staff. And we're looking for another man who is apparently not even in the hotel. That sounds like a prosperous night's work," Stephano said.

"You're in a bad mood, so you're obviously feeling better," Rodrigo observed, ordering more brandy for himself and one for his friend. "Miri's yellow goo may offend the nostrils, but one has to admit its effectiveness."

"I don't like leaving our friends on their own," said Stephano. "Not with demons around. I keep thinking about that poor murdered girl—"

"Lower your voice," Rodrigo said quietly.

Stephano picked up the snifter of brandy, drank it, and motioned for a refill. "God! I wish I hadn't seen her!"

"It was pretty awful," said Rodrigo, pouring more brandy.

"I've seen worse on the battlefield," said Stephano, tossing down the biting liquid. "But I keep thinking about what Father Jacob said, about that man drinking her blood—" He poured himself another glass.

"You might want to take it easy on the brandy," said Rodrigo.

"This is the last," said Stephano. A clock in the hallway chimed ten. He drank the brandy and stifled a yawn. "I've got to get some sleep. If Wallace was ever in the hotel, he's probably gone by now."

"I will remain here with this excellent brandy," said Rodrigo, taking his time to savor a mouthful.

Stephano was rising to his feet when the doorman entered to announce that the coach for Count Fairhaven had arrived. The doorman summoned the page, who went dashing up the stairs to alert the count. The landlord, hearing his distinguished visitor was departing for the opera, came out of his office to bid his well-paying and noble guest a good evening.

Stephano decided he might as well wait to see this Count Fairhaven. He glanced at Rodrigo, who raised his eyebrows. They both watched as the count came down the stairs, escorting his female companion.

Stephano studied the count. The brim of his hat and the feathers that adorned it concealed much of the man's face, as did the curls of the white powdered wig and the frilly white lace at his throat. Stephano caught a glimpse of an aristocratic nose and thin mouth, a black mustache and goatee. The count was elegantly dressed in a black silk cloak, a red waistcoat with overlarge sleeves embroidered with gold stitching, an embroidered weskit, lace cuffs, silk stockings, and buckled shoes. He had one hand solicitously on the arm of his lady. He was speaking to her in Rosian, his accent indicating he came from the eastern region, perhaps somewhere around Haerigan. His voice was high-pitched, thin, affected.

"That's not him," said Stephano.

"But that *is* her!" Rodrigo exclaimed.

"Her? What do you mean her?" Stephano asked, puzzled.

"The love of my life," said Rodrigo.

"Oh, good God!" Stephano looked at his friend in exasperation. "You can't be serious."

"I can. I am!" Rodrigo gazed, smitten. "Have you ever seen such a beautiful creature!"

The count's lady was slender and graceful. Long curling locks of blonde hair fell over white-powdered shoulders. She wore an elaborate headpiece with feathers and jewels that artfully concealed her face and was dressed in an exquisite gown. Her eyes, what could be seen of them behind the large feather fan she held, were lustrous. Her face was powdered and rouged, her lips touched with red. She seemed shy and timid, for she clung closely to her companion.

The count and his lady reached the bottom of the stairs

and were crossing the lobby. The count stopped to assist the lady with her cloak, then walked over to exchange greetings with the landlord. The lady stood a short distance from him in front of the parrot's cage. She looked exceedingly pale and nervous. The hand holding the fan trembled.

The parrot had been asleep with his head beneath his wing. A sudden noise—perhaps the landlord's loud laughter at something said by the count—woke the bird. He let out a loud and raucous squawk. At the unexpected sound, the lady gasped and dropped her fan.

Like an arrow shot from love's bow, Rodrigo leaped from his chair and ran to the lady's side. He picked up the fan and, sinking to one knee, held it out to her.

"I give you your fan, my lady," he said and added in a low voice, meant for her ears alone, "And with that fan my heart, if you will take it."

The lady stared at Rodrigo with wide, frightened eyes. She was trembling all over now, probably terrified of her lover. But the count was either not the jealous type or he did not consider Rodrigo a threat. He glanced with some irritation at his lady and said sharply, "The gentleman has picked up your fan, Imogene. Thank him, my dear, and allow him to get up off his knees."

The lady stammered something incoherent. She took the fan from Rodrigo with a hand that was shaking so much that she nearly dropped it again. Rodrigo rose to his feet, made a gallant bow to her. He bowed to the count, who bowed back.

The count took hold of the lady's arm and guided her firmly toward the door and their coach that was waiting outside. Stephano went to join Rodrigo, who was standing by the parrot, gazing after the woman with love and longing.

"She comes into my life for a brief moment and is gone," said Rodrigo.

"Funny how that always seems to happen," Stephano remarked. "I'm off to bed."

He had his foot on the marble stair. Rodrigo remained in the lobby, yearning after his lost love, who was standing on the sidewalk. The coach driver was opening the door, when the count gave a loud shout, "Assassins! Help!"

Men armed with clubs were attacking the count. He had drawn his sword and was fending them off, all the while trying to drag his terrified lady toward the coach. One of the thugs grabbed hold of the woman and tore her away from the count. She cried out in terror and dropped, senseless, to the ground. The other thugs redoubled their attack on the count. He clouted one with his fist and thrust his sword at another.

The doorman rushed out in the street, shouting for the constable. The landlord stood in the lobby wringing his hands. The parrot screeched. The page boys went running to the windows to see the fight. The maids screamed in horrified delight, and Rodrigo went bounding out the door to save the lady.

"Rodrigo!" Stephano cried. "Are you mad? Oh, for the love of— He'll get himself killed!"

Drawing his sword, Stephano ran after his friend.

The count's blade flashed in the lamplight. He jabbed and stabbed with expert skill, but he was hampered by his efforts to protect the lady, who was lying on the pavement. The coachman was on the box, yelling for the count to get in. The horses were stamping, their eyes rolling.

One of the thugs made a dart at the lady and grabbed one arm, apparently with the intention of dragging her away. Rodrigo seized the lady by her other arm and a tug of war ensued, both of them pulling at the poor woman, yanking her back and forth.

"Let her go, you bounder!" Rodrigo cried angrily.

In answer, the thug aimed a blow with his club at Rodrigo's head. Stephano's blade sliced through the meaty part of the man's hand. He dropped the club with a cry, but continued to stubbornly hang onto the lady.

Stephano held his sword poised over the man's arm. "Let go of her or end up minus a hand!"

The thug apparently decided Stephano meant what he said, for he let go of the woman and ran away. Stephano turned to see the count still fending off two attackers.

"Carry the lady to the coach, Rigo," Stephano shouted. "I'll help the count."

Rodrigo endeavored to lift the unconscious woman, only to find the delicate beauty much heavier than he had anticipated. He staggered and nearly dropped her. "You are a sturdy little thing, aren't you my love?" he said, gasping.

Unable to lift her, Rodrigo was forced to half-carry, half-drag the lady to the carriage. He shoved her hurriedly inside and turned to await developments.

"Go to your lady, my lord!" cried Stephano, coming to the aide of the beleaguered count. "I will hold them off."

The count thanked Stephano in a few brief words, then jumped into the coach and slammed shut the door. Stephano shouted at the driver, who cracked his whip. The coach lurched forward and rushed off with such speed that the wheel narrowly missed crushing Rodrigo's foot.

The instant the coach departed, so did the thugs, vanishing into the darkness, taking their wounded away with them. The piercing screech of whistles announced the coming of the constabulary. Rodrigo was standing in the gutter, gazing woefully after his lost love. Stephano seized hold of him and dragged him off down the street.

"But I haven't finished my brandy—" Rodrigo protested.

"If we stay to be questioned by the police, you'll be drinking your brandy in a jail cell," said Stephano.

"Ah, good point," said Rodrigo.

"Walk. Running looks suspicious."

The two sauntered down the street, pausing as any curious bystander would pause to watch the constables race by. An officer skidded to a stop in front of them.

"Did you see where the thugs went, gentlemen?"

"That way, down the alley," Stephano said, pointing. The constable touched his hat and ran off.

Stephano and Rodrigo continued along the street and

were about to cross to the other side, when a small carriage came dashing straight at them, almost running them down. The carriage careened around the corner and was gone.

"Someone's in a hurry," remarked Rodrigo.

He and Stephano walked on, dispirited and downcast.

"This entire venture has been an unmitigated disaster," said Stephano.

"At least we managed to save a damsel from assassins," said Rodrigo. "That brute actually tried to drag her off!"

"Assassins would have just shot the count. Those men were trying to abduct him and the lady, as well," said Stephano.

"I saw him say something to you. What was it?"

"Something about being in my debt. He gave a kind of chuckle and hoped someday I would realize what I'd done."

"That's a rather odd thing to say to someone who has just saved your life."

"I might not have heard him right. It doesn't matter," said Stephano, shrugging.

"I guess not," said Rodrigo. "Though it pained me deeply to see him drive off with the woman of my dreams. I don't suppose we'll ever know what it was all about."

"And I don't suppose we'll ever find Sir Henry Wallace," said Stephano.

"Look at it this way, our luck can't get any worse," said Rodrigo.

"Don't say that," warned Stephano. "You'll jinx us."

Dubois had watched in disbelief as Captain de Guichen rushed in, sword drawn, to save Sir Henry Wallace from being captured by Dubois' agents. Poor Dubois almost lost his faith that night. He was sorely tempted to ask God whose side He was on.

Dubois regained control of himself, however. He did not stay to wait for the constables to find him. He had two carriages stationed around the corner. He ran to one of them. Red Dog peered down at him from the driver's seat.

"Follow that coach!" Dubois ordered, pointing. "Sir Henry's inside. He's probably bound for the docks. Find out what ship he's sailing on and report back to me."

Red Dog nodded, and within moments the carriage was whirling down the street in pursuit. Dubois climbed into the other carriage.

"The Archbishop's residence," Dubois told the driver. "And don't spare the horses!"

Inside his coach, Sir Henry Wallace roused Alcazar from his fainting fit with a couple of smacks across the face.

Alcazar sat up and looked around. "Are we safe?"

"Yes, my love, thanks to your alluring charms," said Sir Henry Wallace, laughing.

He was in an excellent mood. He thought back to Captain de Guichen coming gallantly to the "count's" aid, helping him escape. Sir Henry leaned back in the seat and roared with mirth. Alcazar came near fainting again at the dreadful sound, but Sir Henry reassured him.

"Be merry, my friend. We are now on our way to your brother's ship."

Alcazar realized with a start they weren't alone in the coach. Two people shrouded in black cloaks were seated opposite him. He shrank back into the cushions.

"Who are they?"

"The woman's name is Brianna. She is a friend of mine. Brianna say hello."

"Hello," said the woman.

"The man is known as the 'Duke.' He is, of course, not a duke at all, but he looks well in evening attire."

"Why are they here?" Alcazar asked, quivering.

He noticed, as they passed under a streetlamp, that the man and woman were dressed in the same clothes he and Sir Henry were wearing.

"Because I never leave anything to chance," said Sir Henry. "And don't start whining, or I'll smack you again."

He glanced out the rear window. He did not see anyone following them, but that didn't mean much. Dubois' agents were good at their jobs. Almost as good as his.

Henry sat back in the seat. He put his fingertips together, tapping them, thinking. When he arrived in Freya, he would hand over Alcazar to Mr. Sloan with orders to take the journeyman straight to the armory. Henry would travel to court, report the joyful news to his queen, and receive her praise and thanks. He would then go to his wife. She would be devastated over the loss of the manor house, but he would be able to assure her he would build her a new one, far grander than any other manor house in Freya.

He was thinking these pleasant thoughts; the rocking motion of the coach sending him into a half-doze, when he was awakened by a cannon's boom.

Sir Henry sat straight up. He listened to the echoes of that single cannon shot dying away in the night and swore.

"What is wrong now?" Alcazar asked fearfully. "Is it war?"

Sir Henry Wallace sank back in the seat of the coach that was now taking him rapidly nowhere.

"The port of Westfirth has just been closed," Sir Henry explained in dire tones. "From this moment, no ships can sail in. No ships can sail out."

"Then we're trapped!" Alcazar cried.

"So it would seem," said Sir Henry.

Chapter Thirty-Six

Confusion, misdirection, greed, bright penny blindness—the art of
the confidence man.

—Sir Henry Wallace,
Earl of Staffordshire

DUBOIS' CAB SPED FROM THE FRACAS AT THE
Blue Parrot straight to the Old Fort, the residence of
the archbishop. In his morning meeting, Dubois had told
the archbishop as much as he deemed the man should know
about Sir Henry Wallace and the threat he posed. He had
warned the archbishop that if Wallace eluded capture, the
port would have to be closed. The archbishop had scoffed
at such an idea.

"Nonsense," said the archbishop. "His Holiness can't be
serious!"

The archbishop had heard rumors about Dubois, knew
him to be the grand bishop's trusted and confidential agent,
but had never met him. The archbishop was at first unim-
pressed by the common, shabby little man. Dubois was used
to creating such a deplorable first impression. Indeed, he
fostered such impressions. He liked being underestimated,
forgotten. He found it easier to slip up on his victim un-
awares.

Having been confident he would capture Sir Henry, Dubois had said nothing more at the time. Now the man had

once more escaped him. Dubois found the archbishop host-
ing a private musical evening for several wealthy gentlemen
of the city, hoping to be able to persuade them to donate to
the building of the cathedral. The archbishop was not
pleased at being summoned away from the concert to meet
with Dubois, who was waiting in the shadows of a balcony
outside the salon.

"Well, what is it?" the archbishop demanded. He could
hear, in the distance, the soprano singing one of his favorite
arias.

Dubois explained briefly that Wallace had managed to
escape.

"You must act now, Your Reverence," Dubois concluded.
"Close the port before this extremely dangerous man can
flee to Freya."

"Out of the question," said the archbishop brusquely.
"People will view this as a prelude to war with Freya. Does
His Majesty know about this?"

"The bishop will handle His Majesty," said Dubois. "As
you are aware, I have here the bishop's letter giving me full
power to make this demand."

The archbishop was well aware of the letter. He knew it
was genuine. He could see and touch the grand bishop's
own personal seal that was affixed to it. But the archbishop
was still not convinced. The idea that he was about to unof-
ficially declare war on Freya by closing the port was appalling. He could envision the hordes of angry ship owners
descending on him, howling about lost money. And, the
truth be told, he was worried about the funding for his magnificent cathedral. In the event of war, that funding might
dry up and so would his legacy.

"The Royal Navy would have to be informed—"

"I've already done that," said Dubois coolly.

The archbishop flushed in anger. "You had no right—"

"I have every right," said Dubois. "I refer you, once
again, to the grand bishop's letter."

The archbishop thought this over. The grand bishop's

letter gave Dubois power to deal with any crisis in general. The grand bishop did not say anything specific about the closing of the port.

"I would feel more comfortable if I had a letter in the grand bishop's own hand stating that he was responsible for issuing the decree," said the archbishop. "As you know, I am but his humble servant. I could send a messenger to Evreux by griffin. He would be back by morning two days hence."

"By which time, Sir Henry Wallace will be well on his way to Freya bearing Rosia's doom," said Dubois.

"Hardly *my* fault," said the archbishop with a telling glance at Dubois. "*You* are the one who lost him."

Dubois would have liked to wring the neck of the grand bishop's humble servant. He restrained himself, however. He was thinking he was going to have to get tough with this man, threaten to reveal a certain sordid incident in the arch-bishop's past which Dubois had taken care to discover, just in case. He did not want to resort to such a drastic measure. Not yet. Not if there was an easier way.

"If you will excuse me," said the archbishop, "I am going to return to my guests."

Dubois gazed, frowning, into the night. Hearing voices drifting up from down below, he glanced down over the edge of the balcony.

Silhouetted against the lambent light of stars and half moon, three men were walking the battlements at a slow pace. He could not see their faces in the darkness, but he knew them by their attire: one man in helm and breastplate, one in flowing monk's robes, one in a long black cassock. By their low tones, they were deeply engaged in some impor-tant and serious conversation. He spoke to the back of the departing archbishop.

"Your Reverence," said Dubois, "what would you say if I referred this matter of Sir Henry Wallace to the judgment of the Arcanum?"

The archbishop stopped. He turned around. He looked uneasy. "Why would the Arcanum get involved?"

"Because they have sense enough to understand the danger," said Dubois.

The archbishop followed Dubois' gaze to the battlements, to the man in the black cassock. The archbishop looked from Father Jacob back to Dubois and back to Father Jacob. The archbishop's face went stony. He turned and stalked off.

Dubois smiled and out of habit started eavesdropping on the priest, who had paused right beneath the balcony. He heard Father Jacob tell his Knight Protector that he was planning to order the archbishop to send forces to scour the city in search of one he termed "the Sorceress" and her evil followers. Dubois raised an eyebrow. He had heard of this Sorceress. Was she responsible for the ambush? If so, why had she been attempting to kill both Sir Henry and Father Jacob?

"I need to meet this woman," Dubois said to himself.

The father and his companions moved on and so did Dubois. As he returned to his coach, he saw the harried archbishop trying to explain matters to his guest, the Lord Mayor of the City of Westfirth, who was almost purple with fury. Dubois shook his head and slipped away.

Within the hour, a cannon announcing the closing of the port of Westfirth went off, as constables fanned out across the city, looking for a young man of about seventeen, who might be suffering from a gunshot wound to the foot, and a Freyan woman named Eiddwen, beautiful, with black curling hair. Dubois returned to his room at the Threadneedle Inn to try to get some sleep while he awaited the reports of his agents.

The echoes of the cannon shot were still lingering in the air when Sir Henry Wallace put his new plan into action. He watched out the window and when the coach entered a certain, shadowy street, Henry rose to his feet and rapped on the ceiling of the coach. The coach rolled to a stop. Henry got out and, glancing behind to make certain the street was empty, he spoke to the driver.

"Are we being followed?"

"Yes, Guvnor," said the driver, who knew Sir Henry by a completely different identity. "Small hansom cab. Keeps a block or two behind."

"Come down here," said Henry.

The driver obeyed. The two walked off to an alley, leaving Alcazar, a prey to terror, alone with the woman and the "Duke." He lost sight of Sir Henry in the darkness and was afraid that Monsieur Russo (Sir Henry's alias) had abandoned him. Then, thankfully, Sir Henry and the driver returned. Sir Henry entered the coach. Alcazar was about to say something when he saw the man's face.

"You're not Monsieur Russo!" Alcazar gasped.

"Shut yer yap," said the driver, now wearing the count's cloak.

Sir Henry, wearing the driver's coat, mounted the box, took the reins, and the journey resumed.

Henry glanced several times over his shoulder and finally caught sight of the small hansom cab. He took care so that the cab did not lose him. The original idea had been to throw Dubois off the trail. Now Henry wanted Dubois on it. Dubois had grown annoying. Henry wanted to be rid of him.

Henry drove the coach to a small boarding house located near the docks. He stopped beneath a streetlamp and, in his guise as coach driver, climbed down from the seat to assist the "count" and his "lady" to leave the coach. Alcazar was also about to leave. Henry strong-armed him, shoved him back inside.

"Not a word," said Sir Henry. "Keep an eye on him," he said to the man who had been driving the coach.

The count and his lady swiftly mounted the steps of the house. The count unlocked the outer door, and hurried inside, bringing his lady with him. Sir Henry returned to the driver's seat. He waited a moment to make certain Dubois' agent in the hansom cab had taken note of the movements of the "count," then drove off. Looking back over his shoulder, Henry noted with immense satisfaction that the hansom cab remained parked near the boarding house.

Once more having shaken a tail, Henry drove the coach to his next destination. When the coach stopped, he ordered Alcazar to quit blubbering and get out. Alcazar looked around and saw with dismay that they were in a stinking, refuse-littered, festering street of one of the worst parts of Westfirth.

There being no streetlamps in this squalid section of the city, few people dared venture out after dark. Those who did had their reasons. The sight of an elegantly dressed "woman" descending from a coach brought unwelcome attention. Two rough-looking men approached her. Alcazar was mute with fear. Henry Wallace coolly drew out a monocle that when he touched it a certain way, began to glow with light. He held the light to his face. The two men halted, then backed away precipitously.

"Pardon, Guvnor," said one man, nervously touching his hand to the brim of a filthy hat. "Didn't know it was you."

Henry ordered the driver to leave, then took hold of Alcazar by the arm and escorted him to what was popularly known as a rag and bottle shop. Henry drew out one of many keys he carried with him, fit it into the lock, opened the creaking door and shoved Alcazar inside. Henry followed, closing the door, leaving them in pitch-darkness, for the windows were shuttered. He told Alcazar to stand by the door, not to move.

Sir Henry drew out the glowing monocle and by its light, he wended his way among the stacks of refuse and broken furniture, cracked dishes, bags of hair, bottles, clothing, books, weapons, watches, and anything else that could be bartered or sold by those in desperate need.

The shop's owner, hearing someone rummaging about, came down from his little room above the shop. He was clad in his nightdress and carried a candle in one hand and a stout club in the other.

Henry again allowed the light from the monocle to play upon his face. The owner stared at him keenly, gave a nod, and asked him in a whisper if he needed anything. Henry told him he required food and a bed for the night. The man went back upstairs. Henry continued on his way to a large portmanteau he kept stashed at the very back of the shop. He opened it, rummaged through coats, waistcoats, shirts, boots, hats, gloves, shoes, underclothes, and even handkerchiefs. Henry took off the driver's clothes he was wearing and placed them in the portmanteau and then opened a small metal box. Henry shone his light on a quantity of letters, official looking documents and papers, all expertly forged. He selected those he required, then shut and locked the metal box.

Henry went back to Alcazar and thrust some clothes into his arms and told him to change. Alcazar was so happy to get out of his corset and petticoats and so exhausted by the events of the evening that he complied readily, without complaining, not even when told he would be spending the night in this ghastly place.

The shop owner returned with a large bowl containing some sort of meat floating in congealed gravy. Sir Henry ate ravenously. Alcazar, smelling it, queasily declined. The owner indicated a vacant room next to his own; they could spend the night there. He brought them blankets and pillows, which Henry spread out on the floor. He lay down on the blanket and stretched out comfortably.

Alcazar remained standing.

"Are there rats?" he asked fearfully.

"Big as dogs," said Sir Henry.

After his exertions in aiding the count to escape his kidnappers, Stephano also spent a restful night. The combination of brandy and yellow goo sent him into a deep slumber. His shoulder was stiff and his thigh sore, but both wounds were healing well. He went to check on Dag and found him already up and eating breakfast.

"How are you this morning?" Stephano asked.

"Fine, sir," said Dag, stolidly eating. "The burns weren't serious."

Stephano noted that Dag was sitting awkwardly, making certain his burned back did not come in contact with the chair.

"He's *not* fine," Miri snapped. "He's going to have his bandages changed and more ointment this morning before he goes anywhere."

She slammed a bowl down in front of Stephano and hurled a spoon in his general direction. He caught it on the bounce. Miri stalked off, going back to the galley.

"Bullets flying, Captain," Dag advised. "Keep your head down, sir."

Stephano understood. Miri was in one of her moods. He took a seat and tried to avoid coming under fire as Miri returned carrying a large pot in one hand and a spoon in the other.

"You're having oatmeal," she stated.

Stephano hated oatmeal, but he caught Dag's warning glance and said meekly, "Oatmeal will be fine. Thank you, Miri."

Miri sniffed and dug her spoon into the pot. Stephano reached out to pet the cat, who was curled up in Dag's lap, dozing in the morning sunshine.

"How is the Doctor this morning?"

The cat responded to Stephano's pat by purring loudly.

"Lazy beast," said Miri scathingly.

She flung the oatmeal into the bowl and then pointed the spoon at Dag.

"I'll have you know, Dag Thorgrimson, I found a mouse in the storage room this morning! Ran right over my foot. Mice running rampant all over the ship and that idle cat of yours sits there purring! He better start earning his keep, or I'll throw him into the Breath."

She shook the spoon at the Doctor, spattering him with oatmeal. The cat gave a startled meow and dashed for cover.

"She doesn't mean it," said Stephano.

"I do so too, mean it!" cried Miri, rounding on him. "The same goes for you, Captain Bloody de Guichen! We've flown all this way and for what?"

Miri slammed the pot with the oatmeal onto the table and answered her own question. "Gythe hearing demons. You stabbed and nearly killed. Dag lit on fire. My own boat attacked and almost sunk. What have you to show for it? Well?"

She stood in front of Stephano, hands on her hips, her red hair flaring in the morning sun, her green eyes blazing. Stephano shoveled oatmeal into his mouth as though his life depended on it which, with Miri in her present mood, perhaps it did. Dag had taken his own advice and was keeping his head down.

"I've a mind to hoist the sails and leave right now!" Miri continued, and Stephano could see that she meant it.

"I'm sorry this hasn't turned out well, Miri," he said, shoving what remained of the oatmeal around in the bowl. "We can't sail today anyway. Not until the authorities complete the inspections and issue permits—"

"Permit!" Miri snorted. "As if I needed a blasted permit!"

Generally, Trundlers did not require permits. Having no nationality, they tended to come and go as they pleased; one reason Stephano was fond of conducting operations on a Trundler houseboat. But war with Freya loomed on the horizon, at least that's what everyone was saying. Even Trundlers might find their lives changed during a time of war.

"Give me today to track down this last Alcazar, the one who's the sailor," Stephano pleaded. "If we don't find him or it turns out he has nothing to do with the journeyman, then we can leave."

Miri regarded him with narrowed eyes, then said coldly, "You have today."

She grabbed up the pot and banged her way through the hatch. They could hear her stomping angrily down the stairs.

"She's worried about Gythe, sir," said Dag.

"I know she is," said Stephano. "I'm worried, too."

The door opened a crack. Rodrigo stuck his head out. "Coast clear?"

"She's gone back to the galley," said Dag.

"Did I hear Miri say we are leaving?" Rodrigo asked worriedly, coming out on deck. "We can't leave yet. I have to pick up my new clothes at the tailor's—"

"I don't think now would be a good time to mention your clothes," Stephano said. "Not unless you want to be wearing oatmeal instead of a hat."

"So what's the plan for today, sir?" Dag asked.

"Pick up my clothes," said Rodrigo.

"*You* pick up your own damn clothes," said Stephano. "Dag and I will go to the docks and ask if anyone knows this sailor named Alcazar. If not"—he shrugged—"we pack up and go home. And I tell my mother we failed."

"She might be interested in the demons," said Rodrigo. "And the green magic I'm not supposed to talk about."

"Fine—*you* tell my mother we fled Westfirth because we were attacked by fiends from Hell riding giant bats," Stephano said testily.

Rodrigo thought this over. "I see your point. She already suspects me of being a bad influence on you. She'd probably think I was luring you into opium dens."

Stephano sat jabbing his spoon dejectedly into his slowly congealing oatmeal. Dag lured Doctor Ellington out from under the cannon with a bit of smoked fish. Rodrigo took a turn about the deck, trying to work up the courage to ask Miri to fix him a coddled egg when he came to a sudden halt.

"Stephano! Look there." Rodrigo pointed to the end of the pier, where several men could be seen conferring. Four of the men were Trundlers, one of whom was Miri's uncle, Ehric McPike. Ehric was talking with a well-dressed man wearing a long hunting coat, tall black boots, and a hat.

"Does that man seem familiar?" Rodrigo asked, frowning. "The one in the hunting coat. I have the feeling I know him from somewhere."

"Yeah, me, too," said Dag, squinting against the sun.

Stephano rose to his feet. He eyed the man and then said slowly, "That's the count. From last night."

"By God!" exclaimed Rodrigo, stunned. "You're right! How do you suppose he found us?"

"That's what I'm wondering," said Stephano grimly.

Miri's uncle and the count began walking down the pier in the direction of the *Cloud Hopper*. Dag reached for his musket. He had heard the story from last night, how Rodrigo and Stephano had fought off thugs to save some mysterious count and his lady.

"The love of my life," Rodrigo said in melancholy tones.

"Fetch Miri," Stephano told him, and Rodrigo hurried down below. He returned in a moment with Miri and Gythe, relating again the tale of the previous evening's adventure, just in case they had forgotten.

"How are you this morning?" Stephano asked, smiling at Gythe.

Gythe was pale and wan. Her fingers danced in the air. She touched her ears and shook her head.

"She says the voices are gone," Miri reported.

Gythe regarded her sister hopefully. Her fingers fluttered. Miri shook her head. Gythe sighed and walked forlornly away.

"She seems to be wanting to tell me something," said Miri helplessly. "But I can't understand her. I'm not sure she understands herself. Oh, Stephano, I'm so worried about her!"

"I am sorry, Miri," Stephano said quietly, moving over to squeeze her hand.

"You better be," Miri said, but she said it with a sigh and a half-smile and squeezed his hand back. He knew all was forgiven.

Ehric McPike accompanied the count, serving as his escort. The Trundlers bowed before no king, but they did have their own nation which was wherever a group of Trundler clans docked their houseboats, a tradition that had lasted for centuries. Many Trundler camps were as old or older than the cities near which they were established. Every so often, some enterprising person (such as the archbishop) endeavored to oust the Trundlers, terming them thieves and smugglers. Nothing came of these efforts, however. The archbishop was informed by the head of the constabulary that the Trundlers could not be told to leave Westfirth because they weren't in Westfirth. They docked in the Breath. The city limits of Westfirth ended at the shoreline.

The Trundler camp had their leader and guards. Outsiders were viewed with suspicion and must be approved by a Trundler clan leader before they were permitted to enter the camp and then only with an escort. When the count and Miri's uncle reached the *Cloud Hopper*, Ehric told the stranger to remain on the pier, while he boarded the *Cloud Hopper*. He kissed his nieces, and then turned to Miri.

"This man"—Ehric motioned at the stranger waiting on the pier with a jerk of his thumb—"says he has business with the captain. Will you receive him and take him into your care, Miri? Or should the lads and I escort him back to from where he came?"

The count stood quite at his ease on the pier. He gazed at the boats and their gaily colored balloons and the Trundlers going about their everyday business: hanging out laundry to dry, cooking, sweeping; all the while keeping a wary eye on the stranger in their midst. The count smiled at Stephano with the air of calm and cool self-confidence he'd displayed during the attempt on his life. Reaching up, he tipped his hat with a courtly gesture.

Stephano kept silent. The *Cloud Hopper* was not his boat. It was not his place to say who could come aboard or not.

"He can board," said Miri. "We'll see to him."

"Shout if you need help," said her uncle, as he took his leave.

Miri promised she would. The count came on board. He cast a glance at Dag, who stood stolidly on deck, his musket under his arm and Doctor Ellington on his shoulder. The count turned to Miri, standing on deck with Gythe at her side. The count's eyes widened at the sight of Gythe, whose remarkable beauty tended to have that effect on most men. He spent a moment regarding her in silent admiration. Gythe did not notice; she never did notice men staring at her. Rodrigo saw, however, and he nudged Stephano.

"There's hope for me!" he whispered. "Ask him about his lady friend."

Stephano snorted and stepped forward. The count swept off his hat. He expressed his pleasure at meeting Miri and Gythe and thanked them for permitting him to come aboard.

"I have business with Captain de Guichen," said the count, turning to Stephano with a bow. "Private business," he added gently.

"I'll leave you to it, then," said Miri. "Come along, Gythe. I need your help with the washing up. Try not to get yourself shot," she added in a low voice, walking past Stephano. "I'm running out of herbs for my poultice."

"Let us be grateful for small blessings," said Rodrigo.

Miri and Gythe descended into the hold. Stephano knew quite well she had no intention of washing dishes. She and Gythe would both settle themselves on the stairs on other side of the hatch, where they could comfortably overhear the entire conversation. Stephano nodded at Dag, who stalked off to the bow, out of earshot, but within musket range. Stephano politely invited the count to sit down. Rodrigo brought up a chair and joined them, despite the fact that he had not been invited.

"You're no count, are you," Stephano said, as the stranger took a seat.

Rodrigo blinked. "What do you mean he's not a count?"

"How very clever of you, Captain de Guichen," said the

stranger with that same cool and confident smile. "But then, the son of the Countess de Marjolaine would have inherited his mother's brains."

Stephano's face froze as always when his mother's name was mentioned.

"What is your name, sir?" he asked. "What do you want of me?"

The count reached into an inner pocket. Seeing Dag raise his musket, the count lifted a warding hand. He drew out a piece of paper, which he laid on the table.

"My name is Russo. Here are my credentials, Captain." Monsieur Russo tapped the wax seal on the letter in an odd staccato rhythm, paused, then tapped it again. The seal was the King's Rose, the official emblem of Alaric, King of Rosia. When the stranger tapped the seal, it began to magically change. The rose vanished and was replaced by a thorn, the emblem of a unit of elite undercover operatives tasked with protecting the king.

Stephano cast a glance at his friend.

"Is it genuine?"

"Quite genuine," said Rodrigo. "The hand-tapping activates the magic. Monsieur Russo has to tap the seal in a certain way or the magic won't work."

"What does the Thorn want with me, Monsieur Russo?" Stephano asked.

"You and Monsieur de Villeneuve performed a valuable service to your king last night, Captain de Guichen," said Russo, picking up the letter and returning it to his coat pocket. "I came to thank you."

"I didn't know I was helping the king," said Stephano. "Otherwise I wouldn't have."

Monsieur Russo smiled. "Your mother told me you might be difficult."

Stephano flushed in anger and rose to his feet. "If that is all you have to say, Monsieur . . ."

"You will be interested to know that I have in my care a certain missing journeyman," said Russo.

Stephano shrugged. "Good for you. What has that to do with me?"

Monsieur Russo glanced around the boat, then said quietly, "Is the name Henry Wallace familiar to you?"

"I've heard of him," said Stephano, shooting Rodrigo a warning look, ordering him to keep his mouth shut.

"Your mother told you about him, I assume."

Stephano shook his head. "I've heard his name bandied about town."

"I very much doubt that," said Monsieur Russo with a dry chuckle. He grew serious, his face shadowed. "Henry Wallace is a dangerous foe. He is the man who kidnapped Alcazar. Two days ago, I managed to free Pietro Alcazar from Wallace's clutches. Alcazar's brother, Manuel, is a merchant seaman. We were to sail on his ship, the *Silver Raven*, last night. As we left the hotel, Wallace's bully boys tried to grab Alcazar. You and Monsieur de Villeneuve thwarted that attempt."

Rodrigo was bewildered. "Excuse me, sir, I don't understand. We saved you and a *lady*—"

He stopped talking and stared, aghast. "No! Don't tell me! That beautiful creature! I held her in my arms . . ." Rodrigo paused, then added, "I *did* think the dear girl weighed rather a lot . . ."

Dag, who wasn't supposed to be listening, was seized with a violent fit of coughing. He turned his back to them, his shoulders shaking. Stephano ran his hand over his mouth and rubbed his chin to hide his grin.

Monsieur Russo frowned at them both. "This is *not* a matter for levity, gentlemen."

"So you managed to escape from Wallace with our help," said Stephano, regaining control of himself. "What happened? Why didn't you leave Westfirth?"

"The closing of the port, of course," said Russo impatiently, annoyed by the question. "You *do* know the port was closed, don't you, Captain?"

Rodrigo was saying sadly, "I can't believe it. The woman of my dreams is a man."

At this, Stephano feared Dag was going to rupture something and he said hastily, "Just because the port is closed doesn't mean you and Alcazar can't leave Westfirth. You could travel overland to reach Evreux."

"We could . . . if we were going to Evreux," said Russo.

"Where are you taking Alcazar?"

"Somewhere safe," said Russo evasively. "You do not need to concern yourself with our destination, Captain. The less you know, the better."

"So how can I help you?" Stephano asked. "In case I am inclined to help you. Which at the moment, I'm not."

"Alcazar is in a secure location being guarded by two of my agents." Russo said, then shrugged. "Or at least I thought the location was secure. Last night, I caught sight of one of Wallace's agents outside the house. This morning, I saw several more. We are surrounded. I need you to draw off Wallace's men, while I take Alcazar to safety."

"Where is Wallace?"

"I have no idea," said Russo. "If I had to guess, I would say he is no longer in Westfirth. I received a report that an attempt was made on his life yesterday."

Stephano exchanged glances with Rodrigo. This much of the man's story was true.

"Then who is watching you?" Rodrigo asked.

"One of Wallace's best men—a pudgy, nondescript little fellow. He goes by the name of Dubois. Do you know the name?" Russo asked casually.

"No, Monsieur," said Stephano. "Should I?"

"I thought perhaps your mother might have mentioned him," said Russo.

"My mother doesn't tend to confide in me," said Stephano dryly.

"You saw Dubois, though you probably didn't notice him. He was in the café when you killed another of Wallace's agents, a man named James Harrington. You knew *him* as Sir Richard Piefer—"

"Good God!" Stephano exclaimed, astonished. "I remember. The pudgy fellow I took for a clerk. He ran over to see if Harrington was dead."

Stephano eyed Russo. "But if that was this Dubois, he told me *I* had ruined his chance of *finding* Wallace . . ."

"Ah, he is clever, our little Dubois. He would say that to throw you off the trail."

Stephano sat for a moment thinking this through, trying to sort out the tangle in which no one was who he—or she—claimed to be. "If this Dubois knows where you have Alcazar, why doesn't he try to abduct him again?"

"He will—tonight," said Russo. "He wouldn't dare attempt to drag a lady out of a respectable house on a well-traveled street during the day. The neighbors would call the constables, all very messy."

"How many men does Dubois have?"

Russo shrugged. "Ten or so. Maybe more."

"Ten!" Stephano repeated and then he laughed. "You have a high opinion of me and my comrades, Monsieur. We are good, but not that good."

"I'm not permitted to handle firearms," said Rodrigo by way of explanation.

"I suggest you enlist the aid of the Constabulary," said Russo. "Show them this document. I will leave it with you." He handed over the letter sealed with the King's Rose.

"You could show them the document," said Stephano. "Commandeer a vessel and tell them to sail you and Alcazar to wherever you want to go. You're on the king's business."

Russo quirked an eyebrow and smiled and adjusted his cravat. He appeared slightly embarrassed.

"He can't," said Rodrigo in sudden understanding. "Because the king doesn't *know* it's his business. His Majesty doesn't know Alcazar was kidnapped."

"His Majesty has so many cares," said Russo gravely. "Your mother believes we should not add to them. This letter will be enough to convince the head of the Constabulary that you require his assistance. That and the name of Lord Captain de Guichen, son of the Countess de Marjolaine."

"You mean my *mother's* name will convince them to act," said Stephano coldly.

"Your mother is held in high esteem throughout the world, Captain," said Russo.

Stephano was about to make some scathing remark when the door opened and Miri walked out onto deck. She came over to Stephano and dug her nails into his shoulder, his sore shoulder.

"I don't trust this man," she said coolly. "He knows too much about us."

"I agree," said Stephano. He eyed Russo. "I want to see Alcazar."

"Out of the question," said Russo shortly.

"I see Alcazar or no deal," said Stephano.

Russo fixed Stephano with a cold and glittering gaze. "You are being asked to perform this service by your king, Captain."

"Piss on my king!" said Stephano angrily. "Do we have a deal or not, Monsieur?"

"Dubois knows you—"

"He knows you and *you* came here without being seen. At least, I assume you weren't followed."

Russo gave a faint smile. "No, Captain, I was not followed." He sat frowning, his hand absently tapping the king's letter. Then he said abruptly, "Very well. I will take you to Alcazar."

"You're certain he's a man? Not a woman?" Rodrigo asked plaintively. "A lovely woman, if a trifle on the hefty side?"

"Quite certain," said Russo.

Rodrigo gave a heartfelt sigh. This was too much for Dag, who burst out with a roar of laughter.

Chapter Thirty-Seven

To the unrefined or underbred, the visiting card is but a trifling and insignificant bit of paper; but to the cultured disciple of social law, it conveys a subtle and unmistakable intelligence.

—Rodrigo de Villeneuve

HENRY WALLACE, ALIAS MONSIEUR RUSSO, smiled inwardly as he watched the captain's team, the so-called Cadre of the Lost, make their plans to foil Dubois and prepare to accompany Sir Henry to meet Alcazar. Henry had not been pleased when the captain had set the condition that he must meet the journeyman, but for his own plan to escape Westfirth to succeed, Henry had been forced to give way. The meeting with Alcazar would do no harm and might prove to do some good. Henry was already considering how he might use this to his advantage.

The main danger had been that Stephano would recognize the name Dubois and know him to be the grand bishop's agent, not Wallace's agent as Sir Henry had claimed. But Dubois was a common name in Rosia, like the name "Smith" in Freya. Henry could always claim that his Dubois was not the grand bishop's Dubois. His fears on this score were allayed. Stephano did not appear to have heard of any Dubois.

Lounging on deck, Henry watched Dag swiftly and expertly load a variety weapons. He watched Miri and the beautiful Gythe emerge from the hold wearing gray robes and white wimples, becoming Sisters of Mercy. He saw Miri tuck her corset gun into her stocking. The only weak link in the captain's chain appeared to be Rodrigo de Villeneuve, who was coming along simply because he was bored and had nothing else to do until the tailor's shop opened. Wallace made a mental note.

At last they were ready or so it seemed until Dag bent down to pick up the cat. He placed Doctor Ellington on his shoulder.

"Uh, Dag," said Stephano, glancing sidelong at an amused Sir Henry, "you might want to have the Doctor remain aboard the boat."

"I'm not leaving him behind to be poisoned again, sir," Dag said stiffly.

"What do you mean by that?" Miri demanded, eyes blazing. "Are you accusing me—"

"No," said Stephano quickly. "He's not. We should be leaving."

"We are going to stop by the tailor's, aren't we?" Rodrigo asked. "My new clothes—"

"Yes, yes, Rigo, not now!" Stephano herded everyone down the gangplank.

"Interesting associates you have, Captain," Henry remarked.

"They get the job done," Stephano replied shortly.

The Cadre split up. The "Sisters of Mercy" went off in one direction, while Henry led Stephano, Dag, and Rodrigo along a circuitous route that eventually took them up onto the rooftops, among the chimney pots of the building next door to the boarding house. He indicated that they were to jump from this roof to the next.

"Dubois and his agents will be watching the doors," Henry said by way of explanation. "We can enter unobserved."

Rodrigo stated that he would go first. He made the jump with ease.

"I have done a bit of roof-leaping once or twice before,"

Rodrigo confided. "Comes in handy when a jealous husband is breathing down your neck."

Dag, on the other hand, stood glowering down at the ground that was about four stories beneath them.

"I'm not built for jumping, Captain," Dag said flatly.

Henry pictured the big man in his leather armor and helm attempting to scale the four-foot gap between buildings—with the added impediment of a cat on his shoulders.

"Dubois doesn't know me, sir," Dag added. "I could walk in the front door, take a look, see if I notice anything."

This made sense and Henry agreed.

"Room number 116. Ground floor in the rear. We'll meet you there."

Dag and the Doctor departed, heading back down to street level. Henry and Stephano jumped the gap. Once on the roof, they entered through an access door, hurried down a dark staircase and into a hall. The boarding house catered to single men, no families allowed, this being stipulated by the building's owner, who happened to be Sir Henry Wallace. Single men went to work during the day and tended to mind their own business at night.

"Quiet place," said Stephano.

"I am fond of quiet, Captain," said Henry.

He walked briskly down the hall that led to room 116. The numbers, in fading paint, were barely visible on the door. He knocked in a peculiar manner on the door and waited expectantly.

No reply.

Henry frowned slightly and knocked again, then called out to one of the two agents he'd left to guard Alcazar.

"It's me, Brianna. Russo. Open the door."

His agents had been up all night. They had probably fallen asleep. He drew out his key, inserted it into the lock, and opened the door.

"It's Russo. I'm not alone—"

Henry came to a sudden halt. He stared in amazement so great he was momentarily paralyzed.

His two agents, the man and the woman, were dead. The man lay on the floor in a pool of blood. His pistol was at his side. He'd drawn it, but never had a chance to use it. The woman was sprawled in a blood-soaked chair, her vacant eyes staring at the ceiling. Both had been shot at point-blank range, the man through the head, the woman through the heart.

Rodrigo stood staring at the body of the woman. "Oh, my God! Is that . . . her? I mean him?"

Stephano grabbed his friend and shoved him back out into the hall. "Go fetch Dag. He's coming in the front."

Rodrigo didn't move. "I don't understand—"

"Go!" said Stephano.

"That's him, isn't it?" said Stephano in a grim voice, his gaze on the woman. "That's Alcazar."

Henry, in his first overpowering shock, had made the same mistake. The dead woman was wearing the same clothes as Alcazar; she had been of similar build, height, and weight. But she wasn't Alcazar. Henry began to breathe again.

"No," said Henry. "She's one of my agents."

"Then where—"

Henry pointed.

The apartment had two rooms: living area and bedchamber. The door to the bedchamber was shut. Henry indicated with a gesture that Alcazar might be in there with the killer. He drew his pistol. Stephano reached for his own pistol.

Henry motioned for Stephano to circle around to the left of the door. Henry kept to the right, a route that would take him past the dining table and the small white card propped up against the saltcellar. He palmed the card as he passed.

Dag entered, accompanied by Doctor Ellington, whose nose twitched at the smell of blood. Henry indicated with a jerk of his thumb that someone might be inside the bedroom. Dag nodded and moved silently to join Stephano. Rodrigo remained in the hall with his hands covering his ears.

Stephano and Dag and Henry stood together, pistols raised, hammers cocked. Henry looked at Stephano, who nodded. Henry kicked in the door and the three men ran inside.

The bedroom was empty. Henry glanced first at the window, saw it was shut, the curtains drawn. He breathed an inward sigh of relief.

"Alcazar," Henry called, frowning. "It's me, Russo."

"I'm here," quavered a voice.

"Where?" Henry demanded.

"Under the bed!"

"You can come out now," Henry said. "You are safe. I have friends with me."

"I would, but I'm stuck . . ." Alcazar said plaintively.

Henry rolled his eyes, muttered something beneath his breath. He lowered the hammer on his pistol and thrust it back into his belt. He and Stephano managed to disentangle and then drag Alcazar out from beneath the bed. The journeyman was in a pitiable state, shaking and trembling and barely coherent, for which Henry was grateful.

Alcazar claimed he had been asleep on the bed when he'd been wakened by the sounds of gunfire outside the door. He had been so terrified, he had rolled off the bed and crawled underneath it. He had no idea who had fired the shots. He'd heard the killer leave and close the door, but he'd been afraid the murderer would return for him, so he remained in hiding beneath the bed all morning. Alcazar had not seen the killer. If the killer had said anything, Alcazar had not heard it.

He nearly fainted at the sight of the bodies; particularly when he saw the woman in the same clothes he had been wearing. Rodrigo came to the poor man's aid, pouring wine from a bottle he'd managed to locate for himself.

"Drink this, Madame," said Rodrigo. "I mean, sir. I find this all frightfully confusing," he said in a low voice to Stephano.

"Here are the keys to the room next door," Henry said,

handing the keys to Rodrigo. "Take Alcazar there and keep an eye on him, will you?"

Rodrigo escorted the quivering journeyman and the wine bottle into the adjoining apartment. Henry looked up and down the hall, then shut the door.

"Obviously the killer mistook the woman for Alcazar," said Stephano. "But why would Dubois want to kill Alcazar? That doesn't make sense."

"Remember that this Dubois is an agent for Sir Henry Wallace. Perhaps Dubois was acting on orders. After the attempt on his life, Wallace considered Alcazar a danger, a liability," Henry suggested. "Wallace ordered Dubois to kill him so that he wouldn't talk."

"Maybe . . ." Stephano did not appear convinced. "But if what I hear about Alcazar is true, the value of his discovery is beyond estimation. My mother has told me Wallace is not the type of man who is easily scared."

"Far be it for me to argue with the opinion of the countess," said Henry with a bow and a smile.

Dag, meanwhile, had been examining one of the bodies. "I know this man, Captain. He's the Duke—a knifeman working for one of the bosses, a gent known as the Guvnor. Could be this killing had nothing to do with Wallace *or* Alcazar, sir. Could be a fight between rival bosses."

An excellent idea. Henry wished he'd thought of it.

"I believe you are right, sir," Henry said in admiring tones. "It is quite possible this man was involved in a gang. I knew nothing about him or the woman. I hired them on recommendation."

"There's an easy way to find out," said Stephano. "If Dubois and Wallace's other agents are still keeping an eye on this place, then Wallace wasn't the killer. If they're not there, it means they figure the job is over."

Sir Henry agreed that this made sense. He locked the door to the room containing the bodies. Stephano sent Dag and Doctor Ellington to join Rodrigo keeping watch on Alcazar. Henry accompanied Stephano to the main entryway.

Peering out the window, Henry scanned the street. He saw the two "Sisters" strolling slowly along the avenue. The nuns would stop every so often, studying the addresses on the houses, as though searching for a particular location.

"There," said Henry, pointing. "In the alley. Those two men. The pudgy man in the hat and cloak, that's Dubois. I don't know the name of the other man, but I do know him to be another of Wallace's agents."

"You're right," said Stephano, watching out another window, keeping behind the curtain. "I recognize Dubois. He's the man I saw in the café."

"He's probably come to find out from his agent if Alcazar is still in the building," said Henry.

"So it wasn't Dubois who killed your agents," said Stephano.

"A gangland shooting, as your shrewd lieutenant surmised," said Henry.

"You smuggle Alcazar out by going over the rooftops, the way we came in," Stephano suggested. "We'll keep on eye on Dubois."

"You've met Alcazar, Captain," said Henry dryly. "Picture that quivering mass of jelly leaping gaps and running across rooftops."

"I see what you mean," said Stephano. "Look there. Dubois is leaving."

"His agent assured him Alcazar and I are still inside," said Henry. "He'll be going to make arrangements for our capture. You should follow him."

"Miri and Gythe know what to do," said Stephano complacently.

Miri and Gythe, in their guises as nuns, strolled along down the street after Dubois, keeping some distance behind him. He vanished around a corner and the Sisters disappeared after him.

"Excellent," said Henry. "As we planned, you and your friends will dispose of the agent who is lurking across the street. You will enlist the aid of the Constabulary and take them to arrest Dubois. I will wait here for an hour, just to make certain we are in the clear, then I will take Alcazar to the ship I have waiting."

"I've made a small change in that plan," said Stephano. "I'm leaving Dag here with you and Alcazar. He'll escort you to the ship."

Henry frowned. "That wasn't part of our arrangement—"

"Finding two of your agents dead wasn't part of the arrangement either," said Stephano grimly. "The killer might return. Dag comes in handy during a fight."

Henry was silent, thinking this over.

"Very well, Captain," he said at last. "As you say, your man might be of use to me."

He and Stephano found Rodrigo and Alcazar sitting at the table, sharing the wine, deep in discussion about magic. Alcazar appeared to have recovered from his fright. He seemed relaxed in Rodrigo's company, talking volubly.

Stephano told Dag about the change in plans. Dag agreed. He and the Doctor mounted guard near the door.

"I believe I will stay here with Dag," said Rodrigo unexpectedly. "Monsieur Alcazar and I have a lot in common."

Stephano was startled. "What about your tailor?"

"I can see him later," Rodrigo said with a wave of his hand.

Henry eyed Rodrigo closely, wondering what was going on, not liking it. Everything Henry had heard about this man indicated Rodrigo de Villeneuve lived for wine, women, and song. He was certainly not a threat and, being Stephano's best friend, might prove an asset.

"Your friend appears to be having a calming effect on Alcazar," said Henry. "Perhaps he should remain."

"I think the wine is having the calming effect on both of them," said Stephano. "But Rigo can stay if he wants."

Rodrigo poured out two more glasses of wine, one for himself and one for Alcazar.

"I suppose the cat is staying, too?" Henry said caustically.

Doctor Ellington had jumped down off Dag's shoulder and was roaming about the room in search of food. Not finding anything, he took great interest in a mousehole in the wall. He settled himself in front of the hole and stared at it fixedly.

"See there, Captain," said Dag, pointing. "Tell Miri. The Doctor goes after mice."

"He just never catches them," said Stephano. "Keep an eye on Rigo, will you?"

Dag nodded and settled himself in a chair by the door, his musket across his lap. Stephano departed, heading for the rooftop again. Rodrigo and Alcazar were deep in a technical discussion about magic. The Doctor was gazing hungrily at the mousehole.

"I'll go take a look to see if there's anyone watching the rear of the building," Henry said to Dag, who silently nodded.

Henry walked into the bedroom. He went to the back window and, in the shadow of the curtain, drew out the visiting card, which was the type ladies leave when they make their daily calls on friends. The card was of expensive stock, elegantly engraved with a bit of knot work. A few words had been written on the back.

So sorry to have missed you, Henry. Another time, perhaps.

The note was signed: *Eiddwen*.

Chapter Thirty-Eight

For the love of all that is holy, just give me a straight-up, stand-up sword fight! I hate court intrigue and all the closet-hiding, eavesdropping, secret-liaisoning, lying, and manipulating, who's-watching-who-watching-who bastards that bow and scrape and simper as they slip arsenic into your claret. You can't tell your friends from your enemies from one day to the next.

—Stephano De Guichen

STEPHANO EXITED THE BOARDING HOUSE by the tradesmen's entrance in the back of the building. Coming around the front, he saw without seeming to see the agent Sir Henry had pointed out. The agent was loitering in the shadows in an abandoned mews, leaning up against a wall. Stephano casually crossed the street. He had no reason to think he'd given the agent any cause for suspicion and he wasn't worried about losing him. But when Stephano reached the mews and glanced inside, the agent was no longer there.

The thought: "You're a bloody idiot!" flashed through Stephano's mind.

Half-turning, he saw someone coming at him with a rush from behind. He ducked, and the truncheon that had been aiming for his head missed. Stephano drove his shoulder into his attacker's body and both men went down onto the street. Stephano grappled for his assailant's throat, planning to choke him into submission. Surprisingly, he met no resistance.

The agent was limp, unconscious. Stephano rolled him over to find that the agent had hit his head on the edge of the curb. Stephano examined him. His skull was cracked and bleeding, but he was breathing. Stephano took hold of the man by the shoulders and dragged him into one of the horse stalls and dumped him in the hay. He'd wake up with the world's worst headache, but at least he'd wake up.

Stephano had been toying with the idea of questioning the agent at gunpoint, asking him for information about his boss. That was obviously no longer an option. Stephano left the mews. Looking back toward the boarding house, he could not see Monsieur Russo, but he figured he was watching. Stephano touched his hat and continued down the street, heading in the direction Miri and Gythe had taken as they followed Dubois.

The sisters had a good head start on Stephano, but Gythe would leave a trail for him. When he came to an intersection of two streets and needed direction, he looked about and almost immediately saw a ball of bright white light dancing among the lower branches of a flowering shrub. Known as "fireflies," these sparkling balls were among the first magical spells taught to children, for they could be created by drawing a single, simple sigil on a bit of paper.

The fireflies have no particular use, other than to introduce children to the wonders of magic. (And entertain cats. Doctor Ellington was particularly fond of chasing them around the deck.) Fireflies do not generate heat and are not harmful. Those created by children generally last only a few moments. Gythe's fireflies lasted hours, however. She could even cause them to glow different colors.

Gythe and Stephano had worked out a code, so that he or Dag or anyone else in the Cadre could tell by the number of fireflies what direction the subject had taken, or if Gythe and Miri had lost the subject, or if the subject had entered a building or jumped into a cab, and so on. Anyone seeing the fireflies flickering in a bush or sparkling in a gutter would merely assume that children had been playing with magic and would think nothing of it.

Stephano's main worry was that Wallace's agent, Dubois, would have taken a cab to his destination, in which case they would lose him. Stephano and Rodrigo and Gythe had tried to develop spells that could be thrown onto the back of a cab in order to track it through the streets, but thus far they had met with only limited success. Traffic tended to obliterate or displace any sort of magical markers left on the pavement and if the cab was drawn by a wyvern and took to the skies they'd lost the person for good.

Fortune smiled on Stephano. Dubois walked back to his lodgings, which were not far from the boarding house. Miri and Gythe had no difficulty following him. Stephano followed the firefly directions and found the sisters sitting on a low wall—two weary nuns taking their ease.

"He's in there," said Miri, indicating a small inn in a residential neighborhood.

"For how long, I wonder," Stephano said.

"Oh, he's going to be there for some time," said Miri complacently. "Gythe and I went inside to ask the landlord for a donation to our Home for Wayward Children. We heard this Dubois fellow tell the innkeeper to have his dinner sent up to his room. He also said that if anyone came asking for him, to send them in to him immediately."

"Excellent!" said Stephano, and he added teasingly, "Did you get any money for your wayward children?"

Miri held up a coin. "I figure I've earned it," she said with a wry smile.

"I'm truly sorry I brought all this trouble on you, Miri," said Stephano ruefully. "Am I forgiven?"

"So long as you convince Dag I did *not* poison his cat," said Miri feelingly.

Stephano leaned his head under Miri's wimple and gave her a kiss, causing two women walking past to glare at him in shocked reproof.

"And now," said Stephano, reaching into his jacket to give the dragon pistol a reassuring touch, "let us go ruin the dinner of Monsieur Dubois."

Sir Henry Wallace watched with satisfaction as Stephano removed Dubois' agent. Wallace still had a problem, however, in the form of Dag Thorgrimson. Henry had not counted on Stephano leaving the mercenary and Rodrigo behind with orders to escort Alcazar to the ship. Henry considered shooting Dag, but the mercenary's competence in handling his weapons and the fact that he was holding a loaded musket forced Henry to dismiss that notion. He might try bribing him, but one look at Dag's ugly, loyal face, his stalwart, soldierly mien, and Henry knew bribery was not going to work.

Henry sat at the table, half-listening to Rodrigo and Alcazar talk, considering ways to get rid of Dag.

After imbibing several glasses of wine, Alcazar had recovered quite remarkably from his fright. He and Rodrigo were discussing Alcazar's job as a journeyman with the Royal Armory. Alcazar, aware of Sir Henry's eye on him, had been careful not to mention anything regarding his discovery up to this point. But now the wine had gone to his head. He was chatting away happily when suddenly something seemed to strike him.

"I beg your pardon, Monsieur, but did you say your name was Villeneuve?" Alcazar asked.

"I did, sir," said Rodrigo.

"Rodrigo de Villeneuve? The man who wrote the treatise on *Magic and Metallurgy*?"

"The same," said Rodrigo, delighted. "Have you read it?"

"My dear sir," said Alcazar with emotion, reaching out to clasp Rodrigo by the hands, "it was your brilliant theories that led me to my discovery—"

At the word, "discovery," Sir Henry's attention snapped

back to the conversation. He fixed Alcazar with a hard, glittering stare that froze the words in the journeyman's mouth and ended the conversation in mid sentence. Henry turned his attention to Rodrigo, who was humming a popular aria and accompanying himself on the table, running his fingers over the table as though it were a pianoforte. Rodrigo appeared to be completely self-absorbed, giving no indication that he had heard Alcazar's babbling, much less understood the importance of what he'd said.

But Sir Henry was not fooled. He had caught the quick gleam of intelligence in the brown eyes and the smile of cynical amusement on the sensitive mouth.

"I do not trust you, Monsieur," said Henry Wallace to himself, gazing at Rodrigo from beneath half-closed eyelids. "Captain de Guichen is not the type of man to have a fool for a friend."

Sir Henry rose to his feet. He saw Dag shift his hand to the trigger of the musket.

"I'm only going to take a look outside," said Sir Henry, and he walked to the window.

Several people were moving along the street. Sir Henry dismissed all of them as being unsuitable and eventually settled on a man dressed in shabby clothes who was walking slowly, peering at the houses, as though searching for an address. Henry summoned Dag.

"That man is one of my agents. I'm going to go speak to him. Remain here where I can summon you if I have need."

Dag nodded silently and, putting down the musket and, keeping his hand on a pistol beneath his coat, took up his station near the entrance to the boarding house. Henry hurried outside and ran out into the street. He stopped the man by flinging an arm around the stranger's shoulder.

"I'm sorry to detain you, friend," said Sir Henry. "But there is a silver petal in this for you if you will stand here and converse with me a moment. How do you find the weather? I fear we may have rain this afternoon. There is a smell of thunder in the air. What do you think?"

"I think it is uncommonly hot, sir," said the man, seeing the glint of silver in Sir Henry's palm.

"An astute observation," said Sir Henry. "Here is your money. Off you go."

He clapped the stranger on the shoulder, then turned and walked back into the house, leaving the stranger to stare after him a moment, then shrug and continue on his way.

Sir Henry motioned Dag to accompany him back to the room where Alcazar and Rodrigo were pouring more wine.

"I fear I am the bearer of bad news regarding your friends, the two young women," said Henry. "My agent brought word. Dubois discovered the two women were following him. He and his agents seized them and carried them off. Your help is needed at once."

Dag's face creased in worry. He scooped up Doctor Ellington, settled the cat on his shoulder, then reached for his musket.

"You coming, Rigo?" Dag demanded, glowering.

Rodrigo remained seated.

"Stephano told us to stay here," Rodrigo said, playing a silent sonata.

Dag glowered. "*You* stay, then. God forbid you should get your clothes dirty."

"Dag," said Rodrigo quietly, "I think we should do what Stephano says."

At this, Dag hesitated. He was clearly worried about the welfare of the women, but he was also worried about disobeying Stephano's orders. Henry took charge.

"Captain de Guichen could not have foreseen this development. You should go help your friends, Thorgrimson," said Sir Henry. "Monsieur de Villeneuve and I will remain here until you return."

Dag looked relieved. "Yes, sir. Thank you, sir."

"Dag," said Rodrigo, his voice taking on a note of urgency. "You should stay. This man is—"

Sir Henry reached into his coat, drew a small stowaway

pistol and, using his coat to shield the weapon from Dag's sight, aimed the pistol at Rodrigo's heart.

"This man is what?" Dag asked impatiently.

"—going to fetch another bottle of wine," said Rodrigo.

Dag shook his head in exasperation and hurried out the door, carrying the musket. The Doctor rode on his shoulder, tail switching as he dug in his claws to keep hold.

Rodrigo glanced at the gun and smiled.

"You know who I am," said Sir Henry.

"Although we were never formally introduced, I believe I have the dubious pleasure of addressing Sir Henry Wallace," said Rodrigo.

"Your servant, sir," said Sir Henry.

Alcazar was blinking at them both in drunken confusion. "Sir Henry? Who's that? This man is not Sir Henry. His name is Russo . . ."

Henry gestured at Alcazar with the pistol and told him to shut up. Alcazar stared at the pistol, gulped, hesitated, then pushed himself up from the table.

"I don't feel good," he said and tottered unsteadily toward the bedroom.

Rodrigo looked after him, then looked back at Sir Henry.

"It is true, then. That journeyman, Alcazar, developed a formula for strengthening metal using magic. I theorized it might be possible, you know," Rodrigo added, with a shrug, "But I never put my theories to the test. Too much bother."

He hummed a waltz and ran his hands over the imaginary keyboard. Then he stopped, his fingers hovering. "That confounded theory is the reason you wanted to kill me!"

Rodrigo pondered this a moment, then continued his playing. "Stephano and I both wondered. We couldn't figure out why anyone would go to such lengths to get rid of *me*."

"When the countess figured out that Alcazar had succeeded where so many others had failed and that he was now working for Freya, she would have dug around until she discovered that treatise of yours, then put you to work to re-create the procedure."

"Put me to work . . ." Rodrigo repeated the words with a soft chuckle. "Some things are impossible, sir, even for the countess."

"Once Alcazar is back, we will leave for the docks," said Sir Henry. "I will be requiring the pleasure of your company."

"The harbor is closed," Rodrigo observed. "The authorities will not allow your ship to depart. If you attempt to run, the shore batteries will open fire on your ship."

"Not when I have a hostage on board. Captain de Guichen would certainly never permit a friend of his to come to harm, sir," said Sir Henry.

"And how is Stephano to know I'm aboard your ship?" Rodrigo performed an intricate cadenza.

"Oh, he'll know," predicted Sir Henry with a smile.

Rodrigo thought this over and played a second silent sonata. "A mere former captain doesn't wield much authority with the admirals of the Royal Navy."

"Ah, but the son of the Countess de Marjolaine is not a mere captain, sir," said Sir Henry.

Rodrigo sipped his wine and conceded that this was true. "We are sailing to Freya, I suppose?"

"Some of us are sailing to Freya, Monsieur," said Henry gravely. "One of us, I fear, will be dropped into the Breath. After you are no longer of use to me."

"Ah," said Rodrigo. "Of course. If you don't mind my asking, sir, was it this Dubois person who shot your friends in there?"

"A private quarrel," said Sir Henry with an apologetic air. "I fear I cannot discuss it."

Rodrigo dashed off a saraband. "You appear to have a vast number of enemies, Sir Henry."

"Let us simply say that I will be extremely glad to leave Rosia, Monsieur de Villeneuve," said Henry Wallace with feeling.

Alcazar returned. His coat had been hastily thrown on. None of the buttons were buttoned correctly and his collar stuck up behind his ears.

Sir Henry gestured with the pistol. "Time to go, Monsieur de Villeneuve. Take charge of this drunken idiot. Keep him on his feet."

Rodrigo took hold of the unsteady Alcazar, who was green about the nose and mouth and continuing to mumble that he didn't feel well. On their way out the door, Rodrigo stopped and turned to face Sir Henry.

"I was wondering . . ."

Henry thrust the barrel of the gun into Rodrigo's ribs.

"Yes? What?"

"Could we stop by my tailor?" Rodrigo inquired. "It's on the way."

Stephano and Miri discussed their plans as they walked slowly toward Dubois' lodging. A modest sign referred to this inn as The Ivy, an appropriate name considering that much of the brickwork of the three-story building was covered with green leaves and trailing vines. The inn housed few guests, apparently, for most of the windows to the rooms were closed and shuttered. One window belonging to a corner room on the second floor was open, admitting sunlight and fresh air, and providing an excellent view of the main street and a side street. Stephano kept an eye on the window of that room, but saw no one.

"You have that paper with the king's seal Russo gave you," Miri was arguing. "I think you should summon the constables and have them arrest this Dubois."

Stephano shook his head. "By the time I found the Chief Constable and showed him the paper and convinced him the seal was real and the crisis was real and that *I'm* real and I'm who I say I am, he would have to collect his men and they'd have to march here, by which time Dubois could be on the move again and we'd never catch him. Besides," said Stephano, checking to make certain his pistol was loaded, "I don't exactly trust Monsieur Russo or his paper."

"I gathered that when you left Dag with him," said Miri. "What are we going to do with Dubois once we have him?"

"I will take him along to Monsieur Russo, collect everyone involved in the same room, hold them all at gunpoint, and see if we can sort this out," said Stephano. "We're going to make this apprehension quick and quiet. You and Gythe keep the landlord occupied while I speak to Dubois. Are you ready, Sisters?"

"We're ready," said Miri crisply. "Gythe, dear, time to feel faint."

Gythe smiled and winked at Stephano. She put her hand to her forehead. Her eyes rolled back. She swayed on her feet. Miri cried out in alarm. Stephano lifted Gythe in his arms and carried her inside the inn.

"The sister has fainted," he told the landlord.

"Sister Catherine is feeling ill from the heat," Miri told the landlord. "Could she rest here a moment, Monsieur? This room is so lovely and cool."

"Of course, of course," said the landlord, hovering near. He turned to a servant. "Fetch some brandy for the sister. Take her into the parlor, sir."

Stephano carried Gythe into a room off the main lobby and laid her gently on a couch.

"Thank you for coming to our aid, Monsieur," said Miri.

Stephano bowed. "My pleasure, Sister. I happened to be here myself on business. Do you require my assistance for anything else?"

Miri assured Stephano that he was no longer needed. He turned to the landlord, who was hovering over the young and very beautiful nun, asking if she would like something to eat and shouting once more for the brandy.

"I came to see Monsieur Dubois," Stephano said, interrupting. "What room is he in?"

"What? Who? Oh, room number 6," said the distracted landlord.

Grinning, Stephano dashed up the stairs. He moved swiftly, treading softly. Entering the hall, he found the door with a brass number 6 nailed to it at the top of the stairs. Stephano gently tried the door handle and found it locked. He rapped on the door smartly.

"Who is it?" a mild voice called.

"Your dinner, sir," said Stephano in servile tones.

He heard the shuffling of papers, footsteps, then the key turning. The moment Stephano heard the lock click, he kicked open the door and jumped inside, his pistol drawn and aimed at Dubois.

Stephano came to an abrupt halt. Dubois stood with his pistol aimed at Stephano. The two men faced off, each with a pistol aimed at the other.

Dubois suddenly recognized his assailant.

"Captain de Guichen!" Dubois exclaimed and raised his weapon, pointing the gun at the ceiling. Unfortunately, due to amazement or perhaps out of nervousness, Dubois inadvertently squeezed the trigger. The gun went off, blowing a hole in the plaster.

At the sound of the gunshot, cries and shouts came from below. The landlord was demanding to know what the devil was going on, and Miri was crying out that Sister Catherine had fainted once again. Stephano waved away the smoke, all the while keeping his pistol aimed at Dubois. Miri could be counted on to deal with the landlord.

"What is the meaning of this armed invasion, Captain de Guichen?" Dubois demanded with indignation.

"You can cancel your plans to kidnap Alcazar today, Monsieur," said Stephano in pleasant tones. "Be so good as to inform your master."

"Kidnap! Alcazar!" Dubois gasped. "My 'master,' as you refer to His Eminence, Captain, is trying to *rescue* Alcazar, not kidnap him."

Stephano gestured with the pistol. "Interesting story. Too bad I don't believe it. Come along with me, Monsieur Dubois, and we'll sort all—"

He was interrupted by a scream from below and Miri's

we're-caught-in-a-raging-storm-and-the-mast-is-falling bellow. "Stephano! Company!"

Footsteps pounded up the stairs.

"You bastard," muttered Stephano, eyeing Dubois. "That shot you fired wasn't an accident. It was a signal!"

Stephano turned halfway, just as a man with red hair and beard plummeted through the door and seized hold of his arm, trying to wrest the pistol from his hand. Stephano's pistol went off. Dubois gave a cry and clapped his hand over his shoulder and staggered backward.

Red Dog knocked Stephano to the floor and tried to get his hands around Stephano's throat. Miri entered the room to find the two men wrestling and rolling about. She grabbed hold of a chair and smashed it over Red Dog's head. He groaned and rolled off Stephano, who heaved himself to his feet. Miri bashed Red Dog in the head with the chair's leg. He went down and did not get up.

Below, the landlord was out in the street, blowing a whistle, summoning the constables. More footfalls sounded on the stairs. Stephano motioned for Miri to wait behind the door with the chair leg, ready to bash whoever came in. Stephano hurried over to Dubois, who had collapsed into a chair. He was still conscious, his hand pressed against right shoulder. Blood welled out from beneath his fingers.

Stephano gave the wound a cursory examination. "You'll live. The bullet took out a hunk of meat, that's all. On your feet. We need to get out of here. I'm sure you don't want to deal with the police any more than I do."

Dubois didn't budge. "Left pocket."

"There's no time—" Stephano began.

"Look in my left pocket, Captain," said Dubois sternly, indicating with a nod the coat he was wearing.

Stephano glared at him, then, thinking Dubois might have some sort of document that would placate the authorities, Stephano reached into Dubois' coat.

"The leather case," Dubois instructed. Lifting his left

arm slightly to allow Stephano access, he gasped in pain and kept pressure on the wound. Stephano was drawing out the case, when Dag came running into the room, his musket in his hands.

"Stephano, I heard about Miri—" he cried, just as Miri emerged from behind the door, brandishing the chair leg.

"What are *you* doing here?" Dag gasped, goggling at Miri.

"What are you doing here?" Miri demanded.

Doctor Ellington didn't wait to find out what anyone was doing here. The cat leaped off Dag's shoulder and made a run for the stairs. Gythe, coming in behind Dag, reached down and deftly scooped up the fleeing Doctor before he shot out the door.

"Oh, my God," Stephano groaned.

He had been reading the document he had just removed from the leather billfold. He looked from Dag to Miri to Red Dog, who was rubbing his head and staring around groggily, to Dubois, bleeding on the sofa.

"What's gone wrong now?" Miri demanded in dire tones.

"This man . . . uh . . . works for the Church. He's Grand Bishop Montagne's agent." Stephano heaved a sigh and ran his hand through his hair.

"You just shot an agent for the grand bishop?" Miri cried, scandalized.

"I didn't mean to!" said Stephano.

Gythe frowned, touching her lips and making a face as though tasting something bad.

"Maybe he's lying," Miri translated.

"Read the paper on the desk," Dubois instructed. He closed his eyes and bit his lip against the pain.

"Gythe," said Stephano, "keep watch."

Gythe and the Doctor went over to the window, while Miri hurried to examine the document.

"It's from the grand bishop," said Miri. "The document instructs the archbishop and Lord Mayor of Westfirth to close the harbor. It's signed and sealed . . ."

Her brow furrowed. "But if this man, Dubois, is working for the bishop, then why did Russo tell us that Dubois was working for Sir Henry Wallace?"

"Wallace!" Dubois cried, his eyes opening. He sat up in the chair. "What about Wallace?"

Stephano didn't answer. He was staring at Dag, suddenly realizing amidst the confusion that the mercenary was in the room.

"Dag, what *are* you doing here?" Stephano demanded.

"Russo told me Miri and Gythe had been kidnapped," Dag said wretchedly. "He told me you needed help . . ."

His voice trailed off.

"Where's Rigo?" Stephano asked tensely.

"He didn't come with me," said Dag. "He didn't want me to leave. He must have known. . . . Oh, God, Stephano! Now I know where I've seen that Russo before! I kept thinking he looked familiar. At the ambush at Bitter End! He was the man in the greatcoat . . . I saved his goddamn life!"

"And Father Jacob told us that man was Henry Wallace. So this Russo is really Sir Henry Wallace and now Wallace has hold of Alcazar *and* Rodrigo," said Stephano.

"I'm sorry, sir," said Dag miserably, "That bastard fooled me completely."

"Don't blame yourself," said Stephano. "He fooled all of us."

Gythe, standing at the window, snapped her fingers to draw their attention. She pointed down at the street and made a gesture with her hands intimating the tall hats worn by the constables.

"I think I'll just let them arrest me," said Stephano. "They can charge me with being an idiot. I'll plead guilty."

"You can't stay here. You have to stop Wallace, Captain," said Dubois sharply. "Alcazar must not reach Freya!"

"And how do you propose I do that, sir?" Stephano demanded bitterly. "The constables are on their way up the stairs and Sir Henry Wallace is on his way to the docks and he's holding my friend hostage!"

"That friend would be Monsieur de Villeneuve?" asked Dubois.

"You seem to know all about me," said Stephano grimly. "Yes, my friend is Monsieur de Villeneuve."

"Ironic," murmured Dubois. "It was Sir Henry Wallace who gave the order to have Ambassador de Villeneuve assassinated. I don't suppose your friend knows that."

"No," said Stephano. "Probably just as well he doesn't."

"I will deal with the constables, Captain," said Dubois. "Go into the bedroom. Enter the wardrobe. Inside is a false back that opens onto a staircase which leads to the servants' quarters. Exit through the kitchen door into a secluded garden. From that point, you are on your own."

Stephano motioned for everyone to do as Dubois said. Dag led the way, with Gythe and Miri and the Doctor following. Stephano remained a moment. He could hear the constables pounding up the stairs. "I am sorry I shot you, Monsieur. I don't suppose you have any idea where Henry Wallace might be going?"

Dubois gave a faint smile. "Pietro Alcazar has a brother, Manuel. He serves on a merchant vessel docked in the Foreign Commons. The name of the ship is the *Silver Raven*."

Stephano was halfway through the bedroom door when he stopped, turned around. "You're going to order the navy to sink that vessel, aren't you?"

Dubois inclined his head. "Alcazar must not be permitted to reach Freya alive, Captain."

"Give me a chance," Stephano pleaded. "Let me try to capture the vessel and keep everyone alive, including Alcazar and Rodrigo."

Dubois gave a faint smile. "God go with you, Captain. And give your esteemed mother my regards."

Stephano slammed the door shut behind him and pretended he had not heard. He waited a moment to make certain Dubois did not betray them. He listened to the constables enter. Dubois gave them some sort of story about thieves and told them that the man who had shot him had gone out the window.

Stephano could not risk waiting longer. He entered the wardrobe, passed through the false back, and hurried down the dark and narrow stairs that led from the servants' quarters in the top of the inn to the kitchen area below. He found his friends waiting for him in a garden surrounded by a high wrought-iron fence and tall walnut trees whose intertwined branches effectively shielded them from view of the constables.

Stephano opened the garden gate carefully, afraid the hinges would creak. The hinges were silent, and he noticed they'd been oiled. Dubois thought of everything. Stephano and his friends filed quietly out. The two nuns walked demurely down the street away from the inn. Stephano and Dag with the Doctor back in his accustomed place on his shoulder strolled along behind.

Glancing over his shoulder, Stephano saw constables up on the roof, while others took up positions in the front of the inn. More would be inside, continuing to talk to the grand bishop's agent, Monsieur Dubois, who was going to be giving the order to the Royal Navy to blast Wallace's ship—and Rodrigo—out of the Breath unless Stephano could find a way to stop Wallace before that happened.

"What a rotten day! I wonder what the Hell else can go wrong?" Stephano asked himself morosely.

Chapter Thirty-Nine

Our eyes wept for our emerald Isle as Glasearrach sank into the Breath. Our hearts wept as our brethren fell to their deaths. Our people wept as God cast us out.

—Trundler Ballad,
"The Sinking of Glasearrach"

THE MORNING HENRY WALLACE FOUND EID-DWEN'S visiting card, Sir Ander entered the archbishop's dining room in search of a late breakfast.

Sir Ander and Brother Barnaby had been up much of the previous night, standing on the battlements, observing with interest the naval ships moving swiftly through the Breath to interdict any vessel trying to slip out following the closing of the port. The shore batteries located in the concrete bunkers beneath the battlements were fully manned, though only a few guns had been run out to fire a warning volley of powder and wadding, warning irate ship captains that the port-closing would be enforced. The navy caught several ships trying to escape; mostly small boats loaded with contraband.

Sir Ander had explained the naval strategy to Brother Barnaby, pointing out how the larger naval vessels took key positions around the bay while the city's gunboats moved inside the bay. The smaller gunboats were twenty-four feet long, each mounting a cannon that fired a twenty-four-pound ball. Six armed marines were aboard every gunboat. If a fleeing vessel failed to stop, the marines would fire their muskets. If that failed to persuade the captain, the gunboat would fire the cannon to disable the ship and force it to land. One such vessel was now perched on the roof of a nearby warehouse. Brother Barnaby had never seen such a spectacle, and he had watched in fascinated awe.

Father Jacob had not been on the battlements with them. He had summoned agents of the Arcanum who were currently in Westfirth to the Old Fort, then sent them out to search for the Sorceress and her young disciple known as the Warlock. Father Jacob was hoping that the embargo would keep the Sorceress trapped in this city. Agents were stopping all wyvern-drawn carriages in and out of the city. All overland routes were under surveillance.

Following his meeting, Father Jacob had been engaged in researching the object he had salvaged from the ambush. He had given orders that he was not to be disturbed. At about midnight, Sir Ander had knocked on Father Jacob's door to see how he was faring. His knock receiving no response, Sir Ander had opened the door softly and quietly.

He had seen Father Jacob hunched over a table covered with a white sheet, taking measurements of the blackened lump and recording them in a book. Sir Ander had watched a moment, wondering what Father Jacob had discovered, if anything. Sir Ander had known better than to disturb his friend while he was at work. He had closed the door and gone off to his bed.

This morning, Sir Ander was alone in the dining room. A servant informed him that archbishop had dined early and gone to see how the work was coming on the cathedral. Brother Barnaby had also dined and had left word for Father Jacob that he would be in the archbishop's private chapel, praying. The servant had not seen Father Jacob.

Sir Ander assumed the priest had once again fallen asleep over his work. The servant poured coffee. Sir Ander helped himself from the collation on the sideboard. He was dishing out his favorite: Freyan sausages known as "blood pudding," when he heard Father Jacob's voice resounding through the palace, shouting Sir Ander's name in strident and impatient tones.

Sir Ander sat down at the table and began to eat his sausages. The servant looked at him, startled.

"The priest is calling for you, my lord. Should I tell him you are in here?"

"No," said Sir Ander calmly. "He'll find me soon enough. I plan to finish my breakfast."

Still shouting, Father Jacob burst through the doors with a bang, bounding into the room with such energy that the servant, who was accustomed to the elegant, refined manners of the archbishop, jumped and spilled the coffee.

"Here you are, Ander!" cried Father Jacob in a peevish tone.

"Eating breakfast," said Sir Ander calmly. He pointed to his plate with his fork. "Blood pudding. Excellent. You should have some."

"I've been looking for you everywhere," said Father Jacob.

"And now you've found me," said Sir Ander, savoring his sausage.

"I need you to come with me. Now! Where is Barnaby?"

"In the chapel," said Sir Ander.

Father Jacob asked the servant to prepare a basket of food and a bottle of wine. When the servant left to carry out the order and they were alone, Father Jacob turned to Sir Ander.

"I know you are always armed, my friend," he said gravely. "But it might be wise to take extra precautions."

Troubled by the priest's grim expression, Sir Ander stood up, gulping his hot coffee and burning his tongue.

Father Jacob went off to fetch Brother Barnaby. Sir Ander returned to his room, put on his light chain mail vest, set with the magical constructs and buckled on his sword belt.

He loaded the dragon pistol, placed one of the non-magical pistols in a concealed pocket and thrust the other in his belt. He grabbed his helm.

He found Father Jacob and Brother Barnaby waiting in the entry hall. Father Jacob was on the move immediately, walking in such haste that his long strides caused his cassock to ride up around his shins. Brother Barnaby, armed with his portable writing desk, had to almost run to keep up. He flashed a look at Sir Ander, asking silently if he knew what was going on. Sir Ander shook his head.

Father Jacob strode rapidly through the halls of the Old Fort and headed out for the battlements. Sir Ander thought this was their destination, and he was startled to see the priest keep going.

The battlements extended from one guard tower to another for a distance spanning many hundred feet. In the guard towers, the bored soldiers were relieved to have some amusement to break up the tedium of their watch, observing with interest the attempts by the navy to enforce the blockade. Although the Old Fort had not been occupied for years, the moment the archbishop expressed his desire to move into it, the lord mayor found that he was suddenly extremely attached to the site and did not want the Church to commandeer it. He had taken his grievances to the king, who had gone to the grand bishop. The result was that the Church paid the city of Westfirth handsomely for use of the Old Fort. The soldiers who guarded the Old Fort were under the command of the lord mayor. The archbishop had his own guards, whose main duty was to protect His Reverence's person.

The archbishop's soldiers patrolled the archbishop's living quarters. The Westfirth guards were responsible for the rest. There being no enemy to guard against, the only excitement for either force these days was the occasional skirmish between the Mayor's soldiers and those belonging to the archbishop when one or the other crossed the demarcation line.

The soldiers in the guard towers saw Father Jacob in his black cassock and Sir Ander in his chain mail armor, his sword clanking at his hip, and looked at each other with raised eyebrows. All breathed a little easier when the Arcanum priest passed them by.

"Where are we going?" Sir Ander ventured to ask, as they walked by the third guard tower.

In answer, Father Jacob pointed to top of the cliff, to the Bastion, the crumbling remains of the abandoned outpost that had once belonged to the Dragon Brigade. The outpost was situated high on a peak above the Old Fort. Sir Ander gaped in dismay at the series of winding steps cut into the rock that led up the side of the cliff.

"Beautiful day for a climb, isn't it?" said Father Jacob in hearty tones. "Did you know that the dragon bastions are fairly modern, dating back only about seventy years? The bastions are historically important because they are different from those found in the dragon homeland. I have never had a chance to fully study the Westfirth Bastion. *No one ever goes there now*," he added with emphasis. "More's the pity, eh, Sir Ander? You have long said the Dragon Brigade should have never been disbanded. Let us go take a look."

Sir Ander understood. Father Jacob needed a place to speak to them in absolute privacy, a place where there was not the slightest chance they could be overheard. He braced himself for the climb and was thankful he had decided to wear chain mail and not his heavy breastplate.

The trek up to the top of the cliff did not prove as difficult as Sir Ander had anticipated. The stairs did not ascend straight up, but were cut into the side in a zigzag manner so that the ascent was not particularly arduous. Sir Ander was rewarded for his efforts by a magnificent view of the city of Westfirth and the mists of the Breath in the harbor.

"Humans were stationed here, as well as dragons," said Father Jacob when Sir Ander remarked that the climb was not as bad as he had anticipated. "Your godson, Captain de Guichen, must have made this trek often."

Neither Sir Ander nor Brother Barnaby had been in a dragon bastion before and despite the seriousness of the situation, they both looked about with interest as they walked the empty halls formed of stone laid by dragons. The Bastion was built in a circle with halls and rooms radiating from an enormous courtyard of stone. In the center of the courtyard were traces of a mosaic depicting the emblem of the Dragon Brigade: a blue-green dragon in flight, wings extended, on the background of a red-and-golden sun.

"The dragons and their riders landed and took off here," said Father Jacob. He indicated the courtyard which was open to the skies.

The wind blew continuously from the Breath, shredding the mists, providing excellent visibility. Above them, the sky was a deep, cobalt blue. The Bastion was named "Bastion of the Wind" for this reason. Sir Ander could picture Stephano and his dragon, facing into the wind; the dragon extending his wings, allowing the breeze to lift them. He could picture his godson and his mount soaring out into the Breath, riding the thermals. Sir Ander had never quite understood Stephano's passion for climbing onto the backs of dragons and flying into the sky until now, in this place with the wind on his face, wrapped in silence, the blue vault of Heaven above, all cares left on the ground far below.

"The dragons were quartered in these rooms that extend out from the courtyard." Father Jacob was explaining to Brother Barnaby. "Their riders lived in the barracks over there to the north."

"The rooms and halls don't seem big enough for dragons," Brother Barnaby marveled.

"Dragons are large, but they are extremely flexible," said Father Jacob. "They curl up tail to nose when they sleep. Like foxes and wolves, they feel safe in cozy cavelike rooms. That is why, in even the grandest and most magnificent dragon palaces, you will find the sleeping chambers are small and snug."

"I would like to see a dragon palace," said Brother Barnaby wistfully.

"And so you shall," said Father Jacob, pleased. "I have been wanting to pay a visit to my friends in the dragon realm again, though I fear that pleasure must wait for a time. For now, we have urgent matters to discuss."

Someone—dragon or human—had planted a rose garden in an angle between one hall and another. Sheltered from the constant wind, yet open to the sunshine and rain, the rose garden must have once been lovely. The garden was now overrun with weeds, though here and there a few rosebushes clung stubbornly to life. The three settled themselves on a stone bench and opened the basket of food, all of them feeling in need of sustenance after the climb.

Whatever was on Father Jacob's mind, he refused to discuss it while they were eating. Once they were finished, Brother Barnaby packed away the dishes and scattered the remains of the bread for the birds, then brought out the writing desk and made ready to take notes.

"First, I must relate bad news. The Sorceress has eluded capture," said Father Jacob. "Arcanum agents found where she had been living, but she was gone. There was evidence that she fled in haste."

"She was warned," said Sir Ander grimly. He glanced around. "So that's why we are up here in the clouds. You think someone in the archbishop's household alerted her."

"Someone in the house or one of the guards . . ." Father Jacob shrugged. "I do not know and thus I could not take a chance on anyone overhearing our conversation."

He fell silent, his expression dark and somber.

"*I'd* like to hear our conversation," said Sir Ander, after long moments of continued silence.

Father Jacob stirred. "I'm sorry. I am still trying to make sense of what I have discovered. I hope the two of you can help me. You will recall I managed to retrieve that remnant of the demon's remains yesterday. I spent the night studying it. As I thought, we are *not* dealing with forces of Aertheum or legions from Hell. Though, as I told Captain de Guichen, it depends on how one defines Hell . . ."

He again fell quiet. Sir Ander waited in foreboding, not certain he wanted to hear. Brother Barnaby's pen stopped scratching. The only sound was the wind whistling through the empty hallways.

"The demons are, as I suspected, humans," Father Jacob said at length.

"I don't suppose any of us really believed they were demons," said Sir Ander. He caught Father Jacob's eye. "Well, maybe I did, but just for a moment . . ."

Brother Barnaby was sorrowful, grieving. "I could almost wish they had been demons."

"I know, Brother," said Father Jacob quietly. He regarded the monk with an odd intensity. "It is hard to think that human beings could commit such terrible atrocities as we have witnessed. Yet, there is no doubt. I found a part of a human skull inside the burned helmet."

"Human." Sir Ander shook his head. "But why the elaborate disguise?"

"We are meant to think they are demons. The demonic mask fosters fear," said Father Jacob. "Brother Paul and those sailors all believe they were attacked by demons, which is why I placed them under Seal. If they went around telling people that Aertheum was launching a war against humanity, the panic among the populace would be incalculable. Their demonic aspect is designed to play upon the fears that dwell in our hearts from childhood, the terrors that assail us in the dead of night."

Father Jacob sighed and rubbed his eyes. His shoulders sagged; he was gray with fatigue. "Terrors that are well-founded."

"What do you mean?" Sir Ander asked.

"The helm the man was wearing was made of leather. But these people, whoever they are, did not use animal hide. The leather hide was from a human."

Brother Barnaby dropped the pen. He had gone so pale,

the ebony skin going gray, that Sir Ander hastened to pour him a glass of wine.

"Steady, Brother," said Sir Ander. He flashed an irate glare at Father Jacob.

"He needs to know the truth," said Father Jacob sternly. "These people spoke to him. Remember?"

Barnaby shuddered at the memory, but went on to say that he was all right. He drank the wine at Sir Ander's insistence and managed a smile that was meant to be reassuring. But Sir Ander could see the lingering shadow of horror and loathing in the young monk's eyes; a horror he knew must be a reflection of his own.

"These are not humans, Father. They are monsters!" Sir Ander exclaimed heatedly. "How could you tell if the leather was . . ."

He glanced at Brother Barnaby, trying to hold the pen in trembling fingers and could not say the words. "What you said it was."

"What I have discovered will not be easy to hear, Brother Barnaby."

"I am myself again, Father," said Brother Barnaby. "I will not fail you. Please go on."

He held the pen poised over the paper, his hand steady.

"When I touched the helm, I felt intense pain," said Father Jacob. "The pain did not come from the so-called demon. The pain was from the victim whose skin had been used to make the leather. I had a vision of a man tied to a rock, while other men were flaying the flesh from his bones. He was alive during the heinous procedure."

Sir Ander's gut clenched. He rose to his feet and, wiping his hand over his mouth, took a walk around the garden. Brother Barnaby recorded the information. A tear dropped on the page, but he hastily whisked it away and continued writing.

"Are they Freyans?" said Sir Ander harshly, coming back to resume his seat. "No offense, Father, but I have to ask."

"No, they are not. There are indications—" Father Jacob shook his head and fell silent.

"So who are they?" Sir Ander demanded.

Father Jacob looked again at Brother Barnaby, as though he could provide the answer. The monk was completing a sentence and did not notice. Father Jacob rose to his feet with a grimace and massaged his back.

"You could use the Corpse spell," said Sir Ander abruptly.

"I could," said Father Jacob. "I did."

Sir Ander had witnessed the priest performing the magical spell that could be used to determine the identity of corpses. The energy of a living person remained with the body for a long time after death. Father Jacob used his magic to cause this so-called "ghost" to materialize. The use of such magic was forbidden to all except those of the Arcanum, who were often called to identify bodies that had been burned or mutilated. Unless the bones were too old, the spell could sometimes be used to identify skeletal remains. Contrary to popular opinion, the ghost that was summoned by the magic did not speak to the loved ones. It was not capable of pointing to a murderer, nor did it go flitting about graveyards, fling dinner plates, or dwell in attics. A portrait artist would make a likeness of the ghostly face and, once this was done, the priest would end the spell and the ghost would fade away.

"The spell takes a long time to cast and requires a vast store of energy," said Father Jacob wearily. "I am exhausted."

"What did you find out?" Sir Ander asked. "What did you see?"

Father Jacob continued to regard Brother Barnaby as he spoke. "I saw a man with pallid skin, white as milk, with a sickly yellowish hue. He had unusual eyes, large with enormous pupils. Given the abnormally pale skin and strange eyes, I theorize this person had been born to darkness, had been raised in darkness—"

"The Bottom Dwellers," Brother Barnaby said softly. He let the pen drop. His gaze was abstracted, looking inward.

"Is that what they called themselves?" Father Jacob asked quietly. "When they spoke to you?"

Brother Barnaby nodded. "They said the same to Gythe, only in her language."

Sir Ander was about to interrupt. Father Jacob raised an urgent, warding hand.

"Continue, Brother," he said.

"That's all. I don't know . . ." Brother Barnaby appeared distressed. "Except . . . they hate us . . ."

"Indeed they do," said Father Jacob. "Even after death, the rage felt by the dead man lived on, radiating from the corpse. I had never seen the like before now. I did not know such hatred was possible."

He sighed deeply and said sadly, "Yet, perhaps, they have good reason to hate us."

Brother Barnaby stirred and regarded Father Jacob with wondering anguish. "Who are they, Father?"

"And what bottom do they dwell in?" Sir Ander asked, looking skeptical.

"I do not know for certain," said Father Jacob slowly, seeming to talk to himself, as though thinking his thought process out loud. "But I have my suspicions. Recall your history lessons. Long ago, the nations of Aeronne banded together to rid the world of pirates, who were taking shelter on the Trundler island of Glasearrach. War crafters of both Freya and Rosia and the other nations came together to use powerful magicks to sink the island, dooming the pirates and those innocents who had refused to heed the order to flee to certain death in the foul mists of the Breath below."

Father Jacob raised his eyes. "But what if those people on the island did not die?"

"Merciful God in Heaven!" Sir Ander exclaimed. "You can't be serious, Father? You are saying they live in the depths of the Breath? That is not possible. We know that no one could survive down there!"

"We have long *theorized* that no one could survive," Father Jacob corrected. "We do not know for certain. The pirates were said to be dabbling in contramagic, the reason the Church advocated the sinking of the island to stop the spread of heresy."

Sir Ander swallowed. "Which is why these fiends want to silence the Voice of God."

"And they have the ability to do so," said Father Jacob in grim tones. "They are now quite skilled in contramagic. They sank a naval cutter and toppled stone towers. Imagine what would happen if they turned their weapons on a city . . ."

Sir Ander once more rose from his seat and began to pace restlessly about the garden. Brother Barnaby sat quite still. He had made no move to pick up the pen. When he did, belatedly, Father Jacob stopped him.

"No, Brother. Do not record a word of this. I must confer with my colleagues. It is imperative that I return to the Arcanum. When will the *Retribution* be ready? Why are the repairs taking so long?"

"Master Albert is hopeful we can leave tomorrow," said Sir Ander.

"Tomorrow!" Father Jacob glowered.

"The crafters are working as fast as they can, Father."

"I know, I know. But it is critical that I make my report," said Father Jacob. "The Bottom Dwellers know I am here. They will come after me."

Sir Ander was staring off into the distance.

"What is that?" he asked. "Sorry to interrupt, Father, but look to the southeast. There's something in the sky. I can't make out what it is . . ."

He pointed. Father Jacob turned, as did Brother Barnaby.

"A dragon," said the monk promptly.

"God bless young eyes," said Sir Ander, squinting. "All I can see is a blob."

The dragon was flying rapidly and appeared to be heading in their direction.

"I believe that is our friend from the Abbey of Saint Agnes, Sergeant Hroalfrig," said Brother Barnaby, as the dragon drew nearer.

"You are right," said Father Jacob. "You can see his bad leg drooping. I fear he is the bearer of bad news."

"No one ever flies that fast with *good* news," Sir Ander agreed.

The three hastened to the central courtyard, keeping a safe distance from the landing area, waiting for the dragon. As Hroalfrig began his descent, they could see the dragon appeared immensely tired. He was gasping for breath and came down with a bone-rattling crash, pitching forward onto his nose.

"Are you all right, Sergeant?" Sir Ander hastened forward when there was no danger of being crushed.

The dragon stared in astonishment. "Sir Ander! Father Jacob! Did not expect. You. Here."

"More to the point, Sergeant," said Sir Ander in concern. "What are you doing here?"

Hroalfrig managed to raise himself up. He sucked in huge quantities of air, his rib cage heaving. "Came to warn you, sir. Large flight. Demons."

"Is the abbey under attack again?"

Hroalfrig shook his head, neck, and mane. His tail lashed the ground. "Westfirth. Coming here."

He glanced over his shoulder. "Right behind me."

Sir Ander saw a dark, black cloud rolling toward them, boiling up out of the Breath.

"That's not a storm cloud," said Brother Barnaby tensely.

"No," said Father Jacob. "A cloud of bats. We are too late."

Sir Ander stared. "There must be hundreds of them!"

"Flew as fast as I could manage. . . . Hroalfrig bowed his head. He was still gasping for breath.

"We'll sound the alarm," said Sir Ander. "Thank you, Hroalfrig. You should take cover in the Bastion—"

"Cover!" Hroalfrig glared fiercely. "Never. Catch breath. Ready to fight."

Sir Ander feared the demons (he could not think of them in any other terms) would make short work of the exhausted dragon, but he didn't have time to argue. Father

Jacob had turned and was running for the stairs that led back down the cliff face. Brother Barnaby was hurriedly gathering up paper and ink and replacing them in the portable desk.

"Leave it!" Sir Ander ordered.

"But Father Jacob—"

"We'll come back for it!" Sir Ander said urgently. He didn't like to think what would happen if the demons caught them up here, out in the open. "You can run faster without the desk."

Barnaby quite sensibly agreed, though he did take time to close everything securely in the desk and hide it under a bench. He and Sir Ander hurried after Father Jacob, who was clambering over the stairs, not bothering to use them, but sliding and scrambling straight down the side of the cliff. Brother Barnaby, fleet of foot and extremely agile, soon caught up with Father Jacob. Sir Ander eyed their reckless descent and pictured himself trying to emulate them wearing his sword and chain mail and carrying loaded pistols.

"You go on!" he shouted to Father Jacob. "I'll be right behind you."

Sir Ander began to run down the stairs, taking them two at a time. He glanced at the warships, as he ran. They had not seen the threat or, if they did, they likely thought the cloud was nothing more than an approaching storm. The warships and patrol boats were too busy attempting to enforce the harbor closing to pay attention. Officers on board the gunboats were engaged in shouting matches with the captains of merchant vessels, firing warning shots across the bows of those who tried to slip past.

The guards in the guard towers were hanging out the windows, watching the altercations; their muskets propped against the walls. He thought of the people of Westfirth, going about their business, soon to be caught up in a horror they could never have foreseen. He thought of his godson, Stephano, and his friends.

"God help us!" Sir Ander breathed.

Chapter Forty

Upon inspection, the Guild of Greater Masonry is fully prepared to affirm that the Westfirth large-bore cannon emplacements surpass the requirements specified. Carved directly into the cliff face and faced with stone and concrete, the addition of multiple layers of strengthening and hardening magical constructs has created a virtually impregnable series of defensive positions. Battlements and towers linking the positions add another layer of defense and support. Any enemy foolish enough to attack Westfirth will quickly find themselves overmatched.

—Master Francis Malinbrand, Guild of Greater Masonry,
in a letter to the Rosian Naval Secretary upon
the completion of defensive fortifications in Westfirth

ON BOARD THE *CLOUD HOPPER*, STEPHANO had his spyglass trained on the merchant vessel, *Silver Raven*. He could see signs that the crew was making the ship ready to sail, and he wondered how much Wallace had paid the captain to try to run the blockade. An immense sum, no doubt. Stephano swept the deck with the spyglass, searching for Rodrigo. Wallace could have simply killed him, left him back there in that house with the other bodies.

"Rigo's fine," said Miri, from her place on the forecastle, steering the boat. She flashed Stephano a reassuring smile. "He's Rigo."

"That's what worries me. He must know we're searching

for him," said Stephano. "He could give us a sign. Sail closer, Miri. Maybe he hasn't seen us."

"Wallace knows the *Cloud Hopper*, too," Miri pointed out.

"Bah! He won't notice us," said Stephano. He grinned. "We're selling calvados, like all the rest of these boats out here."

The harbor was surprisingly busy, considering the blockade. Ships were being permitted to enter, just not to leave, which meant that in some cases, arriving vessels had no place to dock. They were now lined up in the harbor, waiting for ships in port to leave so that they could unload their goods. The harbormaster was frantically urging vessels that had been unloaded to vacate the dockyards to allow others to enter. Most furious captains were not in a mood to cooperate and refused, which meant a good deal of confusion in the harbor and on the docks.

Trundlers, ever quick to take advantage of a situation, filled their houseboats with food, water, and calvados—especially calvados—and sailed around from ship to ship, selling their wares to stranded sailors. Merchant captains were notoriously lax when it came to discipline and they could not keep their crews from trading with the Trundlers. Now many of the sailors on board the merchant ships were roaring drunk. Collisions between the hundreds of ships massed in the harbor were inevitable, even if the sailors had been sober. Fortunately, none of the incidents were serious: masts splintered, balloons punctured, the lines of two ships becoming entangled.

The *Cloud Hopper* joined the Trundler Calvados Armada and they were now just one more gaily colored Trundler vessel among many others selling the apple brandy. Miri navigated the *Hopper* expertly in and under and over and around the various ships floating in the harbor to bring the vessel as near the *Silver Raven* as she thought was wise. She kept the tall masts and sails of another vessel between her ship and the *Silver Raven* as cover. Sailors on board the ship, seeing the Trundler boat, yelled and waved for Miri to come closer.

"Captain! Look!" Dag called.

He had his spyglass out, was keeping watch. Stephano had lowered his glass to rub his eyes. He lifted the glass again.

Henry Wallace—the man they had known as Russo— was standing on the deck of the *Silver Raven*. Beside him was Rodrigo, unmistakable in his lavender coat. Wallace was holding a pistol to Rodrigo's head. Rodrigo, seeing them, lifted his hand in a light and airy wave. Stephano swore and lowered the glass.

"Dip the flag, Gythe. Let Wallace know we get his goddam message."

Gythe lowered the *Cloud Hopper*'s flag up and down. Sir Henry waved his hat in return and shoved Rodrigo into a deck chair where a sailor stood guard over him. Sir Henry went to speak to the captain.

Taking advantage of the confusion in the harbor, the *Silver Raven* set sail. Undoubtedly the captain had told the harbormaster he was giving up his place at the docks, and no one paid attention to the *Raven* as she left, maneuvering carefully to avoid running into another ship. The merchant ship would be safe until she tried to run. Then the shore batteries would turn their cannons and their magically guided rockets on her. The navy ships would fire a warning shot across her bows and then, if she kept sailing, ship and shore batteries would both fire in earnest.

The merchant vessel was considerably larger than the *Cloud Hopper*. Designed for long voyages into the deep Breath, the two-decker had two large masts that supported twice the number of balloons as the Trundler vessel. The *Raven* carried a crew of at least forty men, but, being a merchant vessel, she was armed only with swivel guns which were used to fend off pirates. The *Cloud Hopper* was more maneuverable and more heavily armed. Stephano wondered what Wallace was going to do. Was this an attempt to flee made in desperation or did he have some sort of plan?

He has a plan, thought Stephano gloomily. He knows I'll urge the navy to let him go so that he won't harm Rigo. Of course, once he's escaped, he'll kill my friend.

"Keep on him," Stephano told Miri.

"What do you think the navy will do?" Miri asked.

"Knowing the navy," said Stephano bitterly. "Nothing."

During the time required for Miri and Gythe to prepare the *Cloud Hopper* for sailing, Stephano had dispatched an urgent message to the naval flagship, the *Royal Lion*, one of King Alaric's new balloonless ships that relied on the Blood of God, the liquefied form of the Breath, to remain afloat. Stephano had used his name and had even gone to the extreme of invoking his mother's name to tell the navy that the *Silver Raven* was carrying extremely valuable cargo. He pleaded with the admiral not to fire, but to attempt to capture the *Silver Raven* and take all the passengers into custody.

He was not very hopeful the navy would agree. Stephano had few friends in the Royal Navy anymore, especially after the incident at the Estaran fortress and his duel with Hastind, the man who had ordered his guns to fire on Lady Cam. Unfortunately, Hastind was now the Commander of the Westfirth Squadron and the *Royal Lion* was his ship. Hastind would certainly not be inclined to do any favors for Captain de Guichen. Stephano's only hope was Dubois—the man he'd shot. The grand bishop's agent could order the navy to try to seize the vessel, take Wallace alive. But Dubois could also order that the *Silver Raven* be blown out of the skies.

"We could stop the ship, sir," Dag suggested. "Shoot off a spar, puncture the balloons . . ."

Stephano shook his head. "Wallace would kill Rigo."

"Again, sir, I am sorry," said Dag heavily. "This is my fault."

Stephano clapped his friend on his shoulder and managed

a reassuring smile. "It's nice to know I'm not the only person in this boat who screws up. Run out the cannons, make sure they're loaded and ready to fire."

Gythe gestured to the hull of the *Cloud Hopper* and made signs to her sister, who translated. "Gythe says she has replaced the magical defenses. She and Rigo did it together. He showed her how to lay the spells properly this time."

Gythe shifted her worried gaze to the *Silver Raven*. They could see Rodrigo on deck. His lavender coat showed up well against the backdrop of the gray cliffs.

"She wants to know if Rigo will be all right," said Miri.

"He'll be fine," said Stephano, wishing he meant it. He added briskly, "Dag's going to run out the guns. Gythe, you'd best take the Doctor to the storeroom."

"What's the point of running out the guns?" Miri asked, as her sister went to corner the cat, who knew where he was headed apparently, for he ran underneath a deck chair. "Wallace knows you won't shoot his ship."

"The captain of the *Silver Raven* doesn't know that," said Stephano. He paused, then added, "And then there's the naval ships."

Miri stared at him, aghast. "You're planning to take on a naval warship?"

"I won't let anyone harm Rigo, Miri," Stephano said. He turned to face her. "But you have the final say. This is your boat. If you don't want to risk it, I understand. Sail over to shore and let me get off. I'll find some other way—"

"How dare you?" Miri flared.

"How dare I what?" Stephano asked, startled.

"How dare you accuse me of letting someone harm Rigo?" Miri wiped away her tears and blinked her eyes, trying all the while to steer.

Stephano was taken aback. "Miri, I didn't say anything of the kind . . . I just wanted you to know . . ."

"Get off my bridge, Captain de Guichen," said Miri, through clenched teeth. "Go help Dag. Or are you going to get rid of him as well? I suppose you figure you'll take on a sixty-four-gun warship single-handed!"

"Miri, you know I didn't mean it—"

"Go!" Miri ordered.

But instead of going, Stephano put his arm around her and hugged her close.

"Thank you," he said huskily.

"Get along with you!" Miri snapped. "Let me do my job before we smash into that trawler up ahead."

Stephano lifted the glass to his eye to have another look at the *Silver Raven*. Stephano was armed and wearing his heavy flight coat and light chain shirt. The dragon pistol was in its holster on his right side, opposite his rapier. Loaded muskets stood in a weapon stand against the ship's rail. Dag wore his breastplate that still bore the burn marks from the demons' ambush. He had a pair of pistols tucked into his belt. His blunderbuss and his boarding ax were in a nearby weapon stand.

The *Hopper* and the *Silver Raven* were both coming up on the Old Fort, leaving the dockyards and the mass of ships behind. Apparently, no one aboard any of the blockade ships had noticed the *Silver Raven* trying to slip out. The ship glided along, hugging the shoreline, with the *Cloud Hopper* in dogged pursuit.

"He's sinking into the Breath," said Stephano suddenly, alarmed.

"He's leaking air on purpose," said Miri. "The captain is reducing the lift of the ship's balloons; that's why they're flattening out. *Raven* is slowly losing altitude, hoping no one will notice. He's going to hide himself in the mists."

Miri gave a lopsided smile. "We've done that ourselves a time or two, as I recall. It's not a pleasant way to travel by any means, but then he only has to stay down there until he's well away from the patrol ships."

"Keep with him, Miri," said Stephano.

"I'll stay as close as I can, but once he dives down, I'll lose him, Stephano," said Miri. "You remember what it's like in the deep fog. I wouldn't be able to see you if you were right next to me, much less try to keep track of another ship!"

"This is why we had dragons, damn it!" said Stephano, slamming his fist onto the railing. "They could find *Raven*, fog or no fog. Look at Commander Hastind in that great bloody battleship sitting out there, blind as a bat."

"I could fire the swivel gun, sir," said Dag. "Draw the navy's attention."

"And they would fire on the *Raven*," said Stephano.

"There he goes!" Miri called urgently.

The *Silver Raven*'s captain suddenly let all the air out of his forward balloons and dropped the prow of his ship. At the same time he pushed his airscrews to full, propelling the vessel into the mist and out of sight.

"Miri, follow him!" Stephano ordered, but even as he said the words, he knew it was hopeless. Once the *Silver Raven* was deep in the fog, the captain could sail off in any direction and leave them behind, with no way of knowing where he went.

Miri took the *Cloud Hopper* down as rapidly as she dared. Gythe had returned from stashing the Doctor in the storeroom (they could hear his angry yowls) and she and Dag and Stephano leaned over the rail, peering into the thickening mists until their eyes ached. Suddenly Gythe seized hold of Stephano and jabbed her finger.

"Look there!" Dag cried at the same time. He was leaning over the rail at a perilous angle, holding onto a line and peering into the Breath. "A firefly!"

"And it's lavender," said Stephano, smiling.

The small light shone palely, a tiny beacon guiding them through the Breath. The light was far below them. The Silver Raven had gone down rapidly.

"I hope I don't crash into them," Miri muttered, adjusting her course, letting the *Cloud Hopper* fall through the mists. "If I do, we're both finished."

The lavender light continued to glow. Stephano strained

his eyes to see and his ears to hear when out of the mists below them came the sound of shouts and terrified cries and a bang.

"That was a pistol shot," said Dag.

Stephano's brow furrowed. "What the—"

Below in the mists, green light flared. Gythe gave a sudden gasp and a moan and backed up against a mast, cowering in terror. They could hear muffled voices and the sounds of gunfire.

"Get out of here, Miri!" Stephano cried. "Take her up! Fast as you can! Dag—the swivel gun!"

Orange eyes glowed in the mists. A bat flew past the ship, the speed of its flight shredding the mists. Green fire struck the *Cloud Hopper*; the boat's defenses flared blue. Gythe cried out in pain and sank to the deck.

Miri's fingers flew across the helm. Magical energy flowed into the balloons and the wings' lift tanks. The smaller, light *Cloud Hopper* soared up through the mists toward the clear, sunlit sky above. Dag was manning a swivel gun, but, as he said in frustration, he couldn't be expected to hit a goddam blur.

The lavender light had gone out, but they didn't need Rodrigo's signal anymore. The *Silver Raven* was also rising up swiftly out of the Breath. They could see the tops of her masts and the balloons, now fully inflated. Stephano and Dag both crouched tensely at the swivel guns, searching for the demons on their gigantic bats.

The *Cloud Hopper* burst into the sunlight. The boat was well out of the harbor area now, approaching the Old Fort. Stephano looked back toward harbor and saw nothing out of the ordinary. Merchant ships and barges rode at anchor, resignedly waiting for the authorities to come to their senses and lift the blockade. Naval vessels were spread out from the naval station on the southwest edge of the bay, along the southern Rim east to the main harbor area. The northern shore was dominated by the Old Fort and the artillery batteries. The *Royal Lion*, pride of King Alaric and flagship of the western fleet, floated near the mouth of the bay.

"Dag, take the helm!" Stephano called. "Miri, take Gythe below."

But although Gythe was obviously in pain, she refused to leave. Shaking her head, she allowed Dag to help her to a chair on the deck, but that was as far as she would go.

A gunboat, seeing the *Cloud Hopper* suddenly bob up out of the mists, was bearing down on them, though not with any sense of urgency. Trundlers could always be expected to try to slip past a blockade and were generally considered harmless, though the captain's eyes must be opening somewhat wider at the sight of the *Cloud Hopper*'s two cannons, swivel guns, and the frog. Stephano could see no sign the navy had noticed anything out of the ordinary. The sound of the pistol shot fired down in the mists would have gone unheard, muffled by the Breath.

The *Silver Raven* sailed up out of the mists, emerging some distance from the *Cloud Hopper*. The sight of the merchant vessel appearing out of nowhere caused the navy gunboat to shift their attention away from the *Cloud Hopper*. Stephano swept the deck of the *Silver Raven* with his glass. He saw Rodrigo's lavender coat and he gave a sigh of relief. Wallace was there, as well, talking to the captain. By his emphatic gestures and belligerent stance and the fact that he was aiming his pistol at the captain, the discussion was not going well.

"Flagship's signaling, Captain!" Dag called.

Stephano lifted his spyglass, trained it on the *Royal Lion*. He suspected this flurry of signals must have something to do with the sudden and unexpected appearance of the *Silver Raven*. He could not read the flags; the codes were changed frequently so as to confuse any enemy who might be watching. He waited tensely to see if the gunboat, *Capture*, would respond and how it would respond.

The *Capture* fired a warning shot in front of the *Silver Raven*, ordering it to halt.

The *Raven* ignored the warning, continuing to add on sail in an effort to increase speed. The *Cloud Hopper*—now forgotten—trundled along gamely behind. The merchant ship, the gunboat, and the *Cloud Hopper* were now rounding a corner of the Old Fort, coming in view of the battlements and the guard towers and shore battery.

The battlements, made of magic-reinforced concrete and stone, were over a mile long. They ran along the northern Rim of the bay, up a cliff called the Short Step to the Old Fort, stretched along the shore until they reached the foot of the high, jutting cliff known as the Bastion. Beyond the cliff, the topography was wild and uninhabited, made up of hills covered with trees, outcroppings of jagged-edged granite, and spectacular falls of water where rivers cascaded off the continent and plunged into the mists of the Breath.

Stephano could see the long, black muzzles of the cannons of the shore battery thrusting out from the side of the cliff. He waited tensely for the shot that would cripple or sink the merchant vessel.

"Miri, bring us in close," said Stephano. "We're going to board the *Raven*. Dag, you're with me."

"Captain," said Dag. He had his spyglass to his eye and there was a strange, strangled sound to his voice. "Look at that."

Stephano had his pistol drawn and was standing by the port rail, ready to step onto the ship's short wings. Miri was sailing the *Cloud Hopper* closer to the *Silver Raven*. Both of them turned to Dag, then shifted their gazes.

A darkish gray cloud rolled over the hills, moving at incredible speed, lit from within by flashes of green fire and accompanied by an eerie whirring sound—the wings of countless gigantic bats. Hell's Gates had swung wide. Aertheum had sent his legions to attack in force.

Stephano was momentarily paralyzed by the astonishing sight. Then he looked at the naval warships, whose officers were watching the harbor, ready to stop smugglers. He looked at the fortress, at the guards enjoying the show. All unknowing, unaware of the horror about to break over them.

Stephano had to warn Hastind, make him see the approaching danger. He ran to the storage locker on the deck where they stored such objects as signal flags, rope, and patching material for the balloons and sails. He flung it open and dragged out a flag made up of four blocks: red and white on top and white and red on the bottom. The flag's message was terse and to the point: *Standing into Danger*. Stephano hurriedly attached the flag to the lines and ran it up the mast of the *Cloud Hopper*. The question was: Would anyone see it and, if they did, would they pay attention to a flag being flown by a Trundler.

"Dag, fire a gun to get their attention. Miri, all hell is going to break loose, and we're now right in the middle. We need to—"

He paused a moment to look at the *Silver Raven*. The merchant vessel was ahead of them by several hundred yards. Rodrigo would understand the nature of the peril swooping down on them. So would Henry Wallace.

The *Cloud Hopper's* four-pound cannon fired with a boom that reverberated off the towering walls of the fortress. Stephano could imagine all the spyglasses on all the navy vessels now searching for the boat that had fired. He watched Wallace standing on the deck of the *Silver Raven*. The gunshot had caught *his* attention. He would be certain to think that the *Cloud Hopper* was firing on his ship.

Wallace, his expression grim, aimed his gun at Rodrigo.

Raising a speaking trumpet, Stephano bellowed through it. "Demons!" He jabbed his finger in the direction of the approaching swarm.

Rodrigo heard and understood. He looked over his shoulder and even from this distance Stephano could see his friend's horrified expression. This apparently convinced Henry Wallace, for he turned to see the demons closing in. The bats were no longer a homogenous mass. They were individuals, their mouths wide, fangs gleaming. Their riders with their hideous faces twisted in fury, orange eyes glowing, were raising the green-fire, handheld cannons.

Stephano could not see Wallace's face, but he could tell by the fact that he took an involuntary step backward and had to steady himself by grabbing onto a mast that he was astonished and alarmed.

The naval ships had heard Stephano's warning cannon shot and seen his flag. Most captains would summarily dismiss a small Trundler boat signaling danger. A few astute captains might take the signal seriously. Every lookout in the crows' nests above and every officer on deck below would have their spyglasses sweeping the skies, searching for the threat.

They did not have far to look.

The heavy mists of the Breath below the ships shredded. More bats and their demon riders rose from below. The demonic forces were already causing havoc in the harbor, firing their green blasts at the helpless merchant vessels, which were essentially sitting ducks. Already flames were starting to rise from burning hulls and masts. Naval gunboats were racing to their aid, but the navy was now coming under attack, as well.

A flurry of signals sailed up mastheads, captains asking the flagship what was going on. Beating drums on board all the ships sent the gun crews to their stations. The shore batteries were already prepared to enforce the blockade, their gun crews were at their posts, gunports open, guns ready to fire.

"And we're in their sights!" Stephano realized.

Henry Wallace had reached exactly the same alarming thought.

"Miri, take her up!" Stephano shouted frantically.

"Gain altitude!" Wallace yelled.

The ship's balloons billowed with magical energy, giving them full lift capacity. A flag with a blue cross on a white background soared up the mast on board Wallace's ship. The flag meant: "Break off your intentions and communicate with me." Stephano wondered what the hell Wallace was up to. Now was hardly the time to try to open negotiations with the Royal Navy! Probably a mistake, he thought. Some panicked sailor sent up the wrong signal. He was proved right in that the next moment, that flag came down and they sent up a distress signal.

Stephano shouted. "Stay on Wallace's tail! I don't want to lose Rigo."

Miri tossed her red hair. "I'm supposed to sail through an army sent by the Devil himself, keep this boat from going down in flames, and all the while try to fly this boat fast enough to catch a ship that has three times her sail?"

"I have every confidence in you," said Stephano. He grinned as he ran past her.

"You're enjoying this!" she said accusingly.

Stephano considered her statement as he crouched behind the swivel gun and looked down the sights. "Enjoy" wasn't the right word. He didn't enjoy the idea that their boat might come under attack or that innocent people were dying or that he and his people might be blown up at any moment. But he knew what Miri meant.

This was danger he understood. Danger he could fight. No more hiding in the darkness, skulking about alleys or crawling over rooftops. No more getting slammed on the head from behind or sneaking out through wardrobes. No more of his mother's sneaking, underhanded, lying way of doing business. This was war, plain and simple. Stephano knew what to do in war and he knew how to do it and he was damn good at it.

Dag had loaded both the swivel guns. While in Westfirth, he'd found time to buy more canisters of ammunition, for they were stacked neatly on the deck. Dag had said nothing about it, of course. All part of his job.

Stephano looked at Dag: steady, cool, calm, undaunted in the face of danger. He looked at Miri, her lips pressed together in grim determination, her hands flying over the brass helm, paying no heed to the demons or the bursts of green fire or the flashes of fire from the guns of the shore battery. He looked out across the widening expanse between their ship and the *Silver Raven* and saw Rodrigo, seated at his ease in a deck chair while chaos erupted around him. Stephano looked at Gythe, who was now crouched on the deck at the bottom of the mast, terrified nearly out of her wits, but refusing to hide, singing softly to maintain the magic that would protect the *Cloud Hopper*.

Stephano's eyes dimmed with tears, his throat and nose clogged. These were his friends, and he loved them. For a moment, he couldn't see to aim his weapon. He gave himself a mental slap and wiped his eyes in time to witness an astonishing sight.

The Breath boiled and out of it rose a ship. The vessel with its wide beam and a squared bow looked cumbersome and unwieldy. The short forecastle was overshadowed by a high sterncastle that extended out beyond the hull. The Estarans had built ships like this during the Bishops' War, but that was more than one hundred years ago. He'd never actually seen one in person, only in books. Three masts rose from the deck, but none of them supported any balloons. Black sails flapped in the air. In the center of each sail, a human corpse dangled from a rope.

Stephano grabbed a spyglass to get a better look. The ship's hull was covered in leather marked with strange sigils. Glowing green lines ran from sigil to sigil, connecting them all in a grotesque construct. Green energy crackled along the black sails as the ship leveled off.

Miri's eyes widened at the sight. Her hands trembled and the *Cloud Hopper*'s forward speed slowed.

"Miri, whatever that is, it's not after us!" Stephano shouted, hoping he was right. "Keep up with *Raven*."

Miri nodded and turned back to her task. By this time, the *Cloud Hopper* and the *Silver Raven* had gained altitude and were floating above the Old Fort, looking down on the battlements with their shore batteries. The hapless merchant vessels in the harbor and the navy gunboats and warships were all under assault. Smoke and flames rose from the docks.

Stephano wondered how the Trundlers were faring. Probably not well. Unlike the *Cloud Hopper*, few Trundler ships were armed and would be ill-prepared to fend off the demon attacks. Miri was worried about her uncle and family; he could see her cast agonized glances over her shoulder in a vain attempt to see what was happening far away at the Trundler village.

A few demons had been flying toward the *Silver Raven*. The merchant vessel carried a score of large swivel guns to fend off pirates. They had manned their swivel guns and were ready to fire when, surprisingly, the demons broke off the attack and flew, instead, toward the *Cloud Hopper*, which was closing rapidly on the *Raven*.

Sir Henry Wallace was on the deck of the *Silver Raven* with the captain (Wallace was no coward, Stephano had to give him credit for that) watching the demons; a puzzled expression on his face, as though wondering himself why they had not attacked the ship. He actually walked over and said something to Rodrigo, who shrugged his shoulders.

Wallace gazed at the demons flying toward the *Cloud Hopper* another long moment, then he spoke to the captain. He may not have known why the demons had not attacked his ship, but he was quick to take advantage of the fact. The sailors were running to set more sail, increase *Raven*'s speed.

Having fought the demons before, Stephano and his crew were better prepared to deal with them than the sailors on board the naval vessels; many of whom, Stephano guessed, must be in a state of mind-numbing panic. As it was, he and Dag had practice aiming and firing at the giant bats and their demonic riders.

Green fire flared, racing toward the *Cloud Hopper*. Gythe's magical defenses arced blue and the first shots did no damage—except to Gythe. She gave a whimpering cry and put her hands over her ears.

"Gythe! Go below!" Stephano shouted.

Gythe either didn't hear him, or she was pretending she couldn't hear him. He had asked her before what the demons were saying to her, but she had replied that while their words made sense at the time, they didn't make sense when she thought about it. Like voices in a dream.

Stephano watched an approaching bat, waiting for it to fly into his sights, a trick he'd learned in the last battle. Below the *Hopper*, the shore batteries had opened fire on the ungainly black-sailed ship, which was flying straight toward them. The ship was still out of range, and the batteries were trying to find their target. The demonic ship was armed with only a single gun mounted on the high sterncastle. The gun wasn't very big, and Stephano wondered what sort of damage the fiends thought they could do with that.

He fired the swivel gun at a demon and saw it veer rapidly off. He had no idea whether he'd hit it or not. Dag's gun fired almost simultaneously. Dag struck his target; the giant bat shrieked horribly, flipped over, and bat and rider went spiraling down into the Breath. Before Dag could reload, a bat flew up from underneath the hull and dove at Miri. Dag grabbed his musket and fired, just as the demon shot green fire at her. Miri ducked behind the helm. The *Cloud Hopper*'s magic flamed blue. The demon flew off; one arm dangling useless at his side.

Gythe slumped down onto the deck and moaned.

"Dag! Take Gythe below!" Stephano yelled.

Dag tried to persuade her to leave. She shook her head obstinately. Stephano reloaded his swivel gun and Miri left her helm long enough to race over to reload Dag's. Stephano waited tensely for another attack, but none came. Bats that had been flying toward them suddenly veered and flew off. Dag, shaking his head, went back to the gun. Gythe, shivering in fear, remained defiantly on deck.

Miri dashed back to the helm. The fight with the bats had cost them precious time. The *Silver Raven*, now with all sails set and its propellers whirling, was drawing away from the *Cloud Hopper*. Stephano had lost sight of Rodrigo.

"Stay with them!" Stephano yelled.

"I'm trying!" Miri yelled back impatiently. "Something is fouling the main yard control lines. I can't set the mainsail! Port side."

Stephano ran to the port blocks. A quick examination revealed several large splinters of wood lodged in three of the main pulley lines. Stephano used the butt end of his pistol to knock the obstructions free.

The port mainsail filled with air. The *Cloud Hopper* surged forward.

Stephano and Dag remained at the swivel guns, watching the bats and the demonic ship, which was crawling nearer and nearer the shore batteries. Its single gun looked like a child's toy. The shore batteries were firing, attempting to hit the strange ship, but they were having difficulty targeting the vessel.

Stephano and Dag both aimed their swivel guns at the demonic ship, though there was small chance of hitting it. Still, a lucky shot might do some damage. As Stephano stared down the sights, the ship flickered and blurred in his vision, shifting left, then right. The sight made him dizzy and he had to look away. He blinked and tried to aim again, but the same thing happened.

"I can't see to shoot at it!" Dag called.

"Some sort of weird magic," Stephano muttered.

The *Cloud Hopper* was directly above the battlements, flying over them at about twenty feet. A man in a black cassock ran along the top of the wall, followed by a man in armor that shone in the sunlight. Stephano recognized Father Jacob and Sir Ander. Some distance behind the two, he could see their companion, the monk. Movement and the flash of sunlight on scales caught his eye and he looked up at the Bastion and his heart skipped a beat.

A dragon stood poised on the top of the cliff, his wings spread, ready to soar down and join in the fighting. Stephano recognized his old friend, Sergeant Hroalfrig. Stephano waved to try to attract the dragon's attention. Miri had caught sight of Father Jacob and was exclaiming in worry over him.

A green beam shot out from the single gun mounted on the strange ship and struck the concrete bunker housing the guns of the shore battery. The beam was powerful, blinding as though one had looked directly into the sun. All Stephano could see for a moment was the afterimage, yellow tinged with red. The beam blazed for maybe a minute. Green light washed over the concrete and stone and magic walls of the bunker and then the beam went out.

Nothing happened.

No fire, no explosion.

The guns of the shore battery had not ceased shooting. Stephano could hear the booms and see the flashes from the muzzles and the cannonballs flying through the air. He was halfway inclined to laugh at the demonic ship and its little gun, and then he heard a rumbling sound, deep and terrible; the sound of breaking, cracking, smashing.

The side of the bunker crumbled. The stone and concrete walls collapsed, crushing the gun crews. The enormous cannons lurched forward and fell into the Breach, along with a huge portion of the side of the cliff. The walls of the old Fort cracked. The guard towers shook and started to topple.

Stephano tried frantically to see what had happened to Father Jacob and Sir Ander who had been on top of the battlements. Smoke and dust rose up in choking clouds and he lost sight of them. He looked for Hroalfrig and saw the dragon diving straight into the midst of the chaos and then Stephano lost sight of him, as well.

On board the *Cloud Hopper*, everyone was dazed, struck dumb. Sailing above the disaster, they looked down on utter ruin. Even from here, they could hear the screams of the wounded, the dying.

Then Miri gulped and said in a strangled voice, "How did . . . how did that happen!"

"I saw something like this back on the redoubt," said Dag, shaken. He glanced at Stephano. "The fire from your

dragons broke down the magical sigils. My crafter had to
work to restore them. But this . . ." He shook his head,
words failing him.

"This attack didn't break down the sigils," said Stephano
grimly. "This obliterated them."

Gythe gave an eerie animal cry and pulled herself up.
She ran to the railing and was leaning over, staring into the
ravaged fortress. Walls were still collapsing. One of the towers—located directly over the battery—had gone down in a
heap of stone and rubble. Gythe pointed frantically at the
fort.

"She wants to help," said Miri. She didn't say it, but they
all knew Gythe was thinking of Brother Barnaby.

"There's nothing we could do," said Stephano. "We're
not out of this yet ourselves. And we can't abandon Rigo."

Gythe looked at him, her face tearstained and unhappy.
She gave a bleak nod of understanding.

The *Silver Raven* was sailing past the last guard tower,
leaving the Old Fort behind, heading out into the open
Breath. Stephano looked back, fearing pursuit, but the demons were concentrating their attacks on the naval ships.
Smoke and flame shot up from the dockyards and the harbor area. The demonic ship with the green beam was coming about. Another shot would finish the Old Fort, but now
the demons were facing a new threat—the flagship, the
Royal Lion, was bearing down on them.

"Ha, ha!" Miri cried triumphantly, pointing to the *Raven*.
"I knew it!"

Stephano wrenched his gaze away from the battle and
looked at the merchant ship, which had been steadily drawing away from them. He had been wondering dismally how
they were ever going to catch *Raven* when he saw the ship
had slowed considerably. Sailors were rushing about the
deck, where Wallace stood, red-faced and furious, gesturing
wildly.

"What happened?" Stephano asked.

"I knew it!" Miri repeated, exultant. "They were carrying

too much sail in this wind and snapped a yard on the main topsail. They'll have to slow down or risk losing the balloon."

The *Silver Raven* was still sailing, but the *Cloud Hopper* was definitely catching up to her. Stephano turned to look back at the battle. The *Royal Lion*, King Alaric's pride and joy, fired a broadside at the demon ship.

The demon ship took no damage that Stephano could see. The magical sigils on its hull protected the ship much as Gythe's sigils protected theirs. The single gun mounted on the prow fired. The green beam swept over the flagship.

The *Royal Lion* seemed to shudder. Stephano heard a series of cracks and groans. Several small explosions tore through the lower gunports, and then the entire hull on the port side exploded outward. A moment later explosions rocked the starboard side. Flames flared from the quarterdeck and main hatches.

The flames breached the main magazine and ignited the ship's store of powder. The entire bottom half of the ship disappeared in a blinding flash. The flaming remains of the *Royal Lion* fell into the Breath and were gone.

"Dear God in Heaven!" Stephano breathed softly. "Not even for you, Hastind, would I have wished such a fate. God have mercy on you all."

Chapter Forty-One

And on God's palette are the colors of the world, and one of those colors is black. So I will not fear the darkness, for it is of God's making as death is another part of his grand design. My soul will walk in the darkness and shadows and marvel at the night sky. Death is but a journey back to the canvas of my God.

—Requiem

WHEN HE FIRST SAW THE SWARM OF DEMONS flying to the attack, Sir Ander had regretted the fact that his magically reinforced heavy steel breastplate was back in his guest room on the armor stand. Scrambling down the face of the cliff and running along the battlements in the heat of midday, trying to keep up with Father Jacob, Sir Ander no longer regretted the breastplate. He was now starting to regret wearing clothes.

Father Jacob was running across the battlements, shouting at the top of his lungs, "To arms! To arms!"

Guards grabbed their weapons and looked about for the enemy. If the warning had come from anyone except a priest of the Arcanum, the guards might well have shaken their heads and gone back to watching the navy ships harassing merchant vessels.

An officer cried out, "Father, where is the foe?"

Father Jacob did not stop running, but he did slow down. He pointed to the sky above the Bastion.

Sir Ander, who was closing in on the priest, saw the startled look on an officer's face, saw the man's jaw drop, his eyes widen. He could imagine what was going through the man's mind. The officer was about to rush off when Father Jacob grabbed him.

"Tell the . . . battery . . . run out . . . all the guns . . ." Father Jacob gasped. "All of them!"

The officer nodded. Clapping his hand over the sword that was banging against his leg, he dashed off, shouting commands as he went.

Sir Ander's duty was to guard the person of Father Jacob, but he did not forget Brother Barnaby the monk's steps lagged. He stared at the demons. Ander wandered if the fiends were speaking to the monk again. Brother Barnaby saw Ander looking back at him with concern, and he smiled and waved his hand and shouted out, "Tell Father Jacob I'm coming, sir!"

The battlements were divided into four segments, each guarded by a tower manned by twenty soldiers armed with muskets and smaller field artillery. The large batteries were down below—cannons lined up in a long row, each manned by its own crew. Sir Ander had been down to have a look at the batteries when they'd first taken up residence at the Old Fort, and he'd been impressed by the gunnery officers and the men they commanded. The city of Westfirth relied on the shore batteries for its defense; a Freyan attack would undoubtedly come from the Breath, not overland.

A few of the guns had been run out to deal with the merchant vessels. Now they were all being run out. Sir Ander could feel the rumble beneath his feet and picture the activity in the bunker; the gun crews opening the gunports, running out the cannons, swabbing, loading; stacks of cannonballs piled neatly nearby. The demons would find the fortification difficult to attack, for the guns were in a manmade cavern dug out of the side of the cliff, protected by stone, concrete, and magic.

"We should take cover, Father!" Sir Ander yelled, pointing to the guard tower they were fast approaching.

Father Jacob shook his head and kept running. He shouted over his shoulder. "The books!"

Sir Ander understood. The books on contramagic written by the Saints were in Father Jacob's room in the main part of Old Fort and although they were hidden in a safe place, protected by all manner of magical spells, Father Jacob was not about to risk letting them fall into enemy hands.

Father Jacob stopped at the second tower to give the same orders, which proved unnecessary, for drums were beating and the guards were already in position.

"Can we at least . . . stop and rest . . ." Sir Ander gasped, bending over, his hands on his knees to relieve a painful stitch in his side. "And wait for . . . Barnaby."

Father Jacob had no breath left to answer and stood for a moment leaning with his hand on the wall. He and Sir Ander watched in silence as the bats swooped past the Old Fort, flying toward the merchants in the harbor. The guards in the tower were thrown into confusion at the sight of the gigantic bats and their demon riders.

Some cried that they were fiends from Hell and that the world was ending. Throwing down their guns, they fell to their knees and began to pray. Others remained grimly at their posts and fired their muskets, but the fast-moving bats were almost impossible to hit.

"They're human," said Father Jacob testily. "Tell them they're human!"

"They won't believe you," said Sir Ander. He helped himself to water from a barrel, drinking from the community mug that was attached to the wall by a rope.

He offered the water to Father Jacob, who drank gratefully. "And even if they are human, they have the accursed souls of demons, which is how I will always think of them. So why do these Bottom Dweller demons want the books? Why torture Brother Barnaby and Brother Paul to try to find out where they are?"

"A question I would love to be able to answer," said Father Jacob. "They obviously know far more about the use and workings of contramagic than the Saints, who barely understood the true nature of their discovery."

"Perhaps these fiends are afraid we may learn how to combat them through reading these books," Sir Ander suggested.

Father Jacob gave a grim smile. "The Bottom Dwellers have no need to worry. It will take us years and years of study and experiment to even begin to start to understand contramagic. If the Church had not suppressed it . . ."

He shook his head in bitter frustration, then smiled to see Brother Barnaby running up to the guard tower. He drank the water Sir Ander offered and stood panting for breath.

Father Jacob walked over to peer out a murder hole. Gunfire was sporadically going off around them. Most of the Bottom Dwellers were still too far out of range for anyone to hit.

"They are concentrating their attack on the naval ships," said Father Jacob. "Look! There are our friends! That's the *Cloud Hopper!*"

Sir Ander and Barnaby crowded next to him to see.

"They're coming under attack," said Sir Ander.

"Poor Gythe!" said Brother Barnaby unhappily. "She will be terrified."

"God be with them," said Father Jacob softly. He turned to Sir Ander. "We will make a run for it. Are you ready?"

"No," Sir Ander growled, "but I don't suppose that makes any difference."

"You mustn't go out in the open, Father!" cried Barnaby, alarmed. "You should stay here in the guard tower where it is safe!"

Barnaby suddenly winced and put his hand to his ear. He looked distressed.

"You hear the voices . . ." said Father Jacob.

"They are asking about books," said Barnaby in helpless

confusion. "They keep asking me about the books! What books? I don't know what they're talking about!"

Father Jacob and Sir Ander exchanged glances. They had still not told Brother Barnaby about the writings of the Saints. Both men knew the monk would die before revealing any secrets to the foe, whose voices were still in his head. Father Jacob did not want Brother Barnaby to have to make that choice. If the monk could honestly plead ignorance, the Bottom Dwellers might eventually cease to torment him.

Directly below them, the guns of the shore battery had opened fire on the bats. They could feel the ground shake and smell the smoke as it swirled into the tower.

"We should go now while we can use the smoke for cover," said Sir Ander urgently.

The three men made a mad dash across the top of the battlements, Father Jacob in front, Sir Ander running behind him, and Brother Barnaby keeping watch in the rear. The smoke that had concealed their movements began to dissipate. They had reached the center of the battlements and were running along the narrow stone walkway that led from the guard tower to the stolid bulk of the Old Fort ahead of them, when six demons caught sight of them.

Brother Barnaby saw them first; gigantic bats closing in on their prey. He cried out a warning. Sir Ander raised his pistol, aiming at the bat and rider closest to them. He was carrying the pistols that did not rely on magical constructs. Sir Ander blessed Cecile for having given them to him.

"Keep going, Father!" Sir Ander shouted.

He fired his pistol, striking his foe in the chest and blowing it out of the saddle. The Bottom Dweller landed on his back. Sir Ander remembered his experiences at the abbey, when the demon he had thought he'd killed had come most unexpectedly back to life. He ran up to the demon, drew out the dragon pistol, and shot the demon between the orange glowing eyes. He holstered the pistol and turned to look for Father Jacob.

Sir Ander swore beneath his breath. He'd told Father Jacob to keep running, but he had, of course, not listened to the advice. Father Jacob had stopped, turned, and was racing back to Sir Ander. A bat and rider veered away from the pack. They had circled around and were flying at the priest from the rear. The demon was taking aim at Father Jacob with the green-fire cannon.

"Father! Drop!" Sir Ander bellowed, drawing his third pistol.

Father Jacob dove for the pavement. Sir Ander shot the demon, knocking the weapon from its hands. The screeching bat landed on top of Father Jacob as he lay on the ground, digging its claws into his back and trying to sink its teeth into the priest's neck.

Sir Ander remembered the gory lumps of flesh, all that remained of the slaughtered nuns. He could see vividly how they had died as the bat tore a chunk out of Father Jacob's shoulder. Father Jacob was trying vainly to grapple with the creature, but the gigantic bat was heavy, weighing him down, and he could only lash out futilely with his fists.

Sir Ander drew his sword and was running to the priest's aid, when the demon rider rose up in front of him, wielding a wicked-looking dagger with a serrated blade. The demon made a clumsy attempt to stab Sir Ander. He easily parried the strike and sent the dagger spinning out of the demon's hands. His return sword stroke sliced through the demon's neck. Blood spurted and the fiend fell to the ground, flopping and twitching.

Sir Ander jumped over the demon and, reaching Father Jacob, drove his sword into the bat. The creature screeched horribly, gave a hideous gurgle, and died. Sir Ander, his gorge rising, took hold of the beast and dragged it off Father Jacob, who was covered in blood.

"Help me up!" he gasped, holding out his hand.

Sir Ander heaved the priest to his feet. Shielding him with his body, Sir Ander turned, ready to fight. For the moment, he and Father Jacob were safe. The shadow of wings flowed over them. Sir Ander looked up to see the dragon, Hroalfrig, circling protectively above them, while the other demons were coming under fire from several guards in the tower. They had seen the priest and his friends under attack and, led by a quick-thinking soldier, ran to their aid, closing in on the demons from the rear. Two of the soldiers fired their muskets. One shot missed, but the other hit one of the demons and knocked him off his mount.

Another demon fired at the soldiers. The green fire from the handheld cannon struck one of the men in the act of raising his musket. The green fire sparked along the muzzle. The gun blew apart. The soldier screamed in agony. His companion fired, hitting the bat and causing it to fall onto the stone parapet, bounce off, and go tumbling into the Breath.

Barnaby heard the man scream and turned to see the wounded man standing on the battlement, staring in shock at the splintered bones and bloody, mangled flesh that had once been his hands and arms.

"Stay with Father Jacob!" Barnaby cried to Sir Ander. "I'm going back to help!"

Sir Ander did not reply. He was watching the strange black ship that had reared up out of the Breath, the black sails with the bodies hanging from the masts, the archaic design and the single silly-looking gun mounted on the sterncastle.

Brother Barnaby was helping the soldier, who had fallen to his knees, moaning, just as the monk reached him.

The black-sailed ship began to come around, bringing its single gun to bear on the shore battery. Sir Ander looked at the ship. He and Father Jacob looked at each other. The same thought, the same memory came vividly to mind: the pirate ship and the green-beam weapon that had nearly sunk the cutter, *Defiant*.

"Run, Father!" Sir Ander shouted. "Run!"

"Barnaby!" Father Jacob gasped. Blood poured down his arm, soaking the cassock, and dripping off his hand.

"I'll go to him!" Sir Ander yelled. "You save the books."

Father Jacob cast an agonized glance at Brother Barnaby, and then broke into a staggering run, heading for the Old Fort that was only a short distance away.

Sir Ander saw the green-beam gun taking aim at the shore batteries. The green beam that would obliterate every magical sigil and construct it touched. He saw the guard tower, built of stone reinforced by magic, and Brother Barnaby kneeling on the pavement in the shadow of the guard tower, holding the wounded man in his arms.

The green beam blazed from the muzzle of the gun. The light was blinding, the heat overwhelming. Sir Ander could not see anything or feel anything except the terrible heat that was like being roasted alive in an ironmonger's furnace. Hearing a terrible cry, Sir Ander frantically rubbed his eyes, trying to see past blue-and-yellow sparks.

Father Jacob lay sprawled on the pavement some distance away. His eyes were closed, his head lolled, his body was limp. Sir Ander ran to him and knelt beside him, trying to find a new wound. There had been no explosion, only light and heat. Sir Ander thought hopefully that perhaps the gun had misfired.

Then the world shook beneath his feet. Concrete cracked, steel rods buckled, wooden timbers snapped, stone ground against stone. The magic disintegrated. Sir Ander could hear the screams of the men crushed to death as the bunker's walls and ceiling collapsed on top of them.

The guard tower began to sway. Men inside cried that it was going to fall and it did fall, before they got the words out of their mouths. Brother Barnaby was holding the wounded soldier in his arms, trying to drag him to a place of safety, a place that did not exist.

The ground split beneath Barnaby's feet. The wall crumbled.

Sir Ander bellowed, crying out the monk's name in helpless denial.

Barnaby looked up at him and gave a fleeting smile,

then he disappeared in a cascade of tumbling stone. Sir
Ander roared in anger and lunged across the shaking
ground with some wild idea of saving the monk. The pavement began cracking beneath him. He knew it was hopeless. Swearing in anger, he ran back to Father Jacob, who
was either unconscious or dead. Sir Ander picked the
priest up in his arms and carried him through smoke and
fire and a rain of debris across the battlements until they
reached the Old Fort.

Sir Ander tried to go on, to carry Father Jacob inside, but
his strength gave out. He laid the priest on the ground beneath a stone archway and collapsed beside him. He had no
idea what was wrong with Father Jacob. He could find no
wounds other than the bat bite. Yet Father Jacob's breathing was shallow, his skin ashen and chill to the touch.

"Jacob," said Sir Ander urgently, shaking him, trying to
rouse him.

Father Jacob did not move.

Sir Ander shouted for help, and help came. The archbishop's guards ran to his aid. They asked him about Father
Jacob, about what had happened. Ander didn't know. He
couldn't say. They asked Sir Ander if he was hurt. He shook
his head. They brought a litter and placed Father Jacob on
it and bore him to where the healers had established a
makeshift hospital. They wanted to take Sir Ander with
them, but he refused to leave and eventually they quit bad-
gering him and went away, leaving him alone, crouched beneath the arch.

The ground had quit shaking, except for a rumble and
tremor, like a body twitching in its death throes. Sir Ander
wondered if the contramagic weapon was next going to fire
on the Old Fort. If so, he was too exhausted, too numb to
care.

All he could see was Brother Barnaby's face as the monk
realized he was falling to his death. There had been a little
fear, and then a fleeting smile of faith and reassurance.

"God holds me in his hand," Brother Barnaby had seemed to say to his friend. "Do not grieve for me."

Sir Ander closed his eyes and felt the hot tears burn through his lashes. He gave a shuddering sob. How was he going to tell Father Jacob that the gentle monk who had come to him by a saint's command was gone?

Chapter Forty-Two

Stephano is the soul of honor and valor. He is brave, intelligent, but he is not, I fear, very wise. Too often Stephano's restless, reckless heart carries the day. Yet I would not change him! He was born of an illicit love that doomed both his father and myself, yet to my way of thinking, Stephano is proof that God has forgiven us. God gave Julian and me the greatest gift—our brave and noble son.

—Letter from the Countess de Marjolaine to Sir Ander Martel

A DAY AND A HALF HAD PASSED SINCE THE ATTACK on Westfirth. The *Cloud Hopper* had traveled far from the ravaged city, yet they could still see the smoke of burning—a smudge on the horizon, darker than the mists of the Breath of God. Ahead of them, the damaged merchant vessel carrying Henry Wallace, Pietro Alcazar, and Rodrigo was afloat and still sailing. But the *Silver Raven* continued to lose altitude.

"A slow leak somewhere," Miri said. "Probably when the yard and rigging crashed into the mizzen balloon, it damaged the outer skin. Hard to repair when the balloon is at full capacity. They're going to have to land soon and make repairs."

"Land on what?" Stephano asked. "We're in the middle of Nowhere."

They were, quite literally, in the middle of Nowhere, this being a region in the Breath marked "Nowhere" on Trundler maps. Located off the western shore of Rosia between Westfirth and Caltreau, the shoreline for about five hundred miles was wild, desolate, and rock-bound, beautiful to look upon, but deadly if a ship sailed too close. Whipping curls and eddies of the Breath swirled among the crags and tossed against the cliffs. The bones of wrecked ships that had been caught in those eddies could be seen amidst the trees, a most effective warning to stay away.

Miri consulted a map. "The only place for the *Raven* to land would be somewhere in the String of Pearls Islands off to the northwest here." She pointed to a mass of small, floating islands, the larger of which, numbering about a hundred, formed a rough circle that made them resemble a pearl necklace. The "pearls" were surrounded by innumerable small islands; too many to count and too unimportant to chart. Free-floating, drifting among the Breath, the islands frequently collided, causing widespread destruction and making them unfit for human habitation. A ship in desperate straits could set down on one of these islands and make repairs; far safer than risking a smashed hull against the cliffs of Nowhere.

"*Raven*'s altered course. Looks like that's where they're headed," Dag reported, watching the ship through his spyglass.

"The way she's leaking air, she'd best hurry," said Miri.

"Good!" Stephano rubbed his hands. "Maybe luck is with us for once."

"Spit!" Miri ordered, alarmed. "Spit over your left shoulder! Now! You've put the hex on us and you have to lift it!"

"Better turn so you're not facing into the wind, sir," said Dag, trying to keep from grinning.

Stephano rolled his eyes, but he did as he was told. He spit over his left shoulder. Miri then ordered him to swab the deck.

Stephano and Dag began to plan their assault. Miri voiced her opinions from the helm. Gythe sat in a deck chair, singing softly to the Doctor, who lay curled up in her arms. She looked pale and seemed troubled, but insisted she was fine. Stephano asked her if she had heard the voices again. She nodded. He asked if she wanted to talk about it. She shook her head.

"Gythe thinks about things," Miri had said, when Stephano had urged her to force her sister to reveal what she knew. "Turns them over in her mind. She'll tell us when she's ready."

Stephano sighed in frustration. He was curious about the demon raid on Westfirth, wondering about the strategy behind it. The demons had displayed their capability of using awful, terrifying, mysterious power. But, analyzing the attack, he realized that the targets the demons had attacked had been easy, vulnerable targets of opportunity, such as the merchant ships. The demons had attacked major military targets, that was true, but only two—the shore battery and the *Royal Lion*. With the shore battery destroyed, the city of Westfirth had been left completely undefended. But instead of sailing in to finish the foe, set fire to the city, slaughter thousands, the strange demonic ship had vanished, disappearing into the Breath and taking the demon bat riders with her.

"Maybe all they wanted to do was spread fear," suggested Miri and she added somberly, "Maybe that's all they needed to do."

"They could have attacked other cities at the same time," Dag pointed out. "We have no way of knowing."

Stephano had a sudden image of the demonic ship with its green-beam weapon firing on the floating palace. He could picture vividly the terrible destruction, the walls cracking, towers falling as the castle, its magic destroyed, plunged to the ground. He imagined the chaos, the terror of the helpless victims trapped inside. He thought of his mother and he felt a pang of fear and dread.

The feeling startled him and even angered him. He thrust it away and told himself to stop daydreaming. Given a fight between his mother and a demon, he would back his mother. She could take care of herself. She'd managed well enough thus far. Besides, he had the feeling—call it the instinct of a soldier—that Dag was wrong. The attack on Westfirth had been isolated.

"I think it was an experiment," Stephano said. "A test. To see if their weapon worked."

"Then they must have gone back to Hell happy," Dag said bitterly.

"Or maybe," said Miri, "they were after Papa Jake."

"All right, enough about demons," said Stephano curtly, not liking the reminder the fiends were out there, hiding in the Breath, perhaps watching, listening. Undoubtedly waiting . . . "Our problem is how to free Rigo and rescue Alcazar."

While the *Cloud Hopper* had been fending off demons, the *Silver Raven* had managed to rig her boarding nets. Stephano's idea of boarding the ship while sailing the Breath was not going to work.

"It was crazy anyway," was Miri's pronouncement.

"Once the *Raven* lands, we'll—" Stephano stopped. He had no idea what they were going to do.

"We've still got the same problem," Dag pointed out. "Wallace is holding Rigo hostage. We fire at Wallace. He'll kill Rigo."

"You're a crack shot, Dag. Could you shoot Wallace before he shoots Rigo?" Stephano asked.

"Maybe if I had one of those new rifled guns, sir . . ." said Dag, hinting broadly. "Otherwise. . . ." He shrugged and shook his head. "I wouldn't want to chance it."

"We could aim our cannons at them and tell them we're going to kill everyone on board unless they surrender and hand over Rigo and Alcazar," said Miri.

"There are little ones on that ship!" said Dag, shocked.

They had all seen the children playing on the deck. Judging by the fact that they often clustered around Alcazar, they assumed they were part of his family, perhaps the children of his brother, the sailor.

"You know I wouldn't do such a thing," said Stephano.

"I know that. But the crew and the captain don't know you," said Miri. "You could be a bloodthirsty monster. They'll be scared out of their wits."

"Wallace won't let the captain surrender."

Miri snorted. "There are forty of them and one of Wallace! He'll do what they say."

"He could just shoot Rigo," said Dag.

"He won't," Miri argued. "Wallace knows that if Rigo dies, he's a dead man. You *would* burn that ship."

"I don't like it. We're taking a risk with Rigo's life," said Stephano, shaking his head.

"Begging your pardon, sir, but what else we can do?" Dag asked. "The *Raven* has a crew of forty. There's just the two of us."

"Not bad odds," said Stephano with a half-smile.

"True, sir," said Dag coolly. "But if the two of us launched an attack, Wallace might kill Rigo out of desperation. This way, at least we have a chance."

"The *Raven* being crippled is a gift from God," Miri said persuasively. "She's a fast ship and we're a slow one, and if she hadn't been hit, she'd be halfway to Freya by now and we'd have no chance of catching her."

"And you realize, sir, that if they get away from us, Wallace will have no more need of Rigo. He'll toss him overboard," said Dag.

"Much as many of us have wanted to do on occasion," said Miri.

Their conversation was interrupted by the Doctor, who jumped onto Dag's knee and from there to the table where he made himself the center of attention by sprawling out full length on top of the map. Stephano reached out to pet the cat, his mind on his trouble.

Gythe came over to stand beside Miri at the helm and made signs to her sister, who translated.

"Gythe says it's a good plan. Rodrigo will do something to help us."

"Good God! That's just *all* we need," Dag exclaimed, alarmed.

They looked expectantly at Stephano. He sighed and ran his hand through his hair.

"It's not much of a plan—"

"As if our well-laid plans have worked out so very well this trip," Miri said crisply.

Stephano gave in. "All right. We'll make ourselves look bloodthirsty and menacing, as if we slaughter small children every day just for the fun of it."

"We can do that, sir," said Dag.

He picked up the Doctor and placed the cat on his shoulder and gently rubbed him under the chin.

Wispy tendrils of mist swirled around the *Cloud Hopper* as they followed the *Silver Raven* in her slow descent. The mist was not thick enough to block their view of the ship, and they kept up with her as her captain sailed over the coastline, trying to find a clearing in which to land his crippled ship.

Scientific minds theorized that the floating islands known as the String of Pearls had been formed by silt-laden water runoff from the continents interacting violently with the magic of the Breath and exploding, resulting in the formation of these floating landmasses.

This particular island was about twenty miles across, with a single mountain near the center. A massive upheaval centuries upon centuries ago had caused horizontal layers of the rock to shift so violently that they now jutted vertically into the air. The rocky sides of the mountains were devoid of all vegetation except a few scrub pine trees. The rest of the island was thickly forested. The trees were so dense that Stephano had no idea where the captain was going to find a safe place to land.

Fortunately for the sinking ship, a broad stretch of reddish-brown beach came into view. The *Silver Raven* made a rapid descent. The *Cloud Hopper* was close behind. Stephano could see Rodrigo, whose lavender coat was a colorful spot against the brown background of the ship's timber. The merchant ship was traveling light this trip, and Stephano guessed that the only cargo she was carrying was Sir Henry Wallace and the journeyman who knew how to enhance metal with magic.

The *Raven* made a rough landing. They were forced to throw out their anchoring grapnels and slam her airscrews into full speed reverse to slow down, and the ship hit the ground hard in what must have been a bone-jarring, teeth-rattling landing. Miri touched the helm and the *Cloud Hopper* ran out her cannons. Stephano and Dag stood beside her swivel guns, smoke rising from the matches they were holding over the guns, ready to fire. The armaments transformed an otherwise small and inoffensive Trundler houseboat into a gunboat, capable of blasting the helpless merchant vessel into fragments of splintered wood.

Stephano had his spyglass trained on Sir Henry Wallace, who had his spyglass and was looking coolly back at Stephano.

Stephano felt his skin crawl. He had expected Wallace to look angry, thwarted, defeated. Instead, Sir Henry Wallace grinned. Stephano lowered the spyglass and picked up the speaking trumpet.

"Captain of the *Silver Raven*. You will immediately release two passengers, Monsieur de Villeneuve and Monsieur Alcazar. If you do not, we will blow your ship apart."

The captain made a gesture that needed no translation, telling Stephano exactly what he could do with his demand.

"Dag," said Stephano, grim-faced and tight-lipped, "show them we're serious."

"By being careful not to hit anything," Dag muttered.

He was lowering the match to the fuse in the gunport when Sir Henry Wallace raised his hand and pointed toward the mountain.

"As if I'm going to fall for that old trick," said Stephano. "Fire—"

"Stephano!" Miri cried, gulping. "It's not a trick."

The man-of-war sailed out from behind the mountain where the ship had been hiding. Her cannons were run out, her men standing beside them with smoldering matches over the guns' touch holes. The man-of-war mounted thirty-two cannons to the *Cloud Hopper*'s two. Named the *Resolute*, the warship flew the Freyan flag.

Sir Henry Wallace removed his hat and made a bow. "A pleasure knowing you, Captain!"

And as if they had been waiting for the signal, the man-of-war fired on the *Cloud Hopper*.

On board the *Silver Raven*, Rodrigo watched in horror as the Trundler houseboat, struck by the cannon fire, burst into flame and fell precipitously from the sky. He could not see what became of the boat as it disappeared among the thick trees. All he could see was a coil of smoke rising up from the vegetation.

Standing beside him, Pietro Alcazar's face went white. "Those are your friends."

"Yes," said Rodrigo in a voice he didn't recognize.

"I'm sorry," said Alcazar and it sounded as if he was going to cry. "I didn't mean for any of this to happen."

"Oh, for God's sake, quit whining," said Sir Henry.

He rested a hand on Rodrigo's shoulder and added coolly, "Don't worry, Monsieur. The damage to your vessel looks much worse than it is. I told Admiral Baker to see to it that he cripple the boat, not blow it apart. I fancy the houseboat will be difficult to repair, especially given that there are no shipyards on this God-forsaken place. Still, Captain de Guichen is a most resourceful fellow. With your help, he'll find a way to get off this island. Though you might be marooned here for some time, I fear."

Rodrigo watched the smoke rising from the trees, then turned to Sir Henry.

"I don't understand," said Rodrigo, puzzled. "I thought you were going to throw me in the Breath."

"Oh, I was, I assure you," said Sir Henry. "But events have occurred that have led me to revise my plans. Come to my cabin."

The man-of-war floated overhead, casting a shadow upon the *Raven*, whose crew was making her ready to sail. The damage to the vessel had been much more minor than Wallace had made it appear. The crew had already made the necessary repairs. They were waiting only for Sir Henry to give the orders to depart for Freya.

Sir Henry took Rodrigo to what had once been the captain's cabin, but which had been given to him. The cabin was small and dark and smelled strongly of tobacco. Sunlight crept through a small porthole. The cabin was sparsely furnished with a desk and two chairs, a bed bolted to the bulkhead, and a large portmanteau.

"I would invite you to be seated, Monsieur, but this won't take long," said Sir Henry.

He walked over to the portmanteau, leaving Rodrigo standing in the middle of the cabin. Rodrigo could tell by the faint afterglow of magical sigils that the portmanteau had been bound by powerful spells, recently removed. Sir Henry inserted a key, lifted the lid, and took out an object. Shutting the trunk, he carried the object over to Rodrigo.

"Give this to the Countess de Marjolaine when you see her. With my compliments."

He handed Rodrigo a pewter tankard.

Rodrigo regarded the tankard in dazed astonishment. He had been prepared to die and now he was being handed a tankard and told to take it to the countess. He couldn't for a moment think what the elegant Countess de Marjolaine would do with such a lowly object as a pewter tankard when suddenly he realized what he was holding. He gave a soft gasp and looked at Sir Henry for an explanation.

"There's a message that goes with it," said Sir Henry. He was smiling, but only with his mouth. His eyes were cold, in deadly earnest. "Tell the countess: 'The same green fire that sank the *Royal Lion* struck this tankard. As you can see, the green fire had no effect on it whatsoever.'"

Rodrigo blinked. The words meant nothing to him for a moment, jumbled up in his scattered thoughts. When he finally understood, he was so astounded he nearly dropped the tankard.

He looked at Sir Henry. "The demonic weapons had no effect on this tankard. Which means the magically enhanced metal Alcazar designed can withstand—"

Sir Henry waved his hand impatiently. "You should go, Monsieur. Your friends will be concerned for your safety. I am sure you are concerned for theirs."

Rodrigo clasped the tankard tightly and walked toward the door. Once there, he stopped and looked back over his shoulder.

"You know what Rosia will do with this knowledge, sir. We will use it to attack Freya. Why are you giving this to us?"

Sir Henry was silent, his lips compressed, his expression dark. "Others look at the road at their feet. I look far ahead, Monsieur de Villeneuve, to the distant horizon. As Father Jacob and I stood together to fend off the demons, when your country and mine will one day stand back-to-back battling a foe intent on destroying us both. In that eventuality, I want my ally to be as strong as I am. And now, good day to you, Monsieur. Give Captain de Guichen my regards. I trust his little houseboat is not much hurt. Ah, and do accept my condolences on the death of your father."

Rodrigo clutched the pewter tankard and left the stuffy cabin. Climbing the stairs, he emerged, blinking, into the bright sunshine. In the distance, the smoke was still rising from the *Cloud Hopper*.

Rodrigo did not bother to bid good-bye to Alcazar, who stared, openmouthed, at the pewter tankard in Rodrigo's possession. The captain lowered the *Raven*'s gangplank, and Rodrigo walked down it onto the sandy beach. The merchant ship was making ready to set sail, filling the balloons with Breath from the barrels stored in the hold. The captain had deliberately released the air, allowing the ship to give the impression it was crippled. The *Raven* would be accompanied back to Freya by the man-of-war.

Once on the beach, Rodrigo considered going to find his friends. He took one look at the thick and impenetrable forest in which he'd most certainly end up lost, glanced down at his fine leather shoes with the silver buckles and his silk stockings and decided to sit on the beach in the shade of a tree and let Stephano find him.

Rodrigo sat on the beach, waiting to be rescued, and turned the pewter tankard over in his hands, studying its smooth, unblemished surface with wonder. He thought about the treatise in which he had postulated the idea of mixing metal with the Breath of God. He'd written the paper one night after imbibing a bit too much wine and submitted it for publication in a vain effort to keep from being tossed out of University. He had never imagined anyone would take his theory seriously. He thought about the green fire, the demons who wielded it, the destruction of the concrete bunker, the sinking of the *Royal Lion*, and how this tankard had survived unblemished, intact.

Two foes, standing back-to-back, defending against an enemy intent on destroying them both. Rodrigo believed Henry Wallace. The countess would believe him, too, though it might be some time — some considerable time — before he and the Cadre managed to make their way back to Rosia.

"And what will I wear when I do return to court? I never had a chance to pick up my new clothes," Rodrigo wondered sadly.

The *Silver Raven* lifted up off the beach of the unknown, uncharted island and sailed into the Breath, scuttling along in the wake of the enormous man-of-war, a single gosling trailing after an overprotective goose.

In his cabin aboard the *Raven*, Sir Henry gazed out the dirty porthole to watch the ship make her ascent. Far below, among the trees, he could see the wreckage of the *Cloud Hopper*. They were close enough that he could make out Captain de Guichen and the mercenary battling the flames. The captain and his crew wouldn't be going anywhere for a long, long while.

On the deck of the *Raven*, Pietro Alcazar was chatting happily with his brother and his brother's wife. Sir Henry could hear him promising that he would give up baccarat, mend his ways.

Damn right Alcazar will give up gambling, Henry thought, amused.

The genius would have his every wish fulfilled. He would be provided with luxurious living quarters, the finest food and drink, the best tools and equipment, apprentices and journeymen to work under him. And he would be guarded around the clock; soldiers armed to the teeth escorting him, watching his every move.

Sir Henry Wallace yawned and stretched his long frame luxuriously. For the first time since he had opened that package and seen that pewter tankard, he could let down his guard. He crossed to the door, flung it open, and shouted for someone to bring him a bottle of wine from his private stock.

Hard to believe only a few weeks had passed, he reflected. It seemed a lifetime.

He sank into a chair and glanced with distaste around the cabin. He would eventually transfer to more luxurious quarters aboard the man-of-war, but Admiral Baker had been forced to wait two weeks here at the rendezvous point and was liable to be in a very bad mood. Henry would give him time to recover.

As he waited, Sir Henry thought about his wife and hoped she was well. He might be back in time for the birth of his child. He felt ridiculously pleased at the idea of holding his tiny child in his arms.

A sailor brought in a bottle containing the very fine wine he'd bought while in Westfirth. The Rosians might not be good for much else, but they knew how to make wine.

"Set it on the table," he ordered the sailor, who placed the bottle on the table, along with a corkscrew and two glasses.

"Why two glasses?" Henry demanded. "Do you see anyone else, you dolt?"

The sailor stared at him stupidly, apparently not comprehending. Sir Henry dismissed the fool man with a wave. He opened the bottle and poured a glass of the red wine. The fragrance filled the cabin.

I will drink to Dubois, he thought, and chuckled.

The sailor had walked over to the door, but instead of continuing on out the door, the man shut it, locked it, and came back to sit down in the other chair. The sailor faced Sir Henry with cool aplomb.

The fellow was typical of his type, dressed in duck trousers with a loose fitting shirt, sunburned with bare legs and feet. He wore a sort of stocking cap over his head. Henry glared, outraged, but instead of withering beneath his fury, the sailor crossed his bare legs and held out his glass.

"What is the meaning of this, sirrah?" Henry sputtered with fury. "Get back to work before I have you flogged."

In answer, the sailor drew off his cap and shook out his hair. Or rather—she shook out her hair.

Long black curls fell around her slender shoulders. A few tendrils trailed over her face. Her gold-flecked eyes regarded Sir Henry with amusement. She held out her glass, indicating he was to pour the wine.

"Eiddwen!" he gasped.

"Hello, Henry," said Eiddwen.

Chapter Forty-Three

Stephano de Guichen's own true love is the blue sky of dawn, the orange mists of twilight, and the wings of the dragon that carries him to freedom.

No mere female can compete with such a rival.

—Miri McPike

THE DAMAGE TO THE *CLOUD HOPPER* WAS SIGNIFICANT, but not as bad as it might have been. Either the gunners aboard the man-of-war were excellent marksmen or terrible shots, for their cannons could have pounded the houseboat to splinters. Cannonballs wrecked the starboard wing lift tank and smashed several large holes in the hull. In a freak accident, one of these balls struck the galley stove, scattering burning embers while, at the same time, splinters from the hull hit a barrel of flour. The combination of flour dust and burning embers resulted in an explosion. In an ironic twist of fate, one of Miri's healing ointments turned out to be highly flammable and the entire galley was soon burning merrily. The wooden structure of the hull was set with constructs to resist fire and the blaze was contained, but the galley and everything in it, including all their food, was a total loss.

Stephano didn't have time to think about their future during the frantic moment when he, Dag, Miri, and Gythe were engaged in a desperate battle to save their boat. The

sisters filled buckets with water from a nearby lake and
flung them on the flames, while Dag and Stephano worked
to smother the fire and beat out glowing embers, sometimes
with their feet. Stephano saw out of the corner of his eye
the merchant ship, *Silver Raven*, sail off, escorted by the
man-of-war. He did spare a moment—several moments—
to wonder what had become of Rodrigo. Had Wallace killed
him? Stephano considered this likely. Wallace had no use
for Rigo anymore, so why leave him alive? Stephano was
desperate and grieving and furious and he poured his emotions into saving the boat, since he couldn't save anything
else.

When at last the fire was out, Stephano stood gasping for
breath and wiping sweat from his face that was black from
the smoke. He and his friends stood in the water-soaked,
singed, and flattened weeds and brush, staring in mute sorrow at the ruins of the *Cloud Hopper*. They watched the
smoke rise from the smoldering remains of the galley and
trail out the gaping holes in the hull, gazed at the shattered
wing and the broken lift tank and listened in dismay to the
hiss of the magical Breath they would need to lift them
from the island leaking out of the tank. The hard reality of
their dire situation began to sink into all of them, with the
possible exception of the Doctor. Terrified by the noise and
the fire, the cat had leaped from the burning ship the moment it hit ground and disappeared into the surrounding
woods.

Stephano saw Gythe looking stricken and woebegone.
He made an effort to smile and put his arm around her.

"The damage would be a lot worse if not for your magic,"
he told her. "Your protection spells kept the fire from reaching the powder kegs and held us together long enough so
that Miri could make a safe landing."

Gythe gave him a brave smile and an impulsive hug.
Foreseeing the difficult times that lay ahead for all of them,
Stephano felt tears sting his eyes. Muttering that it must be
the smoke, he hurriedly wiped them away.

Miri had stayed at the helm as the ship fell like a crippled bird, steering the *Cloud Hopper* as best she could to a small clearing formed by a large dome of rock thrusting up out of the wilderness, not far from one of the island's many lakes. The landing had been bone-jarring. They had all grabbed hold of anything they could hang onto and ridden the tumbling boat down.

Stephano had heard wood cracking, flames crackling. He'd seen Dag go flying across the deck and heard Miri scream, more in heartbreak than pain at the loss of her beloved ship. They had all managed to come through it without injury, save for Dag, who had an enormous lump on his forehead and bruised ribs.

Stephano flung himself down wearily on the ground. Miri was still standing by the wreckage, tears rolling unchecked down her cheeks, leaving trails in the grime that covered her face. Gythe put her arms around her sister, and both gazed sorrowfully at the ship that had been their parents' only legacy.

Dag came over to sit down beside Stephano and held out a jug. Stephano could smell the sharp odor of calvados.

"Medicinal, sir," said Dag.

Stephano hesitated, then said bleakly, "What the hell. It's not like I'm going anywhere."

He took the jug, put it to his lips, and swallowed. The liquor bit into his throat and filled him with warmth. He coughed and handed the jug back to Dag.

"You all right?"

"Mostly," said Dag in dispirited tones. "Miri and I will inspect the boat, go over the damage and report—"

"No hurry," said Stephano bitterly.

He was quiet a moment, watching the smoke. He took another pull from the jug. "I made a pig's breakfast out of this job."

"It wasn't your fault, sir," said Dag stoutly. "You couldn't know that bastard would have a bloody warship waiting for him."

"My mother warned me about Wallace. Father Jacob warned me. I should have listened to them. But I was so goddamn arrogant, figured I was so goddamn clever that I could outsmart him. Now the *Cloud Hopper* is in ruins and we're stuck here on some godforsaken island with no chance of being found and Rigo's . . . Rigo's . . ."

Stephano couldn't finish. He put his hand over his face.

"He's not dead, sir," said Dag, an odd note to his voice.

"You can't know that," said Stephano.

"Yes, I can, sir. Look there."

Dag rose to his feet, pointing to three bright flares— lavender in color—bursting above the treetops.

"Rigo!" Stephano exclaimed in relief. "He's alive!"

"And expecting us to go save his lazy ass, of course." Dag grumbled, but he was smiling as he said it.

"We have no food," Miri said, coming to report. Her cheeks were streaked with tears and ashes, but she was brisk and matter-of-fact. "I suppose there's wild game— rabbits and deer and such—to be had around here."

She glared at Stephano. Her green eyes glittered in the sunlight. "I should punch you in the nose."

"I wish you would," said Stephano. "I deserve it. I'll find a way to get us out of here. I promise."

"You will that," Miri said fiercely. "And pay for the damage to my boat, too."

"Of course," Stephano said shamefacedly. "Miri, I'm so sorry . . ."

Miri didn't answer. Instead she put her arms around him and hugged him close. Shaking back her red hair, she grinned up at him.

"Look at it this way," she said, tears glimmering in her laughing eyes. "We are now the Cadre of the *Truly* Lost!"

Before he could clear the choking sensation out of his throat, Miri had slipped out of his arms and stood eyeing Dag and Stephano. "You both have burns on your arms and hands. Fortunately, a jar of my herbal mixture survived the flames—"

Dag cast an alarmed glance at Stephano. "Shouldn't we go rescue Rigo, sir?"

"Yes, we should," said Stephano hurriedly. "Bring your musket."

Miri laughed and shook her head at both of them, then asked Gythe to help her haul out the spare sails to be used as makeshift tents. After a brief search, Dag found his musket and loaded it with powder and shot. Stephano retrieved his dragon pistol. Miri was draping sails over tree limbs to form lean-tos and Gythe was carrying blankets up from the smoke-filled hold when Doctor Ellington suddenly shot out of the woods, his fur standing on end, his ruff bristling, his tail three times its normal size, his green eyes wide. The cat leaped onto Dag's shoulder.

"Something's scared him," said Dag, setting down his musket to soothe the terrified cat.

"Probably a mouse," Miri remarked caustically.

Dag was about to make an indignant denial when Stephano ordered sharply, "Dag, don't move!"

Dag froze, which was not easy, trying to hold the squirming cat in his arms.

"Don't anyone move," Stephano reiterated.

Hearing the urgency in his tone, Gythe stopped dead on the deck of the wrecked *Cloud Hopper*. Miri ducked swiftly beneath a sail and peered out.

"What is it?" she asked in a hissing whisper.

"Look there," said Stephano softly. "By the lake."

Gythe and Miri slowly shifted their gaze. Dag was facing the wrong direction. He tried to see, but couldn't quite manage without moving.

"What is it, sir?" he asked urgently. "Pirates?"

"A dragon," said Stephano.

The dragon had apparently been having a cooling swim when he'd been disturbed by the Doctor coming down to the water for a drink. The dragon rose up out of the lake, water cascading from the head and body, which was about twenty-five feet in length, or so Stephano judged. The dragon's scales were crystalline blue, darker than the water. His head was elegantly shaped, the jaw elongated, the nostrils wide, the eyes emerald green, close set, and glittering. His blue mane ran from a central point in his forehead down his neck, all the way down his spine, and onto the tail. He stood in the water, tail lashing slowly back and forth, stirring up waves.

"Maybe the dragon's never seen a cat," said Dag, who had managed to twist his neck in order to see.

"I don't think he's ever seen a human," said Stephano.

"A wild dragon!" Miri exclaimed, awed. "No one knew such creatures existed anymore."

The wild dragon lifted himself out of the water. Unlike his large, ponderous, and civilized cousins, this dragon was smaller, his movements quick and graceful. He kept his keen eyes on the humans. He was curious about them, not afraid of them.

"He doesn't seem to feel threatened by us, sir," said Dag.

"Perhaps because he can squash us like bugs," said Miri.

The wild dragon fluttered his wings in the lake, like a robin taking a bath, sending water splashing high into the air in sparkling droplets. He emerged to stand poised on the shoreline, regarding them with narrowed eyes, his nostrils flaring at the unusual smell of humanity. He seemed uncertain what to do.

"He's a young dragon," Stephano said. His heart ached at the astounding beauty of the creature.

"What do we do?" Dag asked, struggling to hang onto the cat, who was undoubtedly thinking fond thoughts of his storage closet. "We can't stand here all day."

"Yes, we can," said Stephano. "The dragon has to make up his mind about us. He has to decide that we're not a threat and that we're also not dinner."

"And how do we convince him of that, sir?" Dag demanded.

"The old stories tell of the first meeting of humans and dragons," Miri said, her voice quivering with excitement. "Oh, Stephano, this is a dream come true—"

She was interrupted by crashing and blundering sounds emanating from the forest and loud swearing and then Rodrigo emerged from the woods, hot and sweating, his hair bedraggled, his stockings ripped to shreds. He came up short at the sight of his friends and stared at them indignantly.

"I thought you were all dead! And here you are! Perfectly healthy and lolligagging about—"

"Rigo, shut up!" Stephano said furiously, but it was too late.

Perhaps it was Rodrigo's querulous tone or the crashing sounds or maybe the lavender coat. Whatever it was, there was something about him the wild dragon didn't like. He lowered his head, green eyes flaring, and began to slink toward them, gliding rapidly over the ground, his body moving like blue quicksilver.

"Oh, my God!" Rodrigo gulped. "You should have told me you had company. What do I do? Climb a tree?"

Stephano drew his pistol. "Run for the *Cloud Hopper*."

"Don't hurt him!" Miri wailed.

"I'm not going to hurt him!" Stephano said through gritted teeth. He raised the pistol and pointed into the air. "I'm going to try to frighten him. Run! All of you!"

Rodrigo was already on his way. Miri hesitated, then she made a dash toward the boat. Dag dropped the Doctor and snatched up his musket. The Doctor, now feeling brave, hissed at the advancing dragon.

Stephano fired the pistol. The dragon was startled by the boom and stopped short. His head reared. His eyes narrowed to slits. The dragon regarded them warily. He did not take flight, as Stephano had hoped.

"Dag," said Stephano in a low and even tone, "start backing up. Move slowly, make your way to the boat."

"What about you, sir?" Dag asked.

"I'm right behind you," said Stephano.

The two of them began to edge their way slowly toward the *Cloud Hopper*, both of them keeping their eyes on the dragon, who had his eyes on them. Small gouts of flame shot from his nostrils. Tendrils of smoke coiled from his mouth.

"I don't think you made much of an impression, sir," said Dag.

"I'm thinking that myself," said Stephano.

"I could try to wing him—" Dag said, raising his musket.

"Shoot him and I'll shoot you!" Miri shouted angrily.

"She would, too," said Stephano. "If you hurt him, he'll charge. On my word, make a dash for it."

He tensed, ready to run, and then he heard Dag cry hoarsely, "Gythe, Girl dear, no! Get back!"

Gythe was walking calmly down the gangplank, carrying her harp in one hand and her little stool in the other. Stephano was ready to make a lunge for her, grab her, and drag her back.

Miri called out, "Leave her be, you men! She knows what she's doing, far better than you two trigger-happy lunatics! Put away your guns, sirs, and come into the boat now, the both of you."

Dag cast an agonized glance at Stephano. Dag was silently begging him to ignore Miri and carry Gythe out of danger. The big Guundaran did not know much about dragons, however Stephano did. He lowered his pistol and motioned for Dag to lower his musket.

"I think I know what Miri has in mind. We'll go to the boat."

Dag obeyed orders, though with a shake of his head, and went to guard Miri and Rodrigo on the deck of the *Cloud Hopper*. Miri was pale, but confident, standing with her arms crossed, her lips compressed. Dag put his arm around her and held her close.

Gythe calmly placed the little stool on the ground. She sat down, arranged her skirts, shook her blonde hair around her shoulders, placed her harp in her lap, and drew her hands across the strings. The dragon watched her warily all this time. His teeth bared warningly as she came nearer to him. His tongue flickered from between the front fangs.

At the sound of the music, the dragon blinked. Gythe ran her hands over the strings and then began to sing. Stephano recognized the song, one she frequently sang softly to the Doctor.

The dragon did not appear to know what to make of all this. He tilted his head to one side. His eyes narrowed again, but not in anger. He seemed to be enjoying the music.

"When we were invited to visit the houses of the noble dragons, they always loved to hear Gythe sing," Miri said with quiet pride. "As I was about to tell you, the old stories relate that this is how humans and dragons first came to trust each other. Dragons love music, but they cannot make it. Music brought dragons and humans together."

The dragon drew nearer to Gythe. Dag tensed, his hand clasping his musket. Miri rested her hand on his arm.

"Trust me," she said softly. "Trust Gythe."

The young dragon was quite close to Gythe now. His head hung over her. He could bite her in two with a snap of his jaws. Gythe appeared to take no notice of him. Her eyes were half-closed; she was lost in her music. Her fingers plucked and strummed. The harp strings quivered. Her voice—never used for speaking, only for song—rose in a melody, haunting and sweet and sad, that told the story of some long ago Trundler maiden, mourning her lost love.

The dragon lowered his head to the ground, stretched out his body, fixed his shining eyes on Gythe, and listened.

Stephano relaxed. Sweat ran from his forehead and trickled, stinging, into his eyes. He dared not move to wipe it away lest he break the spell. Of course, the time would come when Gythe would have to quit singing and there was no telling what the dragon might do then, but Stephano wasn't worried. The dragon trusted them now. They had to continue to reinforce that trust and show the dragon that they trusted him. Time and patience would be required. Fortunately, Stephano had a lot of both.

Stephano could guess that gaining the trust of wild dragons

would not be easy and that training them to carry riders would be more difficult still, especially after working with the civilized dragons who had been flying with humans for centuries.

The young dragon lay at Gythe's feet and did not stir.

"I know what you're thinking," said Miri, eyeing Stephano, who laughed, albeit softly, so as not to disturb the dragon.

He had hope again, he had a job again, he was going to fly again. Life suddenly looked much, much better.

"All I'm thinking is that we can change the name of our group, friends," he told them. "From now on, we can call ourselves: 'The Cadre of the Not-So-Very-Lost-After-All.'"

Chuckling to himself, Stephano left his friends standing on the deck of the wounded *Cloud Hopper* and, moving slowly, he walked down to take a seat beside Gythe. The dragon was clearly aware of Stephano, but the beast kept his gaze fixed on Gythe.

Rodrigo and Miri and Dag looked at each other in bemusement, seeing what lay ahead, not sure they liked it.

"Welcome to the Dragon Brigade," said Rodrigo.

Saladin Ahmed

Throne of the Crescent Moon
978-0-7564-0711-7

"An arresting, sumptuous and thoroughly satisfying debut."
— *Kirkus* (starred)

"Set in a quasi–Middle Eastern city and populated with the supernatural creatures of Arab folklore, this long-awaited debut by a finalist for the Nebula and Campbell awards brings *The Arabian Nights* to sensuous life. The maturity and wisdom of Ahmed's older protagonists are a delightful contrast to the brave impulsiveness of their younger companions. This trilogy launch will delight fantasy lovers who enjoy flawed but honorable protagonists and a touch of the exotic." — *Library Journal* (starred)

"Ahmed's debut masterfully paints a world both bright and terrible. Unobtrusive hints of backstory contribute to the sense that this novel is part of a larger ongoing tale, and the Arab-influenced setting is full of vibrant description, characters, and religious expressions that will delight readers weary of pseudo-European epics." — *Publishers Weekly* (starred)

To Order Call: 1-800-788-6262
www.dawbooks.com

00570 6006

Patrick Rothfuss

The #1 *New York Times* Bestseller

THE WISE MAN'S FEAR

*The Kingkiller Chronicle:
Day Two*

978-0-7564-0473-4

"This breathtakingly epic story is heartrending in its intimacy and masterful in its narrative essence, and will leave fans waiting on tenterhooks for the final installment."
—*Publishers Weekly* (Starred Review)

To Order Call: 1-800-788-6262
www.dawbooks.com

DAW 101